P9-ARD-234

THE ALEXANDRIA QUARTET

This is the second of four novels that have become known as "The Alexandria Quartet."

But though it deals with many of the same characters and situations as its predecessor, *Justine,* the reader sees them in a subtly altered light, through different eyes and within a slightly altered context of time.

It is Balthazar who is mainly responsible for this. For when Darley, the narrator and lover of Justine, submits what he has written about her, the doctor and dabbler in psychology furnishes him with additional information, even deeper insights into the true character of this most sensual, vibrantly alive but very complex woman....

BALTHAZAR was originally published by E. P. Dutton & Co., Inc., at $3.75.

Not for sale in the British Empire market.

BY LAWRENCE DURRELL

*The Alexandria Quartet
 *Justine
 *Balthazar
 *Mountolive
 *Clea
Bitter Lemons
The Black Book
Prospero's Cell and
 Reflections on a Marine Venus

*To be published by Pocket Books, Inc., in GIANT CARDINAL editions.

Are there paper-bound books you want
but cannot find at your retail stores? You can get any
title in print in these famous series, POCKET BOOKS,
CARDINAL EDITIONS, POCKET LIBRARY and
PERMABOOKS, by ordering from Mail Service Dept.,
Pocket Books, Inc., 1 West 39th St., New York 18, N.Y.
Enclose retail price plus 5c per book for mailing costs;
send check or money order—do not send cash.

FREE CATALOGUE SENT ON REQUEST

Lawrence Durrell

BALTHAZAR

CARDINAL
EDITION

POCKET BOOKS, INC. • NEW YORK

This GIANT CARDINAL edition includes every word contained in the original, higher-priced edition. It is printed from brand-new plates made from completely reset, clear, easy-to-read type.

BALTHAZAR

E. P. Dutton edition published August, 1958

GIANT CARDINAL edition published May, 1961
1st printing.....................March, 1961

Not for sale in the British Empire market.

L

Copyright, ©, 1958, by Lawrence Durrell. All rights reserved. This GIANT CARDINAL edition is published by arrangement with E. P. Dutton & Co., Inc. Printed in the U.S.A.

GIANT CARDINAL editions are distributed in the U.S. by Affiliated Publishers, Inc., 630 Fifth Avenue, New York 20, N.Y.

Notice: GIANT CARDINAL editions are published by Pocket Books, Inc. Trade mark registered in the United States and other countries.

NOTE

The characters and situations in this novel, the second of a group—a sibling, not a sequel to Justine—are entirely imaginary, as is the personality of the narrator. Nor could the city be less unreal.

Modern literature offers us no Unities, so I have turned to science and am trying to complete a four-decker novel whose form is based on the relativity proposition.

Three sides of space and one of time constitute the soup-mix recipe of a continuum. The four novels follow this pattern.

The three first parts, however, are to be deployed spatially (hence the use of "sibling" not "sequel") and are not linked in a serial form. They interlap, interweave, in a purely spatial relation. Time is stayed. The fourth part alone will represent time and be a true sequel.

The subject-object relation is so important to relativity that I have tried to turn the novel through both subjective and objective modes. The third part, Mountolive, is a straight naturalistic novel in which the narrator of Justine and Balthazar becomes an object, i.e., a character.

This is not Proustian or Joycean method—for they illustrate Bergsonian "Duration" in my opinion, not "Space-Time."

The central topic of the book is an investigation of modern love.

These considerations sound perhaps somewhat immodest or even pompous. But it would be worth trying an experiment to see if we cannot discover a morphological form one might appropriately call "classical"—for our time. Even if the result proved to be a "science-fiction" in the true sense.

L. D.
Ascona, 1957

The mirror sees the man as beautiful, the mirror loves the man; another mirror sees the man as frightful and hates him; and it is always the same being who produces the impressions.

Justine
(D. A. F. de Sade)

Yes, we insist upon those details, you veil them with a decency which removes all their edge of horror; there remains only what is useful to whoever wishes to become familiar with man; you have no conception how helpful these tableaux are to the development of the human spirit; perhaps we are still so benighted with respect to this branch of learning only because of the stupid restraint of those who wish to write upon such matters. Inhabited by absurd fears, they only discuss the puerilities with which every fool is familiar and dare not, by turning a bold hand to the human heart, offer its gigantic idiosyncrasies to our view.

Justine
(D. A. F. de Sade)

To

MY MOTHER

these memorials of an unforgotten city

PART

one

1.

LANDSCAPE-TONES: brown to bronze, steep skyline, low cloud, pearl ground with shadowed oyster and violet reflections. The lion-dust of desert: prophets' tombs turned to zinc and copper at sunset on the ancient lake. Its huge sand-faults like watermarks from the air; green and citron giving to gunmetal, to a single plum-dark sail, moist, palpitant: sticky-winged nymph. Taposiris is dead among its tumbling columns and seamarks, vanished the Harpoon Men . . . Mareotis under a sky of hot lilac.

> *summer: buff sand, hot marble sky.*
> *autumn: swollen bruise-greys.*
> *winter: freezing snow, cool sand.*
> *clear sky panels, glittering with mica.*
> *washed delta greens.*
> *magnificent starscapes.*

And spring? Ah! there is no spring in the Delta, no sense of refreshment and renewal in things. One is plunged out of winter into: wax effigy of a summer too hot to breathe. But here, at least, in Alexandria, the sea-breaths save us from the tideless weight of summer nothingness, creeping over the bar among the warships to flutter the striped awnings of the cafés upon the Grande Corniche. I would never have . . .

o o o o o

The city, half-imagined (yet wholly real), begins and ends in us, roots lodged in our memory. Why must I return to it night after night, writing here by the fire of

carob-wood while the Aegean wind clutches at this island
house, clutching and releasing it, bending back the cy-
presses like bows? Have I not said enough about Alexandria? Am I to be reinfected once more by the dream
of it and the memory of its inhabitants? Dreams I had
thought safely locked up on paper, confided to the
strong-rooms of memory! You will think I am indulging
myself. It is not so. A single chance factor has altered
everything, has turned me back upon my tracks. A memory which catches sight of itself in a mirror.

o   o   o   o   o

Justine, Melissa, Clea. . . . There were so few of us
really—you would have thought them easily disposed of
in a single book, would you not? So would I, so *did* I.
Dispersed now by time and circumstance, the circuit
broken forever. . . .

I had set myself the task of trying to recover them in
words, reinstate them in memory, allot to each his and
her position in my time. Selfishly. And with that writing
complete, I felt that I had turned a key upon the doll's
house of our actions. Indeed, I saw my lovers and friends
no longer as living people but as coloured transfers of
the mind; inhabiting my papers now, no longer the city,
like tapestry figures. It was difficult to concede to them
any more common reality than to the words I had used
about them. What has recalled me to myself?

But in order to go on, it is necessary to go back: not
that anything I wrote about them is untrue, far from it.
Yet when I wrote, the full facts were not at my disposal.
The picture I drew was a provisional one—like the picture
of a lost civilisation deduced from a few fragmented
vases, an inscribed tablet, an amulet, some human bones,
a gold smiling death-mask.

o   o   o   o   o

"We live," writes Pursewarden somewhere, "lives based upon selected fictions. Our view of reality is conditioned by our position in space and time—not by our personalities as we like to think. Thus every interpretation of reality is based upon a unique position. Two paces east or west and the whole picture is changed." Something of this order. . . .

And as for human characters, whether real or invented, there are no such animals. Each psyche is really an ant-hill of opposing predispositions. Personality as something with fixed attributes is an illusion—but a necessary illusion *if we are to love!*

As for the something that remains constant . . . the shy kiss of Melissa is predictable, for example (amateurish as an early form of printing), or the frowns of Justine, which cast a shadow over those blazing dark eyes—orbits of the Sphinx at noon. "In the end," says Pursewarden, "everything will be found to be true of everybody. Saint and Villain are co-sharers." He is right.

I am making every attempt to be matter of fact. . . .

○   ○   ○   ○   ○

In the last letter which reached me from Balthazar he wrote: "I think of you often and not without a certain grim humour. You have retired to your island, with, as you think, all the data about us and our lives. No doubt you are bringing us to judgment on paper in the manner of writers. I wish I could see the result. It must fall very far short of *truth:* I mean such truths as I could tell you about us all—even perhaps about yourself. Or the truths Clea could tell you (she is in Paris and has stopped writing to me altogether). I picture you, wise one, poring over *Moeurs,* the diaries of Justine, Nessim, etc., imagining that the truth is to be found in them. Wrong!

Wrong! A diary is the last place to go if you wish to seek the truth about a person. Nobody dares to make the final confession to themselves on paper: or at least, not about love. Do you know whom Justine really loved? You believed it was yourself, did you not? Confess!"

My only answer was to send him the huge bundle of paper which had grown up so stiffly under my slow pen and to which I had loosely given her name as a title— though *Cahiers* would have done just as well. Six months passed after this—a blessed silence indeed, for it suggested that my critic had been satisfied, silenced.

I cannot say that I forgot the city, but I let the memory of it sleep. Yet of course, it was always there, as it always will be, hanging in the mind like the mirage which travellers so often see. Pursewarden has described the phenomenon in the following words:

"We were still two or three clear hours' steaming distance before land could possibly come into sight when suddenly my companion shouted and pointed at the horizon. We saw, inverted in the sky, a full-scale mirage of the city, luminous and trembling, as if painted on dusty silk: yet in the nicest detail. From memory I could clearly make out its features, Ras El Tin Palace, the Nebi Daniel Mosque and so forth. The whole representation was as breath-taking as a masterpiece painted in fresh dew. It hung there in the sky for a considerable time, perhaps twenty-five minutes, before melting slowly into the horizon mist. An hour later, the *real* city appeared, swelling from a smudge to the size of its mirage."

o   o   o   o   o

The two or three winters we have spent in this island have been lonely ones—dour and windswept winters and hot summers. Luckily, the child is too young to feel as I do the need for books, for conversation. She is happy and active.

Now in the spring come the long calms, the tideless, scentless days of premonition. The sea tames itself and becomes attentive. Soon the cicadas will bring in their crackling music, background to the shepherd's dry flute among the rocks. The scrambling tortoise and the lizard are our only companions.

I should explain that our only regular visitant from the outside world is the Smyrna packet which once a week crosses the headland to the south, always at the same hour, at the same speed, just after dusk. In winter, the high seas and winds make it invisible, but now—I sit and wait for it. You hear at first only the faint drumming of engines. Then the creature slides round the cape, cutting its line of silk froth in the sea, brightly lit up in the moth-soft darkness of the Aegean night—condensed, but without outlines, like a cloud of fireflies moving. It travels fast, and disappears all too soon round the next headland, leaving behind it perhaps only the half-uttered fragment of a popular song, or the skin of a tangerine which I will find next day, washed up on the long pebbled beach where I bathe with the child.

The little arbour of oleanders under the planes—this is my writing-room. After the child has gone to bed, I sit here at the old sea-stained table, waiting for the visitant, unwilling to light the paraffin lamp before it has passed. It is the only day of the week I know by name here—Thursday. It sounds silly, but in an island so empty of variety, I look forward to the weekly visit like a child to a school treat. I know the boat brings letters for which I shall have to wait perhaps twenty-four hours. But I never see the little ship vanish without regret. And when it has passed, I light the lamp with a sigh and return to my papers. I write so slowly, with such pain. Pursewarden once, speaking about writing, told me that the pain that

accompanied composition was entirely due, in artists, to
the fear of madness; "Force it a bit and tell yourself that
you don't give a damn if you *do* go mad, and you'll find
it comes quicker, you'll break the barrier." (I don't know
how true this all is. But the money he left me in his will
has served me well, and I still have a few pounds between
me and the devils of debt and work.)

I describe this weekly diversion in some detail because
it was into this picture that Balthazar intruded one June
evening with a suddenness that surprised me—I was going
to write "deafened"—there is no one to talk to here—but
"surprised me." This evening something like a miracle
happened. The little steamer, instead of disappearing
as usual, turned abruptly through an arc of 150 degrees
and entered the lagoon, there to lie in a furry cocoon of
its own light: and to drop into the centre of the golden
puddle it had created the long slow anchor-chain whose
symbol itself is like a search for truth. It was a moving
sight to one who, like myself, had been landlocked in
spirit as all writers are—indeed, become like a ship in a
bottle, sailing nowhere—and I watched as an Indian must
perhaps have watched the first white man's craft touch
the shores of the New World.

The darkness, the silence, were broken now by the
uneven lap-lap of oars; and then, after an age, by the
chink of city-shod feet upon shingle. A hoarse voice gave
a direction. Then silence. As I lit the lamp to set the
wick in trim and so deliver myself from the spell of this
departure from the norm, the grave dark face of my
friend, like some goat-like apparition from the Under-
world, materialised among the thick branches of myrtle.
We drew a breath and stood, smiling at each other in the
yellow light: the dark Assyrian ringlets, the beard of Pan.
"No—I am real!" said Balthazar with a laugh and we embraced furiously. Balthazar!

The Mediterranean is an absurdly small sea; the length

and greatness of its history makes us dream it larger than
it is. Alexandria indeed—the true no less than the imagined—lay only some hundreds of sea-miles to the south.

"I am on my way to Smyrna," said Balthazar, "from
where I was going to post you this." He laid upon that
scarred old table the immense bundle of manuscript I
had sent him—papers now seared and starred by a massive interlinear of sentences, paragraphs and question-
marks. Seating himself opposite with his Mephistophelean
air, he said in a lower, more hesitant tone:

"I have debated in myself very long about telling you
some of the things I have put down here. At times it
seemed a folly and an impertinence. After all, your concern—was it with *us* as *real* people or as 'characters'? I
didn't know. I still don't. These pages may lose me your
friendship without adding anything to the sum of your
knowledge. You have been painting the city, touch by
touch, upon a curved surface—was your object poetry
or fact? If the latter, then there are things which you
have a right to know."

He still had not explained his amazing appearance
before me, so anxious was he about the central meaning
of the visitation. He did so now, noticing my bewilderment at the cloud of fireflies in the normally deserted
bay. He smiled.

"The ship is delayed for a few hours with engine
trouble. It is one of Nessim's. The captain is Hasim
Kohly, an old friend: perhaps you remember him? No.
Well, I guessed from your description roughly where you
must be living; but to be landed on your doorstep like
this, I confess!" His laughter was wonderful to hear once
more.

But I hardly listened, for his words had plunged me
into a ferment, a desire to study his interlinear, to revise
—not my book (that has never been of the slightest importance to me for it will never even be published), but

my view of the city and its inhabitants. For my own personal Alexandria had become, in all this loneliness, as dear as a philosophy of introspection, almost a monomania. I was so filled with emotion I did not know what to say to him. "Stay with us, Balthazar—" I said, "stay awhile. . . ."

"We leave in two hours," he said, and patting the papers before him: "This may give you visions and fevers," he added doubtfully.

"Good—" I said, "I ask for nothing better."

"We are all still real people," he said, "whatever *you* try and do to us—those of us who are still alive. Melissa, Pursewarden—they can't answer back because they are dead. At least, so one thinks."

"So one thinks. The best retorts always come from beyond the grave."

We sat and began to talk about the past, rather stiffly to be sure. He had already dined on board and there was nothing I could offer him beyond a glass of the good island wine which he sipped slowly. Later he asked to see Melissa's child, and I led him back through the clustering oleanders to a place from which we could both look into the great firelit room where she lay looking beautiful and grave, asleep there with her thumb in her mouth. Balthazar's dark cruel eye softened as he watched her, lightly breathing. "One day," he said in a low voice, "Nessim will want to see her. Quite soon, mark. He has begun to talk about her, be curious. With old age coming on, he will feel he needs her support, mark my words." And he quoted in Greek: "First the young, like vines, climb up the dull supports of their elders who feel their fingers on them, soft and tender; then the old climb down the lovely supporting bodies of the young into their proper deaths." I said nothing. It was the room itself which was breathing now—not our bodies.

"You have been lonely here," said Balthazar.

"But splendidly, desirably lonely."

"Yes, I envy you. But truthfully."

And then his eyes caught the unfinished portrait of Justine which Clea in another life had given me.

"That portrait," he said, "which was interrupted by a kiss. How good to see that again—how good!" He smiled. "It is like hearing a loved and familiar statement in music which leads one towards an emotion always recapturable, never-failing." I did not say anything. I did not dare.

He turned to me. "And Clea?" he said at last, in the voice of someone interrogating an echo. I said: "I have heard nothing from her for perhaps two years, perhaps more. Time doesn't count here. I expect she has married, has gone away to another country, has children, a reputation as a painter . . . everything one would wish her."

He looked at me curiously and shook his head. "No," he said; but that was all.

It was long after midnight when the seamen called him from the dark olive groves. I walked to the beach with him, sad to see him leave so soon. A rowboat waited at the water's edge with a sailor standing to his oars in it. He said something in Arabic.

The spring sea was enticingly warm after a day's sunshine and as Balthazar entered the boat the whim seized me to swim out with him to the vessel which lay not two hundred yards away from the shore. This I did and hovered to watch him climb the rail, and to watch the boat drawn up. "Don't get caught in the screw," he called, and, "Go back before the engines start"—"I will" —"But wait—before you go—" He ducked back into a stateroom to reappear and drop something into the water beside me. It fell with a soft splash. "A rose from Alexandria," he said, "from the city which has every-

thing but happiness to offer its lovers." He chuckled.
"Give it to the child."

"Balthazar, good-bye!"

"Write to me—if you dare!"

Caught like a spider between the cross mesh of lights,
and turning towards those yellow pools which still lay
between the dark shore and myself, I waved and he
waved back.

I put the precious rose between my teeth and dog-
paddled back to my clothes on the pebble beach, talking
to myself.

And there, lying upon the table in the yellow lamp-
light, lay the great interlinear to *Justine*—as I have called
it. It was crosshatched, crabbed, starred with questions
and answers in different-coloured inks, in typescript. It
seemed to me then to be somehow symbolic of the very
reality we had shared—a palimpsest upon which each of
us had left his or her individual traces, layer by layer.

Must I now learn to see it all with new eyes, to ac-
custom myself to the truths which Balthazar has added?
It is impossible to describe with what emotion I read
his words—sometimes so detailed and sometimes so briefly curt—as for example in the list he had headed "Some
Fallacies and Misapprehensions" where he said coldly:
"Number 4. That Justine 'loved' you. She 'loved,' if
anyone, Pursewarden. 'What does that mean?' She was
forced to use you as a decoy in order to protect him from
the jealousy of Nessim whom she had married. Pursewarden himself did not care for her at all—supreme logic
of love!"

In my mind's eye the city rose once more against the
flat mirror of the green lake and the broken loins of
sandstone which marked the desert's edge. The politics
of love, the intrigues of desire, good and evil, virtue and
caprice, love and murder, moved obscurely in the dark
corners of Alexandria's streets and squares, brothels and

drawing-rooms—moved like a great congress of eels in the slime of plot and counter-plot.

It was almost dawn before I surrendered the fascinating mound of paper with its comments upon my own real (inner) life and like a drunkard stumbled to my bed, my head aching, echoing with the city, the only city left where every extreme of race and habit can meet and marry, where inner destinies intersect. I could hear the dry voice of my friend repeating as I fell asleep: "How much do you *care* to know . . . how much more do you *care* to know?"—"I must know *everything* in order to be at last delivered from the city," I replied in my dream.

o   o   o   o   o

"When you pluck a flower, the branch springs back into place. This is not true of the heart's affections" is what Clea once said to Balthazar.

o   o   o   o   o

And so, slowly, reluctantly, I have been driven back to my starting-point, like a man who at the end of a tremendous journey is told that he has been sleepwalking. "Truth," said Balthazar to me once, blowing his nose in an old tennis sock, "Truth is what most contradicts itself in time."

And Pursewarden on another occasion, but not less memorably: "If things were always what they seemed, how impoverished would be the imagination of man!"

How will I ever deliver myself from this whore among cities—sea, desert, minaret, sand, sea?

No. I must set it all down in cold black and white, until such time as the memory and impulse of it is spent. I know that the key I am trying to turn is in myself.

2.

Le *cénacle* Capodistria used to call us in those days when we gathered for an early morning shave in the Ptolemaic parlour of Mnemjian, with its mirrors and palms, its bead curtains and the delicious mimicry of clear warm water and white linen: a laying out and anointing of corpses. The violet-eyed hunchback himself officiated, for we were valued customers all (dead Pharaohs at the natron baths, guts and brains to be removed, renovated and replaced). He himself, the barber, was often unshaven having just hurried down from the hospital after shaving a corpse. Briefly we met here in the padded chairs, in the mirrors, before separating to go about our various tasks—Da Capo to see his brokers, Pombal to totter to the French consulate (mouth full of charred moths, hangover, sensation of having walked about all night on his eyeballs), I to teach, Scobie to the Police Bureau, and so on. . . .

I have somewhere a faded flashlight photograph of this morning ritual, taken by poor John Keats, the Global Agency correspondent. It is strange to look at it now. The smell of the gravecloth is on it. It is a speaking likeness of an Alexandrian spring morning: quiet rubbing of coffee pestles, curdled crying of fat pigeons. I recognize my friends by the very sounds they make: Capodistria's characteristic *"Quatsch"* and *"Pouagh"* at some political remark, followed by that dry cachinnation—the retching of a metal stomach; Scobie's tobacco cough *"Teauch,*

Teauch"; Pombal's soft *"Tiens,"* like someone striking a triangle. *"Tiens."*

And in one corner there I am, in my shabby raincoat—the perfected image of a schoolteacher. In the other corner sits poor little Toto de Brunel. Keats's photograph traps him as he is raising a ringed finger to his temple—the fatal temple.

Toto! He is an *original,* a *numéro.* His withered witch's features and small boy's brown eyes, widow's peak, queer *art nouveau* smile. He was the darling of old society women too proud to pay for gigolos. *"Toto, mon chou, c'est toi!"* (Madame Umbada), *"Comme il est charmant ce Toto!"* (Athena Trasha). He lives on these dry crusts of approbation, an old woman's man, with the dimples sinking daily deeper into the wrinkled skin of an ageless face, quite happy, I suppose. Yes.

"Toto—comment vas-tu?"—*"Si heureux de vous voir, Madame Martinengo!"*

He was what Pombal scornfully called "a Gentleman of the Second Declension." His smile dug one's grave, his kindness was anaesthetic. Though his fortune was small, his excesses trivial, yet he was right in the social swim. There was, I suppose, nothing to be done with him for he was a woman: yet had he been born one he would long since have cried himself into a decline. Lacking charm, his pederasty gave him a kind of illicit importance. *"Homme serviable, homme gracieux"* (Count Banubula, General Cervoni—what more does one want?).

Though without humour, he found one day that he could split sides. He spoke indifferent English and French, but whenever at loss for a word he would put in one whose meaning he did not know and the grotesque substitution was often delightful. This became his standard mannerism. In it, he almost reached poetry—as when he said "Some flies have come off my typewriter" or "The car is trepanned today" or "I ran so fast I got dandruff."

He could do this in three languages. It excused him
from learning them. He spoke a Toto-tongue of his own.

Invisible behind the lens itself that morning stood
Keats—the world's sort of Good Fellow, empty of ill intentions. He smelt lightly of perspiration. *C'est le métier
qui exige.* Once he had wanted to be a writer but took
the wrong turning, and now his profession had so trained
him to stay on the superficies of real life (acts and facts
about acts) that he had developed the typical journalist's
neurosis (they drink to still it) : namely that Something
has happened, or is about to happen, in the next street,
and that they will not know about it until it is too late
to "send." This haunting fear of missing a fragment of
reality which one knows in advance will be trivial, even
meaningless, had given our friend the conventional tic
one sees in children who want to go to the lavatory—
shifting about in a chair, crossing and uncrossing of legs.
After a few moments of conversation he would nervously
rise and say "I've just forgotten something—I won't be a
minute." In the street he would expel his breath in a
swish of relief. He never went far but simply walked
around the block to still the unease. Everything always
seemed normal enough, to be sure. He would wonder
whether to phone Mahmoud Pacha about the defence
estimates or wait till tomorrow. . . . He had a pocketful
of peanuts which he cracked in his teeth and spat out,
feeling restless, unnerved, he did not know why. After a
walk he would come trotting back into the café, or barber's shop, beaming shyly, apologetically: an "Agency
Man"—our best-integrated modern type. There was nothing wrong with John except the level on which he had
chosen to live his life—but you could say the same about
his famous namesake, could you not?

I owe this faded photograph to him. (Much later he
is to be killed in the desert, in full possession of his im-
becility.) The mania to perpetuate, to record, to photo-

graph everything! I suppose this must come from the feeling that you don't enjoy anything fully, indeed are taking the bloom off it with every breath you draw. His
"files" were enormous, bulging with signed menus, bands
off memorial cigars, postage stamps, picture postcards. . . .
Later this proved useful, for somehow he had captured
some of Pursewarden's *obiter dicta.*

Farther to the east sits good old big-bellied Pombal,
under each eye a veritable diplomatic bag. Now here is
someone on whom one can really lavish a bit of affection.
His only preoccupation is with losing his job or being
impuissant: the national worry of every Frenchman since
Jean-Jacques. We quarrel a good deal, though amicably,
for we share his little flat which is always full of uncon-
sidered trifles and trifles more considered: *les femmes.*
But he is a good friend, a tender-hearted man, and really
loves women. When I have insomnia or am ill: *"Dis donc,
tu vas bien?"* Roughly, in the manner of a *bon copain.*
"Ecoute—tu veux une aspirine?" or else *"Ou bien—j'ai
une jaune amie dans ma chambre si tu veux. . . ."* (Not
a misprint: Pombal called all *poules* "jaunes femmes.")
*"Hein? Elle n'est pas mal—et c'est tout payé, mon cher.
Mais ce matin, moi je me sens un tout petit peu anti-
féministe—j'en ai marre, hein!"* Satiety fell upon him at
such times. *"Je deviens de plus en plus anthropophage,"*
he would say, rolling that comical eye. Also, his job worried him; his reputation was pretty bad, people were beginning to talk, especially after what he calls *"l'affaire
Sveva";* and yesterday the Consul-General walked in on
him while he was cleaning his shoes on the Chancery
curtains. . . . *"Monsieur Pombal! Je suis obligé de vous
faire quelques observations sur votre comportement of-
ficiel!"* Ouf! A reproof of the first grade. . . .

It explains why Pombal now sits heavily in the photograph, debating all this with a downcast expression. Lately we have become rather estranged because of Melissa.

He is angry that I have fallen in love with her, for she
is only a dancer in a night-club, and as such unworthy
of serious attention. There is also a question of snobbery,
for she is virtually living at the flat now and he feels
this to be demeaning: perhaps even diplomatically unwise.

"Love," says Toto, "is a liquid fossil"—a felicitous epi-
gram in all conscience. Now to fall in love with a banker's
wife, that would be forgivable, though ridiculous. . . .
Or would it? In Alexandria, it is only intrigue *per se*
which is wholeheartedly admired; but to fall in love
renders one ridiculous in society. (Pombal is a provincial
at heart.) I think of the tremendous repose and dignity
of Melissa in death, the slender body bandaged and
swaddled as if after some consuming and irreparable
accident. Well.

And Justine? On the day this picture was taken, Clea's
painting was interrupted by a kiss, as Balthazar says. How
am I to make this comprehensible when I can only visual-
ise these scenes with such difficulty? I must, it seems, try
to see a new Justine, a new Pursewarden, a new Clea. . . .
I mean that I must try and strip the opaque membrane
which stands between me and the reality of their actions
—and which I suppose is composed of my own limitations
of vision and temperament. My envy of Pursewarden, my
passion for Justine, my pity for Melissa. Distorting mirrors, all of them. . . . The way is through fact. I must
record what more I know and attempt to render it comprehensible or plausible to myself, if necessary, by an
act of the imagination. Or can facts be left to themselves?
Can you say "he fell in love" or "she fell in love" without
trying to divine its meaning, to set it in a context of
plausibilities? "That bitch," Pombal said once of Justine.
"Elle a l'air d'être bien chambrée!" And of Melissa, *"Une
pauvre petite poule quelconque. . . ."* He was right, perhaps, yet the true meaning of them resides elsewhere.

Here, I hope, on this scribbled paper which I have woven,
spider-like, from my inner life.

And Scobie? Well, he at least has the comprehensibility
of a diagram—plain as a national anthem. He looks particularly pleased this morning for he has recently achieved
apotheosis. After fourteen years as a Bimbashi in the
Egyptian Police, in what he calls "the evening of his life"
he has just been appointed to . . . I hardly dare to write
the words for I see his shudder of secrecy, can see his
glass eye rolling portentously round in its socket . . .
the Secret Service. He is not alive any more, thank God,
to read the words and tremble. Yes, the Ancient Mariner,
the secret pirate of Tatwig Street, the man himself. How
much the city misses him. (His use of the word "uncanny"!)

Elsewhere I have recounted how I answered a mysterious summons to find myself in a room of splendid proportions with my erstwhile pirate friend facing me across
a desk, whistling through his ill-fitting dentures. I think
his new assignment was as much a puzzle to him as it was
to me, his only confidant. It is true of course that he had
been long in Egypt and knew Arabic well; but his career
had been comparatively obscure. What could an intelligence agency hope to get out of him? More than this—
what did he hope to get out of me? I had already explained in detail that the little circle which met every
month to hear Balthazar expound the principles of the
Cabbala had no connection with espionage; it was simply a group of hermetic students drawn by their interest
in the matter of the lectures. Alexandria is a city of sects
—and the shallowest inquiry would have revealed to him
the existence of other groups akin to the one concerned
with the hermetic philosophy which Balthazar addressed:
Steinerites, Christian Scientists, Ouspenskyists, Adventists.
. . . What was it that riveted attention particularly on

Nessim, Justine, Balthazar, Capodistria, etc.? I could not tell, nor could he tell me.

"They're up to something," he repeated weakly. "Cairo says so." Apparently, he did not even know who his own masters were. His work was invisibly dictated by a scrambler telephone, as far as I could understand. But whatever "Cairo" was it paid him well: and if he had money to throw about on nonsensical investigations who was I to prevent him throwing it to me? I thought that my first few reports on Balthazar's Cabal would successfully damp all interest in it—but no. They wanted more and again more.

And this very morning, the old sailor in the photograph was celebrating his new post and the increase of salary it carried by having a haircut in the upper town, at the most expensive of shops—Mnemjian's.

I must not forget that this photograph also records a "Secret Rendezvous"; no wonder Scobie looks distraught. For he is surrounded by the very spies into whose activities it is necessary to inquire—not to mention a French diplomat who is widely rumoured to be head of the French *Deuxième*. . . .

Normally Scobie would have found this too expensive an establishment to patronise, living as he did upon a tiny nautical pension and his exiguous Police salary. But now he is a great man.

He did not dare even to wink at me in the mirror as the hunchback, tactful as a diplomat, elaborated a full-scale haircut out of mere air—for Scobie's glittering dome was very lightly fringed by the kind of fluff one sees on a duckling's bottom, and he had of late years sacrificed the torpedo beard of a wintry sparseness.

"I must say," he is about to say throatily (in the presence of so many suspicious people we "spies" must speak "normally") , "I must say, old man, you get a spiffing treatment here, Mnemjian really does understand." Clear-

ing his throat, "The whole art." His voice became por-
tentous in the presence of technical terms. "It's all a
question of Graduation—I had a close friend who told
me, a barber in Bond Street. You simply got to graduate."
Mnemjian thanked him in his pinched ventriloquist's
voice. "Not at all," said the old man largely. "I know
the wrinkles." *Now* he could wink at me. I winked back.
We both looked away.

Released, he stood up, his bones creaking, and set his
piratical jaw in a look of full-blooded health. He examined his reflection in the mirror with complacence.
"Yes," he said, giving a short authoritative nod, "it'll do."

"Electric friction for scalp, sir?"

Scobie shook his head masterfully as he placed his red
flowerpot *tarbush* on his skull. "It brings me out in goose
pimples," he said, and then with a smirk, "I'll nourish
what's left with *arak*." Mnemjian saluted this stroke of
wit with a little gesture. We were free.

But he was really not elated at all. He drooped as we
walked slowly down Chérif Pacha together towards the
Grande Corniche. He struck moodily at his knee with
the horsehair flyswatter, puffing moodily at his much-
mended briar. Thought. All he said with sudden petu-
lance was "I can't stand that Toto fellow. He's an open
nancy-boy. In my time we would have. . . ." He grumbled away into his skin for a long time and then petered
into silence again.

"What is it, Scobie?" I said.

"I'm troubled," he admitted. "Really troubled."

When he was in the upper town his walk and general
bearing had an artificial swagger—it suggested a White
Man at large, brooding upon problems peculiar to White
Men—their Burden as they call it. To judge by Scobie,
it hung heavy. His least gesture had a resounding artifici-
ality, tapping his knee, sucking his lip, falling into
brooding attitudes before shop windows. He gazed at the

people around him as if from stilts. These gestures reminded me in a feeble way of the heroes of domestic
English fiction who stand before a Tudor fireplace, im-
pressively whacking their riding-boots with a bull's pizzle.

By the time we had reached the outskirts of the Arab
quarter, however, he had all but shed these mannerisms.
He relaxed, tipped his *tarbush* up to mop his brow, and
gazed around him with the affection of long familiarity.
Here he belonged by adoption, here he was truly at
home. He would defiantly take a drink from the leaden
spout sticking out of a wall near the Goharri mosque (a
public drinking fountain) though the White Man in
him must have been aware that the water was far from
safe to drink. He would pick a stick of sugar-cane off
a stall as he passed, to gnaw it in the open street: or a
sweet locust-bean. Here, everywhere, the cries of the
open street greeted him and he responded radiantly.

"*Y'alla, effendi, Skob.*"

"*Naharak said, ya Skob.*"

"*Allah salimak.*"

He would sigh and say "Dear people"; and "How I
love the place—you have no idea!" dodging a liquid-eyed
camel as it humped down the narrow street threatening
to knock us down with its bulging sumpters of *bercim*,
the wild clover which is used as fodder.

"May your prosperity increase."

"By your leave, my mother."

"May your day be blessed."

"Favour me, O Sheik."

Scobie walked here with the ease of a man who has
come into his own estate, slowly, sumptuously, like an
Arab.

Today we sat together for a while in the shade of the
ancient mosque listening to the clicking of the palms and
the hooting of sea-going liners in the invisible basin
below.

"I've just seen a directive," said Scobie at last, in a sad withered little voice, "about what they call a Peddyrast. It's rather shaken me, old man. I don't mind admitting it—I didn't know the word. I had to look it up. At all costs, it says, we must exclude them. They are dangerous to the security of the net." I gave a laugh and for a moment the old man showed signs of wanting to respond with a weak giggle, but his depression overtook the impulse, to leave it buried, a small hollowness in those cherry-red cheeks. He puffed furiously at his pipe. "Peddyrast," he repeated with scorn, and groped for his matchbox.

"I don't think they quite understand at Home," he said sadly. "Now the Egyptians, they don't give a damn about a man if he has Tendencies—provided he's the Soul of Honour, like me." He meant it. "But now, old man, if I am to work for the . . . You Know What . . . I ought to tell them—what do you say?"

"Don't be a fool, Scobie."

"Well, I don't know," he said sadly, "I want to be honest with them. It isn't that I cause any harm. I suppose one shouldn't have Tendencies—any more than warts or a big nose. But what can I do?"

"Surely at your age very little?"

"Below the belt," said the pirate with a flash of his old form. "Dirty. Cruel. Narky." He looked archly at me round his pipe and suddenly cheered up. He began one of those delightful rambling monologues—another chapter in the saga he had composed around his oldest friend, the by now mythical Toby Mannering. "Toby was once Driven Medical by his excesses—I think I told you. No? Well, he was. Driven Medical." He was obviously quoting and with relish. "Lord how he used to go it as a young man. Stretched the limit in beating the bounds. Finally he found himself under the Doctor, had to wear an Appliance." His voice rose by nearly an octave. "He

went about in a leopard-skin muff when he had shore
leave until the Merchant Navy rose in a body. He was
put away for six months. Into a Home. They said, 'You'll
have to have Traction'—whatever that is. You could
hear him scream all over Tewkesbury, so Toby says.
They say they cure you but they don't. They didn't him
at any rate. After a bit, they sent him back. Couldn't do
anything with him. He was afflicted with Dumb Insolence, they said. Poor Toby!"

He had fallen effortlessly asleep now, leaning back
against the wall of the Mosque. ("A cat-nap," he used to
say, "but always woken by the ninth wave." For how
much longer, I wondered?) After a moment the ninth
wave brought him back through the surf of his dreams
to the beach. He gave a start and sat up. "What was I
saying? Yes, about Toby. His father was an M.P. Very
High Placed. Rich man's son. Toby tried to go into the
Church first. Said he felt The Call. I think it was just
the costume, myself—he was a great amateur theatrical,
was Toby. Then he lost his faith and slipped up and
had a tragedy. Got run in. He said the Devil prompted
him. 'See he doesn't do it again' says the Beak. 'Not on
Tooting Common, anyway.' They wanted to put him
in chokey—they said he had a rare disease—cornucopia
I think they called it. But luckily his father went to the
Prime Minister and had the whole thing hushed up. It
was lucky, old man, that at that time the whole Cabinet
had Tendencies too. It was uncanny. The Prime Minister,
even the Archbishop of Canterbury. They sympathised
with poor Toby. It was lucky for him. After that, he got
his master's ticket and put to sea."

Scobie was asleep once more, only to wake again after
a few seconds with a histrionic start. "It was old Toby,"
he went on, without a pause, though now crossing himself
devoutly and gulping, "who put me on to the Faith.
One night when we were on watch together on the

Meredith (fine old ship) he says to me: 'Scurvy, there's something you should know. Ever heard of the Virgin Mary?' I had of course, vaguely. I didn't know what her duties were, so to speak. . . ."

Once more he fell asleep and this time there issued from between his lips a small croaking snore. I carefully took his pipe from between his fingers and lit myself a cigarette. This appearance and disappearance into the simulacrum of death was somehow touching. These little visits paid to an eternity which he would soon be inhabiting, complete with the comfortable forms of Toby and Budgie, and a Virgin Mary with specified duties. . . . And to be obsessed by such problems at an age when, as far as I could judge, there was little beyond verbal boasting to make him a nuisance. (I was wrong—Scobie was indomitable.)

After a while he woke again from this deeper sleep, shook himself and rose, knuckling his eyes. We made our way together to the sordid purlieus of the town where he lived, in Tatwig Street, in a couple of tumble-down rooms. "And yet," he said once more, carrying his chain of thought perfectly, "it's all very well for you to say I shouldn't tell them. But I wonder." (Here he paused to inhale the draught of cooking Arab bread from the doorway of a shop and the old man exclaimed, "It smells like mother's lap!") His ambling walk kept pace with his deliberations. "You see the Egyptians are marvellous, old man. Kindly. They know me well. From some points of view, they might look like felons, old man, but felons in a state of grace, that's what I always say. They make allowances for each other. Why, Nimrod Pacha himself said to me the other day, 'Peddyrasty is one thing— *hashish* quite another.' He's serious, you see. Now I never smoke *hashish* when I'm on duty—that would be bad. Of course, from another point of view, the British couldn't do anything to a man with an O.B.E. like me.

But if the Gyppos once thought they were—well, critical about me—old man, I might lose both jobs, and both salaries. That's what troubles me."

We mounted the fly-blown staircase with its ragged rat-holes. "It smells a bit," he agreed, "but you get quite used to it. It's the mice. No, I'm not going to move. I've lived in this quarter ten years now—ten years. Everybody knows me and likes me. And besides, old Abdul is only round the corner."

He chuckled and stopped for breath on the first landing, taking off his flowerpot the better to mop his brow. Then he hung downwards, sagging as he always did when he was thinking seriously as if the very weight of the thought itself bore down upon him. He sighed. "The thing," he said slowly, and with the air of a man who wishes at all costs to be explicit, to formulate an idea as clearly as lies within his power, "the thing is about Tendencies—you only realize it when you're not a hot-blooded young sprig any more." He sighed again. "It's the lack of *tenderness*, old man. It all depends on cunning somehow, you get lonely. Now Abdul is a true friend." He chuckled and cheered up once more. "I call him the Bul Bul Emir. I set him up in his business, just out of friendly affection. Bought him everything: his shop, his little wife. Never laid a finger on him nor ever could, because I love the man. I'm glad I did now, because though I'm getting on, I still have a true friend. I pop in every day to see them. It's uncanny how happy it makes me. I really do enjoy their happiness, old man. They are like son and daughter to me, the poor perishing coons. I can't hardly bear to hear them quarrel. It makes me anxious about their kids. I think Abdul is jealous of her, and not without cause, mark you. She looks flirty to me. But then, sex is so powerful in this heat—a spoon-ful goes a long way as we used to say about rum in the Merchant Navy. You lie and dream about it like ice-

cream, sex, not rum. And these Moslem girls—old boy—
they circumcise them. It's cruel. Really cruel. It only
makes them harp on the subject. I tried to get her to learn
knitting or crewel-work, but she's so stupid she didn't
understand. They made a joke of it. Not that I mind. I
was only trying to help. Two hundred pounds it took
me to set Abdul up—all my savings. But he's doing well
now—yes, very well."

The monologue had had the effect of allowing him to
muster his energies for the final assault. We addressed
the last ten stairs at a comfortable pace and Scobie unlocked the door of his rooms. Originally he had only been
able to rent one—but with his new salary he had rented
the whole shabby floor.

The largest was the old Arab room which served as
a bedroom and reception-room in one. It was furnished
by an uncomfortable looking truckle bed and an old-
fashioned cake-stand. A few joss-sticks, a Police calendar,
and Clea's as yet unfinished portrait of the pirate stood
upon the crumbling mantelpiece. Scobie switched on a
single dusty electric light bulb—a recent innovation of
which he was extremely proud ("Paraffin gets in the
food") —and looked round him with unaffected pleasure.
Then he tiptoed to the far corner. In the gloom I had
at first overlooked the room's other occupant: a brilliant
green Amazonian parrot in a brass cage. It was at present shrouded in a dark cloth, and this the old man
now removed with a faintly defensive air.

"I was telling you about Toby," he said, "because last
week he came through Alex on the Yokohama run. I
got this from him—he had to sell—the damn bird caused
such a riot. It's a brilliant conversationalist, aren't you,
Ron, eh? Crisp as a fart, aren't you?" The parrot gave
a low whistle and ducked. "That's the boy," said Scobie
with approval and turning to me added, "I got Ron for

a very keen price, yes, a very keen price. Shall I tell you why?"

Suddenly, inexplicably, he doubled up with laughter, nearly joining nose to knee and whizzing soundlessly like a small human top, to emerge at last with an equally soundless slap on his own thigh—a sudden paroxysm. "You'd never imagine the row Ron caused," he said. "Toby brought the bird ashore. He knew it could talk, but not Arabic. By God. We were sitting at a café yarning (I haven't seen Toby for five whole years) when Ron suddenly started. In Arabic. You know, he recited the Kalima, a very sacred, not to mention holy text from the Koran. The Kalima. And at every other word, he gives a fart, didn't you Ron?" The parrot agreed with another whistle. "It's so sacred, the Kalima," explained Scobie gravely, "that the next thing was a raging crowd round us. It was lucky I knew what was going on. I knew that if a non-Moslem was caught reciting this particular text he was liable to Instant Circumcision!" His eye flashed. "It was a pretty poor outlook for Toby to be circumcised like that while one was taking shore leave and I was worried. (I'm circumcised already.) However, my presence of mind didn't desert me. He wanted to punch a few heads, but I restrained him. I was in Police uniform you see, and that made it easier. I made a little speech to the crowd saying that I was going to take the infidel and his perishing bird into chokey to hand them over to the Parquet. That satisfied them. But there was no way of silencing Ron, even under his little veil, was there, Ron? The little bastard recited the Kalima all the way back here. We had to run for it. My word, what an experience!"

He was changing out of his Police rig as he talked, placing his *tarbush* on the rusty iron nail above his bed, above the crucifix in the little alcove where a stone jar of drinking-water also stood. He put on a frayed old blazer with tin buttons, and still mopping his head went on: "I must say—it was wonderful to see old Toby again after so long. He had to sell the bird, of course, after such a riot. Didn't dare go through the dock area again with it. But now I'm doubtful, for I daren't take it out of the room hardly for fear of what more it knows." He sighed. "Another good thing," he went on, "was the recipe Toby brought for Mock Whisky—ever heard of it? Nor had I. Better than Scotch and dirt cheap, old man. From now on I'm going to brew all my own drinks, thanks to Toby. Here. Look at this." He indicated a grubby bottle full of some fiery-looking liquid. "It's home-made beer," he said, "and jolly good too. I made three, but the other two exploded. I'm going to call it Plaza beer."

"Why?" I asked. "Are you going to sell it?"

"Good Lord, no!" said Scobie. "Just for home use." He rubbed his stomach reflectively and licked his lips. "Try a glass," he said.

"No thanks."

The old man now consulted a huge watch and pursed his lips. "In a little while I must say an Ave Maria. I'll have to push you out, old man. But just let's have a look and see how the Mock Whisky is getting on for a moment, shall we?"

I was most curious to see how he was conducting these new experiments and willingly followed him out on to the landing again and into the shabby alcove which now housed a gaunt galvanised iron bath which he must have bought specially for these illicit purposes. It stood under a grimy closet window, and the shelves around it were crowded with the impedimenta of the new trade—a dozen empty beer bottles, two broken, and the huge chamberpot which Scobie always called "the Heirloom"; not to mention a tattered beach umbrella and a pair of goloshes. "What part do these play?" I could not help asking,

indicating the latter. "Do you tread the grapes or
potatoes in them?"

Scobie took on an old-maidish, squinting-down-the-
nose expression which always meant that levity on the
topic under discussion was out of place. He listened
keenly for a moment, as if to sounds of fermentation.
Then he got down on one shaky knee and regarded the
contents of the bath with a doubtful but intense eye.
His glass eye gave him a more than mechanical expression
as it stared into the rather tired-looking mixture with
which the bath was brimming. He sniffed dispassionately and tutted once before rising again with creaking
joints. "It doesn't look as good as I hoped," he admitted.
"But give it time, it has to be given time." He tried
some on his finger and rolled his glass eye. "It seems
to have gone a bit turpid," he admitted. "As if someone
had peed in it." As Abdul and himself shared the only
key to this illicit still I was able to look innocent.

"Do you want to try it?" he asked doubtfully.

"Thank you, Scobie—no."

"Ah, well," he said philosophically, "maybe the copper
sulphate wasn't fresh. I had to order the rhubarb from
Blighty. Forty pounds. *That* looked pretty tired when it
got here, I don't mind telling you. But I know the proportions are right because I went into it all thoroughly
with young Toby before he left. It needs time, that's
what it needs."

And made buoyant once more by the hope, he led the
way back into the bedroom, whistling under his breath a
few staves of the famous song which he only sang aloud
when he was drunk on brandy. It went something like
this:

> *"I want*
> *Someone to match my fancy*

> *I want*
>   *Someone to match my style*
> *I've been good for an awful long while*
> *Now I'll take her in my arms*
> *Tum ti Tum ti charms. . . ."*

Somewhere here the melody fell down a cliff and was
lost to sight, though Scobie hummed out the stave
and beat time with his finger.

He was sitting down on the bed now and staring at
his shabby shoes. "Are you going to the party Nessim's
giving for Mountolive tonight?"—"I suppose so," I said.
He sniffed loudly. "I'm not invited. At the Yacht Club,
isn't it?"

"Yes."

"He is Sir David now, isn't he? I saw it in the paper
last week. Young to be a lord, isn't he? I was in charge
of the Police Guard of Honour when he arrived. They
all played out of tune but he didn't notice anything,
thank God!"

"Not so young."

"And to be Minister?"

"I suppose he's in his late forties?"

Abruptly, without apparent premeditation (though
he closed his eyes fast as if to shut the subject away out
of sight forever) Scobie lay back on the bed, hands behind his head, and said:

"Before you go, there's a small confession I'd like to
make to you, old man. Right?"

I sat down on the uncomfortable chair and nodded.
"Right," he said emphatically and drew a breath. "Well
then: sometimes at the full moon, *I'm Took*. I come
under *An Influence*."

This was on the face of it a somewhat puzzling departure from accepted form, for the old man looked

quite disturbed by his own revelation. He gobbled for
a moment and then went on in a small humbled voice
devoid of his customary swagger. "I don't know what
comes over me." I did not quite understand all this. "Do
you mean you walk in your sleep or what?" He shook
his head and gulped again. "Do you turn into a werewolf,
Scobie?" Once more he shook his head like a child upon
the point of tears. "I slip on female duds and my Dolly
Varden," he said, and opened his eyes fully to stare
pathetically at me.

"You *what?*" I said.

To my intense surprise he rose now and walked stiffly
to a cupboard which he unlocked. Inside, hanging up,
moth-eaten and unbrushed, was a suit of female clothes
of ancient cut, and on a nail beside it a greasy old cloche
hat which I took to be the so-called "Dolly Varden." A
pair of antediluvian court shoes with very high heels
and long pointed toes completed this staggering outfit.
He did not know how quite to respond to the laugh which
I was now compelled to utter. He gave a weak giggle.
"It's silly, isn't it?" he said, still hovering somewhere on
the edge of tears despite his smiling face, and still by his
tone inviting sympathy in misfortune. "I don't know
what comes over me. And yet, you know, it's always the
old thrill. . . ."

A sudden and characteristic change of mood came
over him at the words: his disharmony, his discomfiture
gave place to a new jauntiness. His look became arch
now, not wistful, and crossing to the mirror before my
astonished eyes, he placed the hat upon his bald head.
In a second he replaced his own image with that of a
little old tart, button-eyed and razor-nosed—a tart of the
Waterloo Bridge epoch, a veritable Tuppenny Upright.
Laughter and astonishment packed themselves into a
huge parcel inside me, neither finding expression. "For

God's sake!" I said at last. "You don't go around like that, do you, Scobie?"

"Only," said Scobie, sitting helplessly down on the bed again and relapsing into a gloom which gave his funny little face an even more comical expression (he still wore the Dolly Varden), "only when the Influence comes over me. When I'm not fully Answerable, old man."

He sat there looking crushed. I gave a low whistle of surprise which the parrot immediately copied. This was indeed serious. I understood now why the deliberations which had consumed him all morning had been so full of heart-searching. Obviously if one went around in a rig like that in the Arab quarter. . . . He must have been following my train of thought, for he said, "It's only sometimes when the Fleet's in." Then he went on with a touch of self-righteousness: "Of course, if there was ever any trouble, I'd say I was in disguise. I am a police-man when you come to think of it. After all, even Lawrence of Arabia wore a nightshirt, didn't he?" I nodded. "But not a Dolly Varden," I said. "You must admit, Scobie, it's most original . . ." and here the laughter overtook me.

Scobie watched me laugh, still sitting on the bed in that fantastic headpiece. "Take it off!" I implored. He looked serious and preoccupied now, but made no motion. "Now you know all," he said. "The best and the worst in the old skipper. Now what I was going to—"

At this moment there came a knock at the landing door. With surprising presence of mind Scobie leaped spryly into the cupboard, locking himself noisily in. I went to the door. On the landing stood a servant with a pitcher full of some liquid which he said was for the Effendi Skob. I took it from him and got rid of him, before returning to the room and shouting to the old man who emerged once more—now completely himself, bareheaded and blazered.

"That was a near shave," he breathed. "What was it?"
I indicated the pitcher. "Oh, that—it's for the Mock
Whisky. Every three hours."

"Well," I said at last, still struggling with these new
and indigestible revelations of temperament, "I must be
going." I was still hovering explosively between amazement and laughter at the thought of Scobie's second
life at full moon—how had he managed to avoid a scandal
all these years?—when he said: "Just a minute old man. I
only told you all this because I want you to do me a
favour." His false eye rolled around earnestly now under
the pressure of thought. He sagged again. "A thing like
that could do me Untold Harm," he said, "Untold
Harm, old man."

"I should think it could."

"Old man," said Scobie, "I want you to confiscate my
duds. It's the only way of controlling the Influence."

"Confiscate them?"

"Take them away. Lock them up. It'll save me, old
man. I know it will. The whim is too strong for me
otherwise, when it comes."

"All right," I said.

"God bless you, son."

Together we wrapped his full-moon regalia in some
newspapers and tied the bundle up with string. His
relief was tempered with doubt. "You won't lose them?"
he said anxiously.

"Give them to me," I said firmly and he handed me
the parcel meekly. As I went down the stairs he called
after me to express relief and gratitude, adding the words:
"I'll say a little prayer for you, son." I walked back
slowly through the dock-area with the parcel under my
arm, wondering whether I would ever dare to confide this
wonderful story to someone worth sharing it with.

The warships turned in their inky reflections—the

forest of masts and rigging in the Commercial Port
swayed softly among the mirror-images of the water:
somewhere a ship's radio was blaring out the latest jazz-
hit to reach Alexandria:

> Old Tiresias
> No-one half so breezy as,
> Half so free and easy as
> Old Tiresias.

o   o   o   o   o

3.

THE sinking sun which had emptied the harbour
roads of all but the black silhouettes of the foreign warships had nevertheless left a flickering greyness—the play
of light without colour or resonance upon the surface
of a sea still dappled with sails. Dinghies racing for home
moved about the floor of the inner harbour, scuttling
in and out among the ships like mice among the great
boots of primitive cottagers. The sprouting tier of guns
on the *Jean Bart* moved slowly—tilted—and then settled
back into brooding stillness, aimed at the rosy heart of
the city whose highest minarets still gleamed gold in the
last rays of the sunset. The flocks of spiring pigeons
glittered like confetti as they turned their wings to the
light. (Fine writing!)
  But the great panels of the brass-framed windows in
the Yacht Club blazed like diamonds, throwing a brilliant
light upon the snowy tables with their food, setting fire
to the glasses and jewellery and eyes in a last uneasy

conflagration before the heavy curtains would be drawn
and the faces which had gathered to greet Mountolive
took on the warm pallors of candlelight.

The triumphs of polity, the resources of tact, the
warmth, the patience. . . . Profligacy and sentimentality
. . . killing love by taking things easy . . . sleeping out
a chagrin. . . . This was Alexandria, the unconsciously
poetical mother-city exemplified in the names and faces
which made up her history. Listen.

Tony Umbada, Baldassaro Trivizani, Claude Amaril,
Paul Capodistria, Dmitri Randidi, Onouphrios Papas,
Count Banubula, Jacques de Guéry, Athena Trasha,
Djamboulat Bey, Delphine de Francueil, General Cer-
voni, Ahmed Hassan Pacha, Pozzo di Borgo, Pierre Balbz,
Gaston Phipps, Haddad Fahmy Amin, Mehmet Adm,
Wilmot Pierrefeu, Toto de Brunel, Colonel Neguib,
Dante Borromeo, Benedict Dangeau, Pia dei Tolomei,
Gilda Ambron. . . . The poetry and history of commerce,
the rhyme-schemes of the Levant which had swallowed
Venice and Genoa. (Names which the passer-by may
one day read upon the tombs in the cemetery.)

The conversation rose in a steamy cloud to envelop
Mountolive whose personal triumph it was and who
stood talking to Nessim, his host, with the gentle-man-
nered expression on his face which, like a lens, betrayed
all the stylised diffidence of his perfect breeding. The
two men indeed were much alike; only Nessim's darkness
was smooth, cleanly surfaced, and his eyes and hands
restless. Despite a difference of age they were well matched
—even to the tastes they shared, which the years had
done nothing to diminish though they had hardly corresponded directly all the time Mountolive had been
away from Egypt. It had always been to Leila that he
wrote, not her sons. Nevertheless, once he had returned, they were much together and found they had as

much to discuss as ever in the past. You would hear the
sharp pang of their tennis racquets every spring afternoon on the Legation court at an hour when everyone
normally slept. They rode in the desert together or sat
for hours side by side, studying the stars, at the telescope
which Justine had had installed in the Summer Palace.
They painted and shot in company. Indeed, since Mountolive's return they had become once more almost in-
separables. Tonight the soft light touched them both
with an equal distinction, yet softly enough to disguise
the white hairs at Mountolive's temples and the crow's-
feet around those thoughtful arbitrator's eyes. By candlelight the two men seemed exactly of an age if indeed
not of the same family.

A thousand faces whose reverberating expressions I do
not understand ("We are all racing under sealed handi-
caps," says a character in Pursewarden's book), and out
of them all there is one only I am burning to see, the
black stern face of Justine. I must learn to see even
myself in a new context, after reading those cold cruel
words of Balthazar. How does a man look when he is
"in love"? (The words in English should be uttered in
a low bleating tone.) *Peccavi!* Imbecile! There I stand in
my only decent suit, whose kneecaps are bagged and
shiny with age, gazing fondly and short-sightedly around
me for a glimpse of the woman who. . . . What does it
matter? I do not need a Keats to photograph me. I do
not suppose I am uglier than anyone else or less pleasant;
and certainly my vanity is of a very general order—for
how have I never stopped to ask myself for a second why
Justine should turn aside to bestow her favours on me?

What could I give her that she could not get elsewhere?
Does she want my bookish talk and amateurish love-
making—she with the whole bargain-basement of male
Alexandria in her grasp? "A decoy!" I find this very

wounding to understand, to swallow, yet it has all the
authority of curt fact. Moreover, it explains several things
which have been for me up to now inexplicable—such
as the legacy Pursewarden left me. It was his guilt, I
think, for what he knew Justine was doing to Melissa:
in "loving" me. While she, for her part, was simply protecting him against the possible power of Nessim (how
gentle and calm he looks in the candlelight). He once
said with a small sigh: "Nothing is easier to arrange in
our city than a death or a disappearance."

A thousand conversations, seeking out for each other
like the tap-roots of trees for moisture—the hidden meaning of lives disguised in brilliant smiles, in hands pressed
upon the eyes, in malice, in fevers and contents. (Justine
now breakfasted silently surrounded by tall black footmen, and dined by candlelight in brilliant company. She
had started from nothing—from the open street—and was
now married to the city's handsomest banker. How had
all this come about? You would never be able to tell
by watching that dark, graceful form with its untamed
glances, the smile of the magnificent white teeth. . . .)
Yet one trite conversation can contain the germ of a
whole life. Balthazar, for example, meeting Clea against
a red brocade curtain, holding a glass of Pernod, could
say: "Clea, I have something to tell you"; taking in as
he spoke the warm gold of her hair and a skin honeyed
almost to the tone of burnt sugar by sea-bathing in the
warm spring sunshine. "What?" Her candid eyes were
as blue as corn-flowers and set in her head like precision-
made objects of beauty—the life-work of a jeweller.
"Speak, my dear." Black head of hair (he dyed it),
lowered voice set in its customary sardonic croak, Balthazar said: "Your father came to see me. He is worried
about an illicit relationship you are supposed to have
formed with another woman. Wait—don't speak, and

don't look hurt." For Clea looked now as if he were pressing upon a bruise, the sad grave mouth set in a childish expresion, imploring no further penetration. "He says you are an innocent, a goose, and that Alexandria does not permit innocent people to. . . ."

"Please, Balthazar."

"I would not have spoken had I not been impressed by his genuine anguish—not about scandal: who cares for gossip? But he was worried lest you should be hurt."

In a small compressed voice, like some packaged thought squeezed to a hundredth of its size by machinery, Clea said:

"I have not been alone with Justine for a year. Do you understand? It ended when the painting ended. If you wish us to be friends you will never refer to this subject again," smiling a little tremulously, for in the same breath Justine came sailing down upon them, smiling warmly, radiantly. (It is quite possible to love those whom you most wound.) She passed, turning in the candlelight of the room like some great sea-bird, and came at last to where I was standing. "I cannot come tonight," she whispered. "Nessim wants me to stay at home." I can feel still the uncomprehending weight of my disappointment at the words. "You must," I muttered. Should I have known that not ten minutes before she had said to Nessim, knowing he hated bridge: "Darling, can I go and play bridge with the Cervonis—do you need the car?" It must have been one of those rare evenings when Pursewarden consented to meet her out in the desert—meetings to which she went unerringly, like a sleepwalker. Why? *Why?*

Balthazar at this moment is saying: "Your father said: 'I cannot bear to watch it, and I do not know what to do. It is like watching a small child skipping near a powerful piece of unprotected machinery.' " Tears came into Clea's eyes and slowly vanished again as she sipped

her drink. "It is over," she said, turning her back upon
the subject and upon Balthazar in one and the same
motion. She turned her sullen mouth now to the discussion of meaningless matters with Count Banubula,
who bowed and swung as gallantly as Scobie's green
parrot ducking on its perch. She was pleased to see
that her beauty had a direct, clearly discernible effect
upon him, like a shower of golden arrows. Presently,
Justine herself passed again, and in passing caught Clea's
wrist. "How is it?" said Clea, in the manner of one
who asks after a sick child. Justine gave the shadow of
a grimace and whispered dramatically: "Oh, Clea—it
is very bad. What a terrible mistake. Nessim is wonderful
—I should never have done it. *I am followed everywhere.*"
They stared at each other sympathetically for a long
moment. It was their first encounter for months. (That
afternoon, Pursewarden had written: "A few hasty and
not entirely unloving words from my sickbed about this
evening." He was not in bed but sitting at a café on the
sea-front, smiling as he wrote.) Messages spoken and
unspoken, crossing and interlacing, carrying the currents
of our lives, the fears, dissimulations, the griefs. Justine
was speaking now about her marriage which still exhi-
bited to the outer world a clearness of shape and context
—the plaster cast of a perfection which I myself had
envied when first I met them both. "The marriage of
true minds," I thought; but where is the "magnificent
two-headed animal" to be found? When she first became
aware of the terrible jealousy of Nessim, the jealousy of
the spiritually impotent man, she had been appalled and
terrified. She had fallen by mistake into a trap. (All
this, like the fever-chart of a stricken patient, Clea
watched, purely out of friendship with no desire to renew
the love she felt for this dispersed unself-comprehending
Jewess.)

Justine put the matter to herself another way, a much

more primitive way, by thinking: up to now she had always judged her men by their smell! This was the first time ever that she had neglected to consult the sense. And Nessim had the odourless purity of the desert airs, the desert in summer, unconfiding and dry. Pure. How she hated purity! Afterwards? Yes, she was revolted by the little gold cross which nestled in the hair of his chest. He was a Copt—a Christian. This is the way women work in the privacy of their own minds. Yet out of shame at such thoughts she became doubly passionate and attentive to her husband, though even between kisses, in the depths of her mind, she longed only for the calm and peace of widowhood! Am I imagining this? I do not think so.

How had all this come about? To understand it is necessary to work backwards, through the great Interlinear which Balthazar has constructed around my manuscript, towards that point in time where the portrait which Clea was painting was interrupted by a kiss. It is strange to look at it now, the portrait, standing unfinished on the old-fashioned mantelpiece of the island house. "An idea had just come into her mind, but had not yet reached the lips." And then, softly, her lips fell where the painter's wet brush should have fallen. Kisses and brush-strokes—I should be writing of poor Melissa!

How distasteful all this subject-matter is—what Pursewarden has called "the insipid kiss of familiars"; and how innocent! The black gloves she wore in the portrait left a small open space when they were buttoned up— the shape of a heart. And that innocent, ridiculous kiss only spoke admiration and pity for the things Justine was telling her about the loss of her child—the daughter which had been stolen from her while it was playing on the river-bank. "Her wrists, her small wrists. If you could have seen how beautiful and tame she was, a squirrel." In the hoarseness of the tone, in the sad eyes and the down-pointed mouth with a comma in each cheek. And holding out a hand with finger and thumb joined to describe the circuit of those small wrists. Clea took and kissed the heart in the black glove. She was really kissing the child, the mother. Out of this terrible sympathy her innocence projected the consuming shape of a sterile love. But I am going too fast. Moreover, how am I to make comprehensible scenes which I myself see only with such difficulty—these two women, the blonde and the bronze in a darkening studio at Saint Saba, among the rags and the paintpots and the warm gallery of portraits which lined the walls, Balthazar, Da Capo, even Nessim himself, Clea's dearest friend? It is hard to compose them in a stable colour so that the outlines are not blurred.

Justine at this time . . . coming from nowhere, she had done one trick regarded as clever by the provincials of Alexandria. She had married Arnauti, a foreigner, only to earn the contempt of society by letting him in the end divorce and abandon her. Of the fate of the child, few people knew or cared. She was not "in society" as the saying goes. . . . Poverty forced her to do a little modelling at so many piastres an hour for the art-students of the Atelier. Clea, who knew her only by hearsay, passed through the long gallery one day when she was posing, and struck by the dark Alexandrian beauty of her face, engaged her for a portrait. That was how those long conversations grew up in the silences of the painter; for Clea liked her subjects to talk freely, provided they stayed still. It gave a submarine life to their features, and filled their looks with unconscious interpretations of thought—the true beauty in otherwise dead flesh.

Clea's generous innocence—it needed something like that to see the emptiness in which Justine lived with her particular sorrows—factual illustrations merely of a mind at odds with itself: for we create our own misfortunes

and they bear our own fingerprints. The gesture itself
was simply a clumsy attempt to appropriate the mystery
of true experience, true suffering—as by touching a holy
man the supplicant hopes for a transference of the grace
he lacks. The kiss did not for a moment expect itself to
be answered by another—to copy itself like the reflections
of a moth in a looking-glass. That would have been too
expensive a gesture had it been premeditated. So it
proved! Clea's own body simply struggled to disengage
itself from the wrappings of its innocence as a baby or a
statue struggles for life under the fingers or forceps of
its author. Her bankruptcy was one of extreme youth,
Justine's ageless; her innocence was as defenceless as
memory itself. Seeking and admiring only the composure
of Justine's sorrow she found herself left with all the
bitter lye of an uninvited love.

She was "white of heart," in the expressive Arabic
phrase, and painting the darkness of Justine's head and
shoulders she suddenly felt as if, stroke by stroke, the
brush itself had begun to imitate caresses she had neither
foreseen nor even thought to permit. As she listened to
that strong deep voice recounting these misfortunes, so
desirable in that they belonged to the active living world
of experience, she caught her breath between her teeth,
trying now to think only of the unconscious signs of good
breeding in her subject; hands still in the lap, voice low,
the reserve which delineates true power. Yet even she,
from her inexperience, could do little but pity Justine
when she said things like "I am not much good, you
know. I can only inflict sadness, Arnauti used to say. He
brought me to my senses and taught me that nothing
matters except pleasure—which is the opposite of happiness, its tragic part, I expect." Clea was touched by
this because it seemed clear to her that Justine had never
really experienced pleasure—one has to be generous for
that. Egotism is a fortress in which the *conscience de soi-*

même, like a corrosive, eats away everything. True pleasure is in giving, surely.

"As for Arnauti, he nearly drove me mad with his inquisitions. What I lost as a wife I gained as a patient—his interest in what he called 'my case' outweighed any love he might have had for me. And then losing the child made me hate him where before I had only seen a rather sensitive and kindly man. You have probably read his book *Moeurs.* Much of it is invented—mostly to satisfy his own vanity and get his own back on me for the way I wounded his pride in refusing to be 'cured'—so-called. You can't put a soul into splints. If you say to a Frenchman 'I can't make love to you unless I imagine a palm-tree,' he will go out and cut down the nearest palm-tree."

Clea was too noble to love otherwise than passionately; and yet at the same time quite capable of loving someone to whom she spoke only once a year. The deep still river of her heart hoarded its images, ever reflecting them in the racing current, letting them sink deeper into memory than most of us can. Real innocence can do nothing that is trivial, and when it is allied to generosity of heart, the combination makes it the most vulnerable of qualities under heaven.

In this sudden self-consuming experience, comparable in its tension and ardour to those ridiculous passions which schoolgirls have so often for their mistresses—yet touched in by the fierce mature lines of nature (the demonic line-drawings of an expert love which Justine could always oppose as a response to those who faced her)—she felt really the growing-pains of old age: her flesh and spirit quailing before demands which it knows it cannot meet, which will tear it to rags. Inside herself she had the first stirrings of a sensation new to her: the sensation of a yolk inside her separating from the egg. These are the strange ways in which people grow up.

Poor dear, she was to go through the same ridiculous contortions as the rest of us—feeling her body like a bed of quicklime clumsily slaked to burn away the corpse of the criminal it covered. The world of secret meetings, of impulses that brand one like an iron, of doubts—this suddenly descended upon her. So great was her confusion of mind that she would sit and stare at the metamorphosed Justine and try to remember what she really looked like on the other side of the transforming membrane, the cataract with which Aphrodite seals up the sick eyes of lovers, the thick, opaque form of a sacred sightlessness.

She would be in a fever all day until the appointed moment when her model met her. At four she stood before the closed door of the studio, seeing clearly through it to the corner where Justine already sat, turning over the pages of a *Vogue* and smoking as she waited, legs crossed. The idea crossed her mind. "I pray to God she has not come, is ill, has gone away. How eagerly I would welcome indifference!" Surprised too, for these disgusts came from precisely the same quarters as the desire to hear once more that hoarse noble voice—they too arose only from the expectation of seeing her beloved once more. These polarities of feeling bewildered and frightened her by their suddenness.

Then sometimes she wished to go away simply in order to belong more fully to her familiar! Poor fool, she was not spared anything in the long catalogue of self-deceptions which constitute a love affair. She tried to fall back on other pleasures, to find that none existed. She knew that the heart wearies of monotony, that habit and despair are the bedfellows of love, and she waited patiently, as a very old woman might, for the flesh to outgrow its promptings, to deliver itself from an attachment which she now recognised was not of her seeking. Waited in vain. Each day she plunged deeper. Yet all this, at any

rate, performed one valuable service for her, proving
that relationships like these did not answer the needs of
her nature. Just as a man knows inside himself from the
first hour that he has married the wrong woman but
that there is nothing to be done about it. She knew she
was a woman at last and belonged to men—and this gave
her misery a fugitive relief.

But the distortions of reality were deeply interesting
to someone who recognised that for the artist in herself
some confusions of sensibility were valuable. "Walking
towards the studio she would suddenly feel herself becoming breathlessly insubstantial, as if she were a figure
painted on canvas. Her breathing became painful. Then
after a moment she was overtaken by a feeling of happiness and well-being so intense that she seemed to have
become weightless. Only the weight of her shoes, it
seemed, held her to the ground. At any moment she might
fly off the earth's surface, breaking through the membrane of gravity, unable to stop. This feeling was so
piercing that she had to stop and hold on to the nearest
wall and then to walk along it bent double like someone on the deck of a liner in a hurricane. This was itself
succeeded by other disagreeable sensations—as of a hot
clamp round her skull, pressing it, of the beating of
wings in her ears. Half-dreaming in bed, suddenly horns
rammed downward into her brain, impaling her mind;
in a brazen red glare she saw the bloodshot eyes of the
mithraic animal. It was a cool night with soft pockets of
chemical light in the Arab town. The Ginks were abroad
with their long oiled plaits and tinselled clothes; the
faces of black angels; the men-women of the suburbs."
(I copy these words from the diary of a female mental
patient who came under Balthazar's professional care—
a nervous breakdown due to "love"—requited or unre-
quited who can say? Does it matter? The aetiology of
love and madness are identical except in degree, and

this passage could serve not only for Clea but indeed for all of us.

But it was not only of the past that Justine spoke but of a present which was weighing upon her full of decisions which must be taken. In a sense, everything that Clea felt was at this time meaningless to her. As a prostitute may be unaware that her client is a poet who will immortalize her in a sonnet she will never read, so Justine in pursuing these deeper sexual pleasures was unaware that they would mark Clea for years: enfeeble her in her power of giving undivided love—what she was most designed to give by temperament. Her youth, you see. And yet the wretched creature meant no harm. She was simply a victim of that Oriental desire to please, to make this golden friend of hers free of treasures which her own experience had gathered and which, in sum, were as yet meaningless to her. She gave everything, knowing the value of nothing, a true *parvenue* of the soul. To love (from any quarter) she could respond, but only with the worn felicities of friendship. Her body really meant nothing to her. It was a dupe. Her modesty was supreme. This sort of giving is really shocking because it is as simple as an Arab, without precociousness, unrefined as a drinking habit among peasants. It was born long before the idea of love was formed in that fragmented psyche of European man—the knowledge (or invention) of which was to make him the most vulnerable of creatures in the scale of being, subject to hungers which could only be killed by satiety, but never satisfied; which nourished a literature of affectation whose subject-matter would otherwise have belonged to religion—its true sphere of operation. How does one say these things?

Nor, in another scale of reference, is it of the slightest importance—that a woman disoriented by the vagaries of her feelings, tormented, inundated by frightening aspects of her own unrecognised selves, should like a soldier

afraid of death, throw herself into the heart of the *mêlée*
to wound those whom truly she most loved and most
admired—Clea, myself, lastly Nessim. Some people are
born to bring good and evil in greater measure than the
rest of us—the unconscious carriers of diseases they cannot cure. I think perhaps we must study them, for it is
possible that they promote creation in the very degree
of the apparent corruption and confusion they spread or
seek. I dare not say even now that she was stupid or unfeeling; only that she could not recognise what passed
within herself ("the camera obscura of the heart"),
could not put a precise frame around the frightening
image of her own meaninglessness in the world of
ordinary action. The sort of abyss which seemed to lie
around her was composed of one quality—a failure of
value, a failure to attach meaning which kills joy—which
is itself only the internal morality of a soul which has
discovered the royal road to happiness, whose nakedness
does not shame itself. It is easy for me to criticise now
that I see a little further into the truth of her predica-
ment and my own. She must, I know, have been bitterly
ashamed of the trick she was playing on me and the
danger into which she put me. Once at the Café El Bab
where we were sitting over an *arak*, talking, she burst
into tears and kissed my hands, saying: "You are a good
man, really a good man. And I am so sorry." For what?
For her tears? I had been speaking about Goethe. Fool!
Imbecile! I thought I had perhaps moved her by the
sensibility with which I expressed myself. I gave her
presents. So had Clea, so did Clea now: and the strange
thing was that for the first time her taste in choosing
objects of *vertu* deserted this most gifted and sensitive
of painters. Ear-rings and brooches of a commonness
which was truly Alexandrian! I am at a loss to understand this phenomenon, unless to love is to become be-
sotted. . . .

But then I don't know; I am reminded of Balthazar's dry marginal comment on the matter. "One is apt," he writes, "to take a high moral tone about these things— but in fact, who will criticise himself for reaching up to pluck an apple lying ripe upon a sun-warmed wall? Most women of Justine's temperament and background would not have the courage to imitate her even if they were free to do so. Is it more or less expensive to the spirit to endure dreams and Petit Mal so that the physician will always find a hot forehead and a guilty air? I don't know. It is hard to isolate a moral quality in the free act. And then again, all love-making to one less instructed than oneself has the added delicious thrill which comes from the consciousness of perverting, of pulling them down into the mud from which passions rise—together with poems and theories of God. It is wiser perhaps not to make a judgment."

But outside all this, in the sphere of daily life, there were problems about which Justine herself needed re-assurance. "I am astonished and a little horrified that Nessim, whom I hardly know, has asked to marry me. Am I to laugh, dearest Clea, or be ashamed, or both?" Clea in her innocence was delighted at the news for Nessim was her dearest friend and the thought of him bringing his dignity and gentleness to bear on the very real unhappiness of Justine's life seemed suddenly il-luminating—a solution to everything. When one invites rescue by the mess one creates around oneself, what better than that a knight should be riding by? Justine put her hands over her eyes and said with difficulty, "For a moment my heart leapt up and I was about to shout 'yes'; ah, Clea my dear, you will guess why. I need his riches to trace the child—really, somewhere in the length and breadth of Egypt it must be, suffering ter-ribly, alone, perhaps ill-treated." She began to cry and then stopped abruptly, angrily. "In order to safeguard

us both from what would be a disaster I said to Nessim,
'I could never love a man like you: I could never give
you an instant's happiness. Thank you and good-bye.' "

"But are you sure?"

"To use a man for his fortune, by God I'll never."

"Justine, what do you want?"

"First the child. Then to escape from the eyes of the
world into some quiet corner where I can possess myself.
There are whole parts of my character I do not understand. I need time. Today again Nessim has written to
me. What can he want? He knows all about me."

The thought crossed Clea's mind: "The most dangerous thing in the world is a love founded on pity." But
she dismissed it and allowed herself to see once more the
image of this gentle, wise, undissimulating man breasting
the torrent of Justine's misfortunes and damming them
up. Am I unjust in crediting her with another desire
which such a solution would satisfy? (Namely, to be rid
of Justine, free from the demands she made upon her
heart and mind. She had stopped painting altogether.)
The kindness of Nessim—the tall dark figure which
drifted unresponsively around the corridors of society—
needed some such task; how could a knight of the order
born acquit himself if there were no castles and no de-
sponding maidens weaving in them? Their preoccupations matched in everything—save the demand for love.

"But the money is nothing," she said; and here indeed she was speaking of what she knew to be precisely
true of Nessim. He himself did not really care about the
immense fortune which was his. But here one should
add that he had already made a gesture which had
touched and overwhelmed Justine. They met more than
once, formally, like business partners, in the lounge of
the Cecil Hotel to discuss the matter of this marriage
with the detachment of Alexandrian brokers planning a
cotton merger. This is the way of the city. We are mental

people, and worldly, and have always made a clear
distinction between the passional life and the life of the
family. These distinctions are part of the whole complex
of Mediterranean life, ancient and touchingly prosaic.

"And lest an inequality of fortune should make your
decision difficult," said Nessim, flushing and lowering his
head, "I propose to make you a birthday present which
will enable you to think of yourself as a wholly independent person—simply as a woman, Justine. This hateful stuff which creeps into everyone's thoughts in the
city, poisoning everything! Let us be free of it before
deciding anything." He passed across the table a slim
green cheque with the words "Three Thousand Pounds"
written on it. She stared at it for a long time with surprise but did not touch it. "It has not offended you," he
said hastily, at last, stammering in his anxiety. "No," she
said. "It is like everything you do. Only what can I do
about not loving you?"

"You must, of course, never try to."

"Then what sort of life could we make?"

Nessim looked at her with hot shy eyes and then
lowered his glance to the table, as if under a cruel re-
buke. "Tell me," she said after a silence. "Please tell me.
I cannot use your fortune and your position and give
you nothing in exchange, Nessim."

"If you would care to try," he said gently, "we need
not delude each other. Life isn't very long. One owes it
to oneself to try and find a means to happiness."

"Is it that you want to sleep with me?" asked Justine
suddenly: disgusted yet touched beyond measure by his
tone. "You may. Yes. O! I would do anything for you,
Nessim—anything."

But he flinched and said: "I am speaking about an
understanding in which friendship and knowledge can
take the place of love until and if it comes as I hope. Of
course I shall sleep with you—myself a lover, and you a

friend. Who knows? In a year perhaps. All Alexandrian
marriages are business ventures after all. My God, Justine, what a fool you are. Can't you see that we might
possibly need each other without ever fully realising it?
It's worth trying. Everything may stand in the way. But
I can't get over the thought that in the whole city the
woman I most *need* is you. There are any number a
man may want, but to want is not to need. I may want
others—you I need! I do not dare to say the same for
you. How cruel life is, and how absurd." Nobody had
said anything like that to her before—had offered her a
partnership as coolly designed, as wholly pure in intention. It must be admired from this point of view. "You
are not the sort of man to stake everything on a single
throw at *rouge et noir*," she said slowly. "Our bankers
who are so brilliant with money are notoriously weak in
the head when it comes to women." She put her hand
upon his wrist. "You should have your doctor examine
you, my dear. To take on a woman who has said that
she can never love you—what sort of temerity is that? Ah,
no!"

He did not say anything at all, recognising that her
words were really not addressed to him: they were part
of a long internal argument with herself. How beautiful
her disaffected face looked—chloroformed by its own
simplicity: she simply could not believe that someone
might value her for herself—if she had a self. He was indeed, he thought, like a gambler putting everything on
the turn of a wheel. She was standing now upon the very
edge of a decision, like a sleepwalker on a cliff: should
she awake before she jumped, or let the dream continue?
Being a woman, she still felt it necessary to pose conditions; to withdraw herself further into secrecy as this
man encroached upon it with his steady beguiling gentleness. "Nessim," she said, "wake up." And she shook him
gently.

"I am awake," he said quietly.

Outside in the square with its palms nibbled by the
sea wind, a light rain was falling. It was the tenth Zu-el-
Higga, the first day of Courban Bairam, and fragments
of the great procession were assembling in their coloured
robes, holding the great silk banners and censers, insignia
of the religion they honoured, and chanting passages from
the litany: litany of the forgotten Nubian race which
every year makes its great resurrection at the Mosque of
Nebi Daniel. The crowd was brilliant, spotted with
primary colours. The air rippled with tambourines,
while here and there in the lags of silence which fell
over the shouts and chanting, there came the sudden jabbering of the long drums as their hide was slowly stiffened
at the hissing braziers. Horses moaned and the gonfalons bellied like sails in the rain-starred afternoon. A
cart filled with the prostitutes of the Arab town in
coloured robes went by with shrill screams and shouts,
and the singing of painted young men to the gnash of
cymbals and scribbling of mandolines: the whole as
gorgeous as a tropical animal.

"Nessim," she said foolishly. "On one sole condition—
that we sleep together absolutely tonight." His features
drew tight against his skull and he set his teeth tightly
as he said angrily: "You should have some intelligence
to go with your lack of breeding—where is it?"

"I'm sorry," seeing how deeply and suddenly she had
annoyed him. "I felt in need of reassurance." He had become quite pale.

"I proposed something so different," he said, replacing
the cheque in his wallet. "I am rather staggered by your
lack of understanding. Of course we can sleep together
if you wish to make it a condition. Let us take a room at
the hotel here, now, this minute." He looked really
splendid when he was wounded like this, and suddenly
there stirred inside her the realisation that his quietness

was not weakness, and that an uncommon sort of sensibility underlay these confusing thoughts and deliberate
words, perhaps not altogether good, either. "What could
we prove to each other," he went on more gently, "by it
or by its opposite: never making love?" She saw now how
hopelessly out of context her words had been. "I'm
bitterly ashamed of my vulgarity." She said this without
really meaning the words, as a concession to his world
as much as to himself—a world which dealt in the refine-
ments of manners she was as yet too coarse to enjoy,
which could afford to cultivate emotions *posées* by taste.
A world which could only be knocked off its feet when
you were skin to skin with it, so to speak! No, she did
not mean the words, for vulgar as the idea sounded, she
knew that she was right by the terms of her intuition since
the thing she proposed is really, for women, the vital
touchstone to a man's being; the knowledge, not of his
qualities which can be analysed or inferred, but of the
very flavour of his personality. Nothing except the act of
physical love tells us this truth about one another. She
bitterly regretted his unwisdom in denying her a concrete
chance to see for herself what underlay his beauty and
persuasion. Yet how could one insist?

"Good," he said, "for our marriage will be a delicate
affair, and very much a question of manners, until—"

"I'm sorry," she said, "I really did not know how to
treat honourably with you and avoid disappointing you."

He kissed her lightly on the mouth as he stood up. "I
must go first and get the permission of my mother, and
tell my brother. I am terribly happy, even though now I
am furious with you."

They went out to the car together and Justine suddenly felt very weak, as if she had been carried far out of
her depth and abandoned in mid-ocean. "I don't know
what more to say."

"Nothing. You must start living," he said as the car

began to draw away, and she felt as if she had received
a smack across the mouth. She went into the nearest
coffee-shop and ordered a cup of hot chocolate which
she drank with trembling hands. Then she combed her
hair and made up her face. She knew her beauty was
only an advertisement and kept it fresh with disdain.
No, somewhere she was truly a woman.

Nessim took the lift up to his office, and sitting down
at his desk wrote upon a card the following words: "My
dearest Clea, Justine has agreed to marry me. I could
never do this if I thought it would qualify or interfere
in any way with either her love for you or mine. . . ."

Then, appalled by the thought that whatever he might
write to Clea might sound mawkish, he tore the note up
and folded his arms. After a long moment of thought he
picked up the polished telephone and dialled Capodistria's number. "Da Capo," he said quietly. "You remember my plans for marrying Justine? All is well." He
replaced the receiver slowly, as if it weighed a ton, and
sat staring at his own reflection in the polished desk.

o   o   o   o   o

4.

IT was now, having achieved the major task of persuasion, that his self-assurance fled and left him face to face
with a sensation entirely new to him, namely an acute
shyness, an acute unwillingness to face his mother directly,
to confront her with his intentions. He himself was puzzled by it, for they had always been close together, their
confidences linked by an affection too deep to need the

interpretation of words. If he had ever been shy or awkward it was with his awkward brother, never with her.
And now? It was not as if he even feared her disfavour—
he knew she would fall in with his wishes as soon as they
were spoken. What then inhibited him? He could not
tell. Yet he flushed as he thought of her now, and passed
the whole of that morning in restless automatic acts,
picking up a novel only to lay it down, mixing a drink
only to abandon it, starting to sketch and then abruptly
dropping the charcoal to walk out into the garden of the
great house, ill at ease. He had telephoned his office to
say that he was indisposed and then, as always when he
had told a lie, began to suffer in truth with an attack of
indigestion.

Then he started to ask for the number of the old
country house where Leila and Narouz lived, but
changed his mind and asked the operator instead for the
number of his garage. The car would be back, they told
him, cleaned and greased by noon. He lay down and
covered his face with his hands. Then he rang up Selim,
his secretary, and told him to telephone to his brother
and say that he was coming to Karm Abu Girg for the
week-end. Heavens! what could be more normal? "You go
on like a chambermaid who has got engaged," he told
himself hotly. Then for a moment he thought of taking someone with him to ease the strain of the meeting
—Justine? Impossible. He picked up a novel of Pursewarden's and came upon the phrase: "Love is like trench
warfare—you cannot see the enemy, but you know he is
there and that it is wiser to keep your head down."

The doorbell rang. Selim brought him some letters to
sign and then went silently upstairs to pack his bag and
briefcase. There were papers he must take for Narouz
to see—papers about the lift machinery needed to drain
and reclaim the desert which fringed the plantations.
Business matters were a welcome drug.

The Hosnani fortunes were deployed in two directions, separated into two spheres of responsibility, and each brother had his own. Nessim controlled the banking house and its ancillaries all over the Mediterranean, while Narouz lived the life of a Coptic squire, never stirring from Karm Abu Girg where the Hosnani lands marched with the fringe of the desert, gradually eating into it, expropriating it year by year, spreading their squares of cultivation—carob and melon and corn—and pumping out the salt which poisoned it.

"The car is here," said the hawk-faced secretary as he returned. "Am I to drive you, sir?" Nessim shook his head and dismissed him quietly, before crossing the garden once more, chin in hand. He paused by the lily pond to study the fish—those expensive toys of the ancient Japanese Emperors, survivals from an age of luxury, which he had imported at such cost, only to find them gradually dying off of some unknown illness—homesickness, perhaps? Pursewarden spent hours watching them. He said that they helped him to think about art!

The great silver car stood at the door with the ignition switch in the dashboard. He got in thoughtfully and drove slowly across the town, examining its parks and squares and buildings with a serene eye, but deliberately dawdling, irresolutely, emptying his mind by an act of will every time the thought of his destination came upon him. When he reached the sea he turned at last down the shining Corniche in the sunlight to watch the smooth sea and cloudless air for a moment, the car almost at a standstill. Then suddenly he changed gear and began to travel along the sea-shore at a more resolute pace. He was going home.

Soon he turned inland, leaving the town with its palms crackling in the spring wind and turning towards the barren network of faults and dried-out lake-beds where the metalled road gave place to the brown earth tracks

along embankments lined with black swamps and fringed
by barbed reeds and a cross-hatching of sweet-corn plantations. The dust came up between his wheels and filled
the air of the saloon, coating everything in a fine-grained
pollen. The windscreen became gradually snowed-up
and he switched on the wipers to keep it clear.

Following little winding lanes which he knew by heart
he came, after more than an hour, to the edge of a spit
flanked by bluer water and left the car in the shadow
of a tumbledown house, the remains perhaps of some
ancient customs-shed built in the days when river traffic
plied between Damietta and the Gulf: now drying up day
by day, withering and cracking under the brazen Egyptian sky, forgotten by its keepers.

He locked the car carefully and followed a narrow
path across a holding of poverty-stricken beanrows and
dusty melons, fringed with ragged and noisy Indian corn,
to come out upon a landing-stage where an aged ferryman awaited him in a ramshackle boat. At once he saw
the horses waiting upon the other side, and the fore-
shortened figure of Narouz beside them. He threw up an
excited arm in an awkward gesture of pleasure as he
saw Nessim. Nessim stepped into the boat with beating
heart.

"Narouz!" The two brothers, so unlike in physique
and looks, embraced with feeling which was qualified in
Nessim by the silent agony of a shyness new to him.

The younger brother, shorter and more squarely built
then Nessim, wore a blue French peasant's blouse open
at the throat and with the sleeves rolled back, exposing
arms and hands of great power covered by curly dark
hair. An old Italian cartridge bandolier hung down upon
his haunches. The ends of his baggy Tukish trousers
with an old-fashioned drawstring, were stuffed into
crumpled old jackboots of soft leather. He ducked, ex-
citedly, awkwardly, into his brother's arms and out again,

like a boxer from a clinch. But when he raised his head
to look at him, you saw at once what it was that had ruled
Narouz' life like a dark star. His upper lip was split
literally from the spur of the nose—as if by some terrific
punch: it was a hare-lip which had not been caught up
and basted in time. It exposed the ends of a white tooth
and ended in two little pink tongues of flesh in the
centre of his upper lip which were always wet. His dark
hair grew down low and curly, like a heifer's, on to his
brow. His eyes were splendid: of a blueness and innocence
that made them almost like Clea's: indeed his whole
ugliness took splendour from them. He had grown a
ragged and uneven moustache over his upper lip, as
someone will train ivy over an ugly wall—but the scar
showed through wherever the hair was thin: and his
short, unsatisfactory beard too was a poor disguise: looked
simply as if he had remained unshaven for a week. It
had no shape of its own and confused the outlines of his
taurine neck and high cheekbones. He had a curious
hissing shy laugh which he always pointed downward
into the ground to hide his lip. The whole sum of his
movements was ungainly—arms and legs somewhat curved
and hairy as a spider—but they gave off a sensation of
overwhelming strength held rigidly under control. His
voice was deep and thrilling and held something of the
magic of a woman's contralto.

Whenever possible they tried to have servants or
friends with them when they met—to temper their shyness; and so today Narouz had brought Ali, his factor,
with the horses to meet the ferry. The old servant with
the cropped ears took a pinch of dust from the ground
before Nessim's feet and pressed it to his forehead before
extending his hand for a handshake, and then diffidently
partook of the embrace Nessim offered him—as someone
he had loved from his childhood onwards. Narouz was
charmed by his brother's easy, comradely but feeling

gesture—and he laughed downwards into the ground with pleasure.

"And Leila?" said Nessim, in a low voice, raising his fingers to his temple for a moment as he did so.

"Is well," said Narouz in the tone that springs from a freshly rosined bow. "This past two months. Praise God."

Their mother sometimes went through periods of mental instability lasting for weeks, always to recover again. It was a quiet surrender of the real world that surprised no-one any longer, for she herself now knew when such an attack was coming on and would make preparations for it. At such times, she spent all day in the little hut at the end of the rose-garden, reading and writing, mostly the long letters which Mountolive read with such tenderness in Japan or Finland or Peru. With only the cobra for company, she waited until the influence of the *afreet* or spirit was spent. This habit had lasted for many years now, since the death of their father and her illness, and neither son took any account of these departures from the normal life of the great house. "Leila is well in her mind," said Narouz again in that thrilling voice. "So happy too that Mountolive is back. She looks years younger."

"I understand."

The two brothers now mounted their horses and started slowly along the network of embankments and causeways which led them over the lake with its panels of cultivation. Nessim always loved this ride for it evoked his real childhood—so much richer in variety and beauty than those few years spent in the house at Aboukir where Leila had moved for a while after their father's death. "All your new lift pumps should be here next month," he shouted, and Narouz chuckled with pleasure; but with another part of his mind he allowed the soft black earthworks of the river with its precarious tracks separating the squares of cultivated soil to lead him steadily back to the remembered treasures of his childhood here. For this was really Egypt—a Copt's Egypt—while the white city, ás if in some dusty spectrum, was filled with the troubling and alien images of lands foreign to it—the intimations of Greece, Syria, Tunis.

It was a fine day and shallow draught boats were coursing among the beanfields towards the river tributaries, with their long curved spines of mast, lateen rigs bent like bows in the freshets. Somewhere a boatman sang and kept time on a finger-drum, his voice mixing with the sighing of *sakkias* and the distant village bangings of wheelwrights and carpenters manufacturing disc-wheels for wagons or the shallow-bladed ploughs which worked the alluvial riverside holdings.

Brilliant kingfishers hunted the shallows like thunderbolts, their wings slurring, while here and there the small brown owls, having forgotten the night habits of their kind, flew between the banks, or nestled together in songless couples among the trees.

The fields had begun to spread away on either side of the little cavalcade now, green and scented with their rich crops of *bercim* and beanrows, though the road still obstinately followed along the banks of the river so that their reflections rode with them. Here and there were hamlets whose houses of unbaked mud wore flat roofs made brilliant now by stacks of Indian corn which yellowed them. They passed an occasional line of camels moving down towards a ferry, or a herd of great black *gamoose*—Egyptian buffalo—dipping their shiny noses in the rich ooze and filth of some backwater, flicking the flies from their papery skins with lead tails. Their great curved horns belonged to forgotten frescoes.

It was strange now how slowly life moved here, he reflected with pleasure as he moved towards the Hosnani property—women churning butter in goatskins suspended from bamboo tripods or walking in single file down to

the river with their pots. Men in robes of blue cotton at
the waterwheels, singing, matrons swathed from crown to
ankle in the light dusty black robes which custom demanded, blue-beaded against the evil eye. And then all
the primeval courtesies of the road exchanged between
passers-by to which Narouz responded in his plangent
voice, sounding as if it belonged to the language as much
as to the place. *"Nabarak Said!"* he cried cheerfully, or
"Said Embarak!" as the wayfarers smiled and greeted
them. "May your day be blessed," thought Nessim in
remembered translation as he smiled and nodded, overcome at the splendour of these old-fashioned greetings
one never heard except in the Arab quarter of the city;
"may today be as blessed as yesterday."

He turned and said "Narouz" and his brother rode up
beside him tenderly, saying "Have you seen my whip?"
Laughing downwards again, his tooth showing through
the rent in his lip. He carried a splendid hippopotamus-
hide whip, loosely coiled at his saddle-bow. "I found the
perfect one—after three years. Sheik Bedawi sent it down
from Assuan. Do you know?" He turned those brilliant
blue eyes upwards for a moment to stare into the dark
eyes of his brother with intense joy. "It is better than
a pistol, at any rate a .99," he said, thrilled as a child.
"I've been practising hard with it—do you want to see?"

Without waiting for an answer he tucked his head
down and rode forward at a trot to where some dozen
chickens were scratching at the bare ground near a herds-
man's cot. A frightened rooster running faster than the
others took off under his horse's hooves: Nessim reined
back to watch. Narouz' arm shot up, the long lash un-
curled slowly on the air and then went rigid with a sudden dull welt of sound, a sullen thwack, and laughing,
the rider dismounted to pick up the mutilated creature,
still warm and palpitating, its wings half-severed from
its body, its head smashed. He brought it back to Nessim

in triumph, wiping his hand casually on his baggy
trousers. "What do you think?" Nessim gripped and admired the great whip while his brother threw the dead
fowl to his factor, still laughing himself, and so slowly
remounted. They rode side by side now, as if the spell
upon their communication were broken, and Nessim
talked of the new machinery which had been ordered
and heard of Narouz' battle against drought and sand-
drift. In such neutral subjects they could lose themselves
and become natural. United most closely by such topics,
they were like two blind people in love who can only
express themselves through touch: the subject of their
lands.

The holdings became richer now, planted out with
tamarisk and carob, though here and there they passed
the remains of properties abandoned by owners too poor
or too lazy to contend with the deserts, which encircled
the fertile strip on three sides. Old houses, fallen now
into desuetude, abandoned and overgrown, stared out
across the water with unframed windows and shattered
doors. Their gates, half-smothered in bougainvillaea,
opened rustily into gardens of wild and unkempt beauty
where marble fountains and rotted statuary still testified
to a glory since departed. On either side of them one
could glimpse the well-wooded lands which formed the
edge, the outer perimeter of the family estates—palm,
acacia and sycamore which still offered the precarious
purchase to life which without shade and water perished,
reverted to the desert. Indeed, one was conscious of the
desert here although one could not see it—melodramati-
cally tasteless as a communion wafer.

Here an old island with a ruined palace; there tortuous paths and channels of running water where the slim
bird-forms of river-craft moved about their task of loading *tibbin* (corn); they were nearing the village now. A
bridge rose high upon mudbanks, crowned by a magnif-

icent grove of palms, with a row of coloured boats waiting for the boom to lift. Here on the rise one glimpsed
for a moment the blue magnetic haze of a desert horizon
lying beyond this hoarded strip of plenty, of green plantations and water.

Round a corner they came upon a knot of villagers
waiting for them who set up cries of "What honour to
the village!" and "You bring blessings!" walking beside
them as they rode smiling onwards. Some advanced on
them, the notables, catching a hand to kiss, and some
even kissing Nessim's stirrup-irons. So they passed through
the village against its patch of emerald water and
dominated by the graceful fig-shaped minaret, and the
cluster of dazzling beehive domes which distinguished
the Coptic church of their forefathers. From here, the
road turned back again across the fields to the great
house within its weather-stained outer walls, ruined
and crumbling with damp in many places, and in others
covered by such *graffiti* as the superstitious leave to charm
the *afreet*—black talismanic handprints, or the legend
"*B'ism'illah ma'sha'llah*" (may God avert evil). It was
for these pious villagers that its tenants had raised on the
corners of the wall tiny wooden windmills in the shape
of men with revolving arms, to scare the *afreet* away.
This was the manor-house of Karm Abu Girg which belonged to them.

Emin, the chief steward, was waiting at the outer gate
with the usual gruff greetings which custom demanded,
surrounded by a group of shy boys to hold the horses
and help their riders dismount.

The great folding doors of the courtyard with their
pistol bolts and inscribed panels were set back so that
they could walk directly into the courtyard against which
the house itself was built, tilted upon two levels—the
ceremonial first floor looking down sideways along the
vaulted arches below—a courtyard with its granaries and

reception-rooms, storehouses and stables. Nessim did not
cross the threshold before examining once more the
faded but still visible cartoons which decorated the wall
at the right-hand side of it—and which depicted in a
series of almost hieroglyphic signs the sacred journey he
had made to bathe in the Jordan: a horse, a motorcar,
a ship, an aeroplane, all crudely represented. He muttered
a pious text, and the little group of servants smiled with
satisfaction, understanding by this that his long residence
in the city had not made him forget country ways. He
never forgot to do this. It was like a man showing his
passport. And Narouz too was grateful for the tact such
a gesture showed—which not only endeared his brother
to the dependants of the house, but also strengthened his
own position with them as the ruling master of it.

On the other side of the lintel, a similar set of pictures
showed that he also, the younger brother, had made the
pious pilgrimage which is incumbent upon every Copt of
religious principles.

The main gateway was flanked on each side by a
pigeon-tower—those clumsy columns built of earthen
pitchers pasted together anyhow with mud-cement: which
are characteristic of country houses in Egypt and which
supplied the choicest dish for the country squire's table.
A cloud of its inhabitants fluttered and crooned all day
over the barrel-vaulted court. Here all was activity: the
Negro night-watchman, the *ghaffirs,* factors, stewards came
forth one by one to salute the eldest brother, the heir.
He was given a bowl of wine and a nosegay of flowers
while Narouz stood by proudly smiling.

Then they went at ceremonial pace through the gallery
with its windows of many-coloured glass which for a
brief moment transformed them into harlequins, and
then out into the rose garden with its ragged and unkempt arbour and winding paths towards the little summer-house where Leila sat reading, unveiled. Narouz

called her name once to warn her as they neared the house, adding, "Guess who has come!" The woman quickly replaced her veil and turned her wise dark eyes towards the sunlit door saying: "The boy did not bring the milk again. I wish you would tell him, Narouz. His mind is salt. The snake must be fed regularly or it becomes ill-tempered." And then the voice, swerving like a bird in mid-air, foundered and fell to a rich melodious near-sob on the name "Nessim." And this she repeated twice as they embraced with such trembling tenderness that Narouz laughed, swallowing, and tasted both the joy of his brother's love for Leila and his own bitterness in realising that he, Nessim, was her favourite—the beautiful son. He was not jealous of Nessim; only heartsick at the melody in his mother's voice—the tone she had never used in speaking to him. It had always been so.

"I will speak to the boy," he said, and looked about him for signs of the snake. Egyptians regard the snake as too lucky a visitant to a house to kill and so tempt ill-luck, and Leila's long self-communing in the little summer-house would not have been complete without this indolent cobra which had learned to drink milk from a saucer like a cat.

Still holding hands they sat down together and Nessim started to speak of political matters with those dark, clever, youthful eyes looking steadily into his. From time to time, Leila nodded vigorously, with a determined air, while the younger son watched them both hungrily, with a heavy admiration at the concise way Nessim abbreviated and expressed his ideas—the fruit of a long public life. Narouz felt these abstract words fall dully upon his ear, fraught with meanings he only half-guessed, and though he knew that they concerned him as much as anyone, they seemed to him to belong to some rarer world inhabited by sophists or mathematicians—creatures who would forge and give utterance to the vague long-

ings and incoherent desires he felt forming inside him
whenever Egypt was mentioned or the family estates. He
sucked the knuckle of his forefinger, and sat beside them,
listening, looking first at his mother and then back to
Nessim.

"And now Mountolive is back," concluded Nessim,
"and for the first time what we are trying to do will be
understood. Leila—he will help us, if it is possible. He
understands."

The name of Mountolive struck two ways. The woman lowered her eyes to her own white hands which lay
before her upon a half-finished letter—eyes so brilliantly
made up with kohl and antimony that to discern tears
in them would have been difficult. Yet there were none.
They sparkled only with affection. Was she thinking of
those long letters which she had so faithfully written during the whole period of their separation? But Narouz
felt a sudden stirring of jealousy in his brain at the mention of the name, under which, interred as if under
a tombstone, he had hidden memories of a different
epoch—of the young secretary of the High Commission
whom his mother had— (mentally he never used the word
"loved" but left a blank space in his thoughts where it
should stand) ; moreover of the sick husband in the wheel-
chair who had watched so uncomplainingly. Narouz' soul
vibrated with his father's passion when Mountolive's
name, like a note of music, was struck. He swallowed and
stirred uneasily now as he watched his mother trembling-
ly fold a letter and slide it into an envelope. "Can we
trust him?" she asked Nessim. She would have struck
him over the mouth if he had answered "No." She simply
wanted to hear him pronounce the name again. Her
question was a prompting, nothing more. He kissed her
hand, and Narouz greedily admired his courtier's smiling air as he replied, "If we cannot trust Mountolive,
who can we trust?"

As a girl, Leila had been both beautiful and rich. The
daughter of a blue-stocking, convent-bred and very much
in society, she had been among the first Coptic women
to abandon the veil and to start to take up the study
of medicine against her parents' will. But an early marriage to a man very much older than herself had put an
end to these excursions into the world of scope where
her abilities might have given her a foothold. The temper
of Egyptian life too was hostile to the freedom of wom-
en, and she had resigned a career in favour of a husband
she very much admired and the uneventful round of
country life. Yet somehow, under it all, the fire had
burned on. She had kept friends and interests, had visited
Europe every few years, had subscribed to periodicals in
four languages. Her mind had been formed by solitude,
enriched by books which she could only discuss in letters
to friends in remote places, could only read in the
privacy of the *harim*. Then came the advent of Mountolive and the death of her husband. She stood free and
breathing upon the brink of a new world with no charge
upon her but two growing sons. For a year she had
hesitated between Paris and London as a capital of residence, and while she hesitated, all was lost. Her beauty,
of which until then she had taken no particular account,
as is the way with the beautiful, had been suddenly
ravaged by a confluent smallpox which melted down
those lovely features and left her only the magnificent
eyes of an Egyptian sibyl. The black hideous veil which
so long had seemed to her a symbol of servitude became
now a refuge in which she could hide the ruins of a
beauty which had been considered outstanding in her
youth. She had not the heart now to parade this new
melted face through the capitals of Europe, to brave the
silent condolences of friends who might remember her
as she had once been. Turned back upon her tracks so
summarily, she had decided to stay on and end her life

in the family estates in such seclusion as might be permitted to her. Her only outlet now would be in letter-writing and in reading—her only care the bringing up of her children. All the unsteadiness of her passions was canalized into this narrow field. A whole world of relations had to be mastered and she turned her resolution to it like a man. Ill-health, loneliness, boredom—she faced them one by one and overcame them—living here in retirement like a dethroned Empress, feeding her snake and writing her interminable letters which were full of the liveliness and sparkle of a life which now the veil masked and which could escape only through those youthful dark eyes.

She was now never seen in society and had become something of a legend amongst those who remembered her in the past, and who indeed had once nicknamed her the "dark swallow." Now she sat all day at a rough deal table, writing in that tall thoughtful handwriting, dipping her quill into a golden inkpot. Her letters had become her very life, and in the writing of them she had begun to suffer from that curious sense of distorted reality which writers have when they are dealing with real people; in the long years of writing to Mountolive, for example, she had so to speak re-invented him so successfully that he existed for her now not so much as a real human being but as a character out of her own imagination. She had even almost forgotten what he looked like, what to expect of his physical presence, and when his telegram came to say that he expected to be in Egypt again within a few months, she felt at first nothing but irritation that he should intrude, bodily as it were, upon the picture projected by her imagination. "I shall not see him," she muttered at first, angrily; and only then did she start to tremble and cover her ravaged face with her hands.

"Mountolive wants to see you," said Nessim, at last, as

the conversation veered round in his direction again. "When may I bring him? The Legation is moving up to summer quarters soon, so he will be in Alexandria all the time."

"He must wait until I am ready," she said, once more feeling the anger stir in her at the intrusion of this beloved figment. "After all these years." And then she asked with a pathetic lustful eagerness, "Is he old now— is he grey? Is his leg all right? Can he walk? That skiing fall in Austria. . . ."

To all this Narouz listened with cocked head and sullen heavy heart: he could follow the feeling in her voice as one follows a line of music.

"He is younger than ever," said Nessim, "hasn't aged by a day": and to his surprise she took his hand, and putting it to her cheek she said brokenly, "Oh—you are horrible, horrible, both of you. Go. Leave me alone now. I have letters to write."

She permitted no mirrors in the *harim* since the illness which had deprived her of her self-esteem; but privately in a gold-backed pocket-mirror, she touched and pencilled her eyes in secret—her remaining treasure—practising different make-ups on them, practising different glances and matching them to different remarks—trying to give what was left of her looks a vocabulary as large as her lively mind. She was like a man struck suddenly blind learning to spell, with the only member left him, his hands.

Now the two men walked back into the old house, with its cool but dusty rooms whose walls were hung with ancient carpets and embroidered mats, and crowded with gigantic carcasses of furniture long since outmoded —a sort of Ottoman Buhl such as one sees in the old houses of Egypt. Nessim's heartstrings were tugged by the memory of its ugliness, its old-fashioned Second Empire pieces and its jealously guarded routines. The steward, according to custom, had stopped all the clocks.

This, in the language of Narouz, said "Your stay with us is so brief, let us not be reminded of the flight of the hours. God made eternity. Let us escape from the despotism of time altogether." These ancient and hereditary politenesses filled Nessim with emotion. Even the primitive sanitary arrangements—there were no bathrooms—seemed to him somehow in keeping with the character of things, though he loved hot water. Narouz himself slept naked winter and summer. He washed in the courtyard—a servant threw water over him from a pitcher. Indoors, he usually wore an old blue cloak and Turkish slippers. He smoked tobacco too in a narguileh the length of a musket.

While the elder brother unpacked his clothes, Narouz sat on the end of the bed studying the papers which filled the briefcase, musing with a quiet intentness, for they related to the machinery with the help of which he proposed to keep up and extend his attack on the dead sand. In the back of his mind he could see an army of trees and shrubs marching steadily forward into the emptiness—carob and olive, vine and jujube, pistachio, peach and apricot, spreading around them the green colours of quickness in those tenantless areas of dust choked with sea-salt. He looked almost lustfully upon the pictures of equipment in the shiny brochures Nessim had brought him, lovingly touching them with his finger, hearing in his imagination the suck and swell of sweet water through pumps gradually expressing the dead salts from the ground and quickening it to nourish the sipping roots of his trees. Gebel Maryut, Abu Sir—his mind winged away like a swallow across the dunes into the Nitrian desert itself—mentally conquering it.

"The desert," said Narouz. "By the way, will you ride out with me to the tents of Abu Kar tomorrow? I have been promised an Arab and I want to break it myself. It would make a pleasant excursion." Nessim was at once delighted at the prospect. "Yes," he said. "But early," said Narouz, "and we can pass the olive plantation for you to see what progress we're making. Will you? Please do!" He squeezed his arm. "Since we started with the Tunisian *chimlali* we haven't had a single casualty. Oh, Nessim! I wish you stayed here. Your place is here."

Nessim as always was beginning to wish the same. That night they dined in the old-fashioned way—so different from the impertinent luxury of Alexandrian forms—each taking his napkin from the table and proceeding to the yard for the elaborate handwashing ceremony which preceded a meal in the country. Two servants poured for them as they stood side by side, washing their fingers with yellow soap, and rinsed them off with orange-water. Then to the table where their only cutlery was a wooden spoon each for dealing with soup—otherwise they broke the flat thin cakes of the country to dip into the dishes of cooked meats. Leila had always dined alone in the women's quarters, and retired to bed early so that the two brothers were left alone to their repast. They ate in leisurely fashion, with long pauses between the courses, and Narouz acted host, placing choice morsels upon Nessim's plate and breaking up the fowl and the turkey with his strong fingers the better to serve his guest. At last, when sweetmeats and fruit had been served, they returned once more to where the waiting servants stood and washed their hands again.

In the interval, the table had been cleared of dishes and set back to make room for the old-fashioned divans to pass through the room and out on to the balcony. Smoking materials had been set out—the long-barrelled narguilehs with Narouz' favourite tobacco and a silver dish of sweets. Here they sat together for a while in silence to drink their coffee. Nessim had kicked off his slippers and drawn his legs up under him: he sat with his chin in his hand wondering how he could impart his

news, the marriage which nibbled at the edge of his
mind: and whether he should be frank about his motives
in choosing for a wife a woman who was of a different
faith from his own. The night was hot and still, and the
scent of magnolia blossom came up to the balcony in
little drifts and eddies of air which made the candles
flutter and dance; he was gnawed by irresolution.

In such a mood every promise of distraction offered
relief, and he was pleased when Narouz suggested that
the village singer should be called to play for them, a
custom which they had so often enjoyed as youths. There
is nothing more appropriate to the heavy silence of the
Egyptian night than the childish poignance of the *ke-
mengeh's* note. Narouz clapped his hands and despatched
a message and presently the old man came from the servant's quarters where he dined each night on the charity
of the house, walking with the slow and submissive step
of extreme old age and approaching blindness. The
sounding-board of his small viol was made from half a
coconut. Narouz sprang up and settled him upon a
cushion at the end of the balcony. There came footsteps
in the courtyard and a familiar voice, that of the old
schoolmaster Mohammed Shebab who climbed the stairs,
smiling and wrinkled, to clasp Narouz' hand. He had
the bright hairy face of a monkey and wore, as usual,
an immaculate dark suit with a rose in his button-hole.
He was something of a dandy and an epicure and these
visits to the great house were his only distraction, living
as he did for the greater part of the year buried in the
depths of the delta; he had brought the old treasured
narguileh mouthpiece which he had owned for a quarter
of a century. He was delighted to hear some music and
listened with emotion to the wild *quasidas* that the old
man sang—songs of the Arab canon full of the wild heart-
sickness of the desert. The old voice, crumpled here and
there like a fragile leaf, rose and fell upon the night;

tracing the quavering melodic line of the songs as if it were following the ancient highways of half-obliterated thoughts and feelings. The little viol scribbled its complaints upon the text reaching back into their childhood. And now suddenly the singer burst into the passionate pilgrim song which expresses so marvellously the Moslem's longing for Mecca and his adoration of the Prophet —and the melody fluttered inside the brothers' hearts, imprisoned like a bird with beating wings. Narouz, though a Copt, was repeating "All-*ah*, All-*ah*!" in a rapture of praise.

"Enough, enough," cried Nessim at last. "If we are to be up early, we should sleep early, don't you think?"

Narouz sprang up too, and still acting the host, called for lights and water and walked before him to the guest-room. Here he waited until Nessim had washed and undressed and climbed into the creaking old-fashioned bed before bidding him good night. As he stood in the doorway, Nessim said impulsively: "Narouz—I've something to tell you." And then, overcome once more with shyness, added: "But it will keep until tomorrow. We shall be alone, shan't we?" Narouz nodded and smiled. "The desert is such torture for them that I always send them back at the fringe, the servants."

"Yes." Nessim well knew that Egyptians believe the desert to be an emptiness populated entirely by the spirits of demons and other grotesque visitants from Eblis, the Moslem Satan.

Nessim slept and awoke to find his brother, fully dressed, standing beside his bed with coffee and cigarettes. "It's time," he said. "I suppose in Alexandria you sleep late. . . ."

"No," said Nessim, "strangely enough I am usually at my office by eight."

"Eight! O! my poor brother," said Narouz mockingly, and helped him to dress. The horses were waiting and together they rode out upon a dawn with a thick bluish mist rising from the lake. Crisp air, inclining to frost— but already the sun was beginning to soak into the upper air and dry up the dew upon the minaret of the mosque.

Narouz led now, down winding ways, along the tortuous bridle paths, and across embankments, quite unerringly, for the whole land existed in his mind like the most detailed map by a master cartographer. He carried it always in his head like a battle-plan, knowing the age of every tree, the poundage of every well's water, the drift of sand to an inch. He was possessed by it.

Slowly they made a circuit of the great plantation, soberly assessing progress and discussing plans for the next offensive when the new machinery should be installed. And then, presently when they had come to a lonely spot by the river, screened on all sides by reeds, Narouz said, "Wait a second. . . ." and dismounted, taking as he did so the old leather game-bag from his shoulders. "Something to hide," he said, smiling downwards shyly. Nessim watched him idly as he turned the bag over to tip its contents into the dark waters of the river. But he was not prepared to see a shrunken human head, lips drawn back over yellow teeth, eyes squinting inwards upon each other, roll out of the bag and sink slowly out of sight into the green depths beneath. "What the devil's that?" he asked, and Narouz gave his little hissing titter at the ground and replied: "Abdel-Kader— head of." He knelt down and started washing the bag out in the water, moving it vigorously to and fro, and then with a gesture turned it inside out as one might turn a sleeve and returned to his horse. Nessim was thinking deeply. "So you had to do it at last," he said, "I was afraid you might."

Narouz turned his brilliant eyes upon his brother for a moment and said seriously: "More troubles with Bed-

ouin labour could have cost us a thousand trees next
year. It was too much of a risk to take. Besides, he was
going to poison me."

He said no more and they rode on in silence until
they reached the thinning edges of cultivation—the front
line so to speak where the battle was actually being
joined at present—a long ragged territory like the edges
of a wound. Along the whole length of it infiltration
from the arable land on the one side and the desert
drainage on the other, both charged with the rotten
salts, had poisoned the ground and made it the image
of desolation.

Here only giant reeds and bulrushes grew or an
occasional thorn bush. No fish could live in the brackish
water. Birds shunned it. It lay in the stagnant belt of its
own foul air, weird, obsessive and utterly silent—the
point at which the desert and the sown met in a death-
embrace. They rode now among towering rushes whose
stems were bleached and salt-encrusted, glittering in the
sun. The horses gasped and scrambled through the dead
water which splashed upon them, crystallizing into spots
of salt wherever it fell; pools of slime were covered with
a crust of salt through which their plunging hooves broke,
releasing horrible odours from the black mud beneath
and sudden swarms stinging flies and mosquitoes. But
Narouz looked about him with interest even here, his eyes
alight, for he had already mentally planted this waste
with carobs and green shrubs—conquered it. But they
both held their breath and did not speak as they traversed this last mephitic barrier and the long patches of
wrinkled mummy-like soil to which it gave place. Then
at last they were on the edge of the desert and they
paused in shadow while Narouz fished in his clothes
for the little stick of blue billiard-marker's chalk. They
rubbed a little chalk under each of their eyelids with a
finger against the glare—as they had always done, even

as children; and each tied a cloth around his head in
Bedouin fashion.

And then: the first pure draughts of desert air, and
the nakedness of space, pure as a theorem, stretching
away into the sky drenched in all its own silence and
majesty, untenanted except by such figures as the imagination of man has invented to people landscapes which
are inimical to his passions and whose purity flays the
mind.

Narouz gave a shout and the horses, suddenly awoken
and filled with a sense of new freedom and space around
them, started their peculiar tearing plunging gallop across
the dunes, manes and tassels tossing, saddles creaking.
They raced like this for many minutes, Nessim giggling
with excitement and joy. It was so long since he had
ridden at this wild gallop.

But they held it, completing a slow arc eastwards
across scrubby land where wild flowers bloomed and
butterflies tippled amongst the waste of dunes and the
dingy tenacious specimens of plant-life. Their hooves
rattled across shingle floors, through stone valleys with
great sandstone needles and chines of rosy shale filling
in the known horizons. Nessim was busy with his memories of those youthful nights camped out here under a
sky hoary with stars, in a booming tent (whose frosted
guy-ropes glittered like brilliants) pitched under Vega,
the whole desert spread around them like an empty room.
How did one come to forget the greatest of one's experiences? It was all lying there like a piano that one could
play but which one had somehow forgotten to touch for
years. He was irradiated by the visions of his inner eye
and followed Narouz blindly. He saw them in all that
immensity—two spots like pigeons flying in an empty sky.

They halted for a short rest in the shadow of a great
rock—a purple oasis of darkness—panting and happy.
"If we put up a desert wolf," said Narouz, "I'll run it

down with my *kurbash*," and he caressed the great whip lovingly, running it through his fingers.

When they set off again, Narouz started a slow tacking path, questing about for the ancient caravan route—the *masrab* which would take them to the Quasur el Atash (Castles of the Thirsty) where the Sheik's men were due to meet them before noon. Once Nessim too had known these highways by heart—the smugglers' roads which had been used for centuries by the caravans which plied between Algiers and Mecca—the "bountiful highways" which steered the fortunes of men through the wilderness of the desert, taking spices and stuffs from one part of Africa to another or affording to the pious their only means of reaching the Holy City. He was suddenly jealous of his brother's familiarity with the desert they had once equally owned. He copied him eagerly.

Presently Narouz gave a hoarse shout and pointed and in a little while they came upon the *masrab*—a highway of camel-tracks, deeply worn in some places into solid rock, but running in a wavy series, parallel from horizon to horizon. And here once more the younger brother set the pace. His blue shirt was now stained violet at the armpits. "Nearly there," he cried, and out of the trembling pearly edges of the sky there swam slowly a high cluster of reddish basalt blocks, carved into the vague semblance (like a face in the fire) of a sphinx tortured by thirst; and there, gibbering in the dark shade of a rock, the little party waited to conduct them to the Sheik's tents—four tall lean men, made of brown paper, whose voices cracked at the edges of meaning with thirst, and whose laughter was like fury unleashed. To them they rode—into the embrace of arms like dry sticks and the thorny clicking of an unfamiliar Arabic in which Narouz did all the talking and explaining.

Nessim waited, feeling suddenly like a European, city-bred, a visitor: for the little party carried with them all

the feeling of the tight inbred Arab world—its formal
courtesies and feuds—its primitiveness. He surprised himself by seeking in his own mind the memory of a painting
by Bonnard or a poem by Blake—as a thirsty man might
grope at a spring for water. In such a way might a traveller
present himself to some rude clan of Scotsmen, admiring
their bunioned feet and coarse hairy legs, but grateful
too that the sum of European culture was not expressed
by their life-hating, unpleasure-loving strength. Here he
suddenly lost his brother, parted company with him,
for Narouz had plunged into the life of these Arabian
herdsmen with the same intensity as he plunged into the
life of his land, his trees. The great corded muscles in his
hairy body were tense with pride, for he, a city-bred
Alexandrian—almost a despised *Nasrany*—could out-
shoot, out-talk and out-gallop any of them. On him
whose mettle they knew they kept a speculative aborigi-
nal eye; the gentle Nessim they had seen in many guises
before, his well-kept hands betrayed a city gentleman.
But they were polite.

A knowledge of forms only was necessary now, not
insight, for these delightful desert folk were automata;
thinking of Mountolive Nessim smiled suddenly and
wondered where the British had found the substance of
their myths about the desert Arab? The fierce banality
of their lives was so narrow, so regulated. If they stirred
one at all it was as the bagpipe can, without expressing
anything above the level of the primitive. He watched
his brother handle them, simply from a knowledge of
their forms of behaviour as a showman handles dancing
fleas. Poor souls! He felt the power and resource of his
city-bred intelligence stir in him.

They all rode now in a compact group to the Sheik's
tents, down long ribbed inclines of sand, through mirages
of pastures which only the rain clouds imagined, until
they came there, to the little circle of tents, manhood's

skies of hide, invented by men whose childish memories were so fearful they had had perforce to invent a narrower heaven in which to contain the germ of the race; in this little cone of hide the first child was born, the first privacy of the human kiss invented. . . . Nessim wished bitterly that he could paint as well as Clea. Absurd thoughts, and out of place.

But the Sheik's tents were extensive, covering nearly two thousand square feet with a tent-cloth woven of goat-hair in broad stitches of black, green, maroon and white. Long tassels hung down from the seams, playing in the wind.

The Sheik and his sons, like a gallery of playing cards, awaited them with the conventional greetings to which Narouz at least knew every response. The Sheik himself conducted them to a tent saying: "This house is your house; do as you please. We are your servants." And behind him pressed the water-carriers to bathe their hands and feet and faces—the latter now somehow dry and blistered by the journey. They rested for at least an hour, for the heat of the day was at full, in that brown darkness. Narouz lay snoring upon the cushions with arms and legs outspread while Nessim dozed fitfully, awakening from time to time to watch him—the effortless progress of sleep which physical surrender to action always brings. He brooded upon his brother's ugliness— the magnificent set of white teeth showing through the pink rent in his upper lip. From time to time, too, as they rested, the headmen of the tribe called noiselessly, taking off their shoes at the entrance of the tent, to enter and kiss Nessim's hand. Each uttered the single word of welcome *"Mahubbah"* in a whisper.

It was late in the afternoon when Narouz woke and calling for water doused his body down, asking at the same time for a change of clothes which were at once brought to him by the Sheik's eldest son. He strode out

into the heat of the sand saying: "Now for the colt.
It may take a couple of hours? You won't mind? We'll
be back a bit late, eh?" Cushions had been set for them
in the shade and here Nessim was glad to recline and
watch his brother moving quickly across the dazzle of
sand towards a group of colts which had been driven up
for him to examine.

They played gracefully and innocently, the tossing of
their heads and manes seeming to him "like the surf of
the June sea" as the proverb has it. Narouz stopped
keenly as he neared them, watching. Then he shouted
something and a man raced out to him with a bridle
and bit. "The white one," he cried hoarsely and the
Sheik's sons shouted a response which Nessim did not
catch. Narouz turned again, and softly with a queer
ducking discretion, slipped in among the young creatures
and almost before one could think was astride a white
colt after having bridled it with a single almost invisible
gesture.

The mythical creature stood quite still, its eye wide
and lustrous as if fully to comprehend this tremendous
new intelligence of a rider upon its back, then a slow
shudder rippled through its flesh—the tides of the panic
which always greets such a collision of human and animal
worlds. Horse and rider stood as if posing for a statue,
buried in thought.

Now the animal suddenly gave a low whistling cry
of fear, shook itself and completed a dozen curious
arching jumps, stiffly as a mechanical toy, coming down
savagely on its forelegs each time with the downthrust.
This did not dislodge Narouz who only leaned forward
and growled something in its ear that drove it frantic
for it now set off at a ragged plunging tossing canter,
turning and curvetting and ducking. They made a slow
irregular circle round the tents until at last they came
back to where the crowd of Arabs stood at the doorway

of the main tent, watching silently. And now the poor
creature, as if aware that some great portion of its real
life—its childhood perhaps—was irrevocably over, gave
another low whistling groan and broke suddenly into the
long tireless flying gallop of its breed, aimed like a
shooting-star to pierce the very sky, and whirled away
across the dunes with its rider secured to it by the powerful scissors of his legs—firm as a figure held by ringbolts
—diminishing rapidly in size until both were lost to sight.
A great cry of approval went up from the tents and
Nessim accepted, besides the curd cheese and coffee, the
compliments which were his brother's due.

Two hours later Narouz brought her back, glistening
with sweat, dejected, staggering, with only enough fight
in her to blow dejectedly and stamp, conquered. But he
himself was deliriously exhausted, dazed as if he had
ridden through an oven, while his bloodshot eyes and
drawn twitching face testified to the severity of the fight.
The endearments he uttered to the horse came from
between parched and cracked lips. But he was happy
underneath it all—indeed radiant—as he croaked for
water and begged leave of half an hour's rest before they
should set out once more on the homeward journey.
Nothing could finally tire that powerful body—not even
the orgasm he had experienced in long savage battle.
But closing his eyes now as he felt the water pouring
over his head, he saw again the dark bleeding sun which
shimmered behind their lids, image of fatigue, and felt
the desert glare parching and cracking the water on his
very skin. His mind was a jumble of sharp stabbing
colours and apprehensions—as if the whole sensory apparatus had melted in the heat like a colour-box, fusing
thought and wish and desire. He was light-headed with
joy and felt as unsubstantial as a rainbow. Yet in less than
half an hour he was ready for the journey back.

They set off with a different escort this time across the

inclining rays of sunlight which threw their rose and purple shadows into the sockets of the dunes. They made good time to the Quasur el Atash. Narouz had made arrangements for the white colt to be delivered him later in the week by the Chief's sons, and he rode at ease now, occasionally singing a stave or two of a song. Darkness fell as they reached the Castles of the Thirsty and having said good-bye to their hosts set off once more across the desert.

They rode slowly at ease, watching the brindled waning moon come up on a silence broken only by the sudden stammer of their horses' hooves on shingle beds, or the far-away ululations of jackals, and now, quite suddenly, Nessim found the barrier lifted and was able to say: "Narouz, I am going to be married. I want you to tell Leila for me. I don't know why but I feel shy about it."

For a minute Narouz felt himself turned to ice—a figure in a coat of mail; he seemed to sway in his saddle as with a delight so forced and hollow that it made his voice snap off short he crabbed out the words: "To Clea, Nessim? To Clea?" feeling the blood come rushing back to his ticking nerves when his brother shook his head and stared curiously at him. "No. Why? To Arnauti's ex-wife," replied Nessim with a controlled, a classical precision of utterance. They rode on with creaking saddles and Narouz, who was now grinning to himself with relief, cried, "I am so happy, Nessim! At last! You will be happy and have children."

But here Nessim's mortal shyness overcame him again and he told Narouz all that he had learned about Justine and about the loss of her child, adding: "She does not love me now, and does not pretend to: but who knows? If I can get her child back and give her some peace of mind and security, anything is possible." He added after a moment "Don't you think?" not because he wished for an opinion on the matter but simply to bridge the silence which poured in between them like a drifting dune. "As for the child, it is difficult. The Parquet have investigated as best they could—and what little evidence they have points to *Magzub* (the Inspired One); there was a festival in the town that evening and he was there. He has been several times accused of kidnapping children but the case has always been dropped for lack of evidence." Narouz pricked up his ears and bristled like a wolf. "You mean the hypnotist?" Nessim said thoughtfully: "I have sent to offer him a large sum of money— very large indeed—for what I want to know. Do you see?" Narouz shook his head doubtfully and picked at his short beard. "He is the one who is mad," he said. "He used to come to Saint Damiana every year. But strangemad. *Zein-el-Abdin*. He is holy too."

"That is the one," said Nessim; and as if struck by an afterthought Narouz reined both horses and embraced him, uttering the conventional congratulations in the family tongue. Nessim smiled and said: "You will tell Leila? Please, my brother."

"Of course."

"After I have gone?"

"Of course."

With the release of this tension and Narouz' ready compliance Nessim suddenly felt a load lifted from his mind. And correspondingly he suddenly felt very tired and on the point of sleep. They travelled briskly but without haste and it was towards midnight when they came once more within sight of the desert's edge. Here the horses put up a startled hare and Narouz made an attempt to ride it down with his whip but he missed it in the half-darkness.

"It is very good news," he cried on returning to Nessim's side, as if the little gallop across the moonlit dunes

had given him all the time and detachment he needed
to come to a considered opinion. "Will you bring her
to us next week—to Leila? I think I must have met her
but cannot remember. Very dark? 'A firefly's light in
darkness for such eyes' as the song goes?" He laughed
his downward laugh.

Nessim yawned sleepily. "Ach! my bones ache. That
is what I get for living in Alexandria. Narouz, before I
fall asleep there was one other thing I meant to ask
you. I have not seen Pursewarden. The meetings?"

Narouz drew a hissing inward breath and turned his
bright eyes to his brother, saying, "Yes. Very well. The
next one is to be at the *mulid* of Saint Damiana, in the
desert." He flexed the great muscles of his shoulders.
"The whole ten families are coming—can you believe it?"

"You will be careful," said his brother, "to see that
everything is done privately and there are no leaks."

"Of course!" he cried.

"I mean," said Nessim, "that in the early stages this
should not have a political character. It must grow
slowly with the understanding of the matter. Eh? I do
not think, for example, it is necessary for you to actually
speak to them, but rather to discuss. We can't risk. You
see, it is not only the British."

Narouz jaunted a leg impatiently and picked his teeth.
He thought of Mountolive and sighed.

"It is also the French—and they are at cross-purposes.
If we are to use them both. . . ."

"I know, I know," said Narouz impatiently. Nessim
looked at him keenly. "Attend," he said sharply, "for
much depends on your understanding just how far we
can go at this stage."

His reproof crushed Narouz. He flushed and joined
his hands together as he looked at his brother. "I do,"
he said in a low hoarse voice. Nessim at once felt ashamed

of himself and took his arm. He went on in his low con-
fiding tone.

"You see, there are mysterious leaks from time to time.
Old Cohen, for example, the furrier who died last month.
He was working for the French in Syria. On his return,
the Egyptians knew all about his mission. How? Nobody
knows. Among our friends we certainly have enemies—
in Alexandria itself. Do you see?"

"I see."

The next morning it was time for Nessim to return
and the two brothers rode out across the fields at a
leisurely pace to the point of rendezvous at the ferry.
"Why do you never come into the town?" said Nessim.
"Come with me today. There's a ball at the Randidis'.
You'd enjoy it as a change." Narouz as always wore a
hang-dog expression when anyone suggested an excursion into the city. "I shall come at carnival," he said
slowly, looking at the ground, and his brother laughed
and touched his arm. "I knew you'd say that! Always,
once a year at carnival. I wonder why!"

But he knew; Narouz' mortal shyness about his hare-
lip had driven him into a seclusion almost as unbroken
as that of his mother. Only the black domino of the
carnival balls permitted him to disguise the face he had
come to loathe so much that he could no longer bear
to see it even in a shaving-mirror. At the carnival ball
he felt free. And yet there was another and indeed unexpected reason—a passion for Clea which had lasted for
years now; for a Clea to whom he had never spoken, and
indeed only twice seen when she came down with Nessim
to ride on the estate. This was a secret which could not
have been dragged out of him under torture, but to
every carnival dance he came and drifted about in the
crowd hoping vaguely that he might by accident meet
this young woman whose name he had never uttered
aloud to anyone until that day.

(He never knew that Clea loathed the carnival season and spent the time quietly drawing and reading in her studio.)

They parted now with a warm embrace and Nessim's car scribbled its pennants of dust across the warm air of the fields, eager to regain the coast road once more. A battleship in the basin was firing a twenty-one gun salute, in honour perhaps of some Egyptian dignitary, and the explosions appeared to make the clouds of pearl which always overhung the harbour in spring, tremble and change colour. The sea was high today, and four fishing-boats tacked furiously towards the town harbour with their catch. Nessim stopped only once, to buy himself a carnation for his buttonhole from the flower-vendor on the corner of Saad Zaghloul. Then he went to his office, pausing to have his shoe-shine on the way up. The city had never seemed more beautiful to him. Sitting at his desk he thought of Leila and then of Justine. What would his mother have to say about his decision?

Narouz walked out to the summer-house that morning to discharge his mission; but first he picked a mass of blooms from the red and yellow roses with which to refill the two great vases which stood on either side of his father's portrait. His mother was asleep at her desk but the noise he made lifting the latch woke her at once. The snake hissed drowsily and then lowered its head to the ground once more.

"Bless you, Narouz," she said as she saw the flowers and rose at once to empty her vases. As they started to trim and arrange the new blooms, Narouz broke the news of his brother's marriage. His mother stood quite still for a long time, undisturbed but serious as if she were consulting her own inmost thoughts and emotions. At last she said, more to herself than anyone, "Why not?" repeating the phrase once or twice as if testing its pitch.

Then she bit her thumb and turning to her younger son said, "But if she is an adventuress, after his money, I won't have it. I shall take steps to have her done away with. He needs my permission anyhow."

Narouz found this overwhelmingly funny and gave an appreciative laugh. She took his hairy arm between her fingers. "I will," she said.

"Please."

"I swear it."

He laughed now until he showed the pink roof of his mouth. But she remained abstracted, still listening to an inner monologue. Absently she patted his arm as he laughed and whispered "Hush"; and then after a long pause she said, as if surprised by her own thoughts, "The strange thing is, I mean it."

"And you can't count on me, eh?" he said, still laughing but with the germ of seriousness in his words. "You can't trust me to watch over my own brother's honour." He was still swollen up toad-like by the laughter, though his expression had now become serious. "My God," she thought, "how ugly he is." And her fingers went to the black veil, pressing through it to the rough cicatrices in her own complexion, touching them fiercely as if to smooth them out.

"My good Narouz," she said, almost tearfully, and ran her fingers through his hair; the wonderful poetry of the Arabic stirred and soothed him in one. "My honeycomb, my dove, my good Narouz. Tell him yes, with my embrace. Tell him yes."

He stood still, trembling like a colt, and drinking in the music of her voice and the rare caresses of that warm and capable hand.

"But tell him he must bring her here to us."

"I will."

"Tell him today."

And he walked with his queer jerky sawing stride to the telephone in the old house. His mother sat at her dusty table and repeated twice in a low puzzled tone; "Why should Nessim choose a Jewess?"

o   o   o   o   o

5.

So much have I reconstructed from the labyrinth of notes which Balthazar has left me. "To imagine is not necessarily to invent," he says elsewhere, "nor dares one make a claim for omniscience in interpreting people's actions. One assumes that they have grown out of their feelings as leaves grow out of a branch. But can one work backwards, deducing the one from the other? Perhaps a writer could if he were sufficiently brave to cement these apparent gaps in our actions with interpretations of his own to bind them together? What was going on in Nessim's mind? This is really a question for you to put to yourself.

"Or in Justine's for that matter? One really doesn't know; all I can say is that their esteem for each other grew in inverse ratio to their regard—for there never by common consent was any love between them as I have shown you. Perhaps it is as well. But in all the long discussions I had with them separately, I could not find the key to a relationship which failed signally—one could see it daily sinking as land sinks, as the level of a lake might sink, and not know why. The surface colouring was brilliantly executed and so perfect as to deceive most observers like yourself, for example. Nor do I share

Leila's view—who never liked Justine. I sat beside her at the presentation which Narouz organised at the great *mulid* of Abu Girg which falls towards Easter every year. Justine had by then renounced Judaism to become a Copt in obedience to Nessim's wish, and as he could only marry her privately since she had already once been married, Narouz had to be content with a party which would present her to the great house and its dependants whose lives he was always anxious to cement into the family pattern.

"For four days then a huge encampment of tents and marquees grew up around the house—carpets and chandeliers and brilliant decorations. Alexandria was stripped bare of hothouse flowers and not less of its great social figures who made the somewhat mocking journey down to Abu Girg (nothing excites so much mocking amusement in the city as a fashionable wedding) to pay their respects and congratulate Leila. Local mudirs and sheiks, peasants innumerable, dignitaries from near and far had flocked in to be entertained—while the Bedouin, whose tribal grounds fringed the estate, gave magnificent displays of horsemanship, galloping round and round the house firing their guns—for all the world as if Justine were a young bride—a virgin. Imagine the smiles of Athena Trasha, of the Cervonis! And old Abu Kar himself rode up the steps of the house on his white Arab and into the very reception-rooms with a bowl of flowers. . . .

"As for Leila, she never for one moment took those clever eyes off Justine. She followed her with care like someone studying a historical figure. 'Is she not lovely?' I asked as I followed her glance and she turned a quick bird-like glance in my direction before turning back to the subject of her absorbed study. 'We are old friends, Balthazar, and I can talk to you. I was telling myself that she looked something like I did once, and that she is an adventuress; like a small dark snake coiled up at the centre of Nessim's life.' I protested in a formal manner at this; she stared into my eyes for a long moment and then gave a slow chuckle. I was surprised by what she said next. 'Yes, she is just like me—merciless in the pursuit of pleasure and yet arid—all her milk has turned into power-love. Yet she is also like me in that she is tender and kindly and a real man's woman. I hate her because she is like me, do you understand? And I fear her because she can read my mind.' She began to laugh. 'My darling,' she called out to Justine, 'come over here and sit by me.' And she thrust upon her the one sort of confectionery she herself most loathed—crystallized violets —which I saw Justine accept with reserve—for she loathed them too. And so the two of them sat there, the veiled sphinx and the unveiled, eating sugar violets which neither could bear. I was delighted to be able to see women at their most primitive like this. Nor can I tell you very much about the validity of such judgments. We all make them about each other.

"The curious thing was that despite this antipathy between the two women—the antipathy of affinity, you might say—there sprang up side by side with it a strange sympathy, a sense of identification with each other. For example when Leila at last dared to meet Mountolive it was done secretly and arranged by Justine. It was Justine who brought them together, both masked, during the carnival ball. Or so I heard.

"As for Nessim, I would, at the risk of over-simplification, say something like this: he was so innocent that he had not realised that you cannot live with a woman without in some degree falling in love with her—that possession is nine points of the jealousy! He was dismayed and terrified by the extent of his own jealousy for Justine and was honestly trying to practise something new for him—indifference. True or false? I don't know.

"And then, turning the coin round, I would say that

what irked Justine herself unexpectedly was to find that
the contract of wife undertaken so rationally, and at the
level of a financial bargain, was somehow more binding
than a wedding-ring. One does not, as a woman (if
passion seems to sanction it) think twice about being
unfaithful to a husband; but to be unfaithful to Nessim
seemed like stealing money from the till. What would you
say?"

My own feeling (*pace* Balthazar) is that Justine became slowly aware of something hidden in the character
of this solitary endearing long-suffering man; namely a
jealousy all the more terrible and indeed dangerous for
never allowing itself any outlet. Sometimes . . . but here
I am in danger of revealing confidences which Justine
made to me during the period of the so-called love affair
which so much wounded me and in which, as I learn
now, she was only using me as a cover for other activities.
I have described the progress of it all elsewhere; but if
I were now to reveal all she told me of Nessim in her own
words I should be in danger, primo, of setting down
material perhaps distasteful to the reader and indeed
unfair to Nessim himself. Secundo: I am not sure any
more of its relative truth since it might have been part
of the whole grand design of deception! In my own
mind even those feelings ("important lessons learned,"
etc.) are all coloured by the central doubt which the
Interlinear has raised in my mind. "Truth is what most
contradicts itself . . ."! What a farce it all is!

But what he says of the jealousy of Nessim is true,
however, for I lived for a while in its shadow, and there
is no doubt about the effect it had on Justine. Almost
from the beginning she had found herself followed, kept
under surveillance, and very naturally this gave her a
feeling of uncertainty: uncertainty made terrible by the
fact that Nessim never openly spoke of it. It rested, an
invisible weight of suspicion dogging and discolouring

her commonest remarks, the most innocent of after-
dinner walks. He would sit between the tall candles gently
smiling at her while a whole silent inquisition unrolled
reverberating in his mind.

The simplest and most sincere actions—a visit to a
public library, a shopping list, a message on a place-card
—became baffling to the eye of a jealousy founded in
emotional impotence. Nessim was torn to rags by her
demands; she was torn to rags by the doubts she saw
reflected in his eyes—by the very tenderness with which
he put a wrap around her shoulders. It felt as if he were
slipping a noose over her neck. In a queer sort of way
this relationship echoed the psycho-analytic relationship
described in *Moeurs* by her first husband—where Justine
became for them all a Case rather than a person, chased
almost out of her right mind by the tiresome inquisitions
of those who never know when to leave ill alone. Yes,
she had fallen into a trap, there is no doubt. The thought
echoed in her mind like mad laughter. I hear it echo
still.

So they went on side by side, like runners perfectly
matched, offering to Alexandria what seemed the perfect
pattern of a relationship all envied and none could copy.
Nessim the indulgent, the uxorious, Justine the lovely
and contented wife.

"In his own way," notes Balthazar, "I suppose he was
only hunting for the truth. Isn't this becoming rather a
ridiculous remark? We should drop it by common consent! It is after all such an odd business. Shall I give
you yet another example from another quarter? Your
account of Capodistria's death on the lake is the version
which we all of us accepted at the time as likely to be
true: in our own minds, of course.

"But in the Police depositions, everyone concerned
mentioned one particular thing—namely that when they
raised his body from the lake in which it was floating,

with the black patch beside it in the water, his false
teeth fell into the boat with a clatter, and startled them
all. Now listen to this: three months later I was having
dinner with Pierre Balbz who was his dentist. He assured
me that Da Capo had an almost perfect set of teeth and
certainly no false teeth which could possibly have fallen
out. Who, then, was it? I don't know. And if Da Capo
simply disappeared and arranged for some decoy to take
his place, he had every reason: leaving behind him debts
of over two million. Do you see what I mean?

"Fact is unstable by its very nature. Narouz once said
to me that he loved the desert because there 'the wind
blew out one's footsteps like candle-flames.' So it seems
to me does reality. How then can we hunt for the truth?"

o   o   o   o   o

Pombal was hovering between diplomatic tact and the
low cunning of a provincial public prosecutor; the con-
flicting emotions played upon his fat face as he sat in
his gout-chair with his fingers joined. He had the air
of a man in complete agreement with himself. "They
say," he said, watching me keenly, "that you are now
in the British *Deuxième*. Eh? Don't tell me, I know
you can't speak. Nor can I if you ask me about myself.
You *think* you know that I am in the French—but I
deny the whole thing most strenuously. What I am
asking is whether I should have you living in the flat. It
seems somehow . . . how do you say? . . . Box and Cox.
No? I mean, why don't we sell each other ideas, eh? I
know you won't. Neither will I. Our sense of humour . . .
I mean only *if* we are in the . . . ahem. But of course,
you deny it and I deny it. So we are not. But you are
not too proud to share my women, eh? *Autre chose.*
Have a drink, eh? The gin bottle is over there. I hid it
from Hamid. Of course, I know that something is going

on. I don't despair of finding out. Something . . . I wish I knew . . . Mountolive, eh?"

"What have you done to your face?" I say to change the subject. He has recently started to grow a moustache. He holds on to it defensively as if my question constituted a threat to shave it off forcibly. "My moustache, ah that! Well, recently I have had so many reproofs about work, not attending to it, that I analysed myself deeply, *au fond*. Do you know how many man-hours I am losing through women? You will never guess. I thought a moustache (isn't it hideous?) would put them off a bit, but no. It is just the same. It is a tribute, dear boy, not to my charm but to the low standards here. They seem to love me because there is nothing better. They love a well-hung diplomat—how do you say *faisandé*? Why do you laugh? You are losing a lot of woman-hours too. But then you have the British Government behind you—the pound, eh? That girl was here again today. *Mon Dieu,* so thin and so uncared for! I offered her some lunch but she would not stay. And the mess in your room! She takes hashish, doesn't she? Well, when I go to Syria on leave you can have the whole place. Provided you respect my firescreen—isn't it good as for art, *hein?*"

He has had an immense and vivid firescreen made for the flat which bears the legend "LÉGÈRETÉ, FATALITÉ, MATERNITÉ" in poker-work.

"Ah well," he continues, "so much for art in Alexandria. But as for that Justine, that is a better barbarian for you, no? I bet she—eh? Don't tell. Why are you not happier about it? You Englishmen, always gloomy and full of politics. *Pas de remords, mon cher.* Two women in tandem—who would want better? And one Left-Handed—as Da Capo calls Lesbians. You know Justine's reputation? Well, for my part, I am renouncing the whole—"

So Pombal flows in great good humour over the shal-

low river bed of his experience and standing on the
balcony I watch the sky darkening over the harbour and
hear the sullen hooting of ships' sirens, emphasising our
loneliness here, our isolation from the warm Gulf Stream
of European feelings and ideas. All the currents slide
away towards Mecca or to the incomprehensible desert
and the only foothold in this side of the Mediterranean
is the city we have come to inhabit and hate, to infect
with our own self-contempts.

And then I see Melissa walk down the street and my
heart contracts with pity and joy as I turn to open the
flat door.

o   o   o   o   o

These quiet bemused island days are a fitting commen-
tary to the thoughts and feelings of one walking alone
on deserted beaches, or doing the simple duties of a
household which lacks a mother. But I carry now the
great Interlinear in my hand wherever I go, whether
cooking or teaching the child to swim, or cutting wood
for the fireplace. But these fictions all live on as a pro-
jection of the white city itself whose pearly skies are
broken in spring only by the white stalks of the minarets
and the flocks of pigeons turning in clouds of silver
and amethyst; whose veridian and black marble harbour-
water reflects the snouts of foreign men-of-war turning
through their slow arcs, depicting the prevailing wind;
or swallowing their own inky reflections, touching and
overlapping like the very tongues and sects and races
over which they keep their uneasy patrol: symbolising
the western consciousness whose power is exemplified in
steel—those sullen preaching guns against the yellow
metal of the lake and the town which breaks open at
sunset like a rose.

o   o   o   o   o

PART
two

6.

"PURSEWARDEN!" writes Balthazar.

"I won't say that you have been less than just to him—only that he does not seem to resurrect on paper into a recognisable image of the man I knew. He seems to be a sort of enigma to you. (It is not enough, perhaps, to respect a man's genius—one must love him a little, no?) It may have been the envy you speak of which blinded you to his qualities, but somehow I doubt it; it seems to me to be very hard to envy someone who was so single-minded and moreover such a simpleton in so many ways, as to make him a real original (for example: money terrified him). I admit that I regarded him as a great man and I knew him well—even though I have never, to this day, read a single book of his, not even the last trilogy which made such a noise in the world, though I pretend to have done so in company. I have dipped here and there. I feel I don't need to read more.

"I put down a few notes upon him here then, not to contradict you, wise one, but simply to let you compare two dissimilar images. But if you are wrong about him, you are not less wrong than Pombal who always credited him with an *humeur noire* so dear to the French heart. But there was no spleen in the man and his apparent world-weariness was not feigned; while his cruelties of tongue were due to his complete simplicity and a not always delightful sense of mischief. Pombal never recovered I think from being nicknamed *'Le Prépuce Bar-*

bu'; and if you will forgive me neither did you from
Pursewarden's criticism of your own novels. Remember?
'These books have a curious and rather forbidding streak
of cruelty—a lack of humanity which puzzled me at first.
But it is simply the way a sentimentalist would disguise
his weakness. Cruelty here is the obverse of sentimentality.
He wounds because he is afraid of going all squashy.'
Of course, you are right in saying that he was contemptuous of your love of Melissa—and the nickname he gave
you must have wounded also, suiting as it did your
initials (Lineaments of Gratified Desire) . 'There goes
old Lineaments in his dirty mackintosh.' A poor joke, I
know. But all this is not very real.

"I am turning out a drawer full of old mementoes and
notes today in order to think about him a bit on paper;
it is a holiday and the clinic is closed. It is risky work, I
know, but perhaps I can answer a question which you
must have put to yourself when you read the opening
pages of the Interlinear: 'How could Pursewarden and
Justine . . . ?' I know.

"He had been to Alexandria before twice, before he
met us all, and had once spent a whole winter at
Mazarita working on a book: but this time he came back
to do a course of lectures at the Atelier, and as Nessim
and I and Clea were on the committee, he could not
avoid the side of Alexandrian life which most delighted
and depressed him. In a letter to Mountolive:

" ' My dear David,

" 'I see you are named in today's papers as the new
Plenipot. I wish I had known you were coming. I might
have stayed instead of giving ground and being upon the
point of departure myself. Damn! But frankly Egypt is
an unenviable post at present with the break-up of the
High Commission. Terrible dog-fights between fragments
of the old agencies and no one to arbitrate. You will
have headache-size decisions to make if you indeed are

coming—I suppose early spring? I am as usual in disfavour
for neglect of duty and trenchant opinions about the way
things should be. I have nothing really to lose. And your
Chancery is full of queer fish. Errol, a Labour peer, that
strangest of all animals, aflame with zeal and ignorance,
and Donkin who has grown a beard and turned Moslem.
. . . But I won't frighten you too much. My contract is
hinged for April, my views most unwelcome here, so that
I foresee a move. Frankly I would not mind. But it would
be fun to welcome you to this policy cockshy where everything is upside down. But if the work side is horrid, you
will still have Alexandria as it was and ever will be; a
Babylon of Buhl. Nessim, Narouz and their invisible and
eccentric mum . . . I could tell you a deal about them,
but not on paper. If I get sacked I'll try and reach you
through the Bag Room. When do you leave Russia? Post-
card please. I must have a talk to you before you set off,
as there is quite a lot going on under the surface here
to which I am privy, and about which your blissful
Chancery knows nothing.

" 'Yours,

" 'L.P.'

"Physical features, as best I remember them. He was
fair, a good average height and strongly built though not
stout. Brown hair and moustache—very small this. Extremely well-kept hands. A good smile though when not
smiling his face wore a somewhat quizzical almost impertinent air. His eyes were hazel and the best feature of
him—they looked into other eyes, into other ideas, with
a real candour, rather a terrifying sort of lucidity. He
was somewhat untidy in dress but always spotlessly clean
of person and abhorred dirty nails and collars. Yes, but
his clothes were sometimes stained with spots of the red
ink in which he wrote. There!

"Really, I think his sense of humour had separated him
from the world, into a privacy of his own, or else he had

discovered for himself the uselessness of having opinions
and in consequence made a habit of usually saying the
opposite of what he thought in a joking way. He was
an ironist, hence he appeared often to violate good sense:
hence too his equivocal air, the apparent frivolity with
which he addressed himself to large subjects. This sort
of serious clowning leaves footmarks in conversation of
a peculiar kind. His little sayings stayed like the paw-
marks of a cat in a pat of butter. To stupidities he would
respond only with the word '*kwatz.*'

"He believed, I think, that success was inherent in
greatness. His own lack of success (he made very little
money from his work and it all went to his wife and two
children who lived in England) was inclined to make
him doubt his powers. Perhaps he should have been
born an American? I don't know.

"I remember going down to the dock to meet his boat
with the panting Keats—who proposed to interview him.
We were late and only caught up with him as he was
filling in an immigration form. Against the column
marked 'religion' he had written '*Protestant—purely in
the sense that I protest.*'

"We took him ashore for a drink so that Keats could
interview him at leisure. The poor boy was absolutely
nonplussed. Pursewarden had a particular smile for the
Press. I still have the picture Keats took that morning.
The sort of smile which might have hardened on the face
of a dead baby. Later I got to know this smile and
learned that it meant he was about to commit an outrage
on accepted good sense with an irony. He was trying to
amuse no-one but himself, mind you. Keats panted and
puffed, looked 'sincere' and probed, but all in vain. Later
I asked him for a carbon copy of his interview which he
typed out and gave me with his puzzled air, explaining
that there was no 'news' in the man. Pursewarden had
said things like 'It is the duty of every patriot to hate his

country creatively' and 'England cries out for brothels';
this last somewhat shocked poor Keats who asked him if
he felt that 'unbridled licence' would be a good thing in
England. Did Pursewarden want to undermine religion?

"I can see as I write the wicked air with which my
friend replied in shocked tones: 'Good Lord, no! I would
simply like to put an end to the cruelty to children
which is such a distressing feature of English life—as well
as the slavish devotion to pets which borders on the
obscene.' Keats must have gulped his way through all
this, dotting and dashing in his shorthand book with
rolling eye, while Pursewarden studied the further horizon. But if the journalist found this sort of exchange
enigmatic, he was doubly puzzled by some of the answers
to his political questions. For example, when he asked
Pursewarden what he thought of the Conference of the
Arab Committee which was due to start in Cairo that
day, he replied: 'When the English feel they are in the
wrong, their only recourse is to cant.' 'Am I to understand that you are criticising British policy?' 'Of course
not. Our statesmanship is impeccable.' Keats fanned himself all the harder and abandoned politics forthwith. In
answer to the question 'Are you planning to write a novel
while you are here?' Pursewarden said: 'If I am denied
every other means of self-gratification.'

"Later Keats, poor fellow, still fanning that pink brow,
said, 'He's a thorny bastard isn't he?' But the odd thing
was that he wasn't at all. Where can a man who really
thinks take refuge in the so-called real world without
defending himself against stupidity by the constant exercise of equivocation? Tell me that. Particularly a poet.
He once said: 'Poets are not really serious about ideas or
people. They regard them much as a Pasha regards the
members of an extensive *harim*. They are pretty, yes.
They are for use. But there is no question of them being
true or false, or having souls. In this way the poet

preserves his freshness of vision, and finds everything miraculous. And this is what Napoleon meant when he described poetry as a *science creuse*. He was quite right from his own point of view.'

"This robust mind was far from splenetic though its judgments were harsh. I have seen him so moved in describing Joyce's encroaching blindness and D. H. Lawrence's illness that his hand shook and he turned pale. He showed me once a letter from the latter in which Lawrence had written: *'In you I feel a sort of profanity—almost a hate for the tender growing quick in things, the dark Gods. . . .'* He chuckled. He deeply loved Lawrence but had no hesitation in replying on a post-card: *'My dear DHL. This side idolatry—I am simply trying not to copy your habit of building a Taj Mahal around anything as simple as a good f——k.'*

"He said to Pombal once: *'On fait l'amour pour mieux refouler et pour décourager les autres.'* And added: 'I worry a great deal about my golf handicap.' It always took Pombal a few moments to work out these non-sequiturs. *'Quel malin, ce type-là!'* he would mutter under his breath. Then and only then would Pursewarden permit himself a chuckle—having scored his personal victory. They were a splendid pair and used to drink together a great deal.

"Pombal was terribly affected by his death—really over-come, he retired to bed for a fortnight. Could not speak of him without tears coming into his eyes; this used to infuriate Pombal himself. 'I never knew how much I loved the blasted man,' he would say. . . . I hear Purse-warden's wicked chuckle in all this. No, you are wrong about him. His favourite adjective was 'uffish'! or so he told me.

"His public lectures were disappointing, as you may remember. Afterwards, I discovered why. He read them out of a book. They were someone else's lectures! But once when I took him up to the Jewish school and asked him to talk to the children of the literary group, he was delightful. He began by showing them some card tricks and then congratulated the winner of the Literary Prize, making him read the prize essay aloud. Then he asked the children to write down three things in their notebooks which might help them some day if they didn't forget them. Here they are.

"1. Each of our five senses contains an art.

"2. In questions of art great secrecy must be observed.

"3. The artist must catch every scrap of wind.

"Then he produced from his mackintosh pocket a huge packet of sweets upon which they all fell, he no less, and completed the most successful literary hour ever held at the school.

"He had some babyish habits, picked his nose, and enjoyed taking his shoes off under the table in a restaurant. I remember hundreds of meetings which were made easy and fruitful by his naturalness and humour but he spared no one and made enemies. He wrote once to his beloved DHL: *'Maître, Maître, watch your step. No one can go on being a rebel too long without turning into an autocrat.'*

"When he wished to discuss a bad work of art he would say in tones of warm approbation, 'Most effective.' This was a feint. He was not interested enough in art to want to argue about it with others ('dogs snuffing over a bitch too small to mount') so he said, 'Most effective.' Once when he was drunk he added: 'The effective in art is what rapes the emotion of your audience without nourishing its values.'

"Do you see? Do you see?

"All this was brought to bear on Justine like a great charge of swan-shot, scattering her senses and bringing her for the first time something she had despaired of ever encountering: namely laughter. Imagine what one touch

of ridicule can do to a Higher Emotion! 'As for Justine,'
said Pursewarden to me when he was drunk once, 'I
regard her as a tiresome old sexual turnstile through
which presumably we must all pass—a somewhat vulpine
Alexandrian Venus. By God, what a woman she would
be if she were really natural and felt no guilt! Her behaviour would commend her to the Pantheon—but one
cannot send her up there with a mere recommendation
from the Rabbinate—a bundle of Old Testament ravings.
What would old Zeus say?' He saw my reproachful glance
at these cruelties and said, somewhat shamefacedly, 'I'm
sorry, Balthazar. I simply dare not take her seriously. One
day I will tell you why.'

"Justine herself wished very much to take him seriously but he absolutely refused to command sympathy or
share the solitude from which he drew so much of his
composure and self-possession.

"Justine herself, you know, could not bear to be alone.

"He was due, I remember, to lecture in Cairo to several
societies affiliated to our own Arts Society, and Nessim,
who was busy, asked Justine to take him down by car.
That was how they came to find themselves together on
a journey which threw up a sort of ludicrous shadow-
image of a love-relationship, like a clever magic-lantern
picture of a landscape, created by, strangely—not Justine
at all—but a worse mischief-maker—the novelist himself.
'It was Punch and Judy, all right!' said Pursewarden ruefully afterwards.

"He was at that time deeply immersed in the novel he
was writing, and as always he found that his ordinary
life, in a distorted sort of way, was beginning to follow
the curvature of his book. He explained this by saying
that any concentration of the will displaces life (Archi-
medes' bath-water) and gives it bias in motion. Reality,
he believed, was always trying to copy the imagination
of man, from which it derived. You will see from this

that he was a serious fellow underneath much of his clowning and had quite comprehensive beliefs and ideas. But also, he had been drinking rather heavily that day as he always did when he was working. Between books he never touched a drop. Riding beside her in the great car, someone beautiful, dark and painted with great eyes like the prow of some Aegean ship, he had the sensation that his book was being rapidly passed underneath his life, as if under a sheet of paper containing the iron filings of temporal events, as a magnet is in that commonplace experiment one does at school: and somehow setting up a copying magnetic field.

"He never flirted, mind you; and if he started to approach Justine it was simply to try out a few speeches and attitudes, to verify certain conclusions he had reached in the book before actually sending it to the printer, so to speak! Afterwards, of course, he bitterly repented of this piece of self-indulgence. He was at that moment trying to escape from the absurd dictates of narrative form in prose: 'He said' 'She said' 'He cocked an eye, shot a cuff, lifted a lazy head, etc.' Was it possible, had he succeeded in 'realising' character without the help of such props? He was asking himself this as he sat there in the sand. ('Her eyelashes brushed his cheek.' *Merde alors!* Had he written that?) Justine's thick black eyelashes were like . . . what? So it was that his kisses were really warm and wholehearted in an absent-minded way because they were in no way meant for her. (One of the great paradoxes of love. Concentration on the love-object and possession are the poisons.) And he discovered to her the fact that she was ridiculous, with a series of disarming and touching pleasantries at which she found herself laughing with a relief that seemed almost sinful. As for her: it was not only that his skin and hair were fresh and that his love-making was full of a lazy, un-blushing enterprise; he was wholly himself in a curious way. It aroused in her an unfamiliar passionate curiosity. And then, the things he said! 'Of course I've read *Moeurs* and had you pointed out a hundred times as the tragic central character. It's all right, written by a born *lettré*, of course, and smells fashionably of armpits and *eau de javel*. But surely you are making yourself a little self-important about it all? You have the impertinence to foist yourself on us as a problem—perhaps because you have nothing else to offer? It is foolish. Or perhaps it is that the Jew loves punishment and always comes back for more?' And suddenly, but completely, to take her firmly by the nape of the neck and force her down into the hot sand before she could find time to measure the extent of the insult or form a response in her mind. And then, while he was still kissing, to say something so ludicrous that the laughter and tears in her mind became one and the same sort of things, a mixture of qualities hard to endure.

" 'For God's sake!' she said, having decided to behave as if outraged. He had been too quick for her. He had surprised her while she was half-asleep in her mind, so to speak.

" 'Didn't you want to make love? My mistake!'

"She looked at him, a little disarmed by the mock-repentance of his expression. 'No, of course not. Yes.' Something inside her repeated 'Yes, yes.' An attachment without fingerprints—something as easy as sailing a boat or diving into deep water: 'Fool!' she cried, and to her own surprise started laughing. A conquest by impudence? I don't know. I am only putting down my own views.

"She explained this to herself later by saying that for him sex was the nearest thing to laughter—quite free of particularity, neither sacred nor profane. Pursewarden himself has written that he thought it comic and sinister and divine in one. But she could not grasp and define the thing as she wished, for when she said to him, 'You

are hopelessly promiscuous, like I am,' he was really
angry, really outraged. 'Imbecile,' he replied, 'you have
the soul of a clerk. For those who love poetry there is
no such thing as *vers libre*.' She did not understand this.

" 'O stop behaving like a pious old sin-cushion into
which we all have to stick the rusty pins of our admiration,' he snapped. In his diary he added drily: 'Moths
are attracted by the flame of personality. So are vampires.
Artists should take note and beware.' And in the mirror
he cursed himself roundly for this lapse, a self-indulgence
which had brought him what most bored him—an inti-
mate relationship. But in the sleeping face he too saw
the childish inhabitant of Justine, the 'calcimine imprint
of a fern in chalk.' He saw now how she must have
looked on the first night of love—hair torn and trailing
over the pillow like a ruffled black dove, fingers like
tendrils, warm mouth inhaling the airs of sleep; warm
as a figure of pastry fresh from the oven. 'Oh damn!' he
cried aloud.

"Then in bed with her in a hotel crowded with
Alexandrian acquaintances who might easily observe
their rashness and carry their gossip back to the city they
had left together that morning, he swore again. Pursewarden had much to hide, you know. He was not all he
seemed. And at this time he did not dare to prejudice
his relations with Nessim. The Bloody woman! I hear
his voice.

" '*Écoute. . . .*'

" '*Rien—silence.*'

" '*Mais, chéri, nous sommes seuls.*' She was still sleepy.
Cast an eye to a bolted door. She felt a momentary disgust
at this bourgeois fear of his; afraid of intruders, spies, a
husband?

" '*Qu'est-ce que c'est?*'

" '*Je m'écoute moi-même.*' Yellow eyes without a trace
of discernible divinity in them; he was like a slender

rock-god, with ruffled moustache. Past lives?' *Le cœur qui bat.*' Derisively he quoted a popular song.

" '*Tu n'es pas une femme pour moi—pas dans mon genre.*'

"This made her feel like a whipped dog specially as a moment ago he had been kissing her, breaking her down into successive images of pain and pleasure with an importunity which belonged, she now knew, only to his passion and not to himself.

" 'What do you want?' she said, and struck him across the face to feel at once the stinging retort on her own cheek—like spray dashing over her. And now he began to fool again until she could not prevent herself from laughing. All this is there in the third volume—the passage with the prostitute is based on these incidents. I came upon it in my dipping.

"This weird translation of feelings into gestures which belied words and words which belied gestures, confused and disoriented her. She needed someone to tell her whether to laugh or to cry.

"As for Pursewarden, he believed with Rilke that no woman adds anything to the sum of Woman, and from satiety he had now taken refuge in the plenty of the imagination—the true field of merit for the artist. This is perhaps what made him seem to her somehow cold and unfeeling. 'Somewhere inside you there is a nasty little Anglican clergyman,' she told him and he considered the remark gravely on its merits. 'Perhaps,' he said, and added after a pause, 'But your humourlessness has made you an enemy of pleasure. *The* enemy. You have a premeditated approach to experience. I am a truer pagan.' And he began to laugh. Great honesty can be crueller than anything else.

"He was sick, I think too, of all the 'mud thrown up by the wheels of life'—so he writes. He had done his best to scrape off as much as he could, to tidy himself up.

Was he now to be saddled with the inquisitions and ardours of a Justine—the marshy end of a personality which in a funny sort of way he had himself transcended? 'By God, no!' he told himself. Can you see what a fool he was?

"His life had been a various and full one, and he had held a number of contract posts for some political branch of the Foreign Office, largely, I gather, connected with cultural relations. This work had taken him to several countries and he spoke at least three languages well. He was married and had two children although he was separated from his wife—and indeed never spoke about her without stammering—though I gather they corresponded affectionately and he was always most scrupulous in sending her money. What else? Yes, his real name was Percy and he was somewhat sensitive about it because of the alliteration, I suppose; hence his choice of Ludwig as a signature to his books. He was always delighted when his reviewers took him to be of German extraction.

"I think what frightened and delighted Justine about him most, however, was his somewhat contemptuous repudiation of Arnauti and his book *Moeurs*. Mind you, this too was overdone—he actually admired the book very much. But he used it as a stick to belabour Justine, describing her ex-husband as a 'tiresome psychonalytical turnkey with a belt full of rusty complexes.' I must say, this delighted her. You see, here was someone who set no store by jargon and refused to regard her as a Case. Of course Pursewarden, the silly fool, was simply trying to get rid of her and this was not a very good way. Yet as a doctor I can testify to the therapeutic effects of insults in cases where medicine is at a loss to make any headway! Indeed, had Justine succeeded in making herself really interesting to him, she might have learned a lot of valuable lessons. Odd, isn't it? He really *was* the right man for her in a sort of way; but then as you must

know, it is a law of love that the so-called 'right' person
always comes too soon or too late. As for Pursewarden, he
withdrew his favours so abruptly that there was hardly
time for her to measure the full force of his personality.

"But at the time of which I am writing he was busy
insulting her in his somewhat precise idiosyncratic English or French (he had a few pet neologisms which he
used with pleasure—one was the noun 'bogue' which he
had coined from 'bogus'; *c'est de la grande bogue ça*
or 'what bloody bogue') —he insulted her, if one can use
the expression, simply to discourage her. I must say I
can hardly repress a laugh when I think of it: you could
as easily discourage Justine as an equinox, and she was
not disposed to abandon this experiment before she had
learned as much as possible about herself from it. Preda-
tory Judaic characteristic! Pursewarden was like Doctor
Foster in the nursery rhyme.

"For her, his easy detachment gave him freshness of
heart. Justine had never had anyone who *didn't* want or
who could do without her before! All kinds of new res-
onances sprang out of making love to such a person.
(Am I inventing this? No. I knew them both well and
discussed each with the other.) Then, he could make her
laugh—quite the most dangerous thing to do to a woman
for they prize laughter most after passion. Fatal! No,
he was not wrong when he told himself in the mirror:
'Ludwig, thou art an imbecile.'

"Worse, the mockery of his cruelty hurt her, and after
making love, say, made her think something like this:
'What he does is simple as a domestic impulse become
habit—cleaning his shoes on a mat.' Then unexpectedly
would come some terrible mocking phrase like 'We are
all looking for someone lovely to be unfaithful to—did
you think you were original?' Or else 'The human race!
If you can't do the trick with the one you've got, why—
shut your eyes and imagine the one you can't get. Who

knows? It's perfectly legal and secret. It's the marriage of true minds!' He was standing at the washbasin cleaning his teeth in white wine. She could have murdered him for looking so gay and self-possessed.

"Coming back from Cairo they had several rows. 'As for your so-called illness—have you ever thought it might be just due to an inflamed self-pity?' She became so furious that she nearly drove the car off the road into a tree. 'Miserable Anglo-Saxon!' she cried, on the point of tears—'Bully!'

"And he thought to himself: 'Great Heavens! Here we are quarrelling like a couple of newly-weds. Soon we shall marry and live in filthy compatibility, feasting on each other's blackheads. Ugh! Dreadful isogamy of the Perfect Match. Perce, you gone and done it again.' I can reconstruct this because he always spoke to himself in cockney when he was drunk as well as when he was alone.

"'If you try to hit me,' he said happily, 'we shall have a crash.' And he thought of a bitter little short story into which he might insert her. 'What we need to establish for sex in art,' he muttered, 'is a revulsion coefficient.' She was still angry. 'What are you muttering about?—'Praying.'

"For her, the moiety which remained after love-making then was not disgust or despair as it usually was, but laughter; and though furious with him she nevertheless found herself smiling at some absurdity of his even as she realised with a pang that he could never be achieved, attained as a man, nor would he even become a friend, except on his own terms. He offered an uncompanionate, compassionless ardour which in a funny sort of way made his kisses thrilling. They were as healthy as the bite of a hungry child into a cooking-apple. And regretting this, with another part of her mind (there was an honest woman somewhere deep down) she found herself hoping he would never abandon this entrenched position, or

retreat from it. Like all women, Justine hated anyone
she could be certain of; and you must remember she
had never had anyone as yet whom she could wholly
admire—though that may sound strange to you. Here at
last was someone she could not punish by her infidelities
—an intolerable but delightful novelty. Women are very
stupid as well as very profound.

"As for Justine, she was surprised by the new emotions
he seemed capable of provoking. Quite simple things—
for example she found her love extending itself to in-
animate objects concerned with him, like his old meer-
schaum pipe with the much basted stem. Or his old hat,
so battered and weather-stained—it hung behind the door
like a water-colour of the man himself. She found herself
cherishing objects he had touched or thrown aside. It
seemed to her an infuriating sort of mental captivity to
find herself stroking one of his old notebooks as if she
were caressing his body, or tracing with her finger the
words he had written on the shaving-mirror with his
brush (from Stendhal): 'You must boldly face a little
anatomy if you want to discover an unknown principle'
and 'Great souls require nourishment.'

"Once, when she discovered an Arab prostitute in his
bed (while he himself was shaving in the other room and
whistling an air from Donizetti) she was surprised to
find that she was not jealous but curious. She sat on the
bed and pinning the arms of the unfortunate girl to the
pillow set about questioning her closely about what she
had felt while making love to him. Of course, this scared
the prostitute very much. 'I am not angry,' Justine repeated to the wailing creature, 'I am puzzled. Tell me
what I ask of you.'

"Pursewarden had to come in and release his visitant
and they all three sat on the bed together, Justine feeding
her with crystallized fruit to calm her fears.

"Shall I go on? This analysis may give you pain—but

if you are a real writer you will want to follow things to their conclusion, no? All this shows you how hard it was for Melissa. . . .

"If he succeeded in infuriating her it was because he could feel concern about her without any real affection. He did not always clown, or stay beyond her reach; that is what I mean by his honesty. He gave intellectual value for money—in fact he told her the real secret which lay hidden under the enigma of his behaviour. You will find it in one of his books. I know this because Clea quoted it to me as his most profound statement on human relationships. He said to her one night: 'You see, Justine, I believe that Gods are men and men Gods; they intrude on each other's lives, trying to express themselves through each other—hence such apparent confusion in our human states of mind, our intimations of powers within or beyond us. . . . And then (listen) I think that very few people realise that sex is a psychic and not a physical act. The clumsy coupling of human beings is simply a biological paraphrase of this truth—a primitive method of introducing minds to each other, engaging them. But most people are stuck in the physical aspect, unaware of the poetic *rapport* which it so clumsily tries to teach. That is why all your dull repetitions of the same mistake are simply like a boring great multiplication table, and will remain so until you get your head out of the paper bag and start to think responsibly.'

"It is impossible to describe the effect these words had on her: they threw her life and actions into relief in an entirely new way. She saw him all of a sudden in a new light, as a man whom one could 'really love.' Alas, he had already withdrawn his favours. . . .

"When he next went to Cairo he elected to go alone and, made restless by his absence, she made the mistake of writing him a long passionate letter in which she clumsily tried to thank him for a friendship of whose

real value to her he was *completely unaware*—that is true
of all love again. He regarded this simply as another attempt to intrude upon him and sent her a telegram.
(They corresponded through me. I have it still.)

*'First nobody can own an artist so be warned. Second
what good is a faithful body when the mind is by its
very nature unfaithful? Third stop whining like an Arab,
you know better. Fourth neurosis is no excuse. Health
must be won and earned by a battle. Lastly it is honour-
able if you can't win to hang yourself.'*

"Once she happened upon him when he was very drunk
at the Café Al Aktar; I gather that you and I had just
left. You remember the evening? He had been rather
insulting. It was the evening when I tried to show you
how the nine-point proposition of the Cabal worked. I
did not know then that you would type it all out and
send it to the Secret Service! What a marvellous jest!
But I love to feel events overlapping each other, crawling
over one another like wet crabs in a basket. No sooner
had we left than Justine entered. It was she who helped
him back to his hotel and pushed him safely on to his
bed. 'Oh, you are the most despairing man!' she cried
at that recumbent figure, at which he raised his arms
and responded 'I know it, I know it! I am just a refugee
from the long slow toothache of English life. It is terrible
to love life so much you can hardly breathe!' And he
began to laugh—a laughter which was overtaken by
nausea. She left him being sick in the washbasin.

"The next morning she went round early with some
French reviews in one of which there was an article
about his work. He was wearing nothing but a pyjama
jacket and a pair of spectacles. On his mirror he had
written with a wet shaving-stick, some words from Tol-

stoy: 'I do not cease to reflect upon art and upon every form of temptation which obscures the spirit.'

"He took the books from her without a word and made as if to shut the door in her face. 'No,' she said, 'I'm coming in.' He cleared his throat and said: 'This is for the last time. I'm sick of being visited as one might visit the grave of a dead kitten.' But she took him by the arms and he said, more gently: 'A definite and complete stop, see?' He had been having some interviews in Cairo.

"She sat down on the end of the bed and lit a cigarette, considering him, as one might a specimen. 'I am curious, after all your talk about self-possession and responsibility, to see just how Anglo-Saxon you are—unable to finish anything you start. Why do you look furtive?' This was a splendid line of attack. He smiled. 'I'm going to work today.'

" 'Then I'll come tomorrow.'

" 'I shall have 'flu.'

" 'The day after.'

" 'I shall be going to the Zoo.'

" 'I shall come too.'

"Pursewarden was now extremely rude; she knew she had scored a victory and was delighted. She listened to his honeyed insults as she tapped the carpet with her foot. 'Very well,' she said at last, 'we shall see.' (I am afraid you will have to make room in this for the essential comedy of human relations. You give it so little place.) The next day he put her out of his hotel-room by the neck, like a pet cat. The following day he woke and found the great car parked once more outside the hotel. '*Merde*,' he cried and just to spite her dressed and went to the Zoo. She followed him. He spent the morning looking at the monkeys with the greatest attention. She was not blind to the insult. She followed him to a bench where he sat, eating the peanuts which he had originally bought to feed the monkeys. She always looked splendid

when she was angry, with her nostrils quivering, and clad
in that spotless sharkskin suit with a flower at her lapel.

" 'Pursewarden,' she said, sitting down.

" 'You won't believe me,' he said, 'you bloody tiresome
obsessive society figure. From now on you are going to
leave me alone. Your money won't help you.'

"It is a measure of his stupidity that he could use such
language. She was delighted at making him so alarmed.
You, of course, know how determined she is. But there
was a reason—and underneath the insults she detected a
genuine concern—something that did not bear at all on
their relationship such as it was. Something else. What?

"You have already noted that she was an unerring
mind-reader; and sitting beside him, watching his face,
she said like someone reading a badly-written manuscript
—'Nessim. Something to do with Nessim. You are afraid
. . . not of him.' And then in a flash the intuitive contact
was made and she blurted out: 'There is something regarding Nessim which you cannot afford to compromise:
I understand.' And she heaved a great sigh. 'O Fool,
why did you not tell me? Am I to forfeit your friendship
because of this? Of course not. I don't care whether you
want to sleep with me or not. But you—that is different.
Thank God I've discovered what it was.'

"He was too astonished to say anything. This mind-
reading performance surprised him more than anything
about her. He simply stared at her and said nothing, for
a long time. 'O, I am glad,' she went on, 'for that is so
easily arranged. And it will not prevent us from meeting.
We need never sleep together again if you don't wish it.
But at least I shall be able to see you.' Another category
of the 'love-beast,' one which I am unable to define. She
would have gone through fire for him by now.

"The silences of Nessim had already assumed huge
proportions in her mind. They stretched away on every
side like the desert itself—unnerving her. And since her

own conscience was by its nature and even without reason, a guilty one, she had already begun to build up a defensive circle of friends whose harmless presences might obviate suspicion of her—the little court of homosexuals like Toto and Amar, whose activities and predispositions were sufficiently well-known to everybody to offer no cause for heart-burnings. She moved now like some sulky planet in the social life of the town, accepting the attentions of these neuters purely as a defence. In this way a general will utilize the features of a town he wishes to defend by building up ring within ring of earthworks. She did not know, for example, that the silences of Nessim betokened only despair and not suspense—for he never broke them.

"In your manuscripts, you hardly mention the question of the child—I told you once before that I thought Arnauti neglected that aspect of affairs in *Moeurs* because it seemed to him melodramatic. 'To the childless all things are without resonance,' says Pursewarden somewhere. But now the question of the child had become as important to Nessim as to Justine herself—it was his sole means of enlisting the love he desired from her—or so he thought. He fell upon the central problem like a fury, thinking that this would be the one means of penetrating the affective armour of his beautiful tacit wife; the wife he had married and hung up in a cobwebbed corner of his life, by the wrists, like a marionette on strings! Thank God I have never 'loved,' wise one, and never will! Thank God!

"Pursewarden writes somewhere (again from Clea): 'English has two great forgotten words, namely "helpmeet" which is much greater than "lover" and "lovingkindness" which is so much greater than "love" or even "passion." '

"Now Justine one day overheard part of a telephone conversation which led her to believe that Nessim had either located the missing child or knew something about it which he did not wish to reveal to her. As she passed through the hall he was putting down the telephone after having said: 'Well then, I count on your discretion. She must never know.' Never know what? Who was the 'she'? One can be forgiven for jumping to conclusions. As he did not speak of the conversation for several days she taxed him with it. He now made the fatal mistake of saying that it had never taken place, that she had mis-heard a conversation with his secretary. Had he said that it related to something quite different, he would have been all right, but to accuse her of not hearing the words which had been ringing in her ears for several days like an alarm bell, this was fatal.

"At one blow she lost confidence in him and began to imagine all sorts of things. Why should he wish to keep from her any knowledge he might have gained about her child? After all, his original promise had been to do what he could to discover its fate. Was it then too horrible to speak of? Surely Nessim would tell her anything if in-deed he knew anything? Why should he hold back a hypothetical knowledge of its fate? She simply could not guess but inside herself she felt that in some way the information was being held as a hostage is held—against something—what? Good behaviour?

"But Nessim, who had destroyed by this last clumsiness the last vestiges of regard she had for him, was grappling with a new set of factors. He himself had set great store by the recovery of the child as a means to the recovery of Justine herself; he simply did not dare to tell her—or indeed himself, so painful was it—that one day, after he had exhausted all his resources in an attempt to find out the truth, Narouz telephoned to say: 'I saw the Mag-zub by chance last night and forced the truth out of him. The child is dead.'

"This now rose between them like a great wall of

China, shutting them off from any further contact, and making her afraid that he might even intend her harm. And this is where you come in."

Yes, this alas is where I come in again, for it was approximately now that Justine must have come to my lecture on Cavafy and thence carried me off to meet the gentle Nessim; simple "as an axe falling"—cleaving my life in two! It is inexpressibly bitter today to realise that she was putting me to a considered purpose of her own, the monster, trailing me before Nessim as a bull-fighter trails a cloak, and simply to screen her meetings with a man with whom she herself did not even wish to sleep! But I have already described it all, so painfully, and in such great detail—trying to omit no flavour or crumb which would give the picture the coherence I felt it should possess. And yet, even now I can hardly bring myself to feel regret for the strange ennobling relationship into which she plunged me—presumably herself feeling nothing of its power—and from which I myself was to learn so much. Yes, truly it enriched me, but only to destroy Melissa. We must look these things in the face. I wonder why only *now* I have been told all this? My friends must all have known all along. Yet nobody breathed a word. But of course, the truth is that nobody ever does breathe a word, nobody interferes, nobody whispers while the acrobat is on the tight-rope; they just sit and watch the spectacle, waiting only to be wise after the event. But then, from another point of view, how would I, blindly and passionately in love with Justine, have received such unwelcome truths at the time? Would they have deflected me from my purpose? I doubt it.

I suppose that in all this Justine had surrendered to me only one of the many selves she possessed and inhabited—to this timid and scholarly lover with chalk on his sleeve!

Where must one look for justifications? Only I think

to the facts themselves; for they might enable me to see now a little further into the central truth of this enigma called "love." I see the image of it receding and curling away from me in an infinite series like the waves of the sea; or, colder than a dead moon, rising up over the dreams and illusions I fabricated from it—but like the real moon, always keeping one side of the truth hidden from me, the nether side of a beautiful dead star. My "love" for her, Melissa's "love" for me, Nessim's "love" for her, her "love" for Pursewarden—there should be a whole vocabulary of adjectives with which to qualify the noun—for no two contained the same properties; yet all contained the one indefinable quality, one common unknown in treachery. Each of us, like the moon, had a dark side—could turn the lying face of "unlove" towards the person who most loved and needed us. And just as Justine used my love, so Nessim used Melissa's. . . . One upon the back of the other, crawling about "like crabs in a basket."

It is strange that there is not a biology of this monster which lives always among the odd numbers, though by all the romances we have built around it it should inhabit the evens: the perfect numbers the hermetics use to describe marriage!

"What protects animals, enables them to continue living? A certain attribute of organic matter. As soon as one finds life one finds it, it is inherent in life. Like most natural phenomena it is polarized—there is always a negative and a positive pole. The negative pole is pain, the positive pole sex. . . . In the ape and man we find the first animals, excluding tame animals, in which sex can be roused without an external stimulus. . . . The result is that the greatest of all natural laws, periodicity, is lost in the human race. The periodic organic condition which should rouse the sexual sense has become an absolutely useless, degenerate, pathological manifestation."* (Pursewarden brooding over the monkey-house at the Zoo! Capodistria in his tremendous library of pornographic books, superbly bound! Balthazar at his occultism! Nessim facing rows and rows of figures and percentages!)

And Melissa? Of course, she was ill, indeed seriously ill, so that in a sense it is melodramatic in me to say that I killed her, or that Justine killed her. Nevertheless, nobody can measure the weight of the pain and neglect which I directly caused her. I remember now one day that Amaril came to see me, sentimental as a great dog. Balthazar had sent Melissa to him for X-rays and treatment.

Amaril was an original man in his way and a bit of a dandy withal. The silver duelling-pistols, the engraved visiting-cards in their superb case, clothes cut in all the elegance of the latest fashions. His house was full of candles and he wrote for preference on black paper with white ink. For him the most splendid thing in the world was to possess a fashionable woman, a prize greyhound, or a pair of invincible fighting-cocks. But he was an agreeable man and not without sensibility as a doctor, despite these romantic foibles.

His devotion to women was the most obvious thing about him; he dressed for them. Yet it was accompanied by a delicacy, almost a pudicity, in his dealings with them —at least in a city where a woman was, as provender, regarded as something like a plateful of mutton; a city where women cry out to be abused.

But he idealized them, built up romances in his mind about them, dreamed always of a complete love, a perfect understanding with one of the tribe. Yet all this was in vain. Ruefully he would explain to Pombal or to myself: "I cannot understand it. Before my love has a chance to crystallize, it turns into a deep, a devouring *friendship*. These devotions are not for you womanisers, you wouldn't understand. But once this happens, passion flies out of the window. Friendship consumes us, paralyses us. Another sort of love begins. What is it? I don't know. A tenderness, a *tendresse,* something melting. *Fondante."* Tears come into his eyes. "I am really a woman's man and women love me. But—" shaking his handsome head and blowing the smoke from his cigarette upwards to the ceiling he adds smiling, but without self-pity, "I alone among men can say that while all women love me no one woman ever has. Not properly. I am as innocent of love (not sexual love, of course) as a virgin. Poor Amaril!"

It is all true. It was his very devotion to women which dictated his choice in medicine—gynaecology. And women gravitate to him as flowers do to the sunlight. He teaches them what to wear and how to walk; chooses their scents for them, dictates the colour of their lipsticks. Moreover, there is not a woman in Alexandria who is not proud to be seen out on his arm; there is not one who *if asked* (but he never asks) would not be glad to betray her husband or her lover for him. And yet . . . and yet. . . . A connecting thread has been broken somewhere, a link snapped. Such desires as he knows, the stifling summer desires of the body in the city of sensuality, are stifled among shop-girls, among his inferiors. Clea used to say, "One feels a special sort of fate in store for Amaril. Dear Amaril!"

Yes. Yes. But what? What sort of fate lies in store for such a romantic—such a devoted, loving, patient student of women? These are the questions I ask myself as I see him, elegantly gloved and hatted, driving with Balthazar to the hospital for an operation. . . .

He described to me Melissa's condition adding only: "It would help her very much if she could be loved a bit." A remark which filled me with shame. It was that very night that I had borrowed the money from Justine to send her to a clinic in Palestine much against her own will.

We walked together to the flat after having spent a few minutes in the public gardens discussing her case. The palms looked brilliant in the moonlight and the sea glittered under the spring winds. It seemed so out of place—serious illness—in this scheme of things. Amaril took my arms as we climbed the stairs and squeezed them gently. "Life is hard," he said. And when we entered the bedroom once more to find her lying there in a trance with her pallid little face turned to the ceiling and the *hashish* pipe beside her on the table, he added, taking up his hat: "It is always . . . don't think I blame you . . . no, I envy you Justine . . . yet it is always *in extremis* that we doctors make the last desperate prescription for a woman patient—when all the resources of science have failed. Then we say, 'If only she could be loved!'" He sighed and shook his handsome head.

There are always a hundred ways of justifying oneself but the sophistries of paper logic cannot alter the fact that after reading these passages in the Interlinear, the memory of those days haunts me afresh, torments me with guilts which I might never have been aware of before! I walk now beside the child which Melissa had by Nessim during that brief love-affair (was it "love" again, or was he trying to use her to find out all he could about his wife? Perhaps one day I shall discover): I walk beside the child I say on these deserted beaches like a criminal, going over and over these fragments of the white city's life with regrets too deep even to alter the tone of voice in which I talk to her. Where does one hunt for the key to such a pattern?

But it is clear that I was not alone in feeling such guilt: Pursewarden himself must have been feeling guilty —how else can I explain the money he left me in his will with the express request that it should be spent with Melissa? That at least is one problem solved.

Clea too, I know, felt the guilt of the wound we were

all of us causing Melissa—though she felt it, so to speak,
on behalf of Justine. She took it, so to speak, upon herself—appalled at the mischief which her lover was causing
to us both for so little cause. It was she who now became
Melissa's friend, champion and counsellor and who remained her closest confidante until she died. The selfless
and innocent Clea, another fool! It does not pay to be
honest in love! She said of Melissa: "It is terrible to
depend so utterly on powers that do not wish you well.
To see someone always in your thoughts, like a stain
upon reality. . . ." I think she was also thinking, perhaps,
of Justine, up there in the big house among the tall
candles and the oil-paintings by forgotten masters.

Melissa also said to her of me: "With his departure
everything in nature disappeared." This was when she
was dying. But nobody has the right to occupy such a
place in another's life, nobody! You can see now upon
what raw material I work in these long and passionate
self-communings over a winter sea. "She loved you,"
said Clea again, "because of your weakness—this is what
she found endearing in you. Had you been strong you
would have frightened away so timid a love." And then
lastly, before I bang the pages of the manuscript shut
with anger and resentment against Balthazar, one last
remark of Clea's which burns like a hot iron: "Melissa
said: 'You have been my friend, Clea, and I want you
to love him after I am gone. Do it with him, will you,
and think of me? Never mind all this beastly love business. Cannot a friend make love on another's behalf? I
ask you to sleep with him as I would ask the Panaghia to
come down and bless him while he sleeps—like in the old
ikons.'" How purely Melissa, how Greek!

On Sundays we would walk down together to visit
Scobie, I remember; Melissa in her bright cotton frock
and straw hat, smiling and eager at the thought of a full
holiday from the dusty cabaret. Along the Grande Cor-

niche with the waves dancing and winking across the bar,
and the old horse-drawn cabs with their black jarveys in
red flowerpots driving their dilapidated and creaking
"taxis-of-love"; and as we walked past they would call
"Love-taxi sir, madam. Only ten piastres an hour. I
know a quiet place. . . ." And Melissa would giggle and
turn away as we walked to watch the minarets glisten
like pearls upon the morning light and the bright
children's kites take the harbour wind.

Scobie usually spent Sundays in bed, and in winter
nearly always contrived to have a cold. He would lie
between the coarse linen sheets after having made Abdul
give him what he called "a cinnamon rub" (I never
discovered what this was) ; with some formality, too, he
would have a brick heated and placed at his feet to keep
them warm. He had a small knitted cap on his head.
As he read very little, he carried, like an ancient tribe,
all his literature in his head and would, when alone,
recite to himself for hours. He had quite an extensive
repertoire of ballads which he thundered out with great
energy, marking the beat with his hand. "The Arab's
Farewell to his Steed" brought real tears to his good eye,
as did "The harp that once through Tara's Halls"; while
among the lesser-known pieces was an astonishing poem
the metre of which by its galloping quality virtually
enabled him to throw himself out of bed and half-way
across the room if recited at full gale force. I once made
him write it out for me in order to study its construction
closely:

"By O'Neil close beleaguered, the spirits might droop
  Of the Saxon three hundred shut up in their coop
  Till Bagnal drew forth his Toledo and swore
  On the sword of a soldier to succour Portmore.

His veteran troops in the foreign wars tried,

Their features how bronzed and how haughty their
   stride,
Step't steadily on; Ah! 'twas thrilling to see
That thunder-cloud brooding o'er Beal-an-atha-
   Buidh!

Land of Owen Aboo! and the Irish rushed on.
The foe fired one volley—their gunners are gone.
Before the bare bosoms the steel coats have fled,
Or despite casque and corslet, lie dying or dead.

And the Irish got clothing, coin, colours, great store,
Arms, forage, and provender—plunder *go leor.*
They munched the white manchets, they champed
   the brown chine,
Fuliluah! for that day how the natives did dine!"

Disappointingly, he could tell me nothing about it; it
had lain there in his memory for half a century like
a valuable piece of old silver which is only brought out
on ceremonial occasions and put on view. Among the
few other such treasures which I recognised was the
passage (which he always declaimed with ardour) which
ends:

> *"Come the four corners of the world in arms,*
>   *We'll shock 'em.*
> *Trust Joshua Scobie to shock 'em!"*

Melissa was devoted to him and found him extraordinarily quaint in his sayings and mannerisms. He for
his part was fond of her—I think chiefly because she always
gave him his full rank and title—Bimbashi Scobie—which
pleased him and made him feel of consequence to her
as a "high official."

But I remember one day when we found him almost

in tears. I thought perhaps he had moved himself by a recital of one of his more powerful poems ("We Are Seven" was another favourite) ; but no. "I've had a quarrel with Abdul—for the first time," he admitted with a ludicrous blink. "You know what, old man, he wants to take up circumcision."

It was not hard to understand: to become a barber-surgeon rather than a mere cutter and shaver was a normal enough step for someone like Abdul to want to take; it was like getting one's Ph.D. But of course, I knew too Scobie's aversion to circumcision. "He's gone and bought a filthy great pot of leeches," the old man went on indignantly. *"Leeches!* Started opening veins, he has. I said to him I said, 'If you think, my boy, that I set you up in business so as you could spend your time hyphenating young children for a piastre a time you're wrong,' I said to him I said." He paused for breath, obviously deeply affected by this development. "But Skipper," I protested. "It seems very natural for him to want to become a barber-surgeon. After all, circumcision is practised everywhere, even in England now." Ritual circumcision was such a common part of the Egyptian scene that I could not understand why he should be so obviously upset by the thought. He pouted, tucked his head down, and ground his false teeth noisily. "No," he said obstinately. "I won't have it." Then he suddenly looked up and said, "D'you know what? He's actually going to study under Mahmoud Enayet Allah— that old butcher!"

I could not understand his concern; at every festival or *mulid* the circumcision booth was a regular part of the festivities. Huge coloured pictures, heavily beflagged with the national colours, depicting barber-surgeons with pen-knives at work upon wretched youths spread out in dentists' chairs were a normal if bizarre feature of the side-shows. The doyen of the guild was Mahmoud himself, a large oval man, with a long oiled moustache, always dressed in full fig and apart from his red *tarbush* conveying the vague impression of some French country practitioner on French leave. He always made a resounding speech in classical Arabic offering circumcision free to the faithful who were too poor to meet the cost of it. Then, when a few candidates were forthcoming, pushed forward by eager parents, his two Negro clowns with painted faces and grotesque clothes used to gambol out to amuse and distract the boys, inveigling them by this means into the fatal chair where they were, in Scobie's picturesque phrase, "hyphenated," their screams being drowned by the noise of the crowd, almost before they knew what was happening.

I could not see what was amiss in Abdul's wanting to learn all he could from this don, so to speak, of hyphenation. Then I suddenly understood as Scobie said, "It's not the boy—they can do him for all I care. It's the girl, old man. I can't bear to think of that little creature being mutilated. I'm an Englishman, old man, you'll understand my feelings. I WON'T HAVE IT." Exhausted by the force of his own voice, he sank back upon his pillow and went on, "And what's more, I told Abdul so in no uncertain terms. 'Lay a finger on the girl,' I said, 'and I'll get you run in—see if I don't.' But of course, it's heart-breaking, old man, 'cause they've been such friends, and the poor coon doesn't understand. He thinks I'm mad!" He sighed heavily twice. "Their friendship was the best I ever had with anyone except Budgie, and I'm not exaggerating, old man. It really was. And now they're puzzled. They don't understand an Englishman's feelings. And I hate using the Influence of My Position." I wondered what this exactly meant. He went on. "Only last month we ran Abdel Latif in and got him closed down, with six months in chokey for unclean razors. He was spreading syphilis old man. I had to do it, even though he was a friend. My duty. I warned him countless times to dip his razor. No, he wouldn't do it. They've got a very poor sense of disinfection here old man. You know, they use styptic—shaving styptic for the circumcisions. It's considered more modern than the old mixture of black gunpowder and lemon-juice. Ugh! No sense of disinfection. I don't know how they don't all die of things, really I don't. But they were quite scared when we ran Abel Latif in and Abdul has taken it to heart. I could see him watching me while I was telling him off. Measuring my words, like."

But the influence of company always cheered the old man up and banished his phantoms, and it was not long before he was talking in his splendid discursive vein about the life history of Toby Mannering. "It was he who put me on to Holy Writ, old man, and I was looking at The Book yesterday when I found a lot about circumcision in it. You know? The Amalekites used to collect foreskins like we collect stamps. Funny isn't it?" He gave a sudden snort of a chuckle like a bull-frog. "I must say they were ones! I suppose they had dealers, assorted packets, a regular trade, eh? Paid more for perforations!" He made a straight face for Melissa who came into the room at this moment. "Ah well," he said, still shaking visibly at his own jest. "I must write to Budgie tonight and tell him all the news." Budgie was his oldest friend. "Lives in Horsham, old man, makes earth-closets. He's collected a regular packet from them, has old Budgie. He's an FRZS, I don't quite know what it means, but he has it on his notepaper. Charles Donahue Budgeon FRZS. I write to him every week. Punctual. Always have done, always will do. Staunch, that's me. Never give up a friend."

It was to Budgie, I think, the unfinished letter which was found in his rooms after his death and which read as follows:

*"Dear old pal, The whole world seems to have turned
against me since I last wrote. I should have"*

Scobie and Melissa! In the golden light of those Sundays they live on, bright still with the colours that
memory gives to those who enrich our lives by tears or
by laughter—unaware themselves that they have given
us anything. The really horrible thing is that the com-
pulsive passion which Justine lit in me was quite as
valuable as it would have been had it been "real";
Melissa's gift was no less an enigma—what could she
have offered me, in truth, this pale waif of the Alexandrian littoral? Was Clea enriched or beggared by her
relations with Justine? Enriched—immeasurably enriched,
I should say. Are we then nourished only by fictions, by
lies? I recall the words Balthazar wrote down somewhere
in his tall grammarian's handwriting: "We live by
selected fictions," and also: "Everything is true of everybody. . . ." Were these words of Pursewarden's quarried
from his own experience of men and women, or simply
from a careful observation of us, our behaviours and their
result? I don't know. A passage comes to mind from a
novel in which Pursewarden speaks about the role of the
artist in life. He says something like this: "Aware of every
discord, of every calamity in the nature of man himself,
he can do nothing to warn his friends, to point, to cry
out in time and to try to save them. It would be useless.
For they are the deliberate factors of their own unhappiness. All the artist can say as an imperative is: 'Reflect
and weep.'"

Was it consciousness of tragedy irremediable contained
—not in the external world which we all blame—but in
ourselves, in the human condition, which finally dictated
his unexpected suicide in that musty hotel-room? I like
to think it was, but perhaps I am in danger of putting
too much emphasis on the artist at the expense of the
man. Balthazar writes: "Of all things his suicide has re-

mained for me an extraordinary and quite inexplicable freak. Whatever stresses and strains he may have been subjected to I cannot quite bring myself to believe it. But then I suppose we live in the shallows of one another's personalities and cannot really see into the depths beneath. Yet I should have said this was surprisingly out of character. You see, he was really at rest about his work which most torments the artists, I suppose, and really had begun to regard it as 'divinely unimportant'—a characteristic phrase. I know this for certain because he once wrote me out on the back of an envelope an answer to the question 'What is the object of writing?' His answer was this: 'The object of writing is to grow a personality which in the end enables man to transcend art.'

"He had odd ideas about the constitution of the psyche. For example, he said, 'I regard it as completely unsubstantial as a rainbow—it only coheres into identifiable states and attributes when attention is focused on it. The truest form of right attention is of course love. Thus "people" are as much of an illusion to the mystic as "matter" to the physicist when he is regarding it as a form of energy.'

"He never failed to speak most slightingly of my own interests in the occult, and indeed in the work of the Cabal whose meetings you attended yourself. He said of this, 'Truth is a matter of direct apprehension—you can't climb a ladder of mental concepts to it.'

"I can't get away from the feeling that he was at his most serious when he was most impudent. I heard him maintaining to Keats that the best lines of English poetry ever written were by Coventry Patmore. They were:

> *The truth is great and will prevail*
> *When none care whether it prevail or not.*

"And then, having said this, he added: 'And their true beauty resides in the fact that Patmore when he wrote them did not know what he meant. *Sich lassen!*' You can imagine how this would annoy Keats. He also quoted with approval a mysterious phrase of Stendhal, namely: 'The smile appears on the skin outside.'

"Are we to assume from all this the existence of a serious person underneath the banter? I leave the question to you—your concern is a direct one.

"At the time when we knew him he was reading hardly anything but science. This for some reason annoyed Justine who took him to task for wasting his time in these studies. He defended himself by saying that the Relativity proposition was directly responsible for abstract painting, atonal music, and formless (or at any rate cyclic forms in) literature. Once it was grasped they were understood too. He added: 'In the Space and Time marriage we have the greatest Boy meets Girl story of the age. To our great-grandchildren this will be as poetical a union as the ancient Greek marriage of Cupid and Psyche seems to us. You see, Cupid and Psyche were facts to the Greeks, not concepts. Analogical as against analytical thinking! But the true poetry of the age and its most fruitful poem is the mystery which begins and ends with an *n*.'

" 'Are you serious about all this?'

" 'Not a bit.'

"Justine protested: 'The beast is up to all sorts of tricks, even in his books.' She was thinking of the famous page with the asterisk in the first volume which refers one to a page in the text which is mysteriously blank. Many people take this for a printer's error. But Purse-warden himself assured me that it was deliberate. 'I refer the reader to a blank page in order to throw him back upon his own resources—which is where every reader ultimately belongs.'

"You speak about the plausibility of our actions—and

this does us an injustice, for we are all living people and
have the right as such to take refuge in the suspended
judgment of God if not the reader. So, while I think of
it, let me tell you the story of Justine's laughter! You
will admit that you yourself never heard it, not once, I
mean in a way that was not mordant, not wounded. But
Pursewarden did—at the tombs in Saqarra! By moonlight,
two days after *Sham el Nessim*. They were there among
a large party of sightseers, a crowd under cover of which
they had managed to talk a little, like the conspirators
they were: already at this time Pursewarden had put an
end to her private visitations to his hotel-room. So it
gave them a forbidden pleasure, this exchange of a few
hoarded secret words; and at last this evening they came
by chance to be alone, standing together in one of those
overbearing and overwhelming mementoes to a special-
ised sense of death: the tombs.

"Justine had laddered her stockings and filled her shoes
with sand. She was emptying them, he was lighting
matches and gazing about him, and sniffing. She whispered she had been terribly worried of late by a new
suspicion that Nessim had discovered something about
her lost child which he would not tell her. Pursewarden
was absently listening when suddenly he snapped his
fingers which he had burnt on a match and said: 'Listen,
Justine—you know what? I re-read *Moeurs* again last week
for fun and I had an idea; I mean if all the song and
dance about Freud and your so-called childhood rape
and so on are true—are they? I don't know. You could
easily make it all up. But since you knew who the man
in the wretched eyepiece was and refused to reveal his
name to the wretched army of amateur psychologists
headed by Arnauti, you must have had a good reason
for it. What was it? It puzzles me. I won't tell anyone,
I promise. Or is it all a lie?' She shook her head, 'No.'

"They walked out in a clear milk-white moonlight

while Justine thought quietly. Then she said slowly: 'It wasn't just shyness or an unwillingness to be cured as they called it—as he called it in the book. The thing was, he was a friend of ours, of yours, of all of us.' Pursewarden looked at her curiously. 'The man in the black patch?' he said. She nodded. They lit cigarettes and sat down on the sand to wait for the others. Feeling that everything she confided in him was absolutely secure she said quietly: 'Da Capo.' There was a long silence. 'Well, stap me! The old Porn himself!' (He had coined this nickname from the word 'pornographer.') And then very quietly and tentatively, Pursewarden went on: 'I suddenly had the idea of re-reading all that stuff, you know, that if I had been in your shoes and the whole damn thing wasn't just a lie to make yourself more interesting to the psychopomps—I'd . . . well, I'd bloody well try and sleep with him again and try to lay the image that way. The idea suddenly came to me.'

"This betrays, of course, his total ignorance of psychology. Indeed, it was a fatal step to suggest. But here, to his own surprise, she began to laugh—the first effortless, musical laugh he had ever heard her give. 'I did,' she said, now laughing almost too much for speech, 'I did. You'll never guess what an effort it cost me, hanging about in the dark road outside his house, trying to pluck up courage to ring the bell. Yes, it occurred to me too. I was desperate. What would he say? We had been friends for years—with never of course a reference to this event. He had never referred to *Moeurs* and, you know, I don't believe he has read it ever. Perhaps he preferred, I always thought, to disregard the whole thing—to bury it tactfully.'

"Laughter again overtook her, shaking her body so much that Pursewarden took her arm anxiously, not to let her interrupt the recital. She borrowed his handkerchief to mop her eyes and continued: 'I went in at last.

He was there in his famous library! I was shaking like
a leaf. You see, I didn't know what note to strike, something dramatic, something pathetic? It was like going
to the dentist. Really, it was funny, Pursewarden. I said
at last, "Dear Da Capo, old friend, you have been my
demon for so long that I have come to ask you to exorcise
me once and for all. To take away the memory of a
horrible childhood event. You must sleep with me!" You
should have seen Da Capo's face. He was terribly thrown
off guard and stammered: *"Mais voyons, Justine, je
suis un ami de Nessim!"* and so on. He gave me a whisky
and offered me an aspirin—sure that I had gone out of
my mind. "Sit down," he said putting out a chair for me
with shaking hands and sitting nervously down opposite
me with a comical air of alarm—like a small boy accused
of stealing apples.' Her side was hurting and she pressed
her hand to it, laughing with such merriment that it
infected him and involuntarily he began to laugh too.
'Poor Da Capo,' she said, 'he was so terribly shocked and
alarmed to be told he had raped me when I was a street
arab, a child. I have never seen a man more taken aback.
He had completely forgotten, it is clear, and completely
denied the whole thing from start to finish. In fact, he
was outraged and began to protest. I wish you could
have seen his face! Do you know what slipped out in the
course of his self-justifications? A marvellous phrase, *"Il
y a quinze ans que je n'ai pas fait ça!"* ' She threw herself now face downward on to Pursewarden's lap and
stayed a moment, still shaking with laughter; and then
she raised her head once more to wipe her eyes. She said,
'I finished my whisky at last and left, much to his relief;
as I was at the door he called after me, "Remember you
are both dining with me on Wednesday. Eight for eight-
fifteen, white tie," as he had done these past few years.
I went back home in a daze and drank half a bottle of
gin. And you know, I had a strange thought that night

in bed—perhaps you will find it shockingly out of place; a thought about Da Capo forgetting so completely an act which had cost me so many years of anxiety and indeed mental illness and had made me harm so many people. I said to myself, "This is perhaps the very way God himself forgets the wrongs he does to us in abandoning us to the mercies of the world." ' She threw back her smiling head and stood up.

"She saw now that Pursewarden was looking at her with tears of admiration in his eyes. Suddenly he embraced her warmly, kissing her more passionately perhaps than he had ever done. When she was telling me all this, with a pride unusual in her, she added: 'And you know, Balthazar, that was better than any lover's kiss, it was a real reward, an accolade. I saw then that if things had been different I had it in me to make him love me—perhaps for the very defects in my character which are so obvious to everyone.'

"Then the rest of the party came chattering up among the tombs and . . . I don't know what. I suppose they all drove back to the Nile and ended up at a night-club. What the devil am I doing scribbling all these facts down for you? Lunacy! You will only hate me for telling you things you would prefer not to know as a man and prefer perhaps to ignore as an artist. . . .These obstinate little dispossessed facts, the changelings of our human existence which one can insert like a key into a lock—or a knife into an oyster: will there be a pearl inside? Who can say? But somewhere they must exist in their own right, these grains of a truth which *'just slipped out.'* Truth is not what is uttered in full consciousness. It is always what 'just slips out'—the typing error which gives the whole show away. Do you understand me, wise one? But I have not done. I shall never have the courage to give you these papers, I can see. I shall finish the story for myself alone.

"So from all this you will be able to measure the despair of Justine when that wretched fellow Pursewarden went and killed himself. In the act of being annoyed with him I find myself smiling, so little do I believe in his death as yet. She found this act as completely mysterious, as completely unforeseen as I myself did; but she poor creature had organised her whole careful deception a-round the idea of his living on! There was nobody except myself in whom to confide now; and you whom, if she did not love, God knows she did not hate, were in great danger. It was too late to do anything except make plans to go away. She was left with the 'decoy'! Does one learn anything from these bitter truths? Throw all this paper into the sea, my dear boy, and read no more of the Interlinear. But I forget. I am not going to let you see it, am I? I shall leave you content with the fabrications of an art which 'reworks reality to show its significant side.' What significant side could she turn, for example, to Nessim who at that time had become a prey to those very preoccupations which made him appear to everyone—himself included—mentally unstable? Of his more serious preoccupations at this time I could write a fair amount, for I have in the interval learned a good deal about his affairs and his political concerns. They will explain his sudden changeover into a great entertainer—the crowded house which you describe so well, the banquets and balls. But here . . . the question of censorship troubles me, for if I were to send you this and if you were, as you might, to throw this whole disreputable jumble of paper into the water, the sea might float it back to Alexandria perhaps directly into the arms of the Police. Better not. I will tell you only what seems politic. Perhaps later on I shall tell you the rest.

"Pursewarden's face in death reminded me very much of Melissa's; they both had the air of just having enjoyed a satisfying private joke and of having fallen off to sleep

before the smile had fully faded from the corners of the
mouth. Some time before he had said to Justine: 'I am
ashamed of one thing only: because I have disregarded
the first imperative of the artist, namely, create and
starve. I have never starved, you know. Kept afloat doing
little jobs of one sort or another: caused as much harm
as you and more.'

"That night, Nessim was already there in the hotel-
room sitting with the body when I arrived, looking extraordinarily composed and calm but as if deafened by
an explosion. He had been telephoning to Mountolive
in the summer residence on the hill. Perhaps the impact
of reality had dazed him? He was at this time going
through that period of horrible dreams of which he had
a transcript made, some of which you reproduce in your
MS. They are strangely like echoes of Leila's dreams of
fifteen years ago—she had a bad period after her husband
died and I attended her at Nessim's request. Here again
in judging him you trust too much to what your subjects
say about themselves—the accounts they give of their
own actions and their meaning. You would never make
a good doctor. Patients have to be found out—for they
always lie. Not that they can help it, it is part of the
defence-mechanism of the illness—just as your MS. betrays the defence-mechanism of the dream which does
not wish to be invaded by reality! Perhaps I am wrong?
I do not wish to judge anyone unjustly or intrude upon
your private territory. Will all these notes of mine cost
me your friendship? I hope not, but I fear it.

"What was I saying? Yes, Pursewarden's face in death!
It had the same old air of impudent contrivance. One
felt he was play-acting—indeed, I still do, so alive does
he seem to me.

"It was Justine first who alerted me. Nessim sent her
to me with the car and a note which I did not let her
read. It was clear that Nessim had either learned of the

intention or the fact before any of us—I suspect a telephone call by Pursewarden himself. At any rate, my
familiarity with suicide cases—I have handled any number for Nimrod's night-patrol—made me cautious. Suspecting perhaps barbiturates or some other slow com-
pound, I took the precaution of carrying my little
stomach-pump with me among my antidotes. I confess
that I thought with pleasure of my friend's expression
when he woke up in hospital. But it seems I misjudged
both his pride and his thoroughness for he was thoroughly and conclusively dead when we arrived.

"Justine raced ahead of me up the staircase of the
gaunt hotel which he had loved so much (indeed, he
had christened it Mount Vulture Hotel—I presume from
the swarm of whores who fluttered about in the street
outside it, like vultures).

"Nessim had locked himself into the room—we had to
knock and he let us in with a certain annoyance, or so
it seemed to me. The place was in the greatest disorder
you can imagine. Drawers turned out, clothes and manuscripts and paintings everywhere; Pursewarden was lying
on the bed in the corner with his nose pointing aloofly
at the ceiling. I paused to unpack my big-intestine kit—
method is everything in moments of stress—while Justine
went unerringly across to the bottle of gin on the corner
by the bed and took a long swig. I knew that this might
contain the poison but said nothing—at such times there
is little to say. The minute you get hysterical you have to
take this kind of chance. I simply unpacked and unwound
my aged stomach-pump which has saved more useless
lives (lives impossible to live, shed like ill-fitting garments) than any such other instrument in Alexandria.
Slowly, as befits a third-rate doctor, I unwound it, and
with method, which is all a third-rate doctor has left to
face the world with. . . .

"Meanwhile Justine turned to the bed and leaning

down said audibly: 'Pursewarden, wake up.' Then she
put her palms to the top of her head and let out a long
pure wail like an Arab woman—a sound abruptly shut
off, confiscated by the night in that hot airless little
room. Then she began to urinate in little squirts all over
the carpet. I caught her and pushed her into the bathroom. It gave me the respite I needed to have a go at his
heart. It was silent as the Great Pyramid. I felt angry
about it, because it was clear he had resorted to some
beastly cyanide preparation—favoured, by the way, by
your famous Secret Service. I was so exasperated that I
clipped him over the ear—a blow he had long merited!

"All this time I had been aware that Nessim was
suddenly active, but now I recovered, so to speak, and
could turn my attention to him. He was turning out
drawers and desks and cupboards like a maniac, examining manuscripts and papers, tossing things aside and
picking things up with a complete lack of his usual
phlegm. 'What the hell are you doing?' I said angrily,
to which he replied, 'There must be nothing for the
Egyptian Police to find.' And then he stopped as if he
had said too much. Every mirror bore a soap-inscription.
Nessim had partly obliterated one. I could only make out
the letters OHEN . . . . . . ASTINE. . . .

"It was not long before there came the familiar knocking at the door and the faces and tumult inseparable
from such scenes everywhere in the world. Men with
notebooks, and journalists, and priests—Father Paul of
all people turned up. At this, I half-expected the corpse
to rise up and throw something . . . but no; Pursewarden
remained with his nose cocked to the ceiling, in his
amused privacy.

"We stumbled out together, the three of us, and drove
back to the studio where the great failed paintings soothed
us, and where whisky gave us new courage to continue
living. Justine said not a word. Not a mortal word."

7.

I TURN now to another part of the Interlinear, the passage which Balthazar marked: "So Narouz decided to *act*," underlining the last word twice. Shall I reconstruct it—the scene I see so clearly, and which his few crabbed words in green ink have detonated in my imagination? Yes, it will enable me to dream for a moment about an unfrequented quarter of Alexandria which I loved.

The city, inhabited by these memories of mine, moves not only backwards into our history, studded by the great names which mark every station of recorded time, but also back and forth in the living present, so to speak—among its contemporary faiths and races; the hundred little spheres which religion or lore creates and which cohere softly together like cells to form the great sprawling jellyfish which is Alexandria today. Joined in this fortuitous way by the city's own act of will, isolated on a slate promontory over the sea, backed only by the moonstone mirror of Mareotis, the salt lake, and its further forevers of ragged desert (now dusted softly by the spring winds into satin dunes, patternless and beautiful as cloudscapes), the communities still live and communicate—Turks with Jews, Arabs and Copts and Syrians with Armenians and Italians and Greeks. The shudders of monetary transactions ripple through them like wind in a wheatfield; ceremonies, marriages and pacts join and divide them. Even the place-names on the old tram-routes with their sandy grooves of rail echo the unfor-

gotten names of their founders—and the names of the
dead captains who first landed here, from Alexander to
Amr; founders of this anarchy of flesh and fever, of
money-love and mysticism. Where else on earth will you
find such a mixture?

And when night falls and the white city lights up
the thousand candelabra of its parks and buildings,
tunes in to the soft unearthly drum-music of Morocco
or Caucasus, it looks like some great crystal liner asleep
there, anchored to the horn of Africa—her diamond and
fire-opal reflections twisting downwards like polished
bars into the oily harbour among the battleships.

At dusk it can become like a mauve jungle, anomalous,
stained with colours as if from a shattered prism; and
rising into the pearly sky of the sunset falter up the
steeples and minarets like stalks of giant fennel in a
swamp rising up over the long pale lines of the sea-shore
and the barbaric cafés where the Negroes dance to the
pop and drub of a finger-drum or to the mincing of
clarinets.

"There are only as many realities as you care to
imagine," writes Pursewarden.

Narouz always shunned Alexandria while he loved it
passionately, with an exile's love; his hare-lip had made
him timid to visit the centre, to encounter those he might
know. He always hovered about its outskirts, not daring
to go directly into the great lighted heart of it where
his brother lived a life of devoted enterprise and *mon-
danité*. He came into it always humbly, on horseback,
dressed as he was always dressed, to fulfil the transactions
which concerned the property. It took a great effort to
persuade him to put on a suit and visit it by car, though
when absolutely necessary he had been known to do this
also, but reluctantly. For the most part he preferred to
do his work through Nessim; and of course the telephone
guarded him from many such unwelcome journeys. Yet

when his brother rang up one day and said that his agents had been unable to make the Magzub tell them what he knew about Justine's child, Narouz felt suddenly elated—as if fired by the consciousness that this task had now devolved on him. "Nessim," he said, "what is the month? Yes, *Misra*. Quite soon there will come the feast of *Sitna Mariam,* eh? I shall see if he is there and try to make him tell us something." Nessim pondered this offer for so long that Narouz thought the line had been cut and cried sharply, "Hallo—hallo!" Nessim answered at once. "Yes, yes. I am here. I am just thinking: you will be careful, won't you?" Narouz chuckled hoarsely and promised that he would. But he was always stirred by the thought that perhaps he might be able to help his brother. Curiously, he thought not at all about Justine herself, or what such information might mean to her; she was simply an acquisition of Nessim's whom he liked, admired, loved deeply, indeed automatically, because of Nessim. It was his duty to do whatever was necessary to help Nessim help her. No more. No less.

So it was that with soft stride, the awkward jaunty step (rising and falling on his toes, swinging his arms), he walked across the brown dusk-beshadowed *meidan* outside the main railway station of Alexandria on the second day of *Sitna Mariam.* He had stabled his horse in the yard of a friend, a carpenter, not far from the place where the festivities of the saint were held. It was a hot rank summer night.

With the dusk that vast and threadbare expanse of empty ground always turned first gold and then brown —to brown cracked cardboard—and then lastly to violet as the lights began to prick the on-coming darkness, as the backcloth of the European city itself began to light up window by window, street by street, until the whole looked like a cobweb in which the frost has set a million glittering brilliants.

Camels somewhere snorted and gnarred, and the music and odour of human beings came across the night towards him, rich with the memories of the fairs he had visited with his parents as a child. In his red *tarbush* and work-stained clothes he knew he would not be singled out by the crowd as one different from themselves. It was characteristic too that, though the festival of *Sitna Mariam* celebrated a Christian Coptic saint, it was attended and enjoyed by all, not least the Moslem inhabitants of the town, for Alexandria is after all still Egypt: all the colours run together.

A whole encampment of booths, theatres, brothels and shops—a complete township—had sprung up in the darkness, fitfully lit by oil and paraffin stoves, by pressure lamps and braziers, by candle-light and strings of dazzling coloured electric bulbs. He walked lightly into the press of human beings, his nostrils drinking in the scent of aromatic foods and sweetmeats, of stale jasmine and sweat, and his ears the hum of voices which provided a background to those common sounds which always followed the great processions through the town, lingering on the way at every church for a recital of sacred texts, and coming gradually to the site of the festival.

To him all this scattered novelty—the riches of bear-dancers and acrobats, the fire-swallowers blowing six-foot plumes of flame from up-cast mouths—the dancers in rags and particoloured caps—everything that to the stranger would have been a delight was so to him only because it was utterly commonplace—so much a belonging part of his own life. Like the small child he once was he walked in the brilliance of the light, stopping here and there with smiling eyes to stare at some familiar feature of the fair. A conjurer dressed in tinsel drew from his sleeve endless many-coloured handkerchiefs, and from his mouth twenty small live chicks, crying all the time in the voice of the seabird: *"Galli-Galli-Galli-Galli*

Houp!"; Manouli the monkey in a paper hat brilliantly rode round and round his stall on the back of a goat. Towering on either side of the thoroughfare rose the great booths with their sugar figurines brilliant with tinsel, depicting the loves and adventures of the creatures inhabiting the folk-lore of the Delta—heroes like Abu Zeid and Antar, lovers like Yunis and Aziza. He walked slowly, with an unpremeditated carelessness, stopping for a while to hear the storytellers, or to buy a lucky talisman from the famous blind preacher Hussein who stood like an oak tree, magnificent in the elf-light, reciting the ninety-nine holy names.

From the outer perimeter of darkness came the crisp click of sportsmen at singlestick, dimly sounding against the hoarse rumble of the approaching procession with its sudden bursts of wild music—kettle-drums and timbrels like volleys of musketry—and the long belly-thrilling rolls of the camel-drums which drowned and refreshed the quavering deep-throated flute-music. "They are coming. They are coming." A confused shouting rose and the children darted here and there like mice among the stalls. From the throat of a narrow alley, spilled like a widening circle of fire upon the darkness, burst a long tilting gallery of human beings headed by the leaping acrobats and dwarfs of Alexandria, and followed at a dancing measure by the long grotesque cavalcade of gonfalons, rising and falling in a tide of mystical light, treading the peristaltic measures of the wild music—nibbled out everywhere by the tattling flutes and the pang of drums or the long shivering orgasm of tambourines struck by the dervishes in their habits as they moved towards the site of the festival. "All-*ah* All-*ah*" burst from every throat.

Narouz took a stick of sugar-cane from a stall and nibbled it as he watched the wave moving forward to engulf him. Here came the Rifiya dervishes, who could

in their trances walk upon embers or drink molten glass
or eat live scorpions—or dance the turning measure of
the universe out, until reality ran down like an over-
wound spring and they fell gasping to the earth, dazed
like birds. The banners and torches, the great openwork
braziers full of burning wood, the great paper lanterns
inscribed with texts, they made staggering loops and patterns of light upon the darkness of the Alexandrian night,
rising and falling, and now the pitches were swollen
with spectators, worrying at the procession like mastiffs,
screaming and pulling; and still the flood poured on
with its own wild music (perhaps the very music that the
dying Antony in Cavafy's poem heard) until it engulfed
the darkness of the great *meidan,* spreading around it
the fitful contours of robes and faces and objects without context but whose colours sprang up and darkened
the edges of the sky with colour. Human beings were
setting fire to each other.

Somewhere in that black hinterland of smashed and
tumbled masonry, of abandoned and disembowelled
houses, was a small garden with a tomb in it marking
the site which was the sum and meaning of this riot. And
here, before a glimmering taper would be read a Christian
prayer for a Christian saint, while all around rode the
dark press and flood of Alexandria. The dozen faiths
and religions shared a celebration which time had
sanctified, which was made common to all and dedicated to a season and a landscape, completely obliterating its canon referents in lore and code. To a religious
country all religions were one and while the faithful
uttered prayers, for a chosen saint, the populace enjoyed
the fair which had grown up around the celebration, a
rocking carnival of light and music.

And through it all (sudden reminders of the city itself and the full-grown wants and powers of a great
entrepôt) came the whistles of steam-engines from the

dark goods-yards or a sniff of sound from the siren of a
liner, negotiating the tortuous fairways of the harbour
as it set off for India. The night accommodated them all
—a prostitute singing in the harsh chipped accents of the
land to the gulp and spank of a fingerdrum, the cries of
children on the swings and sweating roundabouts and
goose-nests, the cock-shies and snake-charmers, the freaks
(Zubeida the bearded woman and the calf with five
legs), the great canvas theatre outside which the muscle-
dancers stood, naked except for loin-cloths, to advertise
their skill, and motionless, save for the incredible rippling
of their bodies—the flickering and toiling of pectoral,
abdominal and dorsal muscles, deceptive as summer
lightning.

Narouz was rapt and looked about him with the air of
a drunkard, revelling in it all, letting his footsteps follow
the haphazard meanderings of this township of light. At
the end of one long gallery, having laughingly shaken
off the grasp of a dozen girls who plied their raucous
trade in painted canvas booths among the stalls, he came
to the brilliantly lighted circumcision booths of which
the largest and most colourful was that of Abdul's master,
Mahmoud Enayet Allah, splendid with lurid cartoons
of the ceremony, painted and framed, and from whose
lintel hung a great glass jar cloying with leeches. The
doyen himself was there tonight, haranguing the crowd
and promising free circumcision to any of the faithful
too poor to pay the ordinary fee. His great voice rolled
out and boomed, while his two assistants stood at attention behind the ancient brass-bound shoe-black's chair
with their razors at the alert. Inside the booth, two
elderly men in dark suits sipped coffee with the air of
philologists at a congress.

Business was slack. "Come along, come along, be puri-
fied, ye faithful," boomed the old man, his thumbs behind the lapels of his ancient frock-coat, the sweat pour-

ing down his face under his red *tarbush*. A little to one
side, rapt in the performance of his trade sat a cousin
of Mahmoud, tattooing the breast of a magnificent-look-
ing male prostitute whose oiled curls hung down his back
and whose eyes and lips were heavily painted. A glass
panel of great brilliance hung beside him, painted with
a selection of designs from which his clients could choose
—purely geometric for Moslems, or Texts, or the record
of a vow, or simply beloved names. Touch by touch he
filled in the pores of his subject's skin, like a master of
needlecraft, smiling from time to time as if at a private
joke, building up his *pointilliste* picture while the old
doyen roared and boomed from the step above him
"Come along, come along, ye faithful!"

Narouz bent to the tattooist and said in a hoarse voice:
"Is the Magzub here tonight?" and the man raised his
startled eye and paused. "Yes," he said, "I think. By the
tombs."

Narouz thanked him and turned back once more to
the crowded booths, picking his way haphazardly among
the narrow thoroughfares until he reached the outskirts
of the light. Somewhere ahead of him in the darkness lay
a small cluster of abandoned shrines shadowed by leaning
palms, and here the gaunt and terrible figure of the
famous religious maniac stood, shooting out the thunderbolts of a hypnotic personality on to a fearful but fascinated crowd.

Even Narouz shuddered as he gazed upon that ravaged
face, the eyes of which had been painted with crayon
so that they looked glaring, inhuman, like the eyes of a
monster in a cartoon. The holy man hurled oaths and
imprecations at the circle of listeners, his fingers curling
and uncurling into claws as he worked upon them, dancing this way and that like a bear at bay, turning and
twirling, advancing and retreating upon the crowd with
grunts and roars and screams until it trembled before

him, fascinated by his powers. He had "come already into his hour," as the Arabs say, and the power of the spirit had filled him.

The holy man stood in an island of the fallen bodies of those he had hypnotized, some crawling about like scorpions, some screaming or bleating like goats, some braying. From time to time he would leap upon one of them uttering hideous screams and ride him across the ring, thrashing at his buttocks like a maniac, and then suddenly turning, with the foam bursting from between his teeth, he would dart into the crowd and pick upon some unfortunate victim, shouting: "Are you mocking me?" and catching him by his nose or an ear or an arm, drag him with superhuman force into the ring where with a sudden quick pass of his talons he would "kill his light" and hurl him down among the victims already crawling about in the sand at his feet, to utter shrill cries for mercy which were snuffed out by the braying and hooting of those already under his spell. One felt the power of his personality shooting out into the tense crowd like sparks from an anvil.

Narouz sat down on a tombstone to watch, in the darkness outside the circle. "Fiends, unclean ones," shrieked the Magzub, thrusting forward his talons so that the circle gave before each onslaught. "You and You and You and You," his voice rising to a terrible roar. He feared and respected no-one when he was "in his hour."

A respectable-looking sheik with the green turban which proclaimed him to be of the seed of the Prophet was walking across the outskirts of the crowd when the Magzub caught sight of him and with flying robes burst through the crowd to the old man's side, shouting: "He is impure." The old sheik turned upon his accuser with angry eyes and started to expostulate, but the fanatic thrust his face close to him and sank those terrible eyes into him. The old sheik suddenly went dull, his head

wobbled on his neck and with a shout the Magzub had
him down on all fours, grunting like a boar, and dragged
him by the turban to hurl him among the others.
"Enough," cried the crowd, outraged at this indifference
to a man of holiness, but the Magzub twisted round and
with flickering fingers rushed back towards the crowd,
shrieking: "Who cries 'enough,' who cries 'enough'?"

And now, obedient to the commands of this terrible
nightmare-mystic, the old sheik rose to his feet and
began to perform a lonely little ceremonial dance, crying in thin bird-like tones: "Allah. Allah!" as he trod a
shaky measure round the circle of bodies, his voice suddenly breaking into the choking cries of a dying animal.
"Desist," called the crowd, "desist, O Magzub." And the
hypnotist made a few blunt passes and thrust the old
sheik out of the ring, heaping horrible curses upon him.

The old man staggered and recovered himself. He was
wide awake now and seemed little the worse for his experience. Narouz came to his side as he was readjusting
his turban and dusting his robes. He saluted him and
asked him the name of the Magzub, but the old sheik
did not know. "But he is a very good man, a holy man,"
he said. "He was once alone in the desert for years." He
walked serenely off into the night and Narouz went back
to his tombstone to meditate on the beauty of his surroundings and to wait until he might approach the
Magzub whose animal shrieks still sounded upon the
night, piercing the blank hubbub of the fair and the
drone of the holy men from some nearby shrine. He had
as yet not decided how best to deal with the strange
personage of the darkness. He waited upon the event,
meditating.

It was late when the Magzub ended his performance,
releasing the imprisoned menagerie about his feet and
driving the crowd away by smacking his hands together
—for all the world as if they were geese. He stood for a

while shouting imprecations after them and then turned abruptly back among the tombs. "I must be careful," thought Narouz, who intended using force upon him, "not to get within his eyes." He had only a small dagger which he now loosened in its sheath. He began to follow, slowly and purposefully.

The holy man walked slowly, as if bowed down by the weight of preoccupations too many to number and almost too heavy for a mortal to bear. He still groaned and sobbed under his breath, and once he fell to his knees and crawled along the ground for a few paces, muttering. Narouz watched all this with head on one side, like a gun-dog, waiting. Together they skirted the ragged confines of the festival in the half-darkness of the hot night, and at last the Magzub came to a long broken wall of earth-bricks which had once demarcated gardens now abandoned and houses now derelict. The noise of the fair had diminished to a hum, but a steam-engine still pealed from somewhere near at hand. They walked now in a peninsula of darkness, unable to gauge relative distances, like wanderers in an unknown desert. But the Magzub had become more erect now, and walked more quickly, with the eagerness of a fox that is near its earth. He turned at last into a great deserted yard, slipping through a hole in the mud-brick wall. Narouz was afraid he might lose trace of him among these shattered fragments of dwellings and dust-blown tombs. He came around a corner full upon him—the figure of a man now swollen by darkness into a mirage of a man, twelve foot high. "O Magzub," he called softly, "give praise to God," and all of a sudden his apprehension gave place, as it always did when there was violence to be done, to a savage exultation as he stepped forward into the radius of this holy man's power, loosening the dagger and half-drawing it from the sheath.

The fanatic stepped back once and then twice; and

suddenly they were in a shaft of light which, leaking
across the well of darkness from some distant street-lamp,
set them both alive, giving to each other only a lighted
head like a medallion. Dimly Narouz saw the man's arms
raised in doubt, perhaps in fear, like a diver, and resting
upon some rotten wooden beam which in some forgotten
era must have been driven into the supporting wall of a
byre as a foundation for a course of the soft earth-brick.
Then the Magzub turned half sideways to join his hands,
perhaps in prayer, and with precise and deft calculation
Narouz performed two almost simultaneous acts. With
his right hand he drove his dagger into the wood, pinning
the Magzub's arms to it through the long sleeves of his
coarse gown; with his left he seized the beard of the
man, as one might seize a cobra above its hood to prevent
it striking. Lastly, instinctively, he thrust his face forward, spreading his split lip to the full, and hissing (for
deformity also confers magical powers in the East) in almost the form of an obscene kiss, as he whispered: "O
beloved of the Prophet."

They stood like this for a long moment, like effigies of
a forgotten action entombed in clay or bronze, and the
silence of the night about them took up its palpitating
proportions once more. The Magzub breathed heavily,
almost plaintively, but he said nothing; but now staring
into those terrible eyes, which he had seen that evening
burning like live coals, Narouz could discern no more
power. Under the cartoon image of the crayon, they
were blank and lustreless, and their centres were void of
meaning, hollow, dead. It was as if he had pinned a man
already dead to this corner of the wall in this abandoned
yard. A man about to fall into his arms and breathe his
last.

The knowledge that he had nothing to fear, now that
the Magzub was "not in his hour," flooded into Narouz'
mind on waves of sadness—apologetic sadness: for he

knew he could measure the divinity of the man, the
religious power from which he took refuge in madness.
Tears came into his eyes and he released the saint's beard,
but only to rub the matted hair of his head with his hand
and whisper in a voice full of loving tears, "Ah, beloved
of the Prophet! Ah! Wise one and beloved"—as if he
were caressing an animal—as if the Magzub now had transformed himself into some beloved hunting-dog. Narouz
ruffled his ears and hair, repeating the words in the low
magical voice he always used with his favourite animals.
The magician's eye rolled, focussed and became bleary,
like that of a child suddenly overcome with self-pity. A
single sob broke from his very heart. He sank to a kneeling position on the dry earth with both hands still
crucified to the wall. Narouz bowed and fell with him,
comforting him with hoarse inarticulate sounds. Nor was
this feigned. He was in a passion of reverence for one
who he knew had sought the final truths of religion
beneath the mask of madness.

But one side of his mind was still busy with the main
problem, so that he now said, not in the tender voice of
a hunter wheedling a favourite, but in the tone of a
man who carries a dagger: "Now you will tell me what I
wish to know, will you not?" The head of the magician
still lolled wearily, and he turned his eyes upwards into
his skull with what seemed to be a fatigue which almost
resembled death. "Speak," he said hoarsely; and quickly
Narouz leaped up to reclaim his dagger, and then, kneeling beside him with one hand still laid about his neck,
told him what he wanted to know.

"They will not believe me," moaned the man. "And I
have seen it by my own scope. Twice I have told them.
I did not touch the child." And then with a sudden flashing return in voice and glance to his own lost power, he
cried: "Shall I show you too? Do you wish to see?"—but
sank back again. "Yes," cried Narouz, who trembled

now from the shock of the encounter, "yes." It was as if an electric current were passing in his legs, making them tremble. "Show me."

The Magzub began to breathe heavily, letting his head fall back on his bosom after every breath. His eyes were closed. It was like watching an engine charge itself, from the air. Then he opened his eyes and said, "Look into the ground."

Kneeling upon that dry baked earth he made a circle in the dust with his index finger, and then smoothed out the sand with the palm of his hand. "Here where the light is," he whispered, touching the dust slowly, purposefully; and then, "look with your eye into the breast of the earth," indicating with his finger a certain spot. "Here."

Narouz knelt down awkwardly and obeyed. "I see nothing," he said quietly after a moment. The Magzub blew his breath out slowly in a series of long sighs. *"Think to see in the ground,"* he insisted. Narouz allowed his eyes to enter the earth and his mind to pour through them into the spot under the magician's finger. All was still. "I conceive," he admitted at last. Now suddenly, clearly, he saw a corner of the great lake with its interlinking network of canals and the old palm-shaded house of faded bricks where once Arnauti and Justine had lived—where indeed he had started *Moeurs* and where the child. . . . "I see her," he said at last. "Ah," said the Magzub. "Look well."

Narouz felt as if he were subtly drugged by the haze rising from the water of the canals. "Playing by the river," he went on. "She has fallen"; he could hear the breathing of his mentor becoming deeper. "She has fallen," intoned the Magzub. Narouz went on: "No-one is near her. She is alone. She is dressed in blue with a butterfly brooch." There was a long silence; then the magician groaned softly before saying in a thick, almost gurgling tone: "You have seen—to the very place. Mighty is God. In Him is my scope." And he took a pinch of dust and rubbed it upon his forehead as the vision faded.

Narouz, deeply impressed by these powers, kissed and embraced the Magzub, never for one moment doubting the validity of the information he had been granted in the vision. He rose to his feet and shook himself like a dog. They greeted one another now in low whispers and parted. He left the magician sitting there, as if exhausted, upon the ground, and turned his steps once more towards the fair-lights. His body was still shaking with the reaction as if afflicted by pins and needles—or as if an electric current were discharging through his loins and thighs. He had, he realised, been very much afraid. He yawned and shivered as he walked and struck his arms against his legs for warmth—as if to restore a sluggish circulation.

In order to reach the carpenter's yard where his horse was stabled, he had to traverse the eastern corner of the festival ground, where despite the lateness of the hour there was a good deal of hubbub around the swings, and the lights still blazed. It was the time when the prostitutes came into their own, the black, bronze and citron women, impenitent seekers for the money-flesh of men; flesh of every colour, ivory or gold or black. Sudanese with mauve gums and tongues as blue as chows'. Waxen Egyptians. Circassians golden-haired and blue of eye. Earth-blue Negresses, pungent as wood-smoke. Every variety of the name of flesh, old flesh quailing upon aged bones, or the unquenched flesh of boys and women on limbs infirm with desires that could be represented in effigy but not be slaked except in mime—for they were desires engendered in the forests of the mind, belonging not to themselves but to remote ancestors speaking through

them. Lust belongs to the egg and its seat is below the
level of psyche.

The hot blank Alexandrian night burned as brightly
as a cresset, reaching up through the bare soles of the
black feet to incorrigible hearts and minds. In all this
frenzy and loveliness Narouz felt himself borne along,
buoyant as a lily floating on a river, yet burrowing deeply into the silence of his own mind as he went to where
the archetypes of these marvellous images waited for him.

It was now that he saw, idly, a short scene enacted before his eyes—a scene whose meaning he did not grasp,
and which indeed concerned someone he had never met
and would never meet: except in the pages of this writing
—Scobie.

Somewhere in the direction of the circumcision booths
a riot had started. The frail canvas and paper walls with
their lurid iconography trembled and shook, voices
snarled and screamed and hobnailed boots thundered
upon the impermanent flooring of duck-boards; and then,
bursting through those paper walls into the white light,
holding a child wrapped in a blanket, staggered an old
man dressed in the uniform of an Egyptian Police
Officer, his frail putteed shanks quavering under him as
he ran. Behind him streamed a crowd of Arabs yelling
and growling like savage but cowardly dogs. This whole
company burst in a desperate sortie right across Narouz'
tracks. The old man in uniform was shouting in a frail
voice, but what he shouted was lost in the hubbub; he
staggered across the road to an ancient cab and climbed
into it. It set off at once at a ragged trot followed by a
fusillade of stones and curses. That was all.

As Narouz watched this little scene, his curiosity
aroused by it, a voice spoke out of the shadows at his
side—a voice whose sweetness and depth could belong to
one person only: Clea. He was stabbed to the quick—
drawing his breath sharply, painfully, and joining his

hands in a sudden gesture of childish humility at the sound. The voice was the voice of the woman he loved but it came from a hideous form, seated in half-shadow— the grease-folded body of a Moslem woman who sat unveiled before her paper hut on a three-legged stool. As she spoke, she was eating a sesame cake with the air of some huge caterpillar nibbling a lettuce—and at the same time speaking in the veritable accents of Clea!

Narouz went to her side at once, saying in a low wheedling voice: "Oh my mother, speak to me"; and once more he heard those perfectly orchestrated tones murmuring endearments and humble blandishments to draw him towards the little torture-chamber. (Petesouchos the crocodile goddess, no less.)

Blind now to everything but the cadences of the voice he followed her like an addict, standing inside the darkened room with eyes closed, his hands upon her great quivering breasts—as if to drink up the music of these slowly falling words of love in one long wholesome draught. Then he sought her mouth feverishly, as if he would suck the very image of Clea from her breath— from that sesame-laden breath. He trembled with excitement—the perilous feeling of one about to desecrate a sacred place by some irresistible obscenity whose meaning flickered like lightning in the mind with a horrible beauty of its own. (Aphrodite permits every conjugation of the mind and sense in love.)

He loosened his clothing and pressed this great doll of flesh slowly down upon the dirty bed, coaxing from her body with his powerful hands the imagined responses he might have coaxed perhaps from another and better-loved form. "Speak, my mother," he whispered hoarsely, "speak while I do it. Speak." Expressing from this great white caterpillar-form one rare and marvellous image, rare perhaps as an Emperor moth, the beauty of Clea. Oh but how horrible and beautiful to lie there at last, squeezed out like an old paint-tube among the weeping ruins of intestate desires: himself, his own inner man, thrown finally back into the isolation of a personal dream, transitory as childhood, and not less heartbreaking: Clea!

But he was interrupted, yes; for now as I read these scenes in the Interlinear, my memory revives something which it had forgotten; memories of a dirty booth with a man and woman lying together in a bed and myself looking down at them, half-drunk, waiting my turn. I have described the whole scene in another place—only then I took the man to be Mnemjian. I now believe it was Narouz. "They lay there like the victims of some terrible accident, clumsily engaged, as if in some incoherent experimental fashion they were the first partners in the history of the human race to think out this peculiar means of communication."

And this woman, with her "black spokes of toiling hair," that lay in Narouz' arms—would Clea or Justine recognise themselves in a mother-image of themselves woven out of moneyed flesh? Narouz was drinking Clea thirstily out of this old body hired for pleasure, just as I myself wished only to drink Justine. Once again "the austere, mindless primeval face of Aphrodite!"

Yes, but thirst *can* be quenched like this, by inviting a succubus to one's bed; and Narouz later wandered about in the darkness, incoherent as a madman, swollen with a relief he could barely stand. He felt like singing. Indeed, if one cannot say that he had completely forgotten Clea at this moment, one can at least assert that the act had delivered him from her image. He was wholly purged of her—and indeed would have had at this moment even the courage to *hate* her. Such is the polarity of love. "True" love.

He went back slowly, by winding ways, to his carpenter friend and claimed his horse, after first rousing the family to reassure them that it was not a thief who was making a noise in the stable at this hour.

Then he rode back to his lands, the happiest young man alive, and reached the manor as the first streaks of dawn were in the sky. As no-one was about he wrapped himself in a cloak and rested on the balcony until the sun should wake him up. He wanted to tell his brother the news.

But Nessim listened quietly and seriously to his whole story the next morning, wondering that the human heart makes no sound when the blood drains out of it drop by drop—for he thought he saw in this piece of information a vital check to the growth of the confidence he wished to foster in his wife. "I do not suppose," said Narouz, "that after so long we could find the body but I'll go over with Faraj and some grapnels and see—there can be no harm in trying. Shall I?" Nessim's shoulders had contracted. His brother paused for a moment and then went on in the same level tone: "Now I did not know anything before about how the child was dressed. But I will describe what I saw in the ground. She had a blue frock with a brooch in the shape of a butterfly." Nessim said, almost impatiently: "Yes. Perfectly true. It was the description Justine gave to the Parquet. I remember the description. So, well, Narouz . . . what can I say? It is true. I want to thank you. But as for the dragging—it has been done at least a dozen times by the Parquet. Yes, without result. There is a cut there in the canal and a runaway with a strong undercurrent."

"I see," said Narouz, cast down.

"It is difficult to know." But Nessim's voice sharpened its edge as he added: "But one thing, promise me. She must never know the truth from your lips. Promise."

"I promise you that," said his brother as Nessim turned aside from the hall telephone and came face to face with his wife. Her face was pale and her great eyes searched his with suspense and curiosity. "I must go now," said Nessim hurriedly and put down the receiver as he turned to face her and take her hands in his. In memory, I always see them like this, staring at each other with clasped hands, so near together, so far apart. The telephone is a modern symbol for communications which never take place.

o   o   o   o   o

8.

"I TOLD you of Scobie's death" (so wrote Balthazar) "but I did not tell you in detail the manner of it. I myself did not know him very well but I knew of your affection for him. It was not a very pleasant business and I was concerned in it entirely by accident—indeed, only because Nimrod, who runs the Secretariat, and was Scobie's chief at three removes happened to be dining with me on that particular evening.

"You remember Nimrod? Well, we had recently been competing for the favours of a charming young Athenian actor known by the delightful name of Socrates Pittakakis, and as any serious rivalry might have caused a bad feeling between us which neither could afford on the official level (I am in some sense a consultant to his department) we had sensibly decided to bury our jealousy and frankly share the youth—as all good Alexandrians should. We were therefore dining *à trois* at the *Auberge Bleue* with the young man between us like the filling in a meat sandwich. I must admit that I had a slight advantage over Nimrod whose Greek is poor, but in general the spirit of reason and measure reigned. The actor, who drank champagne in stout all evening—he was recovering he explained from a wasting malady by this method—in the last analysis refused to have anything to do with either of us, and indeed turned out to be passionately in love with a heavily moustached Armenian girl in my clinic. So all this effort was wasted—I must say Nimrod was particularly bitter as he had had to pay for this grotesque dinner. Well, as I say, here we all were when the great man was called away to the telephone.

"He came back after a while, looking somewhat grave, and said: 'It was from the Police Station by the docks. Apparently an old man has been kicked to death by the ratings of H.M.S. *Milton*. I have reason to believe that it might be one of the eccentrics of Q branch—there is an old Bimbashi employed there. . . .' He stood irresolutely on one leg. 'At any rate,' he went on, 'I must go down and make sure. You never know. Apparently,' he lowered his voice and drew me to one side in confidence, 'he was dressed in woman's clothes. There may be a scandal.'

"Poor Nimrod! I could see that while his duty pressed him hard, he was most reluctant that I should be left alone with the actor. He hovered and pondered heavily. At last, however, my finer nature came to my rescue just when I had given up hope. I too rose. Undying sportsmanship! 'I had better come with you,' said I. The poor man broke into troubled smiles and thanked me warmly for the gesture. We left the young man eating fish (this time for brain fag) and hurried to the car park where Nimrod's official car was waiting for him. It did not take us very long to race along the Corniche and turn down into the echoing darkness of the dock-area with its cobbled alleys and the flickering gas light along the wharves which makes it seem so like a corner of Marseilles circa 1850. I have always hated the place with its smells of sea-damp and urinals and sesame.

"The police post was a red circular building like a Victorian post office consisting of a small charge-room and two dark sweating dungeons, airless and terrible in that summer night. It was packed with jabbering and sweating policemen all showing the startled whites of their eyes like horses in the gloom. Upon a stone bench in one of the cells lay the frail and ancient figure of an old woman with a skirt dragged up above the waist to reveal thin legs clad in green socks held by suspenders and black naval boots. The electric light had failed and a wavering candle on the sill above the body dripped wax on to one withered old hand, now beginning to settle with the approach of the rigor into a histrionic gesture —as of someone warding off a stage blow. It was your friend Scobie.

"He had been battered to death in ugly enough fashion. A lot of broken crockery inside that old skin. As I examined him a phone started to nag somewhere. Keats had got wind of something: was trying to locate the scene of the incident. It could only be a matter of time before his battered old Citroën drew up outside. Obviously a grave scandal might well be the upshot and fear lent wings to Nimrod's imagination. 'He must be got out of these clothes,' he hissed and started beating out right and left with his cane, driving the policemen out into the corridor and clearing the cell. 'Right,' I said, and while Nimrod stood with sweating averted face, I got the body out of its clothes as best I could. Not pleasant, but at last the old reprobate lay there 'naked as a psalm' as they say in Greek. That was stage one. We mopped our faces. The little cell was like an oven.

"'He must,' said Nimrod hysterically, 'be somehow got back into uniform. Before Keats comes poking around here. I tell you what, let's go to his digs and get it. I know where he lives.' So we locked the old man into his cell: his smashed glass eye gave him a reproachful, mournful look—as if he had been subjected to an amateur taxidermist's art. Anyway, we jumped into the car and raced across the docks to Tatwig Street while Nimrod examined the contents of the natty little leatherette handbag with which the old man had equipped himself before setting out on his adventure. In it he found a few coins, a small missal, a master's ticket, and a packet of those old-fashioned rice-papers (one hardly ever sees them now) resembling a roll of cigarette paper. That was all. 'The bloody old fool,' Nimrod kept saying as we went. 'The bloody old fool.'

"We were surprised to find that all was chaos in the old man's lodgings, for in some mysterious way the neighbourhood had already got to hear of his death. At least, so I presumed. All the doors of his rooms had been burst open and cupboards rifled. In a sort of lavatory there was a bathtub full of some brew which smelt like *arak* and the local people had apparently been helping themselves freely, for there were prints from countless wet feet on the stairs and wet hands on the walls. The landing was awash. In the courtyard, a boab dancing round his stave and singing—a most unusual sight. Indeed, the whole neighbourhood seemed to wear an air of raffish celebration. It was most uncanny. Though most of Scobie's things had been stolen, his uniform was hanging quite safely behind the door and we grabbed it. As we did so, we got a tremendous start for a green parrot in a cage in the corner of the room said in what Nimrod swore was a perfect imitation of Scobie's voice:

> *'Come the four corners of the world in arms,*
> *We'll (hic) shock 'em.'*

"It was clear that the bird was drunk. Its voice sounded so strange in that dismal empty room. (I have not told

Clea any of this, for fear that it would upset her, as she too cared for him very much.)

"Well, back to the police post with the uniform, then. We were in luck, for there was no sign of Keats. We locked ourselves into the cell again, gasping at the heat. The body was setting so fast that it seemed impossible to get the tunic on without breaking his arms—which, God knows, were so frail that they would have snapped off like celery, or so it seemed: so I compromised by wrapping it round him. The trousers were easier. Nimrod tried to help me but was overtaken by violent nausea and spent most of the time retching in a corner. He was indeed much moved by the whole thing and kept repeating under his breath, 'Poor old bugger.' Anyway, by a smart bit of work, the scandal he feared was averted, and hardly had we brought your Scobie into line with the general proprieties than we heard the unmistakable rumble of the *Globe* car at the door and the voice of Keats in the charge-room.

"I must not forget to add that during the following few days there were two deaths and over twenty cases of acute *arak* poisoning in the area around Tatwig Street so that Scobie may be said to have left his mark on the neighbourhood. We tried to get an analysis of the stuff he was brewing, but the Government analyst gave up after testing several samples. God knows what the old man was up to.

"Nevertheless the funeral was a great success (he was buried with full honours as an officer killed in the execution of his duty) and everyone turned out for it. There was quite a contingent of Arabs from around his home. It is rare to hear Moslem ululations at a Christian graveside, and the R.C. Chaplain, Father Paul, was most put out, fearing perhaps the *afreets* of Eblis conjured up by home-made *arak*—who knows? Also there were the usual splendid inadvertencies, so characteristic of life here (grave too small, grave-diggers strike for more pay in the middle of widening it, Greek consul's carriage runs away with him and deposits him in a bush, etc., etc.). I think I described all this in a letter. It was just what Scobie would have desired—to lie covered with honours while the Police Band blew the Last Post—albeit waveringly and with a strong suggestion of Egyptian quartertones—over the grave. And the speeches, the tears! You know how people let themselves go on such occasions. You would have thought he was a saint. I kept remembering the body of the old woman in the police cell!

"Nimrod tells me that once he used to be very popular in his *quartier,* but that latterly he had started to interfere with ritual circumcision among the children and became much hated. You know how the Arabs are. Indeed, that they threatened to poison him more than once. These things preyed upon his mind as one may understand. He had been many years down there and I suppose he had no other life of his own. It happens to so many expatriates, does it not? Anyway, latterly he began to drink and to 'walk in his sleep' as the Armenians say. Everyone tried to make allowances for him and two constables were detailed to look after him on these jaunts. But on the night of his death he gave them all the slip.

" 'Once they start dressing up,' says Nimrod (he is really utterly humourless), 'it's the beginning of the end.' And so there it is. Don't mistake my tone for flippancy. Medicine has taught me to look on things with ironic detachment and so conserve the powers of feeling which should by rights be directed towards those we love and which are wasted on those who die. Or so I think.

"What on earth, after all, is one to make of life with its grotesque twists and turns? And how, I wonder, has the artist the temerity to try and impose a pattern upon it which he infects with his own meanings? (This is

aimed slightly in your direction.) I suppose you would
reply that it is the duty of the pilot to make comprehensible the shoals and quicksands, the joys and misfortunes, and so give the rest of us power over them.
Yes, but. . . .

"I desist for tonight. Clea took in the old man's parrot;
it was she who paid the expenses of his funeral. Her
portrait of him still stands I believe upon a shelf in her
now untenanted room. As for the parrot, it apparently
still spoke in his voice and she said she was frequently
startled by the things it came out with. Do you think
one's soul could enter the body of a green Amazon parrot
to carry the memory of one forward a little way into
Time? I would like to think so. But this is old history
now."

9.

WHENEVER Pombal was grievously disturbed about
something *("Mon Dieu!* today I am decomposed!" he
would say in his quaint English) he would take refuge
in a magistral attack of gout in order to remind himself
of his Norman ancestry. He kept an old-fashioned high-
backed court chair, covered in red velveteen, for such occasions. He would sit with his wadded leg up on a foot-
stool to read the *Mercure* and ponder on the possible reproof and transfer which might follow upon his latest
gaffe whatever that might happen to be. His whole
Chancery, he knew, was against him and considered his
conduct (he drank too much and chased women) as
prejudicial to the service. In fact, they were jealous be-

cause his means, which were not large enough to free
him altogether from the burden of working for a living,
permitted him nevertheless to live more or less *en prince*
—if you could call the smoky little flat we shared prince-
ly.

As I climbed the stairs today I knew that he was in a
decomposed state from the peevish tone in which he
spoke. "It is *not* news," he was repeating hysterically.
"I forbid you to publish." One-eyed Hamid met me in
the hall which smelt of frying, and waved a tender hand
in the air. "The Miss has gone," he whispered, indicating
Melissa's departure, "back six o'clock. Mr. Pombal very
not good." He pronounced my friend's name as if it
contained no vowels: thus: Pmbl.

I found Keats was with him in the sitting-room, his
large and perspiring frame stretched awkwardly across
the sofa. He was grinning and his hat was on the back
of his head. Pombal was perched in his gout-chair, looking mournful and peevish. I recognised the signs not
only of a hangover but of yet another committed *gaffe*.
What had Keats got hold of now? "Pombal," I said,
"what the devil has happened to your car?" He groaned
and clutched his dewlaps as if imploring me to leave the
whole subject alone; obviously Keats had been teasing
him about just that.

The little car in question, so dear to Pombal's heart,
now stood outside the front door, badly buckled and
smashed. Keats gave a snuffle-gulp. "It was Sveva," he explained, "and I'm not allowed to print it." Pombal
moaned and rocked. "He won't tell me the whole story."

Pombal began to get really angry. "Will you please
get out?" he said, and Keats, always easily discounte-
nanced before someone whose name appeared on the diplomatic list, rose and pocketed his notebook, wiping the
smile off his face as he did so. "All right," he said, pun-
ning feebly, *"Chacun à son gout*, I suppose," and clam-

bered slowly down the stairs. I sat down opposite Pombal and waited for him to calm down.

"Another *gaffe*, my dear boy," he said at last, "the worst yet in the *affaire Sveva*. It was she . . . my poor car . . . you have seen it? Here, feel this bump on my neck. Eh? A bloody rock."

I asked Hamid for some coffee while he recounted his latest mishap with the usual anguished gesticulations. He had been unwise ever to embark on this affair with the fiery Sveva, for now she loved him. "Love!" Pombal groaned and twisted in his chair. "I am so weak about women," he admitted, "and she was so easy. God, it was like having something put on one's plate which one hadn't ordered—or which someone else had and which had been sent to one's table by mistake; she came into my life like a *bifteck à point,* like a stuffed eggplant. . . . What was I to do?"

"And then yesterday I thought: 'Taking everything into account, her age, the state of her teeth, and so on, illness might very well intervene and cause me expense.' Besides, I don't *want* a mistress in *perpetuum mobile*. So I decided to take her out to a quiet spot on the lake and say good-bye. She went mad. In a flash she was on the bank of the river where she found a huge pile of rocks. Before I knew what to say *Piff Paff Pang Bong*." His gestures were eloquent. "The air was full of rocks. Windscreen, headlights, everything . . . I was lying beside the clutch screaming. Feel this lump on my neck. She had gone mad. When all the glass was gone, she picked up a huge boulder and began to stove the car in screaming the word '*Amour. Amour*' to punctuate each bang like a maniac. I never want to hear the word again. Radiator gone, all the wings twisted. You have seen? You would never believe a girl could do such a thing. Then what? Then I'll tell you what. *She threw herself into the river*. Figure to yourself my feelings. She can't

swim, nor can I. The *scandal* if she died! I threw myself
in after her. We held each other and screamed like a pair
of cats making love. The water I swallowed! Some policemen came and pulled us out. Long *procès-verbal*, etc.
I simply dare not ring the Chancery this morning. Life
isn't worth living."

He was on the point of tears. "This is my third scandal
this month," he said. "And tomorrow is carnival. Do you
know what? After long thought I have evolved an idea."
He smiled a wintry smile. "I shall make sure about the
carnival—even if I do drink too much and get in a scrape
as I usually do. I shall go in an impenetrable disguise.
Yes." He rinsed his fingers and repeated, "An impenetrable disguise." Then he considered me for a moment
as if trying to decide whether to trust me or not. His
scrutiny seemed to satisfy him for he turned abruptly
towards the cupboard and said: "If I show you, you'll
keep my secret, eh? We are friends after all. Fetch me the
hat from the top shelf in there. You will get a laugh."

Inside the cupboard I found an immense, old-fashioned
picture-hat of the 1912 variety, trimmed with a bunch
of faded osprey feathers and secured by a thick hatpin
with a large blue stone head. "This?" I said incred-
ulously, and he chuckled complacently as he nodded.
"Who will ever recognise me in this? Give it here. . . ."

He looked so funny with it on that I was forced to sit
down and laugh. He reminded me of Scobie in his own
absurd Dolly Varden. Pombal looked . . . it is quite indescribable what this ridiculous creation did to his fat
face. He began to laugh too as he said, "Wonderful, no?
My bloody colleagues will never know who the drunk
woman was. And if the Consul-General isn't in domino I
shall . . . make advances to him. I shall drive him out of
his mind with passionate kisses. The swine!" His face
set in a grimace of hate looked even more ludicrous. As

with Scobie, I was forced to plead: "Take it off, for God's sake!"

He did so and sat grinning at me, consumed by the brilliance of his plan. At least, he thought, such indiscretions as he might commit would not be attributable to him. "I have a whole costume," he added proudly. "So look out for me, will you? You are going, aren't you? I hear that there are two full-scale balls going so we shall weave about from one to the other, eh? Good. I am a bit relieved, aren't you?"

But it was this fatal hat of Pombal's which led directly to Toto de Brunel's mysterious death next evening at the Cervonis'—the death which Justine believed her husband had reserved for her and which I. . . . But I must follow the Interlinear back upon my tracks.

"The question of the watch-key," writes Balthazar, "—the one you helped me hunt for among the crevices of the Grande Corniche on that winter day—turned out oddly. As you know, my timepiece stopped and I had to order another little gold ankh to be made for it. But in the interval the key was returned under strange circumstances. One day Justine came into the clinic and, kissing me warmly, produced it from her handbag. 'Do you recognise this?' she asked me smiling, and then went on apologetically, 'I am so sorry for your concern, my dear Balthazar. It is the first time in my life that I have been forced to turn pickpocket. You see, there is a wall-safe in the house to which I was determined to gain access. At first glance the keys seemed similar and I wanted to see whether your watch-key fitted the lock. I had intended to return it next morning before you had time to worry, but I found that someone had removed it from my dressing-table. You won't repeat this. I thought that perhaps Nessim himself had caught sight of it, and had suspected my motive, and had therefore confiscated it in order to try it in the lock of his safe himself. Fortunately (or unfortunately) it does not fit, and I could not open the little safe. But, nor could I make a fuss about the thing for fear that he had not in fact seen it; I did not want to draw his attention to its existence and its similarity to his own. I asked Fatma discreetly and went through my jewel-cases. No luck. Then two days later Nessim himself produced it and said he had found it in his stud-box; he recognised its similarity to his own but did not mention the safe. He simply asked me to give it back to you, which I herewith do, with genuine apologies for the delay.'

"I was of course annoyed, and told her so. 'And anyway, why should you wish to poke about in Nessim's private safe?' I said. 'It seems to me unlike your normal behaviour, and I must say I feel a good deal of contempt for you after the way Nessim has treated you.' She hung her head and said, 'I only hoped to discover something about the child—something which I think he is hiding from me.' "

o   o   o   o   o

10.

"I SUPPOSE" (writes Balthazar) "that if you wished somehow to incorporate all I am telling you into your own Justine manuscript now, you would find yourself with a curious sort of book—the story would be told, so to speak, in layers. Unwittingly I may have supplied you with a form, something out of the way! Not unlike Pursewarden's idea of a series of novels with 'sliding panels' as he called them. Or else, perhaps, like some medieval palimpsest where different sorts of truth are thrown down one upon the other, the one obliterating or perhaps supplementing another. Industrious monks scraping away an elegy to make room for a verse of Holy Writ!

"I don't suppose such an analogy would be a bad one to apply to the reality of Alexandria, a city at once sacred and profane; between Theocritus, Plotinus, and the Septuagint one moves on intermediate levels which are those of race as much as anything—like saying Copt, Greek and Jew or Moslem, Turk and Armenian. . . . Am I wrong? These are the slow accretions of time itself on place. Just as life on the individual face lays down, wash by successive wash, the wrinkles of experiences in which laughter and tears are utterly indistinguishable. Wormcasts of experience on the sands of life. . . ."

So writes my friend, and he is right; for the Interlinear now raises for me much more than the problem of objective "truth to life," or if you like "to fiction." It raises, as life itself does—whether one makes or takes it—

the harder-grained question of form. How then am I to manipulate this mass of crystallized data in order to work out the meaning of it and so give a coherent picture of this impossible city of love and obscenity?

I wish I knew. I wish I knew. So much has been revealed to me by all this that I feel myself to be, as it were, standing upon the threshold of a new book—a new Alexandria. The old evocative outlines which I drew, intertwining them with the names of the city's exemplars —Cavafy, Alexander, Cleopatra and the rest—were subjective ones. I had made the image my own jealous personal property, and it was true yet only within the limitations of a truth only partially perceived. Now, in the light of all these new treasures—for truth, though merciless as love, must always be a treasure—what should I do? Extend the frontiers of original truth, filling in with the rubble of this new knowledge the foundations upon which to build a new Alexandria? Or should the dispositions remain the same, the characters remain the same—and is it only truth *itself* which has changed in contradiction?

All this spring on my lonely island I have been weighed down by this grotesque information, which has so altered my feelings about things—oddly enough even about things past. Can emotions be retrospective, retroactive?

So much I wrote was based upon Justine's fears of Nessim—genuine fears, genuinely expressed. I have seen with my own eyes that cold speechless jealousy upon his face—and seen the fear written on hers. Yet now Balthazar says that Nessim would never have done her harm. What am I to believe?

We dined so often together, the four of us; and there I sat speechless and drunk upon the memory of her actual kisses, believing (only because she told me so) that the presence of the fourth—Pursewarden—would lull Nes-

sim's jealous brain and offer us the safety of chaperonage! Yet if now I am to believe Balthazar, it was I who
was the decoy. (Do I remember, or only imagine, a
special small smile which from time to time would
appear at the corner of Pursewarden's lips, perhaps cynical or perhaps comminatory?) I thought then that I was
sheltering behind the presence of the writer while he
was in fact sheltering behind mine! I am prevented from
fully believing this by . . . what? The quality of a kiss
from the lips of one who could murmur, like a being sub-
mitting its body to the rack, the words "I love you." Of
course, of course. I am an expert in love—every man believes himself to be one: but particularly the Englishman.
So I am to believe in the kiss rather than in the state-
ments of my friend? Impossible, for Balthazar does not
lie. . . .

Is love by its very nature a blindness? Of course, I
know I averted my face from the thought that Justine
might be unfaithful to me while I possessed her—who
does not? It would have been too painful a truth to accept, although in my heart of hearts I knew full well,
that she could never be faithful to me for ever. If I
ever dared to whisper the thought to myself I hastily
added, like every husband, every lover, "But of course,
whatever she does, I am the one she truly loves!" The
sophistries which console—the lies which keep love going!

Not that she herself ever gave me direct reason to
doubt. I do however remember an occasion on which
the faintest breath of suspicion roused itself against
Pursewarden, only to be immediately stilled. He walked
out of the studio one day towards us with some lipstick
on his mouth. But almost immediately I caught sight of
the cigarette in his hand—he had obviously picked up a
cigarette which Justine had left burning in an ashtray
(a common habit with her) for the end of it was red.
In matters of love everything is easy to explain.

The wicked Interlinear, freighted with these doubts, presses like a blunt thumb, here and here, always in bruised places. I have begun to copy it whole—the whole of it—slowly and painfully; not only to understand more clearly wherein it differs from my own version of reality, but also to catch a glimpse of it as a separate entity—as a manuscript existing in its own right, as the determined view of another eye upon events which I interpreted in my own way, because that was the way in which I lived them—or they lived me. Did I really miss so much that was going on around me—the connotation of smiles, of chance words and gestures, messages scribbled with a finger in wine spilt upon a table-top, addresses written in the corner of newspapers and folded over? Must I now re-work my own experiences in order to come to the heart of the truth? "Truth has no heart," writes Pursewarden. "Truth is a woman. That is why it is enigmatic. Of women, the most we can say, not being Frenchmen, is that they are burrowing animals."

According to Balthazar, I have misread the order of Justine's fears in so far as they concerned Nessim. The incident of the car I have recorded elsewhere; how she was racing towards Cairo one night to meet Pursewarden when the lights of the great moth-coloured Rolls went out. Blinded by darkness she lost control of it and it swarmed off the road, bouncing from dune to dune and throwing up spouts of sand like the spray thrown up by the death-agonies of a whale. Then "whistling like an arrow" it buried itself to the windscreens in a dune and lay trembling and murmuring. Fortunately, she was not hurt and had the presence of mind to switch off the engine. But how had the accident come about? In telling me of it she said that when the car was examined the wiring was found to have been filed down—by whom?

This was, as far as I know, the first time that her fears concerning Nessim, and a possible attempt on her own life, became articulate. She had spoken of his jealousy before, yes; but not of anything like this, not of anything so concrete—so truly Alexandrian. My own alarm may well be imagined.

Yet now Balthazar in his notes says that some ten days before this incident, she had seen Selim from the studio window walk across the lawn towards the car, and there believing himself unobserved, lift the bonnet to take out from under it one of the little wax rollers which she thought she recognised as part of the equipment belonging to the dictaphone which Nessim often used in the office. He had wrapped the object in a cloth and carried it indoors. She sat at the window for a long time, musing and smoking before acting. Then she took the car out on to the desert road to a lonely place the better to examine it. Under the bonnet she found a small apparatus which she did not recognise but which seemed to her to be possibly a recording machine. Presumably a wire lead connected it to a small microphone buried somewhere among the coloured coils of the dashboard wiring, but she could not trace it. With her nail file, however, she cut the wire at several points while leaving the whole contrivance in place and apparently in working order. It was now, according to Balthazar, that she must by accident have disturbed or half-severed one of the leads to the car's headlights. At least, this is what she told him, though she gave me no such explanation. If I am to believe him, all this time, while she went on and on about the heedless folly of our public behaviour and the risks we were taking, she was really drawing me on— trailing me before the eyes of Nessim like a cape before a bull!

But this was only at first; later, says my friend, came something which really made her feel that some action against her was contemplated by her husband: namely the murder of Toto de Brunel during the carnival ball

at the Cervonis'. Why have I never mentioned this? It
is true that I was even there at the time, and yet somehow the whole incident though it belonged to the atmosphere of the moment escaped me in the press of other
matters. Alexandria had many such unsolved mysteries
at that time. And while I knew the interpretation Justine
put upon it I did not myself believe it at the time. Nevertheless, it is strange that I should not have mentioned it,
even in passing. Of course, the true explanation of the
matter was only given to me months later: almost when
I myself was on the point of leaving Alexandria for ever
as I thought, with the child of Melissa—Nessim's child
by her. Clea one night told me the truth with her own
lips!

The carnival in Alexandria is a purely social affair—
having no calendar relationship to the other religious
festivals of the city. I suppose it must have been insti-
tuted by the three or four great Catholic families in the
place—perhaps vicariously they enjoyed through it a sense
of identity with the other side of the Mediterranean,
with Venice and Athens. Nevertheless, there is today no
rich family which does not keep a cupboard full of
velvet dominoes against the three days of folly—be it
Copt, Moslem or Jewish. After New Year's Eve it is perhaps the greatest Christian celebration of the year—for
the ruling spirit of the three days and nights is—utter
anonymity: the anonymity conferred by the grim black
velvet domino which shrouds identity and sex, prevents
one distinguishing between man and woman, wife and
lover, friend and enemy.

The maddest aberrations of the city now come boldly
forward under the protection of the invisible lords of
Misrule who preside at this season. No sooner has darkness fallen than the maskers begin to appear in the streets
—first in ones and twos then in small companies, often
with musical instruments or drums, laughing and sing-

ing their way to some great house or to some night-club
where already the frosty air is bathed in the nigger
warmth of jazz—the cloying grunting intercourse of saxophones and drums. Everywhere they spring up in the
pale moonlight, cowled like monks. The disguise gives
them all a gloomy fanatical uniformity of outline which
startles the white-robed Egyptians and fills them with
alarm—the thrill of a fear which spices the wild laughter
pouring out of the houses, carried by the light offshore
winds towards the cafés on the sea-front; a gaiety which
by its very shrillness seems to tremble always upon the
edge of madness.

Slowly the bluish spring moon climbs the houses, sliding up the minarets into the clicking palm-trees, and with
it the city seems to uncurl like some hibernating animal
dug out of its winter earth, to stretch and begin to drink
in the music of the three-day festival.

The jazz pouring up from the cellars displaces the
tranquil winter air in the parks and thoroughfares,
mingling as it reaches the sealine with the drumming
perhaps of a liner's screws in the deepwater reaches of
the estuary. Or you may hear and see for a brief moment
the rip and slither of fireworks against a sky which for
a moment curls up at the edges and blushes, like a sheet
of burning carbon paper: wild laughter which mixes with
the hoarse mooing of an old ship outside the harbour
bar—like a cow locked outside a gate.

"The lover fears the carnival," says the proverb. And
with the emergence of these black-robed creatures of the
night everywhere, all is subtly altered. The whole tem-
perature of life in the city alters, grows warm with the
subtle intimations of spring. *Carni vale*—the flesh's farewell to the year, unwinding its mummy wrappings of
sex, identity and name, and stepping forward naked into
futurity of the dream.

All the great houses have thrown open their doors upon

fabulous interiors warm with a firelight which bristles upon china and marble, brass and copper, and upon the blackleaded faces of the servants as they go about their duties. And down every street now, glittering in the moonlit gloaming, lounge the great limousines of the brokers and gamblers, like liners in dock, the patient and impressive symbols of a wealth which is powerless to bring true leisure or peace of mind for it demands everything of the human soul. They lie webbed in a winter light, expressing only the silence and power of all machinery which waits for the fall of man, looking on at the maskers as they cross and recross the lighted windows of the great houses, clutching each other like black bears, dancing to the throb of nigger music, the white man's solace.

Snatches of music and laughter must rise to Clea's window where she sits with a board on her knees, patiently drawing while her little cat sleeps in its basket at her feet. Or perhaps in some sudden lull the chords of a guitar may be plucked to stay and wallow in the darkness of the open street until they are joined by a voice raised in remote song, as if from the bottom of a well. Or screams, cries for help.

But what stamps the carnival with its spirit of pure mischief is the velvet domino—conferring upon its wearers the disguise which each man in his secret heart desires above all. To become anonymous in an anonymous crowd, revealing neither sex nor relationship nor even facial expression—for the mask of this demented friar's habit leaves only two eyes, glowing like the eyes of a Moslem woman or a bear. Nothing else to distinguish one by; the thick folds of the blackness conceal even the contours of the body. Everyone becomes hipless, breastless, faceless. And concealed beneath the carnival habit (like a criminal desire in the heart, a temptation impossible to resist, an impulse which seems preordained) lie the germs of something: of a freedom which man has

seldom dared to imagine for himself. One feels free in
this disguise to do whatever one likes without prohibition.
All the best murders in the city, all the most tragic
cases of mistaken identity, are the fruit of the yearly
carnival; while most love affairs begin or end during
these three days and nights during which we are delivered from the thrall of personality, from the bondage
of ourselves. Once inside that velvet cape and hood, and
wife loses husband, husband wife, lover the beloved. The
air becomes crisp with the saltpetre of feuds and follies,
the fury of battles, of agonizing night-long searches, of
despairs. You cannot tell whether you are dancing with
a man or a woman. The dark tides of Eros, which demand full secrecy if they are to overflow the human soul,
burst out during carnival like something long dammed
up and raise the forms of strange primeval creatures—
the perversions which are, I suppose, the psyche's aliment
—in forms which you would think belonged to the
Brocken or to Eblis. Now hidden satyr and maenad can
rediscover each other and unite. Yes, who can help but
love carnival when in it all debts are paid, all crimes
expiated or committed, all illicit desires sated—without
guilt or premeditation, without the penalties which conscience or society exact?

But I am wrong about one thing—for there is one distinguishing mark by which your friend or enemy may still
identify you: hands. Your lover's hands, if you have
ever noticed them at all, will lead you to her in the
thickest press of maskers. Or by arrangement she may
wear, as Justine does, a familiar ring—the ivory intaglio
taken from the tomb of a dead Byzantine youth—worn
upon the forefinger of the right hand. But this is all, and
it is only just enough. (Pray that you are not as unlucky
as Amaril who found the perfect woman during carnival
but could not persuade her to raise her hood and stand
identified. They talked all night, lying in the grass by

the fountain, making love together with their velvet faces touching, their eyes caressing each other. For a whole year now, he has gone about the city trying to find a pair of human hands, like a madman. But hands are so alike! She swore, this woman of his, that she would come back next year to the same place, wearing the same ring with its small yellow stone. And so tonight he will wait trembling for a pair of hands by the lily-pond—hands which will perhaps never appear again in his life. Perhaps she was after all an *afreet* or a vampire—who knows? Yet years later, in another book, in another context, he will happen upon her again, almost by accident, but not here, not in these pages too tangled already by the record of ill-starred loves. . . .)

So then you walk the dark streets, serene as a murderer unidentified, all your traces covered by the black cowl, feeling the fresh wintry airs of the city upon your eyelids. The Egyptians you pass look askance at you, not knowing whether to smile or be afraid at your appearance. They hover in an indeterminate state of mind when carnival comes on—wondering how it should be taken. Passing, you give them a burning stare from the depths of your cowl, glad to see them flinch and avert their faces. Other dominoes like yourself emerge from every corner, some in groups laughing and singing as they walk towards some great house or to neighbouring nightclubs.

Walking like this towards the Cervonis', across the network of streets by the Greek Patriarchate you are reminded of other carnivals, perhaps even in other cities, distinguished by the same wildness and gaiety which is the gift of lost identities. Strange adventures which befell you once. At one corner in the Rue Bartout last year the sound of running feet and cries. A man presents a dagger to your throat, crying, like a wounded animal,

"Helen, if you try and run away tonight I swear I'll kill . . ." but the words die as you raise your mask and show your face, and he stammers an apology as he turns away only to burst into sobs and throw himself against an iron railing. Helen has already disappeared, and he will search for her the whole night through!

At a gate into a yard, weirdly lit by the feeble street-lamps, two figures in black are grappling each other, fighting with a tremendous silent fury. They fall, rolling over and over from darkness into light and then back into darkness. Without a word spoken. At the Étoile there is a man hanging from a beam with his neck broken; but when you get close enough you see that it is only a black domino hanging from a nail. How strange that in order to free oneself from guilt by a disguise one should choose the very symbol of the Inquisitor, the cape and hood of the Spanish Inquisition.

But they are not all in domino—for many people are superstitious about the dress and, besides, it can be hot to wear in a crowded room. So you will see many a harlequin and shepherdess, many an Antony and Cleopatra as you walk the streets of the city, many an Alexander. And as you turn into the great iron gates of the Cervonis' house to present your card and climb into the warmth and light and drunkenness within, you will see outlined upon the darkness the feared and beloved shapes and outlines of friends and familiars now distorted into the semblance of clowns and zanies, or clothed in the nothingness of black capes and hoods, infernally joined in a rare and disoriented gaiety.

As if under pressure the laughter squirts up to the ceiling or else, like feathers from a torn quilt, drifts about in clumps in that fevered air. The two string bands, muted by the weight of human voices, labour on in the short staggered rhythms of a maniac jazz—like the steady

beating of an airpump. Here on the ballroom floor a million squeakers and trumpets squash and distort the sound
while already the dense weight of the coloured paper
streamers, hanging upon the shoulders of the dancers,
sways like tropical seaweed upon rock-surfaces and trails
in ankle-high drifts about the polished floors.

On the night in question, the first night of carnival,
there was a dinner-party at the great house. On the long
hall sofas the dominoes waited for their tenants while
the candlelight still smouldered upon the faces of a
Justine and Nessim now framed among the portraits
which lined the ugly but imposing dining-room. Faces
painted in oils matched by human faces lined by preoccupations and maladies of the soul—all gathered together,
made one in the classical brilliance of candlelight. After
dinner Justine and Nessim were to go together to the
Cervoni ball according to the yearly custom. According
to custom too, Narouz at the last moment had excused
himself. He would arrive upon the stroke of ten, just in
time to claim a domino before the whole party set off,
laughing and chattering, for the ball.

As always, he himself had preferred to ride into the
city on his horse and to stable it with his friend the
carpenter, but as a concession to the event he had struggled into an ancient suit of blue serge and had knotted a
tie at his collar. Undress did not matter, since he too
would later be wearing a domino. He walked lightly,
swiftly across the ill-lit Arab quarter, drinking in the
familiar sights and sounds, yet eager for the first sight
of the maskers as he reached the end of Rue Fuad and
found himself on the confines of the modern town.

At one corner stood a group of shrill-chattering women
in domino bent upon mischief. From their language and
accent he could detect at once that they were society
women, Greeks. These black harpies caught hold of every
passer-by to shout jests at him and to pluck at his hood

if he were masked. Narouz too had to run the gauntlet: one caught hold of his hand and pretended to tell his fortune; another whispered a proposition in Arabic, setting her hand upon his thigh; the third cackled like a hen and shouted "Your wife has a lover" and other unkindnesses. He could not tell if they recognised him or not.

Narouz flinched, shook himself and burst smiling through their number fending them off good-naturedly and roaring with laughter at the sally about his wife. "Not tonight, my doves," he cried hoarsely in Arabic, thinking suddenly of Clea; and as they showed some disposition to capture him for the evening, he began to run. They chased him a little way, shouting and laughing incoherently down the long dark street, but he easily outdistanced them, and so turned the corner to the great house, still smiling but a little out of breath, and flattered by these attentions which seemed to set the key for the evening's enjoyment. In the silent hall his eye caught the black of dominoes and he put one on before edging open the door of the drawing-room behind which he could hear their voices. It disguised his shabby suit. The cape lay back upon his shoulders.

They were all there by the fire, waiting for him, and he took their cries of welcome greedily and seriously, making his round to kiss Justine on the cheek and to shake hands with the rest in an agony of awkward silence. He put on an artificially sincere expression, looking with distaste into the myopic eyes of Pierre Balbz (he hated him for the goatee and spats) and those of Toto de Brunel (an old lady's lap-dog); but he liked the over-blown rose, Athena Trasha, for she used the same scent as his mother; and he was sorry for Drusilla Banubula because she was so clever that she hardly seemed to be a woman at all. With Pursewarden he shared a smile of easy complicity. "Well," he said, expelling his breath

at last in relief. His brother handed him a whisky with
mild tenderness, which he drank slowly but all in one
draught, like a peasant.

"We were waiting for you, Narouz."

"The Hosnani exile," glittered Pierre Balbz ingra-
tiatingly.

"The farmer," cried little Toto.

The conversation which had been interrupted by his
sudden appearance closed smoothly over his head once
more and he sat down by the fire until they should be
ready to leave for the Cervoni house, folding his strong
hands one upon the other in a gesture of finality, as if
to lock up once and for all his powers. The skin at
Nessim's temples appeared to be stretched, he noticed,
an old sign of anger or strain. The fullness of Justine's
dark beauty in her dress (the colour of hare's blood)
glowed among the ikons, seeming to enjoy the semi-dark-
ness of the candlelight—to feed upon it and give back
the glitter of her barbaric jewellery. Narouz felt full of
a marvellous sense of detachment, of unconcern; what
these small portents of trouble or stress meant, he did
not know. It was only Clea who flawed his self-sufficiency,
who darkened the edges of his thought. Each year he
hoped that when he arrived at his brother's house he
would find she had been included in the party. Yet each
year she was not, and in consequence he was forced to
drift about all night in the darkness, searching for her
as aimlessly as a ghost, not even really hoping to encounter her: and yet living upon the attenuated wraith
of this fond hope as a soldier upon an iron ration.

They had been talking that night of Amaril and his
unhappy passion for a pair of anonymous hands and a
carnival voice, and Pursewarden was telling one of his
famous stories in that crisp uninflected French of his
which was just a shade too perfect.

"When I was twenty, I went to Venice for the first

time at the invitation of an Italian poet with whom I had been corresponding, Carlo Negroponte. For a middle-class English youth this was a great experience, to live virtually by candlelight in this huge tumbledown palazzo on the Grand Canal with a fleet of gondolas at my disposal—not to mention a huge wardrobe of cloaks lined with silk. Negroponte was generous and spared no effort to entertain a fellow-poet in the best style. He was then about fifty, frail and rather beautiful, like a rare kind of mosquito. He was a prince and a diabolist, and his poetry happily married the influences of Byron and Baudelaire. He went in for cloaks and shoes with buckles and silver walking-sticks and encouraged me to do the same. I felt I was living in a Gothic novel. Never have I written worse poetry.

"That year we went to the carnival together and got separated though we each wore something to distinguish each other by; you know of course that carnival is the one time of the year when vampires walk freely abroad, and those who are wise carry a pig of garlic in their pockets to drive them off—if by chance one were to be encountered. Next morning I went into my host's room and found him lying pale as death in bed, dressed in the white nightshirt with lace cuffs, with a doctor taking his pulse. When the doctor had gone he said: 'I have met the perfect woman, masked; I went home with her and she proved to be a vampire.' Then drawing up his nightshirt he showed me with exhausted pride that his body was covered with great bites, like the marks of a weasel's teeth. He was utterly exhausted but at the same time excited—and frightening to relate, very much in love. 'Until you have experienced it,' he said, 'you have no idea what it is like. To have one's blood sucked in darkness by someone one adores.' His voice broke. 'De Sade could not begin to describe it. I did not see her face, but I had the impression she was fair, of a northern

fairness; we met in the dark and separated in the dark.
I have only the impression of white teeth, and a voice
—never have I heard any woman say the things she says.
She is the very lover for whom I have been waiting all
these years. I am meeting her again tonight by the
marble griffin at the Footpads' Bridge. O my friend, be
happy for me. The real world has become more and more
meaningless to me. Now at last, with this vampire's love,
I feel I can live again, feel again, write again!' He spent
all that day at his papers, and at nightfall set off, cloaked,
in his gondola. It was not my business to say anything.
The next day once more I found him, pale and deathly
tired. He had a high fever, and again these terrible bites.
But he could not speak of his experience without weeping
—tears of love and exhaustion. And it was now that he
had begun his great poem which begins—you all know
it—

> 'Lips not on lips, but on each other's wounds
> Must suck the envenomed bodies of the loved
> And through the tideless blood draw nourishment
> To feed the love that feeds upon their
>   deaths. . . .'

"The following week I left for Ravenna where I had
some studies to make for a book I was writing and where
I stayed two months. I heard nothing from my host, but
I got a letter from his sister to say that he was ill with
a wasting disease which the doctors could not diagnose
and that the family was much worried because he insisted on going out at night in his gondola on journeys
of which he would not speak but from which he returned
utterly exhausted. I did not know what to reply to this.

"From Ravenna, I went down to Greece and it was
not until the following autumn that I returned. I had
sent a card to Negroponte saying I hoped to stay with
him, but had no reply. As I came down the Grand Canal
a funeral was setting off in choppy water, by twilight,

with the terrible plumes and emblems of death. I saw
that they were coming from the Negroponte Palazzo.
I landed and ran to the gates just as the last gondola in
the procession was filling up with mourners and priests.
I recognised the doctor and joined him in the boat, and
as we rowed stiffly across the canal, dashed with spray
and blinking at the stabs of lightning, he told me what
he knew. Negroponte had died the day before. When
they came to lay out the body, they found the bites:
perhaps of some tropical insect? The doctor was vague.
'The only such bites I have seen,' he said, 'were during
the plague of Naples when the rats had been at the
bodies. They were so bad we had to dust him down with
talcum powder before we could let his sister see the
body.'"

Pursewarden took a long sip from his glass and went
on wickedly. "The story does not end there; for I should
tell you how I tried to avenge him, and went myself at
night to the Bridge of the Footpads—where according
to the gondolier this woman always waited in the shadow.
. . . But it is getting late, and anyway, I haven't made
up the rest of the story as yet."

There was a good deal of laughter and Athena gave
a well-bred shudder, drawing her shawl across her
shoulders. Narouz had been listening open-mouthed, with
reeling senses, to this recital: he was spellbound. "But,"
he stammered, "is all this true?" Fresh laughter greeted
his question.

"Of course it's true," said Pursewarden severely, and
added: "I have never been in Venice in my life."

And he rose, for it was time for them to be going, and
while the impassive black servants waited they put on
the velveteen capes and adjusted their masks like the
actors they were, comparing their identical reflections
as they stood side by side in the two swollen mirrors
among the palms. Giggles from Pierre and sallies of wit

from Toto de Brunel; and so they stepped laughing into the clear night air, the inquisitors of pleasure and pain, the Alexandrians. . . .

The cars engulfed them while the solicitous domestics and chauffeurs tucked them in, carefully as bales of precious merchandise or spices, tenderly as flowers. "I feel fragile," squeaked Toto at these attentions. "This side up with care, eh? Which side up, I ask myself?" He must have been the only person in the city not to know the answer to his own question.

When they had started, Justine leaned forward in the car and plucked his sleeve. "I want to whisper," she said hoarsely though there was little need for Nessim and Narouz were discussing something in harsh tones (Narouz' voice with the characteristic boyish break in it) and Athena was squibbling to Pierre like a flute. "Toto . . . listen. One great service tonight, if you will. I have put a chalk-mark on your sleeve, here, at the back. Later on in the evening, I want to give you my ring to wear. Shh. I want to disappear for an hour or so on my own. Hush . . . don't giggle." But there were squeaks from the velvet hood. "You will have adventures in my name, dear Toto, while I am gone. Do you agree?"

He threw back his cape to show a delighted face, dancing eyes and that grim little procurer's smile. "Of course," he whispered back, enraptured by the idea and full of admiration. The featureless hood at his side from which the voice of Justine had issued like an oracle glowed with a sort of death's-head beauty of its own, nodding at him in the light from the passing street-lamps. The conversation and laughter around them sealed them in a conspiracy of private silence. "Do you agree?" she said.

"Darling, of course."

The two masked men in the front seats of the car might have been abbots of some medieval monastery, discussing theological niceties. Athena, consumed by her own voice, still babbled away to Pierre. "But of course."

Justine took his arm and turned back the sleeve to show him the chalk-mark she had made. "I count on you," she said, with some of the hoarse imperiousness of her speaking-voice, yet still in a whisper. "Don't let me down!" He took her hand and raised it to his Cupid's lips, kissing the ring from the dead finger of the Byzantine youth as one might kiss the holy picture which had performed a miracle long desired; he was to be turned from a man into a woman. Then he laughed and cried: "And my indiscretions will be on your head. You will spend the rest of your days. . . ."

"Hush."

"What is all this?" cried Athena Trasha, scenting a joke or a scandal worth repetition. "What indiscretions?"

"My own," cried Toto triumphantly into the darkness. "My very own." But Justine lay back in the dark car impassively hooded, and did not speak. "I can't wait to get there," said Athena, and turned back to Pierre. As the car turned into the gate of the Cervoni house, the light caught the intaglio, throwing into relief (colour of burnt milk) a Pan raping a goat, his hands grasping its horns, his head thrown back in ecstasy. "Don't forget," Justine said once more, for the last time, allowing him to maul her hand with gratitude for such a wonderful idea. "Don't forget," allowing her ringed fingers to lie in his, cool and unfeeling as a cow which allows itself to be milked. "Only tell me all the interesting conversations you have, won't you?" He could only mutter "Darling, darling, darling" as he kissed the ring with the ovarian passion of the sexually dispossessed.

Almost at once, like the Gulf Stream breaking up an iceberg with its warm currents, dispersing it, their party disintegrated as it reached the ballroom and merged with the crowd. Abruptly Athena was dragged screaming into the heart of the press by a giant domino who gobbled and roared incomprehensible blasphemies in his hood. Nessim, Narouz, Pierre, they suddenly found themselves turned to ciphers, expelled into a formless world of adventitious meetings, mask to dark mask, like a new form of insect life. Toto's chalk-mark gave him a few fugitive moments of identity as he was borne away like a cork on a stream, and Justine's ring as well (for which I myself was hunting all that evening in vain).

But everything now settled into the mindless chaotic dance-figures of the black jazz supported only by the grinding drums and saxophones, the voices. The spirits of the darkness had taken over, you'd think, disinheriting the daylight hearts and minds of the maskers, plunging them ever deeper into the loneliness of their own ir-recoverable identities, setting free the polymorphous desires of the city. The tide washed them up now onto the swampy littorals of their own personalities—symbols of Alexandria, a dead brackish lake surrounded by the silent, unjudging, wide-eyed desert which stretches away into Africa under a dead moon.

Locked in our masks now we prowled about despair-ingly among the company, hunting from room to room, from floor to lighted floor of the great house, for an identifiable object to direct our love: a rose pinned to a sleeve, a ring, a scarf, a coloured bead. Something, any-thing, to discover our lovers by. The hoods and masks were like the outward symbols of our own secret minds as we walked about—as single-minded and as dispossessed as the desert fathers hunting for their God. And slowly but with irresistible momentum the great carnival ball gathered pace around us. Here and there, like patches of meaning in an obscure text, one touched upon a familiar identity: a bullfighter drinking whisky in a corridor greeted one in the lisping accents of Tony Umbada, or Pozzo di Borgo unmasked for an instant

to identify himself to his trembling wife. Outside in the
darkness on the grass by the lily pond sat Amaril, also
trembling and waiting. He did not dare to remain unmasked lest the sight of his face might disgust or dis-
appoint her, should she return this year to the promised
assignation. If one falls in love with a mask when one is
masked oneself . . . which of you will first have the
courage to raise it? Perhaps such lovers would go through
life together, remaining masked? (Racing thoughts in
Amaril's sentimental brain. . . . Love rejoices in self-
torture.)

An expressive washerwoman dressed in a familiar picture-hat and recognisable boots (Pombal, as ever was),
had pinned a meagre-looking Roman centurion to a corner of the mantel-piece and was cursing him in a parrot-
voice. I caught the word "*salaud.*" The little figure of the
Consul-General managed to mime his annoyance with
choppy gestures and struggles, but it was all in vain, for
Pombal held him fast in his great paws. It was fascinating
to watch. The centurion's casque fell off, and pushing
him to the bandstand Pombal began to beat his behind
rhythmically upon the big drum and at the same time
to kiss him passionately. He was certainly getting his own
back. But as I watched this brief scene, the crowd closed
down upon it in a whirl of streamers and confetti and
obliterated it. We were packed body to body, cowl to
cowl, eye to eye. The music drove us round and round
the floor. Still no Justine.

> *Old Tiresias*
> *No-one half so breezy as,*
> *Half so free and easy as*
> *Old Tiresias.*

It must have been about two o'clock that the fire
started in one of the chimneys on the first floor, though

its results were not serious and it caused more delight
than alarm by its appropriateness. Servants scurried of-
ficiously everywhere; I caught a glimpse of Cervoni,
running unmasked upstairs, and then a telephone rang.
There were pleasing clouds of smoke, suggesting whiffs of
brimstone from the bottomless pit. Then within minutes
a fire-engine arrived with its siren pealing, and the hall
was full of fancy-dress figures of *pompiers* with hatchets
and buckets. They were greeted with acclamation as they
made their way up to the scene of the fireplace which
they virtually demolished with their axes. Others of the
tribe had climbed on the roof and were throwing buckets
of water down the chimney. This had the effect of filling
the first floor with a dense cloud of soot like a London
fog. The maskers crowded in shouting with delight,
dancing like dervishes. These are the sort of inadvertencies which make a party go. I found myself shouting
with them. I suppose I must have been rather drunk by
now.

In the great tapestried hall the telephone rang and
rang again, needling the uproar. I saw a servant answer
it, lay the receiver down, and quest about like a gun-dog
until presently he returned with Nessim, smiling and
unmasked, who spoke into it quickly and with an air of
impatience. Then he too put the receiver down and came
to the edge of the dance-floor, staring about him keenly.
"Is there anything wrong?" I asked, lifting my own
hood as I joined him. He smiled and shook his head.
"I can't see Justine anywhere. Clea wants to speak to her.
Can you?" Alas! I had been trying to pick up the distinguishing ring all evening without success. We waited,
watching the slow rotation of the dancers, keenly as
fishermen waiting for a bite. "No," he said and I echoed
"No." Pierre Balbz came up and joined us, lifting his
cowl, and said, "A moment ago I was dancing with her.
She went out perhaps."

Nessim returned to the telephone and I heard him say, "She's here somewhere. Yes, quite sure. No. Nothing has happened. Pierre had the last dance with her. Such a crowd. She may be in the garden. Any message? Can I ask her to ring you? Very well. No, it was simply a fire in a chimney. It's out now." He put down the receiver and turned back to us. "Anyway," he said, "we have a rendezvous in the hall unmasked at three."

And so the great ball rolled on around us, and the firemen who had done their duty now joined the throng of dancers. I caught a glimpse of a large washerwoman being carried, apparently insensible, out into the conservatory by four demons with breasts amid great applause. Pombal had evidently succumbed to his favourite brand of whisky once more. He had lost his hat but had had the forethought to wear under it an immense wig of yellow hair. It is doubtful whether anyone could have recognised him in such a rig.

Punctually at three Justine appeared in the hall from the garden and unmasked herself: Pierre and I had decided not to accept Nessim's offer of a lift home but to stay on and lend our energy to the ball which was beginning to flag now. Little parties were meeting and leaving, cars were being rallied. Nessim kissed her tenderly and said, "Where's your ring?" a question which I myself had been burning to put to her though I had not dared. She smiled that innocent and captivating smile as she said: "Toto pinched it from my finger a few minutes ago, during a dance. Where is the little brute? I want it back." We raked the floor for Toto but there was no sign of him and at last Nessim who was tired decided to give him up for lost. But he did not forget to give Justine Clea's message, and I saw my lover go obediently to the telephone and dial her friend's number. She spoke quietly and with an air of mystification for a few moments, and I heard her say: "Of course I'm all right," before bidding Clea a belated good night. Then they stepped down together into the waning moonlight arm in arm, and Pierre and I helped to tuck them into the car. Selim, impassive and hawk-featured, sat at the wheel. "Good night!" cried Justine, and her lips brushed my cheek. She whispered "Tomorrow" and the word sang on in my mind like the whistle of a bullet as we turned together back into the lighted house. Nessim's face had been full of a curious impish serenity as of someone resting after a great expenditure of energy.

Someone had heard a ghost murmuring in the conservatory. Much laughter. "No, but I assure you" squealed Athena, "we were sitting on the sofa, Jacques and I, weren't we, Jacques?" A masked figure appeared, blew a squeaker in her face and retired. Something told me it was Toto. I dragged his cowl back and up bobbed the features of Chloe Martinengo. "But I assure you," said Athena, "it moaned a word—something like . . ." she set her face in a grim scowl of concentration and after a pause sang out in a lullaby voice the expiring words *"Justice . . . Justice."* Everyone laughed heartily and several voices mimicked her: *"Justice,"* roared a domino rushing away up the stairs. *"Justice!"*

Alone once more, I found that my irresolution and despondency had turned to physical hunger, and I traversed the dance-floor cautiously in the direction of the supper-room from which I could hear the thirsty snap of champagne corks. The ball itself was still in full swing, and dancers swaying like wet washing in a high wind, the saxophones wailing like a litter of pigs. In an alcove Drusilla Banubula sat with her dress drawn up to her shapely knees, allowing a pair of contrite harlequins to bandage a sprained ankle. She had fallen down or been knocked down it would seem. An African witch-doctor wearing a monocle lay fast asleep on the couch behind her. In the second room a maudlin woman in evening dress was playing jazz on a grand piano and singing to herself while great tears coursed down her cheeks. An old fat man with hairy legs hung over her, dressed as the Venus de Milo. He was crying too. His belly trembled.

The supper-room however was comparatively quiet, and here I found Pursewarden, uncowled and apparently rather tipsy, talking to Mountolive as the latter walked with his curious gliding, limping walk round the table, loading a plate with slices of cold turkey and salad. Pursewarden was inveighing somewhat incoherently against the Cervonis for serving Spumante instead of champagne. "I should watch it," he called out to me, "there's a headache in every mouthful." But he had his glass refilled almost at once, holding it with exaggerated steadiness. Mountolive turned a speculative and gentle eye upon me as I seized a plate, and then greeted me by name with evident relief. "Ah, Darley," he said, "for a moment I thought you were one of my secretaries. They've been following me around all evening. Spoiling my fun. Errol simply refuses to violate protocol and leave before his Chief of Mission; so I had to hide in the garden until they thought I had left, poor dears. As a junior I have so often cursed my Minister for keeping me up on boring evenings that I made a vow never to make my juniors suffer in the same way if I should ever become Head of Mission." His light effortless conversation with its unaffectedness of delivery always made him seem immediately sympathetic, though I realised that his manner was a professional one, the bedside manner of the trained diplomat. He had spent so many years in putting his inferiors at their ease, and in hiding his spirit's condescension, that he had at last achieved an air of utterly professional sincerity which while seeming true to nature could not, in reality, have been less false. It had all the fidelity of great acting. But it was annoying that I should always find myself liking him so much. We circled the table slowly together, talking and filling our plates.

"What did you see in the garden, David?" said Pursewarden in a teasing tone, and the Minister's eye rested speculatively on him for a minute, as if to warn him against saying something which would be indiscreet or out of place. "I saw," said Mountolive smiling and reaching for a glass, "I saw the amorous Amaril by the lake—talking to a woman in a domino. Perhaps his dreams have come true?" Amaril's passion was well-known to everyone. "I do hope so."

"And what *else?*" said Pursewarden in a challenging, rather vulgar tone, as if he shared a private secret with him. "What else, *who* else did you see, David?" He was slightly tipsy and his voice, though friendly, had a bullying note. Mountolive flushed and looked down at his plate.

At this I left them and made my way back, equipped with loaded plate and glass. I felt a certain scorn in my heart for Pursewarden, and a rush of sympathy for Mountolive at the thought of him being put out of countenance. I wanted to be alone, to eat in silence and think about Justine. My cargo of food was nearly upset by three heavily-rouged Graces, all of them men to judge by the deep voices, who were scuffling in the hall. They were attacking each other's private parts with jocular growls, like dogs. I had the sudden idea of going up to the library which would surely be empty at this time. I wondered if the new Cavafy manuscripts would be there, and whether the collection was unlocked. Cervoni was a great collector of books.

On the first floor, a fat man with spindly legs, dressed in the costume of Red Riding Hood, was hammering on a lavatory door; servants were sucking the soot from the carpets of the rooms with Hoovers and talking in undertones. The library was on the floor above. There

was a noise in one of the bedrooms, and from the bathroom below I could hear someone being chromatically
sick. I reached the landing and pressed the airtight door
with my foot, and it sucked open to admit me. The long
room with its gleaming shelves of books was empty save
for a Mephistopheles sitting in an armchair by the fire
with a book on his knees. He took his spectacles off in
order to identify me and I saw that it was Capodistria.
He could not have chosen a more suitable costume. It
suited his great ravening beak of a nose and those small,
keen eyes, set so close together. "Come in," he cried. "I
was afraid it might be someone wanting to make love
in which case . . . *toujours la politesse,* I should have felt
bound. . . . What are you eating? The fire is lovely. I
was just looking up a quotation which has been worrying
me all evening."

I joined him and placed my loaded plate as an offering
between us to be shared. "I came to see the new Cavafy
manuscript," I said.

"All locked up, the manuscripts," he said.

"Well."

The fire crackled brightly and the room was silent
and welcoming with its lining of fine books. I took off
my cape and sat down after a preliminary quest along
the walls, during which Da Capo finished copying something out on to a piece of paper. "Curious thing about
Mountolive's father," he said absently. "This huge eight-
volume edition of Buddhist texts. Did you know?"

"I had heard," I said vaguely.

"The old man was a judge in India. When he retired
he stayed on there, is still there; foremost European
scholar on Pali texts. I must say. . . . Mountolive hasn't
seen him for nearly twenty years. He dresses like a *saddhu*
he says. You English are eccentrics through and through.
Why shouldn't the old man work on his texts in Oxford,
eh?"

"Climate, perhaps?"

"Perhaps." He agreed. "There. That's what I was hunting for—I knew it was somewhere in the fourth volume." He banged his book shut.

"What is it?"

He held his paper out to the fire and read slowly with an air of puzzled pleasure the quotation he had copied out: "The fruit of the tree of good and evil is itself but flesh; yes, and the apple itself is but an apple of the dust."

"That's not Buddhist, surely," I said.

"No, it's Mountolive père himself, from the introduction."

"I think that. . . ."

But now there came a confused screaming from somewhere near at hand, and Capodistria sighed. "I don't know why the devil I take part in this damned carnival year after year," he said peevishly, draining his whisky. "It is an unlucky time astrologically. For me, I mean. And every year there are ugly accidents. It makes one uneasy. Two years ago Arnelh was found hanging in the musicians' gallery at the Fontanas' house. Funny eh? Damned inconsiderate if he did it himself. And then Martin Fery fought that duel with Jacomo Forte. . . . It brings out the devil. That is why I am dressed as the devil. I hang about waiting for people to come and sell me their souls. Aha!" He sniffed and rubbed his hands with a parchment sound and gave his little dry cachinnation. And then, standing up and finishing the last slice of turkey, "God, have you seen the time? I must be going home. Beelzebub's bedtime."

"So should I," I said, disappointed that I could not get a look at the handwriting of the old poet. "So should I."

"Can I lift you?" he said, as the sucking door expelled us once more into the trampled musical air of the landing.

"Useless to expect to say good-bye to our hosts. Cervoni is probably in bed by now."

We went down slowly chatting into the great hall where the music rolled on in an unbroken stream of syncopated sound. Da Capo had adjusted his mask now and looked like some weird bird-like demon. We stood for a moment watching the dancers, and then yawning he said: 'Well, this is where to quote Cavafy the God abandons Antony. Good night. I can't stay awake any longer, though I am afraid the evening will be full of surprises yet. It always is."

Nor was he to be proved wrong. I hovered for a while, watching the dance, and then walked down the stairs into the dark coolness of the night. There were a few limousines and sleepy servants waiting by the gates, but the streets had begun to empty and my own footfalls sounded harsh and exotic as they smacked up from the pavements. At the corner of Fuad there were a couple of European whores leaning dispiritedly against a wall and smoking. They called once hoarsely after me. They wore magnolia blossoms in their hair.

Yawning, I passed the Étoile to see if perhaps Melissa was still working, but the place was empty except for a drunk family which had refused to go home despite the fact that Zoltan had stacked up the chairs and tables around them on the dance-floor. "She went off early," the little man explained. "Band gone. Girls gone. Everyone gone. Only these *canaille* from Assuan. His brother is a policeman; we dare not close." A fat man began to belly-dance with sugary movements of the hips and pelvis and the company began to clap to mark the time. I left and walked past Melissa's shabby lodgings in the vague hope that she might still be awake. I felt I wanted to talk to someone; no, I wanted to borrow a cigarette. That was all. Afterwards would come the desire to sleep with her, to hold that slender cherished body in my arms, inhaling its sour flavours of alcohol and tobacco-smoke, thinking all the time of Justine. But her window was dark; either she was asleep or was not yet home. Zoltan had said that she left with a party of business-men disguised as admirals. *"Des petits commerçants quelconques,"* he had added contemptuously, and then turned at once apologetic.

No, it was to be an empty night, with the frail subfusc moonlight glancing along the waves of the outer harbour, the sea licking and relicking the piers, the coastline thinning away in whiteness, glittering away into the greyness like mica. I stood for a while on the Corniche snapping a paper streamer in my fingers, bit by bit, each fragment breaking off with a hard dry finality, like a human relationship. Then I turned sleepily home, repeating in my mind the words of Da Capo: "The evening will be full of surprises."

Indeed, they were already beginning in the house which I had just left, though of course I was not to learn about them until the following day. And yet, surprises though they were, their reception was perfectly in keeping with the city—a city of resignation so deep as almost to be Moslem. For nobody in Alexandria can ever be shocked deeply; among us tragedy exists only to flavour conversation. Death and life are both simply the hazards of a chance which cannot be averted, and merit only smiles and conversations made more animated by the consciousness of their intrusion. No sooner do you tell an Alexandrian a piece of bad news than the words come out of his mouth: "I knew. Something like this was bound to happen. It always does." This, then, is what happened.

In the conservatory of the Cervoni house there were several old-fashioned *chaises-longues* on which a mountain of overcoats and evening-wraps had been piled; as the dancers began to go home there came the usual shedding

of dominoes and the hunt for furs and capes. I think it
was Pierre who must have made the discovery while
hunting in this great tumulus of coats for the velvet
smoking-jacket which he had shed earlier in the evening.
At any rate, I myself had already left and started to
walk home by this time.

Toto de Brunel was discovered, still warm in his
velvet domino, with his paws raised like two neat little
cutlets, in the attitude of a dog which had rolled over
to have its belly scratched. He was buried deep in the
drift of coats. One hand had half-tried to move towards
the fatal temple but the impulse had been cut off at
source before the action was complete, and it had stayed
there raised a little higher than the other, as if wielding
an invisible baton. The hatpin from Pombal's picture
hat had been driven sideways into his head with terrific
force, pinning him like a moth into his velvet headpiece.
Athena had been making love to Jacques while she was
literally lying upon his body—a fact which would under
normal circumstances have delighted him thoroughly.
But he was dead, *le pauvre Toto*, and what is more he
was still wearing the ring of my lover. *"Justice!"*

"Of course, something like this happens every year."

"Of course." I was still dazed.

"But Toto—that is rather unexpected, really."

Balthazar rang me up about eleven o'clock the next
morning to tell me the whole story. In my stupefied and
sleepy condition it sounded not merely improbable, but
utterly incomprehensible. "There will be the *procès-
verbal*—that's why I'm ringing. Nimrod is making it as
easy as he can. One dinner-party witness only—Justine
thought perhaps you if you don't mind? Good. Of course.
No, I was got out of bed at a quarter to four by the
Cervonis. They were in rather a state about it. I went
along to . . . do the needful. I'm afraid they can't quite
sort it all out as yet. The pin belonged to the hat—yes,

your friend Pombal . . . diplomatic immunity, naturally. Nevertheless, he was very drunk too. . . . Of course it is inconceivable that he did it, but you know what the Police are like. Is he up yet?" I had not dared to try and wake him at such an early hour, and I said so. "Well anyway," said Balthazar, "his death has fluttered a lot of dovecotes, not least at the French Legation."

"But he was wearing Justine's ring," I said thickly, and all the premonitions of the last few months gathered in force at my elbow, crowding in upon me. I felt quite ill and feverish and had to lean for a moment against the wall by the telephone. Balthazar's measured tone and cheerful voice sounded to me like an obscenity. There was a long silence. "Yes, I know about the ring," he said, and added with a quiet chuckle, "but that too is hard to think of as a possible reason. Toto was also the lover of the jealous Amar, you know. Any number of reasons. . . ."

"Balthazar," I said, and my voice broke.

"I'll ring you if there's anything else. The *procès* is at seven down in Nimrod's office. See you there, eh?"

"Very well."

I put down the phone and burst like a bomb into Pombal's bedroom. The curtains were still drawn and the bed was in a terrible mess suggesting a recent occupancy, but there was no other sign of him. His boots and various items from the washerwoman's fancy dress lay about the room in various places, enabling me to discern that he had in fact got home the night before. Actually his wig lay on the landing outside the front door: I know this because much later, towards midday, I heard his heavy step climbing the stairs and he entered the flat holding it in his hand.

"I am quite finished," he said briefly, at once. "Finished, *mon ami*." He looked more plethoric than ever as he made for his gout chair as if anticipating a sudden attack of his special and private malady. "Finished," he repeated, sinking into it with a sigh and distending. I was confused and bewildered, standing there in my pyjamas. Pombal sighed heavily.

"My Chancery has discovered everything," he said grimly setting his jaw. "I first behaved very badly . . . yes . . . the Consul-General is having a nervous breakdown today. . . ." And then all of a sudden real tears of mixed rage, confusion and hysteria sprang up in his eyes. "Do you know what?" he sneezed. "The *Deuxième* think I went specially to the ball to stick a pin in de Brunel, the best and most trusted agent we have ever had here!"

He burst out sobbing like a donkey now, and in some fantastic way his tears kept turning into laughter; he mopped his streaming eyes and panted as he sobbed and laughed at one and the same time. Then, still blown up by these overmastering paroxysms he rolled out of his chair like a hedgehog on to the carpet and lay there for a while still shaking; and then began to roll slowly to the wainscot where, shaken still with tears and laughter, he began to bang his head rhythmically against the wall, shouting at every bang the pregnant and magnificent word—the *summa* of all despair: *"Merde. Merde. Merde. Merde. Merde."*

"Pombal," I said weakly, "for God's sake!"

"Go away," he cried from the floor, "I shall never stop unless you go away. Please go away." And so taking pity on him I left the room and ran myself a cold bath in which I lay until I heard him helping himself to bread and butter from the larder. He came to the bathroom door and tapped. "Are you there?" he said. "Yes." "Then forget every word I said," he shouted through the panel. "Please, eh?"

"I have forgotten already."

"Good. Thank you, *mon ami*."

And I heard his heavy footfalls retreating in the direction of his room. We lay in bed until lunch-time that

day, both of us, silent. At one-thirty, Hamid arrived and
set out a lunch which neither of us had the appetite to
eat. In the middle of it, the telephone rang and I went
to answer it. It was Justine. She must have assumed that
I had heard about Toto de Brunel for she made no
direct mention of the business. "I want," she said, "my
dreadful ring back. Balthazar has reclaimed it from the
Police. The one Toto took, yes. But apparently someone
has to identify and sign for it. At the *procès*. A thousand
thanks for offering to go. As you can imagine, Nessim
and I . . . it's a question of witnessing only. And then
perhaps my darling we could meet and you could give
it back to me. Nessim has to fly to Cairo this afternoon
on business. Shall we say in the garden of the Aurore
at nine? That will give you time. I'll wait in the car. So
much want to speak to you. Yes. I must go now. Thank
you again. Thank you."

We sat once more to our meal, fellow bondsmen, heavy
with a sense of guilt and exhaustion. Hamid waited
upon us with solicitude and in complete silence. Did he
know what was preoccupying us both? It was impossible
to read anything on those gentle pock-marked features,
in that squinting single eye.

o   o   o   o   o

11.

IT was already dark when I dismissed my taxi at Mohammed Ali square and set out to walk to the sub-de-
partment of the Prefecture where Nimrod's office was. I
was still dazed by the turn events had taken, and

weighed down by the dispiriting possibilities they had raised in my mind—the warnings and threatenings of the last few months during which I had lived only for one person—Justine. I burned with impatience to see her again.

The shops were already lit up and the money-changers' counters were crowded with French sailors turning their francs into food and wine, silks, women, boys or opium—every kind of understandable forgetfulness. Nimrod's office was at the back of a grey old-fashioned building set back at an angle to the road. It seemed deserted now, full of empty corridors and open offices. All the clerks had gone off duty at six. My lagging footfalls echoed past the empty porter's lodge and the open doors. It seemed strange to walk about so freely in a Police building unchallenged. At the end of the third long corridor I came to Nimrod's own door and knocked. There were voices inside. His office was a large, indeed rather grandiose room befitting his rank, whose windows gave out on to a bare courtyard where some chickens clucked and picked all day in the dried mud floor. A single tattered palm stood in the middle offering some summer shade.

There was no sign from within the room so I opened the door and stepped in—only to stop short: for the brilliant light and darkness suggested that a cinema-show was taking place. But it was only the huge epidia-scope which threw upon the farther wall the blazing and magnified images of the photographs which Nimrod himself was feeding into it one by one from an envelope. Dazzled, I stepped forward and identified Balthazar and Keats in that phosphorescent penumbra around the machine, their profiles magnetically lighted by the powerful bulb.

"Good," said Nimrod, half-turning, and, "sit you down," as he abstractedly pushed out a chair for me. Keats smiled at me, full of a mysterious self-satisfaction

and excitement. The photographs which they were studying with such care were his own flashlight pictures of the
Cervoni ball. At such magnification they looked like
grotesque frescoes materialising and vanishing again
upon the white wall. "See if you can help on identification," said Nimrod, and I sat down and obediently
turned my face to the blaze in which sprawled the silhouettes of a dozen demented monks dancing together.
"Not that one," said Keats. The white light of the
magnesium had set fire to the outlines of the robed
figures.

Blown up to such enormous size the pictures suggested
a new art-form, more macabre than anything a Goya
could imagine. This was a new iconography—painted in
smoke and lightning flashes. Nimrod changed them slowly, dwelling upon each one. "No comment?" he would
ask before passing another bloated facsimile of real life
before our eyes. "No comment?"

For identification purposes they were quite useless.
There were eight in all—each a fearful simulacrum of a
death-feast celebrated by satyr-monks in some medieval
crypt, each imagined by de Sade! "There's the one with
the ring," said Balthazar as the fifth picture came up and
hovered before us on the wall. A group of hooded figures,
frenziedly swaying with linked arms, wallowed before us,
expressionless as cuttlefish, or those other grotesque
monsters one sometimes sees lurking in the glooms of
aquaria. Their eyes were slits devoid of meaning, their
gaiety a travesty of everything human. So this is how
Inquisitors behave when they are off duty! Keats sighed
in despair. One of the figures had a hand upon another's
black-robed arm. The hand bore a just recognisable dash
of white to indicate Justine's unlucky ring. Nimrod described it all carefully to himself with the air of a man
reading a gauge. "Five maskers . . . somewhere near the
buffet, you can see the corner. . . . But the hand. Is it de

Brunel's? What do you think?" I stared at it. "I think it must be," I said. "Justine wears the ring on another finger."

Nimrod said "Hah" triumphantly and added, "A good point there." Yes, but who were the other figures, snatched thus fortuitously out of nothingness by the flash-bulb? We stared at them and they stared expressionlessly back at us through their velvet slits like snipers.

"No good," said Balthazar at last with a sigh, and Nimrod switched off the humming machine. After an instant's darkness the ordinary electric light came up in the room. His desk was stacked up with typed papers for signature—the *procès-verbal* I had no doubt. On a square of grey silk lay several objects with a direct relationship to our brimming thoughts—the great hatpin with its ugly blue stone head, and the eburnine ring of my lover which I could not see even now without a pang.

"Sign up," said Nimrod, indicating the paper, "when you've read your copy, will you?" He coughed behind his hand and added in a lower tone, "And you can take the ring."

Balthazar handed it to me. It felt cold, and it was faintly dusted with fingerprint powder. I cleaned it on my tie and put it in my fob-pocket. "Thank you," I said, and took a seat at the desk to read through the Police formula, while the others lit cigarettes and talked in low voices. Beside the typewritten papers lay another, written in the nervous shallow hand of General Cervoni. It was the invitation list to the carnival ball, still echoing with the majestic poetry of the names which had come to mean so much to me, the names of the Alexandrians. Listen:

Pia dei Tolomei, Benedict Dangeau, Dante Borromeo, Colonel Neguib, Toto de Brunel, Wilmot Pierrefeu, Mehmet Adm, Pozzo di Borgo, Ahmed Hassan Pacha, Delphine de Francueil, Djamboulat Bey, Athena Trasha,

Haddad Fahmy Amin, Gaston Phipps, Pierre Balbz, Jacques de Guéry, Count Banubula, Onouphrios Papas, Dmitri Randidi, Paul Capodistria, Claude Amaril, Nessim Hosnani, Tony Umbada, Baldassaro Trivizani, Gilda Ambron. . . .

I murmured the names as I read through the list, mentally adding the word "murderer" after each, simply to see whether it sounded appropriate. Only when I reached the name of Nessim did I pause and raise my eyes to the dark wall—to throw his mental image there and study it as we had studied the pictures. I still saw the expression on his face as I had helped to tuck him into the great car—an expression of curious impish serenity, as of someone resting after a great expenditure of energy.

o   o   o   o   o

12.

DESPITE the season the seafront of the city was gay with light—the long sloping lines of the Grande Corniche curving away to a low horizon; a thousand lighted panels of glass in which, like glorious tropical fish, the inhabitants of the European city sat at glittering tables stocked with glasses of mastic, aniseed or brandy. Watching them (I had eaten little lunch) my hunger overcame me, and as there was some time in hand before my meeting with Justine, I turned into the glittering doors of the Diamond Sutra and ordered a ham sandwich and a glass of whisky. Once again, as always when the drama of external events altered the emotional pattern of things, I began to see the city through new eyes—to examine the shapes and contours made by human beings with the detachment of an entomologist studying a hitherto unknown species of insect. Here it was, the race, each member of it absorbed in the solution of individual preoccupations, loves, hates and fears. A woman counting money on to a glass table, an old man feeding a dog, an Arab in a red flowerpot drawing a curtain.

Aromatic smoke poured from the small sailor taverns along the seafront where the iron spits loaded with a freight of entrails and spices turned monotonously back and forth, or bellied from under the lids of shining copper cauldrons, giving off hot gusts of squid, cuttlefish and pigeon. Here one drank from the blue cans and ate with one's fingers as they do in the Cyclades even today.

I picked up a decrepit horse-cab and jogged along by the sighing sea towards the Aurore, drinking in the lighted darkness with regrets and fears so fugitive as to be beyond analysis; but underneath (like a toad under a cool stone, the surface airs of night) I still felt the stirrings of horror at the thought that Justine herself might be endangered by the love which "we bore one another." I turned the thought this way and that in my mind, like a prisoner pressing with all his weight upon doors which denied him an exit from an intolerable bondage, trying to devise an issue from a situation which, it seemed, might as well end in her death as in mine.

The great car was waiting, drawn up off the road in the darkness under the pepper-trees. She opened the door for me silently and I got in, spellbound by my fears.

"Well," she said at last, and giving a little groan which expressed everything, sank into my arms and pressed her warm mouth on mine. "Did you go? Is it over?"

"Yes."

She let in the clutch and the driving wheels spurned the gravel as the car moved out into the pearly nightfall and began to follow the coast road to the outer desert. I studied her harsh Semitic profile in the furry light flung back by the headlights from the common objects of the roadside. It belonged so much to the city which I now saw as a series of symbols stretching away from us on either side—minarets, pigeons, statues, ships, coins, camels and palms; it lived in a heraldic relation to the exhausted landscapes which enclosed it—the loops of the great lake: as proper to the scene as the Sphinx was to the desert.

"My ring," she said. "You brought it?"

"Yes," I polished it once more on my tie and slipped it back once more on to its appropriate finger. Involuntarily I said now: "Justine, what is to become of us?"

She gave me a wild frowning look like a Bedouin woman, and then smiled that warm smile. "Why?"

"Surely you see? We shall have to stop this altogether. I can't bear to think you might be in danger. . . . Or else I should go straight to Nessim and confront him with. . . ." With what? I did not know.

"No," she said softly, "no. You could not do it. You are an Anglo-Saxon . . . you couldn't step outside the law like that, could you? You are not one of us. Besides, you could tell Nessim nothing he does not guess if not actually know. . . . Darling," she laid her warm hand upon mine, "simply wait . . . simply love, above all . . . and we shall see."

It is astonishing now for me to realise, as I record this scene, that she was carrying within her (invisible as the already conceived foetus of a child) Pursewarden's death: that her kisses were, for all I know, falling upon the graven image of my friend—the death-mask of the writer who himself did not love her, indeed regarded her with derision. But such a demon is love that I would not be surprised if in a queer sort of way his death actually enriched our own love-making, filling it with the deceits on which the minds of women feed—the compost of secret pleasures and treacheries which are an inseparable part of every human relation.

Yet what have I to complain of? Even this half-love filled my heart to overflowing. It is she, if anyone, who had cause for complaint. It is very hard to understand these things. Was she already planning her flight from Alexandria then? "The power of woman is such," writes Pursewarden, "that a single kiss can paraphrase the reality of man's life and turn it . . ." but why go on? I was happy sitting beside her, feeling the warmth of her hand as it lay in mine.

The blue night was hoary with stars and the attentive desert stretched away on either side with its grotesque amphitheatres—like the empty rooms in some great cloud-mansion. The moon was late and wan tonight, the air still, the dunes wind-carved. "What are you thinking?" said my lover.

What was I thinking? Of a passage in Proclus which says that Orpheus ruled over the silver race, meaning those who led a "silver" life; on Balthazar's mantelpiece presumably among the pipe-cleaners and the Indian wood-carving of monkeys which neither saw, spoke nor heard evil, under a magic pentacle from Pythagoras. What was I thinking? The foetus in its waxen wallet, the locust squatting in the horn of the wheat, an Arab quoting a proverb which reverberated in the mind. "The memory of man is as old as misfortune." The quails from the burst cage spread upon the ground softly like honey, having no idea of escape. In the Scent Bazaar the flavour of Persian lilac.

"Fourteen thousand years ago," I said aloud, "Vega in Lyra was the Pole Star. Look at her where she burns."

The beloved head turned with its frowning deep-set eyes and once more I see the long boats drawing in to the Pharos, the tides running, the minarets a-glitter with dew; noise of the blind Hodja crying in the voice of a mole assaulted by sunlight; a shuffle-pad of a camel-train clumping to a festival carrying dark lanterns. An Arab woman makes my bed, beating the pillows till they fluff out like white of egg under a whisk; a passage in Pursewarden's book which reads: "They looked at each other, aware that there was neither youth nor strength enough between them to prevent their separation." When Melissa was pregnant by Nessim Amaril could not perform the abortion Nessim so much desired because of her illness and her weak heart. "She may die anyway," he said, and Nessim nodded curtly and took up his overcoat. But she did not die then, she bore the child. . . .

Justine is quoting something in Greek which I do not recognise:

Sand, dog-roses and white rocks
Of Alexandria, the mariner's sea-marks,
Some sprawling dunes falling and pouring
Sand into water, water into sand,
Never into the wine of exile
Which stains the air it is poured through;
Or a voice which stains the mind,
Singing in Arabic: "A ship without a sail
Is a woman without breasts." Only that. Only that.

We walked hand in hand across the soft sand-dunes, laboriously as insects, until we reached Taposiris with its tumble of shattered columns and capitals among the ancient weather-eroded sea-marks. ("Reliques of sensation," says Coleridge, "may exist for an indefinite time in a latent state in the very same order in which they were impressed.") Yes, but the order of the imagination is not that of memory. A faint wind blew off the sea from the Grecian archipelago. The sea was smooth as a human cheek. Only at the edges it stirred and sighed. Those warm kisses remain there, amputated from before and after, existing in their own right like the frail transparencies of ferns or roses pressed between the covers of old books—unique and unfading as the memories of the city they exemplified and evoked: a plume of music from a forgotten carnival-guitar echoing on in the dark streets of Alexandria for as long as silence lasts. . . .

I see all of us not as men and women any longer, identities swollen with their acts of forgetfulness, follies, and deceits—but as beings unconsciously made part of place, buried to the waist among the ruins of a single city, steeped in its values; like those creatures of whom Empedocles wrote, "Solitary limbs wandered, seeking for union with one another," or in another place, "So it is that sweet lays hold of sweet, bitter rushes to bitter, acid comes to acid, warm couples with warm." All members of

a city whose actions lay just outside the scope of the plotting or conniving spirit: Alexandrians.

Justine, lying back against a fallen column at Taposiris,
dark head upon the darkness of the sighing water, one
curl lifted by the sea-winds, saying: "In the whole of
English only one phrase means something to me, the
words: 'Time Immemorial.' "

Seen across the transforming screens of memory, how
remote that forgotten evening seems. There was so much
as yet left for us all to live through until we reached the
occasion of the great duckshoot which so abruptly, con-
cisely, precipitated the final change—and the disappearance of Justine herself. But all this belongs to another
Alexandria—one which I created in my mind and which
the great Interlinear of Balthazar has, if not destroyed,
changed out of all recognition.

"To intercalate realities," writes Balthazar, "is the
only way to be faithful to Time, for at every moment in
Time the possibilities are endless in their multiplicity.
Life consists in the act of choice. The perpetual reserva-
tion of judgment and the perpetual choosing."

From the vantage-point of this island I can see it all
in its doubleness, in the intercalation of fact and fancy,
with new eyes; and re-reading, re-working reality in the
light of all I now know, I am surprised to find that my
feelings themselves have changed, have grown, have
deepened even. Perhaps then the destruction of my private Alexandria was necessary ("the artifact of a true
work of art never shows a plane surface") ; perhaps
buried in all this there lies the germ and substance of
a truth—time's usufruct—which, if I can accommodate it,
will carry me a little further in what is really a search
for my proper self. We shall see.

o   o   o   o   o

13.

"CLEA and her old father, whom she worships. White-haired, erect, with a sort of haunted pity in his eyes for the young unmarried goddess he has fathered. Once a year, however, on New Year's eve, they dance at the Cecil, stately, urbanely. He waltzes like a clockwork man." Somewhere I once wrote down these words. They bring to mind another scene, another sequence of events.

The old scholar comes to sit at my table. He has a particular weakness for me, I do not know why, but he always talks to me with humorous modesty as we sit and watch his beautiful daughter move around the room in the arms of an admirer, so graceful and so composed. "There is so much of the schoolgirl still about her—or the artist. Tonight her cape had some wine on it so she put a mackintosh over her ball gown and ate the toffees which she found in the pockets. I don't know what her mother would say if she were alive." We drank quietly and watched the coloured lights flickering among the dancers. He said, "I feel like an old procurer. Always looking out for someone to marry her. . . . Her happiness seems so important, somehow . . . I am going the right way about to spoil it I know, by meddling . . . yet I can't leave it alone . . . I've scraped a dowry together over the years. . . . The money burns my pocket. . . . When I see a nice Englishman like you my instinct is to say: 'For God's sake take her and look after her.' . . . It has been a bitter pleasure bringing her up without a mother. Eh?

No fool like an old fool." And he walks stiffly away to the bar, smiling.

Presently that evening Clea herself came and sat beside me in the alcove, fanning herself and smiling. "Quarter of an hour to midnight. Poor Cinderella. I must get my father home before the clock strikes or he'll lose his beauty-sleep!"

We spoke then of Amar whose trial for the murder of de Brunel had ended that afternoon with his acquittal due to lack of direct evidence.

"I know," said Clea softly. "And I'm glad. It has saved me from a *crise de conscience*. I would not have known what to do if he had been convicted. You see, I know he didn't do it. Why? Because, my dear, I know who did and why. . . ." She narrowed those splendid eyes and went on. "A story of Alexandria—shall I tell you? But only if you keep it a secret. Would you promise me? Bury it with the old year—all our misfortunes and follies. You must have had a surfeit of them by now, must you not? All right. Listen. On the night of the carnival I lay in bed thinking about a picture—the big one of Justine. It was all wrong and I didn't know where. But I suspected the hands—those dark and shapely hands. I had got their position quite faithfully, but, well, something in the composition didn't go; it had started to trouble me at this time—months after the thing was finished. I can't think why. Suddenly I said to myself, 'Those hands want thinking about,' and I had the thing lugged back to my room from the studio where I stood it against a wall. Well, to no effect, really; I'd spent the whole evening smoking over it, and sketching the hands in different positions from memory. Somehow I thought it might be that beastly Byzantine ring which she wears. Anyway, all my thinking was of no avail so about midnight I turned in, and lay smoking in bed with my cat asleep on my feet.

"From time to time a small group of people passed outside in the street, singing or laughing, but gradually the town was draining itself of life, for it was getting late.

"Suddenly in the middle of the silence I heard feet running at full speed. I have never heard anyone run so fast, so lightly. Only danger or terror or distress could make someone put on such a mad burst of speed, I thought, as I listened. Down Rue Fuad came the foot-steps at the same breakneck pace and turned the corner into St. Saba, getting louder all the time. They crossed over, paused, and then crossed back to my side of the street. Then came a wild pealing at my bell.

"I sat up in some surprise and switched on the light to look at the clock. Who could it be at such a time? While I was still sitting there irresolutely, it came again: a long double peal. Well! The electric switch on the front door is shut off at midnight so there was no help for it but to go down and see who it was. I put on a dress-ing-gown and slipping my little pistol into the pocket I went down to see. There was a shadow on the glass of the front door which was too thick to challenge anyone through, so I had to open it. I stood back a bit. 'Who's there?'

"There was a man standing there, hanging in the corner of the door like a bat. He was breathing heavily for I saw his breast rising and falling, but he made no sound. He wore a domino, but the headpiece was turned back so that I could see his face in the light of the street-lamp. I was of course rather frightened for a moment. He looked as if he were about to faint. It took me about ten seconds before I could put a name to the ugly face with its cruel great hare-lip. Then relief flooded me and my feet got pins and needles. Do you know who it was? His hair was matted with sweat and in that queer light his eyes looked enormous—blue and childish. I realized that it was that strange brother of Nessim's—the one nobody ever sees. Narouz Hosnani. Even this was rather a feat of memory: I only remembered him vaguely from the time when Nessim took me riding on the Hosnani lands. You can imagine my concern to see him like this, unexpectedly, in the middle of the night.

"I did not know what to say, and he for his part was trying to articulate something, but the words would not come. It seemed he had two sentences jammed together in the front of his mind, like cartridges in the muzzle of a gun, and neither would give place to the other. He leaned inwards upon me with a ghastly incoherence, his hands hanging down almost below his knees which gave him an ape-like silhouette, and croaked something at me. You mustn't laugh. It was horrifying. Then he drew a great breath and forced his muscles to obey him and said in a small marionette's voice: 'I have come to tell you that I love you because I have killed Justine.' For a moment I almost suspected a joke. 'What?' I stammered. He repeated in an even smaller voice, a whisper, but mechanically as a child repeating a lesson: 'I have come to tell you that I love you because I have killed Justine.' Then in a deep voice he added, 'O Clea, if you but knew the agony of it.' And he gave a sob and fell on his knees in the hall, holding the edge of my dressing-gown, his head bowed while the tears trickled down his nose.

"I didn't know what to do. I was at once horrified and disgusted, and yet I couldn't help feeling sorry. From time to time he gave a small harsh cry—the noise of a she-camel crying, or of some dreadful mechanical toy, perhaps. It was unlike anything I have seen or heard before or since. His trembling was communicated to me through the fringe of my gown which he held in two fingers.

"'Get up,' I said at last, and raising his head he croaked: 'I swear I did not mean to do it. It happened before I could think. She put her hand upon me, Clea, she made advances to me. Horrible. Nessim's own wife.'

"I did not know what to make of all this. Had he

really harmed Justine? 'You just come upstairs,' I said, keeping tight hold of my little pistol, for his expression was pretty frightening. 'Get up now.' He got up at once, quite obediently, and followed me back up the stairs, but leaning heavily against the wall and whispering something incoherently to himself, Justine's name, I think, though it sounded more like 'Justice.'

" 'Come in while I telephone,' I said, and he followed me slowly, half-blinded by the light. He stood by the door for a moment, accustoming himself to it, and then he saw the portrait. He exclaimed with great force: 'This Jewish fox has eaten my life,' and struck his fists against his thighs several times. Then he put his hands over his face and breathed deeply. We waited like this facing one another, while I thought what there was to be done. They had all gone to the Cervoni ball, I knew. I would telephone them to find out if there was any truth in this story.

"Meanwhile Narouz opened his fingers and peeped at me. He said: 'I only came to tell you I loved you before giving myself up to my brother.' Then he spread his hands in a hopeless gesture. 'That is all.'

"How disgusting, how unfair love is! Here I had been loved for goodness knows how long by a creature—I cannot say a fellow-creature—of whose very existence I had been unaware. Every breath I drew was unconsciously a form of his suffering, without my ever having been aware of it. How had this disaster come about? You will have to make room in your thoughts for this variety of the animal. I was furious, disgusted and wounded in one and the same moment. I felt almost as if I owed him an apology; and yet I also felt insulted by the intrusiveness of a love which I had never asked him to owe me.

"Narouz looked now as if he were in a high fever. His teeth chattered in his head and he was shaken by spasms of violent shivering. I gave him a glass of cognac which he drained at one gulp, and then another even larger one. Drinking it he sank slowly down to the carpet and doubled his legs under him like an Arab. 'It is better at last,' he whispered, and looking sadly round him added: 'So this is where you live. I have wanted to see it for years. I have been imagining it all.' Then he frowned and coughed and combed his hair back with his fingers.

"I rang the Cervoni house and almost at once got hold of Nessim. I questioned him tactfully, without giving anything away. But there seemed nothing wrong, as far as could be judged, though he could not at that moment locate Justine. She was somewhere on the dance-floor. Narouz listened to all this with staring surprised eyes, incredulous. 'She is due to meet them in the hall in ten minutes' time. Finish your drink and wait until she rings up. Then you will know that there has been some mistake.' He closed his eyes and seemed to pray.

"I sat down opposite him on the sofa, not knowing quite what to say. 'What exactly happened?' I asked him. All of a sudden his eyes narrowed and grew small, suspicious-looking. Then he sighed and hung his head, tracing the design of the carpet with his finger. 'It is not for you to hear,' he whispered, his lips trembling.

"We waited like this, and all of a sudden, to my intense embarrassment and disgust, he began to talk of his love for me, but in the tone of a man talking to himself. He seemed almost oblivious of me, never once looking up into my face. And I felt all the apologetic horror that comes over me when I am admired or desired and cannot reciprocate the feeling. I was somehow ashamed too, looking at that brutal tear-stained face, simply because I could not feel the slightest stirring of sympathy within my heart. He sat there on the carpet like some great brown toad, talking; like some story-book troglodyte. What the devil was I to do? 'When have you seen me?' I asked him. He had only seen me three times in his life, though frequently at night he passed through the street to see if my light was on. I swore under my breath. It was so unfair. I had done nothing to merit this grotesque passion.

"Then at last came a reprieve. The telephone rang, and he trembled all over like a hound as he heard the unmistakable hoarse tones of the woman he thought he had killed. There was nothing wrong that she knew of, and she was on her way home with Nessim. Everything was as it should be at the Cervoni house and the ball was still going on at full blast. As I said good night I felt Narouz clasp my slippers and begin kissing them with gratitude. 'Thank you. Thank you,' he repeated over and over again.

" 'Come on. Get up. It's time to go home.' I was deathly tired by now. I advised him to go straight back home and to confide his story to nobody. 'Perhaps you have imagined the whole thing,' I said, and he gave me a tired but brilliant smile.

"He walked slowly and heavily downstairs before me, still shaken by his experience, it was clear, but the hysteria had left him. I opened the front door, and he tried once more to express his incoherent gratitude and affection. He seized my hands and kissed them repeatedly with great wet hairy kisses. Ugh! I can feel them now. And then, before turning into the night, he said in a low voice, smiling: 'Clea, this is the happiest day of my life, to have seen and touched you and to have seen your little room.' "

Clea sipped her drink, nodding into the middle distance for a moment with a sad smile on her face. Then she looked at her own brown hands and gave a little shudder. "Ugh! The kisses," she said under her breath and with an involuntary movement began to rub her hands, palms upward, upon the red plush arm of the

chair, as if to obliterate the kisses once and for all, to
expunge the memory of them.

But now the band had begun to play a Paul Jones
(perhaps the very dance in which Arnauti first met
Justine?) and the warm lighted gallery of faces began to
fan out once more from the centre of the darkness, the
brilliance of flesh and cloth and jewels in the huge gaunt
ballroom where the palms splintered themselves in the
shivering mirrors: leaking through the windows to where
the moonlight waited patiently among the deserted
public gardens and highways, troubling the uneasy water
of the outer harbour with its glittering heartless gestures.
"Come," said Clea, "why do you never play a part in
these things? Why do you prefer to sit apart and study
us all?"

But I was thinking as I watched the circle of lovely
faces move forward and reverse among the glitter of
jewellery and the rustle of silks, of the Alexandrians to
whom these great varieties of experience meant only one
more addition to the sum of an infinite knowledge hus-
banded by their world-weariness. Round and round the
floor we went, the women unconsciously following the
motion of the stars, of the earth as it curved into space;
and then suddenly like a declaration of war, like an ex-
pulsion from the womb, silence came, and a voice crying:
"Take your partners please." And the lights throbbed
down the spectrum to purple and a waltz began. For
a brief moment at the far end of the darkness I caught a
glimpse of Nessim and Justine dancing together, smiling
into each other's eyes. The shapely hand on his shoulder
still wore the great ring taken from the tomb of a
Byzantine youth. Life is short, art long.

Clea's father was dancing with her, stiffly, happily, like
a clockwork mouse; and he was kissing the gifted hand
upon which the unwanted kisses of Narouz had fallen

on that forgotten evening. A daughter is closer than a wife.

"At first," writes Pursewarden, "we seek to supplement the emptiness of our individuality through love, and for a brief moment enjoy the illusion of completeness. But it is only an illusion. For this strange creature, which we thought would join us to the body of the world, succeeds at last in separating us most thoroughly from it. Love joins and then divides. How else would we be growing?"

How else indeed? But relieved to find myself once more partnerless I have already groped my way back to my dark corner where the empty chairs of the revellers stand like barren ears of corn.

o   o   o   o   o

14.

In the early summer I received a letter from Clea with which this brief memorial to Alexandria may well be brought to a close. It was unexpected.

"Tashkent Syria

"Your letter, so unexpected after a silence which I feared might endure all through life, followed me out of Persia to this small house perched high on a hillside among the cedars and pines. I have taken it for six months in order to try my hand and brush on these odd mountains—rocks bursting with fresh water and Mediterranean flowers. Turtle doves by day and nightingales by night. What a relief after the dust. How long is it—two years or more perhaps? Ah, my dear friend, I trembled a little as I slit open the envelope. Why? I was afraid that what you might have to say would drag me back by the hair to old places and scenes long since abandoned; the old stations and sites of the personality which belonged to the Alexandrian Clea you knew—not to me any longer, or at any rate, not wholly. I've changed. A new woman, certainly a new painter is emerging, still a bit tender and shy like the horns of a snail—but new. A whole new world of experience stands between us. . . . How could you know all this? You would perhaps be writing to Clea, the old Clea; what would I find to say to you in reply? I put off reading your letter until tonight. It touched me and reply I must: so here it is— my own letter written at odd times, between painting sessions, or at night when I light the stove and make my dinner. Today is a good day to begin it for it is raining—and the whole mountain side under the hush of the rain and the noise of swollen springs. The trees are alive with giant snails.

"So Balthazar has been disturbing you with his troublesome new information? I am not sure that I approve. It may be good for you, but surely not for your book or books which must, I suppose, put us all in a very special position regarding reality. I mean as 'characters' rather than human beings. No? And why, you ask me, did I never tell you a tithe of the things you know now? One never does, you know, one never does. As a spectator standing equidistant between two friends or lovers one is always torn by friendship to intervene, to interfere— but one never does. Rightly. How could I tell you what I knew of Justine—or for that matter what I felt about your neglect of Melissa? The very range of my sympathies for the three of you precluded it. As for love, it

is so paradoxical a creature and so satisfying in itself
that it would not have been much altered by the intervention of truths from outside. I am sure now, if you
analyse your feelings, you will find you love Justine
better because she betrayed you! The whore is man's
true darling, as I once told you, and we are born to love
those who most wound us. Tell me, wise one, am I wrong?
Besides, my own affection for you lay in another quarter.
I was jealous of you as a writer—and as a writer I
wanted you to myself and did so keep you. Do you see?

"There is nothing I can do to help you now—I mean
help your book. You will either have to ignore the data
which Balthazar has so wickedly supplied, or to 'rework
reality' as you put it.

"And you say you were unjust to Pursewarden; yes,
but it is not important. He was equally unjust to you.
Unknown to either of you, you joined hands in me! As
writers. My only regret is that he did not manage to
finish the last volume of *God Is a Humorist* according to
plan. It is a loss—though it cannot detract from his
achievement. You, I surmise, will soon be coming into
the same degree of self-possession—perhaps through this
cursed city of ours, Alexandria, to which we most belong
when we most hate it. By the way, I have a letter from
Pursewarden about the missing volume which I have
carried around with me among my papers for ages, like
a talisman. It helps not only to revive the man himself
a bit, but to revive me also when I fall into a depression
about my work. (I must go to the village to buy eggs.
I shall copy it out tonight for you.)

"Later. Here is the letter I spoke about, harsh and
crabbed if you like, but none the less typical of our
friend. Don't take his remarks about you too seriously. He
admired you and believed in you—so he once told me.
Perhaps he was lying. Anyway."

" '*Mount Vulture Hotel*
" '*Alexandria*

" 'My dear Clea:

" 'A surprise and delight to find your letter waiting
for me. Clement reader thank you—not for the blame or
praise (one shrinks from both equally) but for being
there, devoted and watchful, a true reader between the
lines—where all real writing is done! I have just come
hotfoot from the Café Al Aktar after listening to a long
discursion on "the novel" by old Lineaments and Keats
and Pombal. They talk as if every novel wasn't *sui generis*
—it is as meaningless to me as Pombal generalising about
"les femmes" as a race; for after all it isn't the family
relationship which really matters. Well, Lineaments was
saying that Redemption and Original Sin were the new
topics and that the writer of today. . . . Ouf! I fled, feeling
like the writer of the day before yesterday, and unwilling
to help them build this sort of mud-pie.

" 'I'm sure old Lineaments will do a lovely novel
about Original Sin and score what I always privately
call a suck-eggs *d'estime* (it means not covering one's
advance). In fact, I was in such despair at the thought of
his coming fame that I thought I would go straight off
to a brothel and expiate my unoriginal sense of sin right
away. But the hour was early, and besides, I felt that I
smelt of sweat for it has been a hot day. I therefore returned to the hotel for a shower and a change of shirt
and so found your letter. There is a little gin in the
bottle and as I don't know where I shall be later on I
think I'll just sit down and answer you now as best I
can until six when the brothels start to open.

" 'The questions you ask me, my dear Clea, are the
very questions I am putting myself. I must get them a
little clearer before addressing myself to the last volume
in which I want above all to combine, resolve and har-
monise the tensions so far created. I feel I want to sound

a note of . . . affirmation—though not in the specific terms of a philosophy or religion. It should have the curvature of an embrace, the wordlessness of a lovers' code. It should convey some feeling that the world we live in is founded in something too simple to be over-described as cosmic law—but as easy to grasp as, say, an act of tenderness, simple tenderness in the primal rela-tion between animal and plant, rain and soil, seed and trees, man and God. A relationship so delicate that it is all too easily broken by the inquiring mind and *con-science* in the French sense which of course has its own rights and its own field of deployment. I'd like to think of my work simply as a cradle in which philosophy could rock itself to sleep, thumb in mouth. What do you say to this? After all, this is not simply what we most need in the world, but really what describes the state of pure process in it. Keep silent awhile and you feel a compre-hension of this act of tenderness—not power or glory: and certainly not Mercy, that vulgarity of the Jewish mind which can only imagine man as crouching under the whip. No, for the sort of tenderness I mean is utterly merciless! "A law unto itself," as we say. Of course, one must always remember that truth itself is always halved in utterance. Yet I must in this last book insist that there is hope for man, scope for man, within the boundaries of a simple law; and I seem to see mankind as gradually appropriating to itself the necessary information through mere attention, *not reason,* which may one day enable it to live within the terms of such an idea—the true mean-ing of "joy unconfined." How could joy be anything else? This new creature we artists are hunting for will not "live" so much as, like time itself simply "elapse." Damn, it's hard to say these things. Perhaps the key lies in laughter, in the Humorous God? It is after all the serious who disturb the peace of the heart with their antics— like Justine. (Wait. I must fix myself a ration of gin.)

" 'I think it better for us to steer clear of the big oblong words like Beauty and Truth and so on. Do you mind? We are all so silly and feeble-witted when it comes to living, but giants when it comes to pronouncing on the universe. *Sufflaminandus erat.* Like you, I have two problems which interconnect: my art and my life. Now in my life I am somewhat irresolute and shabby, but in my art I am free to be what I most desire to seem —someone who might bring resolution and harmony into the dying lives around me. In my art, indeed, through my art, I want really to achieve myself shedding the work, which is of *no importance,* as a snake sheds its skin. Perhaps that's why writers at heart want to be loved for their work rather than for themselves—do you think? But then this presupposes a new order of woman too. Where is she?

" 'These, my dear Clea, are some of the perplexities of your omniscient friend, the classical head and romantic heart of Ludwig Pursewarden.'

"Ouf! It is late and the oil in the lamp is low. I must leave this letter for tonight. Tomorrow perhaps, if I am in the mood after my shopping, I shall write a little more; if not, not. Wise one, how much better it would be if we could *talk.* I feel I have whole conversations stacked inside me, lying unused! I think it is perhaps the only real lack of which one is conscious in living alone; the mediating power of a friend's thoughts to place beside one's own, just to see if they match! The lonely become autocratic, as they must, and their judgments *ex cathedra* in the very nature of things: and perhaps this is not altogether good for the work. But here at least we will be well-matched, you on your island—which is only a sort of metaphor like Descartes' oven, isn't it?— and I in my fairy-tale hut among the mountains.

"Last week a man appeared among the trees, also a

painter, and my heart began to beat unwontedly fast. I felt the sudden predisposition to fall in love—reasoning thus, I suppose: 'If one has gone so far from the world and one finds a man in that place, must he not be the one person destined to share one's solitude, brought to this very place by the invisible power of one's selfless longing and destined specially for oneself?' Dangerous self-delusive tricks the heart plays on itself, always tormented by the desire to be loved! Balthazar claimed once that he could induce love as a control-experiment by a simple action: namely telling each of two people who had never met that the other was dying to meet them, had never seen anyone so attractive, and so on. This was, he claimed, infallible as a means of making them fall in love: they always did. What do you say?

"At any rate, my own misgivings saved me from the youth who was, I will admit, handsome and indeed quite intelligent, and would have done me good, I think, as a lover—perhaps for a single summer. But when I saw his *paintings* I felt my soul grow hard and strong and separate again; through them I read his whole personality as one can read a handwriting or a face. I saw weakness and poverty of heart and a power to do mischief. So I said good-bye there and then. The poor youth kept repeating: 'Have I done anything to offend you, have I said anything?' What could I reply—for there was nothing he could do about the offence except live it out, paint it out; but that presupposed becoming conscious of its very existence within himself.

"I returned to my hut and locked myself in with real relief. He came at midnight and tried the door. I shouted 'Go away,' and he obeyed. This morning I saw him leaving on the bus, but I did not even wave good-bye. I found myself whistling happily, nay, almost dancing, as I walked to town across the forest to get my provisions. It is wonderful whenever one can overcome one's treacher-

ous heart. Then I went home and was hardly in the
door when I picked up a brush and started on the
painting which has been holding me up for nearly a
month; all the ways were clear, all the relations in play.
The mysterious obstacle had vanished. Who can say it
was not due to our painter friend and the love affair
I did not have? I am still humming a tune as I write these
words to you. . . .

"Later: re-reading your letter, why do you go on so,
I wonder, about Pursewarden's death? It puzzles me, for
in a way it is a sort of vulgarity to do so. I mean that
surely it is not within your competence or mine to pass
an open judgment on it? All we can say is that his art
overleaps the barrier. For the rest, it seems to me to be
his own private property. We should not only respect his
privacy in such matters but help him to defend it against
the unfeeling. They are his own secrets, after all, for
what we actually saw in him was only the human disguise that the artist wore (as in his own character, old
Parr, the hopeless sensualist of volume two who turns
out in the end to be the one who painted the disputed
fresco of the Last Supper—remember?) .

"In much the same sort of way, Pursewarden carried
the secret of his everyday life over into the grave with
him, leaving us only his books to marvel at and his ep-
itaph to puzzle over: 'Here lies an intruder from the East.'

"No. No. The death of an artist is quite unassailable.
One can only smile and bow.

"As for Scobie, you are right in what you say. I was
terribly upset when Balthazar told me that he had fallen
down those stairs at the central Quism and killed himself. Yes, I took his parrot, which by the way was inhabited by the old man's spirit for a long time afterwards.
It reproduced with perfect fidelity the way he got up in
the morning singing a snatch of *'Taisez-vous, petit ba-
bouin'* (do you remember?) and even managed to imi-

tate the dismal cracking of the old man's bones as he got out of bed. But then the memory gradually wore out, like an old disc, and he seemed to do it less often and with less sureness of voice. It was like Scobie himself dying very gradually into silence: this is how I suppose one dies to one's friends and to the world, wearing out like an old dance tune or a memorable conversation with a philosopher under a cherry-tree. Being refunded into silence. And finally the bird itself went into a decline and died with its head under its wing. I was so sorry, yet so glad.

"For us, the living, the problem is of a totally different order: how to harness time in the cultivation of a style of heart—something like that? I am only trying to express it. Not to force time, as the weak do, for that spells self-injury and dismay, but to harness its rhythms and put them to our own use. Pursewarden used to say: 'God give us artists resolution and tact'; to which I myself would say a very hearty Amen.

"But by now you will think that I have simply become an opinionated old shrew. Perhaps I have. What does it matter, provided one can get a single idea across to oneself?

"There is so little time; with the news from Europe becoming worse every day I feel an autumnal quality in the days—as if they were settling towards an unpredictable future. And side by side with this feeling, I also feel the threads tightening in our sleeves, so to speak, drawing us slowly back towards the centre of the stage once more. Where could this be but to Alexandria? But perhaps it will prove to be a new city, different to the one which has for so long imposed itself on our dreams. I would like to think that, for the old one and all it symbolized is, if not dead, at least meaningless to the person I now feel myself to be. Perhaps you too have changed by the same token. Perhaps your book too has changed. Or perhaps

you, more than any of us, need to see the city again, need
to see us again. We, for our part, very much need to see
you again and refresh the friendship which we hope
exists the other side of the writing—if indeed an author
can ever be just a friend to his 'characters.' I say 'we,'
writing in the Imperial Style as if I were a Queen, but
you will guess that I mean, simply, both the old Clea and
the new—for both have need of you in a future which. . . ."

There are a few more lines and then the affectionate
superscription.

CONSEQUENTIAL DATA

Some shorthand notes of Keats's, recording the Obiter Dicta of Pursewarden in fragmentary fashion:

(a)

"*I know my prose is touched with plum pudding, but then all the prose belonging to the poetic continuum is; it is intended to give a stereoscopic effect to character. And events aren't in serial form but collect here and there like quanta, like real life.*"

(b)

"*Nessim hasn't got the resources we Anglo-Saxons have; all our women are nurses at heart. In order to secure the lifelong devotion of an Anglo-Saxon woman one has only to get one's legs cut off above the waist. I've always thought Lady Chatterley weak in symbolism from this point of view. Nothing should have earned the devotion of his wife more surely than Clifford's illness. Anglo-Saxons may not be interested in love like other Europeans but they can get just as ill. Characteristically, it is to his English Kate that Laforgue cries out: 'Une Garde-malade pour l'amour de l'art!' He detected the nurse.*"

(c)

"The classical in art is what marches by intention with the cosmology of the age."

(d)

"A state-imposed metaphysic or religion should be opposed, if necessary at pistol-point. We must fight for variety if we fight at all. The uniform is as dull as a sculptured egg."

(e)

Of Da Capo: "Gamblers and lovers really play to lose."

(f)

"Art like life is an open secret."

(g)

"Science is the poetry of the intellect and poetry the science of the heart's affections."

(h)

"Truth is independent of fact. It does not mind being disproved. It is already dispossessed in utterance."

(i)

"I love the French edition with its uncut pages. I would not want a reader too lazy to use a knife on me."

(j)

In a book of poems: "One to be taken from time to time as needed and allowed to dissolve in the mind."

(k)

"We must always defend Plato to Aristotle and vice versa because if they should lose touch with each other we should be lost. The dimorphism of the psyche produced them both."

(l)

"To the medieval world-picture of the World, the Flesh and the Devil (each worth a book) we moderns have added Time: a fourth dimension."

(m)

"New critical apparatus: le roman bifteck, guignol *or* cafard."

(n)

"The real ruins of Europe are its great men."

(o)

"I have always believed in letting my reader sink or skim."

(p)

On reading a long review of God Is a Humorist: *"Good God! At last they are beginning to take me seriously.*

This imposes a terrible burden on me. I must redouble my laughter."

(q)

"Why do I always choose an epigraph from de Sade? Because he demonstrates pure rationalism—the ages of sweet reason we have lived through in Europe since Descartes. He is the final flower of reason, and the typic of European behaviour. I hope to live to see him translated into Chinese. His books would bring the house down and would read as pure humour. But his spirit has already brought the house down around our ears."

(r)

"Europe: a Logical Positivist trying to prove to himself by logical deduction that he exists."

(s)

"My objects in the novels? To interrogate human values through an honest representation of the human passions. A desirable end, perhaps a hopeless objective."

(t)

"My unkindest critics maintain that I am making lampshades out of human skin. This puzzles me. Perhaps at the bottom of the Anglo-Saxon soul there is a still small voice forever whispering: 'Is this Quaite Naice?' and my books never seem to pass the test."

SCOBIE'S COMMON USAGE

Expressions noted from Scobie's quaint conversation, his use of certain words, as:

Vivid, meaning "angry," ex.: "Don't be so vivid, old man."

Mauve, meaning "silly," ex.: "He was just plain mauve when it came to, etc."

Spoof, meaning "trick," ex.: "Don't spoof me, old boy."

Ritual, meaning "habit, form," ex.: "We all wear them. It's ritual for the police."

Squalid, meaning "very elated," ex.: "Toby was squalid with joy when the news came."

Septic, meaning "unspeakable," ex.: "What septic weather today!"

Saffron Walden, meaning "male brothel," ex.: "He was caught in a Saffron Walden, old man, covered in jam."

Cloud Cuckoo, meaning "male prostitute," ex.: "Budgie says there's not a cloud cuckoo in the whole of Horsham. He's advertised."

WORKPOINTS

"How many lovers since Pygmalion have been able to build their beloved's face out of flesh, as Amaril has?" asked Clea. The great folio of noses so lovingly copied for him to choose from—Nefertiti to Cleopatra. The readings in a darkened room.

o   o   o

Narouz always held in the back of his consciousness the memory of the moonlit room; his father sitting in the wheel-chair at the mirror, repeating the one phrase over and over again as he pointed the pistol at the looking-glass.

o   o   o

Mountolive was swayed by the dangerous illusion that now at last he was free to conceive and act—the one misjudgement which decides the fate of a diplomat.

o   o   o

Nessim said sadly: "All motive is mixed. You see, from the moment I married her, a Jewess, all their reservations disappeared and they ceased to suspect me. I do not say it was the only reason. Love is a wonderfully luxuri-

ant plant, but unclassifiable really, fading as it does
into mysticism on the one side and naked cupidity on
the other."

o   o   o

This now explained something to me which had
hitherto puzzled me; namely that after his death Da
Capo's huge library was moved over to Smyrna, book
by book. Balthazar did the packing and posting.

NOTES

From Eugène Marais's *The Soul of The White Ant.*

Bantam Spectra Books by Sheri S. Tepper
Ask your bookseller for the ones you have missed.

P9-ARR-308

Beauty

A novel by

sheri s. tepper

BANTAM BOOKS
NEW YORK · TORONTO · LONDON · SYDNEY · AUCKLAND

All of the characters in this book are fictitious,
and any resemblance to actual persons, living or dead,
is purely coincidental.

This edition contains the complete text
of the original hardcover edition.
NOT ONE WORD HAS BEEN OMITTED.

BEAUTY

A Bantam Spectra Book / published by arrangement with Doubleday

PUBLISHING HISTORY
Doubleday edition published 1991
Bantam edition / April 1992

SPECTRA and the portrayal of a boxed "s" are trademarks of Bantam Books,
a division of Bantam Doubleday Dell Publishing Group, Inc.

All rights reserved.
Copyright © 1991 by Sheri S. Tepper.
Cover design copyright © 1991 by Ron Zinn.
Cover border art copyright © 1991 by Joseph Scrofani.
No part of this book may be reproduced or transmitted in any
form or by any means, electronic or mechanical, including
photocopying, recording, or by any information storage and
retrieval system, without permission in writing from the publisher.
For information address: Doubleday, 1540 Broadway, New York, NY 10036

If you purchased this book without a cover you should be aware that this
book is stolen property. It was reported as "unsold and destroyed" to the
publisher and neither the author nor the publisher has received any
payment for this "stripped book."

ISBN 0-553-29527-6

Published simultaneously in the United States and Canada

Bantam Books are published by Bantam Books, a division of Bantam Doubleday Dell
Publishing Group, Inc. Its trademark, consisting of the words "Bantam Books" and the
portrayal of a rooster, is Registered in U.S. Patent and Trademark Office and in other
countries. Marca Registrada. Bantam Books, 1540 Broadway, New York, New York
10036.

PRINTED IN THE UNITED STATES OF AMERICA

OPM   0 9 8 7 6

*To Malcolm Edwards,
who is wisely
responsible for
these empty pages*

———

Foreword

[In the pages that follow, there are certain interpolations written by me, Carabosse, the fairy of clocks, keeper of the secrets of time. When I stand on the bridge above my Forever Pool, I see all past and future things reflected, near or far, dim or plain. If I invite others to stand beside me, they too may see.

That which we do, we do because we see.

This journal is written by Beauty, daughter of the Duke of Westfaire, recipient of many pleasant gifts. Though it is regrettable that no one gave her the gift of intelligence (a gift not highly valued in Faery) she has a practicality that often makes up for that lack.

Intelligent or not, she is the coffer that hides our treasure.

Intelligent or not, Beauty is all our hope.]

Beauty

The Journal

of

Beauty

daughter of
The Duke of Westfaire

G etting started on this writing, I cut five different quills and ruined them all. Father Raymond finally cut this one for me. I told him he must, since he gave me the book as a reward for good progress in Latin, rhetoric, and composition, and for going a whole month without complaining. Now I have a place to write all the things I cannot say to anyone, except to Father Raymond, and sometimes he is too busy to listen. It is my intention to tell the story of my entire life so when I am aged I can read it and remember everything. Old people often do not remember things. I know because I have asked them, at least the ones around here, and they usually say something like, "Beauty, for heaven's sake, child, I just don't remember."

If I had a mother I would ask her. I never knew my mother. That is probably as good a place to start as any.

1

My Life
in Westfaire

I never knew my mother. My father never speaks of her, though my aunts, his half sisters, make up for his silence with a loquacity which is as continuous as it is malicious. The aunts speak no good of her, whoever she was and whatever has happened to her, specifics which they avoid, however much ill they find to mutter about else. I have always thought they would not waste so much breath on her if she were dead, therefore she is probably alive, somewhere. *De mortuis nil nisi bonum,* Father Raymond says, but that only applies to dead people.

When I was very young I used to ask about her. (As I think any child would. It wasn't wickedness.) First I was hushed, and when I persisted, I was punished. Nothing makes me angrier or more intent upon finding out things than having people refuse to tell me. I don't mind when people don't know, not really, but I hate it when they just won't tell. It's not practical, because it just makes others more curious. It was the aunts whispering about things that started me upon

the habit of listening behind doors and dallying outside open windows. Father Raymond reproaches me
for this when I confess it, though he admits it is not a
very great sin. It was my own idea to confess it because
it felt slightly wicked, but perhaps curiosity is not really a sin at all and I need not feel guilty about it. I will
try not confessing it for a while, and see.

Sometimes I hear my mother's name, Elladine, and
references to "the Curse," or "the Curse on the
Child." The Child is presumably me. If I had known
what a curse was during my more tender years, I might
have been irremediably warped or wounded. As it
was, I knew no more what a curse was than what a
mama was, except that most children had not the one,
but had the other, and that I had had both without
getting any discernable good out of either. Now that I
am older and know what a curse is, though not the
particulars as they may relate to myself, I am used to
the idea and I do not find being cursed as frightening
as I probably should.

(I know I am being loquacious. Father Raymond
says I am very loquacious and affected. I don't really
think I am affected, unless it is by the aunts, and if it is
by the aunts, how could I help it? All these words are
something I was born with. Words bubble up in me
like water. It is hard to shut them off.)

I have resolved to find out all about Mama (and
the curse) as soon as I can. So far I have not found out
much. I do know that Mama was very beautiful, for
one of the older men-at-arms said so when he told me
I look much like her around the eyes though the rest
of me seems to be purely Papa. Papa is an extremely
handsome man, and therefore I am very beautiful. It is
not conceit which makes me say so. It is a fact. One
must face facts, or so the aunts are fond of saying,
though they don't do it at all. They say many things
they don't do. I've noticed that about people. The fact
is that I shall be ravishing when I grow up if I continue
in good habits and do not take to drink.

Aunt Lovage, I regret to say, is a tippler, though
the other aunts are quite abstemious.

Father Raymond took over teaching me when I was ten or eleven years old, but my earliest memories are of an education supervised by the aunts. I learned cookery from Aunt Basil and wines from Aunt Lovage, sewing from Aunt Marjoram (who was herself educated by the Sisters of the Immediate Conception at St. Mary of Perpetual Surprise) and music from Aunt Lavender who, though tone deaf, plays upon the lute with great brio and a blithesome disregard for accuracy. She refers to her style as "spontaneous," and urges me to emulate it.

I have found I can play the right notes quite as easily as the wrong ones, though to satisfy Aunt I do flap my arms rather more than the music requires. I am quite talented in music. I am told I sing nicely.

When I was four or five, Aunt Tarragon taught me my letters in order that I could read improving works and be confirmed in the faith. Some of the writings I like best do not feel very improving, though whenever Aunt Terror is around I pretend I am reading religious books. I was confirmed when I was nine, rather late in life, truly, though Father Raymond considered it soon enough. Even then I thought some bits and pieces of doctrine were unlikely at best. Aunt Tarragon is very pious. The other aunts call her the Holy Terror—a play upon her name. They say things like, "Where's the Holy Terror gone?" and collapse in silly laughter.

It was my grandfather's notion to name his seven daughters after herbs, a black mark in the heavenly score book which was no doubt wiped clean by his death or enslavement at the age of seventy-four while on his way to Rhodes to offer his services to the Knights Hospitaler of St. John. We are a long lived family, so Papa says, and Grandfather was still very hale and fervent at that age. Grandfather's ship was blown off course in a storm and was taken subsequently by Mamluks, so Grandmama was informed by an escaped survivor. From what Papa and the aunts say about him, I doubt Sultan al-Maluk an-Nazir had any pleasure of Grandfather.

Luckily, Grandfather's demise or disappearance

came long after he brought home the builders who saw to the reconstruction of Westfaire Castle. Some say the architects were pagans from the Far East, and some say they were inheritors of the Magi, but they could not have been anything evil to have built so beautiful a place. There is no other castle like it in England; there may be no building like it in the world. Westfaire is without peer. Even those who have traveled to the far corners of the earth, as Father Raymond did in his younger years, say it is of matchless beauty.

Grandfather's first wife had no sons and two daughters. They are eldest of my aunts, Aunt Sister Mary Elizabeth and Aunt Sister Mary George, who are nuns at the Monastery of St. Perpituus in Alderbury. The sisters do not visit us often. I believe they took holy orders simply to escape being called Tansy and Comfrey, though it is possible they were summoned by God. Sister Mary Elizabeth was rather infirm when I last saw her, though it is likely Sister Mary George will go on forever, getting a little leaner and drier with every passing year.

Grandfather's second wife had no sons and five daughters. Aunt Lavvy, at fifty-eight, is the youngest of them. Aunt Love is sixty. Aunt Terror is sixty-two. Aunts Bas and Marj are twins of sixty-five. I am almost sixteen, and the difference in our ages (as well as their reticence about things I want to know) seems an impenetrable barrier between us. They often fail to perceive the things I perceive, and this makes communication between us exceedingly difficult. I cannot say that there is more than a superficial affection on either side of our relationship. Father Raymond talks about filial duty, but it seems to me there should be something more in a family than that.

Grandfather's third wife, my father's mother, died soon after Grandfather vanished, of grief it is said, though in my opinion she died of simple exasperation. I sometimes imagine what it would be like to be wife to a man and mother to a son who are always off on pilgrimage, as well as being stepmother to seven daughters, all of them considerably older than I. I would die of it, I think, just as Grandmama did. She was only fifteen when she married Grandfather, after all, and about thirty-five when he was killed. What had she to look forward to but decades more of the herbal sisters, all of them dedicated to eccentric celibacy? Buried among all those stepdaughters, Grandmama would have been unlikely to find a second husband, especially since there was nothing left of either her dowry or her dower. Grandpapa used everything rebuilding Westfaire: all the dowries of his three wives, all his own money, and all the considerable fortune he had somehow obtained in the Holy Land, about which people say very little, making me believe Grandfather may not have been quite ethical in amassing the treasure. Grandmama was left with nothing to attract suitors, and death might have seemed a blessed release. At least, so I think.

I spend a lot of time thinking about people. If one leaves out religion, there is very little to think about *except* people. People and books are just about all there is. I don't have anyone much to talk with and only Grumpkin to play with, so . . . so I spend a lot of time thinking. It comes out in words. I can't help that.

I do read everything I can get hold of. Books and my own writings are a comfort to me in the late hours of the night when all in Westfaire are asleep but me, and I am awake for no reason that I know of except that my legs hurt (Aunt Terror says it is growing pains) or the owls are making a noise in the trees, or my head is full of things I have do not have enough words for yet—there must be such things!—or my chest burns as it sometimes does, as though I had swallowed a little star. It burns and burns, just behind my collar bone, as though it were trying to hollow me out to make a place for itself. I do not know what it is, but it has always been there.

So, I sit up in my bed with the bed curtains drawn tight, the candle on one side and Grumpkin snoring into his paws on the other, and make lists of new words I have heard that day or write pages to myself about all the things I do not understand. Grumpkin lies on his back with his tummy up, his front feet folded over his chest or nose and an anticipatory smile on his face, as though he is dreaming of mice. I wish I could sleep like cats do.

2

DAY OF ST. PATERNUS, BISHOP, CONVERTER OF
DRUIDS, APRIL, YEAR OF OUR LORD 1347

When I was quite young, about eight or nine, I purloined some boy's clothes from a line near the woods-
man's hut, leaving a silver coin in their place. I had
gone out of my way to steal the coin, too, because I
had no money of my own, and I thought that though
God might forgive my robbing the well-to-do, he
would not forgive my increasing the distress of the
poor. Dressed in these uncouth garments, dirt on my
face, and with my hair twisted up under a grubby cap,
I presented myself at the stables asking for whatever
work Martin, the head groom, could give me. I am
fairly sure Martin knew who I was, but we both preserved the fiction that I was a boy from the countryside, one Havoc, a miller's son, whom Martin
employed in order to take advantage of youthful enterprise. If we had ever been found out, I would have
sworn on the Holy Scripture that he was guiltless, so
grateful to him I was, and I believe he relied upon my
protection in the event our game was discovered.

It was in the stable I learned to ride long before the
aunts had me dressed in voluminous skirts and
perched upon a sidesaddle, one of Grandfather's in-
ventions. I do not think the sidesaddle will catch on.

Most women ride sensibly astride, and I cannot imagine their giving it up for something both so uncomfortable and of such doubtful provenance. According to the stable boys, the sidesaddle was designed to protect a maiden's virginity, while risking the maiden's neck. Risking rather much for rather little, I thought at the time, though of course I knew nothing practical about the matter then and scarcely more today.

Martin sometimes asked me to exercise the horses and take them down through the little wood to the stream for water. It was there I first met the pointy-eared boy. He came strolling out of the copse, introduced himself as Puck, and asked my name. When I told him Havoc, he laughed. "I know that's you, Beauty," he said. When I asked him what he was doing in *my woods,* he told me he was keeping an eye on me for someone. I assumed Martin had sent him, simply because I couldn't think of anyone else who might care to have me looked after. After that, I saw him every now and then. Once in a while he would tell me stories. They were not like the stories anyone else told. He spoke of God, but not as Father Raymond did. Some of the things he said sounded greatly like blasphemy to me, and I told him so. I assumed he was some woodcutter's son, told off to watch me whenever I left the stables, which wasn't often because that's where things were going on and people talking about things I might not have learned about otherwise.

It was in the stables that I learned about animal procreation and saw enough of stable boy anatomy to draw certain useful parallels. Though the boys' equipment suffers by comparison to that of the stallions, the similarity of function cannot be ignored. I think it odd that the aunts have never said anything about this matter. There are a great many things they simply do not discuss with me. They did not even tell me about the way of women, and when it happened I thought God was punishing me for having certain feelings about a certain person by letting me bleed to death. It was Doll who found me weeping and told me it was all very ordinary and had nothing to do with sin.

Doll is Martin's wife. Doll is short for Dorothy. She was named for St. Dorothy who was a virgin martyr known for her angelic virtue. Doll says she wishes she had been named for someone a little less angelic and a bit more muscular. She is one of the women who keeps the castle swept and the cobwebs pulled down, and that takes muscle. I'm sure she has always known what I was up to in the stables, but she has never told on me. Doll and one of the other women make clothes for me, too, and I thank God for that. If it were up to the aunts or Papa, I'd always be dressed in things out of the attic made for ancient female relatives in their latter years. Doll and Martin are my first two friends.

My third friend is Giles.

Giles is one of the men-at-arms. He is a year or two older than I, well-grown for his age, very broad in the shoulder and slender though well-made in the hip and leg. He has a frank and open countenance and much soft brown hair which falls over his forehead at odd times, making him look like a much younger person. His eyes are blue, deep blue, like an evening sky. His lips . . . He has very nice features. I have had certain thoughts about him from time to time, thoughts which I have not even told Father Raymond about, because I would blush to do so. Besides, I don't have any polite words to use because either there aren't any or no one has taught them to me. I know how the stableboys talk, but Father Raymond definitely would not appreciate that. Nonetheless, when I see Giles, I think of the stallions and their way with the mares, and I get all flushed feeling.

Also, I see the way he watches me sometimes— Giles, not Father Raymond—which lets me know he feels those same feelings. He is of good birth, but he is only a young man without fortune or rank, and there is no question about his being a suitable prospect for the daughter of a duke. He is not. I know that, and he knows it as well, but he is nice to me. He is thoughtful and kind and has never, even by so much as a word, done anything improper toward me. Sometimes, after a lengthy rain, I will find my bench in the garden care-

fully dried off and a rose laid upon it. I'm sure it is
Giles who does it, but he doesn't say anything, nor do
I. Still, he is my friend. He would not act so otherwise.
My other friend is Beloved.

Her mother calls her Beloved, though her name is
actually Mary Blossom. She is the daughter of Dame
Blossom, an artisan freeholder, a weaver, in the village. Dame Blossom is very much respected by everyone because she is a midwife and can heal wounds and
set bones. If there is trouble, better get Dame Blossom
and stay away from doctors, everyone says. It's true.
From time to time one or the other of the aunts has
consulted a physician, and all the great scholars ever
did was sniff at their piss, bleed them dry, and give
them some dreadful mixture that—so says Martin—
would kill the old ladies off a few years before their
time. Beloved is my personal maid. She is also my
friend and almost certainly my half sister, almost my
half-twin.

Not that Beloved is the only young one running
about the castle who looks a lot like me. Everyone
pretends not to notice, but I would have to be blind
not to see. When two mares who do not look alike
throw foals that look exactly alike, you know the same
stallion has been at them, so it's clear my Papa has
been at Dame Blossom. That was sixteen or more
years ago, of course, when she was younger and prettier. I remember her when I was a little girl. She was
quite slender and gay then. She has put on weight
since, and become very grave, which is a suitable style
for a respected matron.

So, Beloved is my half sister, born on the same day
I was, and she looks enough like me to be my twin.
Sometimes I love her and sometimes I hate her because she has a mother and I don't. We sometimes
dress up as each other and Beloved will take my place
in the castle, in the dining hall or sewing with the
aunts, and they never know the difference. She can
spend all day in the castle without anyone guessing
that she isn't me. But, if I go down to the village pretending to be the weaver-woman's daughter, Dame

Blossom takes one look at me and says, "Beauty, it isn't nice of you to tease me this way. Go tell my silly daughter to come home."

That always makes me feel like crying for some reason. Maybe because she always knows right away I'm not Beloved. You have to notice people to be that sure about them. Though I have thought that maybe it is because she can see the burning thing in me. I know Beloved doesn't have one of those, because I asked her. She wondered if it was like dyspepsia, and I told her it was not.

3

DAY OF STS. PETER AND JAMES,
MAY, YEAR OF OUR LORD 1347

Yesterday my father, who is thirty-seven years of age, returned from pilgrimage to Canterbury—he has already made pilgrimages to the tombs of St. Francis of Assisi, St. Martin of Tours, St. Boniface at Fulda, and St. James at Compostela, as well as to Glastonbury, Lindisfarne, Walsingham, Westminster, St. Albans, and all places else where there are relics of note. Immediately upon his arrival, he told us he intends to marry again. He told us his intended wife will arrive shortly with a small retinue, and that they will all stay for the betrothal ceremonies. Her name is Sibylla de Vinciennes d'Argent. I detested her from the moment I saw the miniature of her that Papa insisted we all admire.

You must not think this rejection of a stepmama is provoked by hostility toward another woman who will take a beloved mama's place. I have heard tales like that, but I don't know whether I would have loved Mama or not; she has given me no opportunity to find out. As for Sibylla's taking my place in my father's affections, she can't take what I have never had. Though I am almost sixteen, he has done none of the things one expects of a loving papa. He made no pro-

vision for my education, merely leaving me to the
mercies of the aunts. If Father Raymond hadn't taken
me over, I should be as woefully ignorant about many
important things as they. Papa has made no effort to
arrange a marriage for me. When I've raised the subject with him, he has said, "Wait until—well, until
you're sixteen, Beauty. Then we'll discuss it." Not
likely! I can count upon the fingers of one hand the
number of "discussions" I've had with Papa, count
them and quote them from memory.

"Ah, Beauty," he says. "Doing well with your
studies/cooking/music/herbary?"

"Yes, Papa."

"Good girl. Always do well with your studies/cook-
ing/music/herbary."

Once in a great while, when I have been greatly
troubled, I've gone all the way to his rooms to talk
with him. This isn't a journey to take lightly! Starting
in my rooms, which are off the long corridor behind
the kitchens, I go up one flight of stairs to the corridor
outside the small dining hall. This is the tall one hung
with crusaders' weapons and banners and with panel-
ing carved all over with birds and flowers and fish.
Then I go through the little suite between and into the
large dining hall, an even taller room, where the ceiling is decorated with stone rosettes dependent from
the multiple arches, each like lacework, where the long
wall is one tall window after another—all looking over
the garden with the apricot tree that Beloved and I get
all the fruit from because the people in the kitchens
always forget it is there—and the other walls are hung
with tapestries telling stories of gods and goddesses,
most of them naked. At the far end of this dining hall,
I come out into the great hall, under the dome. Father
Raymond says it is not unlike a cathedral dome,
though smaller. Since I've never seen a cathedral, I see
it as the inside of a lovely shiny melon, pressing up
toward the sky, round windows set about it like gems
in a ring, poking up in the center to make the high
lantern visitors say they can see from miles away as
they approach on the north road. They look for it, they

say, as the first sight of the most beautiful building in the world!

The floor of the great hall is marble, laid in designs. When I was little, I used to play there, walking along the designs as though they were paths in a garden. From the great hall, two curving stairs follow the walls up behind a graceful stone balustrade, joining at the center before three arches with statues of veiled women set beneath them. No one alive made the statues. Grandfather brought them from a country across the sea from the Holy Land, from a man who had dug them up from an ancient city, and Papa says Grandfather did it because the architects of Westfaire told him to. From either side of the arches, other corridors lead left and right, and at the far end of the leftward one, up another flight of curving stairs, are Papa's rooms. All the floors, except the one in the small dining hall, which is made out of tiny woven strips of walnut wood, are laid in mosaics, ribbons and leaves and flowers and fruits bordering all the walls. It's hard to walk over them without stopping to look at them. It's hard to climb the stairs without listening to the way my clothes trail along the steps, the way the smooth stone feels under my hand. It's hard to go anywhere in Westfaire without stopping and staring, sometimes for a long, long time. Besides, it's just a very long way to Papa's rooms, so I don't go there very often, only when I'm desperate.

And when I do go, when I get there, I knock on Papa's door and call, "Papa, may I talk to you?"

"Not now, Beauty," he always replies over the sound of female giggles. "I'm very busy just now. Later on, perhaps."

Now that is what our filial relationship amounts to! I don't think that's enough of one for the new stepmama to threaten.

I am not jealous of whatever attention Sibylla may receive from the aunts, either. I heartily hope she will take my share along with her own. They pay entirely too much attention to me, all the time, without being in the least comforting or kind.

No, my revulsion at the idea of a stepmama is not jealousy. It arises from the pictured face itself, a pale, rather long face with a simpering mouth over large teeth and with something thoughtfully devious about the eyes, the kind of face that might result if a rabbit mated with a weasel.

And perhaps I am jealous of the fact that she will be mistress of Westfaire Castle.

No, that is *not* honest. If I am going to write things to remember when I am old, I should at least tell the truth. I am sickened at the thought of her being mistress of Westfaire. Though I have always known it will be my fate to marry and leave it, still I love Westfaire hopelessly. I love the lowe of sunset on the lake at our back, the blossoming trees in the orchard close, the gentle curve of the outer walls resting in the arms of the forest. I love the towers, the shining dome, the delicate buttresses, and the lacy windows. From a hill not far away (we always go there on the first of May to collect herbs and wildflowers) one can look down on Westfaire and see it whole. Whenever I look at it thus, the burning within me grows into a fire, closing my throat, catching at my heart, as though Westfaire and I burned with the same holy light. If I turn in time to catch the aunts staring down, their faces have a look not unlike mine, though not so pained, as though they, too, love the place so much they cannot bear to leave it. I've always refused to think about leaving Westfaire, but it is probable my dislike of Sibylla comes from nothing more than simple grief at what she will gain and I will inevitably lose.

Feeling beauty must be rather like feeling arms and legs. Some of the old men-at-arms talk about losing an arm or a leg in battle and how, ever after, one feels it is still there, even while one grieves over the loss. So I know it will be when I lose Westfaire. I will feel it in me forever, even while I grieve endlessly over losing it.

I still don't want to think about that. Instead, I keep telling myself that a wedding offers to be an interesting event which can be anticipated with an observer's relish of novelty. It will not make much

immediate difference to me, personally, so I can resolve to enjoy it as spectacle.

*[I find it interesting that she feels the truth, without
understanding it in the least.*

*I said as much to Israfel and he remarked that it
would be better if she didn't understand it. "Much of
life," he said to me, "depends on our being ignorant of
reality. If we understood reality, we would never go
on."]*

4

ST. MONICA'S DAY,
MAY, YEAR OF OUR LORD 1347

When I wrote that Papa's marriage would make little difference to me, personally, I had failed to perceive Sibylla's capacity for inventive malice.

She arrived yesterday with her mama and assorted female relatives in a great bustle of boxes and flutter of veils. They trotted briskly through the castle, visiting each of my aunts in her own rooms, which are in various parts of the castle, though not in the long wing where Papa lives, which is virtually empty. We had all assumed the visitors would be quartered there, where the extravagant, lacy vaulting reaches its perfect expression (says Father Raymond) and the tall windows admit the most light. The rooms are comfortably furnished with high, enclosed beds and plenty of benches and hangings and carpets. Besides, in expectation of company, that wing had been given an extraordinarily thorough cleaning. Doll has been at it for days.

Our assumption was mistaken. According to Sibylla's mama—a woman who always looks as though she has a mouthful of something nasty which only courtesy prevents her spitting out—Sibylla could be happy only in the rooms near the kitchens which I have occupied since my earliest memory. It was not, in her mama's words, fitting for Sibylla to be housed too near her intended bridegroom lest some indecency occur prior to the blessing of Mother Church. I turned my mind from the indecency which would undoubtedly occur subsequent to that blessing. Far better, Sibylla's mama went on, for Sibylla to be as far from her intended husband as possible, in the bosom of the aunts, getting to know them better.

Strangely enough, I was rather cheered by all this. It was pleasant to be given a reason for hating her, and this immediate assault upon the daughter of the house by the putative bride told me how right I had been. The rabbit *had* mated with a weasel, and that right gladly. I was furious, of course, but justified. Beloved and I whispered about it, resolving upon mutiny, after which I smiled at the committee which was delegated to approach me, aunts and all, and declined to move.

Aunt Taragon had a few pious words to say concerning Christian resignation and turning the other cheek. I suggested that she convey this message to Sibylla, for whom it could do nothing but good. While this was going on, Beloved hid behind my bed curtains and made faces at me behind Aunt Terror's back. When she left, we collapsed on the bed, giggling. Though Beloved was supposed to be my maidservant, I never ordered her to do anything for me. What she did, she did because she wanted to, such as caring for my clothes because sometimes she wore them while I wore hers.

Aunt Basil was the next to arrive and remind me I had always thought my rooms were so near the kitchens that the smell of aged grease overcame the spices in the clothes press. I suggested she tell Sibylla, who would no doubt change her mind about wanting my rooms. Beloved and I had another giggle over that.

Aunt Lovage came to promise me (or rather Beloved, since by that time we'd changed clothes and were being each other) a bottle of a very special vintage and a picnic on the sward. Beloved suggested we have the bottle and the picnic anyway. This was not a particularly clever rejoinder. Beloved and I look ex-

actly alike, but I am much cleverer. I tried to teach
Beloved to read and write, but she isn't interested. She
doesn't even care. She sometimes watches me reading
and studying, and she says it is a dreadful burden being clever and well-schooled, and she is glad she does
not have to carry it.

Aunt Marjoram promised to make me a new cloak,
but Beloved told her my old one will last years yet. It
will, though it is already faded. Perhaps I will make
myself a new one.

And finally, Aunt Lavender promised to play a
new song for me, one she had learned from a traveling
minstrel. I was being myself by then since it was late
afternoon and Beloved had gone home. Since I had
spent more time with the minstrel than aunt had and
already knew all his songs, I declined.

I had thought they might appeal to Aunt Sister
Mary Elizabeth and Aunt Sister Mary George, but
Papa gave them no time for that. In the afternoon
Papa sent a servant to bring me to the small room
where he does business with his bailiff, and there he
told me to get myself moved by dark or he'd send me
to Alderbury to join my two eldest aunts as a nun.

I would move, I said gayly. I would move happily. I
had always felt my rooms were rather too close to the
kitchens. What had given Papa the idea I was reluctant
to move? I dimpled and curtsied, then rounded up
three serving maids, including my old friend Doll, and
made a clean sweep of it before Sibylla or her mama
could say a paternoster, being sure that everyone
heard me chirping happily away about the whole
thing.

There were no rooms left except the ones in Papa's
wing, including the suite we had intended for Sibylla.
All the rooms there were huge. The corridor was obviously one used frequently by Papa's . . . friends,
whom I did not want to meet going and coming. I sat
on my baskets and told Doll that was the last place I
wanted to go, feeling quite put out now that my little
drama had been played and Sibylla had been installed

where I had lately been, in my cosy rooms beside the
garden, with my carpet and my bed curtains.

"There's the room your mama used sometimes,"
said Doll. Doll is older than most of the other servants,
and she was present when my mama was still in residence. "Up in the dove tower," she said, raising her
eyebrows up under her hair and jerking her head back.
Doll is stout and red-cheeked and has more energy
than any five other women. She stood there, looking at
me intently, hands on hips.

The dove tower is slender and tall, the tallest of all
the castle towers, its top decorated with spiky finials
and a long pole for flying banners. Around it the white
doves make a constant cloud of wings and a liquid
tumult like water falling into a fountain.

"Up in the dove tower, then," I agreed, and we all
went back through the hall and wound ourselves here
and there through little side passages until we came to
the tower door. It screamed when we opened it, like a
goose being killed, and the dust on the stairs puffed
under our feet as we crept up, round and round and
round until we were dizzy. The door at the top hung
loose with great nails sticking out of it, and the room
itself was filthy with bits of bird nest and veils of spider
web. Doll sent a girl to ask Martin to come up and fix
the shutters and the door, and he did that while one of
his boys unstuffed the chimney and two of the women
scrubbed the floor and walls and another one swept
the mess down the stairs. Martin threw the carpet
down into the yard, for it was eaten to rags by moth
and mouse. The doves from the cote below had made
somewhat free with the space, but under the dirty coverlet the bed was all right, and so were the bed curtains we found in the carved armoire, once they'd been
shaken free of dust and well brushed and hung. I
cleaned out the armoire myself (finding something interesting in the process) and put my clothes in it. Then
I sat on the chair and felt important. It has arms! Only
Papa and Aunt Terror have chairs with arms. Everyone else sits on benches or stools. While I sat there, I
examined the thing I'd found in the armoire, but there

wasn't time really to figure out what it was, so after a time, I put it under the chair seat, which lifts up to make a storage place, and told myself I would examine it later on.

Doll showed me the privy closet over the moat. The door is in the wainscot beside the fireplace. I'll have it all to myself. I can see the lake through the little windows. The tiny panes of glass are quite intact and clear now that the bird droppings have been washed away. There are three windows in a row, and the middle one goes all the way to the floor and opens on a balcony where a kind of pole juts out over the stableyard. Martin calls it a spar, and says he'll fix the pulley and put a rope on it tomorrow, so that water and firewood can be hauled up from the stableyard below. By late afternoon everyone was finished with the cleaning and went off, leaving the room neat and sweet-smelling with my lute hung on the wall, a pitcher of water and a bowl to wash in on the chest, a kettle by the fire for hot water, the woodbox filled, all my things tucked away, and me here alone, looking around at the sky like a bird from its nest.

Without a carpet or rushes, the floors will be very cold. Without tapestries, the walls will be even colder. Still, the hooks are still there to put wall hangings on, if I can find some, and the worst of the cold weather is over. It will be warm enough for a night or two, until Sibylla leaves and I can steal my carpet back from my old room. I must stop writing and go down to supper.

Though we made a noisy enough bustle getting the tower room cleaned, it seems the tower is so high and remote no one heard us. None of the aunts noticed where I went; they all spoke as though I'd moved into a room in Papa's wing. I suppose Sibylla and her mama think that's what I've done. At table this evening she peered at me as a chicken does at a bug, acting very discontented and disappointed, as though she had been counting on my making a fuss about moving, perhaps, which would have given her something to complain to Papa about. Poor fool woman. She doesn't know Papa.

"All settled?" he asked them vaguely, not waiting for an answer. "Good. It's always good to get settled." Then he went back to talking with Father Raymond about the pilgrimages he intends to make before and after the wedding while Sibylla sat there, caparisoned like a tournament horse, playing with a slice of overdone venison and staring at the back of his neck. I thought of telling her that's mostly what she's going to see of him. The back of his neck as he plans some journey or the back of all of him as he rides away.

[The device Beauty found in the tower room was one I, Carabosse, had left there for her: a clock. It has my name on it, and I hope it will serve as an introduction so she will not be completely surprised, later, when we meet. We plan for her to leave Westfaire, which is conspicuous now and will be even more so, and go to another place, a hidden place where she is unlikely to ever encounter the Dark Lord. Thus far, things are progressing precisely as Israfel and I expected they would, as the Pool showed they would. The immediate future is usually quite clear in the Pool, and we had foreseen Sibylla. We had anticipated the succession of events leading to Beauty's occupation of the tower. I had even foreseen her pleasure in it.

What I had not anticipated are my own feelings. I fear I am growing fond of the girl. She has something none of her fairy godmothers gave her, something that came entirely from her human heritage. It is a kind of courage. An indomitability. Like a buoyant little boat, she pops to the top of every wave. Loquacious though she is (and Father Raymond was perfectly right about that), even a little arch at times (and why shouldn't she be? Most of her aunts have exactly that manner), still, she has something attractive about her. Perhaps it is the outward sign of what we did to her, Israfel and I.]

5

ST. ETHELREDA'S DAY,
MAY, YEAR OF OUR LORD 1347

After Sibylla left, in the days between the betrothal
and the wedding, which is supposed to take place very
soon, I got the tower arranged to suit me. Martin and I
stole my carpet from my old room and replaced it with
one out of the attic. Laid over a nice layer of straw, it
made the floor much warmer. We could find no wall
tapestries in the attic, but we did find some painted
wall cloths up there, blue background with a design of
little starry flowers in silver, quite good enough to take
the chill off the stone. Also, Martin put up a new firewood rope.

After that, I had time to really look at the thing I
found. It is round, like a wheel, about as big across as
the palm of my hand, and as thick through as four of
my fingers held together. It has four little feet like
lion's paws. It is made of shiny metal which could be
gold, for it is very heavy for its size. The round front is
made of glass. Under the glass are nine numbers, Roman numbers, set in a circle. The numbers start at the
top right with fourteen, and go on around the circle to
twenty-two, which is at the top. There is a lacy golden
arrow starting in the middle and pointing to the four-

teen. Well, actually pointing about halfway between the fourteen and the fifteen.

On the back of it is a place like a keyhole, but there is no key. On the top is a handle, like two dragons, fighting or kissing or just being heraldic. And that's all.

Except the noise it makes. I can only hear it at night when things are very quiet, but I can hear it then. The tiniest ticking, the faintest crepitation, like something very small inside there, breathing or tapping its toe.

Oh, on the front of it, twining all around the numbers is a design of leaves and vines, and I think they are meant to spell out letters. Sometimes I look at them for a long, long time, trying to make the letters out. Two, I'm almost sure, are Ss. Two, I'm almost sure, are As. I think there's a B and a C, but I can't be sure. Since I don't know what it is, I call it my mysterious thing, and it sits on the chest with my other things.

I like the tower very much.

As it happened, Papa had gone off somewhere before the aunts even found out where I am living. When they found out, there was much consternation, buzzing, and confabulation. The aunts wanted to know who suggested such a thing?

No sense getting Doll in trouble. I told them it had been my own idea.

More wide eyes, open mouths, and thrown up hands. More fussing and steaming and orders to move here, move there.

"My mother lived up there," I said to them at last. "If you want me to get out of it, you'll have to tell me why!"

Which settled them down in a hurry. Not one of them is willing to say why or what or when. Since Papa is off viewing decayed bits of saints' bodies, he isn't available to offer an opinion. Aunt Sister Mary Elizabeth and Aunt Sister Mary George, whose thoughts on the matter were solicited by Aunt Terror in a thick letter sent by messenger, have replied that they are unaware of anything ungodly about the tower room.

This sent the aunts into a frenzy of calculation, trying to decide whether either of the elderly nuns was present at Westfaire at any time when my mother was here.

I stood it as long as I could, and then I went to Doll. "Doll," I asked her, "tell me what this is all about." I've asked her about my mother many times over the years, and she has always shaken her head at me. Still, the last time I'd asked had been a long time ago, when I was a child.

"Be my gizzard's worth," she said. "Be worth my life and soul if they found out." She wrung her hands, one in the other, trying not to look at me.

"Not from me," I swore, spitting in my hand and making a cross on my chest with ashes from the cookfire.

She wrung her hands again, staring over my shoulder. Finally she gave a kind of sigh and a shrug and said, almost in a whisper, "When your papa insisted on makin' a great celebration out of your Christenin', she invited some relatives of hers, and when your papa found out about that, they fought about it. I don't know what it was about because I couldn't hear anythin' except them yellin'. Then, when the Christenin' was over, your papa took you away and gave you to a wetnurse down in the village, then he locked your mama in her room up there in the tower. He nailed the door shut, and he went up every day to yell at her through the door, tellin' her the whole thing had been her fault and she'd had no business marryin' him without tellin' him."

"What did he mean?"

She flushed and twisted her hands together. "It's not something I'd speak of, Beauty. Besides, I don't know for sure. None of us common folk knows for sure. Third day after your mama was locked up, your papa got no answer when he yelled at her, so the carpenter jerked the door open and they found her gone."

"Jumped?" I asked, thinking Doll knew something she wasn't telling me. Her face was red, like she was

holding something back, but I didn't want to push her
too much or she'd refuse to talk about it at all.

"Too high to jump," she said.

"Went down the firewood rope."

"Your papa took the firewood rope down first
thing he put her in there."

"Flew away?" I offered as a jest, watching in
amazement as Doll crossed herself.

"There's those that say she did exactly that."

"I did get christened, didn't I?" I asked, wondering
why Mama had made such a fuss about it.

"Of course you did, silly," she snorted, going back
to her cleaning, obviously not wanting to talk about it
anymore. Needless to say, this has given me a great
deal to think about.

6

ST. LADISLAS DAY,
JUNE, YEAR OF OUR LORD 1347

Yesterday Papa came back from his trip full of plans
for the wedding, which he seems in a monstrous hurry
to accomplish, and this has given the aunts something
else to worry about besides where I am housed. None
of them chose to be the one to tell him I am living in
the tower, and I'm certainly not going to tell him.

The weather has been having a sulky spell, with
gloomy clouds and chill rain. I've kept the shutters
closed and a fire going, to make a warm shadowy
space. What with the wall hangings and the carpet and
the low ceiling (though it is vaulted up from five stone
piers to join in a carved rosette high in the middle), it
stays warmer than my old quarters did, even though
the fireplace is a tiny little thing next to the door
where the stairs go down behind the one straight wall.
Though it took him several days to get used to it,
Grumpkin has come to like the tower room, both for
sleeping and for prowling about on the balcony. I love
it. I can practice on the lute without anyone's hearing
or learn new songs or read, all by the light of the fire
with the one candle making strange shadows.

Which led me to my discovery. This afternoon I
saw that a shadow on the chimney piece looked ex-

actly like a face. One of the stones was a nose. I went
over and stroked it, watching the shadow of my hand,
feeling the nose shake a little. The stone was loose. I
fiddled with it and jiggled at it until it slid out into my
hands, not heavy at all. It was only a thin piece shaped
to fit into the front of a little space. And behind the
stone was a box.

I took the box out, replaced the stone, and sat
down before the fire to look at it. The box is well-
made of a pale satiny wood, and though it has a keyhole, it wasn't locked. Inside was a packet of needles
and three hanks of thread, a ring with a carved stone,
and some tightly rolled sheets of parchment. These I
unrolled and found the top sheet was a letter directed
to me.

> Dear Beauty:
> Since you have not had a mother's love, my
> child, I believe you deserve at least a mother's ex-
> planation.
> I did not leave my own country with the inten-
> tion of marrying anyone like your father. I met the
> duke quite by accident; he wooed me with great
> ardor; I fell under the spell of his passion.
> As it happens with my people, from the moment
> of the wooing, my memory of my past existence
> was dimmed. I was first enveloped by your father's
> encompassing desires and later smothered by his
> overwhelming aunts. The former caused me to lose
> my memory and virginity, though temporarily; the
> latter have caused me almost to lose my mind. I
> hope this is also temporary.
> Time passed and I learned that I was pregnant. I
> was not unhappy about this. As I grew large, how-
> ever, your father began to absent himself. I should
> say, absent himself more frequently, as it is com-
> mon knowledge in this household that your father
> is a libertine. As I grew larger yet, he left me com-
> pletely to myself. Among my family, celibacy re-
> stores both memory and virginity, a useful attribute
> under certain conditions—if one wishes to trap a

unicorn, for example. To say I was horrified at what I had done is to say both too much and too little. I regretted the liaison as being beneath my dignity, but at the same time, I delighted in the prospect of having a child. Children have a very special meaning to our people.

Then you were born. Your father planned to have you christened. I considered this unnecessary and demeaning. His religion is stealing our birthright, day by day and year by year! Why should I take part in it! However, your father insisted not only upon the ceremony itself, but upon making it a cause for semipublic display.

Since all your father's aunts would be attending this ceremony, however, fairness dictated that my own aunts be offered the same opportunity. They would have been mightily offended otherwise.

I let the letter fall into my lap as I considered these confusing words. How very strange. I reread the first of the letter, but it made no more sense the second time. I shook my head and went on.

I did not invite Aunt Carabosse. She came uninvited! For some inexplicable reason of her own, she laid a curse upon you, my child. Upon your sixteenth birthday you were to prick your finger upon a spindle and die.

I crushed the letter to my breast in sudden horror. My sixteenth birthday was only days away. I forced my eyes back to the parchment where it trembled in my hands.

No one heard this except your great aunt, Joyeause, who was standing beside the cradle at the time. She came to me after the guests had departed to tell me she had modified the curse as best she could. The curse now implements as follows: "When Duke Phillip's beautiful daughter reaches her sixteenth year, she shall prick her finger upon a

spindle and fall into a sleep of one hundred years,
from which she will be wakened by the kiss of a
charming prince." Or perhaps it was Prince
Charming. I have been much upset by all this and
did not pay proper attention to what she was telling me. No one knows what Aunt Joyeause has
done but me—and you, if you read this letter before your birthday, as I am confident you will do
for I have set a timely discovery spell upon it.

*[Most of the above is nonsense. Joyeause did over-
hear what I said, since she was closest to me at the time.
What I said was that the duke's daughter would be
pricked by a spindle and fall into an enchanted sleep.
All that bit about the hundred years and the prince is
pure invention. I never said the child would die, and if
Joyeause tried for a thousand years she couldn't change
one of my spells. Joyeause has always been a dilet-
tante.]*

Your father, already offended by Carabosse's attendance at an event to which she was not invited,
became outraged. He raved at me, and I had no
time to remonstrate with him before he dragged
me off to this tower! He says he has hidden you
away and will hide all the spindles in the castle,
perhaps all those in the dukedom. He castigates
himself for marrying one of my race, and me for
being what I am. Men are like that. They marry for
reasons that have nothing to do with what they expect from matrimony and then damn their wives
for not being what they want later. They marry for
beauty and charm and sex, and then expect their
wives to be sensible, parsimonious and efficient.

Now that memory and virginity are restored, I
need not remain here to be insulted. I choose to
return to my ancestral lands. My powers at the moment have been considerably diminished by the
time I have spent here, and I cannot find you to
take you with me. You will find this letter when
you are old enough. If you cannot come to me be-

fore the curse takes effect, come as soon thereafter
as you can. I have left you the means to do so.
Keep safe the box in which you find this.

I put down the letter and wiped my face where the
tears were running down, making an itchy mess of my
eyes and nose. I did have a mama. And evidently I was
not to die on my birthday, though the fate Grandaunt
Joyeause had planned did not seem a thrilling alterna-
tive. I could not understand how Mama expected to
see me after the curse, since even mothers did not, as a
general rule, live more than one hundred years. The
letter continued briefly on a separate page.

My dear daughter, too long separated from me,
be assured of my affection. *Come to me with all
haste before you grow any older.* I will await you
with a joyous heart.

Your loving mama,
Elladine of Ylles.

You can imagine my amazement. I was struck by
how clean the parchment looked upon which all this
had been written. It could have been delivered that
very afternoon. The more I looked at it, the more I
thought that in a sense it had been delivered that very
afternoon. After reading the letter several times, both
pages of it, I replaced it in the box and the box in its
hiding place, sliding the stone carefully into place. Set
well in, it cast no protruding shadow. I could only believe she had left it sticking out so that I would see it.
It had been put there for me, and me alone, to find.
Mama.

I climbed into my bed, pulled the bed curtains shut,
propped myself upon my pillows, and pulled the coverlets up to my chin. This was something that required
thinking about, though thoughts were slow and reluctant to come. The first one to emerge teasingly into the
forefront of my mind was that even though the letter
had been written almost sixteen years before, my
mother was alive, just as I had always supposed. I

thought of Beloved's mother, how she had known at once I was not hers, and something lurched in me, just behind my breastbone.

My next thought was that Elladine had said she had left me the means to find her, though I could not imagine what she meant. The contents of the box included only the ring, the packet of needles and the three hanks of thread. Which led to the fleeting suspicion that Mama, however lovely, might not have had all her wits about her. This would explain the aunts' attitude, certainly. Even women as reconciled to the holy will as the aunts might bridle at having a madwoman in the family. It would also explain papa's locking her in the tower, since such is known to be the fate of madwomen and madmen whenever madness and towers occur in appropriate contiguity. Towers, or, in a pinch, attics.

The letter, however, far from seeming the ravings of lunacy, had been odd but well-reasoned. I was sure that Mama was not mad. Absent, yes, and for reasons that seemed sufficient to her, but not mad. I would have to figure out how to find her.

My final thought was that the name of the wicked aunt was Carabosse. The two adjacent Ss in that name reminded me of something. I got my mysterious thing off the chest and looked at it. One of the letters could be a B, and another an R. Is this the gift she gave me? Is it her name upon it? And if so, what is it?

["Wicked aunt" indeed. I confess, that hurts to read.]

7

DAY OF THE VISITATION,
JULY, YEAR OF OUR LORD 1347

My thoughts and worries concerning my own future
have been somewhat interrupted because the wedding
guests have started to arrive. The day after I found
Mama's letter, Weasel-Rabbit and her entourage came
down the roadway on horseback and in two carriages,
followed by an enveloping cloud of dust. Other parties
arrived thereafter, both large and small, some of them
with marquees they have set up in the meadow as
though they had come to a tourney. All the aunts have
moved together into one suite, and their rooms have
been reserved for various countesses and barons. Poor
Father Raymond is dithering about, trying to remember where he put the festive vestments. The wedding is
to take place in our own chapel; the abbot from St.
Paternus (a great, rich, important abbey down the lake
a bit, near the main road to London) will officiate.
Father Raymond will assist him.

Down in the kitchens, the head cook is screaming
at the kitchen boys and having the tantrum he usually
has whenever he has to cook for more than just the
family. The whole place smells of roasting meat and
baking cakes, spices and stewed fruit. There will be a
banquet each night, three nights running, with the ab-

bot attending the banquet the night before the wedding.

I have resolved to be very good, for the sake of my soul. Aunt Tarragon always goes on about the state of my soul, much more than Father Raymond does, which is odd. Over the past few days I have stayed out of Weasel-Rabbit's way and out of the aunts' way and out of Papa's way in the easiest manner imaginable, by putting on my boy rags and working in the stables. Besides, that lets me see what kind of horses everyone has and whether they look well-treated or not. Weasel-Rabbit has horses which look ill fed and badly groomed, not at all consonant, I feel, with her rather extravagant equippage. Her carriages have tall painted wheels and a suspended, woven bed with soft pillows to sit upon, very elegant. Such carriages would indicate (though the matter had certainly not been discussed with me) that Papa is marrying into a fortune. Since I can not see why anyone would willingly marry Weasel-Rabbit otherwise, it explains a great deal. Supporting five half sisters takes a bit of doing all by itself, and helping get up a new crusade (which Papa talks of from time to time) is frightfully expensive. Just maintaining Westfaire involves constant outlay. Papa needs a wealthy wife, though I can't figure out why such a wealthy woman should have such poorly cared for horses unless she is at the mercy of idle grooms simply because she does not know the difference.

8

The preliminary banquets went quite well. There are enough minstrels about that Aunt Lavender has not felt called upon to entertain us upon the lute. Indeed, all five aunts-in-residence spend most of their time with Sibylla's mama, and I am left largely to myself.

There was one noteworthy encounter in the cloister garth this afternoon. I had gone down to the chapel with Grumpkin, not intending to pray, you understand, but simply to see if Father Raymond ever found the vestments he was looking for. He had. They were stored in a chest in the muniments room and he had finally remembered putting them there himself. While I was talking to Father, Grumpkin fell asleep on one of the prie-dieux so I knelt down at the next one. The chapel was so peaceful, the light in it so rarified and the smell of it so—well, the chapel has a certain smell, though only I seem to be aware of it. I have asked Beloved about it, and I have asked Doll, and even the aunts, but none of them notice it. Perhaps it is only the candles or the incense, though it seems different from that to me. More illusive. Less natural. It is very pleasant to me. It makes me want to go on sniffing at it, as though it were a flower.

At any rate, the chapel smelled so whatever-it-is that I prayed a small prayer and determined to behave myself and not absolutely hate Weasel-Rabbit. I knelt for some time getting this resolution firmly in mind, and then Grumpkin woke up and meowed to go elsewhere. I have noticed that cats are little impressed by religion. We went out of the cool, gray light into the brightness of day. Grumpkin was trailing along as usual, batting at my skirts, when we confronted Sibylla coming out the passageway that leads to the kitchen gardens. She took one look at Grumpkin and let out a howl one might have heard as far as Alderbury. "A cat," she screamed. "A cat."

I should have thought the matter self-evident. There is nothing uncatly about Grumpkin. He is a red and cream-colored tabby of most ferocious mien, and I picked him myself from among the litter the stable mouser kindled three years ago. He is called Grumpkin because his furry eyebrows make him seem always frowning or, at the least, very thoughtful about things. He is indeed a cat, and the matter does not usually occasion remark.

"Get it out of here," screamed Sibylla. "It'll have to be killed. I can't bear cats."

I seized Grumpkin up and went off in the opposite direction, trying very hard to hold on to my resolution not to hate her. I think perhaps I could have persevered in a state of grace if Weasel-Rabbit hadn't gone immediately to Papa, demanding Grumpkin's execution.

I'm not sure Papa even paid much attention. So far as Papa is concerned, horses are simply things one rides upon and dogs are simply things one hunts with and cats are simply animals that infest the stable and are tolerated because they dispose of vermin. I don't think Papa has ever had a pet, but if he ever has, he has long since forgotten it. I'm sure the fact I love Grumpkin never entered his mind. At any rate, he listened to Weasel-Rabbit and then told his scribe to take care of the matter. The scribe told one of the men-at-arms, and the man-at-arms, laughing, mentioned it to Giles. Giles knew how I felt about Grumpkin, even though I'd never said a word to him about it. Well, he watched me, sometimes, so he would know, wouldn't he? People who really look at you do know how you feel. Giles told the other man he'd take care of it and came to find me. He bowed, quite formally, and explained the situation. We talked it over, with me trying very hard not to cry and mostly succeeding, and Giles suggested that he take Grumpkin down to the stables to live with Martin for a time and then report the cat disposed of, which he would have been, in a sense.

Since the feelings I have about Giles are often very hot and tempting ones, I usually try to stay as far away from him as I can. Usually I manage it fairly well, but this time I was so grateful to him about Grumpkin I did not stand a distance from him. I stood very close, where I could smell the warmth of him, and handed Grumpkin to him, telling my good cat to be patient and wait for me. Giles touched my arm when he took Grumpkin from me, not meaning to, I think. I can still feel the place he touched.

All of which made the whole matter even more troublesome and upsetting! It seems that Weasel-Rabbit was determined to take everything away from me. First my room and then my cat! I tried to think what else I might have that Weasel-Rabbit would want, but I couldn't think of anything at all, which just shows how naive I was. The rest of her plan emerged late this afternoon, before the final banquet.

I am not supposed to go into the small anteroom adjacent to the muniments room, which is between the small and large dining halls. The anteroom is a cosy warm place where Papa's steward and bailiff and the scribe work during the daytimes and where male guests sometimes retire after dinner to play at dice or cards or chess and talk about their travels in ways they cannot do while the aunts are present. Hidden behind the tapestries is a little oriel window, covered over because it lets in the cold, and under it a low seat just large enough for me. Sometimes I go there to hide. It is the one place no one has ever found me. If one can bear the boredom of hearing the same stories over and over, one can learn quite a bit about swiving and having one's pleasure and what men of Papa's sort think of various classes and types of women. I have learned that men talk about women quite a lot, when they aren't talking about hunting or fighting, though considering that they use the same words and the same expressions for all three things, perhaps there is not much difference.

I hid there because I wanted to be alone. I was upset over Grumpkin; I was upset over how I felt about Giles; I was trying to keep my resolution, trying very hard to exercise Christian forbearance, which Father Raymond constantly suggests that I do. At any rate, there I was in the oriel window when I heard voices through the tapestry. One, which I had learned to know well, was Sibylla's mama. The other I assumed was the abbot, for Sibylla's mama cooed at him in a tone she uses only with royalty and people of importance.

"Sibylla feels that she cannot take responsibility for the girl, Your Reverence. We have all heard about her mother." The words "her mother" were said in a very low, meaningful voice, the same tone of voice in which Aunt Tarragon talks about certain bodily functions, as though they were both repellent and inevitable. "Sibylla will undoubtedly bear children. She would not want those children exposed to . . . well, you understand. Sibylla feels, and I must concur, that it would be wisest to send Beauty to the convent where her aunts are. She can be with her kindred there. As a nun, she may perhaps expiate some of her mother's . . . well, you understand."

Evidently the abbot did understand. He hemmed and hawed, but he said he would discuss the matter with Phillip, Duke of Monfort, Westfaire, and Ylles, that is, Papa, and see if something couldn't be arranged.

Sibylla had not been content to have only my room and my cat. She also intended to have my future.

Somehow, without even intending it, I found myself back here in my tower room, at my work table with a new quill, a pad of ink, and a bottle of water. Spread out before me was the second page of the letter from mama, which I had rolled backwards to make it lie flat. Mama's writing is not unlike my own. We both write a fine, curly hand. There was plenty of room at the top of the page, and the words seemed to flow out of the pen of their own accord. "This first day of July, year of our Lord, thirteen hundred and forty seven." The wedding was scheduled for the following day, the fifth. Dating mama's letter back to the first allowed four days for the letter to have been on the way from somewhere before reaching me. When the ink was dry, I folded the parchment up and addressed it to "Beauty, the daughter of Duke Phillip of Monfort and Westfaire and the Lady Elladine of Ylles." I sealed it and marked the wax with the signet ring from the box. It shows a winged being which I take to be an angel.

I feel rather glum as I look at what I am to wear to the banquet, a dress provided by Aunt Lavender which has all too obviously been made over from something previously worn by someone else. It has achieved a pallid limpness much like that of the cleaning rags which are always drying on the kitchenyard wall.

I must not succumb to vanity. It does not matter how I look.

9

LATER, MIDNIGHT

As I was about to put on the limp dress, Doll knocked on my door and came in with a gown. It was of heavy India silk, the color of a deep pink rose, worked with silver and seed pearls at the neck and at the edges of the full oversleeves. Beneath the long sleeves were tight sleeves of silver cloth and the underskirt was of silver cloth as well, with roses embroidered in a border at the bottom. It had belonged to my mama, Doll said. All this time it had been folded away in clean linen in one of the attics, awaiting an opportunity to be worn again.

I looked across my room to the dress provided by Aunt Lavender. It was poor, ugly stuff, compared to this. Doll saw my glance and nodded.

"I saw what you were goin' to wear," she said. "Thought it wasn't nice enough. Your mama'd have a fit, seein' you in that. All her clothes are up there in the attic, and you should make use of them."

"Did you like my mama?" I asked Doll.

"Nicest lady ever," she said. "And I don't care what they all say, she wouldn't kill herself."

Well, I'd never thought she had! But there was no time to talk about it, for Doll set about getting me dressed and doing up my hair in a knot in back, with part of it flowing down. Most of the women would be wearing wimples and or headdresses with peaks or wings and veils flowing from them. I hate headdresses because they muffle up my head, but then I wash my hair a lot and most women don't. Washing the hair is dangerous because it fevers the brain, they say, but I'd never noticed mine being anymore fevered than usual.

"There now," Doll said when she was finished with me. "You look a lot like her around the eyes."

I caught her eye in the mirror, and we stared at one another, each knowing exactly what the other was thinking. She had piled my silver-gilt hair up, making it look plentiful and curly. She'd told me before that my eyelashes were as thick and black as Mama's, and my mouth curved just the way Mama's did. The dress fit like a glove, so I knew I was built the way Mama was, too, slender in the waist and nicely plump other places. I even guessed I knew why Doll had found the dress for me. She had got me up to look rather like Mama to remind Papa of Mama because Doll didn't think Mama was dead. I smiled at her and winked. She winked back.

There was no pocket in the pink gown, but it had long, full oversleeves. I broke the seal upon the letter and pinned the letter inside my sleeve.

When I came into the hall, Papa gave me a puzzled look, as though he might have seen me somewhere before. After a bit his face cleared and I knew he had remembered. Then he looked at Weasel-Rabbit for a while, frowning. I could see him thinking that his second wife was a paltry substitute for his first. All the aunts gasped when they saw me, but they didn't dare say anything with the abbot right there at the table. I simply smiled and sat in my place. So there we all were: Sibylla and her mama and my papa and five aunts, also the abbot and Father Raymond and a little princeling from somewhere as guest of honor, looking at me with admiration and saying courtly things. As luck would have it, I was sitting between the princeling and the abbot.

My friend, Giles, was at a table just below me. I

saw him watching me, and I blushed and nodded at
him, letting him know I thanked him for what he had
done. Father Raymond saw me see Giles, and he saw
me blush and nod. I know because his brow furrowed
up, the way it sometimes does, and he looked first at
me, then at Giles, several times.

I waited until everyone was eating hungrily and the
musicians were playing and the wine steward was going around for the second time. Then I said to the
abbot, quite loudly, "Your Reverence, I have the most
amazing news. Today I have received a letter from my
mama."

Silence. Everyone had heard me but Papa, who
was busy telling Aunt Terror about a pilgrimage, and
everyone stopped chewing or talking except Papa.

I said, "It's the most wonderful thing, Your Reverence, though I'm sure you've heard many wonders in
your life. I brought it to show you." And with that I
tugged it out of my sleeve and spread it out on the
table, using his wine flagon to hold it down flat. Everyone was whispering to everyone else. Weasel-Rabbit
had gone dead pale. Her mama had little sweat beads
all over her forehead. The princeling was very attentive, ready to enjoy whatever happened.

The abbot read the letter. He handed it to Father
Raymond. Father Raymond read it, flushed, and gave
it back to the abbot, his mouth in a funny little quirk
as though he couldn't figure out whether to laugh or
frown. The abbot read it again, mumbling it out loud,
then it went to someone else. By this time, Papa had
some idea that something was more than merely a little wrong.

The abbot rose to his feet. "I cannot unite in matrimony a man who already has a living wife," he said,
loud enough for everyone to hear him well below the
salt. He got Papa's attention at last. "Your daughter
has received a letter from her mother. It is dated only
four days ago, and thus we know you have a wife still
living."

"Impossible," said Papa, going very pale.

"Ridiculous," said one or two aunts.

"I knew it," cried Aunt Terror. "I always knew she'd come back just at the wrong time!"

I need say no more about the banquet. Papa was so angry he could not speak. It wasn't an hour after I had come back up to my room that I was startled by the carpenter nailing my door shut. Over the years that poor door has had more than its share of spikes driven through it.

"You thankless wench," Papa cried. "You'll not go off like that flighty witch, your mother."

I feel I have achieved considerably more than I had intended. Disrupting the marriage seemed a good idea, merely to get even with Sibylla. Making Papa furious at me wasn't part of the plan. Papa gets so silly when he gets furious. He puts people in the dungeon and then just forgets about them. We used to have a perfectly marvelous goldsmith who made the most wonderful things. Papa got irritated at him and put him in the dungeon. A month later, Papa wanted the man to make him a new salt, but when they took him out, he was almost dead and didn't recover. Papa was fully capable of going off on another pilgrimage and just leaving me locked in the tower to die. Then, when he got back, having happened on an advantageous marriage opportunity for me, he'd probably ask, "Where's Beauty?"

Remembering what Doll said about the time Mama was nailed up in here, I went out and took the firewood rope down from the spar and coiled it up under my bed. Then I lighted a splinter at the coals of the fire and the candle from the splinter and read Mama's letter again, the first page. The page I had used ended up with the princeling. He purloined it from the abbot, probably intending to take it back to court and share it with everyone, including the King. On reading the first page over, the story of the curse sprang out at me.

Maybe I've reminded Papa of the curse and he has nailed me into the tower to protect me!

It would be nice to believe that, nicer than believing he has shut me up to starve out of pure pique.

However, if Mama's Aunt Carabosse managed to get to my christening without an invitation, it is unlikely she would be forestalled by my being locked in a tower.

I do *not* want to spend the next hundred years lying in this tower room, waiting for some prince to happen by, however charming he may be. The idea is intensely unpleasant and frightening!

Now Papa is down in the stableyard, shouting at Martin. I can see him through a crack in the shutters, pointing up and yelling, while Martin holds up the lantern and shrugs his shoulders as though to say there hasn't been any rope there since I moved in. Good old Martin.

I may as well get a night's sleep. There is nothing I can do until tomorrow.

[We had foreseen all this, down to the details of dress and the menu served at dinner. We had looked deep into the Pool, Israfel and I, and we had foreseen it all.]

10

Early this morning, before light, I got dressed up in my stableboy's clothes (the latest of the several sets I've had since I was eight), put the firewood rope back on the pulley, and let myself down into the stableyard after first letting down all the things I thought I'd need, including Mama's box. I have always had a good head for heights, gained through climbing tall trees on a dare when I was very young, which is a good thing for the tower is extremely tall. Almost as though we'd planned it, Doll and Martin were waiting for me.

"I thought that's what you were thinkin, missy," Martin said, wrinkling his nice face at me. "Clever girl. Just like your mama. She was clever. Nice, too." Then he handed me Grumpkin who settled down in my arms and began to purr.

"Doll," I asked, "did my mama leave anything for me here in the castle? Did she leave money for or anything. A map, maybe?"

"I never heard of any such thing, dearie," she said. She sometimes called me "dearie," though no one else did.

"In the letter, she said she'd left me the means to go find her, but I don't know what she meant."

Doll looked at her feet and turned red in the face and squirmed her hands around in her apron. Martin said, "Tell her, Doll. Somebody's got to tell her."

"You mean about Mama being a witch?" I asked, flushing. "Papa said that when he nailed my door shut."

"She warn't no witch," said Doll, firmly.

"What was she then?" I asked. Looking back on it, I was frightfully stupid, but I really hadn't figured it out. It's not the kind of thing that ordinarily occurs to one.

"She was a fairy," Doll said. "And I heard the abbot talkin' to your aunts this mornin' about havin' your papa's marriage set aside because a fairy can't enter into holy matrimony, anyhow. I've never heard that was so, but you know who gave the abbot that idea."

I did know who had given the abbot that idea. Sibylla or her mama, one or both. A fairy! I should have realized that myself! How could her aunts have been anything but fairies to go about making and changing curses. And how could she have escaped from the tower if she were not a fairy herself? It certainly explained the attitude of the herbal aunts. Fairies would be repugnant to my aunts, I suppose, totally concerned as they are with food or drink or religion. Mama's being a fairy also explained why Weasel-Rabbit wanted me shut up in a convent, and it helped explain Mama's letter. When she'd gotten involved with a mortal, she'd lost her memory of being a fairy. I suppose that's about the only way a fairy could survive married to someone like Papa, or married to any mortal. She could accept it only as long as she didn't remember anything else. Then when Papa had gone off and left her, she'd gradually regained her memory, that and the other thing.

"Am I—am I half fairy?" I asked Doll and Martin. "Does that mean anything?"

They looked at one another and shrugged. It was the kind of question I couldn't expect them to answer.

In fact, the only one who might be able to answer it was Father Raymond.

"Never mind," I said as I turned and left them. I found Father Raymond at last, sitting in the orchard close. I remember the bees making such a sound when I asked him if he knew. He gave me and my boy's clothes a long look, maybe wondering how I'd escaped, but then he smiled. Father Raymond sometimes had a very gentle smile for such an old, creased face, like a sweet stalk of sunshine growing through rough clouds.

"Yes, Beauty, I knew your mama was a fairy," he told me. "She didn't tell me before she married your papa, because she didn't remember. Later, she did tell me, when the matter of your christening came up. I intended to discuss it further with her after the ceremony, just to set her mind at rest, but Duke Phillip had her locked away before I had the chance."

"Why did Mama object to my being baptized?" I asked.

He pursed his lips and made the *hmming* noise in his nose that he makes before he answers complicated questions. "I've always understood that fairies were made when the angels were. Long before men, at any rate. There has been conjecture that there's been some mixing, since. It's said that Cain's wife was a fairy. Since the Scriptures give us no account of God creating him a human wife, it stands to reason he must have married something else, and it's unlikely an angel would have lowered herself so. On the other hand, if people have inherited fairy blood, it would explain the fascination . . ." He looked off into the distance. "Your mother had some other objection. She said something to me about the church stealing her birthright. . . ."

Mama had said that in her letter, though I did not know what she meant. "What about my baptism?" I reminded him.

"Oh. Well, fairies, being separately created, were not tainted by the original sin of our first parents, so baptism—for them—wouldn't be necessary. So much

of what the Lady Elladine had to say was correct. On
the other hand, if the duke is your father, and I have
no real doubt of that," he blushed, obviously remembering that Papa seemed to have sired half the children in Westfaire village, "you are half mortal, and
that half needed to be baptized, which your Mama had
not considered, and it was properly done."

"Holy water and the white cloth around my head
and everything?"

"Exactly so. Exorcised, annointed, and the chrisom
bound round your head."

"Are they Christians?" I asked him. "F . . . that
is, my mother's people? Or are they infidels?"

"Well now," he wrinkled his brow at me. "I don't
think that question would mean much to ah . . .
them. If they are immortal, then they don't die. If they
don't die, they don't fear hell. If they don't fear hell,
then they aren't stained by sin. If they aren't stained
by sin, why would they need to be Christians? Or you
can argue it frontwards to the same effect. The question of their being infidels doesn't apply, does it?"

Which just shows you that even though Father
Raymond was old and a little dithery he was still capable of reasoned argument.

*[Which just goes to show you how much sheer fan-
tasy exists even outside Faery.]*

"Then Mama wasn't trying to keep me from being
a Christian?" I asked. "When she told Papa it wasn't
necessary?" There was more to this than he had told
me, but I had no idea what it was. Mama had seemed
to blame religion for something to do with her people,
and nothing Father Raymond had said had explained
that.

"I think it more likely she just made a oversight in
theology," Father Raymond said. "She thought it
wasn't necessary, forgetting you were half mortal. We
can't blame her, after all. I don't imagine fairies spend
much time studying catechism. In any case, I was there
and I heard your fairy aunts giving you some very nice

gifts, and you've always been a very good girl, so don't worry your head about it."

"What nice gifts did they give me?" I asked, though Mama had already told me.

"Oh, they gave you a good nature, for one thing. And charm."

I hadn't known about those, particularly the good-nature one. Sometimes I didn't feel at all good-natured.

"By the way, Beauty," he said. "I wanted to be the one to tell you that Giles has gone away on a journey for me."

"Giles," I said stupidly. "Giles?" wanting to cry.

"He'll be away for a year or so," he said, watching me intently. I didn't say anything. After a moment he asked, "Is there something you need to tell me?"

I just stared at him, hating him. Then not hating him, just blank inside. There was a hole there that nothing would fill, ever. Father Raymond had done it for me, because he thought it was best, but I wished he hadn't.

I shook my head at him, "No, Father." I had nothing to tell him, nothing at all. There was a lump in my throat, and I could hardly get the words out. There was nothing I wanted to tell him ever again.

"Well then," he said, trying to be comforting. "Well then."

By the time Giles comes back, I will either be dead, or married, or asleep for a hundred years, or gone off looking for my mama, and who knows if I will ever return.

11

[When Elladine of Ylles had written her letter to her daughter, my hand had helped move the quill. Not that Elladine is incapable of either writing a letter or loving a daughter, but when she writes she is prolix and when she loves she is sentimental rather than sensible. She gave no thought to what would be involved in loving a half mortal child. Elladine is like others in Faery who have taken the easy way. Like Joyeause, she dabbles. Power is painful, in the getting and the keeping, and Elladine has never thought it worth the pain. So, she flutters and travels and glamorizes and enchants and now and again falls in love, sometimes with mortals. Knowing this, I inserted some words in her letter and removed many others and put the box in her hand already equipped.

Israfel and I were counting on the love of a child for its mother. We had no mothers; we have born no children; so we take the matter largely on faith, but we counted on it nonetheless. Beauty would long to see her mother, off she would go to the place we'd prepared for her, a place remote from the real worlds, a place where the Dark Lord would not think of going for any reason, in short: Chinanga.

Chinanga is one of the imaginary worlds, well off the mainline of invention. It had taken me a long time to find it, and I'd been looking for it. No one who was

*not looking for it would be likely to stumble over it.
Elladine would get there only shortly before Beauty
herself arrived (Israfel and I had arranged that, as
well); once there they could get to know each other, safe
in a place time could not touch. So we planned.*

*Further, we planned—deviously, dangerously—for
Beauty to leave Westfaire without anyone knowing she
was gone. She would make use of the things in the box,
and when the time was right, she would be ready!*

*Unfortunately, we had overlooked who she is and
what she is carrying and what Westfaire is, as well. We
overlooked the forces that bound them together!*

*Beauty did not make ready to go off in search of her
mother! Instead, she found reasons for delay!]*

ANOTHER TIME. ANOTHER DAY.
I DON'T KNOW WHEN, YET.

In the days that followed Giles's departure, while I
was still supposedly nailed into the tower, I moved
freely about the stables, fretting about the three significant events soon to occur: my approaching birthday
(which I was determined to survive without being victim of the curse), Papa's postponed marriage to Sibylla
(to take place when he got matters straightened out
with the church), and my departure in search of my
mama, happenings that would occur, I presumed,
more or less in that order even though I *knew* I should
forget about the birthday *and* the wedding and just *go*,
now, while I had the chance. Good sense said go,
voices in my head said go, dreams said go, but my
stomach said stay.

I found myself making excuses to go into the great
hall and look at the dome, excuses to walk along the
walls, peering at the mosaic floors, excuses to go upstairs and downstairs, slowly, listening to the sounds,
smelling the smells. I found myself crying at odd moments at the thought of leaving Westfaire at all, and
besides, as I frequently told myself, it is hard to plan a
journey when one has no idea where one is going.

I'd never felt quite so alone and lost before. Always before, in the back of my mind, Giles had been there, sturdy and dependable. I'd always known I could go to him if there was real trouble. Or, Father Raymond had been there. Now Giles was gone, and since Father Raymond had sent him away, I couldn't count on him either. Papa and the aunts were just useless. Martin didn't have time to help. Doll was busy, bustling around, directing the other maids who were carrying water up and chamber pots down. I grabbed her arm and made her listen to me.

"Mama said she left me means to find her, but all she left me was this box," I told Doll. "I can't find anything helpful in it." I showed it to her. She looked at it and its contents, quickly, between doing two other things, at the packet of needles and at the signet ring with what I now recognized as a fairy on it and the three hanks of thread: heavy brown, medium black, and fine, silken white. She shook the box to see if there was anything else inside, but there was no secret compartment. It is just a wooden box, and not a very big one.

"If the Lady your mother said she left something for you, then she did," said Doll. "And if this box is all you have, then this box is what she meant. You keep it safe. Sooner or later, you'll find out what it's for." She turned away from me to tell a new servant not to use the Duchess's Staircase, which is what they called the wide curving graceful flight which comes up from the great hall.

"I wish I knew what to do with it," I complained, wishing Doll would pay attention to me. Wishing somebody would.

"Well, you could sew with it," suggested Doll, glaring at me. "That's what people usually do with needles and thread, and it would keep you from bothering me while I get this work done." She ran off after the new maid, who'd gone in the wrong direction.

My feelings were hurt, but the suggestion made sense. I went into one of the attics and scruffed around, discovering some lengths of black tussah silk, probably left over from Grandma's time. I took them and a handful of nuts and some dried apples into the empty stall I'd been occupying to keep me out of the aunts' way and sat myself down on a pile of straw to sew, which was one thing I'd learned to do pretty well in sixteen years, believe me. In the winter there's not much else to do. I've done enough cushion covers and mended enough tapestries to stretch from Westfaire to East Sawley, plus all the hours spent with Aunt Marj mending bodices or starting new tapestries that won't get finished for a hundred years. I told myself that if the curse got me, and if they went on working while I was asleep, the tapestries might be finished in time for my awakening a century from now, in 1447. The fifteenth century!

For the first time, I realized what that meant! If I slept for a hundred years, all the aunts and Papa would be dead. Papa would probably die before Sibylla did. With him gone, Sibylla would probably store my sleeping body in a cellar somewhere, if she didn't go ahead and bury me, out of spite! And then, when Sibylla died, who would come after her?

I imagined Westfaire abandoned, wrecked, sold off to pay Sibylla's debts, and I wanted to scream. And who was going to take care of a sleeping person for a hundred years? I simply couldn't see Sibylla or her children caring whether I lived to wake up or not!

I made myself stop thinking about it by laying out the fabric and the thread and measuring both carefully to see whether there was enough to make a cloak. Straight cloaks are very easy. Father Raymond taught me the pattern, because they're almost the same as the monks wear, except the monks' don't open down the front. First you cut one flat piece as long as from your shoulders to your heels and wider across than your shoulders, for the back. Then you cut four more pieces, the same length and half that wide. Two of these are for the front. The third one gets cut in half, and then each piece folded in half again for sleeves. The last one gets cut in half, and one of the halves gets folded with one end sewed shut for the hood. The hood piece gets gathered on at the neck, which is the hardest part, and if you're not careful it leaves an ugly bunch of puckers on the inside. If you want to get fancy, you can use the other sleeve-sized piece to make pockets. Since I had a lot of time on my hands, I got fancy and made great deep pockets on both sides. By noon, I had it mostly done except for sewing braid around the hood and down the front to finish it off. I'd used the sides of the cloth, what Dame Blossom calls the self-edge, for the edges of the sleeves and front, so all I had to do was hem up was the bottom. I heard Doll's voice outside, so I put it on and went out to show her.

I stood there, turning around for her to admire me, and she looked right through me at Martin and said, "Where's Beauty?"

"Don't know," said Martin. "Haven't seen her since this morning early."

"The whole herb garden met and decided they didn't dare let her out of the tower because of her Papa," said Doll. "They say he'll be home for her birthday celebration and he'll let her out then."

I walked a little closer to Doll, flapped my cloak arms at her. She didn't even blink.

"But then they decided she might starve by then," Doll went on. "They're in there now, tryin' to decide what to do about that."

"How do they expect to feed her?" Martin snorted. "Send nut meats up by pigeon?"

Martin didn't see me. Doll didn't see me. They weren't pretending not to see me; they really didn't see me. It took me a moment, but I finally realized why. The black thread had sewn a cloak of invisibility, which is something a fairy gift might be expected to do. It was all perfectly logical. I went back in the stall and took the cloak off, wrapped it in the sack I'd brought my things down in, then came out again carrying the mostly finished cloak wrapped in a neat bundle.

"There you are, Beauty," Doll said at once. "Your aunts decided they couldn't let you loose without making your father murderous at them, but they're not planning on letting you starve, either, though you'd be a bit hungry by the time they agree on how they'll get you fed. No point in having Martin haul you back up there, far's I can see. Do you want to hide out here in the stables or up in the servant's quarters? There's empty rooms up there."

I said I'd stay in the stables, as it was airier and cooler than the attics where the maids lived, though the flies were much worse. The fact that the aunts wouldn't turn me loose made me very curious as to what was going on, so I went around the corner, put my new cloak back on and wandered into the castle to hear what I could hear. Not surprisingly, no one noticed me. No one at all except Grumpkin, who insisted on trailing along, batting at my skirts just as he always did. Fairy things don't impress cats. Fairy things and holy things. Cats are, perhaps, a separate creation.

I drifted along to my old rooms near the kitchen, wanting to know just what Sibylla was up to, and a good thing I did, for the little Weasel-Rabbit was up to nothing good.

"She has to die," she was snarling to her mother as I sneaked in through the slightly open door. "Duke Phillip's daughter must die."

She disliked calling me, "Beauty," I'd noticed. She usually referred to me as "Duke Phillip's daughter." There were certainly a lot of people wanting me dead. Evil fairy aunts. Wicked stepmothers.

"I had thought," her mother said in a fussy little coo, "I really had thought that having her enter the convent at Alderbury would be sufficient."

"Not at all," said Weasel-Rabbit. "I've spent all morning going over things with Phillip's steward. In the marriage agreement between Phillip and Elladine, she tied up her dowry for her children. If that girl goes into a convent, the convent will claim Elladine's estate as dowry. They certainly won't let the girl into the convent without one!"

"I thought their marriage could be set aside!"

"If the marriage is set aside, the Duke will have *no* right to the estates in Ylles. If there had been no marriage, there could have been no dowry. If the one did not exist, certainly neither did the other!" Sibylla stamped her foot in vexation. "No, the only way is if she dies. With her dead, Phillip will inherit everything she owns."

"Why is it so important? Surely there is enough here . . ."

Sibylla laughed, a long, mirthless laugh. "Oh, Mother, we have miscalculated most stupidly. There is little or nothing left here. Affairs are in a shocking state. The estates in Ylles and Castle Westfaire itself are virtually the only property the man has not pledged to the moneylenders. The only reason he hasn't pledged the estates in Ylles is that he has not been free to do so. Beauty seems to own them, though I believe she is not aware of that fact. The Duke never talks to her about anything, thank God. He scarcely knows she is alive except when she annoys him. He will not grieve greatly when she is gone."

I found myself crouching along the wall, my face wet. I knew what she said was the truth, but it was very hard to hear.

"It is unheard-of to pledge land," Sibylla's mama whined. "No nobleman of honor would pledge land. Why has he not sold his villeins their freedom instead? Or pledged the crops?"

Even I knew the answer to that question, but I remained silent, wiping at my eyes, as Weasel-Rabbit answered.

"He has done all that. I think he would have sold his soul if it had brought him a few guineas. Evidently there was an indebtedness left from the rebuilding of Westfaire in a previous generation. Phillip's father speculated in order to clear this indebtedness and succeeded only in increasing it. Phillip himself goes to shrines and prays for a fortune. He feels only divine intervention will save him."

"Perhaps we had best try again, with someone better off."

"We haven't the time or money to try again," snarled Sibylla. "The estates at Ylles have good revenues, and though we have not seen them, undoubtedly they will do well enough!"

"Ah," said Weasel-Rabbit's mother in a discontented voice. "I suppose it must be done before Phillip finds out your own dowry is as much fakery as the wealth he promised us. He won't be impressed by hired carriages for long."

Well, well, I thought as I wandered out into the corridor again. Here was a pretty mess. Papa wanted to marry a fortune. Sibylla wanted to marry a fortune. Both pretended to have one, and both were as poor as lackeys. Who had the fortune? I did. Or rather, Mama did, since she was alive and well, assuming she was alive and well, which I did assume. Though there had been no recent word of her (despite the letter I had misdated), I simply knew that she had suffered no harm. Something inside me declared this to be incontrovertibly so. She was waiting for me, and I had to go to her.

As I was lost in contemplation, Sibylla came out into the hallway and let out a screech to wake the dead. Grumpkin was there, playing with an invisible something, and Sibylla shrieked for someone to come kill the animal at once. I swept him up, hiding him in a fold of the cloak, and went back out to the stables while she had hysterics behind me, screaming about a cat that had disappeared. My only thought was that my life wasn't worth a fig in that place.

"Where is Ylles?" I asked Martin.

"Eels?" he queried. "In the river, Beauty, some seasons. And in the sea others, so I hear."

"Not the fish, Martin. The place. A town, maybe?"

Doll came out just then, so I asked her as well. She didn't know.

"Mama signed her letter 'Elladine of Ylles,' " I told her. "That means it has to be a place, somewhere."

No one knew. I told Doll to ask Aunt Terror and Aunt Basil, but neither of them had ever heard of Ylles, except as an adjunct to Mama's name, and they got quite offended at being asked by a servant. So I went to the anteroom where Papa's steward keeps things. He wasn't there, or the scribe either, for which I was very grateful. The man always wanted to touch me, just a little. Hand on wrist. Arm against arm. Brushing against me in the hall. You know the kind of thing. Whenever I smiled at him, he melted down into a puddle and just lay there, quivering with inarticulate desire. There is something intensely repugnant about people wanting you in that way. That is, unless you want them back.

I could find nothing that helped. So far as the contracts were concerned, none of them gave direction to Ylles. By the time I had looked through all the dusty scrolls that seemed at all likely to tell me anything, I was starving.

I stopped in the kitchens to sneak some supper. Cold game pie and a lump of cheese out of the firkin in the storeroom. In the stables I chewed and stared at the other hanks of thread, a brown one and a white one. The brown thread was heavy and waxy. It looked familiar to me, and after a time I figured out that it looked like the thread the shoemaker in the village used. Thread to sew leather, which could mean anything at all. I had no way of knowing what. Something kept teasing at me, as though someone might be trying to whisper words in my ear, and I shook my head in annoyance. If I was half fairy, it had to be my bottom half, for my head told me nothing useful. I put the thread down, and found myself picking it up again. Put it down, pick it up. At length I got tired of thinking about it and went to sleep in the hay with Grumpkin curled up beside me.

[I have said elsewhere that Beauty is not particularly intelligent. The sewing kit was the simplest, easiest method Israfel and I could think of to let her seek her mother with the magical powers to which she was born. She has already sewn a cloak; common sense should dictate that the other threads will sew other magical garments! Stories of such garments are current in every hamlet! I cannot recall ever having felt quite so frus-

trated before. She will need the other garments very soon! I keep whispering, "Use the thread and needles," but all she does is yawn!]

I was so weary from it all that I didn't wake up until the middle of the night when I heard people shouting. They were shouting because the dove tower was burning. Of course, I wasn't in it, though no one but Doll and Martin knew that. Except for my carpet, nothing I treasured was in it, which was a good thing because there was little enough left of the tower when the flames were finally extinguished.

I went to Father Raymond, being very cool and dignified, and told him I'd escaped sure death because I hadn't been in my room. I said I believed Sibylla had set the fire. I told him why. I said my life wasn't worth a rotten apple in that place anymore, and I was going away very soon to join my mama. I said that, once I was well away, he could tell everyone I'd gone on a pilgrimage. That would prevent Sibylla laying hands on my dowry lands. He asked me where, and I said I wasn't sure, but I'd figure it out when I got started.

"Oh, Beauty," he sighed at me. "I suppose I might have expected it." He reached for my hand, but I stepped away from him. He had sent Giles away without talking to me about it, and therefore he was no longer really my friend.

"I'm not going until after my birthday, though," I said in a formal voice which only shook a little. "Which is day after tomorrow."

"If you're determined to go, I should think going before would be safer," he advised me. "Just in case there's something to the curse. Or another fire."

"There is undoubtedly *something* to the curse," I said, "Just as there is undoubtedly *something* to Sibylla's burning the tower. However, I will simply not be driven from my home before I am ready to go!" The truth was that the thought of leaving made me so panicky and scared I couldn't do it. I kept putting it off, until this, until that.

"What shall I tell your aunts?" he asked. "They'll wonder why you aren't dead?"

"Tell them I escaped certain death through a miracle. An angel wakened me and opened the door to let me out." I thought I was being pert, but he told them exactly that. Sometimes I think Father Raymond doesn't take things as seriously as he pretends to. Except love. He saw I loved Giles, and he took that seriously. I did love Giles. I do love Giles.

Between the fire and Father Raymond's mention of the curse, I decided it was time to make a few defensive plans. While Sibylla and her mama muttered in the corner and I sat safely among the aunts, being exclaimed over for having occasioned divine intervention, I came up with a stratagem.

The working of it was dependent upon the fact that Beloved knew nothing at all about the curse. It was not something that had been generally discussed (though the aunts had whispered about it when they thought I couldn't hear). Even I had not known of it until I read the first page of Mama's letter, but no one knew about that page of the letter but me. Add to this the fact that Beloved adored parties. She loved being "me." As a result, on the following day, she eagerly fell in with my plan that she play my part on my birthday in order that for a few hours I might escape—so I told her—the edge of Sibylla's tongue. We had spent hours talking over every aspect of the Sibylla matter, and Beloved liked her no better than I did.

Papa was to be home for the celebration. Of the neighboring nobility, a few of the nearest had been invited to a modest banquet in honor of the occasion. Beloved and I spent some time going over the guest list so that she would know who they were and how to address them. She loved to speak the affected Frenchiness of the aristocracy rather than the uncouth but lively tongue of the common people, and she did it so well that no one knew she had not been reared in the castle. We shared this ability of mimicry, she and I, which we must mutually have inherited from Papa, though I had never known him to make use of it.

Very early on our birthday morning, she came to my room—the room I was using in Papa's wing, though I had slept in the stables overnight, just to be safe—and put on my clothes. I told her to be careful of her language and not to look for me until dark. Then I went out, put on my cloak and waited halfway down the Duchess's Staircase to see what happened. As I had more or less expected, by midmorning Beloved was being fussed over and adorned and prepared for the banquet, while the aunts peered into corners (looking for spindles no doubt) and made little cooing calls to the Virgin for protection against evil as they fingered their missals in their pockets.

Grumpkin was not fooled. He knew who was who, and he insisted upon following me about in a worried fashion, so I tucked him into one of the deep pockets, his large, scowling face peering out, visible to me but invisible to anyone else. Though he was a big, heavy cat, I preferred to do this rather than shut him up in the stables. Later, of course, I was to thank God that I had done so. God. Or someone.

[Not I! Israfel and I had never concerned ourselves with her cat!]

Afternoon came. The guests began to arrive for the banquet, which Aunts Lovage and Basil had arranged to be held in the late afternoon or very early evening in order to allow the guests to get home before full dark. The aunts buzzed about in a flurry of hospitality, and I saw Beloved, momentarily ignored, looking annoyed, as though she had a pain. I saw her yawn and lick her teeth. I followed her as she wandered back through the large dining hall and opened the door leading to the enclosed garden outside the high windows.

I knew then that her expression had been the result of simple hunger. She had been so busy being dressed and fussed over, she hadn't had any lunch, and now she was starved and had remembered the apricot tree in that garden. We'd spent many stuffed and sticky

July afternoons there, fighting the wasps for the fruits.
The moment the door opened, I smelled them, heavy
as incense, more fragrant than I had ever known them
to be before.

Grumpkin muttered something and put a paw on
my hand. I stopped to hush him before following her.
"Be still," I said. "You don't want her to know we're
here." Then I went out after Beloved, arriving just in
time to hear a fading burst of cackling laughter and
catch a glimpse of a pair of burning eyes disappearing
in midair.

*[I had let myself be seen. Now surely she would
leave Westfaire and go in search of Elladine. I had put
the thread in her hands a dozen times! Surely now she
would go where we had planned for her to go, where we
could protect what she carried, forever if need be. I
faded into invisibility and remained there, watching,
mentally urging her to go.]*

Beloved was facing me, weaving a little on her legs,
a look of faint astonishment in her eyes. Though she
could not have seen me, her right hand was extended
as though to hand me something. It was a spindle, precisely as it had been described to me: a spiky thing that
looked rather like a spinning top. I put my hands behind my back. The spindle fell even as I moved toward
her, and she went down with it, crumpling, knees and
hips and then shoulders and arms, falling in a loose
pile, like washing. I kicked the spindle thing away and
knelt beside her. Her face was quite peaceful, as
though she was sleeping, as indeed she was, though a
sleep of a strange and terrible depth. Her breast barely
moved. Her skin was chill. A pallor had fallen over her
skin so that she seemed to be carved of ivory.

For a moment, I could not think at all. My mind
was blank. I straightened Beloved out, pulled her
skirts down and folded her hands on her breast, my
tears spotting the satin of her bodice. I left the spindle
where I had kicked it, not daring to touch it. I hadn't
really. . . . I had thought the curse wouldn't function

if it couldn't find me. . . . I had never considered that. . . . Or had I? I didn't know. Had I planned it, or not? The wording of the final curse referred to "Duke Phillip's daughter on her birthday." She was as much his daughter as I was. It was her birthday as much as mine. I had known that!

I fled back through the dining room, seeking help, and was sent sprawling when I tripped over the body of one of the footmen lying beside a trayload of scattered flagons. In my daze, I assumed he had seen what happened to Beloved and had fainted. Even when I reached the hallway and began to find other bodies, I did not immediately realize what had happened. Only when I found Aunt Lavender fallen prone across her lute did I realize that the malediction had been modified by Aunt Joyeause not only to send Duke Phillip's daughter to sleep, but to include everyone at Westfaire. I had worried about what people would do with a princess who slept for a hundred years! It seemed they would do nothing at all, for she was not to sleep alone. When she regained consciousness, a hundred years in the future, all her court would still be around her, though it was not Beloved's court, but mine.

I found Doll and Martin asleep in the stables and Dame Blossom asleep at her loom. In the village, everyone slept. The shoemaker and the tailor and the potter and the tanner and all. I howled for some little time, as frightened as I have ever been, while I ran about through the barns and stables, the armory, the dormitories of the men-at-arms, the kitchens, the granary, the orchards, through every house in the village by the walls. Everyone was asleep, guests and all. Every living thing. The cattle in the byre were asleep, and the chickens in their pens, and the swine, the piglets laid out like rows of barely breathing bottles at their mother's swollen teats. Wasps slept on the fruit on the sunlit walls. Spiders slept in their webs. The weevil slept at the heart of the rose. Papa's dogs lay indolently in the sun, as unmoving as the painted wooden saints in the chapel.

And in that chapel Father Raymond slept beside

Papa—who had arrived home only that morning—
both of them on a bench, propped upright by each
others bodies. Papa's mouth was open and the faint,
infrequent breaths hissed across my ear when I leaned
down to shake him. I inadvertently dislodged him so
that he fell sidewise, onto the bench, but his sleep did
not break, nor did that of Father Raymond when I
clung to him, wetting his surplice with my tears. He
held a piece of paper in his hand. Evidently something
he and Papa had been looking at. It caught my eye
because I saw my name on it.

It was addressed to Father Raymond. "Tell Beauty
that I love her forever," it said. "Tell her I honor her
always. Tell her I would never have done anything to
hurt her. Tell her no matter what distance separates
us, I will love her still." It was signed by Giles. Father
Raymond had not shown it to me. He had shown it to
Papa! I hated them both for that, but I could not stand
there doing it. I put the letter in my pocket and ran on.

The sleepers included even Sibylla and her mother.
I found them in the scribe's office, lying atop Mama's
marriage contract in an uncomfortable looking heap. I
left them that way, hoping when they woke they would
have cramps. Of all living things in all the lands of
Westfaire, only Grumpkin and I were free to move
about because we were cloaked in magic and invisible
to the enchantment. Grumpkin wanted to leave my
pocket, but I did not dare let him go.

I cannot remember what I did then for a while.
Though a few other guests had been expected, none
arrived. It was as though the castle had been set aside
from mortal lands. The sun sank slowly, and I with it.
For a time I huddled on the stairs, crying, Grumpkin
patting my face with his paws and making the small,
trilling noise he makes when he seeks catly companionship, his love call. I clung to him and wept. I reread
Giles's letter and wept.

Tears changed nothing. Eventually, my eyes dried
and I realized I had no choice but to go. There was no
way I could stay in this place. No way I could maintain
myself. I made myself think carefully about going

away, made myself consider calmly the things I would need to take with me, gritting my teeth so hard that later my jaws hurt. I needed money. The keys to Papa's chest were around his neck, and the coin he had available, poor though Sibylla had said he was, was locked in the chest in his room. Also in the chest were two warrants making claims upon usurers in London, and I took them both. Papa or his man-of-business had evidently tried to delay the final reckoning by deferring payment of current expenses and putting current income into the hands of the Jews to collect interest. Usury was a sin for Christians, but then so was lust, and Papa had not balked at that. I think anything done to excess must be sinful, including pilgrimages, but if so the poor man was paying for his sins. If he had not neglected Mama, I kept telling myself, none of this would have happened.

The aunts had some jewels, which I did not hesitate to purloin. They would not need them for one hundred years, and I needed them now. There was the Monfort parure of emeralds and diamonds that Papa intended to give Sibylla for a wedding gift. I took that, too, though I suspected the gems might not be the real ones. Surely Papa had sold them, poor as he was. I wondered how much Papa had received for the jewels when he had sold them and what he had spent it on. If, indeed, Grandfather had not sold the emeralds in his own time and put the money into rebuilding Westfaire.

The last thing I did before I left was to drag Beloved in from the garden. I could not carry her up the stairs into my tower room, which seemed most fitting, but then, what is fitting at such a time? Where are Sleeping Beauties supposed to lie? Towers come inevitably to mind. Towers or perhaps bowers or enchanted tombs of glass. I could manage none of them. Half fairy or no, I had no powers that I was aware of. Perhaps my mama would have managed better. Besides, the tower was burned and there was nothing there except my mysterious thing, sitting untouched upon the window ledge, with charcoal all about it.

As it was, I got Beloved onto the table in the small
dining room and covered her with a brocade hanging,
bringing it neatly up under her chin, placing a cushion
under her head, doing what I could to make her long
sleep a comfortable one. I wondered if she would turn
over in that sleep and found myself giggling hysterically at the thought. "I'm sorry Beloved," I cried.
"Sorry!"

It was pure hypocrisy. Suppose I had known what
was going to happen, wouldn't I have done the same
thing again? I may even have known what would happen without admitting it to myself. Even then I caught
myself thinking, better Beloved than I. She would be
thrilled to be awakened by a prince, and why not? It
was a far finer fate than a weaver's daughter could
ordinarily expect.

As I stood looking at her, I was aware of two
things: first, that Westfaire was redolent of that odor I
had always associated with the chapel; and second,
that there was an aura of glamour which flowed from
Beloved's form in a swelling tide. When I went out
into the hall, the aura came after me, a shining mist of
silent mystery, an emanation of the marvelous. Every
stone of the hallway throbbed with it, giving my footsteps back to me like the slow beat of a wondrous
drum or some great heart that pulsed below the castle,
making the very stones reverberate with its movement.
Above me the lacelike fan vault sparkled like gems;
through the windows the sunbeams shimmered with a
golden, sunset glow. Once outside, I looked up at the
towers and caught my breath, for they had never
seemed so graceful. Over the garden walls the labur-
num dangled golden chains, reflowered on this summer evening as though it were yet spring. In fact,
springtime had miraculously returned. In the corners
the lilacs hung in royal purple trusses, and roses filled
the air with a fragrance deep as smoke.

All around me beauty wove itself, beauty and the
strange, somehow familiar smell of the place. Westfaire became an eternal evening in an eternal May, the
sun slanting in from the west as though under a cloud,

making the orchards and gardens gleam in a green as marvelous as the light in the gems I carried. Slowly the sun moved down, and I feared it would not rise again on Westfaire for a hundred long years.

I took myself away from the castle, across the wide gardens and lawns to the tall inner walls built when the castle was renewed. Outside these walls the moat reached around from the lake on one side to the lake on the other, filled by its waters. The heavy bridge was down. My footfalls thudded on the timbers as I crossed, then fell silent in the dust of the village street. Little shops and houses huddled in quiet, thatch glowing like gold, walls flushed by sun. Beyond the village lay the paddocks and the commons, and past them the outer walls, all that was left of the first Westfaire, built so long ago that men had forgotten when—low, massive ramparts with squat watchtowers and a fanged portcullis—and beyond that the final bridge and the road leading to the outside world.

I went out, hearing my lonely footsteps, remembering the sounds of carriages and horsemen, listening in the silence for a sound that did not come. Beyond the last bridge, at the limit of the castle lands, I stopped in amazement to confront a waist-high hedge of briar rose which rustled with savage and implacable life, pulsing in the smell of magic as it grew ever taller. Was this part of the curse or part of the amelioration? To either side of me the hedge stretched in a wide circle, enclosing the outer walls, reaching back on either side to the shores of the lake, hiding what had always been my home.

I pushed my way through, crying out as the thorns tore at my arms, thankful for the thick fabric of the cloak I wore. Once outside the limits of the enchantment, I took off the cloak and changed my clothes. It would not do for a woman to walk about on the roads alone, though it was safer in the country than in the cities, where gangs of youths roamed about seeking unprotected women to abuse and ruin. I had already decided to wear my grubby boy clothes, which would attract no one's interest. Then, tears still running down

my face, with my hair twisted up under a grubby cap,
and with everything I owned in a sack over my shoulder, I went away from there. At the roadside not far
distant stood a pale arm of stone which emerged from
the forest in a tumbled wall topped by a rock shaped
like a cat's head. Under that rock was a little cave
Grumpkin and I had discovered long ago. We called it
the cathole. It was a place to secrete treasures, a place
for Grumpkin to hide in, a place I had hidden in once
or twice myself as a little child, though I had outgrown
it long since. Now I stopped and put most of the
wealth I carried inside it, stopping the opening with a
few head-sized stones well wedged into place with
smaller bits of rock. The aunts had often warned
against the robbers at large in the world, robbers and
ruffians and villains of all sorts. Hiding a part of what I
had would save it against later need.

I kept some coin in my sack. Though they might
not be real, I kept the emeralds wrapped up in rags:
collar, circlet, two brooches, and a bracelet. I kept one
warrant on a usurer. The rest of the jewelry and coin
and the other warrant, I secreted away. Once this was
done, I started on my way again, wishing I had a horse.
It had been a weary and frightening day.

As I came from behind the stone, I saw a shattered
gleam of sun on the flower-gathering hill, as though a
man in armor had moved and reflected the light. I
thought of Giles, my heart leaping up. He had known I
needed him and had come home! Grumpkin cried, and
I held him in my arms as I ran toward that gleam of
light, telling myself it was Giles, it couldn't be Giles,
perhaps it was only a knight, but perhaps he had a
spare horse he might let me ride, or even a horse and
saddle I might buy. I had not gone far before
Grumpkin snarled, sensing presences I did not. He
would not have snarled at Giles.

*[We had not foreseen this! We had planned on
Mary Blossom taking Beauty's place, but we had not
foreseen this!]*

The men and women I came upon were doing something incomprehensible. They moved among contrivances, among strange apparatus, boxes which hummed and winked and made noises like the midnight peeps of startled birds. There were five persons, some men, some women, though it was hard to tell which were which. They were clad much alike, and my impression of maleness and femaleness came more from stance and stature than from any other regard.

I saw them before they saw me. I should have stopped, turned, gone somewhere else, but it is a measure of my distraction and pain that I simply kept walking, mouth open, eyes fixed on them, wondering vaguely who they were and what they were doing on the May flower hill.

[Nothing in our calculations had included this! These people came from a time the Pool could no longer reach, a time beyond the veil, where I could not see. . . .]

"Did you get time lapse shots of the hedge?" the oldest of the men cried, his voice urgent.

"Time lapse, hell," answered the tallest, heaviest man, his eye fixed to the end of the convoluted box he held upon his shoulder. "It's fast enough to show without lapse. Look at the damn thing! It's fairly crawling into the sky!"

I turned. The hedge had grown up behind me and was now higher than my head. Tendrils at the top reached upward like hands, clutching at the clouds. I felt a sob pressing upward and choked it down. Now was no time to give way, however much I needed to do so.

"What are you doing?" I cried, stepping from behind the bush.

[I actually reached out to stop her, but she moved too quickly.]

They turned, mouths open, staring. Almost simultaneously, two who had not spoken before said:

"Oh, shit!"

"That's torn it. Hell!"

Not a polite greeting, considering everything, though not necessarily hostile.

"What in the bloody hell are you doing here?" asked one of the women in an offended voice. "There's not supposed to be anyone here!" Her accent was strange. It took me a moment to figure out what she had said.

I shook my head, almost unable to respond. "Coming home," I mumbled. "From market."

I saw them mouthing the words, having the same difficulty I had had in understanding what they heard. Evidently my tongue was not their native speech.

The oldest man turned to one of others, throwing up his hands. "What do we do about this, Alice?"

"How the hell am I supposed to know, Martin," the one called Alice replied. "If this shows up on the monitors, they'll have our guts for dinner."

"What's your name, boy?" Martin asked. His gray hair was combed back from his face, almost as short as the woman's.

"I am Havoc, the miller's son," I mumbled. It was the name I had used with Martin since I was tiny. There was no time or need to invent another.

"Damn," he said again, thrusting parts of his apparatus into cases. "Jaybee, you got enough footage? Bill, ready? There are only minutes left."

The man addressed as Bill turned his face toward me, grimacing. He was shorter than I, the height of a child, with hair the color of ripe apricots, and he wore the same kind of singlet and trousers as the others. "Ready," he said, staring at me with something like pity in his eyes.

I did not understand the word "footage."

"Janice?"

The other woman looked into the eyes of her contrivance and nodded. "Plenty," she said in a cold voice. Her hair was white as snow, but she was not an old woman. Her eyes when she looked up at me were hard and black, like fowls' eyes.

"What are you doing here?" I wanted to know.

The white-haired woman laughed, a quick bark of laughter. "A documentary, boy. We are recording the vanishment of magic from England—and from the world. Now, do you know any more than you did before?"

"That isn't true," I said, shaking my head. "No."

"Not yet," she smiled. "But soon."

The one called Jaybee stared at me as he had been since I came from behind the bush. His jaw moved restlessly, like that of a boar pig, and I resolved to stay away from him, for tushes or no, he had that look to him which says all pigs are sows to him. "We need to get rid of this kid," he said, glaring at me. "I'll do it."

"No!" shouted the Alice one. "Killing him would show up on the monitors. Don't! We've only got a minute left."

Jaybee sneered at her and grabbed me by the shoulder. When he jerked me, my hat fell off and my hair tumbled down. He shouted, then laughed and grabbed me up from behind, one great hand clamped on each arm near the shoulder, holding my arms tight as he turned me toward a thing standing behind us, like a great barrel with a door in it. On my shoulder, Grumpkin snarled and scratched at him, but he paid no heed. Both of us were thrust through the door and the others tumbled in after us, all of them shrieking at Jaybee, telling him to put me out, and him fending them off while holding onto me.

Alice staggered to a certain part of the barrel where there were buttons and a flickering of light. She bent over them, muttering. Then we were all twisted inside out. I was. I presume the others were, for Janice cried out and then cursed. Grumpkin screamed. So did I. It felt as though I were being slowly torn apart from inside by rats.

[As was I, for I took hold of the thing she was in and went with her. Or tried. A barrier stretched from

*the bottom of the world to the top, from side to side.
Impenetrable. My powers were absorbed by it, like a
sponge. I could not move it. I could not get through. I
was being sucked dry, sucked out, killed. I felt Beauty
leaving me and could do nothing about it at all. And
then she was gone. What she carried was gone with her.
All our hopes gone. I was still there, sitting on the hill
and weeping when Israfel found me, I who had not
wept since the fountains of the deep were sealed.]*

Then everything stopped. Quiet came. The pain
went away. The others began to stir and bend and
mutter. And the little man, Bill, opened the door into
the twenty-first century.

12

My Life in
the Later Centuries

"I want her," said Jaybee. "She's mine." His fingers were making holes in my arms.

"No," Alice snarled at him, her voice like a whip. "You've gotten us all into enough trouble. You were a stupid fool to drag her along. They're already watching you! Risk your own life all you like, but you're not going to get me killed. Get out of here! Do something to distract the guards at the door, and maybe they won't see there's an extra person!"

"Let Bill take her," said Martin. "Nobody'll bother Bill. I'll see to the guards." He pushed me at the little man and then walked away behind the scowling Jaybee, talking loudly, gesturing, making people look at him.

Bill held me by one wrist. He gave me no time to see anything. I had an impression of grayness, of round things like lance shafts hung across a wall. All sounds echoed, dwindling away in reverberations, as though we were in a great stone hall. I remember a mighty clamor of voices. Some were ours and echoes,

but there were others. One of the women said, "Get
that animal out of sight. Hide her hair."

Choking down a curse, I put Grumpkin under my
shirt and held him there, feeling his ragged breathing
against my belly and his claws in my skin. Bill bundled
up my hair and pushed my cap down on my head. He
must have picked it up when it fell off.

"Now! The guards are looking the other way! Get
her out of here, hurry."

The little man pulled me along with amazing
strength. He was not much larger than Papa's fool, but
he was very powerful. He dragged me up a flight of
stairs that clanged under our feet like swords upon
armor.

The women were behind us. One of them said,
"God, there's a pop-patrol." I heard it as one word,
"popatrol." I looked for it, thinking it must be some
kind of dangerous animal, but saw nothing except
heads and legs, people moving in all directions, up and
down and across, all dressed alike, all looking alike.
The surface we walked upon was full of tiny holes.
Another such surface was above. There were feet
above us, tramping down on us, thousands of feet. Below us were the heads of people, moving fast or slow,
thousands of heads, arms swinging below them, feet at
the bottom, and below them, more heads and arms
and feet. There were people on all sides. I wanted to
scream. I think there were beggars, for some of the
people rattled canisters beneath our noses as they
cried, "Fidipur, fidipur."

"Get off here," the woman said from close behind.

Bill jerked me to one side. We ran down a corridor
that moved beneath our feet, weaving through clots of
people moving more slowly. I stumbled when the corridor ended, only to be hauled up and dragged onto
another one. There were several more corridors that
moved slow or fast. People stared at me curiously. I
lost my footing and fell down and was jerked upright
by my panting escort. Suddenly we were standing on
an unmoving surface in front of a door. Bill put his
hand flat on a place at the side of it. The door opened,

and we were inside somewhere with the door shut behind us and the noise mostly gone, though I could still feel it rumbling in my feet. I felt the scream bubbling in me.

"Home-sweet-home," said Bill. Much of what he said was unintelligible, and I've doubtless got a lot of it wrong, but I know he said "home-sweet-home," because he always said it, whenever he came in.

"And what's your name again?" he asked me.

I swallowed the scream and started to say, "Havoc." No point in that. He knew I was a girl. "Beauty," I said, in a kind of mumble, trying to see on all sides of me at once. I would not have called it home-sweet-home. It was tiny, half the size of my tower room, full of complicated surfaces, with more of those ropes on the walls, very straight, like lances. When we brushed them with our bodies, they clanged.

"Mind the pipes," said Bill. "You'll knock off a steam valve, and then where'll we be?"

I shook my head at him, signifying I did not know either where we were or would be or what a pipe or a steam valve was. I must have looked frightened, for he became less cheerful and tried to soothe me. "It's all right," he murmured. "Just sit down and relax. Sit down. It's all right."

Grumpkin heard him if I did not, for the cat came out from under my shirt all in one movement and crouched at my feet yowling.

"He's hungry," I said. I knew he was, because I was. We had not eaten during all that grieving time at Westfaire. And now—I had the feeling much time had passed.

"What do they eat?" he asked me, pointing to the cat.

I could not imagine anyone not knowing what cats eat. "Milk," I told him. "Meat. Eggs. What any animal eats."

"Milk," he said, laughing. "Meat. Eggs. Ha, ha. Ha."

It was not amused laughter. It was bitter laughter, the kind Papa's fool sometimes got up to when he remembered his wife who had run away with his children.

"You don't have any?" I asked.

"Have none. Have never seen any. Would not know any if I saw them."

"What do you feed your animals? What do you eat?" I asked him in amazement.

"We have no animals. We couldn't have both animals and Fidipur. We eat orange one and two. Green one through four. Red one through five, though I don't much care for three. The original white series, all ten of them." He turned to open a door in the wall and take from it a bowl of things. Wafers. Little flat cakes. Orange ones, and dead green, and pottery red, and white, with numbers stamped upon them. He waved the bowl at me, offering. "It doesn't take much to feed me, so I've got more than I need. 'Balanced protein and fiber with all necessary vitamins and minerals.' "

I didn't know what he meant, but I took a green thing and nibbled at it. It did not taste like anything, and yet I could not honestly say it tasted nasty. I would not have thought it was food, yet I could tell it would stifle hunger. I gave a piece of it to Grumpkin. He sniffed at it, crunched a bit of it, then yowled again.

"They go better," Bill said, "if you have a bit of water along with them. White one and two actually have taste."

"I would prefer beer or wine to water," I said.

"Ha," he muttered. "Ha, ha. Ha."

"You have no beer or wine?" I guessed. Only fools drank water. One could grow ill, drinking water.

"No wine. No beer. Nothing that takes food to make. The food must go directly to Fidipur."

A god, I thought. Some kind of religious being? Perhaps an ogre or dragon that demanded sacrifice? Had I fallen among the heathen? Or were they Christians still? I felt it might be dangerous to ask that question.

"And you have no meat or milk?"

"That would take grain, also, which must go directly to Fidipur." He gazed at me. "How old are you."

"Sixteen," I replied, honestly enough. As of today, I was sixteen. Only, of course, it wasn't today.

"Oh, God," he sighed. "A minor."

"No," I told him. "I am a miller's son." I wasn't, but Havoc was, so to speak.

"I mean you're not yet eighteen," he explained. "In our society, you're not considered a full citizen until you're eighteen."

"What am I then?" I asked.

He shrugged. "A person we don't want to come to the attention of the pop-patrol, that much I know. If they find you, they'll find you don't have an implant. Then they'll wonder how anybody could get here without an implant. Then they'll question you with the truth machines and find out how you got here, and then it will be my neck. Mine and the rest of the team. They'll claim Janice did sloppy research, or one of us fouled up on the trip, and it'll be the disposal chutes for all of us. There wasn't supposed to be anyone around while we were filming. We can't be seen, not that far back, or we risk upsetting history, changing it! No one was supposed to see us."

If I had not subverted the curse, there would not have been anyone around. His trouble was my fault, if anyone's. "Tell me again why no one was supposed to see you?" I asked.

He explained at great length, waving his arms and striding to and fro across the tiny room. It had to do with history, with changing things that had already happened, which might change other things in the now. He used words I didn't know. Permutations of the possible. Linked events. Making a closed loop that would pinch off. I didn't understand much of it. He glared at me and shouted, "I don't know what to do with you. Jaybee and Martin expect me to put you down the disposal chute, but I don't want to do that. We'll have to talk about it and decide."

"I think you should put me back where I was," I said, trying to keep calm. "I don't like it here."

"Ha," he muttered. "Ha, ha." He went on striding, talking, muttering, waving his arms. After a time, I grew weary and my eyes closed. It had been long since we had slept, Grumpkin and I. I heard the little man talking, through a veil, as though he were far away.

Then his hands were on me, gently enough, pulling off my shoes, taking off my cap, feeling my chest.

I sat up, my hair spilling down my back.

"You're a very pretty girl," he accused me, putting his hand back on my chest to make sure I was a girl. "We have very little prettiness anymore, and that makes you noticeable, which makes things difficult."

I drew away, offended. "Actually," I told him through a fog of weariness, "I'm a duke's daughter." I don't know why I told him this. Perhaps it was because I had just been wakened. Perhaps it was to reassure myself that I was really myself.

He buried his head in his hands. "That butcher, Jaybee. He's sick. The things he does, the way he thinks! Not that Alice is that different. She's the only one who can handle him. They both ought to be put down the chutes, but he's a genius, so they don't, they haven't, and now he's dragged you along, they'll put us all down the chutes. What am I going to do?"

"Put me back," I suggested again. "I won't tell anyone. No one would believe me, anyhow."

"I can't," he said. "I don't have an authorization code. We can't use the machine without an authorization code. Even if I could use it, I couldn't put you back at the same time. The tolerances aren't close enough. If we make a closed loop, it will pinch off and everything will collapse!"

He wrung his hands for a while, then told me, "Go on, go to sleep. I've got to think. I've really got to think."

I lay sidewise on the bed I was sitting on, a narrow bed to be sure but no harder than the one I slept upon in Westfaire. Grumpkin lay beside me, munching on the strange biscuit with an expression of remote disdain upon his face. I took a fragment of the biscuit and put it in my mouth, letting it dissolve there. It had sustenance in it but no pleasure. I could live on it, but if it were all there was to eat, I thought living might not much be worth it.

13

The day after my arrival, Bill went away, returning
sometime later very strange in his manner. "All for
nothing," he cried at me, as though something had
been my fault. "Why wouldn't you let us finish it?" He
slammed around the tiny place for a while and then
went out again, giving me an intense, wondering look
as he left. When he returned, he was giggling and staggering a little, happier, for some reason. He seemed to
have forgotten whatever had bothered him before, and
I did not ask him what the trouble had been.

In the days that followed, I grew to know the un-
taste of the biscuits and the boundaries of the tiny
room all too well. It had many folding places in it: a
folding place to wash, a folding place to relieve oneself, folding places to store things. The bed slid into a
pocket, the table slid into another pocket, each thing
became something else. Bill went away each day, telling me to stay out of sight. He locked the door behind
him and unlocked it when he returned. There was no
window. I complained of this, and he told me the room
was deep inside a great redoubt; windows would
merely have looked into other rooms. There were no
windows anywhere, he said, for there was nothing for
them to see but more rooms and more rooms. He
taught me to use the screen, instead, and gave me a
great pile of "documentaries" he had helped make.

They made my head hurt, but I watched them none-theless. It was something to do. I learned to under-stand the language of the place that way, watching the images on the screen as they flowed and danced. It was my own language, more or less, though strangely changed. Often it was easier to understand the printed words that surged across the picture than the spoken ones.

There were other films, as well. I could watch some of the "porno-mance" ones, but the "horro-porn" ones I could not watch. Jaybee had filmed some of them. I threw them down the disposal chute, but every few days more were delivered from the supply chute. There was no end to them, each one full of pain and blood. I learned very soon there was nothing beautiful in that place. Even the things they watched were not beautiful. There was no contrast between beauty and ugliness. There was only ugliness.

I suppose it was more practical for them. If there had been any beauty at all, people might have wanted that instead. As it was, they didn't know there was any such thing, so the lack did not bother them. I knew, though. I hurt all the time with such a longing. My chest burned, as though I would die of it.

Grumpkin learned to make his mess on paper, which I threw down the disposal chute thing where my own waste went. Everything worn out or used up went down the chute, said Bill. His name was William, Wil-liam Picte. "Pic-tee," he said, spelling it for me. He was a writer of what he called scripts, which I learned were stories for the pictures I had watched on the ma-chine. He was a man of mature years, thirty at least. He came up to my shoulder. His hair was the color of apricots, and his skin was very pale, covered over with freckles. The hair on his body was the same as the hair on his head. I saw it when he washed himself. He had nowhere else to go to wash himself. The room we were in was the only room he had. We slept together on the narrow bed, our heads at opposite ends. He did not try to do anything to me, and I was grateful for that.

"Take me with you," I begged him one day when

he was about to set out. "I want to see something else."

"There isn't anything else," he told me. "It's all like this. Except for Fidipur's farms, but nobody can go there except the people who work there."

"Let's go to the ocean," I suggested. "To the sea." I had never seen the sea, but Papa had, many times.

"There isn't any sea," he said. "Except the farms for Fidipur."

"A forest then," I begged, growing frantic. Sometimes I thought if I had to spend one more day in this little closet I would die. "Take me to the forest."

He shook his head. "You don't understand. There isn't any forest anymore. No forest, no prairie, no mountains, no jungle, no swamp, no animals, no birds, no fish. It all went to Fidipur. This is all there is. Rooms like this one. Full of people like me."

"Where do you go when you go out?" I begged.

"To the area supply station to get the daily ration of food wafers," he snarled at me. "I get the same as a full-size person, which is why there's enough left over for you. Then I go to the area work station to check in each day so they will know I am still alive and my room occupied. Then to the area water station to punch in so they'll know I'm still alive and using water. To the required school for continuing education, which is a laugh, because there's nothing left to teach anyone that matters. There aren't any books; they take up too much room. There aren't any teachers. There's one technical university, and only the people who run things get to send their children there, so they can keep on running things."

"You do that every day?"

"Except the sabbath. On the sabbath I go to the required religious observance of my choice. We're very religious, hadn't you noticed. Ha. Ha. Ha."

None of it was reasonable, so I thought he lied. One day I opened the door and stepped out. There were people everywhere, small people. I hadn't noticed the first time, but almost all of the people were small. Still, they filled up the moving corridors and stairs. All of them wore much the same sort of clothes, and it was hard to tell men from women. Some of them saw me looking out, and stopped to stare, muttering, the noise level rising like a disturbed hive. I was afraid the noise would bring some official to see what was going on. I went back in, hastily, and stayed inside after that.

All this time the thing inside me kept flaming away as though it had to burn its way out. It wasn't pain, it wasn't that kind of burning, but there was such a dreadful urgency about it. I felt stretched thin. Like parchment stretched around a flame, trying to contain it, getting hotter and hotter all the time.

Even though he had said there was no wine, Bill came home another time acting giggly and happy, as though he had been drinking. If there wasn't wine, there was something like it, because his face was flushed and the pupils of his eyes were tiny, like dots. He giggled at me, like a drunken baby, waving his finger, and took a box out of one of the hidden closets. The box had women's clothes in it, and he put them on. There were stockings like cobwebs, but full of holes, a silky black blouse, a red and black striped skirt, a slim underbodice without sleeves. Around his shoulders he wrapped a fleece, a sheepskin, with the wool out, as though it had been fur, then he staggered around on high-heeled red shoes. All the things were old and stained, like the clothes the aunts had given me to wear.

I told him the things weren't very nice.

"I know," he said. "Oh, I know. Women don't wear clothes like these anymore. We all dress alike. Men and women. Nothing silky anymore. Nothing lacy or soft. Just these," and he pinched up a handful of the trousers he had discarded, the harsh wrinkled fabric of them pulling up in mountain peaks beneath his fingers. "I brought the silky clothes back from a time-trip, a long time ago. When we went to take pictures of whales."

I thought he would have liked living at Westfaire. My father wore soft things, velvets and satins. "Please take me home," I begged him. "You can go with me. There are many nice fabrics at home. You would love the gowns."

"Beauty," he said to me, pushing me down on the couch and squatting on the floor in front of me like some great lady frog, the soiled silk lying in loose folds on his flat chest. "Listen to me. I am a member of a work crew. The work crew is assigned to make certain kinds of films, like the ones you've been watching. There are five of us. Alice Fremont is the travel technician. She takes us places to film things. Martin Duboise is the director. He tells the cameraman—Jaybee Veolante—what pictures to get. He usually talks to me about that also, because I write the scripts, the words, you know?"

I knew he did. I had seen him at work, at a fold down place with a screen to show words and a thing to print paper.

He said, "Janice Saintjohn is the researcher."

I asked him what that was.

"Researchers find things out. They learn about other people, other places, other times. The researcher tells us where we might be able to get good film. The director decides if we'll do it. I write the script, Alice takes us there, Jaybee photographs it. We do maybe three stories a year, and that's how we earn our keep. Until they assign us some other story, we can't go near that machine. I don't know how to run it anyhow. Alice would have to run it."

"Ask Alice to run it," I demanded. "You said I'm dangerous to you here. So, I'm dangerous to her, too. Ask her to run it and put me back where I belong."

Some days I thought if I had to eat one more of those wafers or spend another day shut up in this cell called home-sweet-home I'd die. I burned and sweated and tried to keep from screaming. One morning, after I'd been restless and nightmare-ridden half the night, I woke up with an idea. I don't know why I hadn't thought of it before. As soon as Bill left, I found the sheepskin thing he had worn around his neck and some scissors he used to cut his scripts and piece them together and I cut the fleece to make a pair of boots.

I knew how to do it. I had watched the shoemaker in the village many times. I knew how to cut the sole and make the upper part and sew the two parts together. It would have been better if I'd had some stiff leather, but on the other hand, stiff leather would have been hard to sew without the right tools. The sheepskin was very soft. I put the wool part inside. I used the thick needle and the heavy brown thread from the box my mama had left. It had come to me in the night what the thread was for. It was shoemaker's thread, so it had to be for seven-league boots. It had to be. Seven-league boots which would take me back to my own time!

When they were done I put them on, and my cloak, with my things in one pocket and Grumpkin in the other, and I opened the door and went out into the hall. "Take me to my mother," I said, closing my eyes and waiting for the boots to work.

When I opened my eyes, there were people standing all around me, staring at me. The boots hadn't worked. The cloak didn't work! They could see me!

I got back inside and fell down on the hard, narrow bed and cried. I was still there, still crying, when Bill got home.

He made me tell him what I'd tried to do.

"You little fool," he sneered at me. "There's no magic left today. The fairies are all gone, and there's no magic left. Put those things away, and don't do anything so foolish again. If someone official had seen you, you'd be down the chutes by now!"

We lay on the bed, head to toe, and I listened to the sound of the world. A clangor, a constant sound of metal, distant and yet all around me. It was like being inside a gong, gently struck by an erratic wind, the reverberations coming and going without rhythm or predictability. Over that the sound of voices, a buzz, a hum, like some great hive. Over that the sound of feet, shuffling, stepping, never together, never marching, but moving endlessly up and down the corridors of the world. One listened and listened, waiting always for something significant in that sound. Some voice one knew. Some sound one recognized. There was never anything but the constant roar of everyone, everything, closing in and closing in. I put the blanket around my ears and wept while Grumpkin licked my eyes.

I cried so hard and so long that Bill said he would bring Alice to talk with me. Next time he went out, I waited for a long time walking back and forth, back and forth, like the lion one of Papa's friends had brought back from the Holy Land with him, to and fro in my cage as he had gone to and fro in his, action that his body demanded even when his mind was hopeless, to and fro until he died at last, his feet stretched out and worn through to the blood beneath, as though he had walked himself to death, trying to get home.

At last voices spoke outside the door. I hid myself in the disposal closet until I was sure it was Bill. The woman Alice was with him. So was Jaybee Veolante. He stared at me. I realized almost at once that my hair was down and my singlet was tighter than the shirt I had worn when he saw me. He grunted, and I thought again of a boar pig.

"So," he said as his eyes devoured me, "what've you been up to with her, Billy-boy?"

I found my shirt and put it on. The way he looked at me was frightening. As though he wanted to swallow me. Which was not unlike the way the woman was looking at me.

"You remember Alice," Bill said to me. "Alice Fremont?"

She was a little older than he, I thought. Her face was pale and thin, like the carved face of a saint sanctified through many stringencies, but alive and hungry withal. She was looking at me hungrily, too, and I shifted uncomfortably.

"I told Alice what you suggested," Bill said to me. "About her taking you back. Us, back."

"Us," sneered Jaybee. "All or none."

"Jaybee, uh, overheard us," Bill explained. "He

wants to be included." He shifted nervously, watching Jaybee from the corners of his eyes.

"Included, right." Jaybee's jaw moved as though he were chewing something. His teeth made an audible gnashing.

Alice sat down on the bed. Bill pulled a seat out of the wall and sat confronting her. Jaybee lounged against the door, as though to prevent anyone escaping. I stayed where I was, with Grumpkin behind my legs, his head against my ankle.

"Before we technicians do a trip with a team," Alice explained, "we always do a check-trip, to be sure the machine's working right. The check-trip is always a hundred years, give or take a few. The tech is supposed to be the only one aboard during the check-trip. That's part of the reason we only go a hundred years, so if something's wrong with the machine, only the tech gets abandoned, and the time is recent enough a person could probably get along."

Bill slumped on his chair. "What are you saying, Alice? Tell me what you're saying."

"I'm saying, any tech can get into the complex anytime to make a check-trip. If I could get you in there with me, I could take you back with me."

"A hundred years?" I asked. "That's no good! I want to go home! That's what? Seven hundred at least, isn't it?"

"Seven hundred forty-two," she said. "There's no way to do that. The machine is energized for trips over a hundred only on receipt of a trip-authorization number from the powers that be, but it's always on ready power, that is, energized for a hundred years—roughly. Zero to one day takes a lot of power. That's what they call the Present Horizon. It takes enormous energy to get into that time because nothing is settled yet. People don't know what the hell is happening in the present. Some things that happen are inconsequential and get forgotten almost immediately. Some things that don't happen are thought to have happened; they get recorded or have consequences, and then people think they remember them. The present is fluid. It has to settle before you can travel in it.

"From one day to ninety-eight point something-or-other-years takes almost no power, so they keep the machine hot. That's the Recent Past, and we don't fool with it, either, because we'd be in the lifetimes of living people. Still, it's cheaper keeping the machine powered for the Recent Past than shutting it down between trips and having to power it over the Present Horizon again."

"So you're saying we could go back to the 1900s?" Jaybee asked.

"Talk to Janice about it," Alice suggested. "There are rumors that a lot of people have gone back. We know some have because we've talked to them ourselves when we've been there."

"I met one once," Bill said. "When we did the first shots on the whales. She told me she had come back."

Alice nodded. "I've heard some researchers say it's the last good time. The last years before Fidipur."

Bill stared at me intently. "It would be better than here."

"Yeah," Jaybee muttered. "If we end up there. But we could end up dead. There's guards on the travel-complex. Alice may have a permit, but they won't give me one."

"I said it would work *if* I could get you in," Alice said. "I'm not talking anybody into anything. Bill asked me, I didn't ask him."

"You'd stay?" I asked her. "You'd stay there?"

"Damn right," she said, glaring into my eyes as though determined to find something I didn't know was there. *"If* I can figure out a way to sneak us down there."

"Janice finds things out," I said. "Bill told me so. Ask her to find out who goes where the machine is."

"Janice?" Alice wondered.

Bill looked up alertly. "She might want to go along."

"She'd drag Martin in."

"No," said Bill. "That's why she might go. They

broke up not long ago. He said she was getting weird and filed for separate quarters. Haven't you noticed how they've acted? She's become very strange and religious."

"Then she might want to go." Alice shook her head, ran her fingers through her short hair. "She might. Who's going to ask her?"

"I will," said Bill.

The others said a few more words, then left. As he was going out, Jaybee turned around and gave me one more stare, a long, swallowing look, as though he'd like to hit me. Or eat me.

Bill brought Janice to the home-sweet-home later on. I was asleep when they came. They talked in whispers, and I never really woke up. I was dreaming about Westfaire, and I didn't want to wake up because in the dream I knew if I wakened Westfaire would vanish forever. So I let Bill and Janice talk without letting go of the vision, knowing when Janice left they had come to some kind of agreement. When I woke up, I remembered this very clearly, but there was no one to tell it to but Grumpkin. Grumpkin looked sick. His fur was dull. His eyes looked bleary. He needed outdoors. He needed it no more than I. My legs were jumpy. My skin was breaking out in spots. I dreamed of trees. The burning in me was getting so bad I thought I'd turn to coals and die.

A day or two later, Bill came home with two suits of stiff green clothing that went over everything and closed up the front with fuzzy stuff. He had me put one on. Then he told me Grumpkin was too likely to attract attention, so I'd have to put Grumpkin down the chute. I told him I'd kill him if he ever said such a thing again. We ended up putting Grumpkin in the sack, along with my cloak and things. Bill didn't want to leave his woman clothes behind, but I told him he could buy all the woman clothes he wanted where we were going and I'd even buy him a new fur to make up for the sheepskin I'd cut to pieces. I still had the emeralds, so buying a sheepskin shouldn't be that difficult. I cut a hole in the sack for Grumpkin's nose. The cat

growled, but he stayed put. I think he knew I was trying to get us home.

When we went out, there weren't as many people
as usual. Bill said it was between shifts. Somewhere
along the way, Jaybee joined us. We went down stairs
and around corners. I didn't recognize anything or
anyone from before, but then everyone looked alike.
Almost everyone was the same size, their hair was cut
alike, they wore the same clothes, they had the same
dead, no-expression blanks for faces. We came to a
gate with two men outside who were dressed a little
differently, in high-buttoned jackets and hats with
metal trim on them.

"Cleaning crew," Jaybee said in the bored voice
everyone used.

"You're early," one of the metal-hats complained.

"We're late," said Bill. "Should have been here
last shift. There's a stalled walkway down toward the
nine-hundreds and everybody's jammed up."

The man nodded without paying any attention and
let us through. Inside were more corridors and stairs,
and then Alice came out of a room and walked along
with us. She was carrying a little bag.

"Janice is already down in the control room," she
said.

She was there when we arrived, dressed as we
were. She nodded at us, then we all moved out into the
huge, high room where the machine was. I hadn't really looked at it from the outside before. It looked like
it was made out of rock, like a great tub carved from
stone. The door of it clanged behind us. Alice pushed
some buttons. My insides came out through my nose,
and then back in again.

"Quick," said Alice. "We've only got seconds."

Bill opened the door and we all fell out. When we
turned to look behind us, the machine was shimmering, then it was gone. In its place was a signpost pointing ten miles to a place I had never heard of.

"Nineteen ninety something or other," Janice murmured. "In what used to be the States of America.
And God help us."

[We found her! We feared she had gone forever, except we could feel what was inside her, pulsing a little, like a faraway heart still beating. We knew she was still alive, for I could feel her life, just as I could feel that life dwindling. All we could do was lurk along the borders of that time and hope she would come out. Oh, the pain of living where there is no magic at all. Even humans need a little of it. The Holy One, Blessed be He, knew that. Perhaps it is why he put both our races here to begin with.

Never mind. We've found her. We know where she is. She is in a time of little magic, but there may be enough. We can reach her, slowly, slowly, setting our lures, readying our hooks. We will draw her back to us!]

14

July 1991

We joined the homeless, many of whom are from the twenty-first and slightly later times. Janice said it was odd the authorities of the 1980s never caught on to the fact that the homeless sprouted rather suddenly. Time-travel was perfected in 2080, and the hundred-year limit means that the homeless began showing up in the 1980s, many of them with limited communications skills, covering up by pretending to be crazy. There's a secret finger sign we travelers use among ourselves to tell each other that we're what we call "comebacks," and there are enough real 1980s homeless that we comebacks can hide among them without difficulty.

Evidently the people in this time decided to knock down all the poor people's hovels because they weren't nice enough and close all the asylums for crazy people because they weren't perfect either, but the people who had lived in the hovels and the asylums didn't have any other place to go, so now they live under bridges and places like that. I think we did it better back in the fourteenth. At least we didn't knock down hovels just because they were substandard. It seems to me substandard is better than nothing.

Anyhow, Bill and the rest of us took advantage of

the situation by seeking shelter in an almshouse run by the Church, which did not surprise me at all, though the first time I attended Mass I was considerably astonished. The priest did the whole thing facing us and speaking English, which is what the language is now called. Evidently no one uses Latin anymore. I thought of all those sessions with Father Raymond and could have cried.

Jaybee and Alice and Janice had a big fight, and then Jaybee and Alice left for some big, big city where they can both sort of disappear into the mob. I was so glad when Jaybee went. It was like smelling rain after a long dry spell, just to know he was gone. Bill and Janice have signed up for job training here. You have to, or they won't let you stay in the almshouse, that is, the shelter. After a few weeks of being tutored by Bill in arithmetic and by Janice in geography and current history, which I know nothing about (Bill shakes his head and tells me not to believe half of what Janice tells me), I will be sent to school.

August 1, 1991

Everyone went out to look for work today. They left me in the shelter, by myself except for a few other people who had just come or were too ill to go out. Two of them were a woman and a child who came last night. They were both very pale, very thin, almost like stick people, and the little girl seemed very sad.

I went into their cubicle to see if I could talk to them, maybe cheer the little girl up a bit. The two of them sat on their bed, scarcely moving. On the table was an almost untouched plate of food someone had brought them, the knife and fork laid side by side, a glass half-empty beside it. I got the little girl to play with me. At least, I sat her on my lap and told her stories. She leaned into me, as though she needed the warmth. She put her head against my chest and smiled a tiny smile. I wondered if she felt whatever the burning was. It hadn't been quite so bad since we'd come to the twentieth, but I could feel it, so maybe she did, too.

I told her the story about the gypsy and the prince, and I ended it, "So they lived happily ever after."

"Ever after," said the woman. "Together."

I had not heard her speak before. Her voice was dreadful, like a mechanical echo, with nothing vital in it at all.

"We loved each other," she said. "We said we would be together ever after, together."

"Who's she talking about?" I whispered to the child.

"Daddy," the child whispered back, putting her cheek against my chest and smiling, as though she heard something inside there.

"But the chutes were full," her mother said in her cold, quiet voice. "We were going together, but the chutes were full. Full all the way to the top, the furnaces gone out, bodies jammed in, rotting, stinking, bones sticking out . . ."

"Daddy and mommy and me were going down the chutes," the child said with wide eyes. "To happyland."

I looked at the woman in horror. Her face was very still, her eyes were still. Her mouth moved and the words came out, but there was nothing behind them. It was as though she were dead, already, and the words were bats fleeing from her coffin.

"But we couldn't go, couldn't go, couldn't go," she chanted. "So we walked away, down the corridors where the sidewalks slept, down the aisles where the rot lay thick, down the stairs where the stink rose up like paste, gluing itself inside our lungs, down and down to the room where the machine was, humming to itself, the little machine."

"It was very tiny," the child said. "Only big enough for Mommy and me. Daddy knew it was there. He turned on the big engine that gave it power for more than a hundred years, and he put us in and shut the door. And when we opened the door, we were here."

"Down, down," the woman crooned, "down, to happyland."

I asked the child to come away with me, and after a while she did. Her name was Elaine. She had a lovely laugh. I asked her what year she had been born, and she said 2108. She couldn't remember what year it had been when she got in the tiny machine, but she looked about six to me, which would make it about 2114. We stayed in the corridor, playing ball, playing hide-and-seek.

The last time she hid, I could not find her. Finally, I went back to their cubicle to see if she had gone there, and she had. She was lying beside her mother on the bed. Her mother's hand was still upon the knife, wet with Elaine's quiet blood. Deathwords came from the woman's mouth, a terrible singing, "Down . . . down . . . down . . . to happyland."

I screamed, stood there screaming, screaming until it hurt. The people who manage the shelter came and took the woman away. They wrapped up the little girl's body in black stuff and took it away. Someone gave me a white pill and a glass of water. They said the woman was mad. That she should have been locked up long ago.

I did not tell them that the woman had been locked up, locked up all her life; that in the time she had come from, everyone was locked up forever.

August 12, 1991

Bill brought back a set of his documentaries with him to use as examples of his work. He had to claim they are speculative fiction in order to use them in seeking a job, but evidently they're good examples of his talent, for it didn't take him long to get a position writing for a television station. Janice got work, too, at a library, and then we three rented a house on the corner of Wisdom Street and Seventh Avenue. It's a house about the size of the pigpen at Westfaire.

However, it has flush toilets, which I like, and a garbage disposer. I also like hair dryers and tampons. I do not like telephone salesmen and the way everybody has dogs they let empty themselves just anywhere. In my time commoners didn't have dogs, they couldn't have fed dogs, they'd probably have ended up eating the dogs. I don't like the noise people are allowed to make with radios. It does not sound like music. It sounds savage and makes your ears ring, and afterward it is hard to hear when people speak.

I have a room of my own, with my own things in it. I put my cloak and the boots and Mama's box at the back of the closet shelf. Grumpkin sleeps on my bed. I don't like all the concrete and no trees. I do like hamburgers and french fries and Pepsi, and the kind of chickens they have now with all the meat on them. In the fourteenth, chickens were very skinny and tough. I hate the way the world smells. On balance, I would go back in a minute, but since the boots don't work, I don't have that choice, I'm trying to seek the good in the time I'm in.

From a television show I learned that people like Bill are called transvestites and that Janice is probably frigid (though maybe she's just a religious fanatic) and Jaybee is probably a psychopath. The aunts would have had a fit if they had ever seen the things they talk about on TV, but I think it's good to have words for things.

Everything is all right, except for the dreams I have about the little girl in the shelter. I dream I am with them in the twenty-second. I dream I am trying to find a chute which is not already stuffed full of bodies. I dream I am singing: down, down, down to happyland. And I wake up choking.

August 15, 1991

I met a neighbor girl my age. She's a senior at George Washington High, the school I'll be going to next month. Her name is Candace Maclear, and everyone calls her Candy. She's very friendly. She says I'm really rad, which is good, and offered me some coke (to sniff) and spent all day teaching me to fix my hair. She says I talk funny, so I'm concentrating on sounding more like her.

August 17, 1991

I told Bill about Candy offering me drugs, and he warned me about it when I go to school in two weeks. Everyone here uses them, he says, and it's hard not to. He talked about "peer pressure," which seems to mean letting other people run your life for you. I had enough of that at Westfaire!

August 20, 1991

Candy's brother told me her boyfriend really goes after girls with long hair, and Candy's afraid he'll take to me. I've seen Candy's boyfriend and, believe me, she hasn't anything to worry about. His hair stands up in spikes and he has pimples. I look at him and I think of Giles. I look at all the boys here and I think of Giles. I wonder if they're all like this!

August 21, 1991

Everything here in the twentieth seems very temporary. Nothing lasts. Friendships don't last. Love affairs don't last. Marriages don't last. I've seen men here who people tell me have been married four or five times, and their old wives aren't dead, either. People even change what sex they are, and there are people coming to the door all the time trying to get me to

change my religion and be born again, though I
haven't gotten used to being born the first time yet.
Wouldn't being born again imply I didn't trust God to
have done it right the first time?

Even though I was mad at him, I wish Father Raymond
were here! Janice did get born again, last week,
and there's no living with her. I finally had to tell her I
am a Catholic and please leave me alone. She got very
angry. She doesn't approve of me and she doesn't approve
of Bill. She says he's being sinful to dress up like
he does. I can't see why. He isn't hurting anyone, but
Janice says God intended men to wear trousers and
women to wear dresses. I look at pictures of Greeks
and Scots and aborigines and Jesus, and I can't figure
out how she knows that!

September 6, 1991

Well, I've been to school. I know who sells crack and
who fucks who and which teachers are gay and who
has AIDS. Nobody has asked me to do any arithmetic
or geography at all, so that was a waste of time. I am
taking classes in literature and biology and Spanish.
Bill and Janice decided these were the safest subjects
for me.

Bill took one whole hour to tell me about sexual
diseases, and maybe it's a good thing he did. I do not
want any of their diseases, though, after eavesdropping
on a table of boys at lunch, I don't think I'd be
tempted anyhow. They were talking about this girl
they got drunk or stoned and then they all did it,
watching each other. They were laughing at the way
different ones had done it, making comments about
how long it took this one or that one, like the stableboys used to hang over the paddock, watching the stallion serve the mares, giggling and pointing. I wonder if
that has anything to do with male bonding?

In the fourteenth, we dreamed of chivalry and
courtly love. I remember the oaths of fidelity the

young men-at-arms used to offer their ladies, and they
were no older than these high school boys. These guys
don't offer anything. It's like the women they hit on
are sacrifices to some kind of god that only boys worship. Most of the boys here remind me of Jaybee,
though I'm not sure why.

The twentieth makes me feel very lonely. This isn't
my place. When I remember how beautiful Westfaire
is, was, when I remember Giles, I want to cry. I choke,
my chest burns, I get the hiccups and have to lie down.
The worst part of living here is that nothing is beautiful. There must be something beautiful in the twentieth, and maybe I just haven't seen it yet, but the way
everyone acts, this is all there is. Magic doesn't work.
There is no other way. Some days all I want to do is
cry.

[Some days all I *want to do is cry! We keep trying to
lure her, and she keeps ignoring us. I have thought of
sending Puck. He says he can get there. The problem is,
his doing so might draw attention to her. The Dark
Lord may be watching the Bogles. We don't know who
he's watching! Puck's going there might show up like a
meteorite, burning across the night. Israfel keeps saying,
"Patience, Carabosse."* Patience! *I don't think he sees
the irony of that.]*

October 4, 1991

Today I think I figured out Fidipur. In social studies
class the teacher commented that the recent famines in
Africa are only the beginning of what may turn out to
be worldwide famines of varying degrees of severity.
Then he showed us a film of black people in Africa
dying in large numbers and another one about the
hole in the Van Allen belts. (Father Raymond would
be fascinated!) The teacher explained that very soon
the world would warm up and get dryer, that food
would be harder to produce, and "We won' be able to

fidipur, 'cause there'll be millyuns and millyuns of 'em.''

Fidipur! Feed the poor. The way he said it was exactly the way the beggars in the twenty-first had said it. I asked Bill to explain it to me, and he told me about population growth and the Catholic church and acid rain and cutting down the rain forests to grow more food. Everyone argues about it, he said. Economists and businessmen say nothing is going wrong. Ecologists and population experts say the end is coming. While they argue, things keep changing until we get to the point of no return, sometime during the next hundred years. After that, there'll be no more out-of-doors because every square inch of land will be needed to produce food, and that's why, in the twenty-first, all the people had to be shut up in great tall, half-buried towers where they couldn't move around and interfere with Fidipur's farms.

I said, sensibly I thought, that God gave man the duty to take care of the world, not a contract to wreck the place, and Bill laughed the way he does, ha, ha, ha.

The comebacks say everything starts breaking down sometime late in the twenty-first, with Fidipur's farms playing out and people getting pushed down the chutes a hundred thousand at a time and all the machines breaking down. Elaine may have been the last person who came back, and she came in about 2114.

Bill says the handwriting is already on the wall, we're already doomed. Janice says he shouldn't say "doomed" when so many people will be alive and being fed, so he asked her why she left the twenty-first if it was so great, and she got mad at him. There are tear spots all over this page, and I can't stop.

October 7, 1991

I've stopped thinking about Fidipur. You can't think about things like that all the time. Your body won't let you. Everytime I started to cry about it, my chest would burn like a bonfire. It got so I was afraid to think about it at all. So, I'm trying to think about other things, about trying out for cheerleader—which seems kind of dumb, but all the good-looking girls do it—and going to football games and things like that. I am trying to do as Father Raymond used to suggest and seek the good. Things wouldn't be too bad if Janice would just stop talking about religion and let me alone. I wish I could be nicer to her about it, but her religion is so ugly! So mean!

[We go on transmitting these urgencies, but they have not the volume of the constant music where she is; they cannot be heard above the traffic noises. There are so many distractions in the twentieth, she doesn't hear us. If she would only decide to be a nun! I think possibly we could get through to a nun.]

November 15, 1991

Yesterday we had a special kind of event at school. The event was called "Career Days," and they had people from all kinds of jobs and professions come speak to us about their jobs. One of the men was our teacher's brother, an author, Barrymore Gryme, only he told us all to call him Barry. I've seen his books in the school library, but I've never read one. After the session, when the students were leaving the room, he asked me what my name was. I told him, Dorothy, because that's the name Bill and Janice and I had decided on, after my old friend Doll. We knew enough to realize I couldn't call myself Beauty, not in the twentieth.

"You don't belong in Kansas, do you?" he asked me with a funny smile.

I didn't know what to say, so I just smiled back.

"No, you're the Emerald City all over," he said. Then I knew he was talking about that movie with the singing girl and the straw man. The Yellow Brick

Road one. I'd seen that in the twenty-first, about fifteen times.

"Not that Dorothy," I explained. "I was named
after an old friend."

"Where do you live, old friend Dorothy?" he
asked me. I didn't want to be rude, so I told him.
When I got home that night, there were flowers for me
in the living room, from him. Bill was puzzled, but
Janice was furious.

"What have you been doing when you're supposed
to be at school," she shouted at me. "What have you
been up to?"

I guess my mouth dropped open, because Bill told
her not to yell. When I saw his name on the tag with
the flowers, I was just as puzzled as Bill was.

"I only said about six words to him," I said. "And
there were lots of other people around."

"Where, around?" Janice demanded.

I told her, at Career Day, at school, that he was our
teacher's brother, and after a while she believed it.
When I told her his full name, then she was as puzzled
as Bill.

Bill nodded, his mouth pursed up. Then he sat me
down at the desk and made me write the man a nice
note, saying thank you for the flowers but I'd sent
them to a hospital, because I wasn't allowed to accept
gifts from older men. Bill thought it was "appropriate."

November 17, 1991

I told Candy about the flowers I got from Barrymore
Gryme. I said I couldn't understand why he'd do that,
and she got bright red in the face and said, "Honestly,
Dor, you're so dumb it's just unbelievable." And when
I asked her why, she said look in the mirror for
crysakes.

Well, I've known for a long time I'm beautiful, but
that doesn't explain anything! He's too old for me, and

I'm sure too young for him. Candy thinks I ought to have an affair with Barry Gryme.

I told her she was crazy.

She says just wait. Her aunt told her virginity gets to be more and more of a burden the older you get. She told Candy you get to the point where you don't decide whether you like someone enough to make love to them or not, you only get to the point of wondering whether they're good enough to give it up for. "Aunt Becky says you quit wondering when and start wondering if," Candy said.

Should I have an affair because of Candy's aunt?

[As if Israfel and I did not have enough to worry about already!

We were standing at the Pool, trying our best to get through to the twentieth, when Israfel remarked that, as our magic weakens, the power of the Dark Lord strengthens. I had known that, of course, though I had not let myself consider it deeply. Our departed brother took terror and pain as his portion. It was always a part of what we did. Magic is a perilous thing, and it has its horrifying aspects, but we have always worked with and around these aspects, not making them the focus of our art. The Dark Lord has taken these to the exclusion of all else. He works in pain and prurience, lust and death, ramifying these until they fill his whole canvas. Discontent with his own efforts, he selects minions among men to develop these themes further. Is Jaybee one of these? Is Barrymore Gryme?

Has this man been set upon her, like a hound set upon a hare? We have been so careful. We have done nothing to draw attention to her, letting it seem that she has done everything out of her own motivation, out of her own desires. She has left no magical trail behind, like the slime of a snail, for some inimical creature to follow. Surely, he can't know?

So I say to Israfel, and he to me, trying to convince ourselves.]

November 20, 1991

I got a Barry Gryme out of the school library and tried to read it. I read two hundred pages, then I had to quit because it scared me to death. Everything in it was hopeless and terrible. People kept being mutilated or eaten or destroyed. It was full of sex, too, but there was no pleasure in it. It was . . . it was a lot like the horro-porn films in the twenty-first. If lots of people read things like this, there's something terribly, terribly wrong. . . .

Christmas Morning 1991

Bill and Janice are still asleep. If I were home, I'd be in church, watching Father Raymond moving around at the altar, smelling the incense, hearing his voice with the Latin rolling out, seeing the candles flicker. I'm homesick. There's nothing to do about it, so I'm watching one of Bill's documentaries.

Water, gray and cold, with lights in it as bubbles, rising, bright shadows in the water and vast distances, with everything moving and shifting, so there is no up or down. Singing in the water. Deep, organ tones, one, then two together, then a third. Soft, hurting sounds.

Bill's voice, his deep voice, the one he uses when he does the narrations. "These are the last whales, and this is their last song. Though they are unaware of it, this pod of whales is the last of the great sea creatures to swim the seas of earth. Cells have been saved in the hope that some future time will allow their regeneration, though as things stand today such hope seems dim and distant."

The organ voices again. Incredibly sad. Jaybee's camera focuses on an eye set in a great wrinkled socket. The eye looks at me. Oh, there's knowing there. They know. They know they are the last. All these seas are their tears, they have wept them all. All the oceans of earth are made up of tears. Whale tears, elephant tears, the tears of forests, the tears of flowers, the tears of everything beautiful cried out to make oceans.

We come up. We fly up through the water, we rip through the surface scattering droplets in all directions, we skim over the waves like a flung spear, toward the farms, skeletons on the horizon, with huge blades rotating, with solar collectors like blinding sheets of white fire.

"Fidipur's farms," says Bill's voice. "Here, suspended over the deep, are the mighty wind- and sun-powered pumps that bring the cold harvest of the sea to the surface, where it is dried, powdered, and shipped to the great landside factories of Fidipur."

Ships going and coming, being loaded and leaving, zipping into the loading docks empty, one after the other, by the hundreds. Like beetles. Like wood beetles. Eating everything, all, until nothing is left.

Back across the water, down to the whales again, this time slowly, letting us see them. Their bones show through their flesh. Their eyes are deeply sunk. The thin calf nuzzles its mother hopelessly. There is no milk. They are starving. Fidipur has taken it all.

I'm crying. Janice is calling me to breakfast. I'm not hungry. It's Christmas, but beauty is dying. We're gobbling up the world. I don't ever want to be hungry again.

June 1992

Graduation. At first I didn't think I'd go, but I did. Bill and Janice came, too. We all wore those silly hats and the rented gowns and paraded up to get a piece of paper which isn't even really our diploma. We'll get that later in the mail, after the office checks to see we don't owe any money or library fines or anything. So, big deal, I thought, that's over, so now what will I do?

I got a phone call from Barry Gryme. He wanted

to know if I was old enough yet, and I told him no, I am only seventeen, and I don't go out with married men anyhow (Janice found out he was married), and he said he was divorced.

July 1992

I bought another one of Barry's books, to see if I could read it all the way through. I got about a hundred pages into it and then I had to stop.

I've seen people die. I saw the goldsmith Papa put in the dungeon, when he was almost dead. He had been my friend, and I saw him when they took him out, saw his bones showing through his skin, and the sores on him, and the places the rats had chewed him. I saw a thief whipped to death once. I've seen men hanged. It's horrible, seeing that, but not as horrible as this book, because in this book, you're supposed to *like* seeing it, *like* reading what happens to the people. You can tell the way it's written you're supposed to kind of lick it up, like something juicy.

[We tried again. She was in such a downcast mood, we thought she might hear us, but she didn't. I'm considering sending Puck through to her. She knows him, and possibly she could accept him without headlines resulting: CALIFORNIA GIRL SEES CREATURE FROM OUTER SPACE.

Israfel says be patient just a little longer. I have just about had it with Israfel!]

Christmas 1992

A letter came for me, from Jaybee. I'd almost succeeded in forgetting Jaybee. The letter was gibberish, but frightening gibberish, and it was illustrated with photographs.

At first I couldn't tell what the photographs were. They looked like abstract art, fascinating compositions, dark, light, black, white, with ribbons of red. Then I saw that the dark was shadow, the light a woman's breast, the ribbon of red . . . well, it was blood, wasn't it? You could see the knife, the edge of it, making a design against the nipple. I began to make out what all of the photographs were, flesh, manacled flesh, cut flesh, an eye, half open, staring unbelievingly into the lens, lips which looked swollen with desire until you saw they were bitten half through.

If you turned them upside down, they were fascinating abstracts. Only when you looked at them closely could you see what was really happening. They were mostly pictures of one woman. Sometimes pictures of several. Well, I knew about that kind of thing. I'd taken a psychology course at school. Knowing about it didn't make it less sick, less hateful. I burned them. I didn't know what else to do!

The pictures somehow reminded me of Barry Gryme. Last month he called me to ask if now that I'd started college I was old enough to go out with him. I told him I didn't think I'd ever be old enough, and he laughed. He said he needed to know what I meant, would I just have coffee or a beer with him, so I said yes, I'd have a beer with him between classes the next day.

He showed up, which kind of surprised me. Seeing him sitting there, I tried to switch gears, tried not to be just a college girl, tried to be me, Beauty, someone who knew things he would never really know. He's not bad-looking. He is a charming, funny man. He's full of little jokes and amusing stories. Finally, he asked me what I've got against horror writers.

I said there was real horror in the world. Disease and starvation and torture. I said we needed to feel revulsion for these things, needed to be galvanized into action against them and against all poverty and pain and injustice, but that his books merely made us accustomed to horror, as a recreation.

He wasn't listening. He was looking at my face, at

my shape, smiling a little smile to himself, his head cocked. He was thinking about going to bed with me.

I stopped talking. After a moment, he said, well, his books were popular; they made a lot of money, which bought a lot of nice things; people liked being scared to death, so why not?

One of the teachers came by just then and greeted him by name. Barry got up to go speak with him about some seminar he was doing.

I sat there, wondering why not. I knew there had to be a reason, but I couldn't say what it was. Maybe it was that I knew the world was going to end fairly soon and he didn't. All his horror was going to come true. Here people were, bustling around, speaking of the dangers, creating committees and movements to Save the Whales, Save the Forests, Save the Rain Forests, Save the Condor. How could *these* people become what I had seen? But they would.

They would become habituated to horror. They would read it, see films of it. They would soak it up. It would deaden the sense of terror they needed to stay alive. They would catch a kind of leprosy of the spirit, an inability to feel. I mean, I've seen some of that already. They had a terror they call the Holocaust, and because people are so determined it mustn't happen again, they keep banging on it and banging on it until people have stopped paying attention. The more you talk about it, the oftener you see it, the more it loses its power to shock, its power to disgust.

And in the end, unable to feel terror, mankind will go, we will all go down, down, down to happyland.

"Thank you very much for the drink," I said to him, when he returned to the table. "I'm sorry I couldn't explain better what I meant, but I don't believe you know what horror is."

He got a teasing smile on his face and reached for my hand. I whipped it back, as I would have whipped it from the hand of Death himself. He looked in my face and whitened at what he saw there. I was surprised that he, writing what he does, seemed not to have seen real terror before.

[Jaybee Veolante. Barrymore Gryme. Israfel reads and peers as I do and turns away, sickened. We have already sent Puck, telling him to stay out of sight. We tell ourselves not to panic, that these men may be merely men, not creatures of the Dark Lord, that they may be attracted to her for her physical beauty alone. Israfel has stopped telling me to be patient.]

New Year's,
January 1, 1993

Outside the window I hear singing in the street. A drunk, I think, on his way home from a twenty-four-hour celebration. I am not going to the window to see. I am afraid to go to the window. Instead, I sit here in the Wisdom Street house with Father Raymond's book resting on the table, one bloody hand holding it in place while the other plies the pen and mops at my nose, trying to make it stop bleeding. I think it may be broken.

I am writing to keep from screaming.

Bill is dead. I don't know exactly where Janice is; she said she was going to visit friends somewhere over the holiday and won't be home until day after tomorrow.

Bill has . . . had a gun somewhere. I went looking for it and came upon my cloak and boots and this book instead. It was too late for the gun anyhow.

Short recess there to wash off some of the blood. This is all so stupid and terrible.

Bill and I were having a quiet New Year's Eve. Almost midnight, someone knocked on the door, and Bill went to open it. Jaybee came in, looked at me, and said, "I've come for you, sweetie."

I could tell he was drunk. Bill got in front of me

and said, "Here, now, Jaybee. Let's talk about this."
That's all he had time to say.

Jaybee reached out and snapped. . . . Just that.
Bill's body was there on the floor. Jaybee didn't even
change expression. Then Jaybee knocked me down
and pulled off my clothes and hit me and raped me.
He kept turning me over, coming at me from the front,
then from the back, over and over. I fainted, finally. At
least, I don't remember anything for a while. Then he
went away. He took Bill's body with him, wrapped up
in a blanket, like laundry. The last thing he said when
he left was, "Thank me nicely for cleaning up the
place, sweetie. I'll be back in the morning."

*[Puck has to have arrived by now! Oh, why did we
wait so long? He must be there. He must!]*

Sweet, kind Bill. Dear little man. Oh, he loved it
here where he could dress in lace and silk and satin
and velvet. He would put on a recording and dance, all
dressed up in his heels and stockings and smooth, slick
underwear. I gave him teddies for Christmas gifts.
Teddies and lace panties and garter belts. He was so
kind to me. When I cried because I was lonely, he told
me stories to make me laugh. When I cried out at the
future of the world, he told me nothing was certain,
not even death, and I should never give up hope.

He was the size of a child. He had delicate little
wrists and ankles, a thin little neck, like a tiny woman.
He was strong for his size, but he was tiny! Jaybee
broke his neck with one blow of a great ham hand,
broke it and laughed, and then kicked him where he
lay.

I don't remember very well what I did right after
Jaybee left. I hunted for the gun; I've said that. I found
the book, and Mama's box, and my cloak. The warrant
on the usurer was there, and the emeralds. The box
and the cloak almost pushed themselves into my
hands, as though someone were actually handing them
to me.

Then anger came, out of nowhere, like a fever. I

shook with it, burned with it, bathed in it, soaked it up, wanting nothing else. All I want to do is kill him!

I came to myself crouched over the book here. Anger will have to wait. I'm too sick and weak to plan vengeance, let alone execute it. My nose is battered. There are great bruises on my face. I think one or two ribs are cracked. And the pain in my groin feels as though he pushed a knife up me. I'm bleeding two places down there, too.

I have to get myself together. I have to calm down. To calm down I have to go home, really home. I need quiet to think in.

Something made me start thinking of home, like someone whispering memories in my ear. Maybe it's because I need to escape. Jaybee said he would come back, and I know he will. If stay here, he'll find me. He's inescapable.

So I can't stay here.

LATER:

The boots were in my hand. I couldn't remember picking them up, but there they were. They hadn't worked before, but now? Only it wasn't before, was it? It was future, not past. Now? I didn't know. I thought, maybe they will work. I put them on. I put on the cloak. I put the book in the pocket, and Mama's box.

I went to the window and pressed my eye to the slit in the curtain. There were some people out there, milling around, singing drunkenly. Jaybee was standing on the corner watching my windows, an expression of amusement on his face. I could read that face. He intended to do it again. As soon as the people moved away, he planned to come back in here.

I ran to find Grumpkin. On the shelf of my closet were the boy clothes I had arrived in. They went in one pocket and Grumpkin in the other. He hung there, paws and head protruding, wondering what was happening, growling a little as he caught my mood. As we had arrived together, so we would depart together.

I had just fastened the cloak when the knocking started: a soft, insistent, teasing knock on the door. I stood in a corner, paralyzed. He called me. "Beauty?" Softly, sweetly. "Beauty."

Sickness and terror rose in my throat and Grumpkin moaned in his throat, almost a snarl. "Shh," I told him. "Be still Grumpkin, my cat."

"Beauty?" Jaybee called again. "Let me in or I'll break down the door." He laughed, a liquid, bubbling laugh, like molten lava, molten lead, searing in its vile heat. "I'll huff, and I'll puff, and I'll blow your house down!"

He would. I knew he would, but I couldn't move. He would huff, he would puff, he would blow my house down. All my safety he would rip away. He liked to do that. I leaned down and touched the boots, but still waited, as though I had to *see* him do it. No. It was because I was so afraid the boots wouldn't work. Until I had tried and failed, I could hope. Once I had tried and failed, there would be no hope.

He kicked in the panel of the door with a splintering crash. His hand came through the hole, releasing the latch. Then he was in, grinning, whispering, "Beauty? Beauty?"

"Go!" a voice said in my ear.

He didn't see me! He went past me and didn't see me! He went through the living room into my bedroom. I heard the closet door slam against the wall. He was calling, "Beauty, Beauty, Beauty," as though he was calling a dog or cat. "Don't make Jaybee mad," he sang, like a spell, like an enchantment. But he didn't find me so he became angry, angrier still as he searched everywhere.

"Go!" said the voice again.

I tiptoed toward the broken door. Behind me I heard crashing and breaking. Anything I might have treasured, he would wreck. I heard the shattering, the bellows of rampaging fury.

I got out, onto the sidewalk, onto the lawn. Someone had heard the noise and called for help, for there were sirens at the end of the street.

"Boots," I whispered softly, praying I had not mis-calculated, "take me home."

I took a step. A whirlwind bent down to take me, and I heard Jaybee running past me on the walk. The world spun and dizzied. I was standing on a street corner I recognized, not a block from the house. There was a newsstand beside me and the papers in it were dated August 13, 1981. Only ten years. I trembled. It was probable Jaybee could not find me here, but it was a long way from where I wanted to be. Grumpkin me-owed in the pocket of my cloak. Someone coming along the street looked at me, then away, then back again, as though they saw me but not quite. Jaybee hadn't seen me because of the dark, the shadows. In the daylight, he would have.

"Go," whispered the voice, gently.

"Boots," I whispered again, taking another step.

I was on another street corner, in the midst of a huge crowd. Soldiers were marching in the street. People were screaming and throwing paper. "What year is it?" I asked a man from behind him, hoping he would not turn to answer. He gave me the answer over his shoulder.

"Nineteen forty-five," he cried. "Nineteen forty-five."

"Boots," I sighed.

The next stop was in the early years of the century, then the century before. Each time the boots surged more strongly upon my feet, and I knew that as I went back, the power grew stronger and stronger. There had been none of it in the twenty-first, and little enough in the twentieth. By the time I reached the sixteen hundreds it was strong enough to carry me the rest of the way home. When I said "Boots," there was only wild wind and bent time and the shriek of ghosts sucking all the air away. I gasped. There was nothing to breathe. Everything was dark and bloody red inside my eyes, and then only dark.

[And then only dark, thank God. We stood looking down at her, only now beginning to breathe again.

"Is she all right?" asked Israfel, leaning down to put his hand on her breast. *Can he feel what is there, inside?* "She looks . . . she looks drawn very fine."

"We need to get her to Chinanga," I told him. "To the place of safety we planned for her! Now she'll go to find her mother, and all will be well. If her mother is still there!"

"Oh, Elladine's still in Chinanga," said Israfel. "So far as she's concerned, no time has passed at all. I wish Beauty didn't look so tired."

"She's been through hell," I snapped at him. I leaned down and smoothed the hair back from her brow. *Beauty. My beauty. Poor child.]*

15

I wrote the last few pages when I woke up at the first
light of dawn, on a weedy road looking up at the hedge
of roses, now some sixty or eighty feet high. When I
sat up, I felt dizzy and weak, but the feeling passed, so
I pulled out the book and wrote of Jaybee's wrecking
the house and my escape while I could still remember
everything. It gave me something to do and stopped
my wanting to scream or run or do something else
loud and foolish. I wrote until I was too tired to write
anymore, then I lay back down for a while, the cloak
tight around me, and did not wake again until the sun
was halfway up the sky. I dreamed someone came and
told me I looked tired, smoothing the hair away from
my forehead. Perhaps it was my mama.

When I awoke the second time, I saw the cat's-
head outcropping of stone not far down the road. Beyond that pinnacle was the hill where we had gathered
flowers when I was a child, where I had first met Bill
and the others. To my left was the old well we called
the shepherds' well, where the flocks were watered on
their way to market in East Sawley. Nothing looked
the same, and yet everything looked familiar—oddly
familiar, as though I had only remembered it wrongly.

The pinnacle was too short, the hill too low. The trees were too huge, too vast. There were no trees like these, anywhere, anytime. I leaned against one of them, feeling the scratchy roughness of the bark. No. There had been trees like these, once. It was just that I hadn't seen them for a very long time.

I slipped off the boots and rose to my feet, putting one hand toward the hedge to help myself and withdrawing it with a howl of pain. The rose-wall was furred with thorns, small ones and large, an upholstery of needles. The four-petaled pink blooms were sweetly fragrant, though the scent was faint, more like a smell remembered than one present, like an old sachet, left long in a linen drawer, remini-scent. I turned to see an old horse grazing nearby, one eye watchfully on me. When I moved, he turned to stare at me, ears forward, not yet sufficiently surprised or frightened to move away.

I played games in my head, saying words to myself to see if I knew what they meant. Retreat. Regroup. Realize. Resume. The horse whickered at me, coming forward with its neck stretched out, nostrils wide. I put an arm across his back and together we walked away from the hedge. When I looked back, I was unable to see the top. It seemed to arch away from me at the height, and the farther I walked, the taller the green mass stretched into the sky.

Under the cat's-head stone, I searched for my fortune. There were flowers growing between the stones, and a silver-leafed shrub grown well down among the rocks I had used to stop the hidey-hole. It was clear I had returned some little time after I had gone. The rocks had to be levered out with a dead branch, and they came unwillingly, bound about by roots. Inside the hollow was a scattering of coins and gems, but no sign of the leathern bag that had contained them. A mouse, I thought, finding signs about: a whole company of mice. I picked the coins and jewels up and put them into my sack, feeling here and there for the warrant I had left behind. Parchment, it had been. To a mouse as goodly a chewable as a leather bag! Then something rustled under my hand and I pulled the parchment out, dry and whole, not badly stained, nibbled only at the edges. Perhaps the small creatures had not liked the flavor of the ink.

After retrieving my belongings, I trudged up the wildflower hill, turning at the top to look down on Westfaire as I had done a hundred times in my childhood. There was no Westfaire. There were no towers. No high banners whipping in the wind. Nothing there but an escarpment of green, a great whale-back of verdure, a monstrous and overgrown mound, a spined and impenetrable barrow of roses. If one did not know what was under it, one would think it merely a hill covered with thorns, not worth the scratches it would take to explore.

Something shoved me. I turned to find the old horse nosing at my sack. He whickered at me. I stroked his soft muzzle and he pushed his nose into my shoulder.

"I have no grain. Will you be ridden? Saddle or no?" I grasped a handful of mane and drew him toward a rock, climbing upon it and leaning across his back. He made a sound, almost of pleasure. I slid a leg across. He waited. I lowered my weight upon him, fully expecting to be tossed onto the rocky ground. Instead, he turned to look at me, as though asking, "Where do we go now?"

"Down the River Welling is a little hamlet called Sawley Minor," I said aloud to see how the words sounded, trying for the remembered words and accents of this time. "Where the miller lives. Let us go there." When I had played at being Havoc, the miller's son, Sawley Minor had been the place I imagined as home. If I received no welcome at the mill beside the Sedgebrook, the abbey lay only a little farther down the River Welling, and beyond it the village of East Sawley. East Sawley was a village of some size, occupied by woodsmen and sawyers, and I could undoubtedly find lodging there. I nudged the horse with a leg, showing the way, and he moved slowly down the hill in the direction I had indicated.

When the horse moved, I felt the pain in my groin, like a knife. Jaybee had torn me there. There were raw places, and I could feel warm stickiness on my legs. Getting on the horse had started the bleeding again. I shook with fear and rage and loneliness, and the horse turned his head to fix me with his round, incurious eyes. "My enemy isn't here," I said, convincing myself. "He doesn't have boots, so he can't get here without the machine, and he'd have to go back to the twenty-first to use the machine, and he probably wouldn't dare do that even if he could. Besides, he could not imagine I have returned here. No one knows I had the means to do that."

Grumpkin stirred against my thigh, like a hand, stroking me. That reminded me of Bill, and I felt the blood leave my face. Bill knew. No. Bill didn't know I could come back, that is, he didn't believe I could come back, but he didn't know I thought so. Pray God he didn't mention it to Jaybee.

Then I remembered Bill was dead. Jaybee had killed him. Bill wouldn't mention anything to anyone.

"My enemy isn't here," I whispered again, blinking rapidly to make the tears drain away, keeping my voice flat and level. "Not in this time. Not in this place. Take me somewhere, good horse, where we may rest."

We ambled down the road while the sun moved toward noon. The blood caked on my legs, and my trousers stuck to my skin. When the sun was at its height, we reached the place where the Sedgebrook fell into the Welling beside a tumble of stone and the shattered remnant of a great wheel, moss-hung where it stood beneath the sluice. Scattered among the trees were the stalks of old chimneys and a soggy rubbish of thatch. Sawley Minor was no more. There was no one in the place and nothing to show why they had gone.

Grumpkin crouched beside the water, a paw extended to catch whatever might be swimming there. The horse nibbled at the tall grass beside a broken chimney. I took off my clothes and washed myself and my trousers and changed my underwear and put a folded twentieth-century sock between my legs to keep the blood from coming through my clothes. In this time there were no napkins, ready-made in a box. There were no tampons. At my next "flowering" (Aunt Lovage's word), I would have to go back to rags, worn and washed in cold water, then dried and worn again, as Doll had taught me.

The horse and I drank long at the sluice while I wondered what to do next. Though there was no one at the mill, the road that led beside the ruins was still traveled. There were hoofmarks in the muddy verge, and the grasses at the edges had been bitten back by hungry beasts. It led to the abbey and on to East Sawley, and there would be someone, many someones, at either place. We turned down it, the horse, the cat, and I, moving slowly in the shadow of the leaves.

As we rounded each corner, I found myself looking for the abbey. I had been there a few times, with Papa and Aunt Terror. It had not seemed a lengthy journey, even to a child. When I saw it at last, however, I did not recognize it for what it was.

Empty walls by the lakeside. A few carved pillars, with branching tops, like trees turned to stone. Steps leading upward to a floor littered with blackened, shattered beams and a sooty altar stone. The chapel had been there. The burned beams told of fire and the roof falling in. Around this wreck stood vacant halls where men had once worked and prayed, weedy fields they had once planted. Beyond the chapel floor, in the cemetery of the abbey, lay row on row of crosses, a hundred new ones where once there had been a few dozen old ones.

I slid off Horse's back and walked between the stones of the tumbled wall. Beyond the fallen rock, roses were blooming. Here the abbot's garden had stood. Papa and Aunt Terror and I had had wine and cakes on the pillared porch where briars now tangled themselves beside the steps. In the center of the garden was a fishpond where lilies had bloomed, the roots brought home from distant lands by a crusader, so the abbot had told us. The pond was muddy now, sodden from recent rain and rank with vines.

I heard a sound and turned to see a skulking figure dart away behind a pile of stone. "Hey," I cried. "What happened here?"

There was no answer. I waited where I was, and after a time, an old face peered around a corner. I started toward it and was waved away.

"Stay away," he cried. "Stay away from me. Bring me no death. Stay away."

I stopped. "What happened here," I called again. "Did the place burn down?"

"Dead," he cackled at me, his eyes squinched almost shut. "Dead, all of them. All but half a dozen. Then the fire. Then the ruin. Then those that were left went away to Wellingford, all but me. I'll stay, I told them. Stay and guard the abbey."

"Dead?"

"Where've you come from, boy, that you don't know dead? With the Black Death dancing among us like the vintners upon the grapes until we are squoze, trampling us like the threshers on the straw until we are winnowed. Dead they all were, the abbot among them. Swollen and screaming and dead." He came out from behind the corner, a thin old monk in a ragged habit, capering like a goat and making a thin, screeching sound of lonely agony.

I knew of the Black Death. Of course. I had read of it, heard of it, repressed the information, somehow never dreamed that it had touched anyone I knew. And it had come here! And where else?

"Are there many dead in the nearby towns as well?" I asked. "In the hamlets and villages?"

"Everywhere," he cried, jigging up and down in his fear or fury. "Everywhere. And half of all the world is dead of it, too. Stay away from places, boy. Hide you in the forest. Hide you deep where nothing comes on you. Else you'll join them all. . . ." Something sounded deep within the trees, and he leapt like a startled deer and darted away. When I turned back from the sound, he had gone, leaving me with my dilemma still.

I had no time to nurse it. What had sounded in the

trees was a horn, and what emerged from the trees was a hunting party, two lords, a few huntsmen, and a pack of spotted hounds. The men carried boar spears, so I knew they had been after wild pig, up Trottenham way most likely. I stood aside, humble as salt, and let them come.

He who came up with me was a stone-built man, thick through as a tree. "Ho, boy," he said to me with a bit of threat in his voice. "How came you by that horse?"

I bowed, as common people did. "I came not by it, master," I said. "It came by me. I was on the road, and it came up and nuzzled the sack I carry. When I told him I had no grain, he cared not but bid me ride anyways."

"That's Miller Sedgebrook's horse," said one of the huntsmen. "Miller's been dead over a year."

"Him and all his house," said another. "But one son who'd gone away."

I marked down that the miller had a son who'd gone away. Named Havoc, most likely. "Me," I said. "I've come back."

"Likely the beast was wandering," said the first huntsman. "Lonely for humankind."

"He seemed lonesome indeed," I said, looking at my feet.

"Did no one teach you to take off your cap before your betters?" the lord asked. "And what happened to your face?"

"Aye, s-s-sir," I stuttered, "but I've got my supper in it, and a man beat me, sir, and robbed me." Which was true enough. He had stolen my virginity and my best friend and all my peace. He had robbed me well enough.

Though I had spoken without thinking, what I had said made me cry and them laugh. They felt amused and sorry for me, both at once.

"Get up on old Sedgebrook's horse and come with us, then," the lord said. "You can have a bite of supper that's better than you'll find under your cap, at least, and a place to sleep while you heal."

I gestured at the ruined abbey. "The old one there told me to stay far from people, sir, lest I die."

The lord nodded. "Ah, and well enough he'd have told you last year, boy, or the year before. But there've been few deaths this last twelvemonth, and we've hopes the thing is done with."

"The Black Death, he said?" I wanted confirmation.

They gave me curious looks, and I thought I'd better say less and listen better. Evidently the matter was so well-known it occasioned no comment.

"It seems to have been everywhere," I added, hastily.

They agreed it had indeed and bid me again to ride off with them, which I did, though well behind as was respectful. If I was to keep up my boy's disguise, I'd need to cut my hair shorter or braid it up tightly. The men wore theirs almost to their shoulders, but if I'd taken off my hat, mine was down my back so I could sit on it, which was what had betrayed me first to Jaybee. If they'd seen that, they'd not have long accepted me as a boy.

The place they took me was Wellingford House, a goodly manse set some distance from Wellingford village and with no walls about it. Papa had always called the lords of Wellingford plain fools to have no defenses, but from what was said on the ride, they had survived the Death better than most other places. When I saw the place, I thought I knew why. Whether I'd heard of the Death or not, everyone in the twentieth knew that rats and mice and fleas carried disease, a thing unknown in my own time. Wellingford House was as clean a place as I have seen in that time. Since there were no close walls to hold it in, the stables, kennels and barns were well away from the house with much clean garden between. The house had no rushes on the floor, and maids were kept busy sweeping morning and night. In most lordly places, even some parts of Westfaire, the floors were a midden of old rushes, bones, dog offal and droppings, and other, even more disgusting, dirt. Janet, the chatelaine of

Wellingford House, would have none of that, and I saw only one rat the whole time I was there, and that was near the granary.

Janet was a termagant against fleas, as well, with much beating and sunning of clothing and much flea-bane strewn in the presses. As a result of all this clean-liness, few of them at Wellingford had died. I was not introduced to those who were left, but I was sent to the kitchens, which is as good as an introduction. Never was a cook yet didn't like to talk, so I'd been told by our cook at Westfaire, and in the Wellingford kitchens I found out a good deal about the people, especially after the woman there had seen my battered face and come to feel sorry for me.

The lord was Robert of Wellingford, eldest son of the old earl who'd died some time before. His lady was Janet, and they had four children living, the youngest only three. Robert's two younger brothers lived on the place as well, the youngest, Richard, in the manor it-self and the middle one, Edward, in the Dower House, which was some distance away across the park. There was some shaking of the head and pursing of the lips when they talked of Edward, "Naughty Ned," they called him, "One For The Ladies," who was always "Setting A Bad Example For The People." Janet had told him he must go out of the manor house to the Dower House, where he could have his doxies out of sight and mind.

I nodded and slurped my soup and dipped my bread and begged a bit of meat for Grumpkin and a swatch of hay for the old horse, which was really my horse if I was the miller's son, and asked questions about the countryside. Wellingford village and East Sawley, it seemed, were still there, though the latter was much depleted by the plague. All around the countryside places were in ruin, and there was nobody left to build them up again.

"Sir Robert's been looking for masons and build-ers for over a year now, to put the abbey back to-gether, but there's no men to be had. In the cities, it's worse! There's no one left to do anything at all. We've only enough here to work the fields and the flocks, as is, and there's places hadn't enough men to put seed in the ground! Come harvest time, people'll go hungry, mark me!" She, plump as a pigeon, bustled around the fire in a way that made one doubt hunger existed. Still, if she was right, if there weren't enough people left on the farms to plant grain, hunger would come. I shivered and took another mouthful.

"Sir Robert planted extra this year, so's he can give doles come winter," she fretted. "But it won't be enough. Nothing will be. When the people died, the oxen wandered off, and the horses, like the one you found. Some are probably out there, wandering, but many have been killed and eaten by the poor and the homeless. So, even if we had more men to plant more fields, we'd have no more plowbeasts. And the people, wandering about, taking refuge in old places, they make fires and burn the places down, not meaning to, just out of carelessness. The mill, that's how the mill went. And the abbey. And nothing tastes like anything at all, either." She put her hands on her ample hips and glared at me as though I might have occasioned the plague without knowing it. "There's been no spices all this year. The traders died, too, just like everyone else. We're lucky to have a priest about to keep us in the grace of God; most places have none at all."

I thought of Father Raymond, asleep at Westfaire. It was no time to think of Westfaire.

"What's the year?" I asked, ignorant country boy that I was. "I forget."

"It's the year of Our Lord thirteen fifty," she said. "So says our learned priest. And no Death this year, which makes it a good year, boy, whatever else happens." She gave me more soup and a pat on the head.

I had spent a year and a half in the twentieth, but three years had passed here since I had left. So much destruction and death in three little years.

"If everyone's looking for workers, then maybe there's room for me here?" I asked. "I'm thin, but I'm strong. I'm good with horses. I've done stable work since I was eight."

"I'll tell Sir Robert you want to speak to him," she said.

She was good as her word, and the lord spoke to me the next morning, giving me my keep and space in the stables and a tiny wage for my work, as well. Considering everything, it seemed a good place to stay. Grumpkin agreed. The smells of the horses and the hay spoke to him of home. He made himself a nest in the loft and lay there much of the day, like a lion glorying in his past and future conquests, while I groomed horses and mucked out the stalls and rubbed oil into leather, just as I had used to do long ago, with Martin. He had schooled me well, for no one found fault with my work.

It was a strange time, that next time. Despite all the death around, I felt safe. Despite that the country was in ruins, I felt at home. Despite that I had to hide my hair and my body—easier then, in those loose smocks and unfitted trousers than it would have been in the twentieth—I felt myself. Anger left me, slowly, until I was able to acknowledge what had happened. It had happened, I said to myself. I had been defiled and terrorized, but I was still alive, unmutilated, sound in body and mind. My body had healed. Vengeance, I promised myself, but there was no hurry. I could take a time to simply be Havoc, the miller's son. I had been away, I said when they asked. I had not known my family was gone until I came to the mill itself.

"I didn't know the miller had another son than the three who died," the Lady Janet said.

"Oh, yes," someone said. "He had another son, but I've forgotten what it was about the boy."

"He sent me to his sister when I was only a baby," I told them. "I've been there since." Who was to say I lied? Let them think what they would think anyhow, that Havoc had not been born in wedlock, that he had been the miller's son but not of the miller's wife.

Each day started with a bite of bread and a draft of beer in the kitchen, this through the kindness of the

cook who said I was still a growing boy, for others of
the servants and serfs got nothing until later. Then
exercising the horses out on the meadows, staying
away from the sheep and the cows so they would not
be scattered by the dogs who came running after the
horses, their tongues lalloping out of their mouths as
they ran. Then grooming, and feeding, and taking care
of the saddles and bridles. Some of the leather was
worked in gilt, and the oil would strip it away, so it was
mincy work with a little brush and a rag. The other
stable hands hated it for their big hands were clumsy
with the tools, so I did most of it myself. It was quiet.
There was no one about.

Dinner at midday was bread and beer again, and
salad or a bit of fruit and a bite of stringy mutton
sometimes, or a piece of boiled fowl, sometimes juicy,
sometimes powdery from being in the soup so long,
tasting like the memory of chicken. Then there was
hay to pitch up from the wains, or stalls to muck.
Sometimes Grumpkin would bring me mice, strings of
them, laying them out on the stable floor like toy
soldiers. He was learning to be a real stable cat again.

Supper was in hall, everyone there except the
kitchen servants, and me at the bottom of the lowest
bench of all, quite content to be there, even though I
had lice. No help for it. No way for a stableboy to
avoid other stableboys, no way to get a hot, soapy bath
in the washroom off the kitchen, no way for me to let
my hair down until night, when they all slept and I was
alone in my loft. I itched all the time, but I was content
to be there, nonetheless, listening to the singing sometimes when a jongleur came through, listening to the
lords and ladies talking in their stilted French with English words dotted through it like raisins in a pudding,
while the rest of us bellowed away in that same English, soon enough to be the language of us all, I supposed. Since they'd spoken something like it in the
twentieth, clear enough that it was the tongue to survive.

In the stables, I'd met Lord Richard and Lord Edward: Naughty Ned. Of the two, Ned was the more

interesting. Robert and Richard were both sticks, nice
sticks, but sticks all the same, dry and twiggy and given
to crepitant stretching when they dismounted, every
bone making its own little complaint. Ned was full of
the juices of life, wild and rideaway, with lips that
fairly dripped honey, even to those in the stable. They
had not lied about him. He did have his ladies, no
better, as cook said, than they ought to be, a new one
every few days or weeks. They were not doxies, really.
They were widows mostly, women of a certain class
who took only noble lovers and accepted "presents"
rather than payment, living from invitation to invitation.

Everyone talked about Robert's demand that Ned
get himself married. Ned said no, and Robert said yes,
and it had been that way for a while. Even Lady Janet
had put her voice to work on him, explaining how people were needed to work the estate and how it was
everyone's responsibility to produce children.

Ned only laughed. He'd stand in the stableyard,
telling the head groom about it, saying he scattered his
seed far enough, it wasn't his fault it didn't grow. Scattered among the tares, muttered the chaplain, giving
him long penances when he confessed. I was outside,
praying. I could not confess, for I did not trust the
priest as I had Father Raymond. He might well tell on
me.

I asked about Giles. Sure enough, he had returned
—one of the men-at-arms knew of him—but had gone
away again when he found Westfaire mounded with
roses. That night I wept, wondering where he might be
and how I might find him and whether I dared have
the boots take me to him. He could be anywhere in the
world. He could be married. I was afraid to find out.

It was a time, a few foolish weeks, during which I
returned to the sureties of childhood.

It stopped abruptly one day when the cook asked
me, "Havoc, how long have you been here, now? Five
weeks or more? And not stepped foot in the chapel for
mass yet or gone to confession. . . ."

Five weeks. Surely not. And yet when I counted

up, it was true. I had been there five weeks. My mouth
dropped open in sudden realization.

I had, using Aunt Lovage's word, "flowered" only
two weeks before Jaybee had attacked me. I had not
"flowered" since. Aunt Lovage talked that way when
she was a little drunk. Which, come to think of it, was
better than the other aunts who hadn't talked of it at
all. It hadn't mattered that they hadn't told me however. What I hadn't learned in the stable or from Doll,
I'd learned in school, in the twentieth, about things
like this.

Things like this. Things like probably being pregnant. I wanted to howl, couldn't howl, not with the
cook there, bustling about, not in that soapy, hot-wa-
tery place, all grease and yeasty smelling. I wanted a
howling place, a place of my own.

Evening went, and I went with it, mounted on my
old friend, Horse, and with Grumpkin on my shoulder.
I went back to Westfaire by the light of the moon,
determined to get inside those roses. I remembered
the water gate, where the lake ran into the moat. I
remembered a time Martin and some of the other men
had gone to clean it out, and Havoc had tagged along.
They had gone under the stone bridge which stood at
the shoreline and through a gate into the moat itself.
Roses, so I thought, could not grow on water.

By the light of the moon, I went out into the lake,
then waded up to my neck, holding Grumpkin on the
folded cloak above my head, my shirt making slithery
motions around my thighs. Nothing but roses on the
shore, piled into pinnacles and towers, massive ramparts and flowery battlements, roses and more roses.
But in the water, nothing. I saw the shape of the
bridge, covered with thorny green. Below the bridge,
roses draped down to the very surface of the lake, but
behind those canes was a gaping hole where the water
flowed in. I waded, pushing the canes aside with padded hands. Under the bridge, only water and the soft
lop lop lop of it against the curving mossy sides where
it flowed. At the inside end was an iron grating, like
the portcullis above. That was to prevent people bring-

ing boats into the moat from the lake. I had no key, but the bars were far enough apart that I could slip between them.

Which I did, scratching myself on the rusty iron and discomfiting Grumkin a little. I stroked him while he growled and clung to me, as though I were a tree. There were slippery steps leading up to the little door in the corner of the wall. I went up, and through, and came out dripping wet in Westfaire.

So strange a place. Surrounded by darkness. Only open at the very top, so that the moon shone in, silvering the stones. Within the roses, nothing had changed. Everyone was sleeping still, just as I had left them. I sat down and howled, holding onto my cat, crying my heart out, letting the stones hear my grief. Certainly no one else heard it.

"Mother!" I cried. "I'm pregnant!"

No wind in answer, no song of bird. Not even the squeak of a bat, high in that moon-tunneled darkness. Silence and sleep. I stood amid watching shadows and wept.

[We stood in the darkness and watched her, Israfel and I. I think I cried, I who have wept only once since the fountains of the deep grew dry.

"She was supposed to go from here, into hiding," I said. "To Chinanga, where no one could hurt her!"

"Yes," Israfel nodded. "But she needed a little rest first."

"Perhaps we could take it out of her and hide it somewhere else," I said.

"We'd kill her if we tried," said Israfel. "It has grown into her. She permeates it, now. You can't get it out without killing her."

"Is the Dark Lord looking for it yet?"

"He has been looking for it since he was born. He simply doesn't know what it is."

"And he has not found it yet."

Israfel shook his head to tell me no, the Dark Lord had not found it yet.

I think people sensed it in her. I think Jaybee and

Barrymore Gryme had sensed it, without knowing what it was. Perhaps the Dark Lord had sensed it as well, though he had not found it yet.

"Can we wait until she has the baby?" I asked.

"We must," said Israfel. "Since it was fathered by someone who may be a minion of the Dark Lord himself, who knows what it is likely to be," he said. "She cannot have it in Chinanga. She would remain pregnant forever in Chinanga. She could have it in Faery, but everyone would talk of it and the Dark Lord would surely be curious about it. Better that she have it here, where it will evoke no curiosity, where it will only be another birth among these fecund humans. If it is a monster, we can protect her from it."

"Poor child," I said. I had said that several times recently. Briefly I wondered, if I had known her before we did what we did, would I have done it?

"Yes," said Israfel, reading my mind. "You would."]

There was no answer to my cry. I tried again. "What am I going to do?" Still no answer. The shadows looked like robed figures, watching me. Almost I expected them to speak, but they did not. Instead they wavered, as in a breeze, and became only shadows.

What could I do. Go back to the twentieth. Stay where I was. Go somewhere else. Oh God, oh God, where was Father Raymond? Where was Doll? Asleep, deep asleep.

In the twentieth it wouldn't be much. Women had children all the time, married or not. As Candy would say, not enough to shed two tears over. Except he was there, Jaybee. Wouldn't he love it, making me pregnant. Wouldn't he strut, cock of the walk, cock of the dung heap. Wouldn't he whisper to me, stroking me like a cat, Beauty, Beauty, come with me, Beauty, or else. . . . And what would he do to a child?

I couldn't. I would rather die. Not merely words, those, but truth. If dying were the choice, then I'd do it. Drown myself out in the lake. Swim out until I couldn't swim any farther, then go down, choking, just for a little time, into swimmy depths.

Not to know how it all came out? Not to know where Mama was? Not to know whether it would be a boy, or a girl. Or neither! There was a thought!

Abortion. I could go back and have an abortion! Go to some other place. New York, New York, the wonderful town. Chicago. It didn't have to be the States of America, it could be London! I didn't need to have it. It could be ripped out.

I howled.

I didn't want it to be ripped out. I didn't want it, either, but I didn't . . .

Didn't . . .

Don't, I told myself. Don't do anything. Don't decide anything. You're too tired and upset. Go up to your room and sleep, here in Westfaire. Wrapped in your cloak, you're safe. Sleep.

I did. I went up the winding staircase to my own tower room, finding it miraculously repaired, all signs of the fire gone away. I started to lie down on the bed but found myself lying there already. Someone had brought Beloved up from the room far below where I had put her. Somebody had put her in the tower, where romance and glamour demanded she be. The fairy aunts, like enough. I would have done it had I been all fairy. On the chest beside her my mysterious thing made its quiet noise, and I looked long at it, convincing myself the lacy arrow had moved. Not much, but some. It was now exactly halfway between the fourteen and the fifteen.

"Oh, shit," I said, leaving it there to go thumping my way down the stairs, down to Aunt Lavender's room. She was asleep on the floor. Her bed would be empty, dust free and sweet scented by the herb she was named after. As it was, for Grumpkin and I lay down there, wrapped in the cloak, and slept, deeply and dreamlessly, until morning.

Morning was as strange as night had been. Everything was lost in a green murk. Only at noon, with the sun straight overhead, was there any light, for the roses went up to make a great chimney, open at the top. I could look straight up and see clouds passing, birds flying. "Mama," I called again, thinking she might be about, for perhaps she had helped to move Beloved, "I'm pregnant!"

No answer. Perhaps Aunt Joyeause had moved Beloved. Perhaps they had all come together, riding on doves, to repair the tower and set things properly, as on a stage, and then had gone far away again, where I could not follow for I knew not where they were.

Grumpkin meowed at me, saying he was hungry. In the dairy I milked a sleeping cow and we shared the milk. In the kitchen we found a meat pie and shared that. It was enchanted and therefore did not taste as though it had been sitting there for three years. The smell was still there, and the aura flowed down from the tower. I was in my cloak and did not fall asleep. I put a flap of it over Grumpkin as he ate, and he did not fall asleep, though I thought of setting the cloak aside and lying down there in that familiar place, to sleep for a century or so.

What did I want to do?

I didn't want to go back to the twentieth. It was too uncomfortable and too ugly and too threatening.

I wanted to stay here, where I was.

I didn't want to have a bastard child. Life is very hard for bastard children, even when they aren't called that. Even in the twentieth, life was hard for them.

Well then. I would need a husband. Preferably a wealthy one. Preferably a charming one. Preferably . . .

"I have decided our future," I told Grumpkin at last. "We're going back to Wellingford House and seduce Naughty Ned."

16

I am not an accomplished seductress. I am not a seductress at all. At Westfaire, no man would have dared say a word to me about such matters or even make a gesture toward me. In the twentieth there were words and gestures in plenty, but I rejected all of them, too frightened of diseases to risk getting involved with anyone, perhaps, or, perhaps, simply not interested. Still, I knew well enough how babies were planted. What I had not learned at the stables in Westfaire or at school in the twentieth, Jaybee's assault would have shown me. If Naughty Ned were to be convinced my child was his, I would have to get him to bed with me soon as might be.

And just to bed would not be enough. He would have to want to marry me as well. Unfortunately, there was no reason under heaven he should want to marry Havoc the miller's son. Havoc who smelled. Havoc with his lice and his dirty skin and his filthy boy's clothes.

I considered stealing women's clothes. Often the maids put Lady Janet's linens out to air, and I thought I could make away with some of them, leaving a petticoat or two half over the hedge to suggest the wind had blown them away. Lady Janet was twice my size, however, as well as being shorter than I. And even if I took the underthings, I would still need a gown. No

one at Wellingford was my size, and none of the girls
in the village nearby had nice enough gowns. I could
not even make myself a gown, for how would I hide it
from my stable mates while working on it?

After a time the obvious answer came to me. There
were ladies' clothes aplenty at Westfaire. If one of my
mother's gowns had fit me, then all would fit me. I
made another midnight expedition to bring some of
them out—a few of the dozen I found hung in the
attics—and I hid them away in a kind of cubby over
the stable, still wrapped in the sheet I had carried
them in. I would have been able to do none of it without the horse God had sent me, so I thanked Him by
renaming the beast Angel.

Next it was time, so I thought, to find out what
kind of women Naughty Ned preferred. Every night
for a dozen nights I went to the Dower House, invisible in my cloak, seeking the answer to that question.
There were four ladies during those dozen days. One
left the first night I watched. One came then for three
days. One came then for seven. And one was still there
when I stopped watching. At the end of that time, I
asked my question still, for the ladies were nothing
alike. One was a blonde, two were dark-haired, one
had hair the color of carrots. One was slender, two
voluptuous, one skinny as a rake. Their eyes and
mouths and skins were different as well. I conquered
my blushes to watch what they did in bed as well as
out of it, or beside the bed or on the way to it. It was
nothing any two acrobats could not have done better
with less sweat, though possibly with less enjoyment.
Though, come to think of it, Naughty Ned had not
seemed to enjoy it that much. He had been lively and
yet, if I interpreted his look correctly, somehow unin-
volved.

There was the one woman who had stayed seven
days. He had taken her to bed less often than the others, but she had stayed with him longer than the others. She, though not astonishingly clever, was the
wittiest of the lot. Seeing this gave me a faint ray of
hope. The time came, as I had assumed it would, when

the current lady went away, and there was not yet another lady to take her place. There was not another lady because certain messages had been intercepted or sent mistakenly to people who knew nothing about them. Havoc had been invisibly busy, arranging that letters should go astray.

When the last lady departed, Havoc volunteered to get up at dawn and heat the water for doing the wash, which was done in the same tub and the same room as people bathed in, when they did. It was Beauty who bathed in the water while it was hotting, however, well before dawn and no one knew about that. I washed my hair, as well, and combed the nits out of it before wrapping it up in rags because there are no curlers in this century. The rags I hid under my cap, and I dirtied my face in case cleanliness should cause suspicion. Faces are easy to wash.

When nighttime came, I washed my face again, combed out my dry hair to let it hang in a foamy golden cloud down my back, put on one of Mama's gowns and my cloak, and sneaked away across the meadows. At the Dower House I took off the cloak, hung it carefully over the terrace railing, where I could find it again, and walked down the terrace to the room where Naughty Ned always sat at his ease after his evening meal. I knocked. He came to the tall window himself and let me in, his face a perfect picture of surprise.

"Good evening, Edward," I said. "I am Beauty, the daughter of the Duke of Westfaire. I have come to keep you company and tell you tales to allay your boredom."

Then I sat down by the fire and told him the future of the world. I was witty. I was amusing. I laughed gently and forestalled his advances. I drank but little wine and kept my wits about me. When the bell in the Wellingford chapel rang for Matins, I excused myself and left him there, disappearing into my cloak on the terrace. He came out after me, searching, calling my name. I ran away, down the long terrace and home across the meadows, just in time to put my gown away,

get on my boy clothes once more, and catch a scant
few hours sleep in the hay.

It had been, I told myself, done as well as I could
do it. When I saw how well he liked the wittier lady, I
remembered a book I had read in school in the twentieth. It was called the Arabian Nights, and it was about
Scheherazade who told clever tales for a thousand and
one nights in order to avoid being put to death. I had
nowhere near that long. If I couldn't fascinate him
sooner, the whole thing was hopeless anyhow. Going
to bed with him would not accomplish what I had in
mind. He had done that over and over again with
many women without wanting to be married to any of
them. And though he had tried several times, out of
habit, to interrupt me by suggesting something improper, I had always put him off and gone on with my
tales. I thought possibly the mystery would reach him
where the carnality hadn't.

As Havoc, I watched that day as Edward set off to
ride to Westfaire, which was known by most local resi-
dents to be under an enchantment. I heard Edward
talking about it with the men who were riding with
him. "An enchantment of roses," is the way he put it,
sounding excited. That evening, when he returned, he
looked scratched and frustrated. One of the men told
the head groom that Lord Edward had not been able to
penetrate the roses around Westfaire though he had
repeatedly tried! I considered it a hopeful sign.

That night I put on the second gown—I had
brought only three from Westfaire—and went to the
Dower House again. Again I told him tales until Matins, and again he pursued me when I ran away.

On the third night I took my cloak in with me, set
it beside me on the chair, and in the midst of my discourse sighed and interrupted the tale. When he asked
me why, I told him I was under an enchantment. That
until I was married to a man who would ask me no
questions, I could appear only after dark and the barrier around Westfaire would remain. I said this twice,
being sure he understood it, before I directed his attention to a spurious spy at the window and disap-

peared while his head was turned. He looked around him wildly, cursing and crying my name. I had done it as well as it could be done, I told myself again, making my weary way home across the fields.

The fourth night I did not go at all. Nor the fifth.

On the sixth, I returned in the gown I had worn when he saw me first. He was stalking up and down on the terrace outside his window, clenching and un-clenching his fists, muttering and sighing. This was a good sign. I took off the cloak and sighed loudly, my-self. The moment he saw me, he went to one knee and asked me to marry him. I turned away, thrusting out one hand as though my maidenly modesty had been deeply surprised. He begged. I looked at my hands and wrung them dramatically. He begged the more. At last, on an expiring sigh, I said yes. I would meet him at the Wellingford chapel at dusk, three days after-ward, and marry him there.

He would have time for second thoughts. So did I, when I was awake enough to have any thoughts at all. Lord Robert cursed at me for being asleep in a horse's stall, and Lady Janet told me to wake up when I dozed against the side of the steed she was mounting. Mostly I thought that I did not want to be married. I would not have minded if Giles had been there to marry me, but I did not want to marry Ned. What I really wanted to do and had set out to do was find my mother. I longed for a mother. Someone to tell my troubles to, a shoulder to cry on, a sympathetic hand on my fore-head, a voice saying, "There, there, dear, we'll work it all out." I thought of using the boots, assuming they would take me wherever she was, but the thought of going to my mama pregnant! She had told me to come to her at once, before I grew older. Coming to her in my present condition did not seem appropriate. It would be like going home in disgrace. Despite my fret-fulness, that night I slept like one dead, and in the morning woke to hear the news everyone was bab-bling. Lord Edward was going to be married in three days, but he would not say to whom.

I went in my cloak to keep watch on him that night.

There were no ladies at the Dower House, nor on the night that followed. It appeared he really intended to go through with it.

The Wellingford chapel was a small one, large enough for the family and servants only, served by a resident priest who said daily masses and took care of christenings and burials. Also, three monks had been taken in from the abbey when it was destroyed, and it was they who rang the bells for the holy office. The chapel was set in a graveyard, and there were Wellingfords buried all around and beneath it, the whole place smelling a bit of sanctity and dust and rot, as well as of incense and tallow.

I did not go openly. I went in my cloak, ready to flee if something appeared amiss, and I stood on the porch for a time, looking in at the people. The priest was there, looking grumpy. So were various members of the family, irritably glancing around to catch a glimpse of the putative bride. Ned was there, jumpy as a cat, darting glances at the door every second or two. The priest gave up his unpleasant look to yawn. Ordinarily, Ned and I would have pledged our respective properties and exchanged rings in the church porch. I had no property to exchange, or at least none I was willing to use as dowry. Ned would have to take me as I stood.

I put the cloak down in the porch and walked slowly down the center aisle. Everyone stared at me and murmured. I pretended not to notice the admiring looks cast my way by some of the gentlemen and even a few of the ladies. I had done what I could to look well. There were summer flowers twined in my hair. I had returned to Westfaire for yet another dress, the pink one I had worn at the banquet the night before Papa had intended to marry Weasel-Rabbit. When the priest asked my name, I told him in a clear and carrying voice that all might hear: "Beauty, daughter of Elladine of Ylles and the Duke of Westfaire, under an enchantment which can only be broken by marrying an uninquisitive man."

Ned looked into my eyes and swore to honor and

keep me. He whispered in my ear that he would be uninquisitive. He would not ask questions. He trembled when he took my hand. I looked at his chin and pledged to render him my duty, wondering betime what Father Raymond would have said about all this. Father Raymond had had definite opinions about the sacrament of marriage, and I concluded he would have been disappointed in me, taken all in all. The priest babbled a great deal of comfortable Latin and we took the sacrament together. Ned kissed me, delicately, as though I might break. I curtseyed to his older brother, to Janet, to his younger brother, to other members of the family. Janet gave me a hug, rather quickly, as though she were afraid the enchantment might rub off on her. We left the chapel and walked across to the manor house where the kitchens had been steaming since noon, preparing a feast.

"We didn't have time to prepare anything elegant," said Janet. "Or to think of a proper gift."

"I was given a proper gift," I said in what I fondly hoped were mysterious tones. "A young boy, seeing me approaching the chapel, told me he would give me his dearest possession as a gift for my wedding. The gift is a cat called Grumpkin, he is in the stables, and I would like him brought here."

Someone went for Grumpkin, coming back later rather the worse for wear with my poor cat in a sack. I cursed myself for stupidity in letting anyone else go in my place and turned him loose, giving him a saucer of cut up fowl on the floor at my feet.

"We couldn't find the boy, ma'am," I heard one of the servants saying to Janet.

"He told me he was leaving," I said, my words carrying over the clatter of the diners. "Going away. Never to be seen in these parts again."

It was true, then, so far as I knew. What need had the wife of Edward Wellingford for Havoc, the miller's son.

.   .   .

Remembering what I had seen in the Dower House as
a voyeur, I made no effort to compete in innovation or
athleticism with the women Edward had consorted
with in the past. It was no lie to pretend virginity. It
was no lie to pretend shyness. I felt them both. When,
on the third or fourth night after the wedding, Edward
made love to me at last—I having held him off till then
out of a genuine feeling of revulsion which I managed
to overcome at last only by much purposeful wine-
bibing—I felt nothing much except discomfort and relief when it was over. Jaybee had evidently unsuited
me for the enjoyments of the flesh, though thereafter,
knowing what to expect from Edward, it became easier. I knew it was supposed to be a pleasant experience. Out of curiosity if nothing else, I had read in the
twentieth how a woman can assure that it is pleasant,
but I felt no impetus toward talking with Edward
about it or doing what in the twentieth would have
been called "working at our relationship." It would
have been a lie. I did not want to work at the relationship because I did not love him. I came quite to like
him as the days went by, but I did not discern in myself
even so much affection toward him as I had often felt
toward Bill or so much as I felt toward Grumpkin.
Edward did not know me and never would. Our relationship was built upon a fiction. It was shallow and, I
feared, temporary. I could not visualize myself staying
at Wellingford long after the child was born. The child
itself, I could not visualize at all.

Still, I was carefully gentle and kindly in my mood,
receptive in my manner. So much was owed the man,
after all. I took my wedding vows as seriously as I
might for what time I had. He liked me to look lovely,
so I made a point of that. Even when I became, all too
soon, swollen as a melon, I could smell sweet as any
garden and wear flowing things that rustled gently.

We rode. He insisted I ride sidesaddle, which I
hated. My grandfather's invention evidently had
gained some little reputation among the neighboring
nobility. We read together, he evincing delight that I
knew how to read and write, which, indeed, I did bet-

ter than he. I told him stories, things I had experienced, things I had heard of, and he was mightily amused, wondering how I had come by such a store of tales. I made up a lie about my father's fool, that he was a widely traveled creature with a retentive memory who had fed me on stories from my childhood. It was more or less true. The fool had fed me on stories, right enough, though they had mostly been of a less than salutary kind that made the women he had known the butt of his evil humor.

When we had been married about four months, Edward came in from riding one day to tell me that the roses mounded Westfaire still, that the enchantment remained. He looked hurt.

I was prepared for this. I told him that we knew half the enchantment had been removed, for I was able to appear regularly in the daylit hours, but that since complete lack of inquisitiveness was the *conditio sine qua non* there must be some kernel of curiosity in him still, which prevented the entire enchantment from being broken. He flushed, and I knew I was safe from further conversation on that matter.

Time wore on through the winter to the early spring, and the baby was born. It was early, of course. I made much of that when labor started, saying no, no, it could not be yet. I need hardly have troubled. In that time, babies often came early and were too tiny to live. Often they died. I thought I would die, wished to die, wished I had stayed in the twentieth where there are drugs for such pain, almost screamed out for my boots to take me there, but was drowned out by the midwives' exhortations to breathe, to breathe, to push, to push. I screamed and breathed and pushed. There was a squall, followed by bustling to and fro, then the tiny swaddled creature was laid on my arm while someone messed about between my legs, cleaning up. There was much clucking over the afterbirth, in which the midwives purported to read signs and portents of both good and evil, but they soon gave over and set things to rights. I thought of Aunt Lavvy as they sprinkled oil of lavender about and burned sweet resins in the candles to kill the mudflats, seaside smell of birthing. When Edward was allowed in, we were clean and sweet once more, and he gazed at us both as he might have gazed at heavenly angels.

"What shall we name her," he asked in a whisper, his hand gently upon my arm.

"After my mother," I told him. "Elladine. That was my mother's name." I wanted to love the child. I wanted to remind myself that children need a mother's love.

He added a string of family names, and a day or so later she was taken to the chapel by Janet to be christened. Though she was one-quarter fairy, I made no mention of the fact. My own christening had started all this mess. Better the baby get by as simply as possible with Robert and the Lady Janet as her godparents and the blessing of Holy Church to guard her through life.

After that, time seemed almost to stop. I tried to nurse her myself, rejecting the wet-nurse from the village. I rather liked the feel of it, liked being close to her. The sight and sound of the tiny fuzz-covered head so tight against me, the little star-shaped hands pushing like a kitten's paws, the toothless pink mouth agape like a bird's, all were interesting. Then one morning when she was about two weeks old—it was midmorning, actually, with the sun casting westward beams along the wall at the edge of the heavy curtains —as she was nursing, she opened her eyes and looked at me and it was Jaybee's look, greedy and violent. Her mouth clamped down on me as though strong fingers pinched me. There was blood on my nipple. I gave a cry, and the maids came rushing in. I told them to fetch the wet-nurse, that my breasts would no longer be enough for the child, keeping my voice as calm as I could though inside I bubbled with hysteria. He too had bitten me there. He too had drawn blood.

["Now," I said to Israfel.
"Wait a little," he said. "She is coming to it of her own accord."]

Thereafter they brought her to me once or twice a day, to look at. She was everything tiny, precious, holdable. Everything fragile and sweet. And yet his eyes looked out at me from the infant face, as though he lay within the infant mind, waiting. After that, I could not touch her without an instinctive aversion, a revulsion. The wet-nurse fed her; the nursemaid changed her napkins; and Edward adored her. Seeing his face above the child was like seeing the spring sun rising over the fields. He was so full of love it shone from him.

Edward hovered over me, too, but, as was thought proper in those times, did not invite me to his bed for the forty days I lay with the bedcurtains drawn, seeing neither the sun nor moon until time came to be churched. Father Raymond had always said the churching of women was a ceremony of thanksgiving for a safe delivery, but at Wellingford it seemed quite another thing. There, so the midwives said, a woman was considered unclean and unholy by virtue of the blood she had shed in giving birth, and only the priest's words said over her put her in a state of grace once more. While there were some at Wellingford who disbelieved such nonsense, Lady Janet believed it wholeheartedly, and it was her way the wives forced on me, whether I would or no. In some other time or place I might have made a fuss, but since Edward and his kin were kindly and generally well-disposed toward me, there was no point in making them uncomfortable.

At the end of the "lying in," I went to the chapel, all muffled up in the traditional veils, to take a seat near the altar and have the priest read psalms over me to compensate for my having offended God by bearing a child in holy wedlock. The "chapel smell" was very strong that day, as it had been the night Ned and I were married. I still couldn't identify what it was. When the priest had finished, I was supposedly free of the world again, able to look upon sunshine and stars. I did not tell them I had been sneaking out of bed nighttimes to sit in the window watching the moon and longing for something I could not quite name. My own

mother, I think. Someone of my own, at least, who
could explain to me what I was feeling. Despite all my
good intentions I could not love my own child. It horrified me that I saw Jaybee's malevolence in that tiny
face. She was half me! Surely my half counted for
something! Often though I convinced myself of that,
when I saw her, when she opened her dark eyes and
looked at me, I saw only violence and terror and felt
only a memory of pain.

In addition to her fears about newly delivered
women, Lady Janet also feared the babe would be
taken by fairies, so there were maids about day and
night, hovering over the cradle. Janet told tales of
babes snatched away with changelings left in their
place. No one said why fairies preferred human children to their own, and I considered it unlikely. I had
seen one that Janet spoke of and knew him to be no
changeling but a poor idiot, what the twentieth called
a Down's syndrome child, born to a woman in her
forty-fourth year, but there was no point in arguing the
matter with Janet. It would do little Elly no harm to
have loving people about her, even for a spurious reason.

Though I kept her at a distance from me, she had
no lack of caring hands to help her and gentle arms to
hold her. Ned played with her as if she had been a
novel toy, doing peek-a-baby and pat-a-cake until both
he and Elly were helpless with laughter. More than
once I surprised on his face an expression of grateful
wonder, as though there were something in being a
father he had neither expected nor dared hope for. As
for me, I wavered between resentment that the babe
was not the child of someone I loved and thankfulness
that at least she bid fair to be beautiful and not apish
as Jaybee's child might well have been.

Remembering what I had learned in the twentieth,
I took such precautions as I might to be sure I did not
conceive again. Luck or God was with me. Almost a
year went by and I did not kindle. Remembering
Ned's boistrous talk before our marriage about having
scattered his seed widely without issue, I began to

think he might be sterile. I wished I knew for sure, that I might give up the counting of days and the playing of games, pretending to have headaches or other infirmities to keep him at a distance betimes. Still, the thought gave me some hope that Elly would be our only child.

I took to riding a good deal, for exercise, and to get away from the house. I went often alone, preferring that to being pursued by panting stableboys mounted on fat carthorses, for the master of horse would let them ride nothing better and there were no men to spare to keep an eye on me. One day I had ridden out early, going up into the hills, and I came to a ridge where one could look down, over the burned abbey and the lake and across the lake to the mound of roses where Westfaire slept.

I didn't see the man there until I had dismounted. He moved, and it startled me.

"M'lady," he said. "Do not be afraid."

Oh God, I knew that voice. I turned and went toward him, he looking across at me, at first in curiosity and then, almost, in terror.

"Beauty!" he cried.

"Giles!" I screamed in return. Oh, he was the same, the same. He had hardly aged at all. The same light brown hair, though it was cut short, as though he had spent much time under helm. His eyes were the same when they looked into mine.

"You can't be," he said firmly, like a man turning his back on an enchantment. "Oh no, you can't be!"

"No, I am!" I cried. "I really am. It wasn't me who got enchanted, Giles. I was outside!"

He took my hands. He pulled me close to him and I felt the thunder of his heart. It was the first time he had ever held me, and everything in me turned warm and molten and, oh, I lusted after him. I wanted him, there, then, on the patch of grass beneath that tree. I put my arms about his neck and kissed him, the kissing burning like a fire. We kissed one another, turning our heads this way and that, as though if we found the

proper position we could somehow transcend our sep-
arateness and become one person, fused at the lips.

"No, no," he gasped at last, putting me away from
him. "This is not proper. You are a virgin girl. . . ."

I laughed. I reached for him, clung to him, said I
wasn't. I was married, a mother, married to Edward of
Wellingford. I babbled, holding on to him like a cat to
a tree. He went white. He loosened my hands. He
backed away from me.

"Married," he whispered. It was as though he had
said, "Dead."

I stopped talking and looked into his eyes. There
was no lack of love there, but I knew that, when I told
him I was married, I had lost him. Giles was an honorable man. He was a religious man. He was a chivalrous
man. I had lived so long in the twentieth, I had forgotten about honorable, chivalrous men. But Giles was!
Not merely in words, but in deeds. He would no more
cuckold another man than he would strike an oppo-
nent from behind, for such would not be virtuous, and
he longed for virtue. Would he have obeyed Father
Raymond and gone from me else?

"Giles . . ." I whispered. "Oh, Giles. Don't leave
me. I need you."

He warded me off, as he might have warded a
curse. "I love and honor Beauty, the only woman I will
ever love," he said. "But she whom I loved was a girl
whom I had the right to love." He went away from me,
turned and ran for his horse, and I think I heard him
sobbing as he went.

I screamed his name. I stood there, screaming his
name, the tears running down my face. I threw myself
on the ground and wept. When I looked up next, he
was gone. I thought I might have imagined him, but
then I saw him, far below, riding full tilt across a clearing, away, away.

When I could, I returned to Wellingford, to Elly, to
Ned, to my life. I felt that I had died, and only my shell
was there.

As Elly had grown, so had Ned's love for her. He
loved me, too, but as he might love an ornament, a

thing fragile and fair which he might brag of having, a thing barely utilitarian. He owned a crystal cruet some knight had brought from the Holy Land, and he spoke of that cruet much as he spoke of me. My lovely Beauty. My Beauty without compare. And then, "Mother of my Beloved . . ."

When he said that, something cracked. Anger spurted out like blood from a new wound. So, I was the mother of his beloved. I was always something to do with someone else's beloved. Edward's beloved or my father's beloved. And Giles, my beloved, would not have me because I was the mother of Ned's beloved. I went to my bed and cried, and the longing to get away began to grow in me. The longing for someone of my own kin possessed me.

I remembered that while a year and a half had passed in the twentieth, three had passed in the fourteenth. I wasn't sure how old I was. Was I seventeen? Or nineteen? My mama had said to come before I got any older, but I was older. Still, if I spent some time searching for Mama, it might seem only a little time to little Elly and to Edward, for time was different in different places.

I wrestled with my conscience as Jacob wrestled with the angel of God, paining myself in the sport until I could not sleep at night. I wandered about the place all that night, half the night spent traversing the walk to the chapel, there and back again. I went through the still room stores, counting and recounting the cordials, the jams. Through the cellars, totting up the wine. Through the linen closets. As I was counting the linens, it became too much to bear. I locked the closet and went to the nursery.

She was asleep in her cradle beside the fire. The heat had made her rosy. Her hair tumbled in dark curls about her head. Her thumb was in her mouth. Her eyes were shut, but I knew if she opened them, I would see Jaybee once more.

["Now," I said. "She is coming now."
"She is," said Israfel. "At last."]

I was wearing a simple kirtle. I snatched up my
cloak and took my boots from the pocket, dropping
the linen closet key deep into the pocket as I did so. I
traded the boots for the shoes I had on, putting the
shoes in the pocket also. As I went out the door, I
picked up a sunshade one of Edward's craftsmen had
made for me. It would do to keep off the sun or rain
and to keep dogs at a distance. Outside the front door,
I said, "Boots, take me to my mama."

The vertiginous darkness swept me up in its embrace. I heard Elly crying from a great distance, a
brief, pained cry, and then I knew nothing more.

17

CHINANGA: TIME UNKNOWN,
PERHAPS TIME IRRELEVANT

When at last the darkness passed and the boots were
still, I stood on a spit of sand that extended like a
finger into an expanse of water which seemed, at first
glance, to be limitless as the sky. It was full day with a
hot sun half hidden behind rising mists. Behind me
dark trees full of noises and vines thrust up through
the water to make a shimmering wall. Before me the
water moved slowly, glossed with metallic lights and
sullen ripples. Across the flow were other trees, laced
with more vines and echoing with fainter though similar noises, the water going away among them to sheen
the buttressed trunks with dancing reflections of
greeny light. At a considerable distance to both my left
and right, the trans-riparian growth curved inward to
join the closer jungle behind me. The curve informed
me I sat on the inner shore of a sweeping bend in a
great river.

The nearer trees were decked with orchids, their
cloying fragrance spiced by scents of lemon and clove.
Though the perfume beckoned, the jungle did not welcome, nor did the water. The scene was not there to be
entered but to be observed, like a splendid backdrop
for some as yet unplayed drama. Seen thus, with the

sun filtered through rising veils, the scene was one of
somber loveliness, of profound melancholy, of aching
nostalgia, as though I—or everyone—had known this
place, in youth, or in dream, or in richest imagining.

I had told the boots to take me to my mother. If
she were anywhere near, her presence was hidden
from me. Given that I still wore the boots, I could
have gone striding off in search of her, but all directions seemed equally magnificent and mysterious, and
along with the heady fragrance of the orchids and
spices came the stench of swamps, an odor which recommended caution.

Time in this place was not equivalent to ordinary
time. Hurry had little meaning. Impatience had none. I
resolved to wait upon matters. The cloak hid me well
enough that I was not afraid of predators; the sand spit
was dry and warm; I had set out not long after supper
and I had eaten reasonably well. So I sat down and
waited, bringing my book up to date, letting the slow
surge of the flood before me lull me into a daylong
doze broken only when a tribe of quarrelsome monkeys came down to drink. The water was silent. *Altis-
sima quaeque flumina minimo sono labi,* Father
Raymond had been fond of saying: deep rivers are
quietest. He usually said it when the aunts were chattering. Or when I was. This river was quiet enough to
be very deep.

When something changed at last, I sensed it only
gradually as a remote dissonance adding itself by tiny
increments to the sounds of birds and monkeys. A
splashing sound. A clattering yet liquid noise. Something upon the water, or within it. Something far off to
my right and slightly behind me, in the direction of the
water flow, coming upriver though as yet hidden by
the towering screen of trees.

Should I become visible or remain invisible?
Should I appear miraculously out of nothing? I considered the alternatives without moving as I watched the
bow of a great riverboat emerge from behind the jungle, a tall, many-decked boat with two huge wheels at
its sides, thrashing its methodical way against the flow,

its decks cluttered with folk. In this case invisibility would not aid me. I slipped off the cloak and boots and stood forth in my simple gown to summon attention with my ruffled sunshade.

It was some time before anyone saw me, then everyone saw me at once. The ship shuddered as it changed direction. The riverboat's whistle screamed, making me put my hands over my ears. A small boat was put over the side and came darting in my direction like a water bug, walking upon its oars. The two rowers ran the little boat up onto the sand and then sat in it staring at me as though I were some kind of exotic animal, though I was no more strange in my way than they in theirs, they being dwarfish and dark-skinned men with narrow ears.

"My name is Beauty, Lady Wellingford," I told them. "I have been abandoned here and need transportation to the nearest town or city."

They muttered. I understood them well enough for they spoke a kind of bastard Spanish with a great deal of Latin in it. At last one of them got out of the boat and offered to carry my baggage. I smiled prettily and let him, somewhat astonished to find I had baggage. We got into the boat, they pushed off with the oars, and we went skimming over the water toward the riverboat, which beat slowly at the current, holding itself in place.

The lower deck protruded fore and aft of the upper ones, making the upper decks look rather like the upper layers of a wedding cake set down upon an uncompromising loaf of something darker and more practical, pumpernickel, perhaps. The lower deck carried cargo. The upper ones carried passengers. So much was obvious from the faces peering at me over every rail.

I ascended a ladder to the second deck, then had only time to straighten my skirts before being confronted by the captain, a gold-bedecked, large-headed, stocky person who might as well have been carved out of wood for all the solicitude he expressed.

"Ma'am!" he said, in a threatening tone.

I repeated my self-introduction in a lingua franca of my own, what Spanish I remembered from school plus Latin and a smattering of Saxon and medieval French, at hearing which he glared at the sand spit as though it had been guilty of hatching me of its own malicious will.

"Never before!" he asserted. "I've been ferrying people, man and boy, so many years I can't count, and never before has there been anyone picked up along the way."

"I have some resources if it's a question of payment," I suggested.

He shook his large head, drawing his brows together, considering what this might imply. At last he said, "No need. Traveler in distress is enough reason to stop. Got an empty cabin, so no difference." And he stalked away, muttering mysterious oaths in what I took to be Hebrew and Greek, shaking his head, plunking his stumplike legs down as though to force them through the planks. Despite his assurances, I did not feel welcomed.

There was time to catch only a glimpse of the other passengers: some, behind a barricade, burly and small, brown-skinned and dark-haired, dressed fancifully in what appeared to be ethnic garb; others, walking about the deck, lighter-skinned, dressed in uniforms or simple gowns. It was a colonial group, obviously. The ruled and the rulers.

While those behind the barricade stared and pointed, one of the boatmen led me to the empty cabin, a small, cool room with a wardrobe and dressing table along the inner wall, a narrow, netting-canopied bed, and shuttered windows looking out upon the deck. It was there the captain joined me when he had had time to compose himself and become more cheerful about my rescue. The intervening moments spent alone allowed me time to decide upon a story of kidnapping and abandonment. I had been taken from my home, I did not know by whom. I had been left upon the sandbank, I did not know where. Some of it was more or less true, and the rest could not be disproven.

The captain shook his head at all of it, while claiming he was delighted to be of service. His name was Karon, he told me, and the boat was the *Stugos Queen,* currently bound for Nacifia in the land of Chinanga, which country surrounded us. He asked me if these geographical locutions sounded at all familiar to me, and I could only reply honestly that they did not. I had expected to be in Ylles. I had expected to be in Faery. Perhaps this was Faery. Certainly it was not Ylles.

"Is the land of Ylles near Chinanga?" I asked.

"By St. Frog," he said, "do they have their own land now?"

Wondering if I had heard the oath he had used correctly, I let the matter go. He evidently did not know of Ylles. He led me out upon the deck and introduced me to my fellow passengers before conducting me upon a tour of the vessel. The passengers were more than merely interested in me. I gained the impression that matters in Chinanga were not always amusing. One very old and wizened lady held my hand long in hers, cocking her head to get a good look at me. "Hello, a beauty," I think she said. Surely she could not have said, "Hello, Beauty," for I was introduced as Lady Wellingford. She smiled engagingly, but her manner was a little forbidding in that it was quite intense and focused. She was a stranger, and yet with something familiar about her, as though her voice or face, perhaps, resembled someone else's. Someone I had known well.

The forward hold, said the captain, was full of raw rubber from the plantations downriver. The after hold was stacked with sacks of coca leaves and coffee and stalks of plantain, swarming with flies. At the extreme upriver end of the voyage, she would take aboard exotic fruits and wines from the sunny hill plantations of Baskarone, sent down through Joyafleur.

"Baskarone?" I asked. The word set up a strange reverberation inside me, that almost-recognition I had felt for the old woman. "Baskarone?"

"Our neighboring country," he said. "Up there." He pointed upward with a peculiar gesture. I assumed he meant at a higher altitude, though the river mists prevented my seeing mountains, however close they may have been.

We stood at the rail together. The Stugos was in flood, he said, as it was at least half the time, but the torrential waters were more moody than usual even for floodtime, full of strange eddys and streams of bubbles emitting violet fogs. The crew, he said, seemed to be spending half its off-duty time at the river altar on the taffrail, propitiating one or another of the water devils or begging St. Frog to protect them.

"St. Frog?" I asked, wondering once again if I had heard him correctly.

He nodded. "We bought relics of St. Frog from the Cathedral of Helpful Amphibians last time we were in Nacifia." He scratched his buttocks reflectively, wondering out loud if it might be worth the trip up a tributary river to a particular one of the mighty falls at the very border of Chinanga where one might make an offering at the shrine of Our Toad of the Intermittent Torrents, perhaps, or to Saint Serpent of the Sandbanks.

I was reminded of my father. "Is such a pilgrimage thought to be efficacious?" I asked wearily, a question I had many times asked Papa.

He shook his head gloomily. "Don't know," he replied. "Some say yes, some say no."

He might have explained further, but he was hailed by a crewman and left me to go to the lower deck and put his ear to one of the hatches, listening, no doubt, for the rubber or coca leaves to declare themselves. I knew then that he had lied about what was in the holds.

I stood at the railing, asking myself whether I should put on the boots and go in search of Mama. The old woman stood next to me, as she was to do often in the succeeding days.

"Have you come here to meet someone?" she asked me, a little surprisingly, for surely Chinanga was not the crossroads of the world.

"I have come here to meet my mother," I said. "But I have no idea where she is."

"We arrive in Nacifia in three days," the old woman told me. "You will undoubtedly be able to find out where she is, in Nacifia. Someone there will know."

I thanked her and she smiled at me, a smile of particular pleasure and joy. Nothing in our conversation explained her expression, and I went to my room thinking her even more strange than I had formerly done.

Strange or not, she had told me the truth. On the third day, just before dawn, the dome of the Cathedral of Helpful Amphibians in Nacifia loomed against the fading stars. Our arrival time, which may well have been purposeful, allowed the whistle to be used to maximum effect. While I watched our approach from near the rail, my hands held tightly over my ears, Captain Karon hauled on the whistle rope, hunching his head down between his shoulders to keep the reverberations from rattling his skull. The resultant howl was enough to wake the dead. Certainly the noise could do nothing less than bring the sleeping town to attention.

When he had hauled on the rope a few more times, sending great clouds of pigeons reeling skyward from behind the dome of the cathedral, to be turned into flying rose petals by the pink light of dawn, he evidently felt he had let off enough steam that he could tell the stokers to leave off, rake down, and tie the valves open. By the time we docked, the town was stirring like a disturbed anthill. I spied more than a few rude gestures aimed in our direction. The captain only grinned and hoisted his round belly over the top of his trousers, stroking it with one hand as he might some imperfectly tamed animal, raising the other in an ironic salute in my direction.

I went down onto the lower deck and looked about me with the keenest interest. The passengers were a motley lot, their oddities more evident than usual thus assembled in contiguity to one another, and their

crated belongings were odder yet. Armadillos plated
in gold and decked with jewels; chickens in shades of
vivid emerald and aquamarine; turtles, their eyes
awash with lugubrious tears. There were even stranger
figures upon the pier, leaping men and women with
painted faces, cavorting among the crowd in manic
lunges. I pointed them out to the old woman, who was
standing beside me. She habitually stood beside me.
As though she did not want me to be out of her sight.

"From the clownery," she remarked, pointing to a
brightly painted building along the river as she tapped
her head with a meaningful gesture. "Every now and
again they escape."

"Do you know Nacifia well, madam?" I asked her.

"I have explored it," she said. "Prior to choosing it
as my place of residence for a time. I have a little
house on the hill, there, up the Street of Immaculate
Intentions. Perhaps you will visit me there."

"Perhaps, madam," I murmured.

"Captain! Ho, captain!" The call came from the
pier, slightly below us and to our right. Captain Karon
craned his neck to see the person waving her flowered
umbrella at him. I had not seen her approach, though
she was worth the seeing now she had arrived, a full-
bodied and bright-haired woman, skin glowing ivory in
the creamy shadow of her highly domed parasol. Her
voice was softly rounded, an amorous moo, so solid
and smoothly finished a sound that it seemed to writhe
itself toward his welcoming ear, probably tickling all
the way down as it demanded attention.

"Mrs. Gallimar!" he shouted in return, taking off
his gold-bedecked cap and stumping toward the gangway where passengers were already clotting up like
ants on a mango, waiting to disembark. Captain Karon
slid behind the barrier and down the gangway to meet
the lady on the pier. This was no doubt the lady he had
mentioned to me—and to everyone—so frequently
during the voyage.

She spoke clearly, making no effort to avoid being
overheard. "Oh, Dear Captain Karney. Here you are
again, but so late!" She tapped him on his chest with

an extended forefinger, the finger bending backwards like that of an oriental dancer, flexible as cable, as she looked up at him through fringed eyelashes with an expression of admiring coquetry. "I expected you weeks ago." Her voice lowed, like that of an amorous bovine; it sinuated like a snake—a veritable cow-python of a voice.

The captain flushed and shifted from foot to foot, as though aware of a sudden warmth in various parts of his anatomy. I wagered idly to myself that Mrs. Gallimar, with her smooth skin and her smell like a garden full of flowers, had that effect on most males. "We're right on time," he objected. "Not even a day late."

"Oh, but I was so eager!" She tapped him again, smiling up at him with wide and innocent eyes. I knew those eyes. Candy had had such eyes. Such eyes made a practice both of flirtiness and of not noticing men's response to it. It was a way of telling them not to presume upon what seemed to even the most iron-groined among them to be unmistakeably sexual signals. This contradictory manner probably left most men as it left Old Karney now, opening and closing his hands helplessly and with a distinct shortness of breath. Mrs. Gallimar was, not to be too vulgar about it, a tease. I had seen teases in the twentieth. I put my hand up to hide a knowing smile as she cooed at him. "I'm going with you when you leave!"

He was dumbfounded. His doubt showed in his face, for the lady nodded her head, slowly and emphatically, signifying that he had not misunderstood her in the slightest. "I have to go upriver, Captain. To Novabella."

"Novabella?" He could not help his faint grimace nor I my start of slight surprise. From what I had been told, it was not a town for the likes of Mrs. Gallimar. Novabella, in the crew's opinion, was not a town for anybody much.

"The Viceroy is sending me," Mrs. Gallimar confessed. "It seems there's a gallivant eating the people there, and I'm to take a provisional permit."

"A permit?" he breathed, as though he could not believe it.

"I know it's hard to credit, but a permit it is." She nodded, her lips pursed in a serious and childlike expression, her eyes saying that though one could hardly believe it still it was true.

"A permit," he said again, trying the consistency of the words to see if there was anything believeable in them. During the days of our voyage the matter of permits had come up more than once. Permits, I had been told, were mythical creatures, less common than gallivants. There were bodies lying unburied for generations in Chinanga, for want of permits. There were bastard great grandchildren of couples who had hoped to marry but had not, for lack of permits. To obtain a permit! Ah, what had happened to occasion this?

"How many people has the gallivant eaten?" the captain asked.

Mrs. Gallimar burrowed in her tiny purse, digging a chipmunk tunnel through the contents, bringing out a tiny leather covered notebook with a mother-of-pearl pencil at one side, leafing through it reflectively to find her notes. "Two children," she said sadly. "And at least one adult person. And it has bitten the left buttock and part of a breast off a woman married to someone important." She shook her head as though wondering at the novelty of it as she put the notebook away once more.

"But a permit!" the captain said, still in awe.

"I know." She nodded, seeming to admit the weirdness of it, the notion that a permit even in the abstract would be strange enough without having one in the absolute to deal with.

"So you'll be coming along," he breathed.

"I'll be coming. As well as Colonel Esquivar, just in from the jungle, going to hunt the gallivant. And Mirabeau, the chaperone."

"Aha," said the Captain. *"That's* it! They've found one!"

Mrs. Gallimar nodded. "I think so. What else

would move the Viceroy to issue a permit? They must have found one."

I shifted my position to get the sun out of my eyes, deciding in that moment that I wished to be introduced to Mrs. Gallimar. With the old woman trailing behind me, I went to the gangway and, with a barely audible "excuse me," slid behind the barrier as Captain Karon had done.

"Well, we'll be leaving tomorrow," the captain was saying as I, we, approached. "Or maybe the day after that. As soon as we can discharge the cargo."

I smiled at the captain. He bowed in my direction. I asked to be introduced to the lovely lady of whom I had heard so many fascinating things. For a moment Mrs. Gallimar's hand rested in my own as the captain mumbled, "Mrs. Gallimar, Lady Wellingford. Lady Wellingford, Mrs. Gallimar." The old woman behind me said, "Ahem," and the captain began again. "Mrs. Gallimar, Senora Carabosse; Senora Carabosse, Mrs. Gallimar."

The old woman's name brought me up short. Surely I had heard it before. Surely I had seen that name somewhere.

I was given no time for reflection. Mrs. Gallimar expressed a belief that meeting me was one of the most exciting things that had ever happened to her. Her eyes ate at me with tiny glances, she nibbled at me with her ears, almost twitching at every word I uttered. She wondered if I had breakfasted, and when I told her I had not, she invited me to accompany her to her house, for if the *Stugos Queen* was to leave soon, she would need to see to her packing. She left the captain with a last titillating stroke of her fingers along his arm, and we sauntered up the cobbled street down which she had come, back to the gentle amenities of a little pink house set behind a sheltering wall on the south side of the Street of Immaculate Intentions. Behind us the old woman stumped along, disconsolate, watching me as though she were a fish and I a fly. When Mrs. Gallimar and I went into Mrs. Gallimar's house, Senora Carabosse went on up the street, glancing at me over her shoulder.

While breakfast was being prepared, we sipped passion fruit juice as Mrs. Gallimar toyed with a pet ocelot. The ocelot had been a gift from Colonel Esquivar himself, Mrs. Gallimar remarked, seemingly to the ocelot. The colonel had recently recovered from being poisoned by his wife, the Viceroy's sister, monstrous Malisunde, who was a notoriously inefficient poisoner. It was said the colonel had more to fear from his mistress, the Viceroy's wife, despicable and fecund Flatulina, who had threatened to batter him to death and would no doubt be aided in the attempt by the elder half-dozen of the colonel's numerous bastards. Such a fate had been long predicted. It would scarcely come as a surprise, even to the colonel himself. Did I think such an end was likely?

Unprepared for her including me in the conversation she had been having with her pet, I took a moment to reply that I had not really considered the matter.

She went on to say that very shortly the Viceroy's palace would make the formal announcement of the hunt for the gallivant. Everyone would begin to wonder, just as the captain had, why the Viceroy would have issued the permit at all. By nightfall there was not a creature in Nacifia who would not guess that the people of Novabella had found the virgin. The one everyone had been hunting for. So Mrs. Gallimar told herself and the ocelot, while the ocelot watched me and I watched both of them, listening.

"The virgin?" I asked. Something within me trembled, as a glass will quiver, in resonance with a distant bell.

"A virgin with a difference," she replied almost in a whisper. "The Viceroy has been seeking one for a very long time."

"A virgin with a difference? What difference would that be?"

"One wonders, doesn't one. One has all kinds of strange ideas."

Her softly voiced ruminations were interrupted by the arrival of breakfast, brought in by the two maids, Dulce and Delice, upon a wheeled table and set in the large bay window overlooking the garden. I smelled muffins and my mouth watered. We sat at either side of the table to confront a platter of tiny delicious sausages and breakfast breads oozing with fruit.

As we sat down, I asked, "Have you lived in Nacifia long?"

"As long as one does," she replied. "Sometimes that seems very long indeed." She gave me tea.

"You know, I should suppose, almost everyone?"

"Oh, my dear Lady Wellingford, not almost but definitely everyone. Some better than others, of course, but yes, everyone. Each last wee babe, each tottering elder. And why not? Hasn't there been time enough to know them all?" She passed the tiny buttered muffins, and I took several.

"Does the name Elladine mean anything to you? Elladine of Ylles?" The muffins were spread with sweet butter which clung to the tongue like a lover's kiss. Why was I thinking of lover's kisses?

She thought, furrowing her brow delightfully. "What time-of-life person are we speaking of. Would she be a young-appearing woman?"

I nodded. Elladine would surely be a young woman. Did fairies ever grow old?

"Her appearance?"

"Ah," I murmured. "Very lovely. Very lovely indeed. Rather like me around the eyes."

She examined my eyes, shaking her head firmly. "No, my dear Lady Wellingford. There is no one like you around the eyes in all of Nacifia. I could not be mistaken about that."

I sighed. She passed the marmalade. We went on to speak of other things. She told me while in Nacifia I must see the cathedral, the marketplace, the clownery.

Our enjoyment was interrupted by a firm knock at the door. A moment later, the caller was announced: Licencee of the Bureau of Public Morals, Chaperone First Class, Roland Mirabeau.

Mrs. Gallimar composed her face into an expression of dignified pleasure and rose to greet her guest. He entered, bowing, and stood up to reveal a face which would not have disgraced a classic sculpture. He had stature and presence, a curly moustache and eyes that glittered. I was introduced. He bowed again. He took Mrs. Gallimar's hand and expressed his compliments. Mrs. Gallimar seemed unstimulated by this encounter, and I wondered why.

She signaled to Delice that another chair should be brought to the table and a third place laid.

"Senor Mirabeau," she began.

"Roland," he instructed with a polished smile, which was only very slightly peremptory, as he took a cup of tea. "Though we have not seen one another for a time, lovely Mrs. Gallimar, still, we are acquainted."

"Roland," she began again, returning his smile with one of her own. I knew that smile. Captain Karon had described that smile, the smile flirtatious, which had been known to conquer whole regiments of men while they were merely marching past.

The chaperone assumed an appropriately spellbound expression, but the mechanics of this process were as entirely visible to me as they were to Mrs. Gallimar. Though the face before us went through a series of calculated adjustments indicating enchantment, its owner was not, in fact, enchanted. Mrs. Gallimar recognized this fact as quickly as I did. Her mood changed, and with it her manner. The smile flirtatious was tucked away. "This gallivant," she said in a businesslike voice, "seems to be causing a good deal of trouble."

The chaperone sat back in his chair and said calmly, "Indeed."

"It must have been very difficult for them to obtain even a provisional permit," she said.

"Undoubtedly the people of Novabella offered a sufficient inducement," the chaperone replied, accepting her offer of a cuscumbre muffin. "As you and I both know they must have done, Mrs. Gallimar. Let us not trifle with one another. I have come to inquire what your part in all this may be."

"I am to convey the permit to Novabella," she said. "Prior to providing it to the Gallivant Committee, I am to ascertain that all is as it has been represented. The Viceroy wishes me to do so."

"Is there some doubt that the gallivant has indeed eaten the children it is said to have eaten?" he asked innocently. "If so, how will you be able to tell whether they met their fates by being eaten rather than by some other equally dismembering cause?"

"There is no doubt about the beast. As to the other matter, I will ask questions," she said. "The Viceroy trusts me to come to the truth of the matter. I am confident of my abilities in this regard. Still, you may expect to be paid your proper fee."

"Oh," he said casually, biting into a bit of brown bread, "The fee is the least of the matter. It distresses me that the Viceroy does not think me capable of ascertaining what I am sure you are also being sent to ascertain, Mrs. Gallimar. He wants to make doubly sure that she's truly a virgin, doesn't he."

Mrs. Gallimar flushed, only slightly. "Perhaps the Viceroy felt that . . . well, a woman would be better qualified."

"Nonsense," he said crisply. "Any graduate of the Bureau of Public Morals Institute of Chaperonage is quite capable of knowing on the instant whether One is or One is not."

"Perhaps he is sending me, dear Roland, to keep her company on the return voyage." Mrs. Gallimar pouted prettily and cast her eyes toward her tiny shoes. There was a moment's uncomfortable silence.

"Is it permitted to ask," I inquired, "what sort of difference this virgin is to display?"

Roland's perfect lips lifted slightly away from his white teeth. "Difference, dear Lady Wellingford. How can one define difference. The virgin is to have it, else she will not do. Were she lovely as the dawn and pure as the spring rain, I would still find nothing there of interest to me unless there is also *difference*."

The words set up that odd resonance once more. Something I had heard. Something I had seen. Where had I, myself, encountered reference to a virgin with a difference?

So musing, I almost missed Mrs. Gallimar's grumpy response to the chaperone's comment. "I quite understand," she said.

I felt that I, too, was beginning to understand. Roland Mirabeau was unmoved by women, by any ordinary woman, by any except an extraordinary woman. Mrs. Gallimar knew this, though her customary manner had caused her to overlook it for a few moments. Roland was, in fact, unteaseable, therefore of little interest to her.

He took another bite of brown bread. "We can hope she is as represented, Mrs. Gallimar. If she is, I will know it." He snapped up the last bite with a click of his teeth and a quick lick at his lips. "Since our departure is imminent, I will take my leave, lovely Mrs. Gallimar, in order to put my baggage in order and assure that it is properly stowed."

He bowed himself away from us both, murmuring, "Lady Wellingford, such a delight," while Mrs. Gallimar sat unsmiling and annoyed. I thought as I made my own farewells that for a woman of Mrs. Gallimar's disposition Roland Mirabeau would not be an amusing companion on a lengthy voyage.

["I had hoped to get to know her," I said to Israfel. We sat across from one another in my house on the Street of Immaculate Intentions. We were drinking tea.

"She looks at you and is afraid," he replied. "She senses your interest in her and is put off by it. Your acquaintance is too new. You have offered her your friendship too soon."

"I shall persevere," I told him severely. "Too soon or not, she will need me."]

18

Aboard the *Stugos Queen,* I put on my cloak and went into Nacifia to see all those things Mrs. Gallimar had recommended I see. If we left upon the morrow, there might be no other opportunity to investigate the city.

I went first to the Cathedral of Helpful Amphibians, which was beautiful, outside and in. Though the materials were not ones Gaudi could have used, the place reminded me somewhat of pictures I had seen in the twentieth of a Gaudi cathedral. I sat down near one of the pillars, crystal carved into the likeness of a jet of water, leaping toward the sky. The whole cathedral was a fountain in stone. It was lit from high green windows with a dim, liquescent light, and in the side chapels statues of the helpful creatures sprawled or lay or climbed, each after its own nature.

I took off my cloak for coolness sake when I sat down. It was not long thereafter that I was surprised by a voice behind me saying, "Is there anything I can do for you, daughter, or are you merely sightseeing?"

"Ah . . . Father," I murmured, turning about so I could see him. "Sightseeing. Yes."

"You're the lady rescued from the sandbank," he smiled at me as he came to sit beside me. "What do you think of our cathedral."

"It's very beautiful," I said honestly.

He nodded in agreement, beaming at the pillars.

"At home," I said, struggling for truth without complication. "At home we would think it strange to dedicate a cathedral to . . . ah . . . amphibians."

He seemed slightly startled. "What would you dedicate a cathedral to?"

"A martyr, perhaps," I suggested. "An angel?"

"Were they made by the Creator?" he asked.

I nodded that they were.

"Well, so are these," he said with some asperity, gesturing around him. "Are some parts of creation more worthy than others in your homeland?"

I told him yes, that in my homeland (thinking of the twentieth and twenty-first) only humans were worthy of anything at all. All else was disposable.

He shook his head over me, speechless, his old face suddenly lined with horror. He made a gesture in my direction, which I recognized as being one of aversion, one of fear.

"I didn't say I believed that," I cried.

He made the gesture again, and tottered away into a side chapel where I could see him kneeling at the altar of St. Frog, murmuring in a heartbroken tone. I slipped on my cloak once more, saddened by his rejection.

My next stop was at the clownery, where I wandered invisibly down long hallways, watching the inhabitants at their work or play or whatever it was they were doing. One inmate was packing cockroaches, one hundred to the bag. I do not think the insects were dead, though they were very quiet. Another inmate was constructing a large bust of the Viceroy, so the label said, out of what appeared and smelled to be dung. A third inmate, with the aid of a tall ladder, was writing her autobiography on the walls of the place. She had covered four stories of one stairwell and had extended her tale out into the reception area, where two walls were already covered with obscenities. I followed her story back in time until I reached a door to the roof, where a group of attendants were having morning coffee. Even read in reverse, it had been a novel of violence, abuse, incest, and horror.

I stood on the roof listening to the attendants, who were mostly interested in discussing the fine points of their latest soccer series. When I went down the stairs again, the walls were clean. Another inmate with bucket and brush was washing them, as he sang a lovelorn lament. The inmate with the bags of insects had given them to someone else, who was letting them go. The sculptor was asleep in the shade of his gigantic construction, while six or seven others carried the substance of it away in wheelbarrows. Each madness had been unmaddened.

I made my way next to the macabre heights of Mont Osso Negro where the citadel stood. I had a mind to look upon the Viceroy of this place. I found him striding through arched corridors in search of his daughter Constanzia, whom, as his bellows of rage and accusation testified, he suspected of dalliance with the young men of the garrison. Before his iron-booted feet, legions of scrub women scattered to one side or the other, squawking like chickens, except for one aged crone who scuttered along beside the Viceroy on all fours, attempting to slosh soapy water in his path while muttering, "Beast. Hideous beast. Inhuman dog. Ingrate," calumniations of which the Viceroy took no notice. His long, white face was set in an expression of obdurate annoyance, one, I was to learn, of his two customary expressions, the other being a vacuous stare of terminal ennui.

When his invective became boringly repetitious, I left off following him and went in search of Constanzia herself, a quest which the boots made simple. She was hidden in one corner of the long, vaulted library loft, reading a leather-bound volume with the word "Forbidden" stamped on its cover in age-faded ink. The book was mildewed and fly-specked; the pages were yellowed by time. Still, the gold leaf of the title gleamed bravely in the slim rays which leaked through the owl holes cut in the gables of the loft: *The Diaries of Ambrosius Pomposus, Founder of the State of Chinanga.*

Constanzia's reading was interrupted frequently by

the need to look up words with which she was unfamiliar. I went to and fro with her as she searched for references in various volumes written in a multitude of tongues, a process which ate up the hours. She had managed to get only to page one hundred forty-two of *The Diaries,* and she muttered to herself that it had taken the better part of three rainy seasons to read that far. A sense of fiery purpose emanated from her, like heat from the sun.

When I grew weary of reading, I explored the castle, finding the Viceroy soaking in his tub, a steaming towel wound around his head, leaving only his nose to quest for air, like a tapir's snout, while an intermittent procession of water carriers dipped out portions of the cooling water and poured in equivalent ewers of hot from the boilers in the kitchens below. Obviously, the plumbing no longer functioned, and certain smells wafting from lower regions indicated the drains, too, might be endangered.

Captain Jemez sat on a chair by the window, reading the *Nacifia Noticias,* remarking occasionally upon its contents, while the Viceroy muttered comments from under the towel. After a time, the Viceroy seemed to fall asleep, and Captain Jemez went to the window.

I peered over his shoulder. In the marketplace the fruit stalls were bright with mangos and pollarels, bananas and cuscumbres and chinangarees. On the hills behind the town the goatherds played their pipes, the sound coming faintly over the bleating of their flocks, borne by the soft warm winds down from Baskarone.

"Ah, Baskarone. Sun-kissed Baskarone of the thousand delights," the captain murmured, beginning to sing in a strong tenor voice, "I found my love in lovely Baskarone."

He crossed to the other side of the room to look out across the river, far among the drowned trees where the land sloped up to the range of jungle hills. After the rains, the river would fall, I had been told, into its narrower channel, leaving behind ten thousand little lakes and pools to reflect the blossoms and give a homeland to the frogs.

The captain had similar thoughts. "Bless all frogs and other helpful amphibians," he intoned in plainsong, switching to his baritone register.

"Captain," said a firm voice behind us.

"Madam," he bowed, flushing. I slipped to one side, not to be trampled by the visitor. Flatulina had come into the bathroom and stood considering her husband's recumbent figure as the steam rose gently about him.

"How long has he been in there?" she asked, arms akimbo, massive shoulders raised in inquiry, huge head cocked, its generous features dwarfed by the mane of black hair which boiled from her skull in an uncontrollable torrent.

"Most of the morning, madam."

"Get him out. He'll be all wrinkled." Flatulina's full lips twisted in distaste.

"Madam . . ."

"Get him out. There's an ambassador come. Ambassador Israfel from Baskarone. Tell him I said." And she was gone, leaving the captain to consider how he might best disturb the Viceroy without running the risk of that gentleman's wrath. I followed the woman, much desiring to see Ambassador Israfel from Baskarone.

And he was there. Though I was wrapped tightly in my cloak, he looked up and smiled at me as I came into the room. He was only slightly more marvelous than I supposed any other man might be, anywhere. Looking at him, I felt that I had been changed forever. The thing that burned at the center of me came alight, a fine white flame.

And he went on smiling at me, seeing me though the cloak was tight around me, seeing and approving that flame before he turned away and greeted the Viceroy. I leaned against a pillar in utter confusion. As soon as I could move, I returned to the *Stugos Queen*.

.   .   .

I lay upon my bed, wondering what I had seen, what I had felt. I had loved, still love Giles. That is a human affection, a love that desires, at least partly, some physical consumation: a touch, a glance, something that speaks from one body to another, one heart to another. Even if we were very old, Giles and I, we would want that. We would want to lean together in the gloaming, our cheeks next to one another, our hands clasped, letting our selves say to one another that we loved. I think that would be true. Remembering him now, I think that would be true.

This thing I feel in the presence of the ambassador is something else. This is what I sometimes felt in Westfaire, at certain times when the light fell beneath hovering clouds onto the windows and the grass, lighting them with a mysterious and marvelous effulgence, colors so pure that they made one's eyes ache, or at certain times when the rain dropped in gauzy curtains of mist to half-hide, half-disclose the fine, soaring lines of the castle. It is a longing so deep, an appreciation so rare . . .

In the twentieth I felt it a few times. I went to an opera and heard a woman's voice, like a stream of falling water, the orchestra behind her in a cataract of sound, and I felt it then. I felt it a little when I set my eyes on the jungles of Chinanga for the first time, a kind of perfection that sings inside.

They are both love. If Father Raymond were here, perhaps he would say this other thing is the love of God. But I was not thinking of God when I felt it at Westfaire, and when the woman sang, and when I saw Israfel. I don't think I was.

Night came to Nacifia. The riverbank bloomed bright with torches. The day had been long and hot and full of sights and sounds and tastes. I had no wish to engage in conversation or be introduced to anyone else. After supper, I put on my cloak and moved like a shadow along the quay, looking here, listening there. Captain Karon and his crew scattered themselves among the waterfront tavernas; the people of the town scattered themselves likewise. Constanzia approached the captain with a curtsy and a request from her mama. The captain was known to have certain special luxuries aboard. Would he be inclined to display them?

Display his wares tonight? the captain asked in nicely feigned disbelief. Who would look at his poor goods after sundown?

Certain people, she said, had indicated that they might be persuaded.

The captain demurred. Surely not.

There was so little amusement in Nacifia, she persisted, with a flounce, a sidelong look, and maidenly laugh.

Until, at last, the captain gathered up a dozen torches and set them around the *Stugos Queen* while ordering three of his men to open the hatches of the small, forward hold and bring out what was there.

Cages of silver peacocks and lengths of shining silk. Incense and carved sandalwood boxes. A half-lifesize mechanical ballerina who danced upon her toes, click, click, click, like a cricket, coming to the edge of her stage and raising her tiny hands in mechanical fright before turning to begin her dance again. Pots of perfumed ointment and hand-blown bottles of cologne. Monkeys with gold collars and iguanas in jeweled chains. Lace from the convent at St. Mole and confections from the monastery of St. Cloud. How so many things could come out of the little hold was a wonder to everyone, no less to me. Each thing brought out smelled, too, that old, mysterious smell which I had never identified: the chapel smell, the smell of Westfaire.

Coins changed hands. The Viceroy's wife went home with lengths of sparkling fabric. Other wives contented themselves with the piece goods Flatulina had overlooked. Daughters sniffed at the crooks of their arms where drops of ointment deliquesced in silken folds. The robust Malisunde carried off an ape in a cage, as a substitute for a husband who was never

home said someone, not meaning to be heard. Only
the shadows and I heard, and only we laughed.

In the half-darkness, at the edge of the torchlight, a
young lieutenant stood with Constanzia, murmuring,
"His Excellency, your father, has been somewhat distraught of late."

"Do you think so?" Constanzia asked. "I had
thought he was rather less irritable than usual. This
business in Novabella has quite set him up. He hasn't
tried to kick Grandma for at least a week. Even when
she got soap under his feet and knocked him down in
the long gallery last Friday. And he is sending Mrs.
Gallimar as plenipotentiary. With a provisional permit!"

The lieutenant agreed that the issuance of even a
provisional permit betokened the possibility of novelty, even, perhaps, of change. He was gazing at her as
at a wonder, but she did not seem to notice.

Constanzia nodded thoughtfully. "I believe the
people of Novabella have promised him a virgin with a
difference. He has all the ingredients but that one.
Think what it will mean if she truly is what they say
she is!" She smiled on the young man, at which he
blushed red as a rose. But then, just as he put out his
hand to touch hers, she excused herself and went trotting off up the street toward the citadel. He turned
away in confusion. Poor boy.

I stood sleepily by the gangway of the *Queen* as the
place emptied and night settled. Only a few persons
remained when I, with considerable surprise, saw Constanzia peering around a corner near the square. I
thought again, as I had several times during the evening, how lovely she was. Her face had a spontaneous
liveliness about it. Very dark. Very sexy. Very sly, at
the moment, and cautious not to be heard or seen. She
came out into the street, carrying a basket from which
protruded the dusty cover of the book with the word
"Forbidden" stamped upon it. She came nearer,
slipped up the unguarded gangway onto the *Queen,*
opened a hatch cover, and disappeared below. When

the boat left in the morning, evidently she intended to be aboard.

I heard the stumping footfalls of the captain moving along the quay. I followed him onto the riverbank, where Mrs. Gallimar still sat as she had throughout the evening, bidding for nothing at all, dreamily watching the torchlit flow of the water. The captain was not content to leave her so. He carried a bottle of ruby glass in which, so I heard him say, she might find a wine which a master vintner would envy.

Mrs. Gallimar was so touched with his gift that she suggested they share it then and there. They sat in the flamelit night, watching the reflected flares shimmering on the Stugos, avenues of silken light reaching away from them away into unimaginable darkness where the flood moved silently in the night. As they watched the light, ignoring their glasses, I drank their wine. A divine vintage. One of the wines, perhaps, of Baskarone.

"We are at the center of the universe," purred Mrs. Gallimar. "See how the light reaches out from us in all directions."

Silently, I agreed that it was so. In daylight, things seemed to vanish at the horizon, joining there. Here in the firelit dark, all lines plunged toward us across the waters, ending at our feet, a fan of radiance with ourselves at its center. All things centered upon the observer. I was the axle of a wheel of light. It seemed important to remember this moment when the universe wheeled upon my hub, the moment in which I was impaled upon a fan of light.

"Remember this," said a voice. It was the voice of the ambassador from Baskarone. "Remember this. All things end here, with you, Beauty. Remember this."

"Remember," whispered an old woman's voice. Senora Carabosse. I looked around, but she was nowhere near.

It was a fantasy, no doubt, brought about by the darkness and the wine. Still, I would remember.

"We are," the captain said in a strangled voice, "the very center of everything."

"Until now," sighed Mrs. Gallimar with a softly amorous tone, "I had not looked forward at all to this journey."

"Until now," growled the captain in husky honesty, "neither had I."

I left them there, my lips sweet with the wine, my mind full of wonder at the circled paths of light, resolving, as I returned to my cool cabin on the *Stugos Queen,* never to forget this night. The old woman was standing at the railing, just outside my door. "Good night, dear Beauty," I thought she said, but the wine had made me too giddy to hear her aright.

"Good night, Senora Carabosse," I replied. Though the monkeys were screaming in the flooded jungle once more, I knew that, on this night, I would sleep.

19

Captain Karon, by threats and shouts and hiring a few layabouts to help with the unloading, got the last of the publicly acknowledged cargo off the ship shortly after sunrise. Three inmates from the clownery showed up to see the boat offshore, which delayed matters a bit as they insisted upon helping the passengers with their baggage.

The stokers bent their backs before the boilers, the whistle began to bleat, and the passengers trickled toward the rail to watch the departure. The chaperone emerged onto the deck to motion with one languid hand. Colonel Esquivar, a tall person with sharp squinty eyes, an enormous moustache, and very brown skin—riven by long exposure to the elements—had come aboard during the night, and he staggered out of his cabin bleary eyed, bowed to Mrs. Gallimar, sneered at the chaperone, and said something mildly insulting to the captain before staggering back into his cabin and slamming the door behind him. With a final toot, the *Stugos Queen* moved out into the flood, breasting it with a great shuddering clatter of both monstrous wheels, while the clownery inmates hurtled along the shore in a series of giant cartwheels and balletic leaps, ceasing to follow the ship only when it came opposite the swamps at the mouth of the tributary Rio Apenado.

The stewards began laying the tables in the first-class dining room. The cooks were already ladling out stew for the second-class passengers, the crew, and that part of the cargo needing to be fed at midday. (Was I the only one who noticed food being carried twice each day into the holds? No, the old woman saw it, too. She gave me a significant look and a wink. Who is she? What does she mean?) First-class luncheon would be later, which gave the kitchen boys time to decorate the dessert table with a frilled lizard carved from ice and garlanded with poppies carved from halves of blood-red chinangarees.

I settled easily into the routine of the voyage. Each morning I arrived in the dining room before Roland Mirabeau, who—shaved, dressed, with his hair arranged and moustache trimmed by his servant—arrived shortly after me to drink a glass of cuscumbre juice before sitting down at my table with a steaming cup of coffee or maté or cou, all of which were available, each in several varieties.

Since I was not in the mood or market for a lover and had made this fact clear, Roland accepted me and talked freely in my company. I listened, seldom making any comment that required a reply. The old woman, Senora Carabosse, usually emerged from her room a little later to sit at a neighboring table with her tea, eavesdropping on our talk as she blinked and muttered to herself. Poor old thing. I felt ashamed of my animadversion. She was harmless enough.

[Really!]

After a time, Mrs. Gallimar would come down to breakfast, usually with either the captain or Colonel Esquivar in attendance. There would be a flutter of ribbons and a rustle of sweet, scented flounces, a titter of laughter and a softly modulated voice calling good morning. I would see Roland preparing himself for appropriate reactions, for smiles and courtly bows, for admiring nods and glances, all of which Mrs. Gallimar would expect. One morning he confessed to me that he felt there was something missing in his responses. He felt the lack, as one feels something missing in a flavor which does not fill the mouth but merely lies there upon the tongue as though in anticipation of some more complex savor. So Roland felt a certain lack of sincerity at the core of his acquaintance with Mrs. Gallimar. He did not, in fact, lust after her, although, on an intellectual level, he could appreciate all her lustworthy qualities. She left him chill and untouched, his flesh like tallow, stiff and unwarmed by her welcoming sensuality. So he said, supposing I would understand. This was an unflattering supposition, though I made no remark upon it but merely smiled, cocking my head to solicit further intimations. Behind me, Senora Carabosse chuckled quietly to herself.

Had this been a new sensation, Roland went on, he would have been disturbed by it, but in fact it was his usual feeling with regard to women. Flowers could move him. Sunsets could bring tears to his eyes. The sight of the wind bending the trees at dawn could make him cry out in luxurious sensitivity, but women moved him not at all. There was something about them, some inherent fleshiness, some excess of corporeality which turned him cold. And then there was their smell, whether masked in perfumes or alive upon the air as itself, that fecund stench, that earthy aroma, that mephitic scent, which seemed to come upon them with womanhood.

(I leaned toward him, wondering if he would catch my aroma. Evidently he did not. It was then, I think, that I began to understand the world in which I found myself. I was beginning to find a certain lack of consistency. As though natural laws only partially applied.)

Little girls smelled otherwise, Roland said. He quite liked little girls. He loved their breastless little bodies and their wee buttocks, like two eggs laid side by side. He loved their elven haunches, their dimpled knees, and pink soled feet, but all this adoration was in his eyes only. He did not lust after them. He merely

worshipped them, as he worshipped the egg icons in
the sanctuary of St. Frog, for what they symbolized,
not for what they were. Purity. Oh, Roland adored
purity. Purity and beauty. It was why he had become a
chaperone, after all, in order that he might adore it.
Serve it. Preserve it. And though there was much
beauty, there was little enough of purity in Chinanga,
so he said.

"I sometimes wonder," he remarked to me over
his second cup of cou, "what we would have been like
had we not been condemned to live here in Chinanga.
What would we have been like had we been allowed to
settle in holy Baskarone?"

His remark was overheard by Captain Karon, who
snorted and said, "Better ask what Baskarone would
have been like if we'd lived there. Can you imagine
the Viceroy ruling Baskarone?" Then the captain
flushed and looked around himself quickly to see who
might have overheard. "Meaning no disrespect," he
mumbled, catching Roland's eye. "No disrespect,
Chaperone."

"None taken," mused Roland. "In fact, I appre-
hend your question, Captain. Are we what our environment makes us? Or do we make our environment
what we are? If the latter, then one might ask who
really lives in Baskarone. Do we not say 'Blessed Baskarone'? Do we not speak of Joyafleur as a heavenly
city?"

It was the first time I had heard those words. They
set up a reverberation within me, a humming, as
though some great tuning fork had been thrust down
my spine. A holy city. A blessed country. And the
ambassadors from that region, ah, what were they,
then? I inferred what they were and flushed as I felt
myself longing for angels. Had the ambassador from
Baskarone been an angel?

The captain made a face as though to spit, then
thought better of it. "Well, sir, since we're speaking
frankly, how by all the serpents would I know? Not
having been there. We look up toward Baskarone

from these sweaty lowlands and see it all stretched out there like some great, feathery wing, full of color and design, but who's been there? None of us, that's sure. The border posts, they don't let tourists from Chinanga go up to take a look, now do they?"

I caught Senora Carabosse's eye. She was listening unabashedly, her mouth slightly open, as though ready to bite at some intimation she desperately desired.

Roland murmured, "There have been visitors from there."

"Ambassadors. Oh, yes. Once in a while. Close-mouthed as turtles, too. I met one once, at Mrs. Gallimar's."

"Did you indeed? An ambassador from Baskarone?"

"A great tall, tan fellow with a sunny smile and a ready laugh, not a feather in his wings out of place, and no more information in him than there is good intentions in a woodtick."

Was it the same ambassador from Baskarone? Had he had wings? I could not remember.

"Then what was he doing here?" asked Roland.

"Flew down to find out how many cases of wine we wanted lowered from Joyafleur. Come to find out what we had to trade. Come to find out whether any contraband was getting through, had I been bothered by pirates. Asked if Chinanga was stable, if it was safe if someone wanted to leave something here for a while. Complained a little about a few hunters climbing the wall and falling off. It messes up the trails through there, so they say, and since the wall is known to be impassable, creates a foolishness. That kind of thing. Full of questions, he was. If you ask me, he was here spying, finding out about us, about Chinanga."

"Did you ask him about Baskarone, directly?"

"Well, you know how people will, at a dinner party. 'How're things in Baskarone, Your Excellency?' 'Had any interestin' happenins in Baskarone?' 'How's the weather been in Baskarone?' That kind of question."

"To which he replied?"

"Not at all," said the captain. "Far's I could tell, nothing ever happens at all in Baskarone. He said about six words."

"I wish I'd been there," Roland mused. "I would have asked him directly, 'Tell me about Baskarone.'"

"No you wouldn't," said the captain. "You think you would, but you wouldn't."

"I suppose that's true," sighed Roland, with a side-long glance at me. He sipped the cooling cou as he stared across the undulant waters, letting the silence settle between them.

I thought of the captain's words often in the succeeding days. Did we suit our environments or did we change them to suit ourselves? And in that case, what were we who had lived in the twentieth? And in that case, who were they who lived in Baskarone?

Late that night the *Stugos Queen* tied up at what had once been and would be again, when the floods had passed, the riverbank. There, under the motionless branches of great jungle trees, Captain Karon conducted some hours of quiet business. All the passengers except myself had long been asleep before the captain and the mate opened the hatches to the forward hold and lifted out a number of cages. During the earlier hours of the evening small boats rowed by persons claiming to be from Tartarus and Tophet and Eblis and Gehenna had drawn near to the *Queen,* and now they surrounded the ship. Natives came aboard a few at a time to pick up consignments or to offer Captain Karon bids for his unconsigned merchandise. Cages were lowered into the waiting boats. To unsuccessful bidders, the captain offered his hand and the suggestion that they might have better luck next time. As the first fingers of dawn stroked the sky, the last native boat departed, skimming the water like a swallow, away and into the drowned forest and up one of the tributary rivers, Rio Lamentarse, Rio Abrasador.

The cage tied to its hull shaking from the agitation of those enclosed.

"Is that the lot?" the captain asked the mate.

"That's it. Thirty-seven big cages and thirteen small ones. Only ones left are in the after hold, a dozen of 'em, consigned farther upriver. Erebus, if I remember right. Oh, and there's one little box for Abaddon, up the Rio Desmemoriarse. What do the natives do with them, anyhow?"

"No idea. Long as they do it out of sight, I don't much care. I get paid to ship 'em, and ship 'em is what I do. Load 'em aboard at the Edge and take 'em wherever they're consigned, if they're consigned. Sell the others. Any we don't sell, we drop off in the Great Swamp, but I get paid anyhow." The captain took a deep breath and sighed. "You took a look down in the forward hold, did you, to see none of them got out of the cages?"

"I always do."

"Wouldn't do to have one of those wandering around the *Queen,* now would it. Ugly things. Scare Mrs. Gallimar out of her pretty shoes."

I, who had seen all that the cages contained, had not found them that ugly. Pitiful. Angry. Hopeless. But not ugly.

The mate answered, "No, no escaped ones. I did find something else down there, though."

The captain turned and fixed him with a stern eye. "You found . . . ?"

"This," said the mate, beckoning to one of the boatmen on the lower deck who came up the ladder tugging a struggling young woman along behind him. It was the Viceroy's daughter, Constanzia. I had wondered when she would show up.

"Stowed away," said the mate. "And she's the Viceroy's daughter, to top it all." If he had intended surprise, he had achieved his goal. The captain stared at the young person as though he could not believe it.

"What in the . . . ?"

She shook herself, thrust wild hair back from her broad, low forehead, then smoothed her dress and stood erect, glaring at him. "I have brought money to pay for my passage. The only reason I went down into the hold is that I couldn't let anyone see I was aboard."

"Your father will be very annoyed with me," said the captain throatily. I knew he was thinking of beheading, or of quartering, or perhaps of both. "He was annoyed with me last time, and he will be annoyed with me again."

"Papa will not even know I am gone if you do not do anything foolish, Captain. I have come to see the virgin with a difference, as I seem to remember having done once or twice before, though this time there may really be a difference, which has not happened before now. I thought I might get to know her a little on the return voyage. When we get back to Nacifia, I will disembark quietly, and Papa will think I was merely avoiding him for a time, which I often do."

Captain Karon shook his head, then nodded, then shook it once more, conveying the confusion of his thought. "We're full," he muttered. "There's no cabin space."

"Oh, yes, Captain," I murmured, having taken off my cloak and folded it over one arm. "The young lady is welcome to share my cabin with me."

And so it became possible for me to read even more in the diaries of Abrosius Pomposus.

["She's getting too involved!" I cried to Israfel. "She's thinking too much. How can this be a safe hiding place if she starts analyzing it? She'll pull it to pieces!"

"Hush," said Israfel. "Imaginary lands are hard to destroy."

"They are not hard to disbelieve in," I told him. "She's reading, studying . . ."

"She learned to do that in the twentieth," he said. "It's not something you can stop her doing."

"We may have to talk to her," I said. "Tell her."

"Wait a while," he said. "See what happens."]

"There are slaves down there in the holds," Constanzia cried to me later that night as we prepared for bed, tears coursing down her olive cheeks. "Slaves."

I nodded understandingly. I had seen them.

"Women and children, too," she sobbed. "And men, young ones and old, old ones. It's dreadful."

"Dreadful," I admitted. But there was nothing she could do, nor I. She had evidently not understood the implications of the book she carried with her.

Kindhearted child. She cried herself to sleep.

I went out onto the deck. The old woman, Senora Carabosse, was standing there. I nodded and smiled good evening. In the saloon, I heard a clock strike. Suddenly, with a rush of memory which was almost a physical blow, I knew where I had heard the name before. Carabosse! It was the name on my clock. She was the fairy who had cursed me!

"Is it you!" I said, raising my hand as though I would ward her off or strike her, one. I don't know whether I would have struck her or not. I felt like it.

"Hush," she said, raising her own hand. Mine fell to my side as she gestured at it. "Whatever you think you know about me is probably false, so don't do that."

"You cursed me," I said.

"If you call that a curse. As it turned out, I cursed your half sister, Mary Blossom," said the old woman. "Which I meant to happen, right from the beginning."

"Why?" I cried.

"To get you away without anyone knowing," she said. "Away from Westfaire. Away from England. Away from the middle centuries. To hide you somewhere safe."

"Here?" I looked about me at the wallowing riverboat and laughed. "Here?"

"No one knows you are here," she whispered to me. "Jaybee doesn't know. The Dark Lord doesn't know."

"What Dark Lord?"

"Hush. Men like Jaybee do not spring into existence like spring spinach. They are aided into being by

the Dark Lord. The evil power. The Devil. He who
has taken his portion in horror and pain. That one."

"And you would hide me from him here?"

She repeated patiently what she had said before.
"No one knows you are here. No one knows *here* is
here."

Staring into her old eyes, I suddenly believed her. I
had read Pomposus's books, just as Constanzia had.
The difference between Constanzia and I was that I
had understood what they meant. I knew that
Chinanga was an imaginary world. All the people in it
were imaginary people. It had been dreamed up by
Ambrosius Pomposus—or by some creature or person
calling himself or itself Ambrosius Pomposus. He had
packed it full of all manner of strange things and characters. He had borrowed from myth and legend and
other worlds for some of them.

How would anyone except Ambrosius himself
know anything about this world? And he, I thought,
had possibly died long since.

As though reading my mind, Carabosse said, "I
used the secrets of time to find this place and explore
it. No one else could find it in ten million years. All my
effort, all my care has been directed at bringing you
here. Believe me, Beauty, here you are safe." She patted my hand.

Safe? Why should Carabosse care? I opened my
mouth to ask these questions, and others.

She shook her head at me, much as my aunts had
used to do when I asked questions about sex. No, no,
no, her expression said. You must do without knowing. She drifted away down the deck, leaving me to
wonder at what she had said.

What did I believe?

I believed that I was safe. I believed that she cared
greatly about my safety, though I did not know why. I
believed there was something more she had not told
me. I did not believe, could not believe who it was she
said I was safe from. What would the Dark Lord, under any name, want with me?

.   .   .

The *Queen* arrived at Novabella about noon. Among those assembled for the arrival were a squat and swarthy couple, Emilia and Domenico Sandifor, charged with conveying an official welcome to the Viceroy's plenipotentiary and the chaperone, and, of course, to the captain. Constanzia and I became part of the party by virtue of the fact that no one saw fit to deny us that privilege. If anyone had done so, I am confident that Constanzia would have been equal to the occasion.

"I hope you'll consent to stay with us," Emilia bubbled at Mrs. Gallimar. "Don Masimiliano, the perfect of our province, has requested the honor of your company at the castle, yours and the chaperone's, but I thought you'd want to stay here in the town for convenience's sake."

"I will not have time even to dine with Don Masimiliano," said Roland in a severe voice. "I am to be taken to the person at once for a preliminary survey."

"She's been staying with us," admitted Emilia. "With Jorge on a mat outside her door every moment that she's in her room."

"Windows?" snarled Roland. "What about the windows?"

"They have very heavy gratings, Senor Mirabeau. Quite impenetrable, I assure you."

"Senora, if you had seen some of the things I have seen." He shook his head gloomily to let us know that he had seen the worst that life in Chinanga afforded.

"Well, why don't we get along there now?" Domenico offered.

We strolled along the cobbled street to the Sandifor house, the official delegation in the fore, we unofficial hangers-on following close behind. A tall iron gate admitted us to an acre or so of garden with orange trees and orchids. The house bulked beneath its tiled roof; an outside staircase led us to an upper floor where we found the manservant, Jorge, curled in stupified slumber before a metal-bound door. His bulky form stirred as Emilia took out a large black key, and he woke enough to move aside as she started to insert it into the lock. The key was taken from her by the chaperone before she could turn it.

"If you don't mind," Roland smiled. "I believe this is my affair from now on."

"Not quite," smiled Mrs. Gallimar. "It would be fair to say, our affair. *Quis custodiet ipsos custodes?*"

"Really!" The chaperone was outraged. "I am a licencee of the Bureau of Public Morals!"

"And I am the Viceroy's personal representative. Shall we go in together?"

Which, after a lengthy simmering glance, they did.

Left in the corridor, the Sandifors looked at one another in awe. "What was that she said to him?" asked Domenico.

"I have no idea," his wife replied.

"A quotation," I murmured from behind them. "A question once asked in a similar connection. 'Who will chaperone the chaperones.' "

"Oh," he replied. "Do you suppose we should wait here for them?"

Emilia shook her head. "I want to see what's happening."

She had spoken all our thoughts. We went quietly into the room. Mrs. Gallimar and Roland stood side by side, their backs to us. Before them, sitting on one of the luxuriously padded window seats, a young woman sat reading. She looked up when the two stepped forward.

I was astonished. So astonished I could not move. It was as though I had looked into my own face in a slightly distorting mirror. My hair. My eyes. She looked less like me than Beloved had, but she resembled me in ways Beloved did not. I knew who she was. She was the one I had been seeking. Elladine of Ylles. Who else could she be?

Roland sank to his knees before her. I moved to one side so I could see his face. He was looking at her hair, at her feet, at the delicate rose of her cheeks. At her eyes. The swell of her breasts, like petals belling before spring wind! I saw his eyes flicker. The smell of her! I saw his nostrils dilate.

"You must be the virgin," smiled Mrs. Gallimar with a slightly sceptical tone.

For a moment the young woman could not or would not answer. Then she murmured, "Indeed. At the moment I must be. Are you the Viceroy's representatives?"

"I am the Viceroy's representative. This gentleman is Roland Mirabeau, licencee of the Bureau of Public Morals, a registered chaperone, first class."

The young woman smiled, unspeaking, nodding once. Oh, but she was beautiful. But then, so was I.

"Now." Mrs. Gallimar smiled again, licentiously. "We need to ascertain that you are as represented . . ."

"No," Roland announced, firmly. "It is not necessary to do anything at all. The young woman *is* as represented. As a registered chaperone, I can tell."

Mrs. Gallimar stared at him, unbelieving. He took her firmly by one arm and drew her away. "I can tell, Mrs. Gallimar. By the smell alone. She smells like a six-year-old child after a bath."

Mrs. Gallimar sniffed. "She may, in fact, just have bathed."

"I assure you, I cannot be misled."

"She may have used scent."

"There is no such perfume. She is as she is, Mrs. Gallimar. I know it!" And he turned to confront the young woman who sat looking at him with a lively and precocious interest. "My nose cannot be misled!" It was obvious he believed it was so, and yet this young person was looking at him with unmistakeably sexual interest. "She is a virgin, and with a difference," he murmured abstractedly, turning and looking straight into my face with an expression both of doubt and anxiety. I knew he was wondering whether he was indeed the best person to protect that virginity all the way back to Nacifia.

•   •   •

"Tell me about her," he demanded from Emilia and
Domenico, when we were all sitting in the Sandifor
courtyard.

"She says she was married to a duke. She got tired
of being married to him and left him to go home.
Something interrupted her journey to or from, at that
time or some other, and she ended up in the jungle.
She says she has the feeling she was there for a very
long time. The natives picked her up and brought her
here. That's as far as we've got."

Roland stared at Emilia in disbelief. "This is all
you know? But you've had her for days!"

"She talks a great deal. I can tell you all about the
duke, and his sisters, and where they lived. She puts in
a lot of detail."

"You haven't tried to hurry her any?" Mrs. Gallimar asked.

"Madam. Senor Mirabeau," Domenico interrupted, "perhaps things are different in Nacifia. Perhaps there are many interesting events in Nacifia. Not
here. Things are dull in Novabella. We examine what
we can see of Baskarone through our telescopes. We
eat. We take a nap. We go down and stare at the river,
wondering whether it will rise or fall. We see the little
boats from Abaddon, and we fervently hope they will
keep their distance, or, at worst, try to sell us fruit or
monkeys from the jungle. We eat something else. We
wait for Captain Karon to arrive with something new
in the cargo. We play cards. We grow frightfully . . .
how shall I say? *Pococurante.* You understand what I
am saying?"

"Bored," murmured Roland, who had told me he
was very familiar with the feeling.

"Exactly. Anything new, any new tale, new jest,
new trick, new dress—anything new is delightful to us.
Why would we hasten it away? We have let her take
her time, tell the tale in her own way."

I wondered how much my mother remembered.

How had she come to be lost in the jungle of
Chinanga? How long had she been there?

"You have not heard the end of her story?" I
asked.

Domenico shook his head. "There may be no end
to it. Better if we are left with a little still between our
teeth to chew upon after she is gone."

While the others went on talking, Constanzia and I
went back to visit the virgin. She welcomed us as she
might have welcomed any fairly interesting strangers.
Seeing her face, even younger looking than my own, I
suffered from doubt and fear that she might reject me
when I told her who I was.

"Since my arrival," she confided to us, "I have
been asking what country I have come to, but aside
from telling me the name of the place, the people here
are remarkably evasive. What is it about Chinanga
that occasions such restraint?"

"They are ashamed of their origins," said Constanzia with a blush.

My mother regarded her with the liveliest interest.
Without thinking, I said I felt no origin, however
lowly, should shame a population for more than a generation or two. Constanzia shook her head at me.

"There has been only one generation, Lady Wellingford. I believe that Ambrosius Pomposus, father of
Chinanga, must have been a warlock who traveled in
far and wondrous places, only to fall under the spell of
his own memories, his recollections of tropical lands
full of languor and splendor and luxuriant vegetation,
full of incestuous entanglements and erotic desires, a
place in which time seemed damped in its passage. He
determined to create such a land of his own, so laid
claim to this milieu along the eternal rivers and created in it, Chinanga!" She gestured widely, signifying
all and everything, a great, inclusive gesture which
stopped only at the farthest reaches of her fingertips.

"How do you know this?" asked Elladine.

"She read about it in Pomposus's book," I replied,
to Constanzia's amazement. She had indeed read it
there, though she still did not understand what she had

read. "Though Pomposus may have been only a writer, not a warlock. Writers, too, can create such places."

"I see," breathed Mama.

I went on, "I believe Constanzia has also read that Chinanga is to remain changeless until the Viceroy, while in the company of a virgin with a difference and after the celebration of a certain rite which Constanzia has not yet been able to translate, decides differently."

"I see," said Elladine, who did indeed see, turning to the girl. "Your father wishes to change the country? A revolution, perhaps?"

"A devolution, I believe," whispered Constanzia, coming away from the windows as though suddenly aware of ears which might be pricked at those windows. "He wishes to attain mastery over Baskarone. He speaks of it metaphorically, as the ascent of the lover onto his mistress's balcony, claiming he will do it with love."

"There is ravishment of that kind," said Elladine, dispassionately. "And then there is rape."

Constanzia nodded. "I know. Daddy has grown insensitive and mulish with the centuries. He wishes some great apotheosis."

"I, on the other hand," said Elladine, "merely wish to get home to Ylles."

"Ylles," mused Constanzia. "Ylles. I have heard of Ylles. It is mentioned in *The Diaries*. It is here, in the continuum, part of a larger creation, not far away."

"Roland told me it was an unachievable distance away. Surely he would not lie?"

"Nonsense. A chaperone wouldn't know the truth if it waved its wings at him." Constanzia patted my mother's shoulder. "Never mind. I'll find Ylles for you. When we get home, I'll look it up in the great encyclopedia, if you will only tell me how to spell it."

"Wy," I said to her. "Double *el, ee, ess.*"

"How did you know?" Mama asked me.

"I have seen reference to the place in certain family papers," I replied cunningly. "In Westfaire. My home."

"Westfaire," brooded Elladine. "I remember Westfaire. Then you . . . you must be . . ."

"Your daughter," I answered softly, watching her face.

She gave me a long look, a troubling look. As though she could not believe who I was. At last her lips trembled open, and her eyes lit with . . . was it love? Was it something else?

"Beauty," she cried. "You got my letter!"

Constanzia watched in amazement as we embraced. The embrace itself was not what I expected. It was awkward, a little embarrassing. Mother did not cling. She gave me a brief, almost perfunctory hug, and then stood away from me, looking intently at me, as though trying to find in me some resemblance she had expected. Perhaps our meeting would have seemed more natural if Mama had appeared to be only a little older. Almost at once Constanzia increased my embarrassment by commenting upon Mama's youthful appearance.

"She's a fairy," I told Constanzia. "I imagine she'll always look that way. On the other hand, I am only half fairy. I'm already older than she is." I smiled fondly at Mama. At least, it began as a fond smile. Mama's reaction to it was to turn abruptly away from me with a sigh. Something was not as I had planned or hoped, but I didn't wish to consider what it might be at that moment.

"You're very lovely," said Constanzia, patting me upon my cheek. "You couldn't be prettier even if you were only twenty-three."

Since I thought I was only nineteen or twenty, at least as I counted elapsed time, her words did not greatly cheer me. And, though I considered myself only nineteen or twenty, there were unmistakeable signs about the eyes that I might actually be somewhat older, which reminded me suddenly of what Mama had said in her letter to me. The bit about coming in haste, before I got any older.

My mother reached out a hand to touch me, felt of my breast with her fingertips, drew her hand away as though burned. Perhaps she had felt the mysterious fire within me. Perhaps she could tell me what it was!

Before I could ask her, she spoke, almost abruptly, to Constanzia. "I simply cannot figure out what I am doing here! I had returned to Ylles, I remember quite distinctly. Then something came up, some necessary journey back to Westfaire. I think I was with Aunt Joyeause. Then we were returning to Ylles once more, and suddenly I was caught up, as in some whirling vortex of wind, and deposited on a small, uncomfortable outcropping in the middle of a jungle."

I started to tell her why she had gone back to Westfaire, then realized that would require lengthy explanation. I was saved from saying anything by Constanzia.

"It might have been Daddy who trapped you there," she said. "He's been making black magic to summon a virgin with a difference for years. He may have hit upon something that worked."

I thought this exceedingly unlikely. The Viceroy had not struck me as a competent sorcerer. The spell had been cast by Carabosse, to catch and hold my mother here, to bring me here to join her, to keep me safe. Why was my safety so important?

"But why? Why this obsession . . . ?" my mother asked.

This was a safer subject than the other, and I had been thinking about the matter ever since we left Nacifia. I had come to certain conclusions, and in order not to think about other things, I shared them with Constanzia and my mother.

"Ambrosius Pomposus had only the compass of his own mind to invest in his creation. Each of the beings he placed here in Chinanga partook of his sensitivity and his feeling, and each is, therefore, similar to every other, or if not similar to, at least totally comprehensible by. There are no foreign thoughts, no strangenesses entering from outside. The mystery of the exotic is lacking. The lure of the peculiar, the alien, the inexplicable, all are missing.

"Even in the clownery, which I visited during a

stop in Nacifia, the patients are not truly insane within the totality which is Chinanga. The actions of one are offset by the actions of another; what one creates, another destroys, precisely as errant thoughts in one's own mind are corrected by other thoughts until they result in a personality which, though undoubtedly unique, is entirely familiar to itself. It occurs to me that after long time, all of Chinanga must feel that it knows itself far too well, that it exists as one entity, bound about with invisible and inexorable ties of familiarity, alone, without contrast, in solitary confinement for endless time."

"Years of solitude," Constanzia murmured, nodding in agreement. "Mother has often commented upon it. Endless solitude."

"I first thought of this," I continued, "when I saw how delighted Mrs. Gallimar was to meet me and how little surprised she was about virtually anything else. Everything that can happen in Chinanga must have happened before." I paused for a moment, reflecting that Mama and I—and Carabosse and the ambassador—might be the only real, non-Ambrosius creatures currently in Chinanga. I did not want to say this to Constanzia. She had obviously not considered her own reality or lack of it, and I did not wish to upset her.

I finished my peroration lamely, "Chinanga, though very lovely, remains a singularly inhibited creation."

My mother regarded me with wonder. "The way you talk!"

I chose to take this as fondness and smiled modestly. "I was a college student, majoring in literature."

"What is literature?" she asked.

It was not the time to discuss such things, so I replied only briefly.

"Still," she yawned when I had finished, "if I take your meaning correctly—which is, darling, somewhat difficult to do when you use all those strange words—it might explain why Constanzia's father has summoned me up. The poor Viceroy is simply bored out of his senses."

"I have not yet been able to translate the rites mentioned in *The Diaries,*" Constanzia murmured. "But I think Daddy has done so. He is not alone in being bored. Mother is bored. Colonel Esquivar is bored. Even Roland Mirabeau is bored. I have tried to deny it to myself, but I am bored also. What have we to look forward to except things we know are going to happen but which happen less frequently than others? The *Stugos Queen* arrives less often than do the seasonal festivals, and her arrival is therefore cause for more excitement. The river rises less often than the *Queen* arrives, and the rising is considered cause for celebration. A gallivant causes depredations only once in a very great while and brings, therefore, almost a quality of surprise. I'm amazed the people here at Novabella want the gallivant hunted and killed, for even the woman whose buttock it ate admits it has made an interesting change."

[We did not foresee this. I had never thought the place would be boring. So much life and color and exotic splendor should not be boring. And yet, I suppose, given sufficient time, everything becomes boring.

"We should have known," said Israfel. "We, of all creatures, should have known."]

Constanzia's voice trailed away into silence. She shook her head somewhat petulantly and excused herself, the tiny frown on her face betraying troubled thought. Perhaps she was beginning to realize that Chinanga was an imaginary land, and what the implications of that might be. I reproached myself silently for having said anything about Chinanga within her hearing. I had wanted to impress Mama with my intelligence, and all I had done was make Constanzia apprehensive. It would be better if Mama and I could leave Novabella at once, before I was the cause of any further disruption. I suggested to Mama that since I had the seven-league boots in my pocket, we might depart together, dispensing with any ceremony. She said it was worth a try, so I put them on. "Boots," I said, holding Mama tightly about the waist and refusing to acknowledge that she shrank slightly from my embrace, "take us to Ylles."

[Israfel and I held our breaths. She was not supposed to do this. She was not supposed to try to leave Chinanga! We muttered enchantments and held fast!]

At once the boots attempted to depart with my feet inside them. Mama, however, remained rooted in place. It was as though I had taken hold of one of the great forest trees, a mighty monarch rooted deep through the swampy soil of Chinanga into the eternal substance of whatever lay beneath. Mama could no more move than such a tree could move, but I was being whipped to and fro like a flag attached to an immovable mast, feeling my grip slowly loosened by the force of the fairy shoes.

"Boots," I cried in a strangled voice, "desist!" I fell to the floor, for a moment unable to stand, feeling as though my legs were made of water.

"It will do no good," Mama murmured in my ear. "Whatever spell has caught me here in Chinanga will not let me go. We must find out what the enchantment is before it can be broken."

I did not think it was the Viceroy who had done it. I thought it was more likely Carabosse. I determined to talk to her the next time I saw her, to learn what she was doing to me and why.

In any case, it seemed we must defer our departure until later, and we could not return to Nacifia at once. We had the choice of joining the *Stugos Queen* as it completed its voyage upstream to the wall below Baskarone, or of remaining in Novabella. Since we were assured by everyone that nothing in Novabella was worthy of our attention—except the hunt for the predacious gallivant in which Colonel Esquivar was even now engaged, but which we, as non-hunters, could hardly share—Mama, Constanzia and I decided to go on upriver with the Captain and his remaining passengers.

We shared a large cabin. Roland and Mrs. Gallimar accompanied us upon the trip. Whenever Mama emerged from the cabin, one or both of them were in attendance. Though I was certain Senora Carabosse had been on the ship when we came to Novabella, she was not there when we left.

[I had gone home, to attempt to find out what we were doing wrong!]

Upriver from Novabella, the aspect of the country began to change. The river became swifter and less spread out; the land on either side sloped away more steeply. There were fewer drowned trees and more great rock pillars, accumulating as we traveled into ramparts, escarpments, and pinnacles of stone set well back from the flow but still visible whenever the mists lifted. During the entire voyage, Constanzia scarcely left the rail or the window. Each turn in the river made her exclaim.

"Then there is something new in Chinanga," I teased her, wondering if I had been mistaken about the country's reality. "You have not seen this stretch of country before."

"Oh, yes, yes," she replied. "There have been virgins with a difference reported before, though none were ever genuine. I have stowed away before. Before I knew it was all there was, I traveled all of Chinanga. But those journeys were so long ago I have almost forgotten them."

Once, late in the evening, we looked up to see the stars occulted by a vast shadow with a line of light along its edge and knew we gazed upon the incredible heights of Baskarone.

"I want to go there," Constanzia breathed. "I can think of nothing else. Since I first saw an ambassador from Baskarone, I have longed to go there. It is why I started reading *The Diaries*. To find a way!"

Mama shook her head, biting her lip. "I'm afraid that is impossible, child."

"You don't understand. If you'd ever seen one of them . . ."

"I have," Mama said, her nostrils flaring, her mouth grim. "Several, as a matter of fact. What you say is true. Seeing them makes us long for Baskarone, but we may not go there, no matter how we long. They will not let us in." She turned abruptly and went into her cabin, leaving Constanzia and me to stare after her, wondering at her tone.

I wondered often at her tone. When I was honest with myself, I realized I had expected a mother, my mother, to be like Dame Blossom: a little severe, but unfailingly affectionate in a kindly, nurturant way. Mama was not that. Sometimes I thought she was not even very like the woman who had written the letter. Oh, it was nothing one could put one's finger on. We talked together, took tea together, confided in one another. I told her about Giles. Her eyes filled with tears, and we cried over that together. She understood. She said she had felt that way about my father. I held her hand and was happy. And then, just as I thought I was beginning to know her, I saw on her face an expression of remote untouchability. She looked through me, as though I did not exist. Then, some hours later, she became my affectionate mama again.

This happened more than once on our voyage. I could not explain it. I feared, from time to time, that something I had done or, more likely, had not done, sometimes came to her mind, damaging the feelings between us. Or I feared that something about me put her off. I didn't know what it was. When she was being my mama, I felt as secure as a child held in loving arms. When she looked through me, I felt wavery, as though my very existence was in question. I actually wished for Carabosse, so that I could ask her what she thought was happening.

Another night, with the *Queen* moored at the edge of the water, I saw the last of the cages disposed of. Several times during late-night hours of our journey I had left Mama and Constanzia sleeping and had sneaked into the hold to hold converse with those in

the cages. Ambrosius had read or traveled widely, and
had been interested in the religions of the world. Each
cage had been consigned to a particular hell, and each
cage was full of beings Ambrosius imagined had
learned to fear that special hell, whether one of fire or
ice or eternal separation or mere time-serving prior to
some later reconciliation with whomever or whatever
they considered responsible for their fate. There were
many espousing fundamentalist Christian faiths, all
babbling of the love of God while seething with guilt
and resentment. I suggested to them that, if they could
bring themselves to disbelieve, they might free themselves from their confinement, and a few must have
managed to do so, for several of the consignees from
Erebus complained of light weight when they received
their shipments at last.

When I came up on deck after the last such conversation, the captain was standing at the rail. I was not
wearing my cloak. He nodded at me and grinned apologetically. "Can you believe I used to bring them all
across from the Edge in a rowboat?" he asked. "Of
course, that was before I came to Chinanga. I suppose
it's more interesting now."

"Where did Ambrosius borrow you from?" I
asked.

"The Greeks," he said. "I am their ferryman."

"Of course," I said, remembering things I had
read. "You rowed a boat across the Styx."

"For the coins on the dead men's eyes," he said.
"The work has not changed much."

"And where do the souls come from in the cages?"
I asked.

"Where do the trees come from," he smiled. "And
the snakes and the orchids."

I nodded, thoughtfully, taking his point. "Are you
bored?" I asked. Everyone spoke much of boredom
here in Chinanga.

"Oh yes," he said in a grumpy voice. "I am bored.
So much so that occasionally I long for the simpler
days."

Two days later we reached the falls which came

down from Baskarone and moored along the riverbank, well back from the plunging torrent. We could
not see the top. The roar of the waters and the clouds
of spray extinguished any appreciation of the enor-
mousness of the fall.

In a clearing some distance from this pool the captain found the expected stack of kegs and crates, let
down from above, I supposed, by some unimaginable
windlass. While the crewmen were loading, several
passengers departed, quiet persons with purpose writ
large upon their faces. The captain shook his head after them as they went off toward the great wall.

"Going to try for it, they are," he told me. "Going
to try and climb it. Every time I come up here, there's
a few. Silly creatures. Even if the wall wasn't unclimb-
able, which it is, them from Baskarone aren't going to
let anyone climb there."

I shook my head with him. Poor vagrant creations
of Ambrosius Pomposus, destined to climb so high to
so little purpose.

While they were getting the cargo aboard, Mama
and I hiked to a hilltop some little way apart where we
might see the falls entire. Even at this distance, I could
see only the lower half, though Mama's fairy vision
could see far more than I. She had some ointment in
her pocket, one of the things, she said, that she always
carried with her. She annointed my eyes with it, telling
me to blink several times and wait until the tears
stopped. It stung, but only for a moment. When I
looked up again, I caught my breath in wonder.

The wall was wreathed in rainbow, not puny arcs
such as we sometimes see after a shower, but great
circles and bows, one within another, like the radiance
of a butterfly's wing or the feathers of certain birds
where the light breaks its own color through barbs and
scales to make a glorious aureole. The waterfall was a
silver marvel, tumbling in sprays and droplets, each
catching the light, separating and rejoining in a myriad
braided saults. Above, upon the height, I could see
trees and towers and color where great tracts of flowers bloomed. The angle was wrong, I should not have

been able to see anything there. It was as though the
light itself bent, as it does going around stars, to give
me a glimpse of what lay above.

The vision was more like taste than sight. When I
looked away, my eyes longed for me to look back, as
the tongue longs for savor. Each tree upon the height
was the epitome of tree. Each tower the quintessence
of what towers could be. Everything there seemed to
be the design from which earthly things were made. I
was conscious that the burning presence in my chest
was still. I did not feel it. It was at rest.

In a moment my eyes stung again, perhaps from
the ointment, more likely from tears, and when I
looked back, the vision was gone.

"The ointment is stale," Mama said in an annoyed
tone. "I waited for rescue overlong in that jungle.
Never mind, my dear. When we come to Ylles, you
will learn it is as beautiful as Baskarone." Her words
sounded confident, but her smile, when I turned to
look at her, seemed forced.

I believed her, but still I wiped tears from my eyes
as we returned to the *Stugos Queen.* We were not
alone. Several of the passengers had come along for
the sightseeing, and they, too, seemed depressed and
sad. It seemed almost willfully malicious to let us see
what lay upon the heights and yet forbid us access to
it, but when I said this to Constanzia she rebuked me.

"Such is not the case. It is only from such visions
and temptations that fantastic longing comes. Out of
that vision, a thousand worlds are built. I have heard it
said in Nacifia that it is better to be a climber who falls
to his death from the walls of Baskarone, than to be
king in any other land." She sounded somewhat
doubtful, as though the source of the quotation was
not a trustworthy one. "Any other land," she repeated, as though to convince herself.

"Except Faery itself," I commented to Mama, as a
quiet aside.

"Except Faery itself," she agreed. "Oh yes, dear.
Of course."

When the cargo was aboard, the *Queen* turned

downriver, and we raced with the current instead of against it, achieving in one or two days what had taken ten or twelve to accomplish on the way up. Our speed was such that we felt quite giddy. Before we knew it, we were at Novabella once more, having dinner with Don Masimiliano *(sopa de limon, filetes des pesces del rio, ensalada de los helechos tropicales, plantain tostarse, quarto trasero de gallivant asado*—from the colonel's successful hunt—*pastelillos de frutas,* with *patito-chuleta* as a savory followed by coffee and liqueurs) and then away downstream toward Nacifia.

Mama did not feel well after eating the roast gallivant. She whispered to me that the fauna of imaginary regions were invariably poisonous to beings from her realm. Not binding, necessarily, as were fairy fruits or the pomegranate seeds of Hell, but simply unhealthful. I had felt no such trouble, and therefore decided that my digestive system was probably fully human. When I mentioned this to Mama, she said in a tart voice that it had taken me some little time to arrive at that conclusion. Only then did I realize that she had not had recourse to the personal cabinet at the rear of the ship once since she had come aboard.

"In many imaginary lands, as here, they shit and piss," she advised me. "As on earth, though rather less copiously. But not in Ylles nor, I believe, in Baskarone. Never mind, dearest. When you eat fairy fruits, you will not be bothered with such grossness any longer."

I had not precisely been bothered up until this time, though afterward I seemed to give a great deal of unaccustomed attention to the matter. No doubt this was one of the differences that Roland sensed in Mama. The implications were shattering. How refreshing to have all the joys of love (I write in a literary or conventional sense, rather than from experience) sans consequent familiarity with those anatomical proximities which humans find both so unfortunate and so teasingly attractive. I came to the conclusion that there would be no perversions in Ylles.

We arrived at Nacifia late one night and tied up at

the pier with no sound from the whistle. I thought it might be thoughtfulness on the captain's part until I saw him and Mrs. Gallimar tête-à-tête in the dining room and realized he simply had not wished to interrupt their last evening together. Last, one assumes, for a time, for a long time, though not for all time, since everything in Chinanga repeats itself. Constanzia had already gone ashore. It was one of those evenings when Mama and I felt close and familial, a dear feeling, one that left tears brooding in the corners of my eyes. We stood at the rail with Roland close behind and looked at the sleeping city while we whispered to one another all that we knew, thought and imagined about it. On the pier several escapees from the clownery presented classical tableaux vivants for our edification. They had chosen to portray an ascent to Baskarone, as though achieved by certain historic personages, each tableau occasioning a tiny frisson, as of surprise. If one were not continuously aware of Chinanga's origins, one was continually agitated by little shocks, only to say to oneself a moment later, "But what else would one expect in Chinanga?" Tableaux vivants, of course.

"Beauty," Mama said to me in a serious voice, "when we are taken to the Viceroy's palace tomorrow, stay close to me and do not be surprised at anything I may say or do."

[*"She's going to do something stupid," I said to Israfel.*

"Who?" he asked. "Beauty."

"No. Elladine. She's going to do something silly. I can feel it."]

I kissed Mama on her beautiful cheek and promised her that I would not. We went into the cabin together and so to bed.

20

I had no further thoughts until the morning when the whistle, so long delayed, woke us as well as every living thing within hearing of it. It was not long after breakfast that the Viceroy sent a cart for Mama, one draped in fringed velvet, its curtains held aloft by a tottery framework of gilt staves. I guessed the cart had appeared in festival processions for many seasons, and when I saw the priest from the cathedral wringing his hands on the sidelines, I knew I was correct. Mama had merely replaced St. Frog in being hauled up the cobbled streets by a succession of devotees, including many inmates from the clownery who seemed in a state of unusual excitement.

I walked at the side of the cart, behind Mrs. Gallimar, who moved along with ladylike little steps, acknowledging the plaudits of the assembled citizenry. Beyond her was Senora Carabosse. I resolved to keep her in sight until we had a chance to talk. On the other side of the cart strode Roland Mirabeau, his fine features drawn together in an expression of concentration and resolve. Behind us came another cart bearing the head of the gallivant, preserved in a barrel of Baskaronian wine for this occasion. Colonel Esquivar strode beside this tumbrel, his moustaches waxed into spiral magnificence, with several of his ragged children tagging at his heels. Behind the colonel came the captain and his crew, and after them the ragtag and motley of the town. Outside the gates to the citadel there was a momentary hiatus in our progression, soon remedied when the great gates swung open to the accompaniment of fanfarons and vorticals. Inside the gates a blood-colored carpet led up the vast stony flight to the massive portal, just outside which the Viceroy waited.

He had dressed for the occasion in cloth of gold with diamonds. Flatulina was no less marvelously accoutred, and various of the viceregal children stood here and there, observing our approach with scarcely concealed incredulity. I was not surprised to see Constanzia between two of them, standing attentively immobile, as though she had been there all along. We paused at the foot of the stairs.

"Senorita," the Viceroy began, sweeping his hat before him in the first gesture of a very complicated reverence.

"Senora, actually," Mama said.

The Viceroy came erect all at once, like a poker. He glared at Roland Mirabeau, who shrugged elaborately.

"She is a virgin," the chaperone said. "No matter what she calls herself."

"With a difference?" hissed the Viceroy, coming down the stairs sidewise, like a crab, one hand held threatening before him. Flatulina edged down behind him, her head held slightly forward, like a snake about to strike.

"As you will observe," Roland said calmly, indicating Mama with a nod of his head. She sat at ease, awaiting the Viceroy's approach. When he had come near enough, she held out her hand for him to kiss. He bowed over it. I saw his nostrils quiver. Perhaps he scented the odor of . . . of whatever Roland had sensed. Over the top of his head she gave me a look of sceptical disdain, but when he raised himself again, her face was all sweetness.

"I have been told you require my assistance," she said. "So happy to be of help."

I scarcely heard her. At the top of the stairs, the ambassador from Baskarone emerged from the great doors. My eyes became fixed upon him. They could not turn aside. What business had kept him here so long? What business had brought him here at all? Why ever he had come, his stay had not changed him. The thought occurred to me that ambassadors from Baskarone were, perhaps, among the eternal things which did not change.

He became aware of my stare and smiled at me as though we were friends but lately separated. I blushed and cast down my eyes, released by that smile to come to myself once more. Resolutely I turned my eyes on Mama and the Viceroy. That was where any business pertinent to me would transpire, and Mama might at any moment need my help. When I glanced up a moment later, the ambassador had gone, perhaps away, perhaps inside the castle, who could say. My heart stopped for a moment, then resumed its steady thudding.

The Viceroy awarded a medal to Colonel Esquivar, to much tantara of trumpets and huzzah from the populace. The gallivant head was turned over to representatives from the firm of Pelasges y Plumas, *rellenadores acclamados* to the hunters of Chinanga. The head would hang in the viceregal dining room, said the Viceroy. Considering both its bedraggled state and the bestial glare remaining in the glassy eyes, the *rellenadores* would have their work cut out for them.

Mrs. Gallimar and the chaperone were rewarded and dismissed. A benefice was awarded Captain Karon. Alms were given to clownery inmates loose along the street. Sweets were tossed to the crowd. There was a general departure, and we were left in relative quiet, scarcely more than a two-family party: the Viceroy's numerous one; plus Mama and me. The Viceroy rubbed his hands together and put on a new expression as he winked and nodded at his wife. "I have everything ready," he chortled. "Have had, simply forever, just waiting, don't you know." His eyes glittered with hectic abandon. He was not the same man I had seen before. He was transformed by excitement.

[*"I don't like this at all," I said. "This wasn't supposed to happen."*

"Carabosse, it will happen, whether we like it or not," sighed Israfel. "It has been inevitable, ever since Elladine arrived. This world does not appear in our futures; we misinterpreted that fact, that's all. We had no way of knowing."

"I should have read all The Diaries," *I confessed. "I should have been more careful."*

"Shhh," said Israfel. "Be ready to salvage what we can. . . ."]

I looked across at Constanzia, who shrugged. Evidently her father had gone further in *The Diaries* than she had. Following his urgent beckoning, we entered the castle and paraded down a long, stone-floored corridor between files of uniformed guardsmen, climbed several flights of rocky stairs which twisted and coiled about in the walls of the place, and arrived at last in a tower room set up for the study of astrology, alchemy, or some even more esoteric science. I stooped to one great brass telescope as we passed it, finding it focused upon the heights of Baskarone. The mechanism had not the power of Mama's salve, but one could make out the effulgence of the place.

"At last," the Viceroy said, lighting candles and setting alembics to bubbling. "At last," as he thrust a sword through a ring and suspended both above a chair. "At last," as he bustled about opening books to proper pages, laying out indescribable things upon a stone set in a pentacle. He motioned for Mama to seat herself in the chair. She looked at the suspended weapon with a suspicious eye, but complied even as she summoned me nearer, taking me firmly by the hand.

"If I am not mistaken," she murmured. "The Viceroy is about to turn his universe inside out."

["This world has lasted for centuries," I sighed. "Oh, Israfel, why. Why? Just when we had need of it." Israfel didn't answer me. He had no time to answer.]

Various members of the Viceroy's family were assigned parts in the rite. They were already well-rehearsed. The telescope was evidently part of the ritual, for it was sprinkled with liquids from the alembics, censered with fragrant and bitter smoke, and Mama was asked to put her eye to it as the final words of the spell or invocation were spoken. The words were in no language I knew. I could not even have begun to spell the sounds which issued in gutteral imperatives from the Viceroy's throat.

Silence.

A wind came up from somewhere. Mama gripped my hand. A voice from behind us said, "May I drop you ladies somewhere?" I turned to see the ambassador from Baskarone, smiling at us both. Senora Carabosse stood at his side, looking like a rider whose horse had just died unexpectedly, her face a puzzle of chagrin and impromptu resolution. I looked back at the Viceroy, only to find him vanished, his place taken by an amount of empty and chilly air. So with Flatulina and the children. Constanzia whirled past, her hair a wheel of dark and light as she spun and was gone. She held out her hand toward me, her face pleading.

I cried out to her. "Constanzia . . ."

The ambassador shook his head. "Ambrosius Pomposus did not intend his imaginary world to exist forever. He included in his creation a procedure whereby the inhabitants, when they grew sufficiently bored, could accomplish the rite of dissolution. Some such rite is part of all creations, Beauty. Of Faery. Of the world. It is our misfortune that our own actions have helped un-create this one just now."

He took Mama on one arm and me on the other and began to stride across the clouds that suddenly stretched before us, Senora Carabosse walking effortlessly beside. I thought, irrelevantly, that if she walked so easily, she could not be so old as I had previously thought. My fingers tingled where they touched the ambassador's arm. I heard Mrs. Gallimar's voice saying faintly to someone, "Such a lovely wine. Such a lovely, lovely wine," and then came the retreating wail of the *Stugos Queen*. The clouds opened below us to let us see a great, edgeless river where a lonely boatman looked up from his oars and waved. Chinanga had departed, but the river was still there.

"The Styx was imagined before Chinanga," said the ambassador. "It will be there through many creations yet."

"Ylles, Israfel, if you would be so kind," Mama said in a strained, polite voice.

"Glad to be of service, Elladine," he replied. There was something weary and ironic in his voice.

We were very high up. For a moment I saw the beautiful heights of Baskarone, clear as day. Then they were gone, and so was he.

21

I write the truth when I say that Ylles is an almost-
Baskarone. When one eats fairy fruit, one sees it as
glorious, lovely, utterly beyond compare. Since I had
eaten no fairy fruit prior to arrival, however, my first
glimpse of it was disappointing. It looked rather like a
waste of moorland with some pigpens and hovels scattered here and there. The moment we arrived, Mama
darted away into the bushes, and Carabosse, who was
standing quietly beside me with an expression of deep
pain upon her old face, leaned forward and said,
"Come see me as soon as you can, Beauty. Ask Puck
to bring you." Before I could ask her who Puck was,
she took a step or two down the path toward some
pigpens, sidled a little to the right and was gone. It was
a method of coming and going I was to see much of in
Faery.

Mama emerged from the shrubbery with a handful
of berries which she thrust upon me, urging me to eat
them all as quickly as possible. While I did so, she
gathered others for herself. She chewed them as
though famished, eyes rolled up, jaws working furiously. It was an astonishing sight which kept my eyes
fixed on her for several minutes. When I looked at my
surroundings again, I found myself in true Ylles. Park-
land had replaced moorland; castles stood where the
hovels had been, and over all stretched a sky of late-

evening blue spangled with early stars. The grasses
were also starred with tiny five-pointed flowers of silver, umbels of golden bloom, and tinkling sprays of
bluebells. Though I saw it all quite clearly, Mama was
not content until she had uprooted a small, hairy
stemmed plant and rubbed the juice of its root into my
eyes. It stung horribly for a time, but when the pain
vanished, my eyesight was like that of a falcon.

"Elvenroot," she explained. "It grows only in
Faery, nowhere else. It enables one to see all our mar-
vels."

"Ylles is in Faery?" I asked stupidly, sniffing at an
odor which had caught my nostrils, a familiar scent.

"A province," she said, nodding. "One of many. It
goes from those hills over there," and she pointed, "to
the ocean over there," pointing once more. "I am the
ruler of it, when I'm here. When I'm not here, another
of the Theena Shee takes it over."

I had not understood the word she used. She said it
again, then smoothed a patch of ground and spelled it
out with her finger, in Irish, evidently the only human
language in which the word was written. "Daoine
Sidhe," she said. *"Theena Shee.* My people. The people of True Faery. One of whom takes over rulership
of my province when I am away. Here, I'll show you
the boundaries."

She turned me to face a direction I thought of as
north, where loomed a range of shadowy mountains,
their ridges making a jagged line against the stars. At
the foot of the mountains lay dark folds of forest.
Mama turned me widdershins from the forest to see
the land sloping down to a starlit sea, the white comb-
ers rolling endlessly toward us. Widdershins from the
sea was moorland, covered with low growth and extending as far as I could see. Widdershins from the
moorland brought me facing uplands, where many fantastic and marvelous palaces stood, though none, to
my surprise, as lovely as Westfaire. Whichever direction I turned, the familiar odor came past me on the
wind, as though blown from every quarter.

"Oberon's and Mab's," she said, pointing to the

two closest palaces. "And mine, and a dozen more. It doesn't really matter which part belongs to who. Oberon's realm is next to mine, and he would look after it if I left."

We stood beside a copse which was more or less at the center of all this: tall trees, lacy, silvery, softly susurrant.

"Why would you ever leave it?" I asked, staring in wonder around myself. Truthfully, it was very lovely.

"Oh," she said vaguely. "Sometimes one wants a change."

Every view was one a painter would sell his brushes for. Every aspect thrilled. Every structure was perfect from every angle. The scent of the flowers alone was enough to make one drunk, though it did not mask that other scent. . . .

"Mama, what is that smell?" I asked.

"Smell?" She sniffed delicately. "The flowers?"

"No, the smell on the wind."

She sniffed again, her ivory nostrils dilating to take in the breeze. "Not the sea? Not the pines of the forest?"

"No. The smell . . . the smell that's everywhere."

She laughed, liltingly. "The smell of Faery, silly child. The smell of magic!"

As I was about to pursue that matter, we were interrupted by the sound of horns, tiny horns pitched high as a wasp's buzz. Mama gestured to one side, and I turned to see a troupe passing by, little men mounted on mice, butterfly-winged maidens riding hedgehogs saddled with roses. Elladine called and they answered, their voices like infant bells, waving tiny hands, calling a greeting but not turning aside from their processionary way.

"Trouping fairies," she told me with an indulgent smile.

"Where are they going?"

"Nowhere. Everywhere. They simply go. They camp on the mosses and dance. Then they move on. They are not serious creatures. They have only small enchantments, small as themselves. Sometimes they are seen in the human world, sometimes they are heard. Sometimes their dance floors are seen."

"Fairy rings?"

She nodded. "They are the only fairies with butter-fly wings, the only fairies to inhabit human gardens. Once they were as large as we; once they were worshipped as gods and goddesses, long, oh long, long ago. They had mighty names then: Pomona. Naiad. Dryad. Aurora. Over time they have shrunk. They get smaller with every passing century. Eventually I believe they will vanish into the atmosphere, and we will hear them for a time, like midges, then they will be entirely gone." There was something careless and remote in her voice, a tone I had noted before, a tone I had shuddered to hear.

"Won't you miss them?" I asked, wanting her to say yes, yes, she would miss them because they were fanciful and marvelous.

She didn't answer the question I had asked. "We Sidhe do not need wings, nor mice to serve as steeds. We have our own hunt, our own ways." She sounded eager, almost voracious. There was something uncomfortable in her voice, something like an edge of grass, seeming so soft, cutting so deep, the life's blood following it almost invisibly so that one does not know one is cut until one sees the red. I drew in my breath, waiting for the wound to gape, but she walked away over the verdant meadow, and I followed her, drawn like the tail of a kite, wondering what had happened to her. Even in Chinanga she had seemed more . . . more human. But then, I told myself, Chinanga had been a human imagining, while Faery was not.

We had gone only a little way when we saw the Sidhe coming toward us, a host on horseback, the first among them leading two riderless horses by their bridles. Oh, the horses were fine! All the horses I had seen as a child were nothing to these, and all the tack I had cared for was nothing to what they wore. Milk-white steeds, they were, shod with silver and bridled in gold, with gemmed frontispieces over their foreheads and jeweled taches across their chests. The skirts of the saddles were dagged, with gilded edges, and were gemmed in patterns of flowers and leaves. Broad in the chest, those horses were, and their nostrils flared and their eyes gleamed as though made of fire.

The riders wore green mantles fringed with gold and bright helmets feathered with green plumes. Each one had in his hand a golden spear from which a long, narrow banner flew, the banners coiling across the sky like the writing I had seen on leatherwork brought back to Westfaire by Papa's father, the liquid writing of the heathen in the Holy Land.

"Read the banners," Mama instructed me, laying her hand on my eyes, and in that instant I could understand them, for they spelled words and paragraphs that slipped into my mind as a hand into a well-worn glove. They expressed the language of the djinni, the banner language of the slow-winds which all in Faery know. The words told me it was the King of that place coming to welcome Mama, and with him a whole host of other elvish peoples, all curling their banners to make her name: Elladine.

Behind these male fairies the females rode, clad in bright silks of colors and designs I had never seen, their hair bound in circlets of oak leaves tied with ivy, the ivy leaves dangling beside their pure white brows. Most among them had golden hair, and this was obviously the color preferred. Others, male and female, were smaller, swarthier folk who rode at the sides of the procession, and at the rear, mostly unheeded by the golden-haired. The King wore a high crown tipped with diamonds like drops of dew glittering with inner lights.

Mama bowed when he approached, tugging me into a similar obeisance. He got down from his horse and bowed in return. There was much talk as I was led forward and introduced. Beauty. Daughter of Elladine. Only half fairy, but true to her mother's line. Much murmuring among the ladies. "Elladine's child? But so old!" I tried not to let the shock show on my face as I tucked that away to think on later. There were many glittering eyes among the men. "Elladine's

daughter. Still young enough!" No one explained, but
it was not long before I learned why this difference in
their perceptions.

We mounted the white horses brought out for us. I
had never ridden a horse like that. His feet fell like
feathers upon the grass. His mane tossed like silver
floss, floating upon the air. His gait was smooth, firm,
and steady as a stone, and his eyes were full of intelligence. I had no need to ride. He carried me. Mama
touched me, and I found myself clad as they all were,
silken gown, green mantle, and wreath of leaves. We
rode toward the djinni castle nearest us, one with towers impossibly narrow and high, with conical roofs so
tall I did not know how they could have been built,
topped with banners which reached to the stars.

A fairy woman rode up beside me, and another on
the other side. "Well met, Beauty," they called to me.
"We are your grandaunts. We were at your christening." They waved and rode on, looking at me curiously
over their shoulders with something of the same expression Mama had first shown me. That slight nar-
rowing of eyes, that barely noticeable discomfiture.

Another took their place. "I am your Grandaunt
Joyeause," she introduced herself. "When your
mother and I carried your sleeping body up to the
tower, I had no idea the curse would seem to take such
little time."

"The curse . . ." I faltered. So far as I knew, the
curse was continuing. Mama and Joyeause had gone
back to Westfaire to move my body into the tower,
and it was then, returning to Ylles, that Mama had
been caught by Carabosse's spell. But it hadn't been
my body they had carried up to the tower of Westfaire. With sudden pain I admitted to myself that they
hadn't known the difference!

I turned away, trying not to think of that. "Is it
morning or evening," I asked Mama, gesturing at the
sky.

"It is as it is," she said. "As it always is in Faery.
The sky a dark and glorious blue. The stars just showing. The flowers still visible, and their perfume lying

soft on the air. The grasses cool with evening. The air warm from day just past and the warmed leaves of the trees exuding fragrance. As it always is, in Faery.''

What was the emotion in her voice? I could not place it. Not sadness, not quite. What? I was lost among these people. I could not tell what they were feeling, or why!

"Look there!'' cried Aunt Joyeause.

There were whisperings among the host. "Mab. Queen Mab. Come to greet Elladine.''

A single rider came toward us, clad all in silver with a crown of pearls. Far behind her white horse was another steed ridden by a dark-haired young man. He was dressed in silver, also, but he was not her son or her brother or her lover. They appeared to be of an age, but this was only seeming. She was old as the hills and lovely as the dawn, and he was something other than that.

"Young Tom-lin of Ercildoune,'' they whispered. "See, she's brought young Tom-lin.''

"He fell from his horse, hunting,'' Mama whispered to me. "In time to see Mab riding by. He greeted her, and she snatched him up. She brought him here to Faery, and here he's dwelt since, almost seven Faery years. She longs for him, but though he gives her every reverence, he'll have none of her.'' Mama's nostrils flared, as though in disgust at such ingratitude and impertinence.

"Maybe he longs for home,'' I suggested.

"What has home to compare with this,'' Mama said.

"Why do they call him Tom-lin?'' I asked.

"Because he has ceased to be Tom,'' she said. "Though when he speaks of himself, he calls himself Thomas the Rhymer, still, and writes verses down on bits of paper.''

Mama greeted Queen Mab, evidently a higher ranking queen than herself, though Mab was kindness itself when she spoke to me, welcoming me to Faery.

"You've been long away,'' she said to Mama.

"A hundred mortal years, evidently," Mama said gaily. "Else my daughter would not be with me."

So Mama hadn't known the difference between me and Beloved. So what. I'd been asleep. Or rather Beloved had. And Mama hadn't seen me since I was a baby. How would she have known? Inside me, something said, "Somehow, she should have known."

Queen Mab turned to ride with us to the palace and Tom-lin turned to follow. I caught the full strength of his stare, hungry and demanding. I was careful not to stare back, having the feeling Queen Mab would not much like it, but something in me responded to that stare. Something human and sympathetic.

There was a feast prepared at the castle. We ate and drank. The wine was wonderfully flavored and scented, but it did not make one drunk. The food was wonderfully prepared, but it did not make one full. One could eat and drink forever if one wished, pandering, as Aunt Basil had used to say, to one's palate with no thought for tomorrow's indigestion.

When everyone was weary of eating, we trooped outside. I thought, perhaps, we would walk in the gardens or have music or even dance, but no. In the glades behind the castle streams ran into silver pools, steaming beneath the stars. The water was warm, and my astonishment at this had not faded when I looked up to see the inhabitants of Faery slipping into the pools, naked as eggs, Mama among them.

She called to me in a bell-like voice. I sat on a stone and fumbled with one shoe, trying not to stare. I could see them, males and females both, slender, the woman almost breastless, their vulvas naked of hair, their bodies like little manikins carved from ivory. The males had a kind of sheath, like a dog, or goat, coming from between their legs and a little way up their bellies, and these sheaths seemed covered with golden fur. Nothing dangled. Nothing protruded. Nothing seemed awkward or erotic. Their smooth buttocks folded gently together on either side of a simple, unperforated crease. Mama had told me the truth. They did not piss or shit in Faery.

But I was not built as they were. I had breasts. I had hair on me. If I bent over, as some of them were doing, my parts would show. I was overcome with shame. I blushed.

And every eye was on me, fierce and prurient. Out of the doggy sheathes, little penises protruded, like darting red tongues. On every female face a luxurious interest gleamed, and I saw their hands reach out to stroke one another familiarly.

I stood up and walked away.

Mama was beside me. "When our fairy children are reared here, they do not find our habits strange," she said with a little tinkle of laughter which did not cover her distress. Her tone was as it had been sometimes in Chinanga, when she turned remote and still. "Grown-up children have too much of the world in them. Perhaps, in time . . ." She patted me on the arm and went away, leaving me to walk among the flowers.

Thomas walked there, too, evidently as discomfited as I at the naked licentiousness of Faery. He glanced at me, but did not offer conversation. After a time the fairy folk came to get us, and we went into the palace, to our own rooms, to sleep on beds where soft moss grew instead of mattresses, and coverlets sewn of rose petals kept off the drafts. If there had been any drafts, which there were not. Fountains played in that place, and their music was an unending melody. I was glad to be left alone.

The blue of the sky seemed to deepen, only a little, as though in awareness that most of us slept. The stars crinkled and winked, as though talking. I lay awake, lost in wonder. After a time there came a scratching at my door. I went on silent feet and opened it, and it was Thomas the Rhymer there. He touched me on the arm.

"I did not dare speak to you in the gardens," he said, softly as a whisper, with great longing in his voice. He stared at me closely. "It's true, you're human!"

I let him in and shut the door behind him. I was

dressed in a full, silky robe. I needed only imagine what I wore, and it was there, around me. It had sleeves that fell away from my arms, floor long panels that wafted like spider silk. "I'm half human," I told him. "Elladine is my mama, but my father is human."

He nodded. "I saw those of Faery at the pool, lusting after you. You have a fine smell about you, one that arouses them. You smell of fecundity. They are almost sterile, you know. They seldom have children of their own anymore. They must steal children from cradles, or consort with mortals to bear them."

"Why is that?"

"I do not know. It has something to do with the way they were made, at the beginning of time."

"My mama is disappointed in me." It hurt to say that, but I was sure of it.

He nodded at me soberly. "You noticed that, did you? Well, it is because you are older than most children the Sidhe get. Most half mortals are stolen as babies or are born here, and they can become like the Sidhe, almost entirely. It is too late for you, however. You will never be one of them, and Elladine knows it. Though she longs to love you, she will not let herself become too fond of you. They lust after mortals, but they do not let themselves love them much."

"Not even her own daughter?" I cried in anguish.

"Not even their own children, no. Long ago, at the beginning of time, it was a different matter. They were noble and mighty then. They did not reject the nobility of suffering for love. But things are different now."

"Why?" I cried. "Oh, why?"

"Because they are diminished from what they once were. Or if not diminished, changed. They do not say so, but one learns of it, listening to what they say and do not say."

"I thought only the trooping fairies were diminished."

"Now. As these will be later. Once these were great as gods, but Faery is dwindling, even now. When it becomes small enough, perhaps I could step out of it, but it will be too late for me."

He sounded anguished. There were tears in his eyes. I started to ask him why the diminution of the Sidhe, but there was a sound in the courtyard outside my window, and he slipped away, closing the door behind him. I heard Mab's voice, asking him where he had been, and he told her he had been walking in the courtyard.

"In the courtyard, Tom-lin?" Her voice was like honey and silk, like fire and gall.

"If it please you, Your Majesty."

"You know what would please me, Tom-Lin."

"I cannot, Your Majesty. Such an honor is not for me."

"I could put a spell upon you, Tom, so you'd think it was your Janet you were making love to."

His voice rasped as he said, "Then it would be my Janet I was making love to, Your Majesty. In my heart."

I peeked out through the window. She stood there in all her loveliness, beautiful as a goddess. If she was diminished, it did not show, not in that moment. "If I cannot have your heart and your seed, Tom-lin, then you cannot have your Janet." She turned and went away from him and he stood there in the silence, his shoulders shaking.

I fell onto the bed, deeply disturbed by what I had heard, sure I would not sleep. The next thing I knew, it was morning, or so much morning as ever comes in that land. Mama and I drank little glasses of something warmly sweet and honey-smelling, then rode out in procession to attend a session at the King's court.

"Does the King have a name?" I asked Mama.

"Some call him Oberon," she told me. "Some Finvarra. Some call him the King of Golden Halls. Some, the King of the Hill People. Some the King of the Good Folk or the Gentle Ones. We call him He Who Endures, and we know when he is gone, so will we be." I heard in her voice again that slight remoteness I had heard once or twice in Chinanga, though now, having spoken to Thomas, I thought I understood it.

When we came to the King's court, the news came out to meet us that a delegation was soon to arrive, people of another sort. It was not Faery, according to what they said, and yet it was.

"It is not heaven nor earth," Mama told me mysteriously, "Nor any hell, so it must be Faery, and yet it is not the Sidhe." She would not tell me any more, but merely laughed. None of the folk of that place seemed to take this delegation seriously, yet when the time came for them to assemble in the great hall and hear the words of those who came as envoys, everyone was still and courteous and grave. The glamour lay about us so thick that I could smell it. Mama was on the dais among the royalty, and I stood along the side in dagged velvet and cloth of gold to watch the envoys come in.

Ah, but they were horrible. Hairy and twisted, fanged and dewlapped. Some among them were better-looking, more nearly straight, but as a general rule they gave the appearance of half-made things. One had long toenails that scratched upon the marble floors. One had an eye in the middle of his forehead. Some had batwings and others had rat teeth.

"Who are they," I whispered to my neighbor, trying to keep my voice from shaking.

"The Bogles," he replied. I knew the voice and turned in surprise to find Thomas the Rhymer standing close behind me. "Has your mother taught you to use the power of sight?" he whispered to me, seeing the fear in my eyes.

I shook my head at him.

"Narrow your eyes, and wish to see them true," he said. So I did, slitting both eyes and concentrating on the wish. In the moment I saw them differently, shorter, stouter people than those of the Sidhe, and darker-colored, but certainly not hideous. Somewhat like those who had ridden at the rear of the procession, though more open of face.

"They appear ugly to keep men at a distance," Thomas said. "Unlike those of the Sidhe who appear beautiful to make men come nearer. To men's eternal loss." His voice was bitter, though only a whisper, as he fell silent in order that we could hear the speeches.

My first view of them had been human sight, obviously. But once I had seen them true, I could not bring back the former vision of them. Most surprising, I had seen their leader before, every now and then when I was a child. He was my old friend, the pointy-eared boy! Of course! Puck.

"You've one among you seven years now," he challenged them. "Taken from human kind, Queen Mab. Time's near come for the teind, and you have him still. We've come to see the treaty complied with."

"It is no affair of yours what I do," the Queen replied in a silky voice. "Be back about your swamp dancing, Puck. We've had this talk before." I didn't know what a teind was, but his voice made it something serious.

"There's a new one come, as well," he went on in an even voice. "And she's none of yours," and he turned and looked at me with a wry look as though to say, "Fancy seeing you here."

Mama rose on the dais and beckoned to me. I stepped forward uncertainly. Puck watched me with his green eyes, like water over stones. He had a brown face with great bushy brows and a wide mouth. My old acquaintance. I started to greet him, then, warned by something in his eyes, did not. Still, I was so taken with his familiar face I almost didn't hear what Mama said. "She is ours, Puck. My daughter. Beauty. Borne by me to a human noble and come to Faery to seek her mother."

He looked saddened by this, though why should he? He knew who I was, who I'd always been. Who had sent him to watch over me, back at Westfaire? I had always assumed it was Martin, or maybe Mama. Obviously not, but then who? Carabosse? He shook his head at me and turned to those on the dais. I stepped back to feel Thomas's hand rest lightly on my shoulder.

Puck tried again, "So, sad though it be, she's here by her own will, Mab. Still, there's Thomas the

Rhymer who is not here of his own will. He's not been lastingly harmed as yet, but what use will you make of him?"

"I say it again, Puck. Take your Bogles back to the swamps and the streams. Get back to the crossroads. Tell your brownies to get to their sweeping, your leprechauns to their shoemaking, your kobolds to their mines. There are enough humans out there for you to cosset without worrying over mine."

"He isn't yours," said Puck, something strained in his voice. "Queen Mab . . ."

"All that is mine is mine," she chanted. "And all that is yours is mine as well. If I so choose."

"I beg you not to choose," he said to her holding out his hard, square hands. His words were an entreaty, but she merely laughed, then went on laughing with those about her as the Bogles conferred among themselves. Puck threw up his hands, then turned to leave, the others coming behind him. Except for one very small, plain one with a scythe over his shoulder, who slipped out of their ranks and took me by the hand.

"I am the Fenoderee," he whispered. "If you have need of a friend, call me." Then he, too, was gone.

Thomas spoke in my ear. "Unless you wish to see the Fenoderee destroyed, do not tell anyone he offered to be your friend."

"I won't tell anyone but Mama," I said.

"Then he is surely dead," Thomas said.

I turned on him angrily, but he had gone back into the crowd. Looking at Mama on the dais where she laughed with Queen Mab, however, I decided I did not need to tell her about the Fenoderee. I had not called for a friend, and the little Bogle's offer did not necessarily warrant mention.

The audience seemed to be over. The nobles were coming down off the dais, talking with one another in careless voices. Curiosity would certainly not be out of place, so when Mama came down to me, I asked her what all that had been about.

"Puck and his following tend to be officious," she

said with her remote, careless look. "They have taken it upon themselves to be protectors of man."

"I thought angels were the protectors of man," I said in a puzzled tone, remembering things Father Raymond had taught me.

"Well then," she laughed, with a nasty twist to her amusement. "Puck has taken it into his head to become an angel. It's an old argument, going far back into time."

I hoped she would tell me more, but Oberon came up just then, and we both fell silent as we made our deep reverences to him. He invited us to join him in the hunt, and we went out to mount horses already standing ready in the courtyard. This was in accord with something I had already noticed about Faery. Food was always ready when one was hungry. Horses were saddled and bridled when one wanted to hunt. Water was hot when one wanted to bathe. Possibly the most altogether magical thing about Faery was that we did not have to wait about for other people to do things before we could do the things we wanted.

We rode out, the horses' hooves making a steady drumbeat as we crossed the bridge and came onto the road of velvety dust. I thought that all the soil of this place must be soft, else the silver shoes on the horses would not last. Mama rode up beside me and hissed, "Riding clothes, girl! Have some manners!"

I looked up see everyone clad in riding clothes with high boots and flowing skirts on the ladies and their hair done up in narrow caps with veils flying behind. As soon as I saw it, I was dressed the same as they, but it had taken my perceiving them to do it. I had done it myself. This gave me a momentary exultation followed by a shiver of fear. If I'd been a child when I came here, I'd have done it without even thinking. What else could I do, just by thinking about it?

We hunted white deer that day. Two of them, a stag and a hind. They fled like the wind, and we pursued like the gale. They fled like the hawk, and we came after them like the eagle. They fled like the flame of candles, and we burned their trails like the fire in a forge. At last they wearied and we came up to them. Oberon shot them both with bright arrows, and the huntsmen cut off their heads. When the heads came off, I had a momentary vision of something not right, something frightening and horrid. I turned away only to find Thomas's eyes on me, as though in warning. The huntsmen put the carcasses over a horse, and we returned to the castle, our horses' equipment jingling, a lutist playing, the people singing. When we came near, I had fallen a little behind, and Thomas rode up beside me to say, "Do not eat of the venison served tonight."

I started to ask him why, but he rode on, faster and faster, until he came up beside Queen Mab. She turned and smiled at him, and he smiled in return. A very sad, hopeless smile.

Most of the people went to the hot springs where they bathed. I went to my room. When the door was tight shut behind me, I sat down on the bed and called, "Fenoderee! I need a friend."

He was there in the instant, standing beside me.

I said, "There was something frightening. I can't remember what!"

"Ah, weel," he said to me, "you've not the knack of the *seein'* yet, and your human sight comes through. It wasna only deer they lopped the heads from there in the wood. It was a man and his wife they hunted down, a man and his wife who'd refused to give their child to Queen Mab when she wanted it."

"And they'll *eat* them?" I cried, unable to believe it.

"Ach, no, lass. They'll eat venison right enough. They wouldn't kill or eat human flesh, for that would break the covenant. But it was human flesh they enchanted into deer. So, what is it they eat? Ah? Did they indeed break the covenant? They'll tell you it's venison, and they'll tell you true, but you know what you saw, don't you?"

"Thomas told me not to eat it."

"Then Thomas told you what was good for you."

"Then he saw it, too." What I had seen, that over-lay of human flesh when the heads had come off.

"Aye, he sees. A man so fearful as that will see what's true."

"What's he fearful of, Fenoderee?"

Fenoderee turned himself around like a dog trying to find a place to lie down. "He's fearful Oberon will use him for something forbidden."

"And what's that?" I could not imagine what could be forbidden in this land where cannibalism seemed to be a matter of course.

"Long ago," said Fenoderee, "when man was made, the Holy One asked us of Faery to help man out, for he was a witless thing then, barely able to stand on his two feet. Some of the Sidhe assented, a few. But Oberon was King then, as he is now, and he told them to hold their tongues, that the Sidhe would do it only if the Holy One commanded it.

" 'No,' said the Holy One, 'I could command it, true, but I will not. I have not designed this universe in all its unpredictable glory in order to interrupt it with gratuitous commands and arbitrary miracles. If you honor my request, you do it out of your own will, out of goodness, in thankfulness for what you've been given.' "

"What did Oberon say?"

"He said no, as he'd said before. So then the Holy One said, 'I will not command, but I may destroy some parts of my creation if they threaten other parts. So I will make treaty with the Sidhe. It is I who made the Sidhe immortal, and they may remain so only so long as no man comes to lasting harm at their hands.' And Oberon accepted that."

"Who were the ones who said they'd help man?"

"Israfel and his lot. Oh, and Carabosse. Oberon paid them no attention. They didn't even go on living in Faery; they went off to Baskarone. Since then, we Bogles have called them our Separated Kindred, or the Long Lost. Oberon calls them something else, but then he's not a forgiving sort."

"But the deer," I cried. "The enchanted deer! That

was surely lasting harm to the man and his wife. To be eaten!"

"Sneaky the Sidhe have become," said Fenoderee. "Sneaky and sly. It wasn't the man and his wife that they killed, you see. It was only deer. Sneakiness like that has been going on for some time now. They've kept the letter of the treaty, no matter what they've done to the intentions."

"Why?"

"Because they're proud, lass. The creation of man was a dreadful blow to them. It needn't have been if they'd put their minds to understanding man rather than just resenting him. But then, after the Dark Lord went off and made his own place, he sent whisperers among the Sidhe, telling them how much their pride had been offended. And some time after the treaty was made, Oberon made another one, this one with the Dark Lord, who pledged to teach Oberon ways to keep the Holy One at bay—though the Dark Lord couldn't keep daylight at bay if the Holy One didn't allow it. The payment to the Dark Lord comes every seven years, and it's what is called the teind to hell, for that is what the Dark Lord has made for himself."

"*The* hell?"

"The only one I know of," he said.

"What's the payment?" I asked, my throat suddenly dry.

"The payment is a person," he said. "Of some sort. Oberon's been using us Bogles for the teind, when he can catch us, but we've grown too smart for him and he hasn't caught one of us in recent time. That's why there were so many of us come to court with Puck, to fight them off if they tried to take one of us by force. Oberon knows if he uses one of the Sidhe, it could cause rebellion against him. So he's thinking of defying the treaty and using a human. And the only human resident in Faery now is Thomas the Rhymer. And you, Beauty."

"But I'm half fairy!" I cried.

"No teind is better than half. Half a teind is better than a whole," he said softly. "And once he's used human, half or whole, then the treaty's broken." Then, "Whsst. I'm gone." And he was.

Outside in the hallway I could hear Mama's voice, along with those of the others. She, still laughing at something Oberon had said, came into the room where I was, her nose twitching, like a cat when it smells a mouse.

"I smell Bogle," she cried. "Has that filthy Puck been near?"

I shook my head at her. "I've not seen Puck since the audience, Mama," I said, truthfully enough. She looked me in the face as though to tell whether I was lying or not, and then she said, "We of Faery value truth above all else, Beauty."

"I know you do, Mama," I said, thinking over what I had said to be sure there were no lies in it.

She sat down on the bed beside me. "Do not put yourself in peril, daughter," she said.

"In peril, Mama?"

"If you make cause with the Bogles against us, no place or time will be safe from Oberon's vengeance. The Bogles are always snuggling up to mankind. They mix more than they should."

I thought this a strange thing for her to say, she who had married my mortal Papa. Was that not mixing? Or even snuggling, come to that. Evidently she did not feel the need to be consistent. I had noticed the same thing among the aunts. What they told me to do was not always what they told others, or what they did themselves.

Mama went on. "Oberon will find you if you offend him, no matter where you go."

"Why should I offend any of you, Mama?" I cried. "You're my mother. These are your people." And, indeed, why should I? What did she know that I did not?

Satisfied at what she saw on my face, she told me to create a marvelous dress and come to dinner.

I ate fruit and bread and clotted cream and none of the venison. I drank what would have been too much wine anywhere else. All around me others were eating the meat with good appetite. I don't think anyone noticed that I left it well alone. Once or twice I looked up to find Thomas's eyes upon me and my plate. Once or twice I looked up to see Queen Mab staring at me with curiosity. I smiled carefully back, and cast my eyes modestly down. If she had enchanted a man and his wife for refusing her their child, what might she do to one who entertained Bogles in her bedroom? All the time I was thinking about the doctrine of transubstantiation and wondering if the man and wife were still present in the venison, though they had been enchanted into something else.

After everyone had gone to sleep, I heard the scratching at my door again. This time I knew it was Thomas, and he slipped into my room like a shadow. He was clearly frantic, his hands trembling, his eyes flicking like hummingbirds from one place to another. "I have to get out of here," he said.

"I know," I told him, going on to tell him how I knew.

"Queen Mab says she will neither let me be used as teind nor let me go," he said, his voice shaking. "But Oberon says he will use me as he sees fit. Queen Mab says she will use you, instead, but Elladine is in favor with the King, so he will not permit that. Oh, Elladine is in excellent odor just now for having brought a half-human woman into Faery, even old as you are. They are all in a frenzy over you."

"Can't you just run away?"

"How? In what direction? Are we under the sea or high in the air? Are we deep beneath the earth under a barrow, as some say, or are we in some enchanted land beyond the bounds of earth? In what direction should I go? And when I have gone, what is to keep Mab from turning me into a deer and hunting me down as she did today with those others? I can escape from this place only by human help, and there is none human here but you."

"When is the teind to be paid?" I asked.

"Soon," he whispered. "Faery time is not the time of earth. It flows fast, it flows slow. Sometimes it almost stops, wandering like the tortoise, long hours in the space of a breath. Other times it dives like the hawk, a year in a moment's pace. I only know it is soon.''

He left me then, as quickly as he had come, his face haggard with fear. I lay on the bed, looking out at the sky, scarcely darker now than in midday. Blue, spangled with stars. There had to be a way to help him. Had to be a way.

Mama and I had a picnic together in the meadow. I had asked her for it, as a favor, wanting to, as I put it, "know her better."

"You must tell me some things," I assured her. "Simply must, Mama, or I shall make the most dreadful mistakes. You must tell me what not to say in front of Queen Mab or King Oberon, or any of the others."

"Don't talk of treaties or Bogles and all will be well," she said, not looking me in the eye.

"Can I speak of the teind to hell?" I asked innocently.

She blanched. "It would be wisest not."

"Then you must tell me what it is, so that I will not mention some aspect of it inadvertently."

"It's a payment," she said impatiently. "To the Dark One. For guarding our borders. For keeping out . . . other influences."

"Angels?" I asked. "But, aren't you acquainted with angels?"

She looked around, making sure we were not overheard. "If you are speaking of those from Baskarone, Beauty, then be sure they are not angels. They are no more angelic than we. They are our own kindred who separated from us when man was created, over some fear they have that we or mankind or both of us will do something . . . something irrevocable. Foolishness. Are we not Faery? Are we not wiser than that? Our separated kindred dwell in Baskarone, but they are not angels."

Though I very much wanted to pursue that subject, I had other matters at hand which needed concentration. "I heard some of the Sidhe speaking, Mama. They said I might be used as the teind."

"Nonsense," she cried. "Who would say such a wicked thing." There were tears in her eyes, the first I had seen there on my behalf. So, like it or not, she was fond of me. Or she was afraid. Or she cried for some other reason.

I almost stopped then, not wanting to be disloyal to her, but something made me go on. Perhaps the anguish I'd heard in Thomas's voice. He had been so fearful, so terrorized, so very human. I said, "So I thought. They have a perfectly good teind in Thomas, do they not? And yet, someone said they thought he might escape."

"He cannot escape."

"How do you know?"

"Because I know the spell set upon him. The only way he could escape would be if a human woman were to see him riding by, were to ask for him and hold him tight, despite all the changes Mab could put him through, hold him fast from midnight to dawn, then he could leave Mab and return to the land of mortal men." She said it carelessly, as though it didn't matter.

"That's not very likely, is it?" I asked faintly.

"Not likely at all, which is why Mab thought it up," she said. "So you've nothing to worry about. It is not long until Samhain, All Hallows Eve on earth, the night when the teind is paid. Once that is done, we'll have no more worries for seven Faery years."

"Mama," I asked, changing the subject, "I think it's time I learned some magic. What am I half fairy for, otherwise."

That night I told Tom-lin what Mama had told me. "Have you such a human woman, Thomas?" I asked. "I could attempt it myself, but I'm only half and it might not work. Besides, it would so offend Mama and my other kindred, I could not stay in Faery."

"My fair Janet," he said. "Oh, yes, my fair Janet might well hold fast against all hell."

"Where will I find her," I whispered.

"Near Ercle's Down is a wood, named for the

carter's house which is there and, near the wood, a well. By that well, roses grow, and Janet will come there at sunset to pull a rose in my memory, for it was there I pledged her my love and gave her a rose in troth."

"In what country?" I asked.

"Why," he replied, "in Scotland."

So, in the midnight hours of Faery, it was to Scotland, to Ercle's Down I went, begging my boots in a whisper to take me quietly.

I came there on a late afternoon in summer. I begged directions from a passing shepherd, who directed me to Carterhaugh Wood, and I went there, quickly enough. The well was less easy to find, for there were a number of wells. Only one grew roses, however, the last one I went to, at the edge of the woods. I waited impatiently for evening, watching the shadows lengthen. As it was growing dark, when I had about given her up, she came walking across the downs toward the trees. I was about to go out to her when I felt a tug at my sleeve, and there were Puck and Fenoderee. "Now that you've led us here, best leave it to us," Puck whispered.

I bridled.

"Nae, lass, leave it to us," Puck admonished me. "Ye have none of the language needed, and it has to be set in rhyme."

"Why does it?"

"Because she'll not believe it's from him, otherwise," and he gripped my hand tightly for a moment. I could feel his hand there for a long time after he had gone.

The girl came to the well and pulled a rose, and I heard Puck's voice in fair imitation of Tom-lin's.

> "The Queen of fairies caught me up
>   in a far green land to dwell.
> And though it's pleasant in that land,
>   I've a fearful thing to tell,
> For at the end of seven years
>   they pay a teind to hell;

> *And I'm a fleshy human man,*
>   *that the Dark Lord would like well.*
> *The night is Halloween, my love,*
>   *the morn is Hallowday;*
> *Then win me, win me, if you will,*
>   *as well I know you may."*

It went on for some little time, but was clear enough for all that, despite being interrupted by the girl's questions every line or two. Puck told her how to recognize him, that is, Thomas: right hand gloved, left hand bare, hat cocked up and hair down, riding nearest the town. He also told her where she would encounter the ride (at Miles Cross) and what horrors he would probably turn into, and that she must hold him until dawn. When he had done, we watched the woman go running back across the downs, her hair loose and tangled behind her, then Puck took me by one hand and Fenoderee by the other while I commanded the boots to take me back outside Oberon's castle.

There we stood upon the terrace, looking out across the midnight meadows, listening to the night creatures and the stream, both murmuring.

"That was a courageous thing you did," said Puck. "To help your fellowman."

"Help fellowman, play Faery false," I said bitterly. "One is the same as the other. I am neither nor, Puck. I am confused and wishing myself other than I am."

"Would we could help you, Beauty. Will it help to know you are helping Faery, too?"

"How?" I asked, very sceptically.

"They break the treaty if they give Thomas to the Dark Lord. And that will harm them far more than losing Thomas will do."

I heard him, but was not sure he told the truth. "Would you take me to visit Carabosse?"

"Old Carabosse of the clocks?" asked Fenoderee. "Old tick-tock?"

"Will you?"

"I will," he said. "I will come for you soon," and with that he was gone.

It was Puck who came for me. I was alone when he came. "Get yourself upon a horse," he said, "ride out and call for Fenoderee."

So I had a stableboy saddle me a lovely horse, rode out some distance from the castle, paused beside a large rock and said into the air, "Fenoderee, I need a friend." Immediately, both he and Puck were standing beside the rock, Fenoderee grinning, Puck picking at a toenail. He liked to stand storkwise, on one leg, his fingers playing with the toes of the upraised foot.

"The fairy Carabosse has invited you to tea," Puck informed me.

"Clockwork Carabosse," chanted Fenoderee, cutting a circle about himself with his scythe. "Old gears and ratchets."

"Who calls her that?" I wondered.

"I just did," said Fenoderee. "Lots of the Bogles do."

"Some," admitted Puck. "Not lots."

"Why do they?"

"You'll find out when we get there."

Puck got up behind me on the horse and held me around the waist. It reminded me of all the times Bill had held me in the twentieth, when I was tired or discouraged or didn't know what to do next. Both he and Puck were small, but wiry and strong. Capable. I relaxed and let him guide the horse. Fenoderee bounded ahead like a fawn, disappearing behind clumps of grass and then appearing again, far ahead.

We came to the forest, went along it to the left until we came to a small stream, followed the stream into the woods, up a narrow defile, and then out into a clearing where a cottage stood, smoke rising from its chimney. It was a fairy-tale cottage. Though I don't know much about tales of that kind, I had seen cartoons in the twentieth. This cottage could have appeared in "Hansel and Gretel" or "The Three Bears" or "Red Riding Hood" without any changes at all.

"We'll wait," said Puck. "Just in case you need us when you come out."

I was fairly sure I could find my way back, but company on the homeward ride would be welcome. I dismounted and walked toward the cottage, hearing as I approached a sound like the muttering of rain on dried leaves. It grew louder and louder, and as I stepped onto the stoop, a chime rang, followed immediately by a cacophony of bells, whistles, cuckoos, gongs, all telling the hour with indiscriminate fervor. After a time the noise died away to the murmur once more, which I now recognized as the ticking of countless clocks, and I knocked firmly upon the cracked panels of the door.

"Enter!" cried a cracked old voice.

She was sitting beside the fire, under her tumult of timepieces. They dangled on every wall; they squatted on every flat surface. They made a noise like a storm of rain until she raised her hand and the sound stopped. All the little pendulums swung, all the little hands moved, but they moved in silence.

"So you've come," she said.

"I've come," I agreed. "I've come because you are the only one who knows what's going on, and I cannot go on, not knowing."

"You weren't supposed to know," she muttered. "You weren't supposed to be bothered with it. All we intended to do was keep it safe, inside you, until the proper time comes. . . ." Her voice dragged away into the clock-silence, the endless movement of hands and swinging pendulums, and she stared into the fire.

I did not disturb her. If she would tell me, she would. If she wouldn't, there was nothing I could do.

"Long ago," she said at last, "when man was made, which was long after we were made, I looked into the future and saw an ending there. You have seen that ending."

I had seen it. Of course, I had seen it.

"At that ending is no magic," she said. "At that ending, all beauty stops. There may be some life after,

bacteria perhaps. Small, senseless things moving endlessly on the winds and in the seas. No matter.

"I saw an end. And those of us who could—they
were not many, for most of us have been less than
diligent in learning what may be done—decided that a
certain *thing* should be preserved."

"In Baskarone," I said, suddenly sure of it.

"*Of* Baskarone, partly. Israfel was one of them
who did the preserving. He and his kindred distilled a
thing from. . . . From the necessary materials. They
made it. But then we had to hide it."

And I knew then. "You hid it here," I said, putting
my hand to my breast. "It burns."

She looked at me pitifully. "Does it hurt you?"

I shook my head at her in wonder. No. It did not
hurt. "What is it?"

"It is what it is. It is what Oberon wishes for but
has never been able to hold. It is what the Dark Lord
lusts for. We must keep it from him."

"That's a riddle, Carabosse!"

"It is how we old fairies speak," she said, looking
at me from under her scanty lashes. "If you knew what
was going to happen, you could not behave normally."

"This thing . . . I suppose it's important."

She sat unbreathing. It was as though the universe
had stopped for that instant. At last her breath left her
in a sigh.

"Important," she whispered to herself. "Yes. Important." She sighed again. "We thought no one
would look for it in a child. Then we planned to entice
you into some place where you could live happily for a
long time. We picked Chinanga, the timeless land. No
one had ever aged in Chinanga. Chinanga was poised
there in the always, and we thought it would go on
forever. How long did we need, after all? Only a few
hundred years.

"We planned you would want to leave Westfaire,
that you would think of the boots, that you would
make them and go to Chinanga. Meantime, your
mama would return to Westfaire to move your sleeping body to the tower, and on her way back to Faery

she would be caught by our spells and brought to Chinanga also. By the time you traveled upriver, she would be there to meet you.

"But, you didn't make the boots, and as you were leaving Westfaire, those people came. They came from the twenty-first. We cannot even see into the twenty-first. And when they took you away, we could not reach you. And when you returned you were pregnant. We didn't want you to go while you were pregnant."

"But then Elly was born," I said.

"That was the first good opportunity for you to go to Chinanga," she murmured. "But then, by the time you got to Chinanga, you were too old for your mama to be easy with, and the Viceroy had already heard of this virgin with a difference. Between them, the Viceroy and Elladine, they destroyed the whole place. Imaginary worlds do not show up in my Forever Pool. Elladine has always done things that are quite unreasonable. And now you are here, where we had never intended you should come."

"Why me?" I asked. "Why did you choose me?"

She sighed. "People don't understand about magic. There are always certain limitations and proprieties: certain symbols which must be kept aligned; certain congruities we must observe. *It* was born of magic and could not live unless there was magic around *it*. *It* was born in truth, so the place we put *it* had to be named truly. *It* had to mature in a place where no ugliness is, and that was Westfaire. *It* could not have been set into just anyone or put just anywhere."

"Why didn't you just let it be me there in Westfaire, sound asleep? That would have kept it safe for you."

She shook her head at me. "The rarer a thing is, the more assiduously it is sought. As magic grows rarer and rarer, the more intent the Dark Lord will become at seeking it out. Eventually, Westfaire will gleam like a beacon, the last repository of magic. Do you think he would ignore that? No. Westfaire was intended as misdirection, Beauty. Legerdemain. Even if he seeks it there, he will not find it. Mary Blossom is only a decoy. You were to have been in Chinanga."

"But I'm really here. And so is it."

"True. For a time, I was deeply dismayed at that, but Israfel assures me all is not lost. Your being here is considered to be perfectly natural. You came to see your mama. Why not? Elladine left you the means to visit her, or she thinks she did, and so long as she thinks so, so does everyone else. As for Westfaire, either they believe the curse has run its course or they know about Mary Blossom, but in either case, everything is explainable. We went to great lengths, Israfel and I, to keep everything around you as natural as possible. The use of magic leaves an aura, like a fire leaves smoke, so when we used magic, we seemed to do it openly, obviously. Anyone sniffing the smoke could see our innocent little fire and dismiss it as trivial. What was it, after all? A sleeping enchantment, a cloak, a pair of boots. Mere bagatelles. Even Elladine's stay in Chinanga is explainable—she believes the Viceroy's enchantments brought her there. No one suspects anything odd about you. No one knows except Israfel and the others in Baskarone. And I."

"Puck?"

"No. He is my trusted friend and servant, but he doesn't know. Even though he has done much running about on your behalf, he doesn't know about *it*. None of the Bogles know."

"So what do I do now?"

"We can still preserve that which must be preserved. If you will simply go on, as you are, pretending to be what you would have been had we never met. I have seen that your visit to Faery will end soon. You will go away from here, very naturally. You will be in the world, being yourself, and meantime, Israfel and I will be searching for some other place—something like Chinanga, only less boring."

I didn't say yes, or no. After a time she reached out and took my hand. It felt like a mother's hand, like Dame Blossom's hand. I wasn't sure I believed the business about my visit ending soon, but I chose not to remark upon it.

"Mother doesn't like me," I said, needing her to say it wasn't true.

"That's not entirely true," she said. "Humans make myths about mothers and daughters, fathers and sons. The myths are very strong. I have counted on them myself, but sometimes the two generations are simply not sympathetic. Especially when they resemble, let us say, the other side of the family."

It was true. Except around the eyes, I most resembled Father. I resembled him in other ways. Fleshiness. Corporeality. The thousand stinks and farts that flesh is heir to.

"Can you go on?" she asked me gently.

"Can you take *it* out?" I asked. "Can you put *it* somewhere else?"

She shook her head. I already knew that. It had grown into me. I could feel its roots, down to my toes, down to my finger tips. So I told her I could go on. What else was there to do but go on?

She patted me. She still felt like Dame Blossom.

"I have this problem," I said. And I told her about Thomas the Rhymer. "If I tell him, I am betraying the Faery folk."

She smiled as though she already knew all about it and said what Puck had said. "If you don't tell him, you will betray them far worse." Suddenly, inexplicably, she asked me, "What would you like to do? Right now?"

"Go back to Westfaire," I blurted. "Go back home and find Giles there and be with him."

She gave me a weary little smile. "Keep that thought in mind. I will, too. We'll see how things work out. Until then, go on, Beauty. Just let things happen, as they will. Very naturally."

Puck and Fenoderee were waiting to take me back to Elladine's palace.

There was a time in Faery after that, neither long nor short, but of considerable importance, during which I learned to do enchantments and spells. Mama taught me how to weave magical garments and how to lay geas on swords or jewels to make them fit for questing. There is a good deal of questing in Faery, as a pastime. This one or that one will be enchanted into forgetting who he or she is, and will then be sent off after a sword or a grail or some other marvel. Or they'll do the same thing to humans and follow along, watching it as though it were a movie. According to Mama, nine-tenths of King Arthur was questing and the other tenth was politics.

Mab taught me the magic of trees and caverns and clearings in the forest. She taught me the dwindling spell, by which things may be made tiny, and the Great Spell of Bran, by which giants may be conjured up. Even Oberon, once or twice, taught me something of spell-casting, mostly matters of bewilderment. Oberon is very strong in bewilderment.

He also invited me to his couch, quite openly, making an honor of it, though not demanding an immediate response, for which I was thankful.

Mama was quite excited about that, not least at the thought of my possibly bearing Oberon's child. I did not want to bear anyone's child.

"It wouldn't be private, would it," I half-laughed to hide my embarrassment. If I had imagined myself talking to my mama about anything in the world, it would not have been this. I could not have imagined her urging me to let Oberon . . . or cooperate with Oberon . . . or even enjoy with Oberon. . . .

"Private?" she asked. "If you didn't want anyone to watch, you could say so. I don't suppose anyone would care."

I sat beside him at dinner. He sniffed at me, my breasts, my armpits. He laid his head in my lap and smelled me through my skirts, almost as a dog does. If I had encouraged him even slightly, he would have thrust his nose into my crotch. I moved away, pretending not to notice. This sounds foolish, doesn't it, pretending not to notice. And yet, the others behaved in such very strange ways that it was not as noticeable as it sounds. Still, Israfel would not have behaved so. Perhaps that is part of what Thomas meant, when he said they were diminished from former times.

Later, I said to Mama, "I'm not like you! My body isn't made the way yours is. He'd be disgusted. Either that or he'd have to lose his memory as you did with Papa."

"He would not lose his memory," she said stiffly. "Not here, not in Faery. And the fact that your body is more fleshy, more earthy, that it has smells of animal fecundity, only adds to his interest."

I had been wrong about there being no perversions in Faery. Their perversion was to lust after human bodies, with all their stinks and scattish contiguities.

"Will I offend him greatly if I ask for time to get used to Faery first," I asked, the only excuse I could think of at the moment. "Will you explain to him about things like . . . like . . ."

She snorted, making it plain she thought me a fool, but she told Oberon something that put him off without angering him. I caught him watching me every now and again with a lustful little sparkle in his eyes.

In truth, my body was in rebellion. I felt constantly weak and tired. I could cast the feeling aside by a little concentration, but I often found myself simply sitting, doing nothing, not wanting to move. It was unlikely that lovemaking would have been even tolerable, and I certainly didn't feel in the least lustful. The people of the Sidhe often went about virtually unclothed. Their bodies were fair and glorious to see, but I felt no prurience or desire, though their couplings and uncouplings were very casual. Sometimes they seemed like showoffy children, staring around to see if someone was watching, more concerned with being seen than with what they were doing. I remembered Roland Mirabeau, wondering if I had caught his disease of sexual ennui, but he had at least adored little girls and I didn't seem to adore any of the Sidhe. There was nothing in the smell of them to move me. They smelled like leaves, like moss, like clear seawater, like glass.

One night I found myself walking near Thomas the

Rhymer. There was no one else about, so I told him we had been to his true love, Janet, and had arranged for her to save him. He was to have his right hand gloved and his left hand bare when he rode on All Hallow's eve. "Cap cocked up and hair long," I instructed him. "That's what she'll be expecting."

"You saw her?" he breathed.

"Only in the dark," I said. In truth, I had not seen her well, though she had seemed older than I had expected. Thomas did not stay to chat. Hope lit his face as he left me there, and I stayed, watching the night until the others woke.

Time went by, and suddenly one morning Oberon announced that evening would be All Hallows Eve and we would ride to the Dark One to pay him his teind. There was a flutter of excitement at that. Mab gave Oberon an angry look, which he pretended not to see. Thomas shivered. I could see it across the room. Elladine stared at Oberon until he turned to her and smiled. So. So and So. It had all been arranged. Someone was going to be very angry if Janet was waiting at Miles Cross.

I can recall almost nothing that happened during the day. Along toward evening a group of us walked in a grove we sometimes frequented. At its center is the Pool of Delights, crossed by a carved stone bridge, over the rail of which the people of Faery are wont to peer, admiring their reflections in the water. I remember looking down at myself, smiling up at myself. My hair was twined up in a net of sapphires, and the thin muslin of my dress was embroidered with blue flowers. The face which smiled up at me was very beautiful, and I smiled at my own reflection, not happily, but in appreciation. Mama's face, no less lovely, was beside mine. It is the only thing I can remember happening, all day.

We rode out at evening. As we went from Faery into the world, the sky lightened and turned to rose and salmon and violet. The air suddenly smelled alive. There were sounds of things living and dying all around us. We went down the road, and people, seeing us pass by, crossed themselves and dipped their heads. Oh, we were glorious to see, like smoke, like mist, like visions of glory, the horses like the waves of the sea.

We went through Miles Village and toward Ercle's Down. A mile from the village was the crossroad, with a large cross set up at its center. The fairy host rode by, not seeing the woman huddled there until she came running toward us to throw her arms around Thomas's legs, pulling him from his horse.

"Thomas, True Thomas," she cried. "I'll never let you go!" She was a middle-aged woman, with gray in her hair. Thomas, suddenly no longer young, looked as surprised as anyone else.

Janet could not have said anything more guaranteed to make Mab angry. Thereafter Janet embraced a dragon, a worm, a snake, a spider, a giant many-armed thing from the sea. She held bears and tigers and man-eating lions. She held dogs and hogs and eagles which tore at her eyes. Held them all, crying the while, "I'll never let you, never let you go," the muscles in her arms knotted as though forever and the ugly tears raining from her eyes.

Too much time went by. Oberon cried like a hawk, pointing at the sky. There was a line of gold along it, the night going fast. "Come," he cried. "We must ride." And they fled away, leaving only Janet to struggle with the monsters in her arms. Janet and me. I looked down to see Puck holding the bridle of my horse to keep him from galloping after.

"Get down, my girl," he cried, "for it will not take them long to find you gone."

"I should be with them," I said stupidly. "Mama will miss me."

"And who will they use as a teind with Thomas gone?" Puck asked. "You, Beauty, be your mama ever so fair and ever so wise, and even fond of you a little, still they'll use you rather than one of them. Carabosse never intended you should ride farther than this. Carabosse sent us, and Carabosse says to go home."

I was sensible for the first time of how foolish I had

been to come on this ride. "How will I get away? My cloak, my boots are back in Faery."

"They are here," said Fenoderee, holding them up for me to see. He pulled me down, slapped the horse on its rump to send it galloping after the others, and then shoved the boots on my feet and my shoes in my pocket. "They do not know you are involved in this. Better they do not know."

"Ah, Puck, thank you," I started to say, not really knowing whether thanks were due.

"Go, Beauty," he said. "We'll meet again," and he turned me about, whispering to my boots, "Take this lady home."

Then was the familiar whirlwind, and I was gone and so were they.

22

I stood beside the rose-mound of Westfaire. Tottered, I should say, suddenly dizzy, as though something in my head had gone awry. Embarrassment, I supposed, at the prospect of meeting Edward once more. And little Elladine. She would be two, or perhaps even three by now. She would not know I was her mother, of course. She would think the wet nurse was her mother or, if she had been weaned, the nursemaid. I thought of my daughter as I had seen her last, asleep in her cradle beside the fire, her dark hair bubbling over the pillow, like black water in torrent, already long enough to reach her shoulders. A pretty child. Not one a mother should have fled from.

Though Carabosse had said that mothers and daughters might not be sympathetic. "Particularly if the child resembles . . . the other side of the family."

Well yes, but she was not a devil. Merely a child who resembled her actual father in some respects. Now she would be walking and talking, but her speech would be the speech of Wellingford. She could not possibly sound like Jaybee.

With these thoughts I calmed myself as I stood beside the shepherd's well, leaning against it almost, pulling myself up straight with an unaccustomed ache, looking myself over to see if I was well enough dressed to go straight to Wellingford. I picked at a fold of my gown, stared at it in confusion, caught in dream, nightmare, pulling the fabric through my hands. . . .

Aside from my cloak and the seven-league boots, I was dressed in rags. Scarcely one thread held to another. I put hands to my head in confusion, only to feel oily tangles and squirming locks. I had seen myself in the Pool of Delights only this afternoon, with my hair swept up in a net of sapphires and my dress of fine muslin, embroidered all over with flowers. How had I come to be dressed like this? And my hair so filthy? It stank. It smelled of smoke and grease and less acceptable things. My fingers found small hard specks caught in the coils: nits!

Shock held me motionless for a long, calculating moment. Hush, I told myself. Figure it out later. You are only filthy, after all. Filth can be washed away. Hair can be washed and the eggs of lice combed out. You have other clothes to wear. Hush now and do what needs doing. Comforted by decision, though not greatly, I tottered down toward the lakeside. Making myself look decent would necessitate getting into Westfaire, which meant a trip through the water gate. When I arrived at the water, I did not bother to strip. The rags I was wearing could be thrown away once I was inside. I bundled the cloak and boots atop my head. The water was cold. I thought it must be winter, then reassured myself that there were flowers growing in the woods and the trees were in leaf. Still, the water was very cold and very deep and harder to move against than when last I had come this way.

Inside the water gate the steps were taller, too, and more deeply covered with moss. Everything was more difficult than when I had last been there. The stairs to the attic seemed endless, but I had to go there to get a dress. On my way back to the kitchen I stopped in Aunt Love's room to snatch up a looking glass and the fine toothed comb made of tortoise shell she had used on me when, as a child, I had picked up lice from my acquaintances in the stables. The bath place was next to the kitchens, a small, stone-floored room with a stone-curbed well in the corner, a great wooden tub, and over the hearth a huge hanging kettle with a copper to bail the water in and out. Except for Papa, my aunts, and I, who had had tubs brought to our rooms for occasional use, everyone at Westfaire had bathed in this room, sometimes half a dozen of them at once. There was a similar arrangement at Wellingford, though I had never been able to use it when I was being Havoc the miller's son for fear of being found out. Once I was Edward's wife, there had been no need. I had had my own tub again, filled and emptied by sweating servant girls. At least, I assume they sweated for I did by the time I had filled the huge kettle from the well.

I lit the fire, already laid, tied the belt of my cloak around my neck to keep from falling asleep, took off the cloak itself, and sat down to comb my hair while the water heated. The tangles were deep. The comb pulled and the tangles caught in the teeth. I pulled the wad of hair out and threw it into the fire, combing again. The next time I threw the hair toward the fire, a draft caught it and blew it back at me. Gray hair. Not wheat straw, not silver, but gray.

The looking glass lay face down on the table. I polished it with the rags of my sleeve. An old face looked back at me. No . . . no, not an old face. Just not a young face. A thirty-fiveish, fortyish face. Not old for the twentieth, but old for the fourteenth, when people did not live so long. There were tiny lines around the eyes, not deep ones, but they were there. There were more lines on my forehead, between my brows, furrows, as though I had often thought deeply, worrying over something. Most of my hair was still gold, but at either temple the gray swept upward in silver wings around a face thin as a chicken's breastbone.

I had only been gone a little time! A few weeks in Chinanga! A few weeks in Ylles! Whence came this protruding skeleton, this skull beneath the wrinkled skin? Whence came this hoary hair, this hip-stiff walk, this pale reflection of beauty gone, beauty done, beauty over! I screamed, I think. It was as though I had found a snake in my bed, a spider crouched upon my food, a monstrous devourer slinking close at my back, death, worse than death, for with death it is done soon and over, but with this, with this, I was still alive to know of it.

Panic and tears and wailing. I came to myself later to find the kettle steaming over the fire, the lid dancing upon the roiling waters, a jolly clangor which seemed to say so you're getting old, you're old, you're old. So what? Hills are old and getting older, rocks are older than that, stars are older still, so what?

"So it's gone!", I cried, half in pain, half in fury. "My youth, my beauty, gone. I didn't even use it up and it's gone! I didn't have time to waste it, time to taste it, time to glory in it, and it's gone! Here I am all sunk-cheeked, droopy-chested, flat-butted, and it's gone."

Bingity-bangety went the lid. You're half a fairy, aren't you? You've learned magic haven't you? What does it matter how old you are?

What did it matter? If I chose to use enchantment, no one would know it but me. Was there a difference if no one knew it but me? Oh, yes, I cried to myself. Oh, yes. There was more weeping, more howling, coming to myself at last with my hands buried in my filthy hair.

Old or not, I could not bear the dirt on me. I filled the tub and stripped the rags away. When I got them off, I recognized what they were: the remnants of the dress I had worn when I left Wellingford. A simple kirtle of fine wool. I had stood on the sandspit in Chinanga in that gown. I had traveled to the wall of Baskarone in that gown. I had met the ambassador in that gown. Evidently I had also grown old in that gown. It was gone. Only tatters.

I heard a voice singing.

"Beauty and rag tag and motley are twins.
When the one's gone then the other begins."

Oh, Fenoderee! How could you be so unkind! I looked around for him, but he was not there.

Chunks of soap lay on the shelf beside the copper. Cook had learned how to make it from some Teutonic connection of his, from tallow and ashes and a lengthy stirring. The aunts had been dead set against soap in the bath, thinking it fit only for the washing of filthy clothes, but water and scented oils alone would do nothing for my hair. I washed it, combed it, washed it again. The body was filthy, too. Not "my" body. It did not look or feel like "my" body. When I was done, I pulled the plug from the drain, then filled the tub again from the kettle and the well, lying in it to soak myself until I felt able to go on.

When I was clean, I fed the body. The body, though not at all familiar, was not as bad as I had feared, only very bony and ugly, like photographs I had seen in the twentieth of starvation victims or one of those unfortunate women with anorexia. Whatever I had been eating in Ylles, or thought I had been eating, whatever I had consumed in Chinanga, it had not been sufficient to sustain a half-mortal person. I felt my breast, feeling a warmth there, as though something simmered gently inside. Being half-starved had not injured what I carried.

Damn, I said to myself, Carabosse should have known!

None of my clothing would fit. Aunt Lavvy had been, was, very thin, as I recalled. Wrapped in a sheet from the linen store beside the bathroom, I went upstairs once more to Aunt Lavender's room. I found the kirtle she had used to ride in, plus several more, all of very plain stuff, with full sleeves to show the tightly buttoned sleeves of the underbodice. Aunt Lavvy's underbodices were all the color of dirt or excrement. Mama's underbodices, in the attic, were of prettier colors: madder red, and dark indigo blue, saffron yellow, and hollyhock root, which is a pale blue. They were soft enough that their fullness did not matter. Thieving through other closets, I took Aunt Terror's new cote-hardie, and Aunt Basil's surcote, which was almost new. I had never worn a wimple and veil, but it seemed a good time to start. Particularly inasmuch as the soap had left my hair as wild as a lion's mane. I found some clean headdresses in Aunt Marj's room, along with a leatherbound box in which everything could be packed. I thought of using the boots to take me to Wellingford from where I stood, inside West-faire, but the thought of what all those thorns might do to me *en passant,* as it were, dissuaded me. The boots might take me without injury, but *sapiens nihil affirmat quod non probat,* as Father Raymond used to say, and God knows I didn't know for sure. So I went out into the lake, naked as celery, with the box teetering on top of my head, dried myself off on the shore, and assembled myself as best I might.

I had remembered to bring the looking glass and a comb and I'd taken half a dozen tortoiseshell hairpins from Aunt Lavvy's cupboard. Mama's soft linen underbodice clad me almost to my ankles. I chose the one died with madder, soft and faded pink from washing, and buttoned tightly to the wrists and neck. Over that went Aunt Lavvy's kirtle, made from soft brown wool with a low scooped neck and wide, short sleeves. Buff linen for the wimple and veil, and then Aunt Basil's black and brown striped wool surcote with red lions embroidered in the corners of the front and back panels. When I was put together, I gave myself a looking over—as best I could with the small looking glass —and saw a bony-faced but passable woman, much too thin, who would be handsome if she put on about twenty pounds. I put on cloak and boots and commanded them to take me and my box to Wellingford.

I did not say "the Dower House." I said "Wellingford," and it was to Wellingford the boots delivered me. For a moment, seeing the ruins before me, I thought I had repeated my earlier journey to the abbey. When my eyes had had time to clear, I saw that the place was indeed Wellingford Manor, but that some walls were fallen and others barely standing, that one corner of the roof had partly burned, and that no one lived there anymore. Or perhaps someone did.

In the ruined hallway, I saw the embers of a fire and heard a deep voice mumble angrily, as though awakened from slumber. "Boots," I whispered, "take me to the Dower House."

One stride brought me to the door. The Dower House stood, and though it had much need of a careful hand, it gave evidence of being occupied. Broken casements sagged crazily on their hinges, paving stones tilted, weeds grew around the door, but there was smoke coming from one of the chimneys and chickens cackled in the kitchenyard. *Deo gratias.* I put the boots in my pocket, replaced them with a pair of Aunt Marj's pointed shoes and knocked upon the door.

A voice screamed inside, words I could not make out. Instructions to a servant, perhaps? Abuse hurled at a dog? The door opened to disclose a surly maidservant in a dirty kirtle and filthier apron who stared at me with her mouth half open. It was the hall of a place which had been my home. It did not look like home anymore. There were chicken feathers on the stairs.

"Who is it?" came the screaming voice from somewhere off to my right where the kitchens were. "Who is it?"

Who was it, indeed? Who was I? Not Beauty, wife of Edward, mother of Elladine. I had not thought of using enchantment. I was what I was, someone else, old enough to be an aunt and dressed like one. I borrowed the name of one of Edward's own aunts, adding Papa's title for verisimilitude.

"Lady Catherine Monfort, Edward Wellingford's aunt."

The slovenly servant trudged away. There were further noises offstage, perhaps a slap, then a door slamming. There were back stairs. Perhaps someone had gone up. After considerable time, someone came down, hand trailing upon the bannister.

"Lady Catherine Monfort?"

She could have been a pretty lady. In her thirties somewhere, rather more late than early. Her hair was red as a bonfire, and her chest as white as chalk. Both owed much to alchemy. Both could have benefitted from washing. Still, the expression on her face was open and concerned.

I nodded politely, wondering who this apparition was. "Come to visit my nephew, Edward."

"You hadn't heard!" She reached out her arms toward me with genuine compassion. "Oh, how dreadful. You didn't know that Edward had died."

"Died?" I asked stupidly. It had never occurred to me that Naughty Ned could die. Not so soon. Not in such a short time. Sweet man, dead? Is kindness and compassion rewarded so? "Not dead?"

"When the plague returned," she nodded. "In sixty-one."

"Year of our Lord," I murmured, putting out a hand to catch myself.

"Thirteen sixty-one," she said. "Yes. I am his widow, Lydia. We had only been married a short time when he died. But that was almost six years ago. How could you not have heard?"

"I've been away," I said, wondering where the intervening years had gone. I had left in fifty-one. "Far away. In . . . the Holy Land."

"A pilgrim," she chirruped. "Do come in," she took my arm. "Oh, what a shock it must be."

We went into the little sitting room. It had been my room, with chairs in it, not wainscot chairs against the wall, but real chairs one could move about, with carved arms, made for me by a man who worked for Lord Robert, given me as a wedding gift. They were still there, still with the cushions I had worked when I was pregnant with Elladine. Sadly soiled and worn, those cushions. The fireplace was deep in ashes. Everything was dirty and ragged. Evidently this lady, like my aunts, did not hold with soap.

"His daughter?" I asked. "Little Elly . . . ?"

"Elladine? Oh, she survived, yes indeed. Very healthy child, she was. Is, I should say, though she's not a child any longer."

"How old . . . ?"

"Elladine would be what? Sixteen? Seventeen?

Hard enough to keep track of my own, such an army of them."

"Your own?"

"Gloriana, that's the eldest. Then my oldest son, Harold. Then my second son, Bertram. Then Griselda. Then comes Elladine. Then the two Edward and I had together. Twins. Catherine and young Edward. Your nephew Edward named them. Why, I just thought! Catherine must be named after you?"

I nodded again, feeling lost. Possibly Edward had named his second daughter after his aunt. And possibly the twins were not Edward's children at all. "You were a widow when you married Edward?"

She threw her arms wide, miming woe. "Twice, now. Oh, it's very hard to bear. Very hard, Lady Catherine. Lord Robert died early in the year, then Janet and the children. Then the youngest brother, Richard. Then, soon after we were married, Edward himself. All of Wellingford has fallen to me. I've the care of all of it to see to, and no one to help!"

If her two sons were older than Elladine, then she should have some help. "Your sons," I suggested weakly.

"Mere children," she waved her hand to suggest something inconsiderable. "Striplings. Caring for nothing but gaming and the hunt. Boys. Mere sweet boys."

"Your daughters?" I suggested, a little more strongly.

"So talented," she said. "So very musical. And such graceful girls. A little tall, perhaps, but then so is a willow, and nothing is more graceful, moving in the wind." She mimed wind, swaying at me. "But then, I'm forgetting myself. You must be famished? Thirsty? Weary? I didn't see your carriage?"

"I rode," I said. "Hired a horse in . . . in . . ."

"East Sawley?" she suggested.

I nodded, inventing. "Two horses and a man to carry my box. Sent them back again."

And she was dismayed. "Then you plan to stay?

Not that you aren't welcome. Oh, you're very welcome. It's just such very short notice."

I gestured vaguely, signifying that I would make do. "There's an extra room, surely."

"A very little one," she assented. "Over the kitchen."

It was the warmest room in the house. The one I had used as a nursery after Elly was born. There was a narrow bed in it, as I remembered. Though, after sixteen years . . .

We got my box. I carried it myself. There seemed to be no one else to carry it. The bed was still there, full of mice. The whole room was very dirty. Why was my whole history one of being given dirty rooms to occupy? "If you'll send me up a serving maid or two," I suggested.

"Serving maid," she said vaguely, as though she should know the word but had forgotten it. "Maid?"

"Women. Who clean rooms, who sweep floors."

"Oh. Of course. Yes."

As we had come along the corridor, I had noticed that the little linen room was shut, just as I had left it when I had gone away with the key in my pocket. The key was still in the deep pocket of my cloak where I had thrust it when I left. Though it seemed a wild hope, I went back to the closet and tried the key. Inside were sheets and covers and two clean ticks, and pillow cases and the extra pillows I had made when we killed the geese the last fall I had been in the Dower House. The mice hadn't been at it, or if they had, the chunks of black hellebore root scattered along the shelves had poisoned them. The cupboard hadn't been opened in all those years! No one had wanted to break it open; perhaps there had been no locksmith available. Perhaps Lydia had simply been too lazy to bother. The linens still smelled faintly of lavender as I carried sheets and pillows and one of the ticks back to the nursery in time to meet two maids, one of them the girl who had answered the door, the other an older version. Slatterns, both. They regarded me with insolent immobility, jaws moving like cows.

"You will clean this room," I said quietly. "You will use soap. Scrub the floors. Sweep down the cobwebs. Scrub out the windows. Take that mattress away and bring me clean straw for this one."

They looked at one another, back at me, challenging me to make them move. Aha. Well and a day.

"Else," I smiled, "I will summon a dragon to eat you both." I snapped my fingers and made fire dart at them so that they screamed. It was a fine, hard fireflight, which told me I was in a time when magic flowed strong.

They had no more sense of how to clean a room than of how to fly. I kept coming back and making them do it over, getting a little angrier each time and they getting a little more frantic at the fire biting them. The whole house was evidence of their slipshod ways, theirs and Lydia's. As for Lydia, she had gone upstairs to lie about on a disordered bed with her elder daughters and the twins, playing the lute (tunelessly) and singing (less melodiously than Grumpkin had used to howl) and talking of the future. I put on my cloak for a reconnaissance and overheard them from the hallway. Their plans seemed to consist of selling Wellingford and going to London to live on the fruits of that sale. For a moment I struggled with this idea, certain that Elladine was the heir if all the Wellingford brothers were dead. But, of course, she was not. Young Edward was the heir: the six-year-old monster whom I caught torturing a dog in the stables, and whose britches I set alight to teach him better manners. He looked nothing like Edward. Nothing at all. Edward, my poor sweet fish, taken twice on the same hook!

And where was Elladine? Over an indescribably bad dinner, I asked again for my "grandniece."

"Poor Elladine," Lydia murmured. "Such an unfortunate name to give a child. Not a Christian name, surely."

"But where is she?"

"She goes off. On a horse, sometimes. Sometimes afoot. We're never sure where she is. Poor child. First motherless, then fatherless, I'm sure she'll be so glad to meet any kin at all."

"You and Edward were married in . . . what year?" I asked.

"In the year of the second Death. Almost at once after Robert and Janet died," she said, "together with Robert's youngest brother and all their sons. Edward was the heir, and he felt he needed someone to help him maintain the estate. And, of course, I'd been left a widow and desperately needed someone to help me, as well. Four fatherless children to rear, with people dying everywhere, it is no pleasant Maytime to be alone in such circumstance, believe me. Edward most wanted someone to care for Ella. I told him I would maintain his daughter if he would maintain me. It was not a love match, precisely, though I was fond of Edward."

Poor Edward. Destined always to be a husband of convenience. "How did you meet?"

"Janet was my cousin. I was visiting here when the plague struck. Oh, there were many visitors, then. Robert and Janet had taken in half the countryside who were homeless. I remember Janet going on and on about being unable to keep the place clean."

Which is why the plague had struck Wellingford, I thought. Poor Janet. So charitable. Giving a home to the multitude, with all their fleas.

"Of the Wellingfords, only Edward and Ella were left alive when the dying paused for a time," Lydia said, leading me into the next room as we heard the maids breaking crockery behind us. She went on to give me the details of the dying, with an unnecessary relish in the recounting, interrupting herself to say, "Ah, here she is!"

A ravishingly beautiful young woman came through the door. Sixteen or seventeen, perhaps. Wild dark hair. Wild dark eyes. A bruise on one cheek. Hands coarse and scratched and black around the nails.

"Elladine, this is your father's Aunt Catherine,"

Lydia said in a kindly tone, edged with some emotion I did not quite understand.

"What would she have here, madam? What's left?" the girl asked insolently. It was the same tone in which Candy might have said "So?" or "Big deal!" in the twentieth.

Lydia flinched, giving me an apologetic glance. Discipline wasn't Lydia's forte either, poor thing. I had yet to find what Lydia's forte was. Surely she must have had something to recommend her to Edward. Or was he so distraught at all the dying, he had grasped her as he, drowning, might have grasped at a straw? Ah well, if discipline was not her thing, neither were manners my daughter's.

"Elly, my dear," I said, kissing my child on her unwelcoming face. "I am your great-aunt, from Ylles, come to visit you."

She gave me a look to tell me she did not care. Her face was Jaybee's face, made feminine, made soft, but with broken glass beneath it. Her hand, as she pushed me away, was as hard as his had been. Elladine remained with us only so long as we held her in unwilling conversation, then departed as quickly as she might, and I stared after her, wondering what I could do to make this situation tenable.

I thought, her mouth is wide and sensual. She has hooded eyes. Her figure is as graceful and lithe as mine once was. Her breasts curve like the swell of a sail, and her cheeks are softly rose. She is beautiful, not as I was, but nonetheless, beautiful. I cannot tell if she is intelligent. She is hard as stone.

I wondered, how much of her hardness is my fault? How much of this iron rancor came from doing without a mother's love?

There was no time to weary myself assessing guilt. Someone had to see to her, see to things, and it was obvious that Lydia could not see to boiling an egg. Though Elladine could use a parent, I could scarcely introduce myself as her mother. I had no idea whether Edward settled anything on her or not before he died.

Without a dowry, her future would be unenviable. All I could do under the circumstances was to be her aunt, stay with her, and try to remedy the situation.

LATER

Later yesterday I met Lydia's four older children. The two daughters are awkward and ungainly girls, both with an intransigent dirtiness about them. The younger one, eighteen perhaps, would not be bad looking if she were cleaner, and if she would stand up straight and comb her hair. The older, however, Gloriana, a maiden of some twenty years, is taller than any woman I have ever seen. She has a face that could carve stone and hands as big as a large man's. I knew at once who was responsible for the bruises on Elladine's face. Gloriana's hands twitch, knot, twitch again whenever she looks at Elly, like creatures with a will of their own. She is as full of anger as Elladine is, though from a different cause. An ugly girl who hates girls who are not. When I heard her voice, it was no surprise. Hers was the knife-edged shriek from the kitchen. That both of the girls are slovens simply fills out the picture. Their shifts have not been washed in many a season, their nails are brown with unthinkable dirt, their hair, I warrant, is as full of lice as mine was when I woke at Westfaire.

The boys, Harry and Bert, looked slightly less dirty when I met them. I believe their relative cleanliness may be due to their having been caught in the rain oft times while hunting. Both are beefy boys, red in the face, big in the teeth, with small eyes and large noses. They are even taller than Gloriana. Though Lydia is a woman of average size, her first husband must have been a giant to have begot these monsters.

Of the twins, the least said the better. They have been spoiled so rotten that they smell of corruption. Neither has ever been forced to do anything he or she did not want to do. They have two voices: a whine; a scream. They have no graces at all.

So, if the family is of little use, what about the servants? There are serving women about the place, but I recognize none of them. Besides the two who eventually finished cleaning my room, I found several more, enough to do the washing, sweep out the filthy hall, bring in wood for the fire, heat the kettle and fill the tubs. Lydia's daughters could have bathed. Their clothes could have been scrubbed. I wonder why they choose instead to go about in dirt? Well, they could do as they chose, but the Dower House need not follow their example.

I slept last night in a clean chamber. I rose this morning at dawn. I found the maids still sleeping, routed them out, and set them to work, though they grumbled mightily when I told them to clean the fireplace in Elly's chamber, saying that she always did that herself.

"Elly," I explained sweetly, "is my nephew's daughter. She does not sweep chambers, carry out slops, or make up fires. You do. You do it well and consistently or you will be eaten alive by dragons!" I glared at them and they cowered.

Elly came upon me in mid-dudgeon, carrying a pail of ashes. She shook her head at me angrily. "It won't do any good," she sneered. "Stepmama won't keep after them once you're gone. They're lazy sluts, all of them." I noticed again that her nails were black.

"They certainly won't do it if you do it for them," I suggested. "Go wash your hands."

One of the maids sniggered behind me. I set a small imp to pinch her black and blue, and her howling could be heard for half a mile. It had a salutary effect on the others. I smiled at Elly, who regarded me with dawning interest.

"You know what these sluts call me," she asked. "Ella of the Ashes. Just because I carry out the ashes so I can get the fire in my room to burn. The others are so lazy, they'd rather freeze. They all pile in one bed together to keep each other warm. Like pigs."

"Why won't Lydia exert herself a little?" I asked, truly interested in Elly's perception of the situation.

"She doesn't want to keep Wellingford. She wants to sell it. That's why she doesn't take care of it. It used to be beautiful. It's all ugly now."

"Whether she wants to keep it or not, there is such a thing as pride," I said. "Only those without any are filthy and lazy. Perhaps she needs to be taught."

"When pigs have wings," said Elly with an ugly snort, leaving me.

It was only later I thought what she had said. Ella of the Ashes. Cinder-Ella.

"Puck," I cried.

He was there, looking at me sidelong.

"What is this?" I demanded, half hysterically. "I've been in the twentieth, Puck. I've read books. I've seen Disney, for the love of God. I know the Cinderella story. What is this?"

"Did you think the stories were made up?" he asked me. "Did you think there was no real Beauty, no real Cinderella, no real Goldilocks or Rose Red or . . ."

"But why me? Why my daughter?"

He shrugged. "Did you never notice, in the twentieth, how legends gather around some people. There is the truth about a man, and then the part truths that gather afterward, and then the myths that follow later yet. A legendary man tends to have legendary sons. Power attracts power, so power gathers. It is one of the truths of magic."

"Am I to expect, then, that there will be a prince?"

He shrugged again. "It depends on what story you learned, there in the twentieth. Was it the true tale, or the part truth, or the myth? Do you know?"

I didn't know, but knowing that Elly was at the root of a fairy tale made me have some hope for her future, at least.

ST. MARY MAGDELEN'S DAY,
JULY, YEAR OF OUR LORD 1367

My daughter is the same age I was when I started writing this story of my life. She is not very like me, as I remember being. She is bad-tempered, quick to strike, eager to continue the fray. She hates her step-sisters and brothers with a hot, even anger. She doses their food with nutshells, boils their woolens to elf size, spreads oil upon the floor outside their rooms to make them fall. They detest her, and she glories in their dislike. Her animosity and their slothfulness seem to have kept her alive. If any one of them had been capable of decisive action, he, or she, would have killed Elly. I look at her and I marvel. So like her father. She would rather have passionate hatred than lukewarm affection.

"What are you looking at?" she snarled at me.

"The indomitable human spirit," I replied.

"Go domit somewhere else," she returned. "I'm sick of you always looking at me."

Perhaps I, too, would be sick of someone always looking at me.

"What was it like when your father was alive?" I asked her.

Pain, then, in her face, swiftly passing but sharp while it was there. "He was . . . he was very good to me," she said. "I think he loved me."

"I know he did," I said. "He told me so."

"She says he didn't," she gestured toward her step-mother's window. "She says he only pretended, because I didn't have a mother. She says nobody could love someone as bad-tempered as I am. He only pretended. He thought he owed it to me."

"That's not true. He loved you. Very much. I remember once when you were a tiny baby, only a few months old, I saw him bend over your cradle and tell you that he loved you, and it was not owing, it was real."

She sat very still, like a cat that is too frightened to

move, afraid I would take it back. Her stance made me think of an old friend.

"There used to be a cat here, named Grumpkin," I said. "He was a great favorite of mine. He must have died a long time ago. It's been sixteen years."

"He did die," she nodded. "He was my mother's cat, and Papa said she left him to me when the enchantment took her away."

I gulped. So Edward had told her that! Poor Edward. He had been curious, and knew it. He had blamed himself.

"Grumpkin slept on my bed sometimes. He lived to be very old. I cried when he died. But he fathered lots of kittens, and I've still got one of his sons. Daddy named him Grumpkin the Second as though he were a king." Her voice had changed. All the hostility had left it. It was for that one moment as open and communicative as a child's.

"Why did the enchantment take your mother away?" I asked, wondering if I'd been right.

"Because Papa got curious about her," she said. "He said it was all his fault."

Oh, Edward. Edward. "Let's go see Grumpkin's son," I suggested, getting up from my chair.

"I have to take out the ashes," she said, not thinking, merely expressing her habitual contrariness.

"No," I told her. "Not anymore. While I am here, I will be sure the maids do it."

Brought to herself, her lip curled into its usual sneer. "How come you can tell the maids what to do and what not to do?" she asked. "You're not the mistress of Wellingford. You're only an aunt."

I had figured out who I was that morning. Even I, who had never cared for children's stories, could not have failed to notice what role I was playing. In the twentieth, I had seen Disney, after all. Though Elly and I were not privileged to be attended by singing mice, it did not surprise me greatly that this segment of my life had gained a spurious immortality, a glossy, oversimplified and untruthful half-life.

I shook my head at Elly, trying hard to get her to

smile. "No, my child. You mustn't tell anyone at all, but I'm your fairy godmother."

She laughed at me, thinking I was joking. It was a genuinely amused laugh.

ST. MARTHA'S DAY,
JULY, YEAR OF OUR LORD 1367

I have my Grumpkin back again. The son is like Grumpkin I, except that he has one white foot. When I picked him up, it seemed almost that he knew me, for he reached out his paw to touch my face as the other Grumpkin used to do. As I write, he is beside me, purring, opening his eyes every few moments to be sure I have not gone away. Though Elly values him, she does not care for him. I saw her slap at him, for no reason except to see him blink. Strange. With her, the having is enough. She uses or ignores. She does not maintain. In that, she is more like Lydia than she would like to think.

Though Lydia is too lazy to take charge of Wellingford herself, she does not seem to resent my doing it. In any case, I have not asked her permission. During the past days the maids have ceased to grumble: they, the household, and the household linens are clean. Elladine has had several baths (as have I), the floors have been swept, and the cook has been instructed to feed us something besides porridge and meat pies. There is plenty of food—it has been six years since the plague came and went again—but acquiring victuals from the gardens and orchards, from the sties and the poultry house and the herds, takes a little attention and good sense, neither of which Lydia seems to be capable of supplying. The small caches of coins I left behind me are still here, for the most part, and I have used some of them to purchase necessities. I also have found the warrant upon the usurers of London where I hid it before I left, but I have set it aside against later need.

I have gained several pounds and look less like a

skeleton. Elly's hands have come clean. Her bruises have faded. I set a small spell upon Gloriana that she should get a painful cramp each time she tried to pinch. She, robbed of her usual prey, has turned to accusing a pretty village woman of witchcraft. I will have to do something about that, too. I have not yet decided what to do to extricate Elly from her current problem, but at least the situation has been stabilized, as they would say in the twentieth.

Carabosse asked me, before I left Faery, whether I could just go along, pretending I was only what I am. Here, in this house, I am only what I am. The thing burns beneath my breastbone, but it is no stranger than my heartbeat or the sound of my own breath. It is almost as though I had stayed in Chinanga. Here, as there, no one knows who I am. I am someone else. No one knows I am here.

ST. STEPHEN'S DAY, SEPTEMBER,
YEAR OF OUR LORD 1367

I was not surprised when a herald came to the door yesterday with a pronouncement. I have been expecting something of the kind.

All inhabitants of Wellingford between the ages of sixteen and twenty-five are invited to attend a series of three evening entertainments given in honor of His Royal Highness, Prince Something or Other, by his parents, the ruling family in exile of some tiny kingdom I had never heard of.

I was surprised, however, at the herald's voice. There was something familiar about it. Something that raised gooseflesh, made echoes in my heart. I went out into the courtyard with a cup of wine and offered it to the man. When I saw him, I knew him.

"Your name is Giles, isn't it?" I asked him, keeping my voice even only with a great effort. I wanted to throw my arms about him. I wanted to cry on his shoulder. "You were a man-at-arms in service to the

Duke of Monfort and Westfaire." My voice trembled when I said it.

"My lady?" he asked, getting down from his horse and bowing to me. "Have we met?" He looked just the same. Older, of course, but just the same. His eyebrows quirked in the same way. He had that little turn at the corner of his lips that I had used to watch for. There was a new scar at one side of his brow. "I don't remember . . ."

I waved my hand in front of my face. "Many years ago," I said. "I can scarcely remember the occasion, but your voice sounded familiar." Not only his voice. He stood as I remembered, straight and tall, feet together, one slightly turned out. As though he had been invited to dance.

"Fancy your becoming a herald!" I said. "Why did you leave Westfaire?"

His eyes shut, only briefly, as though remembering an old pain. "The priest there sent me on a journey," he said. "A kind of pilgrimage, it was. To bring some sacred relics back to the chapel at Westfaire. I had to go a wearisome way, and when I returned . . ."

"The enchantment," I murmured.

"The enchantment," he agreed, letting his eyes shut again. "I think . . . I think they're all in there," he whispered. "All of them. One of them got out for a while, but she had to go back. She'd be a widow now."

Well, of course that is what he would have thought. It is, after all, what Edward thought, what Edward told everyone. Not about my being a widow, but about my getting out of Westfaire. "Someone you cared about?" I asked.

"Oh, yes, ma'am. Yes, indeed. Someone I care about."

I breathed deeply, taking note of the present tense. "So then, what did you do?"

"I chose to stay fairly close by, but I sought service where I might. There was plague, as you know. It seemed wisest to stay away from the cities. I lived rough as a man can. I farmed a bit. At least that meant I'd have food. Then, when these little royals took the place over by East Sawley Mill, they offered me good money to be man-at-arms for them. Escort, mostly. And herald."

"Herald," I said with a tremulous laugh.

He laughed with me. "I've got a good loud voice from calling cows, ma'am, and I remember things."

Oh, indeed he did. And so did I. "Can you remember the reason for this widespread invitation?" I teased, letting something of my old childish teasing come into my voice.

He cocked his head and smiled at me, recognizing the tone if not the origin of that flirtiness. "These little royals, they got driven out of their wee country, over near France or some such place so I'm told, but when they came, they brought a fortune with them. They bought land past East Sawley Mill and rebuilt the big old house up there. But they don't know anybody, ma'am. What with the plague and the unsettled conditions since, it's a wonder anybody's left. They told me to ride to all the noble houses in the surrounding land and pronounce the invitation. There can't be more than six or eight great houses left, and that'll be stretching it. Wellingford's not rightly great, not anymore, but I thought I'd stop." He flushed, thinking I might take umbrage, but I only nodded, telling him that I understood.

"Will there be a ball?" I asked, doubtfully.

"Close as they can get. They've got musicians hired. They've got cooks working away, making three days worth of feasts. The boy's coming of age, ma'am, and his mama wants him to have a celebration. She says they've had enough sadness recently."

He handed me back the wine cup. I watched him go with tears in my eyes and a great longing in my heart, or wherever longing resides. I felt it in my stomach, so perhaps that is where. I had wanted to tell him who I was. The only reason I had not was that he did not recognize me. When I looked into the mirror, it was hard for me to know myself. I was afraid he could not love who I had become.

I went to the kitchens to find Harry teasing his

sisters. "It's him," he was telling them. "The prince who's giving the party is the man who came riding by the other day. He's the prince."

Gloriana said, "Oh, Harry, it's not. It couldn't be."

"I tell you it is. The boy with the yellow hair." Harry seized Griselda in one oversized arm and paraded her around the kitchen, stepping on her feet. His hands were the same size as Gloriana's, and even on him they bulked large. He had jowls already, blue as steel, and a bit of a belly sticking out. Not an altogether prepossessing partner for the dance. "The prince was the one with the yellow hair," he bellowed raucously.

"His hair wasn't yellow," said Elly. "It was gold." She was sitting in the chimney corner as she often did, and she said it so quietly that no one heard her. If they had heard her, they wouldn't have paid attention. I had noticed that. No one paid much attention to Elly. Except me, of course. I kept looking for something of Edward in her. His patience. His devotion. Surprising myself, each time, by remembering that he wasn't her real father. And yet he had given her so much. All to be wiped away like this, lost when he was lost.

"You saw the prince, too?" I asked her in a murmur.

She nodded, pressing her teeth together, making a tight-lipped frown. She has yet to smile at me, except at my embarrassments, and at those she laughs.

"Was he handsome?" I asked.

She took a deep breath. She did not need to answer. Her eyes were answer enough. She looked at me hatefully, detesting this self-betrayal.

"Are we going to the ball?" Harold asked his mother. "We'll need new clothes."

"All of you?" Lydia asked doubtfully. "Why, Harry, I don't know. I'm not sure we can even find anyone to make clothes."

"Have to go," he replied, significantly. "Have to show the girls off. You know what he's doing, don't you? He's looking for a wife. That's why all the young ones are invited."

"He invited men, too," Griselda commented.

"Who would the girls dance with, otherwise?"

"Mother, do you suppose he *is*?" asked Gloriana, face suddenly red as a boiled lobster, eyes hot with hope. Oh, poor child, I said to myself. Don't hope for it, no. It isn't fated. It isn't willed. Poor ugly thing. Her skin was rough as her hands, her hair was a jungle, and she smelled like vintage dirt. My heart swelled with pity for her, and for Griselda, and for all other barnyard geese who long to fly.

"Perhaps I can find a seamstress," I suggested. "I used to know the neighborhood rather well."

"Not only a seamstress," Lydia fussed, "but fabric. Since the second Death, there haven't been the merchants there used to be."

"I'll try," I said. Edward had set a store of fabrics by, bought for me, bought in anticipation of Elladine needing dresses. He had ordered them from London or purchased them from travelers. He loved to see me in silk from the Far East, in damask and velvet from Florence. There were boxes of folded materials in the attic, set away in linen sheets, dosed against the mice with hellebore, against the moths with wormwood and southernwood, lavender and rosemary. Boys mix the ashes of southernwood with oil and use it to make their beards grow. Lad's Love and Maid's Ruin, it is called. When I unfolded the linen, I remembered that, remembered Janet telling me. She was full of herbary, Janet. Fuller than the aunts, despite having an ordinary person-name.

There is a great length of mustard-colored silk, enough to make a gown for Gloriana, and enough greeny-blue damask for Griselda. Edward bought both pieces from a merchant who had brought them from Italy. There are other Italian damasks, too, to make cote-hardies for the boys, and velvet for overmantles. There are silks from the Far East for underbodices, and spools of finer silk for the knitting of stockings, if we had time to knit stockings. It seems there will be no time for that, or for embroidered sleeves, but the fabrics are rich enough. There is nothing in any of the

boxes that I like for Elladine. She needs something
light, something bright with her dark hair. White. It
will have to be white, with short, full sleeves and a
slash at the hem to show a bright full-length underskirt. There *will* be flowers embroidered on the
sleeves, if I have to bribe one of Puck's people to do it.

ST. OMER'S DAY, SEPTEMBER,
YEAR OF OUR LORD 1367

The seven-league boots made it an easy trip to London. I went there late at night, stayed half a day, and
returned with white satin and with pairs of silken hose
from Spain. So far as everyone was concerned, I had
found them all in the attics.

"Mama, keep Elly home or she'll spoil everything," I had heard Gloriana saying.

"I don't think Elly should go," Lydia said.

"Oh, I agree," I said to Lydia. "She's far too
young."

"I'm not too young," Elly later screamed into my
face.

"Of course not, child. But you don't want Gloriana
pinching you black and blue between now and then.
And she will, if she thinks you're going. She might
even break an arm or leg for you, or pull all your hair
out, so sulk and be still. All will come right."

She sulked and was still. I suggested to Lydia that
it might be wise to start bathing her daughters a week
or so in advance to get rid of some of the accumulated
grime. She yawned and said she supposed so and did
nothing about it. I began working on Elly's hair,
brushing it every night, doing it up on rags, saying
quiet prayers of thankfulness for Candy's ministrations
which had taught me all this, even though it did not
seem to matter what I did to Elly's hair. Her hair was a
treasure, like tumbling black water, lightless in its
ebon flow. In anticipation of the parties, her eyes were
slumbrous and her lips seemed swollen with invisible
kisses.

While village women struggled with clothing for Lydia's children, I summoned some help for my own child. Sitting on the side of my bed, late at night, I said, "Fenoderee, I need a friend," only to look down and see him there.

"You're lookin' older," he said impudently.

"You knew how old I'd look," I said. "You and Puck, when you sent me back. I heard you chanting at me. Ragtag and motley, indeed!"

"You can look as young as you like," he told me.

"As Elladine does," I said. "As Mab does?"

He looked down at his feet, suddenly discomfitted.

"Fenoderee?" I asked.

"Don't bother him," said a voice, and Puck stepped out from behind the tapestry on the wall. "He's afraid to tell you."

"Tell me what?" I faltered.

"That with Thomas gone and you not there, Queen Mab went into a fury and used your mama as the teind."

There was a moment of soundlessness, and I came to myself lying flat on the floor with both of them bending over me and Fenoderee saying to Puck, "Ach, you fool, she didn't need to know that."

"Yes, she did," said Puck. "Lest she have her boots carry her back to Faery, expecting Elladine to be there. Lest she say something unwary where Oberon could hear. So far he blames us Bogles for getting Thomas loose. So far he doesn't know Beauty was involved. Nobody knows but Carabosse."

"What . . . is Mama dead?" I asked.

Puck shook his head. "Us of Faery can't be killed so easy, Beauty. She's even kin to the Dark Lord. He despises Faery, but it's not Faery he wants to destroy. Carabosse says to tell you like as not, he'll play with Elladine for a time, then turn her loose. He does that with things that amuse him."

They helped me sit up, and Puck gave me a bit of wine from the bottle in the cupboard. He went to it, as though he knew right where it was. As though he had been there before.

272 *Sheri S. Tepper*

"There's nothing you can do about it," he said. "Carabosse says you are not to upset yourself or think of doing *anything*! She says you will understand what she means."

I did understand. If it came to a choice between Thomas, who was a fellowman, or Elladine, who was my mother but did not much care about that, I was not sure where duty lay. In any case, Carabosse was right. I could do nothing about it. Anything I tried to do would only draw attention to me.

"You wanted something or you wouldn't have called us," said Puck.

It seemed foolishness, then, but I told them what I wanted. Someone to make some dresses for Elladine's namesake, my daughter. I had thought of doing it myself, as I had made dresses in Faery, but I felt insecure with the idea. "I want someone who's done it a lot, who knows what they're doing," I told Puck. A kind of look went back and forth between them, and Puck said he'd send someone along. As he was about to go, I asked him, "When I was a child and saw you in the woods, was it Carabosse who sent you?"

He looked at me insolently. "Me?" he asked. "Why would I have been in *your* woods? I'll send you a seamstress."

She came. A Bogle seamstress, to make Elly's gowns. Three bright white dresses: one embroidered with daisies over a yellow underdress; one with periwinkles over blue; one with roses over red. The trader had said the red silk was from the Far East, beyond the Holy Land. It was the only place where the dyers could achieve that color, so much brighter than madder. Cochineal, perhaps. It must have been China, I told myself. Even in the twentieth, some of the finest fabrics came from there. The seamstress also made three spider veils for Elly's hair. One with pearls, one with sapphires, one with rubies. I am keeping everything hidden as a surprise.

ST. LAMBERT'S DAY, SEPTEMBER

When the morning of the first celebration arrived, Gloriana and her sister decided to bathe. Though I stayed as far away as possible, I could not help hearing the screams as tangled hair refused to be combed, and long embedded dirt refused to let go. Elly sat in a corner of my room and smiled remotely, as though she were already far away, dancing with her prince. I spoke to her, cautioning her to keep her temper in check, to smooth the frown lines from her brow. I told her that men like girls who are sweetly spoken. She merely smiled, as though nothing I could say applied to her. It was as though she was fated, and knew it. A small, cold chill made its way down my spine. What could I do?

That evening Harry and Bert rode off with their sisters toward the manor, some seven or eight miles away. I told Lydia that Elly and I were going for a ride also. Instead we repaired to the stables where I had accumulated certain supplies. A pumpkin. A cageful of mice. Six lizards. One fat toad. I had already created a wand, to add to the drama of it all, though a wand is totally unnecessary. With what Mama and Oberon had taught me, I could have done it blind-folded and with my hands tied behind me.

The mice became horses, prancers, matched grays of considerable spirit. The pumpkin made a golden chariot, the like of which no one had yet seen, nor would for several hundred years. It was exceedingly well sprung, and in the fourteenth no one understood springs. The toad became a coachman, and the six lizards the footmen, the one in brown livery and the six in green. Getting the livery just right took almost the last bit of magic I had in me, and I was panting a little as I spoke seriously to Elly.

"Now listen to me. This equippage will get you there in great style. The only reason we're going to all this trouble is to get the prince looking at you. I've cast a spell of glamour over you to keep him looking, and to prevent Gloriana and her sister and brothers from recognizing you. However, none of it will last past dawn. Fairy things often don't. There's a monastery near the prince's dwelling, and when the monastery bell rings for Matins you must leave, or you can't be sure to be home before the sun rises." I was reminded of my listening for the bell when I had been wooing her father who was not really her father, Ned. Matins was supposed to be sung about midnight, but in my experience the monks were often late with it.

"The place is only two hours or so away," she argued with me.

"If you don't have an accident, yes. But if your coachman has to mend a wheel, it could take longer. You must leave a large margin for error."

"I could walk home," she shrugged, giving me one of Jaybee's intransigent, stubborn looks.

"If you don't want to go back tomorrow night, of course you could. It's about eight miles. But if you want to go back tomorrow night, then be home by dawn. I have to reuse what is here." Once things have been enchanted, it takes less effort to re-enchant them. Besides, it had taken me days to catch six lizards. I was not as agile as I had been as a child, and they do not, unfortunately, enchant until one actually has them in hand. I gave her the dress embroidered in daisies (which she examined critically before saying it would do), combed her hair for her, and told her to be on her way.

"Barefoot?" she asked me. "Fine fairy godmother you are. They'll laugh themselves silly."

I had not thought of shoes. I had extended myself on everything else and had not thought of shoes. There was not enough glamour left in me to create three pair. One would have to do. One to go with everything. I meant to make them white. I was tired. They came out transparent, like glass. It shouldn't have surprised me, but it did. In the future, the story would include a hundred false details, but the damned glass slippers were really part of it.

I hated them. Silly, plastic-looking things. Elly had

never seen plastic, so she loved them. "Glass slippers," she cried. "I almost believe you're really a fairy!"

I had turned a toad into a coachman, had turned mice into horses, had invented coach springs several hundred years before their time, but it took glass shoes to make her believe in me! I watched silently, wearily as she departed, then put on the seven-league boots and went where she was going. All I wanted to do, I told myself, was see her have a good time. Expiation of guilt, certainly. I would have done her better service to have had a serious talk with her about reality, but who was I to speak of reality? She was one-quarter fairy, as I was half. Perhaps I could even have taught her some of the things Mama taught me.

Better not, my conscience said. Better not. My conscience sounded much like Father Raymond. Elly would not use such power wisely. Or even kindly. Not until she was older, if then.

The prince's celebration was very minor stuff. A dozen local musicians, scraping and blowing, any one of whom would have made more tuneful sounds killing pigs. Still, there was a certain rude vitality evident which came partly from reliance upon the wine kegs, partly from letting the notes fall where they might, and partly from everyone's determination to have a good time. The tunes they played were well known. They could not have assayed anything else. They took my added voice as the effects of intoxication and played on, rather better than before.

The prince was yellow-haired and quite good-looking, in a sweet, almost feminine way. He had a straight nose and a gentle, delicate mouth, with dark eyes and brows to lend drama. He was slightly taller than Elladine and a head or more shorter than poor Gloriana. His nickname, given him by his mama, was Charme, or "Charming," as we would say in the twentieth, and he suited that name well enough. His mama was fat and fond and indulgent. His papa, the King or Prince or whatever, was taciturn and worried about other things. When Mama did not recall Papa to himself, he sat on his gilded chair and looked into distances I could not see. The loss of a kingdom, even a very small one, would weigh on one, I supposed.

The young prince dutifully danced with all the ladies, even the very ugly ones. Of these, Gloriana was the most, and Griselda a close second. There were three or four rather pretty girls, and the rest were what one might expect if one rounded up a sample of the countryside. Elladine arrived a couple of hours before midnight, driving directly up to the terrace beside the ballroom as I'd suggested. I'd made sure the doors were open, and no one could have missed her arrival. I had assured her that this could only add to the mystery and make her more fascinating. Not that she needed additional glamour. What I had given her was quite enough. In fact, looking back on it, what she had of her own might have been quite enough. She and the prince danced, and then again, and then yet again. Several of the young ladies cast angry glances at their partners and one another. Gloriana was quite red and unhappy. I put a quick spell on several of the young men along the sidelines, to make them attentive to her, but it did no good. Gloriana had eyes for no one but the prince.

After a time, I wearied. I went out onto the terrace, took off my cloak, and sat on a bench there, watching through the windows. The evening was still and warm. I heard the song of a nightingale among the trees.

"Will you dance, ma'am," said a voice at my shoulder.

I looked up. It was Giles. There was no need to speak. I simply rose and let him take me by the hand. We danced, as they danced inside, bowing and circling, only our hands touching. He looked at me, smiling, in his eyes something almost like recognition.

"I did meet you," he whispered. "I wish I could remember where."

"At Westfaire," I agreed. "On some occasion or other. Perhaps at one of the wedding banquets."

He shook his head, laughing. "Oh, ma'am."

"Catherine," I said. "My name is Catherine."

"Oh, Catherine." He bowed and led me in a circle around him, one hand on his hip, his soft shoes making a brushing sound on the stones. "I remember those banquets well. The lady Sibylla, her face all screwed up. Beauty, the duke's daughter, like a rose. All the aunts. If I'd seen you there, I'd have remembered."

When he said "Beauty, the duke's daughter," his voice had been soft and yearning. I could not help it. I let enchantment happen. Not a lot. Not to be sixteen again. But to be beautiful.

He smiled at me, his own face becoming younger. We danced. "You look like her," he said. "Like Beauty. Are you related to those at Westfaire?"

"Oh, yes," I said. "Edward of Wellingford's wife was kin to those at Westfaire. He was Elly's father. And I am her aunt."

"I didn't know anyone got out of Westfaire except Beauty," he said softly. "And she had to go back. I thought they were all there still."

"Some weren't there at the time," I said. "Elly wasn't born yet. And I was elsewhere."

His hand tightened on mine. His eyes feasted on my face. Mine were as greedy. We danced, and he drew me closer to him as hours spun away.

In the nearby monastery, the bell rang for Matins, and I drew away from Giles, reluctantly.

"Tomorrow night?" he asked me.

I nodded, smiling at him. Oh, yes, tomorrow night.

I turned to the window, saw Elly's head come up, listening. She wavered. She knew if she left, the prince would go on dancing with the others. She knew if she stayed, she might not come back the following evening. Prudence won, and she slipped out of the ballroom and across the terrace to the drive where the horses waited. The carriage got halfway to the main road before the prince realized she was not coming back. She, meantime, lay in the rocking carriage and dreamed, a curved and sensual smile on her face, while I watched invisibly from the opposite seat, wishing I were back there on the terrace, dancing with Giles.

We were home in time. I disenchanted my supplies,

storing my mice and lizards away in a box in an empty manger and then sent Elly into the house to sleep. She did not want to rest, so I told her she would be ugly if she did not, and that decided her. I napped myself, then put on my boots about midday and went back to Prince Charming's home, desirous of knowing what he thought and felt and, perhaps more important, what his parents thought and felt. I had seen his papa staring at Gloriana last night and knew there might be some considerations of which I was not aware.

As there were. The prince was in full spate, screaming in a high, trembling voice at his parents.

"She's ugly. She's huge. She's dreadful."

"Her younger brother is heir to a large fortune. He would settle a good bit on her."

"He might settle the moon and all the stars on her, and I would not have her."

"Duty is not always pleasant. If we are to regain the throne . . ."

"Throne! Until the people throw out Uncle Richard, there is no throne to gain. And if there were a throne, would you want me to marry without any possibility of an heir? I swear to you, I could easier mate with a sow in a sty than with that woman, and if I were forced, I would sooner kill myself." He was sulky and vehement.

"But we have no idea who this other girl is. None at all!"

True enough, they did not. Nor would they, until Elly was safe from Gloriana's retaliation. I felt the matter stood well enough for my purposes and went home to sleep.

That night Elly wore blue. That night she begged to be allowed to stay until the bell rang for Lauds. It was too close to dawn, and yet I allowed it. How could I not when she begged me? How could I not, when I wanted to stay, myself. When she arrived at the ball, her eyes were dreamier yet, and her movements more sensual and languorous. The young cock might be pretty as a girl, but he had it in him to stir this little hen. I envied her. Oh, how I envied her. The only true attraction of that kind that I could remember in myself had been toward Giles and toward the ambassador from Baskarone. Even in Ylles, where I had seen what passed for love all around me, I had not cared enough to consummate it. Not so, Elly. If one touched her, she burned. I envied her lust, the lubricious waves she swam upon, the elegant titillation she was prey to.

Envied, and emulated. Giles waited for me on the terrace and we danced again. I taught him a new dance, one I had learned in the twentieth, where one does not parade at arms length but presses tightly against one's partner. I let enchantment happen, let us be wrapped in glamour. I was young, and so was he. We were together. Nothing separated us except the slow movement of the music, and even the music was enchanted. I held up my mouth to be kissed, drowning in his kisses. We put our hands up the sleeves of our outer garments so that nothing was between our hands and our naked flesh but one layer of thin, silky fabric. We pressed our thighs toward one another, between one another's, letting the hours pass in passion which climbed ever higher and was yet unsatisfied.

Matins rung and was ignored. Lauds rung. I tore myself away from him, seeing the dazed look in his eyes and knowing it was on my own face as well.

"Tomorrow," I said. "Oh, tomorrow."

Elly was already running down the stairs toward the carriage when I came out of the shadows in my cloak. I saw the prince running after her and made him trip and fall. We barely made it home before the sun rose, and if I had not been behind the carriage in my boots, hurrying the horses, she would have been too late.

It was early afternoon before she woke. "I need not leave early tonight" she told me. "This is the last night. I will walk home, after."

"If you are in that ballroom when dawn comes," I told her, "all the faery stitches will vanish from your dress and veil. The cloth will fall about your feet, and you will be there naked, with everyone sniggering at

you. Best leave him at Lauds, as you did last night, and
let me act the marriage broker for you."

"Early in the morning," she begged. "When the
bell rings for Prime."

"When Prime rings, the sun is already coming up,"
I told her, pitying her, envying her. "When you hear it
ring for Lauds, you'll know the dawn is coming. You
must run, then, or be caught out. I do not think the
prince's parents will want him to marry a girl who
takes off her clothes in a ballroom."

She promised me. I scarcely heard her, thinking of
my own lover. I went with her once again, and
watched briefly through the windows before Giles arrived. Poor Gloriana had no hope and knew it now.
The prince danced with no one but Elly.

And Giles and I lay in the grass below the terrace,
hidden beneath my cloak.

"Beauty," he sighed, and I did not correct him. I
was. He was. We were. Our bodies moved and
touched and held one another, with nothing between
us. We grasped at stars, once, twice, three times, falling exhausted at last into the warmth of our nest. My
kirtle was somewhere in the grass. My underdress was
around my neck. Giles wore only his shirt. Our secret
flesh was still wet and entangled, one with another's.

A bell rang.

"Matins," I said drowsily.

"Lauds," he said as drowsily. "Matins was hours
ago."

Above me on the terrace, I heard a sound and
looked up to see Elly in the prince's arms.

The little fool was going to let her clothes vanish
and stand there in her skin, begging him to take her, as
well he might. I could not blame her. How could I
blame her? And yet her chance to marry him would be
over. His parents would not permit such an impropri-
ety. Princes had to have virgin brides, lest doubt be
cast upon their heirs. I moved with a strength greater
than my own, wrenched myself away from Giles,
wrapped myself in the cloak, distracted the prince with

a faroff cockcrow, seized Elly up beneath the cloak and bore her away.

She struggled. She was a strong girl. I got her out to the driveway just as the carriage dissolved. The pumpkin rolled there, broken, spilling its seeds. Mice scattered in all directions as the toad hopped away into the brush with a disenchanted croak. Luckily, no one was looking at the assemblage. Everyone was staring at the terrace, where the prince was running about like one demented. Somehow I got the boots on. I put a spell of silence and compliance on Elly, gathered her up in my arms again and said, "Boots, take us to the Dower House stables." As we went, I heard the bell striking for Prime.

When I set her down, her clothing fell around her feet, as I had told her it would. Her breasts were still rosy with desire, her nipples like little rubies. She put one hand between her thighs as though something hurt her, then left it there. She gave me a slow, hating look. "Why did you do that?" she demanded, her hand moving slowly back and forth.

I snatched it from between her legs and shook her. "Do you want him for one night, once? Is that all? One time, then he will marry someone else?"

Her eyes did not focus on me, so I slapped her. That got her attention, and I asked her again what she wanted.

"I want to go to bed with him," she said in a voice like warm honey. "Over and over again."

"Then you must marry him."

She stepped away from me, stumbling. She still wore one of the glass shoes. The other had been dropped in our flight.

"They didn't disappear," she said. "I dropped one on the stairs."

As soon as she said it, I realized why. They were clear. They were glass. There was no appearance to disappear. They might gradually fade, over some weeks, but they would not disappear suddenly. Which is why they had been in the story in the first place.

"Go to bed," I said wearily. "I need to think."

"He'll marry me," she said as though she were God, deciding fate. "He will. He has to. He can't live without me. He said so."

I did not tell her that men often said such things. Even pretty princes said such things. Even Giles had said such things. I went to my room to think. To think and to get dressed. My hair was down around my shoulders. I had nothing on but a stained underdress. I looked like a woman who had been made love to on the grass all night. I could not let myself think of Giles, for whenever I did, I trembled.

While I struggled with myself, events transpired without me. The first I knew of it was when I rose to a sound outside, went to the window, and saw Giles himself below, flourishing a scroll from which he was pretending to read his already memorized message.

"Know all men, by these words, that Prince-So-and-So of Marvella announces his intention of marrying the maiden whose foot fits the shoe he found last night upon the stairs. The prince rides after me, bringing the shoe to try on all maidens of this house." While I watched, Giles accepted a glass of wine from Lydia and told her the tale, looking about himself the while, looking for me, I supposed. I hurried to get myself dressed, thinking betimes that the work of the marriage broker had already been done by someone else. This public pronouncement was almost as good as a betrothal. The prince was determined to have his way, but Elly had no dowry that I knew of and the prince's parents might still have much to say about that.

By the time I got my hair braided and got downstairs, however, Giles had already ridden away. I found Lydia in the garden, agog. When she had finished repeating the tale three or four times, with embellishments, I asked her what marriage portion Edward had settled upon Elladine before he died.

She flushed. "I'm sure he meant to," she said. "He didn't mean to die so soon."

"You mean he didn't provide for her," I challenged. "Surely, then, you intend to make up for his lack of foresight."

She pursed her lips. "I've thought of it," she said, not looking me in the eye. "But it's really up to Edward to say. As soon as he's reached his majority, I'm sure he will do something about it. He won't be of age, of course, for a number of years."

"Fifteen years," I said drily. "Elladine will be a bit old by then. Thirty-some-odd. A confirmed spinster."

"She could enter a convent," Lydia suggested eagerly. "I've been meaning to mention that to her."

Foolishly, I did not advise Lydia that she reconsider and talk with me again before making any such suggestion. While I went on thinking of ways and means, Lydia went straight to Elly and suggested she enter a nunnery. I heard Elly's scream of rage and got there just in time to prevent her killing her stepmother, though not in time to prevent the attack. The expression on Elly's face was one I did not want to see. It was Jaybee's face, as it had been when I had last seen it, full of towering fury and indomitable determination. She could have killed Lydia gladly, and I feared somewhat that she might do so yet, or do something even more dreadful.

The prince arrived with the shoe in midafternoon. Gloriana was first to try it on, able only to get her big toe into it. She retreated in tears, while Griselda tried. I was there, with Lydia. The prince was there, with a couple of his men, but not Giles. Casually, I asked after Giles and was told he had not returned from his heralding, which had somewhat surprised the prince. There was some courtly chit-chat, though not a lengthy conversation, and Griselda gave up the attempt.

I said, "There's another girl in the house who must try it on."

Lydia glared at me, but I sent a maid after Elly, whose voice I could hear in the kitchen.

We were waiting for Elly to appear when we heard the scream. Gloriana's voice. Lydia and I ran. We found Gloriana in the kitchen, the great meat cleaver still in her hand, her left foot cut half through and blood spurting in all directions. Gloriana had done it herself. In the corner, Elly watched with a remote smile.

"What did you do?" I hissed at her.

"I just told her her feet were too big," Elly said indifferently. "That they might fit if she cut them in half." She took the other glass slipper from her pocket and went out to the waiting gentlemen while we struggled mightily to stop Gloriana's bleeding. The huge girl was too strong for us. She fought us off until she had lost so much blood that it was too late to help her. While Elly melted into the arms of her prince outside in the garden, Lydia and those of us in the kitchen gathered around the body of her stepsister and wept. Gloriana was not a pleasant girl. She was a great cow of a girl, with a cow's mute and intransigent hungers. She had little intelligence. Still, there was something monstrously tragical about the manner of her death, not the least that it has shown me what my daughter is. Of the two of them, Elly had been the more brutish.

ST. WILFRID'S DAY, OCTOBER,
YEAR OF OUR LORD 1367

Gloriana was buried in the chapelyard at Wellingford. Elly lay on her bed in her room and dreamed lascivious dreams. The prince had a tantrum in his own suite at his own house, but his parents remained adamant that they would not allow his marriage to a woman without a dowry. It was no more than I had expected. I got the warrant out from the hole where I'd hidden it and took it to London, where I sought the man who had issued it, a Jew named Yeshua ben Levi. Yeshua was dead of plague. I found his son. His house had advised my papa, some years before the first great Death, to use the money in the purchase of grain. During the times of plague the price had soared. The two warrants were now worth so much that Papa could have settled all his debts and found it unnecessary to marry Weasel-Rabbit. I told the House of Levi to keep the other warrant upon their books, for some heir would come to claim it, perhaps hundreds of years later. They stared at me strangely, but one of the bearded sons made a note of it.

When I returned to Wellingford, I carried with me a more than adequate fortune for Elly's marriage portion. I went to the prince's parents and represented Elly's interests. I signed the documents as her guardian, as her father's nearest kin. I arranged the nuptials. I did it all without meeting with her or discussing it with her. The prince's father negotiated with me, his ponderous mind plodding after me, step by step. He was not quick, but he missed nothing. It was like being tracked by a bear. Still, I did not give him everything. I saved some for myself.

I attested to the fact that Elly was a virgin of noble birth. True. She would not have stayed a virgin long, but she was still, technically, a virgin. And yet I lied. I wanted to say, "I fear she is a monster. Her father was a monster, and she is like him. I fear she is both sensual and cruel, a succubus who will twine herself around your son and suck him dry, making him rue the day he ever saw her." I said none of that. For all his intelligence, the prince's father did not ask. He cared only about the money, her virginity, and that she was nobly born.

I should have stopped it, somehow. And yet, wasn't it fated? Hadn't the story been told for hundreds of years? Wasn't my daughter to have her prince and live happily ever after?

While I was there, I asked again for Giles, saying I had known him for many years. He had gone, they said. He had never returned after delivering the glass-slipper message.

I don't know what has happened to him. I don't know where he is. I want more than anything to go looking for him, but I can't do that just now! First I must arrange this wedding. When it is over, I'll find him. Then he and I will come back to Wellingford. There are fields to harvest and geese to pluck. There are apples to store and cider to make. I can't decide what to do next. There's an old pain burning in me and a new love. Between them both, it's hard to decide what to do.

Was this what Carabosse meant when she asked me to be merely ordinary? Is being a mother ever ordinary? Is caring about one's children ever ordinary? Is there always this much pain?

FEAST OF THE HOLY INNOCENTS,
DECEMBER, YEAR OF OUR LORD 1367

Elly became pregnant even before the wedding. I had not thought to tell her anything about that. Neither had anyone else. Now that she understands there is no way to escape it, she has settled into a sullen resentment at the facts of life.

"I don't want it," she told me. "I just wanted the other, not this."

I told her I understood. I did understand, for I had not wanted it either. At least she had enjoyed the begetting.

Her eyes grew dreamy. "I like the other," she said. "I like it a lot. More even than he does."

I think perhaps I blushed. There is something so frankly lecherous in her tone when she talks like this, an insatiable hunger totally untinted with affection or humor. I tried to change the subject.

"It'll be fun for you to have a child. If it's a girl, she'll probably look like you."

"She can't," Elly said flatly. "I won't let her. No one looks like me. She can look like someone else. Someone pale, like him."

"She'll have your dark hair."

"His pale skin. His red lips. This baby can look like that."

"Like that," I agreed, feeling sick inside. On several occasions I have tried to get her to talk with me about other things: religion, gardening, pets. She doesn't care about any of them. She has some lingering affection for Grumpkin, but it is only a passive thing. Except toward the pleasures of her body, she is closed away. She likes warmth and frequent good food, and, most of all, fucking. She does not read, does not think, does not care. She would ride twenty miles in bad weather for her lust's sake, and would not walk twenty paces down a hallway to do a kindness. She emptied her ashes, not out of any sense of cleanliness, but only so her fire would burn so she could be warm. If she wants something, she could kill to get it, and if she does not want something, it might as well not exist so far as she is concerned.

I blame myself for her nature, though I keep coming back to the real cause. She is not like me. She is like Jaybee. Elly should never have been born, and but for him, she would not have been. But for him and for the fact I remembered too well the things Father Raymond used to teach me. I had told myself it was God's will when it was nothing of the kind. It was only man's stupidity.

Mostly, it was Jaybee's fault. I ask myself if I want Jaybee dead, and tell myself, no. Not dead. Not necessarily. Simply . . . simply unable to do to anyone else what he did to me. The more I see of Elly, the more sure I am that he should never father other children!

She sends for me. Every day or so, she sends for me. When I get there, she takes my hand and holds it, as though it were a rope and she were drowning. She looks at her swelling body with terror.

Well, well, I know. She has heard what all women hear in this time, that babies do not come easily nor safely. Women die giving birth. Many of them die. Life comes through the doorway of death in this time, and Elly is in terror of death. So she sends for me, and I sit beside her and hold her hand. After a time, she grows calm, and her eyes grow soft and her mouth loosens. She begins to think of the prince, and then she sends me away.

I want to go looking for Giles. I cannot. Not so long as she needs me.

Daytimes, I go on about my self-imposed duties at Wellingford. Harry and Bert have gone off to London. Some weeks ago I suggested to Griselda that she might look into the convent where Aunts Tansy and Comfrey—"Acquaintances of mine, now dead"—had found so many pleasant years. She did so and liked it. There she will not have to worry about men or clothes or being ugly, though she will have to bathe. Lydia arranged a dowry for her, very quickly, too, considering that young Edward is still a minor, and Griselda left us. Lydia and the two young children are alone with me. I do what I can with the children. The boy seems past help, but the little girl, Catherine, is beginning to respond to consistency and affection, like a flower growing toward the sun.

ST. BENEDICT'S DAY, MARCH 1368

Little Catherine is dead. My so-called "namesake." Sweet Catherine. Winter came, and with it the diseases that always come, and she died and was buried next to her half sister.

From time to time I go to Edward's grave and talk to him, telling him I am sorry. I should not have left him and Elly. It was my duty to stay. Even as I say it, I know it's not true. Nothing I could have done would have changed things. What looks out of Elly's eyes at the world would have been there even if I had been with her every moment of her life, born in her. Her nature will have its way. Love and good intentions simply don't solve everything.

ST. JULIA'S DAY, MAY 1368

Last night I woke at the Dower House, feeling I had heard someone call my name. Elly's voice. I put on the boots and went. She was in a room overwarmed by a roaring fire, with the midwives all around her, wringing their hands. She was screaming as I had done when she was born, as all women do in this time, her eyes bulging. "Mother," she cried. She had never had a mother, but she cried for one. I gave her my hands and would have given her life itself, but it was already too late when I got there. She had waited too long to call my name. She grasped at me, panting.

"White as snow," she panted, her eyes fixed on mine. "Red as blood. Black as death." She pointed to the child the midwives were holding, then died as I held her, sobbing as she had used to do when she was a baby and we put her down for a nap she did not want. The blood ran out of her in a wave. The baby girl had been born early, her white skin bloodied red all over. She did not want to live at all, but the midwives persevered and at last she cried. They washed her and laid her in my arms. Pale as a white rose, with Elly's dark, wild hair.

When I came into the outer room, Elly's young husband wept, but his eyes were full of some other emotion than grief. Was it relief? Was it gladness? He had the look of a man tried past endurance.

I knew what he was feeling. In college, I had read the Victorian poets. I was much enamored of Swinburne. He had spoken of this same feeling, "the delight that consumes the desire; the desire that outruns the delight." Elly's desire had outrun their delight. The prince did not ask how I came there, but his mother gave me a speculative look.

"There is no question of returning the dowry," she said plainly.

"I did not come for that," I told her.

"What then?" she asked.

What had I come for? "I came because she called for me. I would like Elly to be buried beside her father," I said. "He loved her very much. Perhaps if he had lived, she . . . things would have been different."

Red patches came out on her cheeks. She whispered, "I am glad she is dead. She was destroying my son. She was like an evil spirit, sucking his life." It was as though she had to confess it to me, had to receive absolution from me. It came out in a hiss.

I gave her the absolution she wanted. "I know," I said. "It is a hunger she was born with."

"Her daughter . . ."

"It is not in her daughter," I told her. "Her daughter is your son's daughter. You may trust in what I say." I knew it was true. I could sense nothing evil in the child at all. There was nothing there but sweet babyhood, innocent as dawn.

They let me take Elly's body away. I have found a priest to bury her in the Wellingford chapelyard, beside her father.

STS. DONATIAN AND ROGATIAN, MARTYRS

Only the prince came to Elly's internment, to stand dry-eyed while they filled in the grave. When it was over, he laughed, then he cried.

"We are going home," he said. "The people rose up and killed the pretender to the throne. He was my half uncle, Richard, and I am glad he is dead. They have sent word we are to return." His words had a childlike simplicity, and for the first time I really looked at him. He met my gaze innocently, without intention or guile. There was no large intellect there. He had none of his father's ponderous mind.

"Are you taking the child?" I asked.

"Oh, yes," he told me. "My daughter. Mama is very fond of her. So am I. Do not be concerned about her."

"Does she have a name?" I asked.

He gazed at me abstractedly, trying to think of the name. "Mama named her," he confessed at last. "After a spring flower that blooms through the snow. I cannot remember at the moment. Of course, she hasn't been christened yet."

He sighed, then smiled, without meaning, then said, "There was a man of ours you had an interest in. Father said you had asked after him."

"Giles," I said, my mouth falling open.

"He was killed. Someone saw the assault and sent word to my father. It was a group of men assaulted him, while he was riding on our business that day." He flushed, remembering that day. "Father said you had wanted to know."

Giles. Dead. Elly. Dead. Edward. Dead. Oh, God in Heaven. All dead. All I had loved. All I had tried to love.

"Where?" I breathed. "Where is he buried?"

"There," he said, gesturing vaguely eastward. "Where they killed him."

He left me and rode off with his serving men, still smiling his ineffectual smile, while I wept until there were no more tears. I had brought flowers for Elly's and Edward's graves, the roses they both liked. I gripped the bouquet until the thorns sank deep into my hands, knowing it was Giles's grave my flowers should lie upon.

I went back to the Dower House and got my boots. "Take me wherever it was Giles was set upon," I said.

And I was there, a weedy sunken spot by the side of an unfamiliar road, marked by a rough wooden cross. There was a man working in the field nearby, and he came to the fence, looking at me curiously.

"I didn't see you coming on the road," he said. "Are you looking for the place the fellow died?"

I nodded yes.

He pointed at the cross, at the sunken place. "I buried him there. I was over there, on the far side of the field. I saw him coming along, on his horse. They came out of the woods there, and set upon him. Eight or ten, maybe. Too many for me to fight. I saw his horse run off. I went to the village to get help. When we came back, the horse was there, grazing, and the body of the man. Dreadful cut about, he was. They knew him by his horse, though, for it had the King's arms upon the saddle."

I thanked him, and he went back to his work. I laid my flowers on the grave. They were marked with my blood upon their thorns. I sat there for a long time. When night came, I told the boots to take me home.

Perhaps in time I can find a stonecutter to make a monument for Giles. But why? In time even a monument will disappear. I remember the twenty-first and shudder. Why make monuments? Why build beautiful things? Why create anything when Fidipur's billions will tear them all down.

I don't know. I have no emotions at all except a sullen anger, which boils away inside me, building up the pressure. I want vengeance against the cause of all this pain. If I had not been pregnant when I came back, I would not have married Edward, I would not have had Elly. If I had not married Edward, I could have had Giles. We could have married, lived together, that ordinary life Carabosse wanted for me.

If I had not married Edward, if he had not had Elly, Edward might not have died, and he certainly wouldn't have married Lydia. Oh, what Jaybee had done when he raped me was more hurt than even he had planned!

When I left the twentieth—how long ago?—Jaybee was raging about, full of fury that he could not find me to do it all again. If I leave him there, he *will* do it again, to someone else. He will cause this pain again, generations of it, begetting sorrow as a cloud begets rain. It is not fitting that this should be so. I can do nothing for Elly. I can do nothing for Giles. Edward is gone. All I cared for is gone.

And Jaybee lives to make more sorrow.

Beauty can be disappointed of its children. The worst thing about being a woman is that things can be begot on us, things we do not want, cannot manage, cannot control. We swell to fruition with disasters implanted in us against our wills. We spew out tragedy. And all the disaster and the tragedy, though begot upon us against our volition, is part us. How much, we wonder. How much was me? What could I have changed?

Carabosse says I carry importance within me. A kernel of something incorruptible, no doubt. A seed. Yet one begot upon me without my consent. Can even Carabosse be sure of the harvest? Can this seed grow bitter fruit? Can it be twisted and warped, as my own seed was warped?

And is this, perhaps, what the Dark Lord wants?

What Jaybee wanted, whether he knew it or not? To beget horror on innocence? It cannot be borne. It cannot be tolerated. I cannot let it happen again, to anyone.

All my anger focuses upon Jaybee. Even though magic is thin on the ground in the twentieth, my powers will work there, so I believe, even if only weakly, perhaps enough.

Grumpkin is here. And my cloak. And my boots.

[*"What's she doing?" I asked Israfel.*
"She's going back there. Back to the twentieth."
"Beauty! You mustn't. Please. . . ."]

23

January 4, 1993
Wisdom Street

It is not Holy Wisdom, not Hagia Sophia, the street is named for, but William W. Wisdom, who was Manager of Public Works sometime in the forties. Still, I have always liked the name of the street, and seeing it on the sign at the corner gave me a feeling of welcome when the boots set me down only a few feet from our front door. Our front door. Bill's and Janice's and mine.

Bill had been so excited when we rented the house. To him it represented everything he had ever dreamed of: unimaginable amounts of room, safety, warmth, affection, plenty of privacy in which to indulge himself in his harmless eccentricities; all of the things so notably missing in the twenty-first. To me, accustomed to the vaulted spaces and elegant architecture of Westfaire, it had seemed scarcely better than a hovel, though I had agreed it was far better than the twenty-first.

It was, is, a small frame dwelling, white clapboard with blue shutters and a blue roof, surrounded on its corner lot by a white picket fence. Inside the front door a narrow hall leads back to the kitchen. On the left is a combination living-dining room, on the right, two tiny bedrooms and a bath. Some former owner had built another bedroom and a half bath in the basement, and Bill had chosen those rooms for his own. There he had his closet full of silky dresses and lacy underwear, his high-heeled shoes and fluffy parasols, his full length mirror and his private telephone. Though he never went "out" in his women's clothes, he wore them while he talked on the phone, endless high-pitched conversations full of flirtatious little interjections and giggles.

Though the basement rooms had been his place, he hadn't been stingy with his time and effort in the rest of the house. He and I had refinished the kitchen cabinets, taking endless hours to do it, more than the cheap construction was worth. He had sweated over the tiny lawn, fighting the weeds and mowing it twice a week. He had planted the junipers and the Seafoam roses on either side of the door. In summer they were a cloud of white. Now their brown canes poked through the rare light snow, like old bony fingers. I knocked. Janice opened the door as though she'd been standing in the hallway, waiting for someone. She said, "Yes?" in a tone of voice that told me she didn't know me. Well, why would she?

"I've come about Bill," I faltered. "May I come in?"

She stood back, rather grudgingly, to let me enter, her head tilted to one side, her bird's eyes fixed on me as though I were a bug. I had an almost uncontrollable urge to tell her who I was, but I fought it down. Telling her would involve too many explanations, and I couldn't guarantee she'd believe any of them. Besides, I could not depend on her good will. Her relationship with Bill and me had always been a reluctant one. I must have squeezed Grumpkin, for he protested at being held so tightly. I put him down on the floor and he promptly began to sniff his way around the hall.

"That's Dorothy's cat," she said. "Where did you get Dorothy's cat?" Once we had agreed that I was to be "Dorothy," Janice had never used any other name

for me. Bill had always called me Beauty when we
were alone.

"I'm a friend of hers," I said. "She asked me to
come tell you what happened." I made the comeback
sign. Janice would trust a comeback sooner than anyone else, though she didn't trust anyone much. She
looked startled, but she made the sign in return.

"Where is she?" Janice wanted to know. "And
where's Bill?"

"Dorothy's gone away," I said, breathing in
deeply. There was no kind or easy way to tell her what
had happened. "Jaybee broke in here while you were
away. He told Dorothy he'd come for her, Bill got
between them, and Jaybee killed Bill and attacked
Dorothy. He hurt her . . . raped her. She's gone
away."

She stared at me, unbelieving. "How did you
. . . ? I don't understand how you. . . ."

"I was a sort of witness to it," I said. "I was here
when it happened."

She fell back into the chair just inside the door, her
mouth open. "Jaybee? Bill?" Her eyes filled with
tears. "I should have known. Oh God, I should never
have left Bill alone."

Her emotion seemed genuine, though to my certain knowledge she had only tolerated Bill and me.

"He was like my son," she cried, the tears making
red tracks down her face. "My son I was bringing to
God. Oh, I loved him so."

I started to say, "You never let him know that,"
remembering just in time that I wasn't Beauty, wasn't
Dorothy, wasn't who I was. I was older. A lot older. In
the hall mirror I caught sight of myself, a woman in
her sixties, perhaps. All gray-haired. With crepey skin
on my arms. I looked at my hands, seeing the spots on
the backs of them. Time. I had used it up, going back
and forth. Used it up. I started crying, too, partly for
Bill, partly for myself. All I had seemed to do lately
was grieve. Grumpkin came over and extended a paw,
asking his "prrrt." How had he aged so little? I picked
him up, to hug, for warmth, for something.

"Who are you?" she asked. "Do I know you?"

"My name is Catherine Monfort," I said through my tears. "I came because Dorothy asked me to, and because she thought you might let me stay here."

She threw her hands up, shaking her head, no, then realized how inhospitable that looked. Janice couldn't bear to look bad, though she didn't care what she did if no one knew. Finally she nodded, pointing at the front bedroom, tears running down her face. "He was here yesterday. He asked for 'Beauty.' He even asked for Bill. That bastard. He was laughing at me. Oh, God will punish him. Oh yes, God will punish him."

"Jaybee?" I asked, knowing already that's who it was. Yes. Jaybee. Still looking for Beauty. He hadn't given up.

Janice had her hands folded under her chin, her eyes closed, her lips moving. While she cried and prayed, I went into the bedroom. My bedroom. All my things were still there, except the few I'd taken when I'd run away. My clothes, young clothes, for a college girl. Well, I could wear the nightgowns. The panties. The jeans, maybe. The shoes. Not the brassieres. I had little enough to put a brassiere around. My chest had gone flat, not saggy, just flat, like the fairies. Fairy blood, I guess. Sylph blood. Better than flopping, I suppose. Somewhere, I'd have to get some clothes suitable to a woman my age. I hung up my cloak, set my boots in the closet, put away my book and Mama's box in the drawer of the bedside table. Grumpkin jumped up on the bed, kneaded a place soft and lay down, eyes slitted, just as his daddy used to do. I turned to find Janice in the doorway, staring at me.

"Do you have a job?" she asked. She had suddenly realized she might have to support me. Janice wouldn't do that!

I shook my head.

"What can you do?"

"Handle horses," I said.

"Nobody's going to hire you for that, at your age." The words were a sneer. Janice was sounding more like herself.

I nodded, telling her I knew, thinking of Wellingford. "I managed an estate for a family for a while."

"If you could get references, that might be useful."

"I met Dorothy at college. We were both studying the same things. I'm a fair Latinist."

"Maybe we can find something academic. Through the network."

She meant the comebacks' forgery network that provided social security cards, birth certificates, educational documentation, and even jobs for returnees. What I really wanted to do was find Jaybee and follow him around, until I knew what he was doing, what his vulnerabilities were. That might have to wait.

Janice was still crying, wiping her eyes. "What happened to Bill? To his body?"

I tried to tell her and I choked. It was as if it had happened yesterday, rather than a year, two years ago. I finally got it out, about Jaybee having carried his body away.

"That bastard," she whispered again. "Oh, that rotten bastard." Then she wiped her eyes and said firmly, "When the day of judgement comes, he'll be among the damned." Then she went out, shutting the door behind her, leaving me alone.

I lay down on my own bed next to the cat, so tired it was hard to think, hard to move. I was old. Funny, I didn't know where my youth had gone, but I was old. When I looked in the mirror, I expected to see someone else, that younger face, that smooth skin, that unlined brow. Mama was still young. I should be still young. Instead, there was this thin, slightly wrinkled woman with flyaway gray hair who had to lean close to the mirror to see because she was nearsighted. I sat up and stared in the mirror, squinting my eyes as Thomas the Rhymer had taught me, wishing to see true.

It reminded me of one of the songs they had sung in Faery, in Oberon's court. "Lovely the days of your youth, and fleeting as grass. Stay with me forever in Faery, my golden-haired lass. . . ."

And that reminded me of Puck and Fenoderee, my

only friends. I said their names, wishing they were with me.

"Yes?" said Puck. He came out from the wall, from the bookcase, from somewhere near there. Grumpkin opened his eyes for a moment, yawned, then went back to sleep. He wasn't impressed by half-naked Bogles appearing out of the walls. Puck said, "I came to tell you Elladine is back in Faery."

I felt my heart thudding, like a weary hammer. "Is she angry at me?"

"Why should she be angry at you?"

"Because I ran off." I felt guilty about that, had felt guilty ever since I'd done it.

"I ran you off," he said. "Elladine is of Faery, and she's old in years. Age is a powerful protection against such as he. He's not really interested in those of Faery, so he let her go. He wouldn't have let you go."

"Still . . ." I said, tears in my eyes.

"Still, nothing. She risked your life taking you on that Halloween ride. It was sheer arrogance, too. Elladine is arrogant where humans are concerned. All that lot are."

I thought it must be true. "She never comes to me, even though I know she can!" I cried. "She never came to me when I was a child. The only time she came was after the Curse, to move my body, and it wasn't even me!"

What I felt was the same longing I had felt ever since I was a child. I needed someone to care about me. Stubbornly, I could not stop seeking love. I wanted Elladine to love me.

"Beauty, you're such a child," he laughed at me. "Why don't you take affection from those who'd give it to you gladly? Me, for instance." He made a languishing face at me, enough to make me laugh.

"Elladine told me you're trying to be an angel," I said. "Is that why you're here, looking after me? And how come you never came before when I was here?"

He chuckled ruefully. "I was here before. As soon as Carabosse let me come. Who do you think pushed those boots into your hands when that man was coming after you?"

"I didn't see you."

He shrugged. "I know. Carabosse thought it was dangerous for me to show up, in the flesh, so to speak. You knew nothing about Faery then, and she thought you might go silly."

"I wouldn't have," I said indignantly. "If I could get dragged from the fourteenth to the twenty-first, and then back here, if I could go through all that with Jaybee without going silly, why would I go silly seeing you?"

"Magic's thin on the ground here," he said. "She thought perhaps you'd stopped believing in it."

I sniffed to verify the fact. "I can hardly smell it at all. If I put on my cloak in full sunlight, people can almost see me."

"So, don't put on your cloak."

"I need it," I said stubbornly.

"What are you going to do?" he asked.

"I must make sure Jaybee hurts no more women," I told him.

He made a face.

I said, angrily, "I know you think it's only for vengeance, but it's not only that! It isn't vengeance when you kill a poison snake in the yard where children play, to keep it from killing someone else. I need to make sure he hurts no more people, fathers no more children like Elly. After that, I don't know. Maybe I'll go join a nunnery somewhere." What else was there to do? What had been between Giles and me had been quite perfect. I could never love anyone else in that way.

"You should leave Jaybee to Fate, Beauty. It would be safer. Truly. Listen to me. You have a granddaughter, back then. You could live then, be with her."

I shook my head at him. "They don't know I'm her grandmother, Puck. They think I'm a fairly distant relative. I'd be an intruder. She has a grandma, a grandpa, a father. She'll be a princess." I shook my head, firmly. "Are you going to stay here with me?"

"I'll drop in from time to time. I can't stay, though. We're still trying to convert Faery before they all dwindle, though they're a stubborn lot. Well, so are we Bogles."

"Tell me about it," I asked him, curling up on the bed the way I had used to do when I was young. My bones protested, but I persevered, wanting that feeling of having a whole long time to just sit and talk about anything at all, with pillows softening the world, and maybe hot chocolate to drink. That feeling of being in a safe nest where nothing could hurt me. The way I used to cuddle into my tower bed, when I was young. Grumpkin half-opened his eyes, crawled over to put his feet up against my leg, and started kneading me as he went back to sleep.

"What are you and the Fenoderee and the others trying to do?"

He cocked one ear at me, like a horse might do, or a dog. "We want Faery to fight the Dark Lord. On man's behalf, and its own."

I laughed. "I can see Oberon's face."

Puck grimaced. "Well, he's not receptive thus far."

"Why do you want Faery to fight, Puck?"

He settled himself on my bed. "I'll give you my lecture, which I've given the Bogles over and over. I've given it to the Sidhe, too, but they pay no attention. Mind now. Fold your hands in your lap and pay attention:

"When Faery looks at mankind, it sees him as mostly animal, not immortal and far from perfect. Since those of Faery are immortal, it stands to reason they should feel sorry for mankind, right? Poor little sinful, short-lived thing."

I nodded. I'd felt sorry for myself, often enough.

"But there's this unexpected thing about man. He climbs. That's the thing about him. He climbs. Not all of him, oh no, or there'd be no more living with him than with the angels, but now and then there's one who does." Puck folded his legs and leaned against my bedpost, scratching one brown ankle and furrowing his brow. "And when a man or a woman climbs, Beauty, he or she can end up as high as the angels or higher."

"The saints," I nodded, thinking I knew.

"Oh, saints," Puck said. "Whsst. Saints! Martyrs and virgins and what all. Relics in churches, and both the relic and the churches dead as brass. No. I'll tell you who climbs. Gardeners climb. And farmers. And painters. And poets. People who build beautiful things without destroying to do it. The ones who designed Westfaire, them. And people who live with animals and learn of them until they know every twitch of a tail or an ear. Them, too. And those that study atoms and how they move, and stars and how they move. Those who learn about the Holy One by reading his own book of nature and creation, that's who climbs."

"How do you know?" I asked. "How do you know those people climb?"

"Ach," he said, rubbing his head. "You know how, if you sing a note, sometimes a wine glass sitting in a cupboard sings the same note back again?"

I told him I did.

"Well, sometimes you say the name of a man or a woman and it comes back to you out of the air, singing, and you know that man or that woman has climbed up somewhere."

"Dead or alive?" I wondered.

"Either," he said. "Maybe it's only us Bogles that can hear it, but when you're in Faery next, you try it. Say the name of the ones who built Westfaire and listen for it to come back at you."

I didn't know their names, more's the pity. "Why is that, do you suppose?"

"Because that's the way the Holy One wanted things to be, don't you see? The Holy One created the world beautiful and manifold and complicated, and the way it was made was the way He *meant* it to be! He wasn't just playing, making a toy world with the real world somewhere else. No, this is *it*! Anybody with eyes can see the truth of that. The Holy One wanted mankind to understand creation so he could create in his turn, for man's the only one among us who can create anything at all! Angels don't! They burn with a pure flame, like stars, but they don't create. Faery doesn't! It grows and flowers, without much thought, and it doesn't create."

"Faery is beautiful."

He rubbed his head and looked at me with saddened eyes. "Ah, nah, nah, you know better, Beauty. It's all glamour in Faery. All fool-the-eye, like dreams. It's not real. Without elvenroot and fairy fruit, we'd see no palaces nor fairy steeds. In Faery, it's all in the eye, not in the heart or mind. You know that."

"What's the difference," I said, being stubborn. "It's still beautiful."

"The difference is that nobody builds it. It doesn't really stand there. If we leave it, it will vanish. You can't show it to a mortal man, lest you put elvenroot in his eyes, and you do that, he can't see anything else forever. You can't take a picture of it. Sometimes I wonder if even the Holy One can see it."

"You mean if someone mortal gets elvenroot in her eyes, she can see Faery, but nothing else?" I asked in surprise.

"It's only your fairy blood lets you see Faery and still see this world, Beauty, and your granddaughter hasn't enough fairy blood ever to use it safely. If she goes there, she must stay forever. She's only one-eighth, and that's not enough to go back and forth. If you're thinking of taking her to Faery, beware!"

I hadn't been thinking of my granddaughter. I hadn't been thinking of anyone, specially, though I suddenly thought of Jaybee, wondering what a view of Faery would do to him.

"So why do you want Oberon to fight the Dark Lord, Puck?"

"Because it would do what the Holy One asked of Faery in the first place! To help mankind! Help him instead of using him or ignoring him, which has been the usual pattern. Make common cause with him. Join with him.

"And it's so logical," he said. "Man is dying from

being too many. Faery is dying from being too few. We need to mix more, to value our children more. Men have too many of them, they're cheap. The Sidhe have too few, and they seek them like treasure. Man needs what Faery has to give. Fewer children. Longer lives. Less speed. More thought. Mystery and wonder and glamour built in, so to speak, through the slow creation of marvelous things. Less haste and destruction. More appreciation for what's been given. Like man and Faery were two halves of one thing. If the Dark Lord were conquered, it could all come right!"

"Why won't the Sidhe listen? They lust after humans enough."

"Oh aye, they do. But it's that pride again, Beauty. They said no to the Holy One; you think they're going to say yes to a Bogle? And while a little fleshy stink is exciting to them, they won't accept it as a daily thing. It's common. It's not how they see themselves."

"So they won't."

"They won't. Perhaps it's the dwindle, the way our magic is leaking away. And our numbers are falling, too, one here, one there. A forest gets cut down, and the fairies who were born out of that forest are gone. At one time, the glamour would have been strong enough to protect the forest, but not anymore."

"What's causing it, Puck? Why do they dwindle?"

"There's some say it's the Dark Lord's doing. Every time he makes a new horror, it takes hideous magic to do it, all tied up in that terror, like gold dug out of the earth and hid away. There's some say it's the human priests, sucking our magic away to use it in their religion, turning wine into blood and making spells to forgive sins. There's some who say magic came from nature, and with man destroying nature right and left, there's not enough of it left. Whatever the reason, we've been losing it for a few thousand years. The only ones who're holding fast are us Bogles. We can tolerate mankind better than most, maybe because we never went in for glamour like the Sidhe. We can even live in wasteland, where those of Faery can't. But it's hard times for us, too. We watch things dwindle and dwindle, and Oberon forgets what he once knew, forgets his majesty and his dignity and ruts like a goat, laughing and pretending all is well. As though time were forever."

"But you said they're immortal."

"All that means is they don't die. It doesn't mean they can't fade away. They're tied to the forests, Beauty. Tied to the moors. Tied to the seas and rivers. They were drawn from nature and will go when nature goes. They vanish if their forests vanish. Fade away. Like snow, melting."

His face was drawn into a mask of tragedy, the corners of his mouth pulled down with woe. I took his hand in my own and stroked it.

"Right now," he muttered, "if I went to Faery *in this time,* there'd be almost nothing there. It's all shadows and ghosts. No palaces. No enchanted places. What's left has been invaded by *him.* To reach the Faery you know, I have to go back and come in from hundreds of years ago."

I nodded, sadly. "That's what Bill and the crew were photographing when I met them. The end of Faery. The last enchantments. They were getting a picture of Westfaire with the roses growing up."

He sighed. I tried to think of something comforting to say, but someone knocked on my door. I looked up, startled, looked back to find Puck gone.

"Yes?" I said.

Janice opened the door. "I've made some tea. I thought it might do us good."

I nodded, trying to smile as I levered myself off the bed on aching old legs to go have tea, feeling less lonely but more lost than I had half an hour before. Grumpkin purred and stayed where he was. The end of the world does not impress cats.

Janice wiped her eyes and made small talk. She wondered how long I'd been back in the twentieth; she wondered how I'd been getting along, without a job.

"Oh, I had a job until just recently," I said. "Caring for horses. Then, suddenly, I got old. Up until a year or two ago, I wasn't . . . didn't feel old at all."

She sipped and nodded. "That's the way it takes us all, I think. Suddenly, you're not young anymore, and you don't know where it went. And people tell us they don't love us anymore because we're too old. And some of us fight it, and some of us realize in time that it's God's will." Her eyes blazed at me.

"So," I went on quickly, derailing a disquisition on God's will. "I went back to school, and that's where I met your niece."

"You said you were a witness? When Jaybee came?" Her mouth was tight, but her eyes were avid.

I had to make it up as I went along. "Dorothy and I had planned to have New Year's dinner together. I had just arrived, and I'd asked to use the bathroom. I was inside, with the door ajar, when I heard the man come in. I heard it all, but I was afraid if he saw me, he'd kill me. There was nothing I could do. Afterwards, he picked up Bill's body and went, and I helped Dorothy get herself together, then she decided to go away where he couldn't find her. I don't even know where she is." I had to say that. Otherwise Janice would be at me to get the address. Her mouth was still downturned. Was she angry that Dorothy herself hadn't told her? Or was she angry that Dorothy had gotten away?

"She should have called me," she said bitterly. "I'm terribly fond of Dorothy." Her tone belied the words.

"I don't think she was thinking about that." Besides, I didn't believe her. Janice had never approved of me enough to be fond of me. I equivocated, "I'm sure she'll call you. Before she went, she suggested I come here, that you might like the company, that you might not want to be alone."

"Where were you living before?" she asked suspiciously. I knew she was suspecting me of having invented the tragedy for the sake of free rent.

"In an apartment downtown," I extemporized. "The building has been sold, and all the tenants have to move."

It was evidently explanation enough. Janice forgot

to be suspicious of me and returned to her grief. "That bastard," she whispered, tears coming again. "Oh, that horrible man. What will I do when he comes back?"

"Nothing," I said. "Nothing, please. Dorothy said not to do anything."

"I couldn't do anything now anyhow," she said. "I have to get out of town for a while. The team I used to work with is coming from the twenty-first to photograph whales. They'll be—we'll be coming here, to this very town. I was with them. I can't be here when I come. Not this near or it might make a loop."

When I asked for details, she told me the team had come from the twenty-first on January 12, 1993, and had rented a boat named the *Sally Ann,* with its owner as crew. They had gone out into the ocean and photographed migrating whales. She remembered it clearly, almost yearningly. Her expression softened, as though something wonderful had been connected with that trip. "Martin's coming," she whispered.

"And Bill?" I whispered. "Bill's coming?"

"Oh, yes. Bill. And the others." She got up and went into the bathroom, closing the door. I heard her weeping, making loud gulping noises. I didn't think she was weeping over Bill. Something else grieved her.

Alice had talked about staying away from places that had previously been visited through time-travel. None of the team would want to be in this town when their former selves came back. None of them could be, but I could. They hadn't even known I existed on January 12, 1993.

January 8, 1993

Janice trusted me enough to leave me with the keys to the house, money to buy groceries, and the names of some comebacks I'm supposed to call and ask about jobs. She said she'd be back on the eighteenth.

"When you came this time, when the team comes

back this time, will they know about comebacks?" I asked her.

"Oh yes," she said, disapprovingly. "We even talked to one. Or rather, Bill did. I hardly saw her, but I remember, she gave Bill some clothes." She sniffed. Even with Bill dead, she still disapproves of his clothes.

January 12, 1993: Evening

I saw them all. Jaybee, of course. Younger, but with that same red light of destruction burning in his eyes. Janice and Alice. Martin, the director. He and Janice were obviously in love, and that's what she had remembered so longingly. The two of them had no eyes for anyone else. Janice was lovely, too, with a winsome fragility that could age very quickly and lose itself. Perhaps that evanescent beauty was all Martin had cared about.

Bill was there. Young Bill. Much younger than when I first saw him.

It had taken me most of the past several days to find the clothes I remembered Bill having. The sheepskin was the easiest part. I got that at a place they make sheepskin jackets. I finally found the skirt at the Salvation Army store. I took the tags off everything, put them in a paper bag and carried it with me when I went down to the dock, very early this morning, before it was even light. I found the *Sally Ann*. When the owner came along, he unlocked it, then went up on top, toward the front. While he was up there, I went down inside. A stowaway, I guess I was. Like Constanzia.

I heard their voices on the dock, heard their feet as they came aboard, felt the surging as the boat left the dock, the heaving of the ocean. I prayed I wouldn't be sick. After a while, when we were well out on the sea, I came up from inside. I pretended it was an accident. I'd gotten a migraine while fishing on the pier, I told them, so I'd borrowed the boat to lie down in for a moment, and fallen asleep. I apologized profusely and said I wouldn't get in their way.

Bill and Martin exchanged a look and shrugged. Their twenty-first cameras looked enough like twentieth cameras that they assumed I wouldn't know the difference. They were doing shots to be used early in the whale documentary, shots of healthy creatures. The starving mother and calf that appeared in the final shots wouldn't be photographed until later, sometime around 2025 or 2030, after Fidipur's ocean farms had been built and all the krill and plankton was being used up by man.

Bill and Alice and I talked. I told them I was a comeback. They asked what it was like. I told them it was far better than the twenty-first, the last good time. When Alice joined the others, I showed Bill the clothes in the paper bag, stockings, silk blouse, skirt, underthings. High-heeled shoes, the kind I never wear, never have worn. They were way too small for me, but I remembered them on Bill's tiny feet. The fleece was in there, soft and new now, not the way it would be when I cut the boots out of it. I said I'd found the sack on the pier, and I guessed I'd throw them away. He couldn't keep his eyes off the bag after that. I kept fighting down the urge to tell Bill I loved him. That would have confused him utterly.

The day wore on. Janice clung to Martin, not even noticing me. The whales spewed and basked, and Jaybee ran his cameras. He had one that went underwater, like a tiny submarine, guided from a little TV screen with controls. The man running the boat stayed up front and paid no attention to any of us.

All the time I kept arguing with Puck in my head. He had chided me for wanting vengeance. Father Raymond would have said that vengeance belongs to God. I told myself it wasn't vengeance, and it wasn't for myself. It was for some other innocent person. Then I'd argue with myself some more. If Jaybee hadn't been there, right in front of me, I might have talked myself out of it. Every time he looked up at me, though, it was with that dead-eyed, death-making arrogance, an expression that said he was above any law, outside any commandment. It made me hurt inside. Each time I fought down the notion of what I was going to do, he made it come back more strongly.

Finally, I couldn't fight it anymore. When the boat turned back toward land, I asked Bill to introduce me to Jaybee.

Bill said, "Jaybee, here's a comeback lady wants to meet you. She thinks you're fascinating."

"I didn't say that," I bridled. "I said I thought his photography was fascinating."

Jaybee looked up at me and sneered. He didn't care about old women. He was kneeling on the deck, busy packing up his cameras.

"Be nice, Jaybee," Martin said. He was a handsome man, a bit older than the others. He had that power that some men have, of being always center stage, no matter who else is there. He wore boots and a complicated jacket with many pockets. "Be nice."

"I'm busy," Jaybee snarled. "No time for chit-chat."

"Bill and Martin tell me you're a fine photographer," I said.

"There's never been a better one," he said, peering at me, seeing nothing there to interest him, letting his eyes drop away. "I'm good. I'm very good."

"You use oculum root, then, I suppose."

"Never heard of it," he snorted.

"Oculum root?" Bill laughed. "Sounds like a sneeze. What is it?"

I acted surprised. "You don't know about it? Really? I thought all the really great photographers used it. Not that it isn't a bit risky, but all the biggies seem willing to take the risk."

"Oculum root?" Martin frowned. "I think I've heard of it." He hadn't, of course, but he was that kind of man. He ran one hand along the side of a boot, polishing it. Janice put her hand on his and mooned at him.

"For sharpness of vision," I said. "Sometimes it's

called hawkeye root. It lets the human eye see things in a new, fresh way."

"I'd love to try something that did that," Bill laughed. "But I confess I've never heard of it."

"Well, of course," I said, as though surprised at my own stupidity. "Of course, you haven't heard of it. It doesn't exist in the twenty-first. Because of Fidipur."

"Oculum root," he said.

"It's rare, even now," I said, getting off the rail where I'd been perched and dusting my hands. "I understand the supply is extremely limited. Pity. With oculum root, you'd probably be exceptionally good." Then I went off to look over the opposite rail, leaving Jaybee glaring after me. He might not remember. If he didn't remember, well and good. If he didn't remember, and if he gave up trying to find Beauty, nothing would happen. I'd go home. That's the bargain I'd made with myself. It was really up to him.

When we got back ashore, I went off up the pier empty-handed. I had already seen Bill wearing the clothes in the twenty-first, so I knew he would take them with him.

I found an unoccupied alley nearby where I could put on the boots. I told them to take me to Faery. There was a whirling blackness that seemed to go on too long. Then it cleared, showing me the landscape under the evening sky. It was almost the same as I remembered, the blue sky, the spangled stars, the flower-sequined grass. It was more shadowy than before. There were no palaces. No people. From the woods against the mountains came a faroff howling, totally inhuman, with a tone to it that sent a shiver of pure terror up my back. I stayed just long enough to find two of the hairy-stemmed herbs Mama had squeezed into my eyes. They came up easily, soil clinging to their roots. I told the boots to take me to Wisdom Street. The same whirling darkness happened again.

When I got back to the house on Wisdom Street, Puck was waiting for me.

"That was foolish," he whispered to me.

"What was?" I asked him stupidly.

"You went into Faery," he said. "It doesn't take much magic to get there, Beauty. Not now. There's not much of Faery left, and what is left is very close, because it doesn't belong to us anymore. It belongs to him, and he is bringing it close to man. Close as he can."

I shuddered.

"I told you he had taken over," he accused me. "Carabosse is wild with grief over this. She says you've risked so much, and for what? For vengeance. I told you to let it go."

"I could not let him go on!" I said, suddenly angrier than I have ever been. "Who are you, or Carabosse, to tell me to let it go? It wasn't you he did it to!"

He sighed. He turned pale. He looked at the floor, at his bare toes. I was sorry I had spoken so. "Tell Carabosse I'm sorry," I said. "No harm done."

He shook his head. "That may not be so," he said. "Something saw you while you were there. Carabosse doesn't know who or what it was, but something saw you. She wants you to come home."

"I'll come home," I said. "Soon."

"Now," he begged.

"Soon," I said tiredly, looking at the plant in my hands. Evidently my tone of voice was final. I looked up and he was gone.

I went into the kitchen where I'd already put a sack of potting soil and a flowerpot. I planted the herbs, watered them carefully and labeled them with a large, white plastic plant label. If Jaybee has given up trying to find Beauty, he will never see the plant and I will go home. If he hasn't given up, it is likely he will show up here, at Janice's house, within the next three or four days.

January 17, 1993

Several days ago I went to the optometrist and got glasses, bifocals. I hate them. Whenever I eat the line is right where the food is, and I keep spilling things down my front. I went to the beauty shop, too, and had a cut and set to make me look different from the woman Jaybee met on the boat. Younger, a little, though perhaps it is really only neater.

Jaybee showed up this afternoon, drove up with a squeal of tires, parked by the curb, stepped over the picket fence. I was raking the lawn. A kind of memorial for Bill. Jaybee asked me where Janice was, and I told him she'd had to go out of town. He knew that. He'd been out of town himself. That's why he hadn't been here earlier. He asked me where "Dorothy" was, and I told him she'd moved. He asked me where, and I told him I had it written down somewhere in the house. He followed me into the kitchen where I made quite a drama of searching for the address everywhere but where I'd put it.

The flowerpot was sitting on the counter with its huge label. He couldn't miss it: black felt-tipped block letters on white. "Oculum Root," it said. His eyes flicked around the room, looking at everything, as they always did. Photographer's eyes. Always seeing. They came to the plant, flicked away and returned, fascinated, remembering something that had happened a long time ago, something someone had said.

By the time I found the address and gave it to him, his eyes were firmly fixed on the plant label.

"What is this?" he asked, putting one finger on a leaf, as though to be sure it was real.

"Oh, it's a very rare herb," I told him. "Janice learned about it in her research. It's extremely hard to obtain. She's been wanting some of it for a long time, and she located a man who grows it just before she left."

I handed him the scrap of paper with the address on it. He glanced at it and saw it was the address of the college "Dorothy" had been attending. "I've been there," he said. "She didn't come back there after the holidays. She must be somewhere else."

I pretended to be puzzled. "Janice did say something about another address. Maybe it's in Janice's bedroom." I went out into the hall and around the corner into the back bedroom, leaving him alone in the kitchen. I sat down on my bed and waited, stroking Grumpkin, my mind totally empty. Some time went by. Long enough. I heard footsteps, then his car leaving. When I went back to the kitchen, the plant was gone.

I have not done anything. I have not injured him. I have not met violence with violence. All I have done is to put something where he could steal it if he came hunting for a woman he had abused. Now, perhaps, I will not need to do anything else at all.

Am I revenged? It's very strange, but I don't know. Except for the tiny furnace behind my breast bone, I don't feel anything at all.

January 18, 1993

Janice returned from her trip with word of a job for me. The university needs a part time librarian to work evenings who reads enough Latin and medieval English and French to help students. I thanked her, not telling her I won't be here long enough to bother. I was going to leave last night, but my conversation with Puck had reminded me of something I wanted to find out from her.

"Janice," I said, "Dorothy told me how she met you and the others."

"Did she," sniffed Janice, suddenly suspicious once more.

"She told me you were doing a documentary on the last of the fairies, the last magic. You were the researcher on that, weren't you?"

She relaxed. "I was, yes. Piles of old books I had to plow through to find the answers to that one!"

"Where did all the magic go, Janice?"

"The Church took most of it," she said, giving me this strange, wild-eyed glare.

"The Church?" I asked stupidly. It was what Puck had said, but somehow I hadn't believed it.

"Making magic," she said. "All their sacraments are magical. Turning this into that. Making spells to forgive sins. They don't admit it's magic, but that's what it is! *'The recitation of formulae by an elect, resulting in a condition contrary to reality, is magic.'* But there was only so much of it around. The fairies had it, then the Church took it, and now the Church is losing it to something else. The last days are coming. It's been foretold. It's been revealed. . . ."

And she went off into a tirade about the last days, leaving me sitting there with my mouth open, remembering the smell in the chapel at Westfaire. It had been the smell of magic. The same smell as in Faery.

Something she was ranting about caught my attention. "What was that, Janice?" I asked.

"We never finished it," she said. "We never finished that documentary. We tried, later, but they wouldn't let us."

LATER

Our conversation was interrupted by a phone call. It was someone in the comeback network, and Janice talked to them for quite some time. I went in my room and took a nap. When I woke up, hours later, it was evening. She was waiting for me when I went into the kitchen.

"I've had some news of Jaybee," she said.

"Oh?"

"He's blind. Blind and crazy. He can't see anything, but he thinks he does."

I shook my head at her, saying nothing. Janice

drew her face into the expression I call her holy martyr look.

"At least we can take this opportunity to cleanse ourselves of hate," she said, staring me straight in the eye. "We are being given a chance to forgive. We must figure out some way to take care of him."

"We? Take care of him!"

"We comebacks must care for him. He is one of us and we can't afford to have him talking about us."

"Talking about what?" I laughed, a little hysterically, certainly not amused. "If he's crazy, surely no one is going to believe him."

"We'd rather he doesn't talk about us at all," she said. She gave me a sidelong look, that judging, weighing look. "When they called this afternoon, I told them we'll take him in for the time being."

I couldn't believe her. "He killed Bill! He raped Dorothy. You can't be serious!"

She pursed her mouth and folded her hands. That pious, martyred, holier-than-anybody pose. "It's just for the time being. We have Bill's room downstairs that he can stay in. You'll be working evenings and I'm working days. The network will pay you to look after him while I'm at work. If you're going to pay your share of the expenses here, you'll need more pay than the part-time work the library will give you."

"I can't be party to this," I said. "I saw what he did, and I can't be party to it."

Janice wrung her hands, rolled her eyes, became St. Janice facing the lions. "Either someone has to take charge of him or we have to get rid of him. I can't even consider that! I'm a religious woman. I couldn't kill him. We have to forgive him. If he was crazy, he wasn't really responsible for what he did."

"What makes you think I could control him," I said. "He's a hell of a lot bigger than I am."

"They have him on drugs," she admitted. "Enough to keep him quiet. He can take care of himself. It won't be like nursing him, or anything like that."

"I see," I said, sickened. I couldn't stay in this place if Jaybee were here. I'd end up killing him.

Maybe that's what she wanted. I gave her a look, almost understanding her in that instant. Did she know what she was doing? "Give me a few days to think about it."

"No time," she commented. "I think they just drove up outside."

They had, indeed, just driven up outside, two men I had met when I was young Beauty, friends of Janice's and Bill's, with Jaybee between them, being dragged along. I was reminded of the way he had hauled Bill's body away, carelessly, dumping it in his car, driving off. I had been huddled on the floor, my clothes in shreds around me, blood on my face, blood on my hands, blood leaking between my legs, still able to see him out of the corner of the window. So I saw him now, out of the corner of the window, being dragged along. There was a bandage over his eyes.

I went to my room and got my robe on. I put Grumpkin in the pocket. Poor old cat. He was almost used to it. I put my things in the other pocket, the ones I needed. I put the boots on my feet. I heard Janice open the front door, heard her speaking in her pious, all-forgiving voice. "Poor man. Bring him in."

He came in. I went out.

Puck found me in the hotel where I had taken a room. He was panting, and he looked pale.

I asked him what was the matter.

He rubbed his face with his hands. "It's getting harder to get here. Harder every time. When are you coming home? Carabosse wants to know, Beauty. This is getting serious."

"Does she think I'm in danger here?" I asked. I couldn't get interested in Carabosse, for some reason. "Can I still get back from here?"

"You're not in danger. Not immediately. And you can still get back, for a little while."

"Tell her soon."

April 1993

It is easy to get on a board of directors. All one has to
do is give money. Of course, getting the money out of
a warrant over six hundred years old is another matter.

The House of Levi still exists, strangely enough,
though under quite another name, and it still exists
where I found it first, in London. Getting there from
here was my first overseas flight in a plane. I chose to
do it that way, remembering how thin the magic is in
current time. Using the boots to go back, it gets
stronger as I go. Going from place to place in the
twentieth, the boots might work, but they might drop
me off in mid-ocean, as well. I didn't want to risk it.

When I showed the investment house the warrant,
they looked at it in disbelief. They admitted that the
money had been with them all those years. One of
their young men sat down and figured what it was
worth, millions and millions of dollars. I had to prove
my right to it, as the direct descendent of the daughter
of the Duke of Monfort and Westfaire, which, thanks
to the seven-league boots and enough gold to oil
palms here and there, I was able to do. Puck and Fenoderee helped, rather reluctantly, and only in past
time. They didn't have to come here to do it. I'm not
sure they could have. But in former centuries they
were able to forge parish registry entries and put false
birth records among ancient files. Marriages which had
never occurred were recorded. Baptisms were entered
in faded ink in ancient books. Confirmation records
were put there as well. And, above all, wills, passing
the warrant down from generation to generation, seventeen generations in all, to the present day. To Catherine Monfort. I am an heiress. The people of the
House of Levi have been considerably astonished, but
they are standing behind their document, six centuries
old or not.

I called Janice and offered to hire someone to look
after Jaybee. Janice was so angry I could hear her
voice shaking, which confirmed my suspicion that she

wanted to make me responsible for Jaybee. She had transferred her dislike of Beauty—Dorothy—to this new person, me. In Janice's world, there must always be a sinner who is paying for her sin while Janice watches and judges. Since she could no longer get at Dorothy, she wanted to get at me. I was Dorothy's friend and therefore probably guilty of something. In the last analysis, it is probably her own sin she is forever expiating. I don't know what sin that was. Perhaps neither does she.

It turned out, I didn't need to hire someone to care for him. Within hours of the time I left the house on Wisdom Street, she had found another place for Jaybee.

I found an apartment in New York, and I am now on the board of directors of the International Environmental Crisis Committee, a group of very powerful persons dedicated to saving the world. They feel it is going to hell in a handbasket, and I know they're right, though I can't tell them how I know. Many of them have given millions of dollars to this effort, and so have I. I am privy to everything they are doing. They are attempting to put together a coalition of all environmental bodies, all the so-called liberal religious bodies who are more concerned with life than money, all people everywhere concerned with life on earth. We spend endless hours in meetings, trying to build coalitions, networks, trying to agree on lobbying strategies. We argue which candidates to support. I go to bed every night weary and yet unable to sleep. Grumpkin lies beside me and purrs, and eventually the sound of him lulls me into unconsciousness. Then I dream of the child named Elaine, and her mother, and the knife, and the sound of a mad voice singing "Down, down, down," and I wake up again.

January 1994

Almost three hundred species of flora and fauna have
gone extinct since I gave my first dollar to IECC. On
the front page of the newspaper tonight is the announcement of a Mother of the Year Award, given to
a mother of eleven children. I wonder what Father
Raymond would say? Her eleven children can eat
hamburger made from cows who were fed the ephem-
eral grass that comes after rainforest is cut and burned.
They can breathe the already polluted air. They can
look forward to growing up and having spaces of their
own in the new prefabricated apartment houses now
being built in Japan which give each renter one hundred fifty square feet. The article about the apartments
says all the conveniences are built in. Bill's apartment
in the hive in the twenty-first had one hundred square
feet. There isn't far to go.

March 1994

Puck has been back several times, begging me to come
home, each time more frantically. I might as well have
gone. There is no point in my staying here. There was
never any point. Carabosse must have known that. She
knew it was too late. I felt I had to try.

We have been thwarted at every turn by god. Not
the real God. A false one which has been set up by
man to expedite his destruction of the earth. He is the
gobble-god who bids fair to swallow everything in the
name of a totally selfish humanity. His ten command-
ments are me first (let me live as I please), humans
first (let all other living things die for my benefit),
sperm first (no birth control), birth first (no abortions),
males first (no women's rights), my culture/tribe/lan-
guage/religion first (separatism/terrorism), my race
first (no human rights), my politics first (lousy liberals/

rotten reactionaries), my country first (wave the flag, the flag, the flag), and, above all, profit first.

We worship the gobble-god. We burn forests in his name. We kill whales and dolphins in his name. We pave prairies in his name. We have retarded babies in his name. We sell drugs in his name. We set bombs in his name. We worship him everywhere. We call him by different titles and commit blasphemies in the name of worship.

We were given magic to use in creating wonder, and the gobble-god has sucked it dry. His followers reject mystery and madness and marvel. They cannot tolerate questions. They can believe any answer, no matter how false, so long as it is a certainty nailed firmly onto the cross of money. They yearn for the rapture to come, without knowing they have killed rapture forever. Fidipur is what is to come, and the Holy One, Blessed be He, will not forgive mankind for that.

LATER

I called Fenoderee or Puck. I sat on the side of my bed and called them. Neither of them came. After a long, long time, I heard a faint, far voice calling my name. "Not enough," it said. "Not enough magic."

I may have trapped myself. If I am to try and get back, it must be now. There is nothing I can do to stop things. I've spent the last few days turning money into gold and gems—gems mostly, they're lighter—and what antique coins of the period the dealers have on hand. I made up a story about a costume party and had a couple of outfits made, plain, wool, fourteenth-century style, wimple, veils, shoes. It took me an hour to find this book and Mama's box and my cloak and boots where I'd hidden them when I moved into this apartment. I've sewn the gems into the seams of the cloak. I keep thinking I'm hearing things, someone here with me. Grumpkin is in my pocket with the coins. We're going to try.

24

EARLIER: LATER

I didn't think the first jump moved me at all. I was looking at my watch, thinking the date would have moved significantly. After a moment, I realized the first jump had only taken me back two minutes. I didn't look around. I was standing next to the desk where a previous me was sitting, writing, and I knew the other me was there, at the desk. I didn't dare look. I fixed my eyes on the floor and walked into the next room before I tried again. The second jump moved me four minutes, the third a little over eight. I hadn't been in the kitchen all evening, so I went in there in order not to run into myself. The fourth jump took me back half an hour. The fifth a little over two hours. I lost count of how many it took to get me to the sixteen hundreds where the magic was strong enough to bring me back all the way. The huge mound of Westfaire looms against the stars. The smell of magic is strong. The smell of trees is like wine. I'm going to lie down wrapped in my cloak and sleep. I'm very tired, very sore. I feel very old.

LATER: SHORTLY AFTER DAWN

I look very old, at least my hands and arms do. Luckily, I had a good haircut shortly before I left, and that seems to have stayed with me. So did my manicure, nail sealer, no polish. My new clothes fit. I haven't lost any more weight, at least. I'm just a nicely groomed, quite-old woman, miles from anywhere. I have no idea what year it is. Grumpkin was hungry so he caught a mouse or mole, something small and gray, and ate it. He didn't offer to share it. It's all right. I have protein crackers in my pocket, enough to last several days. Someone is bound to come along, sooner or later.

> *["She's back," I said inadequately.*
> *"So I see," said Israfel. He was as weary as I. "Do you think she'll go back there again?"*
> *"No. She's done everything she can do. You were right. It's grown into her. The two of them have become one thing, and she when she fought for it, she was fighting for her own life. I can't blame her. I'd have done the same."*
> *"What do we do now?"*
> *"Let her alone for a while. While we try to see what's going to happen next."*
> *"She looks very frail. I could send a cart, at least."*
> *"Do that. Send a cart."]*

ST. CYRIL'S DAY,
MAY, YEAR OF OUR LORD 1417

A cart came by midmorning, driven by a tinkerish sort of man, with a blowsy woman and several snot-nosed children along. I begged a ride, offering him a halfpenny, which he respected. I was glad of that, not wanting to use magic unless it was absolutely necessary. It was he, the tinker, who told me the year. Fifty years have passed since I was last here. Seventy since the curse fell on Westfaire. By the count of elapsed years, I am eighty-six. There must be some kind of rule in travel of this sort. It doesn't seem to be the lived time that counts, but some other chronological measure. I don't feel eighty-six. Or as I imagine eighty-six should feel!

Elly's daughter, my granddaughter, will be a middle-aged woman, possibly with children of her own. I will introduce myself as an elderly aunt. A wealthy, elderly aunt. Wealthy relatives are always easier to take. That is, if I can find her. If the little kingdom is still there. The tinker says there has been no plague for a considerable time. Still, there may have been a war. Indeed, there is a war. The war that was going on when I was a girl is still going on. The English against the French. Our King trying to take lands there, or reclaim lands there, or hold onto lands there. Their King trying to drive us out, or keep us out. One would think someone could put an end to it, though as I recall from references I picked up in the twentieth, it is to go on for decades yet.

Henry V is King. He will not be king long, poor boy. Edward III was King when I left in 1350. He was succeeded by his grandson, Richard II, and he by his cousin, Henry IV, and he by his son. This current King Henry will die of a flux of the bowels in France, and his son will die in the Tower, having spent a good deal of time, on and off, as a madman. However, Henry Five's widow will have a grandson who will be Henry VII, and it is all very interesting and complicated. I must be careful not to mention any of this lest I seem to prognosticate. According to the tinker, they are still burning poor old women whenever some busybody gets a gnat up her ass and thinks she's been bewitched. I must also be careful not to seem a Lollard. They are also burning Lollards. I'm not sure I remember what Lollards are. I mean, I know what they are but not the things one must not say if one doesn't want to appear to be one, and I am afraid to appear heretically ignorant if I ask.

The other interesting thing the tinker had to say is that the peasants have left the land and gone searching for better pay. I had read about that, but it all seemed frightfully unlikely. Now, here, seeing the vacant fields, I can tell it has really happened. The nobles have tried to put a stop to it, of course, but it's done no good. It used to be that a man could not leave the land, for there would be no place for him elsewhere. Every lord had his own serfs and little need for more. Now, however, the Black Death has killed so many that there are places begging for any good man. Well, I remember that from Wellingford, from the Dower House. It was hard, even then, to get anything done, and the Death has been back several times since then. Strange, isn't it. Men are more valued when there are fewer of us. Which is what I tried to tell them back in the twentieth. Which is what Puck said, too.

The tinker is a youngish man, but he has traveled these roads since he was a child. All Wellingford is empty now, he says. He does not know where the people went who used to live there. He remembers hearing of the King and Queen who were driven from their home over the seas, but he doesn't remember where that home might have been. He will take me within a very short distance of East Sawley Mill, which still stands, and there I will ask about to see if anyone remembers.

ST. JUSTIN, MARTYR,
FIRST DAY OF JUNE,
YEAR OF OUR LORD 1417

I got down from the cart in front of an inn. What passes for an inn in these times. Outside it, sitting on a bench, was a straight, slender old man chatting with a friend. When he saw me standing there in the road alone, he came forward to offer his assistance.

He looked at me for a long time. I felt dizzy from that look.

"Catherine?" he asked. "It is Catherine, isn't it?"

For a moment I didn't know him. When I did, I felt everything whirling, like a tornado of feeling, swirling me around with it. "Giles? Oh, Giles. Is it Giles? But, you're dead. They told me you were dead!"

He held me, and for that moment I was thirty again. My heart was as strong as it had ever been and that instant became an eternity for me. He wasn't dead. Giles wasn't dead. He knew me when he saw me, though I cannot imagine how. He called me by the name he knew me by, Catherine. He put his hand out to touch my face, and he smiled, as though he had expected me. He told me he had expected me every day for the past fifty years. He said he has thought about me every day during all that time, and he knew I was somehow his own lost Beauty come back to him.

I cried when he said this. I cry every time I think about it. We are of an age. He is still straight as a lance, though his stride is shorter than I remember and he does not see as well as once he did. His hair is as white as mine, but it is still full and soft and falls over his forehead as once it did. I wept and begged to know what had happened to him, and he told me a tale of being waylaid by an impress gang, one of whom he had killed, defending himself, before he was overpowered and dragged away. It was that man who had been buried beside the road.

I told him I had gone there and laid flowers on the place, and he laughed, saying I was the only one to grieve over that ruffian. Because the horse was there, with the king's arms upon it, the witness had not considered it might be one of the gang who had died rather than the man they had assaulted.

The impress gang was working for a merchantman who had a royal contract to carry supplies to France and not enough men to man the ships. They kept Giles for months, sailing back and forth across the channel, and when he escaped at last, I was gone. He had dwelt here about East Sawley since, he said, waiting for me to return, knowing that I would.

"If I'd known you were here, I'd have come long ago," I told him. And I would have. I'd have come long, long ago.

"After what had passed between us, no little wait

seemed at all worrisome," he said. "I have lived all my life in the memory of those three nights."

What can any woman say to that? I went into the privy behind the inn and wiped my face, telling myself I'd been a fool to go to the twentieth for vengeance sake when I could have stayed for love's sake, a fool to stay there for pride's sake, thinking there was anything I could do. But then, I never said I was not a fool.

When I spoke of them, Giles remembered the little royals, and he also remembered the name of their kingdom: Ponte Marvella, somewhere in the high mountains where Aragon and Navarre and France come together in a tangle. I told him about Elly marrying the prince and their having a daughter, my granddaughter. He says he will come with me to find her. Here we are, two old pots, though seemingly fairly hale for all that, going off over the seas. The boots would have taken us there in a moment, but now that he is with me we will travel as other persons do, to see the sights. Giles might not like the idea of the boots. Explanations would be complicated, and perhaps too risky. He loves me for what he thinks I am. So I will try to be what he thinks I am.

Giles has taken some of my smaller gems to turn into coin. He will hire a conveyance to take us to Bristol, a three day's journey. Once there, I can have a few more gowns made. The styles have changed somewhat. More people are speaking English, though it sounds very strange to me, because of all the accents clashing up against one another. Before the Death, no one traveled that much. Now everyone moves about, going and coming, here and there. The vowels slide about with the speakers, some say *ae* and some *ai* and some *ao*. It is almost easier to read lips. Giles says some years ago the Parliament attempted to make English the official language, but the lawyers all refused, saying they couldn't argue in it. Pish. Even in the twentieth they say that! They spend their careers making up words so no one will know what they're talking about! If lawyers had to write in plain English, nine-tenths of them would be out of work!

ST. BONIFACE'S DAY,
JUNE 5, YEAR OF OUR LORD 1417

Bristol. The only rooms we could find here are in the pilgrim hostel. There are no ships. King Henry has commandeered them all to carry his army to Normandy. There are pilgrims waiting who have been waiting for weeks, running about each time they hear a rumor that some new ship may have come into port. Remembering Papa, I said something to Giles about such travel being of little use, and he hushed me. Lollards disapprove of pilgrimage, and speaking so may make people think I am a Lollard. I asked Giles, in a whisper, what Lollards are, meaning what are they like, and he told me they are followers first of John Wycliffe, who translated the Bible into English, much to the annoyance of the priests, and later of Sir John Oldcastle, who was condemned for heresy but escaped the Tower and plotted against the King's life. Though his followers were caught and executed, the man himself remains at large.

As to what they believe, Giles says, to my dismay, they believe much as I do. They doubt the efficacy of the sacraments because they are magical, which is just what Puck said. Lollards read the scriptures in English, which I have done for years. They consider works to be as important as faith, and the pursuit of relics to be wasteful of money that could be used to relieve suffering. It is obvious I must not talk about religion or I will be taken as a heretic. I must be still and rather pious appearing. Giles is worried about me. I can tell from the way he strokes my hand when we sit outside the hostel in the evening, drinking a little watered wine and wondering if a ship will arrive tomorrow.

I remember the feelings we had on the terrace that night, that last night we were together. They are as clear in my mind as the sound of the bell from the monastery. I can remember each shudder of delight, each spasm of ecstasy, and yet my body sits calmly while I remember. My mind knows, but my body does not mind.

I told Giles what I was remembering and asked if he ever feels that urgency. He says he felt it last many years ago, remembering me. He remembers it still, sometimes, in dreams. In recent years, the greatest urgency he feels is early in the morning when he must get up quickly or risk wetting his bed.

Perhaps it was the way he said it. We laughed until our sides hurt.

CORPUS CHRISTI DAY

A procession in honor of the Blessed Sacrament came winding through the streets today. Outside the hostel a crazy woman had a fit when she saw it and had to be dragged away, screaming and yelling. I am told her name is Margery Kempe. In the twentieth they would probably give the poor thing tranquilizers and put her to bed, but in this time she is quite notorious. She goes on incessant pilgrimages, falling continually into these hysterical fits, and she has evidently been doing so for years. While there is no doubt she is seriously disturbed, she is also quite lucky about getting where she wants to go. At least, so Giles and I have been told. If we want to get to Aquitaine, it is suggested we keep close watch on Margery Kempe, as she will probably find a ship before the rest of us do. She wants to go to Santiago de Compostela, which is not far from where we want to go.

LATER

A ship has come in from Brittany and is loading for a journey to Coruna, in Spain. The madwoman has bought passage upon it, and so have we. Now the other pilgrims are muttering among themselves, plotting to keep the madwoman from embarking with us, as, so they say, her doing so is a sure invitation to disaster, storm at sea, shipwreck, and all manner of terrors. They have accused her of being a Lollard, so the authorities tell her she must go to Henbury to be examined by the bishop. The other pilgrims hope a wind will come up while she is gone, so they may depart without her.

LATER

Margery is staying with the bishop at his home in Henbury. Evidently he knew her father. There has been no wind.

THREE DAYS LATER

Still no wind. The pilgrims are beginning to regret their hostility. I heard one say today there would be no wind until Margery Kempe returned, that no matter what the pilgrims may think, God is with her.

LATER

We have been waiting ten days for wind. This morning Margery Kempe arrived, escorted by the bishop's retainers, and with her came a stiff breeze. There is no satisfying some people! Now the pilgrims assert she is a witch who can summon storm, and they threaten to throw her overboard if there is not a calm passage. I do not know what power Margery has, but I am tired of this nonsense. Mama taught me how to handle such matters. We will have a calm passage no matter how much I must weary myself in assuring so.

LATER

We have had four days of sailing south in light weather. Grumpkin has much enjoyed the ship. There has been good mousing, and the sailors approve of him heartily. The pilgrims have been put ashore here at

Coruna, where some will go overland and some will take smaller boats down the coast to the port slightly nearer Compostela. Once there, they will ascend into the city, into the great Romanesque church where they can kiss the statue of St. James and receive the title "Pilgrim to St. James." I know all about it. Papa described it to all of us, over and over. It was Santiago Matamoros that most interested Papa, St. James the Moor Killer. Poor Papa. He did want to do something brave and dedicated against the infidel, but it never really worked out.

I told Giles there was no hurry in finding my grandchild and asked him if he wanted to go to Compostela, but he said no. He is no more interested than I in parts of people's dead bodies, saints or not. Saints' bodies are supposed to be incorruptible, but Giles says he has seen mice dried up in a grain sack who were also uncorrupted. We giggle, like naughty children. Old people find odd things funny. He told me about a time during those years we were apart, when he was in Italy to pick up a cargo which included a crate of relics. He was sent to the workshop where they were created, and there he saw them making miraculous shrouds.

"The workman smeared a naked man with flaxseed oil and wine lees," he said, "then the man lay down on a linen strip and it was folded over him and patted gently to take the print of his face and body. Then they hauled him up, without messing the print on the cloth, and put the cloth in the sun. When it had been in the sun for a time, they brushed off the dry lees and it was like a painting."

"Who was he supposed to be?" I asked.

"Oh," said Giles, "he was all different saints. In the crate I took back to the ship there was one shroud of St. Stephen, with lots of arrow wounds painted on afterward, and at least half a dozen of Christ. It was enough to make a man sceptical."

Well, since he does not wish to go to Campostela, we will stay on the ship for another few days as it runs along the south shore of the Bay of Biscay to Bayonne, where we will disembark to begin our search for

Marvella. Bayonne, so everyone says, is as English as
Bristol. We have had it ever since Eleanor married
King Henry II, except for a brief time when the
French took it back during the long war, while I was
away. Despite our people being thoroughly familiar
with the area, they do not seem to be familiar with
Ponte Marvella. No one knows where it is. The captain
of this ship has heard of it, but he has never been
there. Certain other of the travelers aboard have
heard of it. They have never been there. Surely in one
of the larger ports near the mountains, someone will
know how we can reach the kingdom where my granddaughter must be, by now, a plump and contented matron. Unless she was long ago married off to some
petty kinglet. I hadn't thought of that before! She may
not be there at all! Well, if she is not, we will go where
she is. I hope it may be by horseback or in a carriage.
Otherwise, I must use the boots, and we are having
such a sweet and gentle time without.

JULY

While we search for someone to guide us to Marvella
(and our quest so far has met with no success), I am
enjoying seeing what is available in the shops. I have
bought a warm mantle woven from the fine wool of
Spanish sheep, as well as an illuminated book by one
Christine de Pisan, *The Treasure of the City of Ladies,*
which the bookseller highly recommends. He claims
that his copyist is unable to keep up with the demand
for this volume, though it is difficult to say why, since
it is directed at "princesses," by which the author
means the daughters of kings, princes, and dukes.
Though she spares a word for women of lesser rank
(including some of no rank at all!), her audience is to
be found mainly among the nobility. Perhaps there are
more of us than there seem to be. Or perhaps I have
not been traveling in the proper circles.

At any rate, Christine reminds me very much of
Miss Manners. I always read Miss Manners in the

twentieth. Christine explains how to be polite and
kindly and keep everyone happy and oneself in good
odor with the world. It is a pity it was not written until
a dozen years ago. If I had had this book in 1347, it
would have told me at once what Weasel-Rabbit was
up to.

SUMMER: ON THE ROAD
FROM LOURDES

I have lost track of what day it is. Not that it matters.
It is not so late in the season that I am concerned
about the onset of bad weather. The land we are traversing is hospitable and not unlike home. There are
fields and hedgerows and gentle rains and much bur-
geoning growth. We are ascending beside the torrent
of the Pau, having not long ago left the town and castle
of Lourdes, to turn toward the mountain called
"Lost," which, considering what we are going through
to find Marvella, is not badly named. Pica Perdido, it is
called. It is quite high, but we are not going to the top.

In Bayonne, we met with scepticism, not to say
outright doubt, when we told guides and equipage pur-
veyors that we wished to go to Ponte Marvella. No one
knew how to get there. We spoke of it in English; we
spoke of it in French. No one had ever been there.
Finally, as we were about to give up in despair during
the third or fourth day of quite concentrated effort—at
our age it takes concentration to keep doing things
over and over—a man presented himself to us and,
speaking with a strange accent, told us he could guide
us. He is, the French say, a Basque. His name is
Echevaria, or Eskavaria, or some such. He speaks a
language which no one else in the world speaks unless
that person is another Basque. It does not derive from
Latin, as does normal speech. It is not related to the
languages of the heathen. It has no words in common
with other European tongues. Eskavaria says it is the
language used by the angels when they helped God
make the world, the language of Eden, from which all

Basques came directly. He was laughing at me, of course. I thought of teaching him it is unwise to laugh at one who is half fairy, but he is pleasant enough otherwise, so why make a fuss. Besides, he is a very little man, not four feet tall. He reminds me of Bill except that he is less childlike. He is not a dwarf, as my father's fool was. He is simply very small.

As to what he was doing in Bayonne, he did not say. He did say we could take a carriage to the town of Lourdes, not a very great town in this century, on the River Pau. In Lourdes, the river becomes a torrent, plunging down from the heights of the mountains. There, he told us, we would take horses and ride up beside the plunging water toward the highest peak, the "lost one." It is named "lost" in Spanish, that is, Perdido, but not in Basque. In Basque they call it something else. Halfway up the mountain, we will turn aside, so he says, along a valley, and in that valley is the principality of Marvella.

"Not a kingdom?" I asked. I had thought the prince's father was a king.

"It's maybe ten miles long. It's maybe three or four miles wide," Eskavaria replied. "There's two villages and a castle. It has some cows, some sheep, some goats, a few horses. I don't know is it a kingdom, or a duchy, or something else. What I hear them call it is a principality. Whatever it is, it's very small."

"You have never been there," guessed Giles.

"True," said Eskavaria, "but I been close."

"Why haven't you gone there if you've been close?" Giles wanted to know.

Eskavaria shook his head and gave us a half smile. "Perhaps when you get close, you'll decide not to go there." It sounded almost like a recommendation.

Thus far we have done almost everything that Eskavaria has recommended. We took a carriage to Lourdes. Most of the time, Grumpkin rode on top, with the driver. We spent a day sightseeing in the town. The river is very dramatic, as is the new castle set high above it. The next day we bought five horses, three for us and two to carry our supplies, and the day after that we started up the mountain. Grumpkin rides in a basket on one of the packhorses. They are small animals, scarcely larger than ponies, but they are sturdy. Because they are small, they are easier for me to ride than a big horse would be. My legs don't bend as well as they used to. Sidesaddle is actually easier than astride. Except for that, we get along well enough, Giles and I. We are brittle. We ache. But we get along. The early morning is the hardest. That and trying to get comfortable in our blankets at night. Eskavaria is so small he curls up as Grumpkin does.

Days we simply ride, hearing the marmots whistle, hearing the rocks rattle as herds of chamois flee from our horses. The marmots are very curious. They stand on their hind legs and wriggle their noses at us as we pass. Grumpkin stares at them and yawns, thinking them too large for prey and too impudent for acquaintance.

LATER

I asked Eskavaria what day it was. He doesn't know. He neither reads nor writes. He says no one writes in his language. I recall reading of the Basques back in the twentieth, but I don't remember a thing about the language or the people. All I can recall is something about a separatist movement from Spain with some of the terrorism separatists seem to consider requisite. I asked Eskavaria if he had ever blown anyone up, and he seemed quite shocked at the idea.

I have been reading more of the *City of Ladies* book. Christine would have frowned on my love for Giles. She talks of foolish love affairs and says, "If it happens that some young princess or highborn lady is so lacking in knowledge or constancy that she is unable, does not know how, or does not wish to resist the appeals of the man who is trying to attract her by various signs and gestures (as men well know how to do) . . ."

The only sign Giles ever gave me was the love in

his eyes. The only sign I ever gave him was to blush when he looked at me, and for that Father Raymond sent him away. Christine would have approved of that. But she would not have approved of me. She has decided views on the conduct of virgins. When I was a virgin, I was argumentative and outspoken, which she deplores. I enjoyed eating entirely too much. And she says I should simply have relied upon Papa to have arranged a marriage for me, and should never have mentioned it to him or even have thought about it on my own. Her idea of a proper virgin is a bloodless one, I think. It's obvious that Christine de Pisan did not have Faery in mind at all when she wrote this book! That, or feminism.

I wonder what she would have done if a clock fairy and a putative angel had sunk some burning seed beneath her breast? Repudiated it, no doubt.

Oh, sometimes I wish I could.

LATER

About midmorning today we saw smoke rising over a ridge to our right. "Marvella," said Eskavaria, pointing.

"Do you speak their language?" I asked him, suddenly aware that we might not be able to communicate. Though that was a silly thought. I had communicated well enough with them when they were in England.

Eskavaria confirmed this. "They speak French," he said. "Or Spanish. Or English. They're not my people."

He left us at the ridge. Or rather, he stayed while we came on. He told us he would watch for us there, to guide us back. One day. Five. Ten. Whatever it took.

Giles thought it was strange he would not come with us.

As we started down into the valley, I smelled

magic, and knew why it was Eskavaria hadn't come. He might not know what it was, but he sensed the presence of it. This had a hot, wet smell, like metal doused in the forge. This was not merely magic, but something worse than that.

25

As we rode down into the valley, people looked up at us curiously from the fields. Some came to the road and wandered along beside us, feeling of our shoes, staring at the cat. We told the people we were travelers, going over the mountains to Spain. They spoke a kind of French-Spanish-English mix, which Giles and I could halfway comprehend, though evidently we did not speak it well enough to be clearly understood. Some of our followers ran on to tell others, and soon we had a crowd of them at our heels. Peasant people, ordinary people. Several quite good looking men. No women more than ordinary in appearance. A boy herding geese. A girl with a piglet in her arms. Men who had been cutting hay.

We asked if there were somewhere we could stay for the night. They pointed. We looked up to see the castle perched above us, on a crag. Oh no, we said, we're just ordinary travelers. And they smiled and pointed, pushing us, leading us, dragging the ponies along. Evidently we were to go there, like it or not. I looked at Giles, seeing nothing in his face but pleasant expectation. There was sweat along my forehead, next to my hair, but I kept smiling. Looking back the way we had come, I realized we could have seen the castle all along. If we had been looking for it.

I leaned over and whispered to Giles. "When we

are asked for our names, old friend, do not be surprised at what I say."

He gave me a curious look, but nodded. I had originally planned to introduce myself as Lady Catherine of Monfort, the name I had used when negotiating Elly's marriage. Now, something told me it would be better not to claim any former acquaintance with the prince or his daughter. Not until I knew how things stood.

The climb was a hard one. The ponies were sweating heavily when we arrived. Someone rang a bell at the high wooden gates. Someone kissed my hand and gave me a flower. Then they were gone, off down the hillside, chattering with one another, pleased at having delivered us. The gate opened and we were welcomed within. A chamberlain saw to us. He and a couple of serving men. He spoke French, and so did we. He asked if the cat could be taken to the stable, and I said no, it would stay with me. He asked if we were man and wife, and when I said not, he sniffed and escorted us to separate rooms. He told us the servants would bring bathwater. He said the Princess would welcome us at supper.

I laid my hand on his arm as he was ready to depart and said, "A moment. Long ago, I believe I met the ruling family of your realm." It seemed a neutral word, realm, since I did not know what kind of place it was. "The prince had just come of age. It was in England."

He raised his eyebrows at me.

"Is that family still here?"

"Prince Charme?" he asked.

I smiled.

"And his consort," the chamberlain said. "Princess Ilene." He said it *Ee-lay-nay*.

"His daughter?" I asked.

"He has no daughter," the man said.

"Never? Never had a daughter?"

"No children. Not in twenty years," he said. "I have been here that long."

"I am mistaken then," I smiled, trying not to weep.

"It was another family." How many Prince Charmings could there be? More than one, obviously.

The chamberlain was as good as his word about the bathwater, and I soaked in the heat of it, letting it take away some of the soreness of the long ride. He sent a maid to see to our clothes. I had already hidden my cloak and boots away, under the bed. I wanted no foreign maidservants playing about with those. When time came for the meal, he sent a footman to escort us down the stairs and into the hall of the castle. Not the great hall, which we passed through on the way, but a smaller one, paneled in dark wood, with numerous candles, a fire blazing, and many trophies of the hunt hung in the high shadows near the cross-beamed ceiling. A dozen men and women, earls of this and countesses of that, introduced themselves and asked us about our journey. Though some of the men were quite handsome, all of the women were remarkably plain. The chamberlain came to the door and announced His Serene Highness, Prince Charme of Marvella; Her Serene Highness, Princess Ilene. We wouldn't use their names, of course. They would be called, "Your Highness, this," "Your Highness, that." She might be called "ma'am." They made their way slowly across the room toward us, stopping to speak to each of the other guests as they came. Each man bowed deeply, each woman curtsied.

He was much as I remembered him, sweet-faced, rather feminine-looking, though he now had a little gray beard and moustache to cover his gentle mouth and a little tummy to cover his gemmed belt. He was considerably fatter, much softer looking, much, much older. His eyelids made sad little swags of wrinkled flesh, hiding his eyes.

She was taller than he, very regal, very handsome, with a strange, exotic beauty, like a tiger. No. More like a serpent. Sleek. Also deadly. Her hair was dark, rising from a widow's peak to make a double bow of her forehead, a line completed by her pointed chin to make a narrow heart shape. She wore a close fitting gown of blood-colored damask. Her face could have

been twenty-five, her body younger yet. Her eyes were
several hundred. I thought of Queen Mab and knew
that what I saw was not what was really there, then I
carefully blanked out that thought and assumed the
much excited smile of an elderly woman who was, oh,
gracious mercy, right here in the room with royalty
and all.

They came up to us. I curtsied. Lord, how long had
it been since I had curtsied? My old bones barely
made it. Giles bowed. He did it very nicely. He'd had
more practice than I, so much was obvious. The chamberlain announced the names we had given. Lady Lavender of Westfaire. Sir Giles of Sawley. It no longer
mattered what people called me. Beauty. Dorothy.
Catherine. Lavender. I'll be borrowing Aunt Comfrey's name next. Though I had no sure reason why, I
urgently did not want this woman to know who I really
was. Or what I really was.

"We are pleased to welcome you to Marvella,"
said the Prince. His wrinkled eyelids rose, exposing his
tender soul. Like a quivering oyster.

"We are greatly pleased to be so charmingly welcomed," I murmured. "We had not expected such hospitality."

"We have so few visitors," purred the Princess.
"So little news of the outside world." She looked me
up and down, noting the good though plain fabric of
my gown—one of those I'd had made in Bristol before
we left—the simplicity of my wimple and veil. I knew
how I looked. Inoffensive. Her eyes cleared. I was an
acceptable dinner guest and nothing to worry about.
She gave Giles a quick look and dismissed him, as
well. Too old, her eyes said. Not worth the effort.

I felt his hand tremble on my arm. He had caught
her look, and it angered him. Well, it had angered me,
as well.

We were seated near the middle of the long table,
guests but not honored guests. So much the better. I
would not have enjoyed conversing with the Princess.
Or with the Prince. We ate a salmi of duckling, fresh
fruit, roast venison, bananas (grown, so the Prince

said, in the conservatory), salad, river salmon, and finally a soup of almonds and chicken and lemons. I asked my table companion to my left, an aged baron, if dinners in Marvella always ended with soup and was told that they did. "Always with something warm and liquid, to fill any holes previously unfilled, my dear." I remembered a dinner I had eaten when I was young, in Chinanga, with Don Masimiliano. Had that been any less real than this?

We drank wine. I watered mine and kicked Giles, on my right, until he watered his. My left-hand companion was watching me closely, and I murmured something about no longer having the head for wine we had had in our younger years. He was as white headed as I, so we talked about that.

"I've outlived all my generation," he mumbled. "Charme's father, Prince William, was younger than I by a couple of years, but I outlived my half brother."

I had heard his name and title, but had not made the connection. "You're His Highness's uncle," I said. "I'm sorry, I didn't realize . . ."

"Nothing to realize. Uncles don't count for much. Especially half uncles. Prince William was my younger half brother. Our mother was a widow when she married Charme's grandfather, Prince Enrico. No, no," he waved the young squire away who was trying to pour more wine into his cup. "Go give it to the Prince, he needs it worse than I."

I decided to risk it. "I met the His Highness's parents. Years ago, in England."

"During the Usurpation," he nodded, putting a capital letter on it. "The usurper was my older brother, Richard. Richard and I were never in the line of succession, but Richard liked to pretend to have royal blood. Mama didn't have that. All she had was wealth she'd inherited when our father died. We were babies when Mama married Prince Enrico. Then she bore William, the heir apparent. Richard and I more or less grew up with William. He was the only proper heir, but after Prince Enrico died, Richard stirred up a bunch of malcontents and overthrew the throne.

"William and his wife and the boy fled to England. After they'd been gone a while, and after Richard started passing tax laws right and left, everyone here in Marvella realized what they'd allowed to happen, so they hanged Richard from a gibbet down in the market square and begged William to come home. He did, him and his wife and Prince Charme and the little girl. I felt very lucky to keep my neck unstretched, though everyone knew I'd told Richard he was a fool."

"Little girl?" I asked, trying to keep my voice only politely interested while my heart thudded away in a fit.

"Charme's daughter. Galantha. Beautiful little girl," he sighed. "She was about ten when William died. Charme ascended the throne, of course, and everyone was after him to get married again and produce an heir. Put it off a couple of years before he finally married Ilene. Not long after that the little girl got lost in the mountains. Eaten by beasts, they say. No one mentions her anymore, as hearing her name upsets His Highness."

"He's been married to Ilene for how long?" I asked. Giles, next to me, was listening to this conversation with great interest.

"Oh, it would be thirty-some-odd years now, wouldn't it? He was twenty or so when he came back. Around thirty-two when he ascended the throne. He must be seventy now. I'm almost ninety, which is a dreadful great age for a man."

"His wife looks very young," I said, casually, as though it didn't matter.

"Holds her looks," he agreed. "I'm told her family always has held its looks."

"A neighboring kingdom?" I suggested.

He snorted. "Marvella has no neighboring kingdoms, Lady Lavender. Except maybe Nadenada, and it's not really neighboring. We're a what-you-call-it, a holdover, a survival. Some crusader did a favor for the King of Aragon, I think it was, or maybe the King of Navarre. Whoever-it-was rewarded him by making him hereditary Prince of cowplop and sheepclip. The

main road over the mountains is that way," and he
waved toward the west, opposite to the direction we'd
arrived from. "People used to have to hire porters to
carry them down into the gorge, across the river, then
up the other side. Prince William used Mama's money
to build a marvelous bridge across the gorge, and now
Ponte Marvella makes its living charging tolls. From
pilgrims, mostly. Going down from France to Santiago." He sighed heavily. "I told Richard when he
started all the fuss that if he wanted to risk his life
taking over something, it should at least be something
worth taking. Marvella isn't much."

I saw Ilene's eyes fixed on my aged informer, a tiny
frown between her brows. He was talking too much,
too intently, so I laughed with great vivacity, as though
he had told me a funny story. Her glance went on past,
like the course of a comet, burning ice.

We drank wine. We ate fruit and nuts. We retired
to another room and played at cards for a time. The
cards were from Germany and were printed, unlike
the painted ones I was accustomed to in that time. The
Prince enthusiastically told me how it was done, how
the blocks of wood were carved and then painted with
ink and pressed onto the paper. I wondered if
Gutenberg was at this moment playing at games and
being inspired by the unknown carver of playing cards.
Printing would be invented very shortly, and one thing
always led to another. I put the thought down resolutely and paid attention to my hand.

We learned a Spanish game in which players put
together "bodies," that is combinations of six cards
making up a head, two arms, two legs, and a torso, and
then cried *"Hombre"* to the others as they put down
the man entire. It wasn't unlike rummy, which I had
played with Bill in the twentieth, so I learned it rapidly. Giles caught on very quickly, too, and I was glad
to see that he had the same sense I did that it would
not be wise for either of us to win anything at all from
the Princess.

Christine de Pisan hadn't covered the subject of
manners around royalty, but Aunt Lavender had. No

one could leave until the Prince and Princess left, and
they seemed determined to spend the night taking everyone's money. At last the Prince yawned, everyone
stood up, and the royal couple departed. One of the
earls fluttered about settling accounts. I paid what we
had lost, only enough to be polite, no large amount. I
said good night to the baron, my dinner companion,
who was half asleep in his chair by the fire, then Giles
and I went up to our rooms, where yawning servants
waited our arrival and tankards of wash water steamed
gently before the fires. I told the maidservant she
could go on to bed, that I'd take care of myself after I
had taken my cat out. She did not like to let me go
alone, but I insisted, and when she had gone I put on
my cloak, with Grumpkin in the pocket, and let myself
out an unlocked side door.

I waited about near the stables while Grumpkin
found a place that suited him. When he had finished,
he went back in my pocket while we strolled about,
seeing what was to be seen. All the lights in the castle
were out except in one squatty tower, which was so
close to the precipice it seemed to hang over it, like a
vulture perched on a branch. The tower abutted the
flat roof of the castle, so I slipped on the boots—when
I wasn't wearing them, I habitually kept them in the
deep pocket of my cloak—and went there in one step,
interested in knowing who was still up, and why.

The room opened upon the roof through a case-
ment window which stood ajar. Inside the Princess sat
at a table brushing her hair. Her maid was putting her
clothes away in the press. When the maid had finished
with the clothing, she poured a cup of wine for her
mistress and went away, shutting the heavy door behind her. The Princess got up and bolted the door.
Interesting, I thought, wondering what interruption
she feared. Certainly none from Prince Charming. I
had seen no indication he would be inclined to invade
her privacy. He had scarcely looked at her during the
evening.

After a time the Princess stood up, walked to the
far side of the room, and removed a veil or hanging of

some kind. I saw her hand pulling the veil away, but I
could not see what it had covered.

I inched closer to the low, crenelated parapet,
which was the only thing between me and the valley
floor, a quite dangerous distance below. By craning my
neck, I got a better view of her. She was standing naked in front of a tall mirror with wiverns carved about
the frame. I had never seen a mirror that size in the
fourteenth or fifteenth. I didn't know they could make
flat glass that size. The Princess put her hands out,
beautiful hands, then stroked them down her face, and
intoned:

> *"Lord within the glass, declare!*
> *Lord, who holds my beauty thrall:*
> *you have made me passing fair;*
> *am I fairest of them all?"*

A face formed in the glass. A dark face. Not dark
in the sense of color, but dark in the sense of being
hidden. It did not really show itself. It merely hinted at
being. Despite this, I recognized it. It was Jaybee's
face. Not precisely his, but the paradigm of what his
face was and meant in its totality. Seeing it, I could
say, "This is the pattern from which Jaybee's face was
made." When the voice came, it matched the face, full
of a mocking, horrid laughter.

> *"One time you were, and then were not,*
> *but now are fairest once again,*
> *while she whose beauty is forgot*
> *sleeps on among her little men.*
> *Snow white of skin, and black of hair,*
> *with gentle lips flushed sweetly red;*
> *full long has she lain sleeping there,*
> *with all believing she is dead."*

The Princess made a gesture, a stroking of herself,
breast to hip, approving herself. She tilted her head, to
get a better look at the line of her throat. "Full long

she sleeps," she cried in a jubilant voice. "Oh, long time, yes. And will, forever."

In the mirror the dreadful being smiled and glanced my way. I gasped. Beneath my breastbone something flared into life, aware of deadly danger. My foot slipped on the roof, making a sound. The Princess whirled, like a great hunting creature, eyes wide, ears pricked. "Boots," I whispered, "take me to my room."

I was there! I slipped the cloak beneath the bed and myself into it with Grumpkin beside me, pulling my wimple off as I snuggled down, so my white old locks would show. I let the candle burn so she could see me there plainly. I shut my eyes, knowing she would come. Oh, yes, she would come down from her tower to see who had been spying on her. And she would come faster than any ordinary old woman could have come down all those stairs, thinking to find my room empty and me on the way. . . .

She was quick! The door opened. Someone peered in. I turned, as though sleepily, saying, "Whaa?"

The door closed, and she was gone. She believed someone had been outside her room, but she didn't know who. Down the hall, I heard her open Giles's door. And then close it. He really was asleep. I let time pass, scarcely breathing, pretending sleep. She might be watching. She might be hovering outside my window, like an owl. The candle burned to a smoky stub and guttered out.

Would she let it go at that? Would she ask that thing in the mirror who'd been spying on her?

More important, could it tell her?

"Fenoderee," I whispered, "I need a friend."

He slipped into bed beside me, yawning. "I thought you'd never ask," he said. His sickle rattled upon the floor. "Oh, you do need a friend, Beauty. Nastiness here. And you've got old Carabosse half sick with worry."

"Worse than mere worry," said a voice on the other side. Puck.

"What's going on here?" I said. "Who is Ilene?"

"A witch," said Puck, matter-of-factly. "She signed

one of the usual witch contracts with the Dark Lord, her soul and body in return for being young and beautiful for a few hundred years. Of course, he threw a trick into it. He always does."

"A trick?"

Fenoderee nodded; I could feel his head going up and down on the pillow. "Ilene remains beautiful only so long as there is no other female in the kingdom as beautiful as she. She started out in quite a large kingdom, had to dispose of quite a lot of pretty girls, and the word got around. They came after her with hayforks and torches, the Transylvanian kind you use on monsters, you know? So she moved to a smaller kingdom, and then one smaller yet. Here in Marvella, there weren't all that many beauties to start with, and the last one she had to do away with was Galantha."

"Galantha?" I asked.

"Galantha. That little springtime flower, the white one that droops its head."

"Snowdrop?"

"That one, yes."

What a really odd name for a child! Hadn't one fairy tale been enough? Of course, that bit with the mirror had been a dead giveaway. Magic collects magic, Carabosse had said. "My granddaughter?" I asked, trying to disbelieve but not succeeding one whit.

"That's right," said Fenoderee. "Your granddaughter."

"Who isn't really dead!"

"No. Ilene tried, but she couldn't kill Snowdrop. She sent a huntsman to kill her, and he couldn't. She tried a cursed lace, then a poisoned comb, and that didn't work. Snowdrop is one-eighth fairy, after all. Witches can't be allowed to go around killing off fairies, even part ones. No, though Ilene tried several times to get Snow taken care of, everything failed except the apple."

"The apple?" I started to ask. There was a sound outside in the corridor, and my bed was suddenly empty of anyone but me and Grumpkin. The door opened, and I heard Giles whispering to me.

"Beauty? Catherine? Lavender? Are you all right?"

He came in and crouched on the bed beside me. We whispered together as I told him part of what I had seen. It took very little talk between us to decide this place was dangerous and that we wanted to be elsewhere. The Dark Lord had seen me, or sensed me, or at least caught a glimpse of me, so much was clear. What I wasn't sure of was what else he'd seen. In that moment the thing had flared up within me, and I'd felt like a lantern, throwing light in all directions. Had the thing in the mirror seen that?

"How did you get up there?" Giles asked me wonderingly, not waiting for an answer. "I'm not sure we can get out. There's a guard asleep downstairs in the hall, and another one walking up and down outside in the courtyard. And if she has some kind of captive spirit in that mirror. . . ."

I hadn't told him what was really in the mirror, but I was quite sure it wasn't captive.

"We'll get out," I said grimly. "As far as the stables, anyhow."

I had Giles fetch his clothing from his room. I fetched mine out of the press. I put on the boots, held Giles tightly around the waist, with our baggage tied helter skelter and Grumpkin squashed between us, and said, "Boots, take us to the stables."

And there we were, standing beside the horses, an arrival which startled the horses almost as much as it startled Giles. I told him there was no time to explain, and he subsided unwillingly, full of questions we had no time for. Still, he had his wits about him sufficiently to suggest that we tie some sacks around the horses' feet, so their hooves wouldn't make a noise on the cobbles. We waited until the guard moved around the corner, then made a dash for it. Once we were past the courtyard (the gate wasn't even shut and there was no drawbridge), the road was mostly soft dust. We went down through the dark village, silent as mice, then up the other side. When we got to the top of a long rise, we saw a little campfire, and there was Eskavaria sitting beside it, waiting for us.

"Have you been here all along?" I asked.

"Thought you might not stay very long," he said. "Thought I'd take you along to spend the night with my brothers and me."

He wouldn't have thought of that on his own. Who had told him to stay? Puck? Still running errands for Carabosse? I didn't ask.

He brought our packhorses out of the shadows, mounted his own, and we went along through the starlight, with him humming a little song and the water making an accompaniment to it. We wove through rocks and trees. Once he got down and moved a log behind us, hiding the way. We came to the top of a long slope and could see below us the bulk of a house with windows faintly outlined in firelight.

Eskavaria looked up at the stars. "Midnight," he said. "Time we get under cover."

"What happens at midnight?" Giles asked.

"If she knows you're gone, she may come looking for you then," the little man answered, and we trotted down the long slope toward the house beneath the trees. A stable stood next to it, with a door connecting the two. We were beneath the stable roof when we heard the scream from above, a long, shrill cry that was not an owl.

Giles started to go out and look. Eskavaria grabbed his arm and held him. "No," he said. "Never look up when you hear that cry, or she may see you. Faces show up in the dark more than hair or hats do." Then he led us through the door.

It was a simple house, though larger than it had looked from outside, with one big room downstairs and a large open loft. The brothers, all six of them, were asleep up there. None of them were any bigger than Eskavaria. I could tell from the size of the beds. If not dwarves, they were not far from it. I thought of the "little men" the Dark One had mentioned, and knew these were they.

"You know where my granddaughter is," I challenged him.

"I know where someone is. How can I be sure she is your granddaughter?" he challenged me in return.

I couldn't think of an answer. I was very tired. I hurt all over, and I started to cry. Once started, I couldn't stop.

Giles shouted angrily, "Now see what you've done. Damn it, Esky, she's tired! She's come all this way to find her granddaughter, and you say a thing like that!"

This woke up the family, and they all came down, rubbing their eyes and asking what was going on. Among themselves they spoke the other language, Euskara. Evidently other people call them Basques, but they call themselves the Euskaldunak, which gives you a hint as to what the language sounds like. Except for an occasional word that sounded rather Latinish, I couldn't understand any of it, though the tone of the conversation was decidedly argumentative. There was a great deal of pointing up and making the horn sign and staring at us with a mixture of intense curiosity and obvious distrust.

I don't think there was ten year's difference in age from Esky, the youngest, to the oldest. The older ones had beards, the older the longer. Evidently they never trimmed them. The younger three or four were clean shaven. Esky told us all their names, and I promptly forgot them. Couldn't pronounce them, in any case. Not Sneezy. Not Grumpy. My eyes were falling shut. Next thing I knew, they were spreading some quilts on the floor and I was being invited to lie down and sleep.

I didn't wait for a second invitation.

When I woke, hours and hours later, it was full daylight and the house was empty. The door was open. I could hear horses champing away in the stables and the buzz of flies. Otherwise, silence.

I sat up and fumbled with my hair. Giles must have heard me, for he came in from outside, bringing me a cup of something warm. Broth, I finally decided. With some kind of very fine grain cooked in it. Almost like grass seed. I leaned back against a nearby bench and drank it. Or chewed it. It needed salt.

Giles suggested, very sweetly, that since we had a few moments to ourselves, I explain to him what was going on. I did so, mostly. I told him my mother was a fairy, without dwelling on what that made me, and I said she'd given me certain fairy gifts. I said an inimical force was sort of following me around. I didn't mention Jaybee. I couldn't bear to tell him about Jaybee. In Giles's mind, I was Beauty and I was Catherine, both at once, and they were not necessarily the same person. He could accept that Elly had been Edward's child, and Galantha was somehow my granddaughter, without giving up his belief that his first love, Beauty, still virgin and pure, was asleep at Westfaire. I was her, and I wasn't her, so to speak. He had no trouble believing Galantha had been wickedly enchanted by a witch. He believed in witches. In those times, everyone believed in witches.

"I've been to see her," Giles said, looking at his feet.

"Her?"

"Your grandchild. Galantha."

I started to get up. He pushed me back, very gently. "She looks almost like she's asleep, Beauty. Very pale, but not . . . you know, not rotted or anything. They've put her in a kind of case, so nothing will chew on her. I don't think she's dead."

Giles had never seen Disney. This time I did get up.

"I want to see for myself," I said, pulling the pins out of my hair and trying to find my comb. Giles found it for me and helped me braid up my white locks. When I had the wimple pinned tightly, my veil on and my kirtle smoothed out, he led the way outside.

We went up a gentle hill, not the one we had come down the night before, and through a bit of forest, down a much used path, and into the gaping entrance of a mine. She was lying well back inside, in an area lit by torches. The case looked more like a reliquary than anything else, bits of rock crystal and faceted gems pieced together with gold to make a domed lid in a design of flowers and leaves. The leaves were emeralds, I thought. Or maybe jade. Through the flatter, clearer bits I could see her, only a child, twelve or thirteen, perhaps. She was very beautiful, rather like the child Elizabeth Taylor, in that horse movie they always showed late at night on TV in the 1990s. She was incorruptible, as saints' bodies are supposed to be. I thought of Giles and my conversation about mice and shrouds and laughed at myself.

Then I sat down beside the case and let some tears run, not many. After a while, Esky and one of his brothers came in and asked if I'd like the case opened. I said yes, and they unbuckled it at one side and laid the top back. She lay on a satin mattress, with a satin coverlet over her, her hands folded on her breast. She was dressed very simply, in a full white shift with puffy sleeves and a kind of laced bodice over it. Disney had got that part right.

The other brothers came from deeper in the mine, setting their tools down to one side and seating themselves on chair sized stones, one for each of them. From the wear on those stones, I could tell they had sat there like this time and again for years.

Giles took a deep breath. "She looks just like you," he said to me. "When I first saw you."

I looked at the child, considering. She looked something like Elly and something like her father, but a good deal like me. As though I'd passed on my own looks, skipping a generation. Her hair was black, of course, and mine had been gold, but otherwise, we looked much the same.

I nodded. Esky reached out to touch the bones of my cheeks and jaw and nodded. "I see it," he said.

He could see more than I, then, but his brothers all nodded, telling each other how much the child resembled me. The resemblance, whether fancied or real, seemed to allay their suspicions.

"How?" I asked, motioning at them, her, everything, meaning "How did it happen?"

Esky sighed. "One day we heard this screaming

noise, so we went to see what it was. This big huntsman was down on his knees, crying. He said Princess
Ilene had told him she'd kill him unless he took this
little girl into the woods and murdered her. He
couldn't do it. He said he was going to kill a deer and
take its heart back instead. Then he went off and left
the child behind. It was getting dark. Wolves was
howling. We couldn't leave her there. We took her
along home. She was a sweet, pretty girl. Not much
sense, but sweet." He wiped his face with his hand,
sighing.

"Well, some time went by. We got used to having
her around. At first she couldn't do nothing useful. We
taught her. Cookery a little. Gardening a little. If I tell
the truth, Lady Catherine, all of us lusted after her
even though she was just a child. With all of us living
here, we agreed we'd behave decent. We may be her-
mits, so to speak. We may not be very civilized, but
our ma raised us to be decent folk. Right then, we
should have took her over the mountains into Spain.
Or took her back to Lourdes, we could have did that.
Truth is, none of us travels much, except me, and I
didn't want her to go. She was so pretty. . . ."

He rose and went out of the cave. The brothers
muttered among themselves, in their own language.
No one said anything I could understand. After a time,
Esky came back, his face wet.

"So one day we came home and seen her lying
there on the floor. We picked her up and seen her
bodice was laced up tight. It was a new lace."

One of the brothers interrupted, and Eskavaria
nodded to him.

"That's right, a silk lace, one we hadn't seen before. So we unlaced her, and she caught her breath, all
of a sudden. We asked her what happened. She told us
a peddler woman come by. Well, we knew then what
happened. The witch knew she was here."

The little men nodded, agreeing this is the way it
had been.

"Gally wasn't real quick," Esky went on. "All of us
knew that. Even so, we thought since it happened

once, she'd know next time. We told her no more peddler women . . .''

Another interruption, discussion, nodding of
heads.

Eskavaria nodded. "That's right. No more visitors,
no one. We said stay in the house until we come home.
We said then we'd walk with her if she wanted to pick
flowers or something.

"Well, wasn't a whole week passed before we
come home and there she is again. All limp on the
floor. We thought she was dead. We picked her up,
and then a comb fell out of her hair, and she woke up.
It was another peddler woman. Talked her way
around the child, like the first time.

"So we knew we couldn't trust her alone. Right
then we should have took her over the mountains, fast.
We didn't do that. We decided that one of us would
stay with her, to protect her. Then that didn't seem
decent, so we said two would stay, to keep an eye on
each other along with her. And that went along for
quite a long while. . . .''

He turned to his brothers and asked them a question in their own language. They argued for a moment,
then responded. "Almost a year," he went on. "It was
almost a year. Then one day Euskaby found a big gem
deposit back in the mine with a rock in front of it. Big
rock. All of us had to move it. Maybe an hour we left
her, but when we got back she was on the floor again.
This time was no lace, no comb. We undressed her,
took everything off, looked at everything, put everything back. We combed her hair. We cleaned her fin-
gernails and toenails. We looked in her mouth, in her
nose and ears. Nothing.''

"The witch said it was an apple," I said. "I overheard her." It hadn't been the witch who who had said it,
but I wasn't about to explain about Fenoderee and
Puck.

"If it was an apple, it's inside her belly," said Esky.
"There's no way to get it out of her with her living."

And he was perfectly right, of course, in the fifteenth. In the twentieth, it would be minor surgery.

But if I took her to the twentieth, I might not be able
to get back. Or, if I got back, too much time might
have passed, and I might never see Giles again. I
sighed and bit my lip and decided not to decide, not
just yet.

"We're still within the borders of Ponte Marvella,
right?" I asked.

They talked it over and decided that we probably
were right on the border, not really in, not really out.

"Then we need to get her out," I said. "Once we're
outside Marvella, maybe the witch won't bother us,
and we can decide what to do. I don't think my granddaughter's dead. Not really. Perhaps there's a way to
remove the enchantment." In the story it was a
prince's kiss, wasn't it? Or was that only my own
story? Or was it Disney? I simply couldn't remember!

More argument. They weren't sure they believed
me. I wasn't sure it was true. Esky waved his hands
and shouted. Eventually they agreed. Two or three of
them were crying. One thing they did agree upon.
Daytime was the time to move. Nights were dangerous.

So we started out. Galantha's coffin was bound
about with ropes and slung between the two
packhorses. Our supplies went on Esky's horse. All
seven of the little men came along, to be sure we got
out safely, Esky said, but I think they simply were unwilling to let her go. She had become something more
to them than a sleeping little girl. They decided the
safest thing to do was to go down the south side of the
mountains into Spain, since we were nearest the south-
ern border of Marvella. Also, we had to avoid the toll
bridge the baron had told me about. If the Princess
wanted to stop our leaving, that bridge would be
watched.

The idea was good, but the trails were simply not
wide enough for the two horses with the coffin between. This became obvious very quickly, and a shouting match broke out among the little men. Two of
them kept pointing to the ropes and screaming at two
others. I could read their faces if not their words.

"You didn't tie it right. It's all your fault." And the others: "You don't know a damned thing about knots. What do you mean it wasn't tied right?" It went on far too long, and Giles stopped it by bellowing at them, dismounting, untying the coffin, opening it, wrapping the girl in the satin coverlet, and taking her up in his arms. She was as stiff as an image carved from wood. In a way that was a relief. I had worried myself over what the little men might have been doing with her in that mine, all those years. They had done nothing, obviously, that they could not have done as well with an image carved from stone.

The little men muttered at Giles's picking her up, but decided to allow it. Still, they insisted on bringing the coffin along, the bottom and top tied separately onto the backs of two of the horses. It had been made with love, care, and endless hours of labor. The gems and gold alone were worth a fortune, not to speak of the workmanship. It was their gift to their Snowdrop, and they weren't going to abandon it. I shook my head at Giles, and he subsided with a growl.

After a time, we worked out a processional order that worked fairly well. Esky went first with one of his brothers, leading one packhorse, then Giles, then me, then the horses with the coffin led by two brothers, then the other little men coming along single file. We went up for a time, then abruptly down. Giles asked Esky where we were going.

The little man was breathing hard. "There's a place we can get across the gorge and onto the road to Santiago," he said.

Giles looked at me and shrugged. It looked like we were going to St. James's shrine whether we wanted to or not. I wondered if we would run into Margery Kempe. After that, I tried not to wonder anything or think anything except about hanging on. Riding a horse uphill is difficult. Riding a horse downhill is exhausting.

Night came. The little men went off in all directions, looking for a camp site, finding one at last under an overhanging ledge of stone where we could not be

seen from the sky. I thought perhaps they were being
overcareful. We must have come far from Marvella by
this time. Then, late in the darkness, I was awakened
by the same cry we had heard the night before.
Around me I could hear indrawn breaths, silence. The
horses stopped munching outside among the trees. After a time the cry came again, far away to the north,
echoed by the howling of wolves. The little men began
to breathe once more.

"What was it?" I asked Eskavaria.

"Night lammergeier," he said, not meeting my
eyes. The lammergeier are huge vultures of the
Pyranees, sometimes called "bone-breakers" because
of their habit of dropping large bones from great
heights to shatter them and get at the marrow. Ordinarily, I believe, they do not fly at night. I thought it
wisest not to pursue the matter.

Midmorning, this morning, we came to the road to
Santiago. The road is wide enough that the coffin can
be slung between two horses once more. My granddaughter is in it. Eskavaria is leading the packhorse.
His brothers have faded back amongst the trees, tears
running down their faces. A traveler we met coming
up from Spain tells us today is the fifteenth of August.
We have time yet to get to Compostela before fall.

ST. HELENA'S DAY, AUGUST,
YEAR OF OUR LORD 1417

We have traveled for several days on the downward
road, very slowly because of the coffin, seeing no living
things except an occasional herd of ibex, a few skulking foxes, or the ubiquitous marmots. Then, this morning, shortly after we began our journey for the day, we
came upon a large party of noble men and women
together with their servants, all camped among their
wagons beside the road. It appeared they might have
spare mounts, and Giles went to see if he could purchase a packhorse to carry the supplies carried by

Esky's mount. Esky had been walking, and it had slowed our progress somewhat.

Several of the young men came over to us where we waited, looking us over in an insolent manner, until they saw the coffin itself. Then they became quiet. One of them, a boy scarcely fourteen or fifteen years old, pressed his face to one of the transparent bits of crystal and peered within. I thought it best, since he was surrounded by his fellows, not to antagonize him or cause any notice by using enchantment. I had seen similar gangs of young men, though not noble young men, in Bayonne, where they were said to roam the streets at night, seeking unprotected young women they might rape and ruin. It was a kind of game with them, and the insolence of these young nobles seemed also a game: cockiness pushed to its limits.

The coffin-peering youngster stood up, very arrogantly, and asked me who she was.

"My granddaughter, child," I said, unthinking.

One of the other young men started toward me, angrily, but another courtier, a very handsome, slightly older young man, put out his hand and said softly, "The young man who addressed you is Prince Edward. Fourth son of King Zot of Nadenada."

I bowed, as best I could from atop my little horse. "Your Highness," I said to the arrogant lad. The soft-spoken courtier regarded the prince with a worried expression.

"And you are, sir?" I asked the pleasant-voiced courtier.

"Vincent," he told me with a smile, taking his eyes from his master for only a moment. "Vincent d'Escriban."

Giles returned from the encampment shaking his head. No horse for sale. Well, it had been worth the trial.

I bowed again. "We must depart," I said. "It is a long journey to Compostela."

"Is she dead?" the prince asked, taking hold of my horse's bridle to prevent my moving.

"We think not," I said. "She may be under an enchantment."

The young man looked at Vincent and said, "I want her."

Vincent and I exchanged uncertain glances.

"I want her," the boy repeated. "Buy her for me."

"She is a person," I explained softly. "Not a toy. Not a mannequin. She is not something one can buy."

"Buy her for me," screamed the prince, growing very red in the face.

Vincent shrugged an apology toward me and moved to take the young prince in hand by distracting him from his madness. Esky took the right-hand coffin horse by the reins and led him purposefully onto the road. Giles and I followed, on our horses. The prince broke away from his keeper, dashed into the road and threw himself in front of the coffin horses. One horse stumbled. The rope came loose. The other horse bolted. The coffin fell into the road. The lid bounced off. My granddaughter's body rolled out of it into the road and lay there, coughing.

Beside her in the dust lay a piece of apple.

The mad young prince sat up, looked at my granddaughter with great satisfaction, then smiled. "Buy her for me," he said again. "I want to marry her."

I had slipped off my horse and then had been knocked down in all the confusion. Giles was busy picking me up and seeing that nothing was broken. Eskavaria was cuddling Snowdrop and crying. Vincent was remonstrating with the mad young prince. Persons of great self-importance arrived from across the road to see what all the fuss was about and succeeded in making an even larger one. Questions were shouted at me, which I was too confused to answer.

We are now camped at the edge of the forest, being waited upon by the servants of King Zot of Nadenada while the mad young prince and my granddaughter play at shuttlecocks in the road.

"Who is she?" King Zot himself asked me, having been introduced through Giles and Vincent.

His tone was peremptory. I didn't like it.

"She is the daughter of the hereditary Prince of Marvella and his former wife, Elladine, who was the daughter of Lord Edward of Wellingford and granddaughter of the Duke of Monfort and Westfaire," I said with chill hauteur.

"Oh well, that's all right then," he said, glancing at me out of the corner of his eye. "Related to you?"

"My granddaughter."

"Ah," he said, scratching his nose. His manner changed to one of respect. "How old would you say she is?"

"I would say she is . . ." And I paused, wondering for a moment how old she really is. She had been born quite some time ago. "I would say she is twelve or thirteen," I said. "She spent some time under an enchantment, but she did not age during that time."

"Virgin, is she?"

I snorted. "Of course." Though I wouldn't have put it past Esky or one of his brothers to have tried.

"Ah," he said again, and then sat down, leaned forward, and began to tell me about his kingdom.

Nadenada, it seems, is a pocket realm just over the mountains toward France. It is larger than Marvella, but not by much. The mad young prince is a pocket prince, not the heir, but still a prince, and at fourteen it is time he was married. So said King Zot.

"Undoubtedly you will think of alliances when you consider a wife for him," I said stiffly.

He stared gloomily at the dust between his feet, drawing circles in it with an ornamental dagger. "Not much of that kind of thing in Nadenada," he said, summoning Vincent with one hand. He sent the young man for wine and settled himself more comfortably on the chair he had brought over from his camp. Then he drew more circles. "France wouldn't care, far too big and far away. England wouldn't care, they've enough to worry about warring with France. Navarre wouldn't care, nor Aragon; everything is religion with them, and we're not that observant in Nadenada. And the same applies to Castile, come to that."

"Then you're not concerned with alliances."

"Not really, no."

"Some affair of state, perhaps, which could be helped along by a judicious match?"

"Haven't any affairs of state, either. There was the matter of the wool tax, but that's been decided." He gloomed into his linked fingers. "Shepherds said they'd go over the mountains into Spain, so we relieved them of it. Can't have all one's shepherds absconding to Spain."

"It wouldn't look well," I agreed. "No other affairs of state?"

"None I can think of," he said.

"The prince . . ." (I'd almost said "the mad prince," catching myself just in time). "The prince will want a large dowry, undoubtedly."

"Not . . . not really *large*," the King murmured, giving me a straight look. "It's not as though he were in the succession, you understand."

"An elder brother?"

"Three elder brothers."

"Things can happen," I murmured.

"Yes," he said in a plaintive voice. "They can. Put it, then, that he's not *likely* to be in line for the throne."

"So he wouldn't need a very large dowry."

"Not *very* large."

I considered this. "Did you happen to notice the . . . ah . . . case that my granddaughter was traveling in? Before your son dumped her out into the road."

"I had noticed that, yes. Brass, is it? And crystal?"

"Gold," I said. "And gems."

"Ah," he said again. "One wouldn't have known."

I nodded in agreement. One really wouldn't have known. If one hadn't met Esky's brothers, one wouldn't even have thought it likely. I said, "Of course, your . . . fourth son is very young. Perhaps too young to think of marriage."

The King scratched his head again and sweated gently into his beard. "Let me be frank," he said.

"Since the boy became a man, which happened just a year ago, he has been quite . . . quite . . ."

"Urgent?" I suggested.

"Urgent," he agreed. "We are having some trouble keeping maidservants at the castle. His mother and I are agreed it is time he was married."

We parted, each to think about that. Vincent came to summon the mad young prince to lunch. Snowdrop, thus deserted, came to sit by me in the shade.

"Have you been having fun?" I asked.

"Oh, yes," she said. "It's so nice."

"What about the young man?"

"He's so nice," she replied with a happy expression. I offered her some cakes which the King had brought with him, and she took one, eating it greedily. I was reminded of her mother.

"Tell me, Snow," I asked. "Why did you let the witch poison you with that apple when the little men had told you not to let her in?"

She gazed at me wonderingly, her little brow furrowing with the attempt at thought.

"Because I was hungry and it looked so nice."

Her father, Prince Charming, was never long in the brains department, either.

ST. FRANCIS'S DAY, OCTOBER,
YEAR OF OUR LORD 1417

Giles and I are here in Nadenada for the wedding. We are honored guests. Since the Death ravaged all of Europe, no one wonders if fathers and mothers aren't present at weddings. A grandmother does quite well enough, even one so obviously old as I. The Queen even offered her dressmaker in order that I might be suitably clad for the occasion. Prince Charme and Princess Ilene have been invited to the nuptials. I mentioned to the Prime Minister of this place that Ilene was probably responsible for the spell which had been laid on Snowdrop. He talked with the archbishop, and formal charges of witchcraft are being considered. As a princess, she is not subject to the laws of a neighboring kingdom, but the archbishop believes the Church has authority to examine her even if civil authority cannot. I'm not sure how I feel about this. I don't like Ilene, but then I don't much like heresy trials, either, and I certainly don't like anything which might involve Ilene's patron in the mirror. The archbishop has sent someone posthaste both to Avignon and Rome to attempt to get a ruling from one or more of the popes on the matter. I can't remember whether there are three popes at the moment or only two.

If I were wise, and if I had the conviction wisdom should lend me, I would seize Snow up and take her somewhere away from this pathological child she is going to marry. And yet, one asks, where? Where does one take a gloriously beautiful twelve-year-old girl who has not two tiny brains to rub together to make even one wee warm idea in her head? And when one gets her there, what does one do with her? No monastery would take her. No, that's not true, given a sufficient dowry some monastery would, but she'd be miserable there. Marriage is her only hope. And yet . . .

Well. Beauty does not breed true. I said that before, when Elly died. Beauty exists in all ages, but it does not necessarily breed true. Mixed with dross, it becomes dross. I am only her grandmother, after all. I am not God, who presumably made her as she is for some reason!

ALL HALLOWS' EVE

Tomorrow is the wedding. Tonight I was sitting alone in my warm, tapestry-hung room, with my cat on the bed and Giles next door, remembering Mama. I saw her last on Samhain Eve, so long ago, when Thomas the Rhymer got loose from Faery. I wondered if she would care that her great-granddaughter was being married.

"Fenoderee," I whispered.

And he was there, sitting on the window sill, looking out at the night. Puck lounged against the bed, chewing at a fingernail. Call one, get both.

"I was thinking about Mama," I said.

"Ah," said Puck. "Well, she's in Faery, looking well."

I tried to think of something to ask about her, but I couldn't. Instead, I wondered, "Was it the Dark Lord I saw in the witch's glass?"

"It was," said Fenoderee.

"Did he see me?"

"Carabosse thinks he may have. Israfel thinks he did, also. They're both frightened for you, though they say it was probably going to happen, sooner or later. Once you went back to the twentieth, it showed up in the Pool that he would."

Puck added, "They think the Dark Lord will come looking for you, manipulating things. Be careful, Beauty."

"How much do you know about . . ." I started to ask, then shut my mouth, remembering they didn't know.

"About your burden?" Puck asked. "We've known since almost the beginning. It's not her fault, but old Clockwork Carabosse is one of the Sidhe, after all. She can't get out of the habit of thinking of us Bogles as slightly subnormal. She thinks we don't notice what's going on under our noses."

Fenoderee said, "I don't know what made her think we wouldn't see what she was up to. She and Israfel did it right there in front of us."

I sighed. "I'm getting old, you know. I won't last too much longer. They'd better start thinking of somewhere else to hide it."

Puck nodded deliberately. "They're cogitating, looking in the Pool, thinking deep thoughts, the way they do."

"And I'm still just supposed to go along, is that it?" I was surprised to find myself still capable of a little anger!

"For now," said Fenoderee. "Is that why you called?"

I shook my head. "No, it was just I was thinking about Mama. I was thinking of going to Faery to say hello, but when I returned here, wouldn't a lot of time have passed."

Puck nodded. "Oh, yes. No way around that. Your mortal part ages whenever you travel back and forth by magic."

I wanted to see her, but I couldn't risk that. If I died before Carabosse took away my burden, it might be lost forever. Besides, Giles and I couldn't look forward to that much time together. Nor Grumpkin, either. "Could you take a message for me?"

He smiled.

"Tell her . . . I love her," I said.

I think I do. Despite what she is and how she feels, I think I do. In my long life there have been few enough people, mortal or Faery, for me to love.

ALL HALLOWS' NIGHT

Well, we have had a wedding. There was the mad young prince, all dressed up in taffeta and furs with a plumed cap, looking very handsome, and there was Galantha, Snowdrop, in silk and velvet, both of them standing outside the church door, exchanging their pledges. I had hired a local goldsmith to break up the coffin and melt down the gold into nice little ingots. That gave me a goodly sum for her dowry, and the King settled a house and land on his son. They have enough to live on; neither of them is bright enough to get into serious trouble; and I laid a happiness spell on them as a gift. It was the least I could do. The King is quite a jolly fellow, several decades younger than I, but gallant and well-spoken. He says to call him Zot, and that he'll send word to me in England how the children get along. He flirts with me and tells me I don't look a day over eighty.

After the pledging was done and the rings exchanged and the papers signed, we went into the church and had the nuptial mass. And after that was done, we went to the feast, and there was Princess Ilene of Marvella. I'm not sure whether she knew who the bride was. I'm not sure the invitation mentioned the bride's name. If it did, she may have assumed it was someone else by the same name, or that Snow would have aged during the thirty years she'd been asleep, or something. At any rate, when Princess Ilene saw Snow, her eyes bulged. I've never seen that actually happen before, but it happened this time. Ilene was standing beside me at the time, her eyes bulged, and then something quite dreadful happened to her face. It sagged, melted, and began to fall off the skull. She raised her hands, just as she had when invoking the presence in the mirror, and they were all bones. Well, she'd said the Dark Lord held her beauty in thrall, and she'd been safe so long as no one around was prettier than she. However, Snow certainly was prettier and it seemed the Dark One was ending his contract and taking Princess Ilene for his own.

I was the only one who saw what was happening. Ilene crumpled to the floor, very slowly. I'd brought my cloak to the banquet with me, folded over my arm, thinking I might want to escape if things got dull. I spread it like a fishing net, to hide what was left of the Princess. "Fenoderee," I whispered, and there he was. "Take it away," I said. "And put the cloak back under my bed upstairs."

He was gone only for an instant. Then he was back. "Where did you put her?" I whispered.

"Under the church with the other old bones," he whispered back, then made a face at me and departed. Faery folk aren't very respectful, sometimes. That was consecrated ground!

Then I caught myself and realized that was merely another way of saying "magical ground." She could lie there as well as anywhere.

A few moments later, Prince Charming, the hereditary Prince of Marvella came wandering toward me with Snow on his arm and a silly smile on his sweet old face. He was looking for his wife to tell her he'd found his long-lost daughter, but Princess Ilene was nowhere to be found. I helped them look for a while, until I got tired. Then I came up here to bed.

Giles brought me a cup of wine and asked where we would go now.

"Home," I told him. Meaning Westfaire. Or, at least, somewhere near there. I long for home.

NOVEMBER

King Zot of Nadenada gave us an escort to Bayonne. There we found it simple to join a group of travelers who were seeking passage to England. Good weather held. A merchantman presented itself in due course. Five days north, we landed once more at Bristol and found a carriage we could hire to take us to Sawley, where, after inquiries, I found the man who claimed to own Wellingford (though I much doubt his claim would stand a legal test). I paid him a few years' rent on the Dower House.

And in that house we have come to rest, Giles and I, keeping our old bones busy hiring people to refurbish the place and manage the farm land around it, and finding half a dozen women to keep it clean. It is not a wreck, not like some places in the countryside, but it is certainly dilapidated. I converted gems back to cash, and cash into investments with a certain House of Levi in England. This time, just in case I decide to go away and come back in five hundred years, the money is to be paid to whoever knows a few code words. I've had enough of darting about planting forged documents.

SPRING 1418

Winter came and went. Despite the cold, it has been the happiest time of my life. Strange to say that with youth gone and all the pains of age very much with me, but it is true. Giles is a loving, dear companion, a sweet and kindly friend.

A few days ago I decided I wanted to see Westfaire. I told Giles just enough for him to help me, and we went through the water gate together, floating on pigs' bladders, for neither of us is strong enough to push through that deep water. Inside it is just as I left it. We climbed slowly up to the tower, me holding the cloak, Giles clutching the boots to keep us from falling asleep. As we climbed, he paused often to catch his breath. He was not this weak when we were searching for Snowdrop. It must be a very recent thing.

Beloved is still there in the tower, still lovely, still sleeping.

"How long?" Giles wanted to know, reaching out to touch her face. "How long will you sleep?"

"You." Not "she." Oh, Giles. Giles.

Well, according to Joyeause, she will sleep thirty more years, until kissed by a handsome prince, though, according to Carabosse, that wasn't the real curse at all. Supposing that both of them are right (and I do not take Aunt Joyeause so lightly as old Carabosse does), at the end of a hundred years, someone may be able to take Beloved out of Westfaire and kiss her awake. If I am to see that event, I must live to be one hundred and sixteen years old. Looking at myself in the glass, I don't think I'll make it. Still, if and when that day comes, Beloved will know it was all worth it, being my friend. She'll have the best of it then.

I wrote her a note. "Beloved, you are Beauty. And Beauty is gone, long ago. Live her life as well as she would have lived it, or even better."

As I turned toward the stair, I saw my mysterious thing, still sitting upon the chest. It's a clock, of course. One of Carabosse's clocks. The hand has moved to half past fifteen. It does not measure hours but centuries. It ends, as the world will end, with the twenty-second. I leaned close and listened to the sound. The faint ticking. The tiny crepitation of time moving past. On the face of the clock is the word "Carabosse," entwined with the numbered centuries. She cursed me.

But she left me this gift. Sometimes I wish it was all she had left me.

It was easier climbing down. When we got back to the lake shore, we were thoroughly chilled through. Such a stupid thing to do at our age!

LATER

Giles is very ill. I know what he has. He has pneumonia. I could get to the twentieth in an instant, I could steal penicillin, I could be back before he knows I am gone. Maybe. I don't know if I could. I could try!

I told him that. His being sick is all my fault. He would be all right if I hadn't dragged him through the water and up that tower. He must let me help him.

But he won't. He shook his head at me, smiling. "I saw you sleeping in that tower, just the way you were. If I die, let me die remembering that, sweet girl. I want you here, not off somewhere with your boots."

"Giles, we could have years, yet."

"Don't want years that badly," he whispered to me. "I've had years. More years alone than I ever wanted. Don't leave me alone now. I'm tired. It's enough."

He went off to sleep.

Oh, God in Heaven, I could not let him go. I wept and screamed and threw myself about, while he went on sleeping, more deeply, more deeply.

It was that gave me the idea. I called Puck and Fenoderee and put on the boots, and we held him while all of us went, holding onto him we went, through the thorns, through the roses, into Westfaire. Oh, I could have used the boots anytime. So foolish. So stupid. I let my love go through that cold water when we could have used the boots. If they would go through time, what were a few thorns!

I put him in Aunt Lav's bed. I took the boots away. He fell even more deeply asleep. He slept, as all in Westfaire sleep. He will not die. Nothing in Westfaire can die. I know it! That was the curse Carabosse put upon Westfaire. Sleep! Not for a hundred years, but forever! It has to be. It's the only thing that makes sense of everything that's happened!

I asked Puck if I was right, and he nodded, shuffling his toes in the dust as though embarrassed. I asked him why, and he said he didn't know.

26

With Giles gone from me, nothing seems worth it, somehow. Not that we were recent lovers, in a physical sense. All that sort of thing leaves you. You remember it, but your body doesn't urge you toward it. Your body wants comfort and affection and the sweetness of companionship. We weren't lonely, not so long as we were together, but now I am. I go to Westfaire often and sit there, talking to him as he sleeps. Sometimes I pretend he answers me.

It seems to me his breathing is easier. Is he healing? While he sleeps? It would be so easy to summon him up, not really him, you understand, but an enchantment of him. But I don't. I won't. It wouldn't be fair to him. It would be like Chinanga, all a dream, my creation, not really him at all. An enchantment Giles would be incapable of surprising me. He who always surprised me.

It was unfair of him to go before me. I believe I will probably live quite some time yet. Despite all the aches and pains, my heart sounds steady and strong and I breathe easily. I may have years yet to get through.

. . .

When I was a child, my legs used to hurt often. Aunt Terror, I think it was she, used to say it was growing pains. I have the same pain now. Perhaps now they are ungrowing pains. Whenever the pain wakes me in the night, I think of going back to Faery where I don't feel pain.

I called Fenoderee a day or so ago, and he didn't come. He always came before when I called. What's going on in Faery?

I need to talk to Carabosse. What's she going to do with this thing inside me? I would like to see Mama, too, to tell her how sorry I am for what happened to her. Besides, in Faery, I would at least look and feel young.

Remembering the condition I was in when I returned last time, I'll need to make some provision for staying healthy and clean. Going to Faery will do no good if my human flesh is starved while I'm there. I'll have to figure something out.

The solution to staying healthy and clean in Faery is to come out of it every now and then, into the mortal world, and eat, bathe, and reclothe myself. I have hired a woman from the nearby village to go each evening to the kitchen of the ruined manor of Wellingford, to set out food and drink, to build a fire, and to heat water over it. Though the rest of the manor is dilapidated, the kitchen is whole and the roof over it is in good repair. The woman's name is Odile Kent.

Of course, she wants to know why. I have told her it was a promise I had made my husband before he died. A kind of memorial. Service for a ghost. Though the explanation makes no sense, she accepts it. People in this age believe in ghosts, and people in all ages do odd things in memory of loved ones. I told her, also, that the matter was secret, not something to be rumored about the countryside to bring beggars to eat the food she puts out. I called God to witness our contract and bring down fire upon her if she fails me. She looked suitably impressed. My agent in East Sawley will pay her, year on year. My agent in London will check to be sure that he does. Ever since Chinanga, I have put watchers to watch the watchers.

I have also instructed Odile to put a mark on the chimney face at each full of the moon, thirteen marks in a row, starting the next row beneath. In that way I will know how much time has passed. She's a sensible woman, strong and stout and still quite young. She should last longer than I do. I have already carried a pile of clothing over to the kitchen and stored it in a locked chest together with Mama's box. Looking through the box, I came upon that last hank of thread. When I see Mama, I must ask her what it is for.

The key to the chest is around my neck on a ribbon. As soon as I have taken care of a few things here, I am ready to go. I have told Odile to stay in readiness, that I will let her know when she is to start.

LATE JUNE

Surprise! Just as I was about to leave for Faery this very morning, I received a messenger with a letter from King Zot. He says Snow is very pregnant. He says he's much afraid the father may not be the mad young prince, but he's making nothing of that, because it may be for the best. The messenger who brought the letter is the putative father of Snow's baby: that nice young courtier, Vincent, the one who tried so hard to keep his young master in check.

"Well, this is a fine thing," I said, waving the letter at him so the seals and ribbons flapped. "Why on earth?"

He shrugged, blushing. "I didn't mean to," he said weakly. "She's so lovely. And she has no sense of the fitness of things. And her husband was away, hunting, and I was rather drunk. And she gets prettier and prettier."

I should have brought her back and locked her up

in a monastery. I know I should. "She's not intelligent, you know."

"Oh, I know." He sounded guilty about that, too, as he well might. "One is constantly aware of that. It is like making love to a beautiful talking doll. She keeps saying, 'Oooh, that's so nice.' "

"What's the King doing about her?"

"He's sent me away," he said, shamefaced. "And he's appointed all women to look after them from now on. Old women. You know. Past the age when . . ."

"I know," I snarled at him. "What will the King do when the baby arrives?"

"The King plans to send it here to be fostered and educated. The King doesn't want the baby around the prince, just on the chance that . . . I mean . . ."

"I know what you mean," I said. "The child, if it's a boy, might by some chance get into the succession, and the King doesn't want him to be infected with madness. If madness is infectious." It was no time to give Vincent a lesson in genetics. "What are you going to do now?"

"The King heard that your friend died." (I had given it about that Giles had died.) "So I'm to stay here and look after you," he said. "For my sins."

Well! This postpones my return to Faery for a time. I can't wait to see the baby. Also, it will be nice to have a man around again.

FALL 1418

The baby arrived today. King Zot said I was to see to the naming of him and the rearing of him. The King is getting even with me for Snow, I'm sure of it. The baby's name will be Giles Edward Vincent Charming, honoring everyone who deserves to be honored and at least one who doesn't.

Since I knew the baby was coming, I've a wet nurse already hired. The one who came with him wants to go back to Nadenada. I also have a nursery maid and a pleasant young boy who will play with him when he gets a bit older. It isn't good for boys to have only women around them.

Since it is also not good for a young man to be alone, exposed to the temptations of the world, I have arranged a marriage for Vincent. She is the daughter of a local baron, fallen upon hard times, but of impeccable lineage. Her name is Elizabeth. She is quite pretty, extremely intelligent, and, thanks to her father, well-educated. We took her without a dowry, since the poor man had none to offer, and both she and Vincent feel grateful and relieved to be so well arranged for.

Since the Dower House is large enough for all of us, young Giles will grow up in a house with two parents and one old aunt!

CHRISTMASTIDE 1418

I am having such fun with the baby! Elizabeth is a treasure, such a sweet, helpful girl. I hope Vincent loves her as much as I already do. Both of them are quite sweet with baby Giles, almost as though he were their own. I feel fortunate that they are here.

WINTER 1419

Today, while I was telling cook at some length what I wanted prepared for dinner, I surprised upon Elizabeth's face an expression which was so familiar and yet so elusive that I spent a good part of the morning figuring it out. It came to me at last. With considerable shock I realized it is the same expression that I used to feel upon my own face when one of the aunts did something so outrageous that I could not believe it, yet had no recourse but to accept it. It is an expression of bemused fury.

Well, during my converse with the cook, I had changed my mind several times about the menu. I really had. There was a time when that would have annoyed me. The implication is inevitable. I am merely tolerated in my own house! The idea makes me waver between amusement and fury and grief. I have done everything for Elizabeth that a loving mother might have done. I thought she liked me. Well, she does. She simply wishes I were not so much about. If I were at a distance, she could probably like me quite well, or she could hate me without hindrance, whichever she was minded to do at the moment. When I realized this, I cried, then I thought vindictively of sending her and Vincent away—they are living here at my invitation, after all—then I cried again. Oh, I wish Giles had not died! It is only with our own loves that we are more than mere burdens. Neither of a mated pair should ever die first! Or even, as he has done, go to sleep!

Finally, after much weeping and self-examination, I decided that it is time for me to do what I had planned before Vincent arrived: return to Faery. The baby is not mine. He'll be happier if there is no dissention in his home. Tonight I will tell Vincent I am going on a journey. A pilgrimage. I will give him title to the Dower House and surrounding lands, which I purchased some time ago. I will advise him of the income he may expect to receive per annum. My investments, however, remain my own against my return. Unless I do not return.

LATER

"When will you be back?" Vincent asked. "Who are you going with?"

"A party of pilgrims," I told him. "At my age, I may not be back, my boy, but that is no concern of yours. If I do not return in—oh, thirty years, let us say —my great-grandson Giles Edward Vincent Charming will fall heir to what I have. Thirty is a good age to inherit property. One is still young enough to enjoy it, but old enough to have acquired elementary prudence."

"I don't want you to go," he said. "I don't want you to go." Vincent's face was troubled, part duty, part affection. The larger part affection, I think, though one is never sure, is one? Elizabeth had merely said farewell, without protestation.

"But I want to go," I told him with a smile.

I think I really do want to go. Before, when I was in Faery, I knew too little. Now, I may know too much, but I want to see it again. I keep worrying about what Carabosse may be doing. I keep thinking of Mama. "I have lived long enough, having seen one thing, that love hath an end." My favorite poet said that. He was right. Before my end, I need to make it right with her.

I will take my cloak, boots, and book with me. The only thing left to do is to send word to Odile Kent that she is to begin her daily journey to the Wellingford kitchen.

"When are you going?" Vincent asks. "Soon?"

I will be gone before he knows it. One need not pack for Faery.

FAERY, NO TIME, NO DATE

Most things done in Faery have no meaning in the world. However, as I know from when I was last here, words written here are really written. When I go out of this place, they will come with me into the other world. Promises made here are transferable. Songs sung here can be sung out there. Meaning is meaning, whether in the world or in Faery. Only our outward seeming does not go from one place to the other. Here I am young again, and very beautiful. Here I am Beauty once again.

It would be easy to forget to go back. Suppose my mortal half died here, in Faery. Wouldn't my fairy half go on? Perhaps I would be dwindled, as Puck says, but still immortal. Free to dance here, and dine here, and while the endless time away with hunts and feasts. Dwindle. Ride mice. Sleep in flowers. Become one with the origin of my creation.

It is tempting. Enticing. Seductive. I try to summon what Father Raymond would have called my conscience and determine that, whatever happens, I will go back, at intervals, to wash and eat and dress myself and see what time has passed. Perhaps I can remember to do it. Perhaps not.

As I was leaving, I stood by the ruined hulk of Wellingford and peered back through the trees to see the Dower House well-peopled behind me. Its windows were alight and its chimneys sent up fine coils of smoke toward heaven. Let the smoke carry my prayer: pray God that Vincent and Elizabeth stay well, and so baby Giles.

27

WELLINGFORD: ONE STROKE
ON THE CHIMNEYPIECE

A month already? I would have said a day or two. I
am famished. I ate all the bread and cheese and drank
most of the beer. After I have a bath, I will have the
rest of the beer and the meat. My dress is a bit ragged,
but it will do a while longer. I must have a clean underbodice. This one is covered with something dreadful along the sleeves.

Mama had returned to Faery, as Puck had told me.
My boots took me to the flowery meadow at the center
of that world. I put on my shoes and began walking
toward the distant castles, and there she was, standing
all alone. "Hello, daughter," she said, not at all surprised as she turned to walk beside me. "You've come
back." She said not another word, nor did I, until we
reached the castle. She kissed me on the cheek, an
unmeaning kiss, like the kiss of an aunt, then pointed
to a door and said, "Your room is there." How could
one describe her manner? Neither warm nor chill. Neither welcoming nor forbidding. Merely neutral. As
though it made no difference. As though I had been
noticed, but only that. I did not know how to break
through to her. All the words I had been saving were

useless. I felt despair, but then something stubborn in me said to stay and keep trying. So.

Oberon noticed me, too—but only that. He bowed and swept his hat widely, almost a satire upon himself, but did not invite my company on his couch, nor did any of the others. Not that I'd have consented, but it would have been nice to be asked. After a few days of this treatment by all of them, I decided to find out why, not caring greatly except that I like to know what is going on. I thought Puck would tell me, so I wandered off into a copse of lacy trees and called him up. He did not want to tell me, but did, finally. He says I smell differently now. Mortality, he says. Before, I was in the juice and fat of life, but now I know what age is, I have a scent of sootiness, like a candle burned down to its end.

"They can't see it," he said, kissing me on the cheek to take the pain of his words away. "But they can sense it."

"I'm half mortal," I cried angrily. "I've wondered what that means, really. Can't the mortal half die and the other half remain?"

Puck shook his head. "I've known several begot by mortals, half fairy like yourself. If they were born here, or if they came here as wee children to stay, then they seem to partake fully of Faery. If they live in human lands, they seem to grow up mortal. It's as though the heritage is the smaller part, and the rearing is the most of it. You were reared to a good age in the real world, so your fairy half maybe didn't have a chance to develop. Don't ask me, Beauty. I grow less and less sure about things." He looked older to me than he had in the past, if those in Faery can be said to age. Perhaps Bogles do, if they choose.

"You don't blame me, do you?" I asked, needing him as a friend and not wanting him to disapprove of me. "You don't blame me for coming back?"

"Ach, no," he said. "I don't. The Fenoderee doesn't. None of us do. Carabosse wants to see you, when you've time."

"Everything looks much the same," I commented.

"Thus far," he agreed. "Though Oberon is coming close to changing his world. He's bored, I think."

The words set up a dreadful resonance in my mind. I had seen another ruler change his world out of boredom.

"He's gotten sneakier," said Puck, going on with his comments. "He's fallen into this pattern of evasion."

"Evasion?"

"Of the terms of the covenant. You remember his enchanting people into deer, and then killing them? Cleaving to the letter, but not to the spirit? He's doing more things of that kind. No matter what Oberon says, it's at least a small infraction of the covenant. It's like the agreement they made with the Dark Lord, a kind of slyness. It's unworthy of what he once was, is what it is, but you wouldn't dare say that to Oberon now."

"What would a big infraction of the covenant be, then?"

"Well, they almost found out, didn't they, seven years ago, when they set out from here intending to give Thomas the Rhymer to the Dark Lord?" He made a disgusted face. "They came close then!"

I went back to the castle feeling dismayed but trying not to show it. I needn't have bothered. The people of the hills simply weren't paying any attention to me. Partly because of my mortality, I suppose, but partly something else. Some great event due to occur, something that was known of and planned for even before I came back, something mysterious that even Oberon doesn't speak of. There is whispering, something I don't remember from my former visit. In a land in which everything is known, nothing really hidden, in which all veils are merely seeming, what is there to whisper about?

Finding out will be more exciting than sitting in the Dower House growing lame(r) and blind(er) while Elizabeth simmers. So, when I've had my bath and something more to eat, I'll return to Faery.

.   .   .

The Sidhe are as nervous as sparrows, twitching at every sound. Some great doings are abroad in the land, but they will not tell me what they are. There are tents set up in the meadow, as though the Sidhe were expecting guests. Everyone pretends not to notice them.

I have been left much alone since my return, full of doubts and vagrant memories which sometimes overwhelm me. I spend much time thinking of Giles and of my life in the twentieth, wondering what I might have done differently with both. Sometimes I simply sit about, doing nothing purposeful, trying to make meaning of my life. It comes back to Mama, always. Why had I been born? For what? How had I failed her?

At last I begged her to walk with me in the flowery meadow, and among the copses I asked her to tell me what was going on.

"Going on?" She drew herself up and made her eyes glitter at me arrogantly. "Going on?"

"Come on, Mama," I said desperately. "You know what I mean. There's a definite mood of apprehension about."

"I don't know what you mean, Beauty," she said, striking a very dignified attitude. "I have no idea what you can be speaking of." She spoke as though to a stranger.

"Who is it that's coming?" I wanted to know.

She looked suddenly very haggard. "We're not sure who they are now," she admitted. "They were our kindred once."

"Then how do you know they're coming?" I asked.

"We just know," she said, the glitter in her eyes looking more like tears than arrogance. I tried to put my arm around her, and she pushed me away. "You should have come when you were young," she cried. "I told you to come to me when you were young! And when you came at last, you should have stayed. You went away, and now you stink of age and corruption. If you'd stayed when you were young, you'd have stayed young for a long, long time. So long, you'd have forgotten anything but Faery! I smell death on you, and it hurts me! I cannot bear it!"

Puck had told me about my smell, but hearing it from her was like being slapped. I felt totally mortal, unbelievably old. If I could have shrunk into wrinkles and ashes, I would have done. She stood apart from me, her back to me, and it was a time before I could answer her.

"Mama, I had to go away. Thomas the Rhymer was gone. I know you wouldn't have meant for it to happen, but it's likely Mab and Oberon would have used me for the teind if I'd stayed."

"Better me than you, is that it?" She drew herself up, proudly.

"They didn't break the covenant with you, Mama. They would have broken it with me. And you survived. Puck told me when you came back."

"Puck!" she sneered. "I have a daughter who not only betrays me but also associates with Bogles."

"Mama!"

"I should never have given you the gifts I gave you. You're merely mortal! You aren't worthy of them!"

"Mama!"

She turned away, obdurate, angry.

"Take them back," I said. "If that's the way you feel."

She was sobbing. The Sidhe never cry. "No, the gift once made remains. You are what you are because of me. I try, but I can't hate you enough to take the gifts away." And she ran away, back to the courts, leaving me in the meadow staring after her, longing for a mother's strong love and seeing a child's weakness. Perhaps she could have loved a fairy child. She had nothing to give me. She had never had anything to give me. It was the other way around, and I understood for the first time what Puck meant. The Sidhe did not have children in order to give but in order to get. Mortals have a strength that they need.

Ridiculously, what came into my head then was the third hank of thread. I had wanted for a long time to ask her about the third hank of thread. Now I could not ask. She was hurt with me, but hurt with something else as well, something she had been worried about when I returned. Something great and mysterious had them all in an uproar. I had needed her, and she needed . . . what?

"Fenoderee," I whispered. "Take me to Carabosse."

He was there, holding the bridle of a horse. We went together, the same way I had gone before. Puck was waiting for us at the cottage door, and as I knocked I heard the susuration of clocks suspended into sudden silence.

"Come in," she cried. She sat huddled in a chair before the fire. Behind her, all around her, the walls were still covered with clocks. More hung down a hallway I could see through a half-open door, while others stood on the window ledges and in the corners, hung from the rafters, or lay on the table before her with their gears and hands spread out before them.

The only thing I could think of to say was, "There are few, if any, clocks in the fifteenth!"

"Fifteenth what?" she demanded.

"Fifteenth century," I said.

"Fifteenth, twelfth, first, makes no difference to me," she said.

Puck squatted on the carpet and picked at a toenail.

"I don't keep human time," Carabosse said.

It looked to me as though she kept a great deal of human time, but it seemed inappropriate to say so. "What are they for?" I asked.

"Amusement," she said. "Entertainment. A hobby." She got up from her chair, leaning heavily upon a gnarled stick. I sensed little glamour about her. She evidently didn't care what she looked like. Her hair was sparse; her eyes were bloodshot; her forehead was high and corrugated with deep lines. She had a hump on her back and walked bent in half. She pointed her cane to one of the clocks on the wall and said, "That's Oberon's. The one next to it is Mab's."

I looked at them more closely. They were fine clocks, very beautifully made. Italian, I thought, eighteenth-century, perhaps. Enameled bronze and gilt, a matched pair.

"They've about run down," she cackled at me.

"Would you like me to wind them?" I asked politely.

"Would I like you to wind them? Ha, ha. So, you're a jester, are you? Beauty. Come sit by the fire. Have some tea."

She stumped her way back to her chair, and I took the one across from her, a comfortable rush-bottomed chair which fit me exactly. I had a feeling it would suit any guest exactly. For all its small size and sparsity of furnishings, the cottage was warm and comfortable.

She poured and handed me a cup, cream and sugar, the way I like it. There was no tea of this kind in the fourteenth, either, at least not in my part of the world. It seemed unnecessary to comment on that. It was real human tea. So were the biscuits, real. She and Puck seemed determined to feed me real food.

"You're getting older," she said.

I nodded. "That's my inescapable conclusion, Carabosse. Are you doing something about it?"

"About your getting older?"

"About this package I've been carrying about."

"Shhh," she said, glancing sidewise at Puck.

"He's known about it since I was a child," I said. "Puck knows more about me than either my mother or father ever did."

She glared at Puck, and he made a face at her, like an impudent boy.

"More than your father, certainly," she agreed. "Stupid man. Couldn't think of anything but his ridiculous pilgrimages. Wandering about, gazing at pieces of rotted bodies, thinking that conferred some kind of grace, all the time letting Westfaire go to ruin."

"It really wasn't," I contradicted, a little angered by what she had said. "It wasn't going to ruin, I mean. The roof was whole. All the walls were sound."

"Oh, child, I don't mean the beams and the stones. I mean the people who could have kept it and preserved it. You were his only child, and he almost ignored you. He didn't find you a good husband to help preserve Westfaire. Westfaire deserves preserving. That and a good deal else."

"He didn't find me a husband because you had cursed me," I argued, growing a little pink in the face. I could feel it.

"No, no, no," she said, waving her cane. "Before I cursed you. I looked at what he would do if I hadn't cursed you, don't you see? I don't go around doing indiscriminate curses. Besides, it wasn't you I cursed, remember?"

"Wasn't it Aunt Joyeause who changed your curse from death to sleep," I argued, wanting to get this business of the curse straightened out at last. "That's what the letter said."

Carabosse shook her head, to and fro, sipping at her tea, smiling a knowing, half-toothless smile. "Joyeause doesn't have the wits of a bat. She couldn't summon up a fairy gift if her life depended on it. And besides that, she tells lies. She was the only one near when I cursed Duke Phillip's lovely daughter with sleep."

"Duke Phillip's lovely daughter, and Westfaire," I pointed out.

"Well, yes. And Westfaire."

"Forever?"

"Let us say without a stated time of wakening," she said stiffly, warning me with her expression to press the matter no further. "I left immediately thereafter. Joyeause must have gone to your Mama with some fay and follet story about what she thought I'd said or what she invented to say I'd said or what she would have said in my place. It's like her. Such a silly-shee."

"I used to think all fairies were wise," I said sadly. The thought that Carabosse might be lying never entered my head. She was telling the truth, and I knew it.

"Some are and some aren't."

"So, what's happening, Carabosse."

"The Dark Lord saw you, is what's happening. First, in Faery, picking that vengeful herb to get back at that man. Then, later, in that mirror in Marvella. The first time, it meant little to him. The second time, it meant more. Your showing up in both places has a certain resonance to it. He didn't really see what you're carrying, but he scents it perhaps. He wants to put his nose on you and sniff you up, find out what you are."

Hearing it like that, even though I'd known it, in my heart, made me shudder. "Well, Carabosse, you must find somewhere else to put it, that's all."

"True." She sipped and nodded.

I sighed. "I didn't mean what's going on about the Dark Lord, anyhow. I meant, what's going on in Faery."

"The Bogles did a thing," she said, cocking her eyebrows at Puck where he sat on the carpet. "Oh yes, they did a thing."

"What have you done, Puck?" I asked him.

"The Sidhe wouldn't listen to us, so we've tried the only thing left to try. We've sent a message out of Faery."

"How have you done that?"

"How haven't they?" snorted Carabosse.

Puck settled himself for oration. "We've cried out by every hob and boggart, by the gruagach and the selkies, by the killmoulis and every lob-lie-by-the-fire capable of speech. Every pixie and nixie, phouka and glashan have carried our summons. We've sent the aughisky and the banshee out to howl, the bogan and the spriggans out to screech. The gabriel ratchets have honked the call into the sky, and the fuath have bubbled it down into the watery places beneath the sea.

"In the towers of the north, the dunters are grinding our words in their quern until the message rattles the stones beneath the mountains. Even the duergar have been constrained against wickedness and made to write our summons in the smoke of their fires. The cait sith prowls the edges of the world yowling our yowl, and after her come the black dogs, barking our bark. In all the times of earth until now, no such call has gone out from the Bogle-folk, and if there are any left to answer it, surely they will." He finished up with a fine, broad gesture.

"If they'd asked me," said Carabosse, "I'd have told them it wasn't necessary. I'd have told Israfel, and he'd have told his kinfolk. A few quiet words. All this hullabaloo wasn't needed."

"We wanted a hullabaloo," said Puck in a dignified voice.

"And what answer have you had, Puck?" I knew the answer already. What else could it be?

"The Long Lost are coming home," he said. "They're coming back to Faery. The Sidhe don't much like it. Oberon's wrathful and that makes his people edgy. Elladine's people are in no good mood. They're snarly, and snarly folk do stupid things."

"They're snarly, right enough," I said, remembering how Mama had flown at me, over nothing.

Puck replied, "If things get very bad for you there, with them, call me. It might be well for you to come visit my places. I've visited yours often enough."

"Maybe you should come stay with me," suggested Carabosse.

I shook my head, feeling confused and alone. "What am I supposed to do?" I asked. "What will be best?"

"Just go on," she advised me, pursing her old, wrinkled lips, leaning forward to place her hand on my breast, feeling the little fire in there. "Just go on. Being ordinary."

"With the Dark Lord hovering in the wings, sniffing and waiting to pounce?"

"We've talked about that, Israfel and I. If he pounces, we'll be there. Don't worry, Beauty. We're watching. We're good at that."

I tried to get more out of her and got nothing. She was closemouthed as a turtle, glaring at Puck out of the corner of her eyes, as though he had betrayed the secret instead of merely finding out about it.

He and I went out into the world and rode back to the castle. When we came within sight of it, we stopped and merely sat, seeing what was there. Things change about in Faery. What is there one day is often not there the next.

"Why is Oberon's castle always there," I murmured.

"Because Oberon believes it is," said Puck. "As do his courtiers, of course."

"They all believe the mountains are there," I agreed, for the mountains never changed.

"And the sea, and the stretching moors, and the meadow. Yes. This is the land into which they were born. Originally, of course, it was in the world. Then, as men began to encroach, the Sidhe moved it, but this is the evening land of woods and sea that they were made for, and they believe in it."

"Do you?"

He shrugged. "It is the land into which I was born as well. Many of my people dwell in those mountains, beside that sea, at the far edge of that moor. Others of my people remained in the world when Faery was removed, and many of us chose to continue there, but this most resembles our ancestral home."

"But the trees move about. The copses in the meadow are one time here and one time there."

"The copses shift, perhaps, with those who think of them."

"I've noticed one sizeable copse that always stays," I said, pointing to one that shone silver against the dark bulk of the hills.

Puck paled, though I am not sure how I saw any change in his color in that long gloaming. "The Copse of the Covenant," he said. "It was there Oberon stood when he made the pledge to the Holy One, Blessed be He, that no man should come to lasting harm through the Sidhe."

"And everyone remembers it, so it stays there, in that place," I said.

Puck shook his head. "If they remember, it is not willingly. I have seen Oberon try to move that copse away. I have seen him send axemen to cut it down. He cannot touch it. It stands."

"Because everyone remembers it," I repeated.

"Because the Holy One remembers it," he said.

I could imagine how annoyed Oberon would be at that, how it would nag at him, reminding him. Puck forestalled further question by reaching out a hand to stroke mine, then he vanished as he usually does, not in a puff of nothingness, but with a sidle which seems to carry him behind something, even when there is nothing to go behind. It is so all the Bogles come and go, there one minute, gone the next, slipping into ways we mortals—or even half mortals—cannot see. I think they are ways that even full fairies do not often see, for, considering Oberon's hatred of them, if Bogles were easily followed and caught, there would be many fewer of them.

I walked back to the castle, wondering a number of things. Wondering if I could master the Bogle sidle. Wondering why one has to walk or ride in Faery, rather than simply "being" where one wants to be. Wondering, considering the empty feeling at my center, if it might not be time to come back to Wellingford and get something to eat. It seems too much effort. A needless effort.

I summoned all my strength of will and did it.

WELLINGFORD: ONE ROW
ON THE CHIMNEYPIECE
AND SIX STROKES BELOW

The boots brought me here and I stumbled, weak with hunger. Eighteen months since I was last here, though it seemed merely days, a few days. It was hard to summon strength to stagger to the broken-legged table where the bread was set out, covered with a linen napkin. I will stay here a day or two and eat. I may even raid the kitchen at the Dower House. My clothes are rags. I have already discarded them for others. The warm bathwater was welcome. I soaked off dirt and scabs and washed my hair. Thank God I thought to leave a comb with my clothing.

I came so close not to coming back at all.

LATER

I eat like a starved dog, gulping the food down. I did
raid the kitchen at the Dower House, sneaking around
the dairy like a ghost before wraithing it upstairs in my
cloak to have a look at baby Giles. Such a big boy,
now. Vincent has made him a rocking horse, so he
must be walking. Well, of course he's walking; he's
almost two. Grumpkin III was curled beside the baby's
cot. When I came into the room, Grumpkin woke and
came to me, rubbing around my ankles, purring loudly
enough to wake the house. I sat there and held him,
softness beneath my chin, and he reached out a paw to
touch my face. I hated to leave him there. I wanted to
bring him with me. I cannot. He needs to be here,
where there are mice to catch and queen cats to pursue. If I do not return again soon, I will find his child in
his stead, and yet leaving him is like leaving part of
me.

Now I have eaten, and bathed, and dressed myself.
Now that I am fortified, I'm going back once again.
Mostly because of curiosity. I want to know what's
going to happen.

LATER

I had mentioned earlier that Oberon has largely ignored me since my return. This morning, or what
passes for morning in the eternal evening of this place,
he sought me out among the ladies of his court.

"Beauty," he smiled. "Well met."

"Well met, Your Majesty," I curtsied in a flourish
of samite and lace.

"We have come to invite you to join the royal
hunting party this evening," he said.

I curtsied again, wondering if this would be another expedition after enchanted deer, wondering how
I could say no.

"We go to hunt the moonrise," he said smoothly,
silkily, as though he had read my mind. "In the lands

of mortal men. Such a ride may not come again for a lifetime. We beg you to join us."

I acquiesced, smiling, dropping yet another curtsy. Hunting the moonrise seems innocent enough. I went to find Mama to tell her about the invitation, thinking it would please her. I could not find her, not in the castle, not in the gardens, not near the groves and pools where the ladies of the court like to wander. In the stables I found news of her, however. One of the lads told me the Lady Elladine had ridden out on some business of His Majesty's, some message to be carried somewhere.

I went back into the castle. Everywhere I went there were Sidhe walking about with torches from which a heavy, reddish smoke trailed, filling the air. "What's going on," I asked one of them, a tall, white-haired fay named Auspir.

"Smoking out the spies," he said crisply. "The King believes the castle is riddled with them."

"Spies?"

"Bogles," he said.

I started to tell him if the Bogles wanted to get into the castle, they'd do it, despite all the Sidhe could do against them. I thought better of it.

Grandaunt Joyeause came by, and I asked her what was going on.

"My dear," she trilled, "don't ask *me*! I'm always the last to be told, the last at any event. As you should well know!"

"Is it true that Oberon thinks there are Bogle spies in the castle?"

"Oh, very likely," she said with a high flutter of laughter. "He's always thought that, hasn't he?"

The smoke smelled harsh and resinous and made it impossible to stay in the castle. I went out into the paddock and spent the afternoon watching the horses and writing in this book. Soon it will be time to bathe and dress for the moonhunt. I'll take the book with me on the ride, just in case there is a pause during which I can record what a moonhunt amounts to. I wish Mama were here to go with us. It might make an opportunity for us to work ourselves back into sympathy with one another. Mothers care for their children even when the children are dying of loathsome disease, don't they? Though perhaps there is no disease so loathsome as mortality, and that is why the old die first in the world: so they need not see their children succumb to it.

LATER: AT A HALT

This ride is a strange affair. We began by trotting over the flowery meadows of Faery. Hoof-fall and bridlering jingle, a quiet murmur of voices, the stars chiming like glass bells, the wind coming up to blow in our faces and make us feel we are riding faster and faster, fast as the wind itself.

Which we cannot be. Surely not. Surely not as fast as the wind! And yet the meadow goes under the hooves like a great carpet, smoothly pulled from beneath us, and we are suddenly on the heath, where contorted stones come up through the bracken and gorse to stand as enigmatic monuments upon this high plain. I smell the glamour around us, thick as smoke. Afar on one hand is the level line of the sea, glowing with dimly reflected light from the gathered stars, while far ahead on the other hand are barren hills and behind them a jagged bulk of mountains.

Our ride has brought us out into the world. The air is moist and chill. The horses' breath steams, making clouds around their heads and ours. The rutted road winds along the flanks of the downs, its pale track vanishing into a dark fold of hills. Dry leaves skitter across the ruts. Hunched clumps of heather crouch like toads in the lee of the twisted stones. I find myself counting the months. I came to Faery in March. I returned to Wellingford in April. I returned last the following April, plus six. Likely it is October or November of that year here in the world.

The road winds, along this hill and another hill and another hill. One twisted stone and another twisted stone. One glimpse of the star-silvered sea as we come around a corner, then almost darkness for a time until we wind that way again. Silence among the riders. The horses champ and stamp, gusting their breath in great sighs, and the silent hounds run red-eyed among their legs.

At long last we come to a crossroad, with a crude cross set up on a stepped pedestal, roughly squared stones laid by an inexpert hand. Have I seen it before? It seems familiar to me, and yet not, as though I might have seen it years ago, or in some other place. Oberon has dismounted and stands next the cross, staring at the sky, at the stars to see how they move, as though what he does next depends upon their movement. Perhaps the stars make the only clock Faery can depend upon to know when the moon will rise. I sit on the pedestal beside the cross and write, while the Sidhe murmur together like voiced shadows.

Oberon calls, relish in his voice, anticipation. We will ride again. He and Mab and a whole following of fairy folk. But not Elladine.

LATER

At the road's end is a great cavern, tall and dark as a tomb. Inside it is a fire the Sidhe have built, and behind the fire, a door. Oberon and his people are unusually quiet as they wait for the moonrise. There are so many of the Sidhe about that I do not feel I can call for Puck or the Fenoderee without endangering them. Instead I sit and write, an inveterate chronicler, recording each action. The Sidhe seem to me to be in no very contemplative mood.

Ah, now I see the first light on the eastern horizon. The edge of the moon pressing upward, a half-moon. Everyone murmurs at the rising light. As the moon comes higher, it illuminates the cavern where they are all standing, and they come out, into the pale light, leaving the fire behind them.

They murmur, I write. Now they turn toward the

fire for some ritual or other. Oberon gestures. They fall silent.

The door is opening!

I see light within. A face in the light. A face I have seen before, in a tower room in Marvella, looking out at me from a mirror.

Oh, my God. My God. I've been a fool, a fool. Puck said it. He said, "Seven years ago, when Thomas the Rhymer got free!" It is still Halloween. Seven years have passed since Thomas was claimed by his fair Janet. The Sidhe owe another teind to hell, and this time no one has come between themselves and their intended victim. They have brought here the only teind they could lay hands on who is not wholly fairy. One stinking of mortality. An old woman.

"What have you brought me?" the voice in the doorway cries like a whinney, like a howl.

"Beauty," Oberon says, turning his glittering eyes on me where I sit, petrified, writing. "Beauty, daughter of Elladine."

I am glad she was not with them. I can tell myself she would not have let this happen.

And now they are all departing, taking my horse with them, and I have not cloak nor boots nor Mama's box; not Puck, nor the Fenoderee, nor Giles nor any friend but myself, here, all alone. And in the light the face smiles as only that face can smile, and a finger beckons.

A voice by my ear says, "We are here."

I look. Nothing.

"We are here," says the voice. "Do not fear."

Carabosse? Israfel?

The finger beckons again, and my body moves against my will. I cannot go on writing.

Barrymore Gryme is here. Jaybee Veolante is here. Others of their ilk are here. The things they created in their books and pictures are here as well, made real, embodied in flesh, or more than flesh, or less than flesh. It is not proper that they should be here, either

the authors or their creations. It is not timely. I am
half a millennium away from their time. There are no
movies here, no television, no paperback books, no
best-seller list in the *New York Times*. There are no
publishing houses, no editors, no word processors,
none of what it takes to create monstrousness and
evoke horror, none of what it takes to record frantic
lust as it edges its way toward death. And yet they are
here. The ones whose names blazoned the bookstalls
and the ones whose names were whispered over the
counters; those who sold openly and those who sold
covertly.

As I am moved through this place, I see some of
them at desks, writing. Some are directing dramas.
These are the willing ones who have always belonged
to the Dark Lord. Others, the unwilling, who thought
they could trifle with the Dark Lord's works for
amusement only, they are held in cages until time
comes to act out their stories, and then they are let
out. They are costumed, false faces glued to their own,
breasts nailed to their chests if that is needed, their
own genitals cut away or modified as the plot requires,
this one to play that one's wife or son or mother, another one to play the part of the character who will be
slowly eviscerated in the third chapter, another one to
be the child who returns from the dead with sharpened
teeth or the child who is raped and then murdered,
and then, then, they are set upon the stage, their memories wiped clean, and set to the play. Chapter after
chapter, horror after horror, while the Dark Lord ap-
plauds and cries bravo, bravo, bravo.

Others are here, many of them from the twentieth.
Those who forbade birth control and abortion, wor-
shipping the fetus over all other of God's creations.
They are here in their vestments, their religious garb,
their Sunday robes or their everyday dress, carrying
their picket signs and swollen in endless parturition,
for so the Dark Lord commands that they shall be,
endlessly pregnant, endlessly giving birth, endlessly
suckling the demonic life that burgeons out of them,
with no choice in the matter. Having allowed none,

they are now given none, and the Dark Lord roars with amusement.

The nature destroyers are here, the tree-cutters and whale-killers, they are here, some of them willingly. They sit on bare stone and contemplate bare stone and eat bare stone for their sustenance. Surrounded by ten thousand of their like pressed in on every side, they gasp for air and beg for water. What they did, or wrote, or filmed, or believed in life has brought them here. Here there can be no undoing or rewriting. Here one is judged by the words already on paper, the picture already on film, the speech already recorded. Nothing new is written here. Only old things, redone. Old horrors, relived.

Still, I am able to think new words and distill new paragraphs out of the awful silences between the more horrible sounds. Between the screaming, the panting, the *uhng uhng uhng* sounds flesh makes when the pain and terror grow too much for comprehension. To shut out that sound, I think sentences, I spell them into happening, into my book, wherever my book may be, writing them there in shadow letters, willing them to exist, enchanting them into existing, somewhere, to keep myself sane.

Mama stayed here for a time. Mama came away herself still, or almost herself, still. Can I?

He has put Barry and Jaybee in cells next to mine. Cells. One could call them that. Obdurate cloud, frozen pain, structured agony, something not metal nor stone, something not permeable, not tangible, not anything one knows about substance. It isn't substance, but it's there, on all sides, below, above, opening nowhere except when He reaches through with his hand, his finger, his long, sinuous, lascivious, dignity-destroying tongue.

I hear Barry's voice. He says, "Help me, help me, please, oh help me."

I scream at him in fury and pain. "Nothing is happening to you you didn't describe, think of, imagine.

Nothing is happening to you you didn't conceive of and write down. Why do you ask for my help?"

I cannot even help myself.

"We are here," say the voices. They come close, like a cloak, like a bandage, like a barrier between me and what other things are here. There is healing in them. There is quiet in them. Invisibly, they are here. Even when I am being hurt, they are there, between the core of me and Him. The torturer can see my flesh, but not the thing I carry. He can feel my flesh, but not what it conceals.

"We are here," they say. "Hold on."

Jaybee is next door to me, separated only by a veil. If he sees me, he will break through. If I move, or breathe, or blink, he will see me. So I sit, like a statue, immobile, while he prowls there. Clever of the Dark One to think of this. So much worse than merely being raped, or killed. To think one may escape, if one merely doesn't cough. Doesn't breathe. Doesn't move. Doesn't move. Doesn't move.

He is singing, beneath his breath, a happy little hum as he wanders, brushing against the veil. "Down, down, down to happyland . . ."

It would be easier to die.

Except for the voices that gather around me to protect me, to make all quiet. "Hold on," they say. "We are here." How do they stay invisible? Undetectable?

Who are they? Is it really Carabosse, old Carabosse? Is it really Israfel, come to this hideous place? Strangely, I hear more voices than theirs. I do not take time to wonder. When they offer sleep, I sleep.

Once in a while there is the sound of a great gong, the reverberations slowly dying away into nothingness. I tell myself the gong marks the passage of days, or weeks. It has rung twelve or fifteen times since I have been here. It must be to mark the passage of time. What time? Is it like Carabosse's clock, marking the time until the end!

Time. There was a time, I remember a time, when certain things were said to be unthinkable. Persons did not dwell on these thoughts, they cast them aside, exorcising them by crossing themselves, by prayer, by recital of some formula which would wipe out the unthinkable thing. It did not do to dwell on such things. The darkness was too close. The reality of death was too near.

Later came science and electric lights, a time when people sitting in well-illuminated rooms said, "nonsense, we can conceive of anything at all." Any horror. Any disgusting, vomit-making thing. Any garbage. Any offal. Any violence, blood, evisceration, ripping open, heads flying with blood spurting, things emerging from inside the heart with the tissue ripping like paper and the tender inner places laid bare, no defense, no place to hide. "We can think of those things," they said, with a chuckle. "We can think of them."

There were times, I remember, when we said certain things were unspeakable. Fantasies too horrible for words. Imaginings too gross for description. Violence too inhuman to be put in human language. And then came those who said, "We can speak it, we can say it, make stories of it, until there is nothing that is not there on the page for the eye to see, for the mind to comprehend, for the child in each of us to be corrupted and eternally tainted by."

Innocence. Gone, forever, with the unthinkable and the unspeakable. And innocent laughter gone as well. Now only the dirty giggle, the wicked snigger, the game of out-grossing, the playtime of the beasts.

So that when the real death stalks

When the real horror begins

It will all be familiar and we will be able to enjoy it.

·   ·   ·

Barrymore Gryme has been put in the cell with me.

"Do I know you?" he screamed at me.

One eye hung on his cheek, that cheek gnawed open so that the teeth showed through. I shuddered, sickened, put my hands out and healed him. I am half fairy. I can do that. He was naked. His white, pouchy flesh was covered with scabs and bruises. Parts of him are mangled. Touching him is like touching something long dead.

"When did you die?" I asked.

"Die. Die," he screamed at me. "I'm not dead. I wish I were dead."

"You're in hell," I told him. "The hell you made. Did you believe in it, when you made it?"

He turned his face into the corner of wherever we are and wept. I tried to find a way out, but I cannot get away from him. My pain and disgust are part of the teind. They amuse the Dark Lord who is disgusted at nothing, who feels no pain, but who relishes it in others.

"Hold on," the voices say, breathing cool, fresh air upon me. Offering me cool, fresh water.

Later I saw Barry watching me. "You're beautiful," he said in wonder.

"I am not beautiful," I told him, stripping the glamour away so that he could see what I really am. He did not see. The Dark Lord will not let him see. Or perhaps he sees too well.

"You glow. You shine. Don't be afraid," he whispered. "I won't hurt you. I am a decent man."

I laughed. I laughed until I cried.

The Dark Lord cannot create. Faery cannot create. The angels cannot create. Only God, and man. I told Barry this, carefully, making him pay attention to what I was saying. It was hard. The face glued to his own would not let him breathe, the false breasts fastened to his flesh pained him, the shoes he wore had somehow been made part of his feet so he could not take them off. One of the spike heels was broken, and a fractured end of bone protruded from it. He kept reaching down to feel the bone, trying to convince himself it was not there. It was there. I saw it.

He had been playing a character from one of his own books, a woman who moves into a house occupied by a terrible thing from some other dimension of reality. It kills her children, one by one, in horrible ways, then her boyfriend, then comes after her. Barry had played the role well, so I assumed, for I had heard the Dark Lord's bravos ringing through the substance of the cell. One of the added horrors of this place is that one hears everything.

"The Dark Lord cannot create," I told him again. "You have created everything here. You and the others. He has only borrowed it from you."

"It was only a story," he cried. "Only a story!"

I thought of Chinanga once more. That, too, had been only a story, and yet I remembered Constanzia's face as she twirled slowly into nothingness. What are stories, after all, but reflections of a reality we make? Before Jaybee did anything, first he told himself a story about it. First I will go to her house, then I will break in her door, then I will knock her down and lie on top of her, watching her scream, then I will let my weapon out of my trousers and hurt her with it.

"To those who read it, it was real," I told him. "They lived it, while they read it. Perhaps afterward, they lived it. Some believed it. Perhaps one of those who believe it picked up a weapon and did to someone else what you did to a character. Or tried. There was enough belief to give it reality. Otherwise you would not be here."

He won't believe that. He has stopped talking to me.

The cell is open. I go out. Barry comes behind me.

He is playing with us, of course.

We walk, and I think words. Somewhere they are distilled onto a page. We . . . walk. My feet shuffle along. Barry tiptoes, screaming when he does not get high enough on his toes to avoid the broken bone at his heel. This is part of it, of course. Tempting him to walk, to escape, so that he will try this ungainly, ridiculous gait which hurts him so. I shuffle, he tiptoes. Time goes by. We are still surrounded by others. We can feel them on all sides.

An opening. We separate. He goes one way, I another.

I found a river. I came upon a place where space breaks through into something almost real. Like the door in the cavern, like the mirror, this connects to the world. Or to some other world. It is hard to tell. Mists hang heavily over the flow, which is turgid and silent. Nothing moves in the water. There is no shore I can walk along, but only this one space where hell waits on one side and the water on the other.

Still, it is a change. I sit beside the flow, listening, hoping for a sound other than those I have heard for so long. At last it comes. A slow plopping. From somewhere to my right and behind me. Eons pass and the slow sounds are no closer. And then, at last, they are here, in front of me. A rowboat, a rower, a few other figures who are drawn up past me as though made of smoke, fleeing past me into the enormity of this place.

The rower turns to face me, his dark hood shadowing his face.

"Captain Karon," I whisper.

"Lady Wellingford," he smiles. "Fancy seeing you here." His smile is a death's-head grin, and yet there is something of the old captain there. "Back at my old trade, you see. Sometimes I miss the *Stugos Queen*."

"I thought," I say, wondering what I thought. "I thought that you . . ."

"Would vanish, with the rest? With my lovely Mrs. Gallimar? With Constanzia and the Viceroy? No. No, I was not part of that story only. I am part of many things."

"You've thought about who you are, then."

"I've had an eternity of time to think about little

else," he smiled. "Plying across the Acheron, the Styx, the Cocytus, the Lethe, the Dark Waters at the end of all things."

"Who made them, Captain?"

"Men made them, Lady. Made them with magic their religions stole from Faery. Made them and named them and peopled them, too."

"Along with Acheron and Abaddon and all the rest."

"Surely."

"And this hell behind me, Captain? Did men make this one, too?"

"Men and the Dark Lord, Lady. Each helping the other." He sighed. "Is there anything else I can tell you, or do for you, Lady Wellingford?"

"Would you row me away from here? For old time's sake?"

He laughed. "Where to, Lady Catherine?"

"To the other side."

"What other side?" he smiled again, and pushed his boat away. I heard the quiet plops of the oars recede and was then drawn back into the place.

"Never mind," said the voices. "It may be a way out."

Giles. I have found I can almost escape this place by thinking of Giles. The voices give me silence, and I think of him.

When one is young, one thinks of love in romantic or erotic terms. I did. When I was sixteen, I thought of Giles in romantic and erotic terms. Romance when we were in the dining hall. Eros when I was in bed alone in the night hours. There is no innocence so deep as to veil the urgencies of the flesh from one's own youthful awareness. I wanted Giles, very specifically, to do to me what the stallions did to the mares, what the stable boys talked of doing to their sweethearts. I had no experience of it, but my flesh knew. And then, twenty years later, when we did at last what I had longed for, my flesh knew once again. It was the single thing needed, the one thing wanted, the savor and marvel of life.

I could not imagine doing without it. Being without it.

And yet, all those years in the twentieth, I had done without it, been without it. Seventeen, eighteen years old. At the peak of urgency and desire, and yet I had done without it. Because there had been no Giles. I had remembered him, lusted after him, pleasured myself in my bed pretending he was there. He had been necessary to my joy. It would have been nothing without him. So I had thought.

And when we two had come together at last, we had been splendid, but it had been more than the splendor of the flesh. It was we who loved one another. We two. Old Giles laid his hand upon mine and looked sweetly into my eyes, and I loved him no less than I had loved him on the terrace outside the ballroom where Elly and her young prince moved in a dance of another kind.

Our love, mine, was made of such little things. When we traveled to Marvella, he would rise in the morning and find something warm for me to drink. Broth, perhaps. Some herbal concoction. A cup of mulled wine. He would bring it to me, knowing I wake grumpily from the pains of sleep—since I was a child, my legs have bothered me. They pain me especially at night, and many nights I spend half sleepless, turning over and over. So, he would bring me something and sit on the side of the bed while I drank it and call me Beauty, though I was an old, white-haired hag with pouches beneath my eyes and lines around my mouth even then.

And the love would come up from inside me like water rising in a well. Not lust, not romance, but something kindlier than that. The feeling one has watching a sunrise sometimes. The feeling one has watching kittens at play. The feeling one has seeing a rose bloom beside the window. The Baskaronian feeling. A perfection of being.

When we were on the way to Lourdes, each de-

lightful thing that I saw I could not wait to turn to him
to see if he saw it, to point it out, to make some jest, to
evoke some wonder. Things I read that I wanted to
read to him. How we laughed over Christine de Pisan
together.

When he grew sick, he did not want me to go back
to the twentieth to get the medicine for him. He did
not want to go on living if it meant he might outlive
me. If one of us died, he wanted to die first. He knew I
was mean enough and grumpy enough to get along,
someway. He did not think he could live without me.
And he knew I would remember him. Perhaps he
wanted to be remembered.

I wonder if he knew I would remember him in hell,
and for that little time of recollection, hell could not
exist for me.

There are men here. Sometimes, between the howls
and screams and grunts of pain, I hear marching feet
and voices raised in song. Sometimes I hear laughter.
Sometimes I hear whispers, too soft to understand the
words, but full of sly meaning. Sometimes I hear a
shouted name, and know it is a name of someone real,
someone I have read about somewhere. Not only one
name, but several, in a questioning voice, as though a
teacher calls a roll.

Often there is an answer. A voice raised, "I am
here!"

And sometimes almost a chorus singing, their
voices full of a terrible urgency and a dreadful joy,
"Down, down, down to happyland."

I have been down to see Captain Karon once again,
though he tells me simply Charon would suffice.

"Difficult to be captain of a rowboat," he said, as
the newest cargo of ghosts streamed past him into the
place.

"Charon," I said, "if there were another side,

would you take us there? Or an ocean, maybe, that the river empties into."

"Would I go to an end if I could?" He smiled his death's-head smile at me. "Wouldn't you?"

"Are they dead?" I gestured behind me. "Are they all dead?"

"If not, they will be someday," he said. "Who lives forever?"

The Dark Lord, I started to say. Faery. But then I stayed silent, for he had given me the germ, the merest germ of an idea.

"Yes," said the voices in my ear. "Yes, try that. Those words are good words, as good as any."

"They are not magic words," I say, objecting. "They are mortal words."

"Any words can be magic," whisper the voices. "If they meet the need."

"Did you know that I am a fairy?" I asked Barrymore Gryme.

He laughed, spitting pieces of teeth in all directions. I reached out and healed him. He still laughed.

"How else could I heal you?" I asked him. "Fairies can travel through time. Fairies can be taken captive. Still, they are fairies, with powers of their own. I have magic, Barry."

"Much good it's doing you," he muttered through swollen lips, glaring through bruised eyes.

"It's because I'm alone," I said. "I am outweighed by all you others."

"So, you're stuck," he said. "Like the rest of us."

"My point is, I could get some of you unstuck, if you'd help me. There is some magic in each of you, as well. Man has been stealing it from Faery for thousands of years."

A wily look, perhaps hopeful. "How?" he asked.

"I'll teach you some words," I said. "When you see the others, teach them the words. Have them teach still others. When the gong rings the third time from now, everyone say them together and think of the shore of a river. The words are a magic spell. They'll get us out of here. Think of a river shore and a boat, a big boat come to take us away from here."

He does not believe me. Still, he has learned the words I have given him.

"I've heard this before," he complained as I recited to him.

"Spells do not have to be original to be efficacious," I told him. "This one will work. It will draw upon the magic of Faery. If everyone says it at the same time, it will free us. A great skeptic wrote these words. They will work." Perhaps they will. Though, actually, it is hope that will do the most. Optimism. The undying desire of most men to make things come out right!

Time goes by. Eventually, the gong rings. Over its dying reverberations I hear a whisper, as though a thousand voices have said "One."

There is time here when nothing happens, when there are no voices, no sounds. My mind circles, like a dog, trying to find a place to lie down. It runs off in all directions, thoughts flying in and out like bats while I chase after them. I keep losing them, thinking, "What was the thing I was just thinking of," trying to trace it, trying to remember. I become exhausted, unable to think at all. I start to panic!

"Shhh," say the voices. "Lie down. You are soft, in bed. You are comfortable. Your hands are folded on your chest. You do not hurt. What would you like to hear, or read, or watch?"

One of Bill's documentaries, I think. And suddenly, it is there before me. Bill's documentary on the Last Radish.

Fidipur's farms.

Glass houses as far as I can see. The camera plunges down through the glass, and shows shallow tanks, full of green slime, constantly agitated by mechanical fingers and bubbles from perforated hoses. The camera dwells upon these things, tenderly, sensuously. Between the tanks walk robed acolytes, examining the soup, bending to a thermometer with a motion like a genuflection, adjusting a valve with the tips of sanctified, gloved fingers. There is soft, holy music in the background, a choir singing.

Bill's voice: not his regular voice, but his awed voice. "This is one of Fidipur's farms. Here, isolated from any organism which might interfere with a maximized harvest, the soup is grown from which our food is made. It is here, in this particular section, that green one and two are manufactured."

The voice guides the camera as it follows the green soup. It spills down transparent pipes to the great cookers and emerges as a flaccid mush onto a conveyor belt. Knives divide and texture it. The belt moves into drying ovens, emerges once more, goes through a machine which injects other substances.

"Here essential vitamins and minerals are added," Bill says. "Before the mixture goes on into the molding section and the ovens." He does not mention flavor.

The camera follows the belt as it dumps its half-dried goo into a hopper, from which plops of green-gray gum are extruded into depressions in a great steel band. Heated plates come down at the end of stems. There is a sizzle of steam, then the tops rise and the band curves over to dump its cargo of baked biscuits onto another conveyor beneath.

"Food for the billions," Bill says in a proud tone. "But in the past there have still been those who believe they are too special to eat what the billions eat. Until now there have been the elite, who ate old-style, natural growth foods, because of the status it conferred." Montage shots of fat people at tables, toasting each other, eating with knives and forks. Close-up shot of a jaw, chewing. "In the past," Bill says, "some people have robbed Fidipur, but the robbery is at an end. The new managers, elected by you, Fidipur's billions, are harvesting the last of the old-style foods. Tomorrow, one of Fidipur's farms will rise where they have grown."

Camera flies over the glass houses, flits across the multiple towers of a hive, darts downward into an open space where narrow rows of greenery show against brown earth. The camera turns to the side of the field where Martin, the director, stands beside a stout, wrinkle-faced man dressed as everyone dresses in the twenty-first.

Martin says, "It did not seem right that the managerial class be allowed to consume this last vegetable, and there are not enough such vegetables for all of Fidipur's billions to share. So a worldwide lottery was held to find one of Fidipur's billions to have this privilege." Martin turns, beams at the man next to him. "This is Mr. Walford Tupp. What words do you have for us on this occasion, Mr. Tupp?"

The man gapes, smiles, giggles. "Well, gee, I don't know. I mean, it's such a privlige to be here on this momous casion, isn't it?"

"Yes, it certainly is a privilege on such a momentous occasion, Mr. Tupp. Are you ready to harvest the last radish?"

"Well, I don't know. I mean, sure. I mean, that's what I come for, isn't it? Right?"

"Remember, Mr. Tupp. Slowly. We want to be able to catch every nuance of this historic event." Martin smiles his professional smile and pats Mr. Tupp on the shoulder.

Camera on the Tupp feet, walking over brown earth. He is pigeon-toed. The soles of his shoes are worn more on one side than the other. The earth gives under each footfall, little cracks run away around the edges of his soles, leaving prints behind. There is an ant on the ground. He steps on it. Behind him, the ant struggles out of the compressed soil. Now the camera runs ahead of him, finds the radish, brings it up until it fills the screen. . . .

Green leaves, as large as sails. Slightly crinkled,

textured, glossy hillocks separated by darker-veined valleys, the veins running like brooks to join larger veins, these wandering toward the center to join the strong central rib of the leaf. It is like a rib in the vault of a cathedral, curving gently, its size diminishing toward the leaf-tip, growing larger as it plunges down toward the stem, the whole rounded on one side, cupped on the other, the proportions perfectly designed. Light fractures off the leaf. Light falls through the leaf. The rib is darker, becoming wine colored at its base.

And this is only one leaf. The camera pulls back to let me see two, then three, then four. Each a triumph of architecture. Each a wonder, a marvel. The camera pulls back, back, and suddenly the fingers come down. Grasp the leaves. Crunch them together. The microphone picks up that crunch as cells explode, as their tender juices run out onto those fingers. The fingers pull.

Soil shatters. Crumbs of moist soil rain down the sides of a growing cone. There is a volcano of disturbed soil. Out of its top emerges a flame-red, spherical shape, slowly rising, like a great balloon, like the sun, a gleaming ruby, a vast carbuncle brighter than blood, up, slowly, the long, white root trailing behind, tiny hairs on it broken from their home within the earth. It quivers. It almost screams.

The camera follows the fingers, up, and up, and up.

The camera sees a mouth. Opening. The radish is inserted, halfway. Yellowed teeth champ down. Saliva perks at the corners of the lips. The mouth opens again.

"Shit," says Mr. Tupp, spitting. "That's awful." The camera follows the radish as it falls, a bite out of one side, the other still glowing like martyr's blood, wet and miraculous.

The camera sees Martin walking away with Mr. Tupp, his arm around Mr. Tupp's shoulders in comradely fashion. For a moment the camera follows them. Then it turns downward, down to the last radish.

Jaybee always knew what made a good picture. As the camera draws away, and turns, and draws away, the radish becomes a sun on the horizon, an arc eaten out of it by a low brown hill; the leaves around it are a forest, and behind that forest the glowing ruby sun is setting. Forever setting.

The gong rings. Stronger this time, I hear a murmur, as maybe many voices whispering, "Two."

I am alone in my place. Barry is being tortured somewhere else. I am thinking of my mama. And of myself.

I was Elly's mother. Unwillingly. Without intention. Mama was my mother. If not unwillingly, at least without intention. She left me, left me to Westfaire and the Curse, a short span in her life, telling me to come to her when it was over. I left Elly, only for a few years, I thought, intending to return when they were over. So, perhaps, mothers leave children every day, intending to return, only to find they are too late, returning. The thing has happened. The hour has struck. The time has passed when it would have mattered.

So, are they to blame? Am I to blame, for Elly? Is Mama to blame for me?

And if the mother hovers, settles like a hen upon the nest, clucks to her chick beneath her wings and does not let it go; if the mother says, "No, the hour may strike, the thing may happen, and I will not leave you alone"; if the mother does that? What?

The chick struggles, and runs, and hides, wanting to feel the sun on its feathers, the air beneath its wings. And if it runs away and the hawk gets it, whose fault is that?

Is Mama to blame I am in hell? Was I to blame that Elly was in hell from the day of her birth?

The third gong. I wasn't expecting it. The sound came in a great wave. It left in slow vibration, and after it the almost hysterical gabble of thousands of voices moving from a whisper to a grunt to a shout: "Three, three, three."

Then the voices, saying the words I had taught them, words my favorite poet had made long ago, in some other place:

> *"From too much love of living,*
> *From hope and fear set free,"*

The words were ragged. I joined them, shouting, hearing Barry's voice rise up next to mine.

> *"We thank with brief thanksgiving,*
> *Whatever gods may be"*

The words came more strongly, more surely.

> *"That no life lives forever;*
> *That dead men rise up never;"*

A shriek from the Dark Lord. He had heard us. Was he too late to stop us? Did all the victims believe it enough?

> *"That even the weariest river*
> *Winds somewhere safe to sea."*

We were on the river shore! I heard the shriek, the cry, the bellow of the whistle of the *Stugos Queen*. We were standing on the riverbank in Chinanga, watching it come around the bend. From the high deck, Captain Karon waved at me. Around me lay the bodies of some dead, including Barry, who would rise up never, and some living, who now knew they would surely die. And before them was their transportation on their journey toward that final sea, the one the captain had long wished to find.

I heard a cooing voice and looked up to see Mrs. Gallimar clinging to Captain Karon's arm. She looked like Bill. She was Bill.

So, and so. The captain had done some dreaming of his own. Or he had taken my dreams for himself.

There was a swirling darkness behind us. Out of this aching cloud a figure lunged toward me, a scrambling monster, a hurtling shadow: Jaybee, alive. Well. He had not suffered here. He belonged here, and he was coming to get me. It had been too late, and useless. His breath touched my face, his fingers touched me . . .

"May I drop you somewhere," said a voice from behind me. It was Israfel. The ambassador from Baskarone. Jaybee's hand slid away, an empty skin, a sack, something hollow and unliving.

"Ylles, Israfel, if you please," I said in a fair imitation of Mama's tone.

"Faery, Israfel," said another voice. Carabosse.

He took our hands and we went up.

I looked down to see the river winding toward a far horizon, an endless starlit sea. Behind us was a seething darkness which no light penetrated. "He's still there," I said, disappointed that he had not vanished, as Chinanga once had done.

"A great deal of creativity has gone into that hell," said Israfel. "You and Carabosse and I, we made a spell that freed a few of us, but it will take more than a few verses of Swinburne to free him."

He meant the Dark Lord, of course. I meant Jaybee and all who are like him. Perhaps we both meant the same thing.

"Did you plan for him to catch me?" I asked, wondering now that it was over what it had all been about. "Did you plan it?"

"No," said Carabosse. "Oberon planned it, and Mab. But we knew of it and let it happen. If we'd stopped it, he'd have tried something else. He had the scent and wouldn't give up until he knew—or thought he knew. So we let it happen, but we came along to make sure he would not find in you what he was looking for."

"Will he try again?" I asked, wondering if I could last, again.

"No," said Israfel. "He thinks there's nothing there. He thinks he was misled, and he finds you troublesome. Besides, if things go as we believe they will, he'll be too busy." His voice was furry and throat-stopped with grief. He said nothing more.

28

Israfel and Carabosse suggested that I stop in the world. I did so. They waited while I ate, bathed myself, dressed myself. It took forever. I was so slow. I kept dropping things. Finally, I looked at my hands and cried out, hearing the sound of the cry, a tiny shrilling, like a lost bird. My hands were like claws!

"How long?" I cried.

"The bell rang once each year," Israfel told me.

How many times had it rung. Fifteen? Twenty? "How old am I?" I cried.

"About a hundred and three," said Carabosse, adding kindly, "Don't worry about it, Beauty. It won't matter in Faery."

I laughed, a quavery little laugh. "Odile may not live long enough for me to return again. I think I'll take my things with me this time."

"Things?" Israfel asked, smiling his radiant smile.

"There's still one hank of thread left," I said. "And the needles. I'll put them in my pocket."

When I had dressed myself, I got out Mama's box. It still had the letters in it, her letter, and Giles. I left them there. The time was past for letters. I put on the ring with its little winged figure. I put the needles and thread in my pocket. Then Israfel and Carabosse took me by the hands and led me back into Faery, back onto the flowery meadow where the tents had been set up. A dozen of so of the tents were clustered not far distant from us. Their occupants were standing outside, very quietly, as though they had been waiting for us to arrive.

Carabosse sidled sideways and was gone, but Israfel did not leave me as he had done when he brought me from Chinanga. He walked with me toward the clustered tents, holding my hand upon his arm. On either side, the Sidhe bowed, as though reluctantly, as though forced to do so. None of them looked me or Israfel in the eye, I noticed. I stared them down just to make them more uncomfortable, for among them were the riders who had used me for the teind.

My eyes were drawn to the Copse of the Covenant, where it sat afar upon the grass. There, too, a tent had been raised, and there was no question but that it, too, was occupied. The fabric glowed with a blinding effulgence. I looked away, my eyes watering.

"The messenger of the Holy One, Blessed be He," whispered Israfel, as he prepared to introduce me to those who had been standing by the tents. His fellows. His companions. Male and female.

Michael. Gabriel. Raphael. Uriel. They are the eldest, says Israfel.

Aniel, Raguel, Sariel, and Jerahmeel.

Kafziel, Zadkiel, Asrael, and Israfel himself. There are twelve of them all together. The Long Lost. The separated kindred. Twelve who assented when the Holy One asked Faery to help man; those who went away when Oberon said no; those who built Baskarone; those now returned to Faery. Twelve visitors. Plus Carabosse. Plus the Holy One's envoy.

The envoy is a seraph, says Israfel. Not a star-angel but simply a messenger. Come to deliver the word of the Holy One.

"When I was in Chinanga, I thought *you* were angels," I told them, my eyes on my shoes.

Gabriel shook his head. "Nothing so fiery. From time to time men have seen us and have assumed we were angels, but we are merely ambassadors of Bas-

karone." His voice sank to a whisper. "To the worlds.
Whatever and wherever they may be."

That whisper was familiar! It was like the whispers
I had heard in hell, encouraging me, helping me find a
way out. I realized suddenly that they might all have
been there! All twelve of them! Their faces told me I
was right. They had been there. Invisibly, they had
followed me into hell, to keep me safe.

Israfel squeezed my hand, giving me a significant
look, and I understood. They did not want me to speak
of it, not even to thank them. They did not want anyone—anything—to know what they had done. They
did not want anyone—anything—to ask why.

I tried to think of something inconsequential to
say. "Are you ambassadors even to dreamworlds?" I
asked. "Even to places like Chinanga?"

Gabriel laughed. "If one stretches time long
enough, they may all be dreamworlds. The only differences may be in the length of the dream and the
strength of the dreamer. Perhaps we call reality that
which is dreamed the longest, that's all."

I had learned something of cosmology in the twentieth—what anyone who read a popular science maga-
zine might pick up. "You mean the Big Bang?" I said.

"God breathes in, God breathes out," said Gabriel.
"Blessed be the name of the Holy One."

"What is Baskarone?" I asked them. "I thought it
was heaven."

"We have tried to make it so," said Sariel. "By
copying what was here when man came, and the best
of what has been created since. Much of earthly creation had already manifested itself and departed before men came, of course, but we wished to preserve
the work of the creators, somewhere."

She sounded almost as sad as Israfel did, and I did
not ask any further questions. Besides, there would
not have been time. Somewhere a fanfare of trumpets
blew, a silvery shiver of sound I had not heard before
in Faery. More of the Sidhe came out of their castles
and walked slowly down the hills to the meadow
where we stood. These were all the kindred of

Oberon, those who occupied this world. Behind them came the horses of Faery, tossing their lovely heads, their silver manes flying. The dogs came, too, the white dogs with their red ears and red eyes.

From the other directions, Bogles emerged, as they do, making that sideways sidle which brings them into one world or another.

During what followed, I stood with my hand on Israfel's arm, his kindred arrayed behind us, watching them come. Puck came up to us, quite unselfconsciously, nodding to Israfel as though he knew him well. While he watched his fellow Bogles assemble, he whispered to us both, taking an inventory, as it were, jigging from foot to foot with the rhythm of his voice.

*"When the silver trumpets sound to every puck
        and peri,
    From the clustered hills around, come the folk
        of Faery.
    Brownies, brags, bugbears, hags,
        big black dogs and banshees,
    Boggy-boes, hobby-thrusts,
        imps and lianhanshees,
    Kitty-witches, hinky-punks,
        clabber-naps and swaithes,
    Fachans, follets, fays, fiends,
        gallytrots and wraithes,
    Selkies, scrats, spunks, spurns,
        ciuthaches and cowies,
    Nickies, nacks, gholes, grants,
        tutgots and tod-lowries,
    Melch-dicks and come-quicks,
        cors and mares and pixies,
    Pad-fooits and leprechauns,
        chittifaces, nixies,
    Sprets, trows, gnomes, kowes,
        goblins and Peg-powlers,
    Ouphs, brags, nickers, nags,
        nisses and night-prowlers,
    Lubbers, lobs, tantarrabobs,
        cluricans and correds,*

Tangies, trolls, tatterfoals,
  hobbits and hob-horrids,
Mawkins, tints, gringes, squints,
  shellycoats and sprites,
Roanes and ratchets, pinkets, patches,
  grindylows and wights.
When they hear the summons sound, every puck
  and peri
from the clustered hills around gathers into Faery."

He grinned at me, cocking his eyebrows, and I
knew he'd been trying to amuse me. I suppose I must
have been amused, or at least interested, for I'd paid
enough attention to note that he had not mentioned
the Fenoderee in this inventory, which was not inclusive in any case. Puck had ignored thurses, knockers,
kobolds, and a dozen other beings that Fenoderee had
spoken of.

When all the Bogles had ranged themselves on the
seaside in a vast half circle, the Sidhe began to arrive,
gathering on the upland side and leaving a lane clear
to the Copse of the Covenant, which stood toward the
mountains.

I did not see Mama anywhere.

Israfel put his hand on my shoulder and said,
"She'll be here."

And at last she came, from her own castle, which
stood to the south of the upland. She came walking
with one or two of her people, Joyeause and another
aunt, I think it was. There were tears in my eyes. I was
grieving and didn't know why. When she came close
enough, I saw how very beautiful she is. She looked at
me, shaking her head a little from side to side, tears
running down her cheeks. Oberon looked at her, then
away, flushing angrily. He had sent her away when
they gave me as the teind to hell! She hadn't known he
was going to do it.

And it was all right. No matter that I was a hundred and three and all my remaining years had been
used up in hell. It was all right. She hadn't known. She

hadn't wished me ill. Oh, didn't I know it's the best we can do, sometimes, simply not to wish our children ill.

"Get on with it," said Oberon, impatiently.

Gabriel answered him. "There's nothing to get on with, brother. We are not here to make judgements."

"A little late to call me 'brother,' " said Oberon.

"Not at all," Gabriel said. "We were made at one birth, you and I. We were both children of the Covenant. You and your people chose your way and I and my people chose ours. You have done as you have done, and we have done as we have done. Now we will be judged, both, but neither you nor I will do the judging."

As though that had been an introduction, the seraph came out of the tent and moved down the lane between the Bogles and Oberon's kindred. I couldn't tell what the seraph looked like. All I could see was light, not too bright to look at but much too bright to see whatever was inside. Maybe it was all light and nothing else. It was not made for earth, as man and Faery were. "Earth is all we were given," Puck had told me. "Both Faery and mortal man. Earth is all we were given."

"Oberon," said the seraph. The word was really a word, but there was no sound. We all apprehended the word, but we didn't hear it. It seemed to hang within us, somehow, like a sensation. Like a pain.

Oberon didn't speak. He stood, head up, staring at the light, refusing to blink.

"You have broken the Covenant between Faery and the Holy One, Blessed be He."

"Not true," said Oberon in a harsh whisper. "No *human* has come to harm through me."

"She stands before you. Beauty, daughter of Elladine. Half human in birth. Wholly human in life."

"She's here! She isn't hurt! She isn't dead!"

I felt the glamour around me thick as salve. I could tell from the expressions on all their faces that I was beautiful, lovely as the dawn, lovelier than Mama, even. They were all set on making me so. Their eyes were on me, strengthening me, making me glow. I wish

I could have seen me at that moment. Just to remember. I felt myself shining like a star.

Israfel's hands touched the top of my head, came down my head to the shoulders, down my arms, on down my body. I felt the glamour stripped away. Oberon refused to look. The others could not take their eyes away. I saw Mama weeping as though she could not stop. I was so weak, I wanted to lie down. So old. So fragile. So very tired.

And still, I wanted to defend them. I wanted to cry out, "No! They've given more than the pain cost! There's beauty here. There's enchantment here. They've let me have that. I've had a life that's worth more than the lost years. Don't hurt them. Don't hurt my mama. . . ."

I tried to say that. Israfel's hands rested on my thighs, my old, quivering thighs, barely able to hold me up. I gasped for air. I tried to shout and couldn't, tried to intervene and couldn't. I raised one hand, and it trembled.

"Shhh," said Israfel.

I bowed my head, feeling tears. It wasn't only the years they'd taken from me. They'd taken my strength to defend them. The seraph would have listened if I could have spoken. They'd given my love for them away. They'd risked God's displeasure, and for what?

"She has lived only a few years in the world," the seraph said. "And yet her life has been used up. If she had spent it here in Faery, the Holy One would have said little. A pity, perhaps, but at least partly through her own choosing. A few years in Faery can be of great joy to mortal men, teaching them dreams. But among you was one who turned to the darkness of pain, not as a spur to knowledge, but as an end in itself. Among you was one who made a god of horror. Among you was one who turned his imaginings inward, an immortal who lusted after death, who set himself up as a god of death, which had only paltry gods until he came. He has let men come to him, those with similar desires. Together they have built a hell. We do not charge you

with the deaths of those men, for they went to him of
their own will.

"But you have bowed to him, and given him his
teind, and begged him to hold the Holy One at bay.
And so long as it was only yourselves you sacrificed,
the Holy One, Blessed be He, did not call the Covenant in question, not though you were craven, not
though you had fallen far from the glory you were
given."

The seraph's voice grew gentle. "What did you
think to gain?"

Oberon stared at the distant hills and said nothing.
So proud. He would not beg for mercy. Behind me,
Israfel was silent. All that host was silent.

"Had he told you lies?"

Still silence.

"Had he made you promises?"

No answer.

The seraph made a sound, or we apprehended a
sound, or a feeling, a sound of infinite regret, like a
harp string plucked and broken. "Too large a part of
this woman's life has been consumed in your kins-
man's labyrinth, and that was not of her choosing. She
is mortal and has been used to her lasting harm,
Oberon. Not only for this reason, for there are other
reasons, but with this as the cause, the Covenant is
broken."

Israfel's hands came up once more. The glamour
came back. My strength came back as the seraph
turned and went away. Too late to defend them now.
The seraph went into the tent and the light went out.
The tent stood empty. The trees surrounding it began
to blacken. Within moments they had fallen to dust
and the dust had blown away on its own little wind.
This was the copse Oberon had tried so hard to destroy, and now it was gone. Seemingly he could not
take his eyes from the place it had been.

When I looked back at the assembly, all were
weeping and moving away. Only Mama came to me
and put her arms around me, saying, "I didn't know.
Oberon sent me away, Beauty. He fogged the palace

to drive the Bogles away so they couldn't warn you. He didn't tell me. He just took you. . . ."

I patted her shoulder, hugged her close, crying, "I don't understand how Faery could make cause with the Dark Lord. I don't understand how they could."

She wept, and shrugged, looking in that moment like any grieved old washerwoman I'd ever seen at Westfaire, crying over a lost child, a lost man, a lost life. "I don't know," she cried. "He wooed us. He whispered to us. He told us we had enemies. He told us he would defend us against them. He told us of plots against us, and said he had confounded them. He pointed to the religions of men that were sucking our magic away, religions which pretended to worship the Holy One, and he told us the Holy One allowed the worship and had thus betrayed us. He told us he could lead us to victory against the angels, who would soon declare war upon us. Oberon believed him, perhaps, a little. Enough to give him the teind. A small price, we thought."

Simple paranoia, then? A fairy sociopath, crouched in his labyrinth, spewing lies?

I had been there. I knew there was more to it than that. A monstrous ambition. A death-loving ecstasy. A worship of pain. What dwelt in the Dark One's halls was not only of faery, but also of man, a dreadful alliance. Could it possibly be that there was some dark angel there as well? A hideous triumvirate, brooding destruction?

I looked at Israfel over her bent back and asked, "What's going to happen now?"

"The Covenant is broken. We had our immortality through the Covenant. I suppose we don't have it anymore. That's why Oberon is weeping. When he is through weeping, we will see."

"Baskarone," I faltered.

"Baskarone," he said, his voice breaking. "I don't know how long it will last. The seraph didn't say." I noticed for the first time that Israfel looked . . . not older. No. Worn, somehow. As though . . . as though he had spent himself protecting me. None of us had come out of hell unscathed.

"Before it . . . if it . . . can I see it?" I asked him.

He turned to look at the others. Michael nodded first, then Gabriel. Then the others. Israfel took me by the hand.

"Will you come back?" Mama cried, stepping away from me.

"If there's time," I said. "If I have any time left."

"Israfel," she begged, "I was never part of any of this."

He looked at her without expression. His face was calm but unforgiving. "When man stood up beside his fire and the Holy One asked us to help him, there were only thirteen voices who assented. Ours, and old Carabosse. Yours was not among them, Elladine. When Oberon laughed and walked away, you were at his side."

She bowed her head and wept.

Israfel said, "I'll bring her back if there's time."

What shall I write of Baskarone?

Everything that was lovely of the world when men came into it is here. Everything that men made beautiful while they were in it is here. None of the dross, only the glory. Some gardens. Some monuments. There is even an entire town, designed by a woman of great artistry. I had seen a film on it in the twenty-first. It was built early in the twenty-first and then destroyed by the nationalist terrorists in the Great Reunification War of 2043, the same war that killed all the people in Ireland, North and South, and half those in England and Scotland, as well as sinking the lands of Ireland forever beneath the sea.

In the long run, it didn't matter who destroyed the city. Fidipur's ocean farms now cover the place it once stood. If the terrorists hadn't bombed it and thereby started the war, Fidipur would have razed it anyhow. Mortal man is mad.

There are a handful of marvelous mosques in Baskarone, serene and beautiful. An Egyptian temple is here, crowded with painted columns. A mud fortress is here, its walls glistening with bright murals in tiles. There are structures in Baskarone from Ecbatana and Susa. There is a building from Troy. There are two from the States of America, quite small ones, sculptural houses which look as though they grew from the earth.

Cave paintings are here, fleeing horses and lumbering bison. African carvings are here, and so many things from the Orient I could not see them all, including a city from China, lacquered all in red and gold with dragons upon its roofs.

And all these things are set in gardens and woods and forests and prairies. The flowers that bloom in those gardens are the loveliest that ever grew. The trees in those woods are tall and straight. The grasses on the prairies have never been cut, and the little peeping birds run about among their roots.

There are people here as well. The woman who designed the city, the men who built the fortress, the carpenters who carved the dragons. All those who made beauty with their lives, they are here. Those who climbed. Those whose names ring, like a wine glass in a cupboard, hidden but sounding nonetheless.

The dreams of the men who tried to reach the planets, before Fidipur took everything, they are here. I don't know how they are there, but they glitter like sequins in the shade of that place.

"But you can't have the dreams of space explorers here. That hasn't happened yet," I said. "This is still the fifteenth."

"As Chinanga existed in the always, so do these things," Israfel said.

"Surely the Holy One, Blessed be He, won't let this perish," I said. "Just because of what Oberon did."

Sariel was beside us. She sighed. "Things the Creator Himself made have perished, Beauty, because of what someone else does. The Holy One makes a tree that lives for four thousand years, and someone chops it down to make paper to package chewing gum. The Creator makes whales who sing in the deep, and men kill them to put their oil in lipsticks."

"Enough, Sariel," Israfel said. "She knows. She has seen the end of it."

They let me alone to wander where I would. I walked into a great cathedral, down aisles of yearning stone, the great carved branches sweeping upward toward the traceries of the ceiling, so high above that it seemed impossible men built it and stones sustain it in those delicate arches. A bell rang, and the sound of it moved among the pillars, now soft, now loud, repeating and reverberating, plangent as a sigh. Incense burned, and the smoke of it rose in a pure, blue column in the light coming through high, painted windows. All of it, stone and smoke and sound, blending into one thing, one place, one instant in which the beauty of it stops your heart. Men did it purposely, made that space do that purposely. They knew how. They knew what beauty is.

I walked down aisles of trees that spoke of even greater loveliness. Green glades where light slanted down in golden spears, touching blossoms in the grass. There were oaks as red as stained glass, sifting the sun onto ancient groves. When I walked there, I walked quietly, seeing glory all around me. God did that. He knew how. He knew what beauty is. The cathedral was only a copy of this.

Even the Temple of Helpful Amphibians was there. Ambrosius Pomposus, also, had known what beauty is.

I remembered what I had left in the twentieth: gray concrete and miles of scabby houses, featureless towers of glass and miles of parking lots. The glades had been cut down to make pulp for horro-porn. There had been no holy silence but only the rant and howl of the machines the youths carried on their shoulders, a constant rape of the ears.

Here in Baskarone was a silence in which one could hear birds singing and the low of cattle from distant fields. Once on earth there was silence in which a child's laughter could be heard, or the cry of a kingfisher ratcheting overhead or the high shriek of a falcon. Once fish could be heard, plopping in their pools, and the splash of frogs and the hum of bees.

When I had left the twentieth there had been only the *whom a whom a whom a whom,* each sound hitting the ear like a blow, bruising the hearing so that when the sound was gone the ear throbbed with it still, like a wound. There is no birdsong left in that time, and if, by chance, the ear finds silence somewhere it can hear nothing, for it has been mutilated by what it listened to.

And the eye also. If it has never seen beauty, how can it know? It has been mutilated by ugliness, destroyed by horror. And so the mind.

I wanted to stay there, of course, but I had not earned the right. I did not ask. They did not offer. When I had seen all my heart could hold, they took me back to Faery, where I found Puck waiting amid preparations for war.

Puck was sitting on the ground near where Israfel left me. He got up to take me by the hand and help me seat myself on a convenient stone. I noticed for the first time that he rather resembled Giles. Not the face so much as around the eyes. But then he looked a little like Bill there, too. Strange how much there is of people we love in other people we love. He offered me a cup of something warm which he happened to have by him. It tasted suspiciously like worldly chicken soup with barley in it, and he confessed he had stolen it from a mortal kitchen.

"The cook will not miss it," he said. "She had a whole pot of the stuff. Rest, Beauty, and tell me about Baskarone."

I told him what I could, waxing as poetic as it is in me to be. I could see him noting it all down in his head, ready to make a song of it. While we sat there, several Bogles gathered around, including the Fenoderee. When I had told him all I could, I asked him what had transpired in Faery since I had been there last. I did not ask him how long I had been gone. I was afraid to know that.

It was thus I learned of the war.

"Oberon's people are not happy with him," Puck said. The Bogles all nodded at this intelligence, agreeing that indeed the Daoine Sidhe were extremely unhappy with Oberon.

"He has decided, therefore, that it is all someone else's fault."

"Not mine?" I said, horrified. "Not Mama's?"

Puck shook his head and laughed, shortly. "The Dark Lord's fault, Beauty. If the Dark One had not tempted Oberon, then Oberon would not have broken the Covenant on his behalf. Therefore, everything is the Dark Lord's fault, and Oberon is going to fight him. Him and his close kindred, at least." He sounded disapproving.

"But that's what you wanted them to do!" I cried.

"True, though not for that reason," brooded Puck. "The problem is that Oberon and his kindred are not strong enough by themselves to do more than irritate the Dark Lord, but the rest of Faery is too annoyed with Oberon to follow him."

I asked, "What about you, Puck? And Fenoderee? And all the Bogles?"

The Fenoderee answered. "He hasn't asked our help, and fighting isn't our kind of thing. Bogles have never gone to war. Even though there are a few tribes of us capable of violence, by and large we are too individual and eccentric. I think most Bogles will return to the world and live out our lives, such as they are. We may not be immortal any longer, but something tells us we're a long-lived people. Likely even in the twentieth or twenty-first, there'll be folk thinking they've seen a Bogle, or heard one."

"Where will Oberon attack the Dark Lord?" I asked.

"The Dark Lord won't come out," one of the little

folleti piped from the circle around. "So Oberon will have to go in after him."

"Will my mama go with him?"

They nodded, slowly.

"He has many demons there," I cried. Actually, the thought of the demons bothered me less than those other things in hell. Those horrors created by men in the future.

I told the Bogles about some of them, and they shivered where they stood. "I don't know if those things can be killed," I told them. "Men invented them, but the Dark Lord has given them a dreadful kind of life. They may be proof against anything Oberon can do. Can the Dark Lord himself be killed?"

Puck nodded. "He was of the Sidhe, Beauty. His pride led him to break the Covenant. He was so proud he did not realize he would lose his immortality when the Sidhe lost theirs. Both he and Oberon are like the sons of a generous father who are spendthrift with their father's fortune, treating it as though it were their own and limitless, as though they had earned it rather than receiving it as a gift. Then the time comes at last when the father says enough. Then, when the sons are left without the riches, they curse fate and their father, not willing to lay the blame at their own feet. Yes, the Dark Lord can die, just as Oberon now can die."

I stood up and brushed myself off. It was time I saw Mama. I had promised her I would come back. The Bogles took me part way, then left me as I started up the hill toward the castle of Ylles. As I approached, I saw her coming toward me. We met halfway, and she kissed me. This time she didn't mention my smell. I was careful not to mention hers, which was the smell of old flowers, drying and fading.

I told her what I could about the things they would find in the Dark One's lair and begged her not to go with Oberon. She shook her head at me, but she listened carefully to what I had to say, asking me one question and another. She said the things I described had not been there when she had been used as the teind. Barrymore Gryme and his ilk hadn't been there, either. There had been only fairy horrors, things Mama could handle fairly easily. When I had finished telling her, Mama was very pale and seemed rather frightened. I wondered if she would be able to convince Oberon that he should be careful. Oberon had always struck me as being both arrogant and precipitant in his actions.

Mama said she must go talk with him, but even as she turned to go, she clung to my hand. Finally, she pushed me away from her, pointing toward the place where Puck and the Bogles waited. "Your Grandaunt Carabosse wants you to come to tea. She says she will have no time, later on."

I knew she would not. "When does she want me to come?" I asked.

"Now. As soon as you can." Again she made the pushing gesture, telling me to go with Puck.

I didn't want to leave her. "Should I be leaving just now? With this business of Oberon going to battle and your going with him?"

For a third time, she gestured at me to go. "That's why you must go! Oberon is irritated at you. Oh, Beauty, he's irritated at himself for . . . well, you know what for. He looks at you, and it reminds him of how irritated he is. It's not a good time for you to be in Faery."

I stared at her. "It's probably the last time I will be in Faery, Mama. I'm really one hundred and three. Human people seldom live that long. When I go back, I'm gone. This is the last time you and I will be together."

She started to cry again, and I felt dreadful. I patted her on the shoulder. "Never mind. I'll go see old Carabosse. I won't stay long. We'll have some time to ourselves when I come back." As I turned to join the Bogles, she was trudging up the hill toward Oberon's castle.

Nothing had changed at Carabosse's cottage. The clocks still ticked and could still be silenced by her gesture. The only surprise was that Israfel was with her. They were both very quiet. When we had had tea, Carabosse suggested that I look into her Forever Pool and took me out with her and Israfel to the garden. The pool lay beyond it, among a grove of silver trees. The bridge which arched over it reminded me of the one arching the Pool of Delights, and its purpose was the same. We leaned on the railing, Israfel, Carabosse, and I, looking into its depths, seeing our faces dimly reflected on the black water.

Carabosse moved her hand over the water. Darkness. There was only darkness. Israfel moved his. Still only darkness.

Carabosse said, "Now you," and I did, moving my hands as she had moved hers, in a wide double arc above the surface.

Israfel sighed. "There," he said, pointing. I looked where he pointed and saw a glimmer of light, so faint, so dim, as though in the very bottom of the pool some treasure gleamed, softly and infinitely far.

"Well, so," breathed Carabosse. She and Israfel looked at one another, no expression on their faces at all, but I could feel something flowing between them.

We went back into the cottage. "What's going to happen?" I asked them.

"Something other than what we planned," Carabosse whispered. "It is almost as though someone else had done the planning."

"Whatever happens," Israfel said, "we have seen light at the end of time. I will carry word of that to the others. I think it will be enough."

And that is absolutely all he would say, though his hand lingered caressingly upon my shoulder as he bid me farewell. I stayed only a little while longer. When I went out, Puck was standing there with the horse to take me back. We rode through the forest while Puck sang ballads at me and the Fenoderee accompanied him on a lute.

We stopped on the way to have a picnic. More human food: sliced ham and fresh baked bread and fruit. Several of the more interesting Bogles joined us and vied with one another in telling strange tales of humans they had known. I think I slept. I seem to remember sleeping. We stopped in a wonderful glade to pick orchidlike flowers that grew in the trees. Several Bogles came along and lectured me on the flora and fauna of Faery. It was interesting that some of the creatures I had taken as Bogles, they took as animals, and that some of the creatures I had thought were animals definitely were Bogles. There seemed to be no clear way to tell. Black dogs, for example, are Bogles. The Hedly Kowe, however, is an animal. At least, most of the time it is. And so are the Gwartheg y Llyn. I may have fallen asleep again, during one of the lectures.

We stopped again, to look at a waterfall which Puck thought extremely beautiful. There he introduced me to a nixie, and she insisted that we try some of her water-moss wine, which was exceedingly delicious. Could I have fallen asleep again? It seems to me I did.

When Puck suggested we stop for the fourth time, I said, "Puck, you're preventing my getting back, aren't you? I think you should tell me why."

He shook his head at me. "Well, to begin with, there was some talk among Oberon and his close kin about your knowing your way about in the Dark One's halls. Oberon was talking about taking you along, as a guide."

"I don't know my way about," I said, astonished. "The Dark Lord is one of the Sidhe. They would know more about him than I. Every time I moved about in that place, it was different."

"We know that," said Puck. "And so does Oberon by now. We were just giving him time to become sensible, that's all."

"A very long time," I complained, suddenly worried that we had been away too long.

"We could have returned sooner," he replied. "But Israfel suggested we should allow some time for other developments to occur."

With all the picnics and wine tastings and zoological lectures, I felt we had been gone long enough for

most anything to occur. When we came out of the
trees, however, it was apparent that what Israfel had
meant by "developments" was much more than I
could possibly have foreseen. I had rather expected to
see Oberon and his kindred making ready for battle, a
few hundreds of the folk of Faery making a brave but
futile array upon the meadow. What I saw instead was
a sea of lances, the assembling of a mighty host, all in
bright armor with banners coiling slowly overhead.

And there at the center of the host were the twelve
from Baskarone, the Separated Ones. Israfel. Michael.
Gabriel. All. The great swans' wings they wore made
them stand out, glowing like stars.

"Why?" I whispered.

"Hush," said Puck. "Watch now!"

We stood at the edge of the trees as other of the
Sidhe came over the hills and kept coming, more and
more of them, more than I had ever seen or had
known existed. Puck whispered into my ear as they
came, identifying them, telling me about them. These
were Faery folk, though not of Oberon's lineage, and
they came from afar: an army marching from Tirfo
Thuinn, the lands beneath the sea; a mounted troop of
the Plant Annwn, led by their King, Gwyn ap Nud,
and another troop from the Plant Rhys Dwfen; people
of the Gwyllion; Ethal Anbual, the Sidhe king of Con-
naught, galloping down the hill at the head of a great
host of his people, mounted all on golden horses.

The warrior Queen Tyton came. She was armed
with an ebon bow and silver arrows, and she wore the
crescent moon upon her helm. Around her gathered a
host of warrior maidens, all serious-faced and fell, with
knots of red upon their breastplates to show they intended that their blood be shed to the last if need be.
Their banners bore the image of the hoodie crow and
they cried names of Neman, Macha, and Morrigu in
shrill voices. These are the three names of Badb, the
goddess of war.

Came also the seven winter sisters, Cailleach
Bheur of the Highlands, Black Annis of the Dane
Hills, the Loathely Hag of the Midlands, the Gyre-

Carline of the Lowlands, Cally Berry of Ulster, Caillagh ny Groamagh of the Isle of Man, and Gentle Annie of Cromarty Firth (where winter is softer yet more treacherous than most), all in gray robes, their heads wreathed with gorse, and their faces the color of blue-gray stone. They bore triangular banners of gray with a tiny sun in one corner, and their voices were the voice of winter wind calling death upon the world.

"Why do they come?" I cried to Puck again. "I thought it was only Oberon and his folk! Are they all following Oberon?"

Puck shook his head and held my hand tightly. "They are following Israfel and his kindred," he said. "The Long Lost have gone among them, speaking of the end of time. They know why they are fighting, Beauty. See how they look at you out of the sides of their eyes, without seeming to. See how they glance. It is why we came late to this meadow, why we are posed here against the trees. It is so they can see you, Beauty. They will carry your image and your name into battle, like a flag. It is for you, all this array."

I had not noticed the glamour until then. It was around me as it had been when we confronted the seraph, as much, and yet a different thing. A truer thing. I was as beautiful, but they were not seeing me, but what I carried.

"Tss," whispered Puck as he saw the tears in my eyes. "Hold your head high and do not dare to weep. They are going for you, and they must not see you weeping when they go."

It was a very great host. Many faces in that array showed the determination to die quickly for some great cause rather than to die slowly for none.

I, who was dying slowly, could not find it in my heart to abuse them for that.

And still they came, from afar, from the new world as well as the old, from the islands of the sea, from the forests of Africa, from great chasms and mighty rivers, from all the places of the world where Faery had made a home. I did not know the names of a tenth of them. Even Puck did not know them all.

And when the last of them had come, Mama came riding out from the edge of the host, up the long slope toward us. She looked very wan and worn.

"I told Oberon you could not guide us," she said. "So he's left you out of it. Besides, with all this. . . ." She turned to gesture at the host and sighed. "It was funny to watch him when they started coming. He suddenly remembered who he was! He suddenly measured himself against Israfel and did not want to appear unworthy." She said it with a tiny smile, a tiny, mocking smile. "He is Oberon once more, as I remember him from the distant past. Here at the end of things, he is Oberon once more, perilous and puissant."

I threw my arms around her. "Where are you going?" I asked.

"The route we know best," she said. "To the cavern on the heath. The same place the ride took you."

"I'll go with you that far," I said. She nodded and turned back to join the host.

Puck pulled at my leg. I looked down and he whispered to me. "If you ride with them, Beauty, wear your boots, bear your cloak, carry everything that matters to you."

"I don't even know where my things are," I said. "I haven't seen some of them since I was taken to hell."

"They're here," said the Fenoderee. "I gathered them up for you and kept them safe."

And there they were: boots, cloak, and book. He stowed the book in the cloak pocket and slipped the boots on my feet. The cloak I tied behind me, where I could get it in an instant.

"The Dark One hasn't forgotten what you did," Puck whispered again. "You'd be wiser not to go at all."

"It may be the last time," I told him. "The last time I see Mama. I can't just let her ride away without going with her as far as I can. You have to understand about mothers, Puck. I'm one, and I know. You can't always do for your children what you'd like to do. Your children aren't always people you can do for.

But she never meant me ill, Puck. Never once. She must see that the same is true. I've never wished her ill."

The sound of a great horn came thrilling over the meadow, that horn which is said to be Huon's horn, given to Oberon as a token of friendship. And the ride began.

It was so vast, that host, that the Long Lost had reached the world of men before the last of the Sidhe left the meadow. We rode at the tail, Mama and I, with Puck holding to my stirrups and loping beside us. Not far behind I saw Carabosse on a donkey, picking her way along as though going to a fair. Quick though we rode, she kept close behind, though the donkey never went faster than a walk. She waved her stick at me, and I waved in return.

Mama said, "Did you make it up with Aunt Carabosse, then?" And I suddenly recalled that Mama knew nothing of my long association with Carabosse. Nor could I tell her, now.

"She says she never cursed me to death, but only to a sleep. It was Aunt Joyeause who made that up."

Mama nodded thoughtfully. "Joyeause has never cared for truth much. She says whatever comes into her head. I never doubted her at the time, though."

"Once I thought all fairies were wise," I confessed to her as I had to Carabosse.

"Oh, no," Mama said. "Wisdom is not a great thing among the Sidhe. I have heard a legend about that." She settled herself in the saddle and told me the story.

"It is said that the Holy One, Blessed be He, first created mankind as he created the Sidhe, marvelously fair, and he set the first of them in a garden much like Faery except that day and night came there, spring and fall, warm and cool, dry and wet, and every animal which has ever been, and every bird and every fish."

"I think I've heard this tale," I said, remembering Father Raymond.

"Very likely. The story is very old. And it continues that He set in the middle of the garden the tree of the hunger for wisdom, and He told them what it was. 'Eat of it or not,' He said, 'as you choose. Except, you eat of it, you must leave the garden of ever-life, for wisdom brings a terrible price, the price of pain and death and loneliness. But if you will be immortal, do not eat of it, and you may live here forever in peace.''

And she went on to tell me the whole story of Eden, as though she were reading it out of the Bible, as Father Raymond had used to read it to me.

"Until the first woman could bear it no more," said Mama, "and she went to the tree of the hunger for wisdom and picked a fruit from it and ate it. Then she sat down beneath the tree and cried, for all the questions of the world percolated about in her head, like fish she could not catch, and she knew herself and all her children forever would be adrift in mystery, that as soon as one thing was found out another would present itself to be discovered.

"And the man found her there. When she told him what she had done, he took the core of the fruit she had eaten and tasted it and put the seeds in his pocket. 'For,' he said, 'if you must leave the garden, so will I. And if you must die, so will I. I will go with you wherever you go, leaving all the garden behind. And of the tree of knowledge you have given up paradise for, we will take the seeds to plant in every land we come to, and we will find the fruit bitter and we will find the fruit sweet.''

Mama sighed. "And that is why man was cast out to be no better than a beast, dirty and itchy and covered by smuts from the fire. And it is why he creates, and why he may grow wise, and why he is numerous. Though it is said among the Sidhe that both wisdom and children are the burden of men, we have desired only children. We have not much valued wisdom, for we considered it less valuable than the immortality man gave up for it. Which is why I gave you the hank of thread, child. To sew a cap of wisdom if you liked, for you are half mortal and might care about such things."

A thinking cap! Oh, I should have known. Of course. What else could it have been?

We had come to the road which wound among the dun hills. I could see the moonlight on the lances far ahead, for the host was strung out for miles. Here and there I noticed huddled human forms, their faces in their hands, trying hard not to see us. We must have seemed very terrible indeed, awesome and fell. I wondered what stories those people would tell their children about the night they had seen the Fairy Ride, going out in their thousands from the lands below.

Something itched at me. Something I had seen, or thought I had seen. A flicker, perhaps, along the route we were taking. Something or someone upon the hills. I searched, seeing nothing. Mama's eyes were better than mine, and so were Puck's. "Look," I told them. "Along the hills. Is there something there that shouldn't be?"

Both of them scanned the horizon. At first they saw nothing, but then Mama stiffened and pointed. Then Puck saw it, too, and then I did. The gleam of moonlight on metal, high upon a hilltop overlooking the road we were taking. I knew what it was.

"The television crew," I told them both, barking unamused laughter. "Here to film the end of Faery."

"They may be here to film it," said Puck, angrily, "but it will not be filmed." He jumped up behind me and turned my horse aside, and we went behind the hill. I heard a snort behind us and saw Carabosse's donkey following. So there were four of us, Mama, me, Puck, and Carabosse. We circled around the hills, the horses picking their way through the gorse and the tumbled stones as we worked our way higher, toward the ridge. Evidently no one else among the host had seen them. When we came out behind them, they had no idea they had been observed.

"Let me," I suggested in a bleak voice. "I know their language."

Mama nodded. Carabosse snorted, sitting still upon her donkey. Puck sat down cross-legged and waited to see what I would do.

"This sequence," I said loudly, "is expected to complete the documentary on the last fairies."

Bill spun toward me, then Janice and Alice. The machine sat a short distance away, like a great stone tub. Martin stood up from the place he'd been kneeling behind a stone, watching the host pass below. Jaybee turned slowly, letting the camera rest on me. Carabosse did something with one hand, and he cursed, taking the camera off his shoulder.

"Damned lens fogged," he snarled.

"You are filming the departure of magic from the world. However, your premise is false." I was determined to say it, no matter whether it was true or not. Mama was there, and she needed to hear it. "This host, it is true, will leave the world, but magic will return."

"The hell it will," said Janice. "This is the beginning of the end." She laughed, shortly. "From here on out, it's all downhill. Magic is gone. From here on out, it's religion, then romance, then horror, then the end!"

"Whatever comes when," I said, fixing Jaybee with a loathing glare, "you film nothing here today. Nothing at all."

He had the lens wiped off and raised it to his eye once more, only to curse once more, taking it down to stare at it. Carabosse had evidently fixed it so that he could not get a picture.

"Give it up," I told them. "Go home. We're not going to let you do it."

Jaybee got up and stalked toward Carabosse, violence obviously in his mind. When he got there, she wasn't there. She was a hundred feet away, sitting on her donkey. "No," she said firmly, "you'll not show anyone what happened here tonight. No one at all."

"You have no right," blustered Martin. "People have a right to . . ."

"Know only what others choose to let them know about private matters," finished Mama. "These are private matters."

". . . a right to know," he concluded.

"No, they do not," Puck said. "People have no

right to crash private parties, pornographer. And this party is private."

Jaybee sputtered.

"You won't get a picture," I said. "Even if we go away, which we're about to do. You just won't get a picture, that's all. We have decided the world will never see this."

And we rode down the hill to the road, leaving them fuming behind us. Bill hadn't argued. He had just looked at me, stared at me, listening to every word that was said, as though he recognized me. This trip had happened the day after I got to the twenty-first. I remembered his returning from it, angry that we hadn't let them finish. His superiors must have been annoyed with him, laying the fault at his door. Well, the fault was not his, but there would never be a documentary on the last of the fairies. The last whales, the last dog, the last tree, the last radish, yes. No last fairy. Not yet.

We came back into the ride farther forward in the column. We passed the cross I remembered from last time. It was not long after that we came to the great cavern, the one with the door. Some of the Sidhe had already built a fire. Others were watching the eastern horizon. Evidently the door opened at moonrise, whether the Dark Lord would or no. When it opened, they planned to go through.

Mama shivered, and I got down from the horse and went to her. "You're cold," I said, idiotically. We were all cold. The night was crisp and chill. A winter's night. "Take my coat."

She shook her head. "You have nothing heavy enough to warm this chill. I know what's down there."

I stepped away, staring at the fire and at the door behind it. I was the only one who did know what was behind that door, though I had told Mama and she had tried to describe it to anyone who would listen.

"Father Raymond used to say, *'Una salus victis nullam sperare salutem,'* " I told her. "It means that victory can come out of hopelessness." She smiled, only a little.

Israfel came riding back through the quiet host,
looking for me. When he saw me, he turned his horse
and came straight toward me, bowing to Mama, to
Carabosse, even to Puck as he came. When he reached
me, he held out a hand and pulled me up onto his
horse, then rode a short distance away. We both got
down and stood together, looking at the assembled
multitude. He was very quiet.

"I want you to have this," he said, taking a scarf
from around his neck and putting it about mine. It was
crimson silk, with bands of silver and gold at the edges.
"It is real, not enchanted. I wove it, with my own
hands. When we go in, put on your boots and your
cloak and go home, back to Westfaire."

"To Westfaire? But Carabosse said he would look
there."

Israfel kissed me gently. "He would have. Oh, yes,
my love, he would have looked there. But now, we
believe he won't have time."

"I can't let you go in there alone," I said. In that
instant he was Giles, he was Bill, he was anyone who
had ever cared for me. I could not let him go.

"We aren't alone," he said. "Nor are you. And you
have something to do yet, Beauty. Something more
important than going into that hellhole again.
Carabosse knows. I know."

A sound caught his attention, and he turned to
watch. The moon was rising. The door was opening.
He leapt into the saddle and drew me up beside him.
He kissed me again. It felt like Giles's kiss, that night
when we danced on the terrace. He laid his head
against my breast, where the thing burned, whatever it
was. At Mama's side he left me, then rode forward
into the host.

"Someone will come to tell you about it, daughter," she said. "Puck, if no one else. Do not grieve
over us. We've played the proud fools for a very long
time." She leaned down and kissed me, too, on the
cheek. My lips and my face and my chest all burned
from fairy kisses. Then she rode off, down the hill, and
I was left standing beside Puck, holding the reins of

my horse in one hand. Carabosse jogged past, waving to me. Below, the horses were pouring through the doors like water down a drain. In no time at all they were gone. The door closed. The cold moon looked down at me, unsmiling.

I tied Israfel's scarf around my neck. If there was something left for me to do, I could not imagine what. I had very little time left in which to do anything.

Puck was kneeling at my feet, holding the boots. I slipped my feet in, one, then the other.

"I'll see you there," he said.

Perhaps I nodded. Perhaps not. Far off on the top of a hill was a shimmer, a shifting, as of a time machine going back to its own time. I, too, needed to go to my own time.

"Boots," I said, "take me home."

29

I tottered on my feet beside the rose-hedge of Westfaire. Beside me was the shepherds' well. I could
barely see the cat's-head stone. I put out my hands to
catch myself, and they were only bones with a little
flesh bagged about them, blue veins running like root-
lets across their backs and between fingers with nails
all ridged and twisted. I sat down on the coping of the
well and leaned against the post. Israfel had told me to
go to Westfaire. What could I do in Westfaire? Besides, I had no strength to go anywhere.

I sat there for a long time, accumulating strength,
or perhaps losing it. The boots were heavy upon my
feet, and I slipped them off. The cloak was heavy upon
my limbs, and I took it off as well, letting it lie behind
me over the well coping. I sat there in a ragged kirtle,
feeling the sun strike my skin through the rents. Ah,
well. If I got a bit stronger, I could put the boots back
on and go to the Dower House. There might be someone there who remembered me. Or who would take
me in, out of charity.

As I sat up, almost determined to go, something
dropped from the pocket of my cloak. I picked it up
and looked at it, the hank of thread. I reached into the
cloak pocket for the packet of needles and found it
with one unlucky fingertip.

Thread and needles. To sew, so Mama had said, a

cap of wisdom, a thinking cap. If one wanted a thinking cap. Mama hadn't. Wisdom was the curse of man,
she said. In seeking wisdom, we had lost our heritage.
I didn't believe that. We hadn't sought wisdom dili-
gently enough, that's how we'd lost our heritage. We
preferred cleverness to wisdom. Instead of seeking the
truth, we had preferred to believe in easy certainties.
Always so much easier to take the lazy, easy way and
then pretend God had commanded it. I sighed. I
couldn't make a cap. There was nothing to make it of.

One hand went to my face to wipe frustrated tears
away, encountering a corner of the scarf Israfel had
given me. Such luxurious silk. Silk for a princess. Real
world silk.

I could make a cap of that.

That is, I could make a cap if I could thread the
needle. My eyes were weak, half-blind. The needle
was small. I fumbled with the hank of thread, moving
the almost invisible end of thread back and forth. The
needle slipped in my hand; I grabbed at it, pricking
myself; and the thread fell into the well.

I sobbed. Weakly. Without conviction. What had
made me think I could do it in the first place? My back
pressed against the post, I waited to die, believing I
could cry myself to death if I just kept at it. There
wasn't much to me anymore. I probably weighed no
more than eighty pounds. I thought I would leak my
life out through my eyes and then dry up and blow
away. That would be the end to it, and I could quit
trying.

"What's the matter, Grandmother," said a voice. It
was a male voice, a young voice. I couldn't see who
spoke.

"I've dropped my thread," I said hopelessly. "It
dropped into the well."

"I'll get it for you, Grandmother," the voice said. I
hadn't time to wonder how before I heard the plop of
something sizeable dropping into the water. Not a big
enough splash to be a person. Or had it been? A quite
small person, perhaps?

I heard assorted liquid sounds, plashings and gulp-ings, then a scratching and grunting, and finally something wet and cool pressed the soaking hank of thread into my hand.

"I thank you," I said. "But I'm afraid my reach is beyond my grasp. I needed it to sew with and cannot see to thread the needle."

"It's a pity we do not have a fairy about," fretted the voice. "One who would give you keen eyesight as a fairy gift."

I started to agree with the young man, coming to myself with rather a start. I *was* a fairy, one who had been taught such spells, a long time ago. I had learned diminishing spells. The Spell of Bran. Spells for farsight, sure-foot, keen-ear. Perhaps if I blended the former and the latter. Keen-sight was what was wanted.

I tottered to my feet, made a few graceless passes, and chanted the proper words. My vision cleared at once, and I stared at the well coping where a large green frog sat regarding me with bulging eyes. "How marvelous, Grandmother," he said. "We had a fairy after all."

"I am not your grandmother," I snapped. At my age it was not easy to snap. The few teeth I still had seemed loose.

"I know you are probably not really my grandmother," said the frog. "I was only being polite."

Indeed, he was a particularly polite frog. I could not recall, through the fog of my aged memory, that I had ever encountered a frog of such poise before. I cast about for recollections of other frogs, finding such memories sparse and unprofitable, mixed inexplicably with memories of dinners in Bayonne and Lourdes and garlicky servings of something I had preferred to think of at the time as chicken.

"Of course," said the frog. "I am not really a frog, either."

I had already guessed that. "You're a prince disguised as a frog," I hazarded. "To prevent your being killed by your enemies."

He shook his head. Since a frog has little neck, this involved shaking the entire body. The coping was slippery, and he fell into the well once more, emerging moments later very wet and out of breath.

"Actually," he said, "I am a prince enchanted into a frog for some reason which I am utterly incapable of understanding."

I was busy threading the needle and spared only a moment to look inquiringly at him.

"Since you are going to be occupied with your sewing, perhaps you would like me to entertain you with my life's history," the frog suggested.

I nodded. Certainly there was no reason why not. Until I got the thinking cap done, there was nothing else I could do but sit and sew. I was already planning how to make the cap, by folding the scarf into fourths, diagonally, as one does to make a cocked hat out of paper, and then sewing the folded side closed and turning it up to make a brim. Since the frog seemingly had not interpreted my nod as permission to go ahead, I repeated it more firmly as I tied a knot in the thread.

"Ahem," he began, clearing his throat.

"My earliest memories are of a childhood surrounded by loving people. My foster father and mother, my nursemaid, the servants, the young man who was hired to play with me, later my tutor. When I was old enough to be told anything at all, I was told that my true father and mother, a prince and princess, lived far away, in another kingdom from which it was thought advisable I be excluded, inasmuch as I was not an heir to the throne and my presence might serve as an excuse for usurpers to cause dissention and unrest. I was told that this step had been taken in order to assure me a happy and extended life, since claimants to thrones, even legitimate ones, often live shorter lives than other, less exalted persons."

"I have known of such cases," I told the frog. "History is rife with them."

"So I was informed," the frog went on. "Since I am not ambitious, this explanation was satisfactory to me. The allowance my foster parents received for my care was sufficient to guarantee a pleasant life, and the maintenance of the estate on which I was reared was a sufficient career to interest me. I learned agriculture, beekeeping, cattle raising, dairying, egg production, fodder storage, gardening, horsemanship, independence, jar molding, kennel keeping, lamb raising, manpower management, nut growing, orchard keeping, poultry breeding, quarrel quashing (among the serfs), rabbit hunting, sheep grazing, timber cutting, usury, viniculture, wool clipping, xylogliphy, yoke making, and zealotry."

"What is xylogliphy?" I asked, amazed.

"Wood carving," he replied. "It was the only *x* I could think of."

"And zealotry?"

"One must be zealous, mustn't one. About something."

"And you learned usury?"

"To avoid it, Grandmother."

I started to remind him I was not his grandmother, but halted. Dim thought swam through my turgid mind. A fish I could barely see. Something he had said. "Go on with your story," I said.

"My foster father, a good man, and my foster mother, a good woman, though at times impatient, gave every attention to my education. I had the finest tutors from the time I was a child and learned Latin, Greek, French, and the common tongue as well as the trivium and quadrivium, including grammar, rhetoric, logic, mathematics, composition, and history. I learned to play four musical instruments and sing in a pleasing voice a great number of popular ballads and instructive songs."

"How many times have you told this story?" I asked, taken with the well-rehearsed tone of the verbiage he was spewing.

"Many times, Grandmother," he sighed. "More times than I can count. Has it begun to sound overly familiar?"

"A bit more spontaneity might be welcome," I said, turning the seam in the cap I was making. "However, whatever comes most naturally to you will do." I sighed, fretfully, suddenly overcome with hunger.

"What's the matter, Grandmother?" the frog asked.

"I'm starved," I said. "Literally starved. I have been too long in Faery, and my mortal body has not been fed."

"I can find you an apple," the frog said, leaping off the coping and hopping into the woods which surrounded the rose-hedge. I remembered then that there had been an old orchard there, one that had not been used for generations, except by lovers, lying on the sweet grasses. Within a little time, the frog hopped back again, removed a ripe apple from his mouth, and wiped it upon my ragged skirt, apologizing for the only way he had to carry it. I felt a sudden spasm of affection for the frog.

The apple was crisp and sweet. I bit into it, gently, in order that my teeth not come out in the sweet flesh of it, and the juice ran down my throat as the frog continued.

"It's interesting that you're not all fairy. I am not all prince, either. Though, as a child, I was told I had royal blood; the kingdom from which I had come was small and had insufficient fortune to keep me well all my life. Therefore, I was educated with a view to becoming industrious and independent. My foster father told me that, when I was twenty-one, he and my foster mother would return to the tiny kingdom from which he had come, and which he missed agonizingly from time to time, though I cannot say why. The stories he told of it were uniformly boring. It had no natural splendors that he could remember, and its architectural heritage he described as rural revival, though a revival of what, he could not say. Still, I looked forward to the day when I should be master of my own destiny, little knowing that such matters are subject to many reversals totally outside one's own competence.

"When I was about ten, I learned that my mother and father, whom I had never met, had died in an avalanche. I grieved, though not greatly, since I had never known them.

"As do all boys, I came to the age of physical maturity somewhat ahead of any mental or emotional stability with which the physical surges and urges might be controlled. I had a bittersweet and blessedly brief affair with a dairy maid, an unsuitable partner, one might say, though she had a lovely complexion, very pretty hair, and a vocabulary not exeeding one hundred words, most of them to do with cows."

The frog reminded me of someone. I couldn't tell who, but he did. His manner of speaking reminded me of someone.

"I then wooed and won the hand of the fair Elaine," the frog went on. "A very suitable match. We were to be betrothed on my eighteenth birthday. She was some years younger, and it was thought we would be wed when she was fifteen or sixteen and I about twenty-one. In the interim, my foster father was of the opinion I should seek sophistication through travel. While he did not recommend any attempt to go to the Holy Land, then, as you know, held by the infidels, he did recommend a journey to Santiago de Compostela, to which he had journeyed in his youth with great cheer and good company."

Through the murk of memory, the fish swam nearer.

"However," said the frog, "before I could depart on the journey set out for me by my foster father, with due regard for continuing my education and experience in ways that would benefit me, I happened to go riding into the forest and became lost. On attempting to find my way out, I came upon a tower in which a maiden sat singing. Her name was Rapunzel, as I learned when an old and opinionated fairy came out of the underbrush, carrying a clock, and insisted that the maiden let down her hair."

"Carabosse!" I said. "It could only have been Carabosse."

"However did you know, Grandmother? It was indeed the fairy Carabosse. Well, to make a long story short (for I see you have almost completed your sewing), the fairy tricked me in a very unpleasant way, and when I climbed what I thought was a rope of hair securely attached to the head of Rapunzel—a very lovely maiden, indeed—I found the old fairy instead. She harangued me at length upon the subjects of time and beauty, ending her discourse by putting an enchantment upon me that I should become a frog and remain so until kissed willingly by a princess!

"Since that time, it has been my hope that I would first be kissed, then returned to my natural state, though I fear that neither Rapunzel nor the fair Elaine will have waited. Some thirteen years have passed since then. Both of them will be old maids of twenty-five, or buxom matrons, mothers of many." The frog wept briefly. "Though I have spoken to my foster father about the matter, and he assures me the estate will be still be mine when I achieve manhood once again."

I finished the cap and put it upon my head. The elusive fish swam up and looked me in the eyes.

"You are my great-grandson Giles Edward Vincent Charming," I said.

"Well of course, Grandmother," said the frog. "I would not have addressed you so familiarly otherwise."

This was specious, but I did not argue with him. I had been one hundred and three when I had visited Carabosse. If, while I dallied returning to Ylles, she had come immediately to the world of men to enchant my great grandson, as she no doubt had, and if thirteen years had passed since that time, I was now one hundred sixteen years old. The century had passed during which Beauty was condemned to sleep. Or was that in the curse? And which curse? Joyeause's curse, or Carabosse's? Or Disney's? I started to blurt all this out, then stopped. Beneath the thinking cap, faculties long unused—nay, faculties never used before—began to stir.

"At one time," I said, "I think it was in 1417 or the year after, while in Bayonne, I bought a book by Christine de Pisan. It was called, I recollect, *The Treasure of the City of Ladies*. Do you know of it, by chance?"

"I'm sorry, no, Grandmother. I am unacquainted with feminist literature."

"She directs her discourse toward princesses, including in that number the daughters of dukes. Would you agree with her inclusive idea of royalty?"

"The daughters of dukes are certainly very noble, Grandmother. Certainly they might be included among princesses."

"Then let me kiss you, child. I have not seen you since you were two years old."

I leaned forward and kissed the frog. The air shimmered. I felt dizzy. A small earthquake made the stones beneath us shift, ever so slightly. When I looked up, he stood there before me, stark naked, as fine-looking a young man as has ever been my fortune to see, except for his very slightly bulging eyes. No doubt he would outgrow them in time. I enchanted a few leaves into a long shirt for him and told him that would have to do until we got into Westfaire.

"Westfaire," he mused. "I thought Westfaire was mythical, like Faery, like Olympus, like . . ."

"Mythical things frequently aren't," I said tartly. "Focus your mind, boy. Grandmama has need of you."

With Giles Edward Vincent Charming's assistance along the way—let us be clear, mostly he carried me—I got back into my boots and, holding him firmly around the neck, told them to take us through the roses into Westfaire. Once inside, he let loose my hand and promptly fell asleep, as I should have known he would. I was carrying the cloak and the boots and had the magic cap upon my head. He had nothing to protect him from the spell upon the place. Retaining the cap, I thrust the boots inside his shirt and belted it around him with the belt of my cloak. Thus closely associated with magical influences, he woke once more to stare around him unbelievingly. If anything, the hedge had grown taller since I had last been there. Everything within seemed to glow with a light of its own. The glamour was so thick it seemed buttery.

He carried me upstairs for his first look at Beloved.

Once he had seen her, he could not tear his eyes away. He wanted to kiss her, but I would not let him. "No, Giles," I said. "Not yet. We have some thinking to do."

He became almost uncontrollable, so I pulled the cap off my own head and put it on his. He subsided, his mouth falling open as his mental faculties underwent instantaneous enlargement. When he looked completely dazed, I removed the cap and replaced it on my own head. I felt it might take a day or two to explore the full ramifications of the headgear, and I had no time to lose. In passing, I examined Carabosse's clock and verified that it was almost half-past the fifteenth century. The numbers still ended with twenty-two. Though all of Faery had gone to war, nothing had changed. Or perhaps something had. After I had seen light in the bottom of the pool, she had seen fit to leave Faery and enchant my great-grandson. There had to have been purpose in that.

We went first to the barracks, to get Giles Edward some clothing, and then to the kitchens. He prepared food while I sat and thought and thought and sat. We ate together, ignoring the cooks sprawled across the floor. While we ate, I began to tell him the story of my life, referring from time to time to this book, my book, the book Father Raymond gave me so long ago, to remind me of the sequence of occurrences. So it was I found Carabosse's addition to my text and marveled over them. As I read, I realized who it was the frog had reminded me of when he talked. It was myself. I had been a loquacious youngster.

When I grew weary, I gave him the book and let him read for himself while I dozed beneath the cap, aroused occasionally by his exclamations as he encountered something strange or unbelievable or patently impossible.

"I know, I know," I murmured. "But it all happened just as I have said."

I was not really surprised to find that my account of my time in hell was in the book, as I had imagined setting it down. That kind of thing is, has been, usual in Faery.

When we had eaten, we were weary, so I directed him to Aunt Lavvy's room where I had slept before. I had forgotten my Giles was there, but it did not matter. I told young Giles who he was, then lay down beside my love. My great-grandson tucked me into a blanket and rolled himself into a quilt upon the floor, asking if there was any danger we would sleep forever. The question was too close to my thoughts for comfort. I assured him we would not, and in a moment his youthful snores echoed in the room.

I dozed. After a time I woke. The very old do not need as much sleep as younger folk, though they need it more frequently. Like cats, we nap and wake, nap and wake. The thought of cats reminded me of Grumpkin, and I missed him. One of the first things I wanted to do was explore the Dower House stables to see if he had left a son.

I felt somewhat stronger, and wanted to look about me a little. I took the boots from my great-grandson's shirt, replacing them with the cap, and bade them take me to the lakeshore beyond the roses. Instantaneously, I stood there, the cool night wind blowing in my face.

Across the lake were the villages of East and West Moerdyn, where, evidently, they were having carnival time. There were fires on the lakeshore and torches among the trees. All along the lakeshore, from far on my left to far on my right, the little fires flickered and burned and I could hear, as though from another world, voices raised in jollity.

On the surface of the lake, windlessly calm, the reflections of the fires and torches stretched to my feet like a hundred golden roads leading to the edges of the world. I was at the center of a fan of fire, a wheel of golden beams.

I heard, as though in a dream, the voice of Captain Karon saying, "We are at the center of the world."

I saw myself, once again young and beautiful, at the center of a wheel of light.

All light, all beauty, ends at my feet, I told myself. It comes from everywhere, and ends at my feet. For a time a vision possessed me, a great wheel of light which could not be extinguished, which would roll and burn and roll forever.

At length, I came to myself. It was chilly with the moist wind blowing, and the fires had been put out. I bid the boots return me to my bed. There I lay quiet and warm and quite awake, my hand on my Giles's chest, wondering if Carabosse had foreseen what I would attempt to do.

When my great-grandson woke, I told him to put the cap on his head while I explained what was in my mind. When I told him the world, or at least all life was to end in the twenty-second century, at first he protested. However, the thinking cap exerted its influence, and he admitted it was inevitable, given the nature of men. When I told him that Faery might end very soon, he wept. Despite having been turned into a frog by the fairy Carabosse, he had gentle feelings for most of fairykind. After that, he simply nodded, concentrating on my plan.

"It might be done, Grandmother," he said. "If one really wished to do it." He looked very wistful, however.

"You're thinking of the girl upstairs," I said.

He admitted that he was.

"I am sure we can work something out," I told him. "But everything else must be done first."

"It may take years," he sighed.

"I think not," I told him. "I'm sure help is available. But, even if it should take years, remind yourself that you are one-sixteenth fairy, a sufficient share of fairy blood to guarantee you an extremely long life."

"How old are you, Grandmother?"

"One hundred sixteen," I said, thinking what a brief time it all seemed.

He sighed, but he was a good, sensible boy. Thank God he was Vincent's son, and not the child of the mad young prince. Thank God he took after his father rather than his mother. Thank God he took after his great-grandma, at least a little. Perhaps beauty does, in time, breed true. I knew he would do as I asked.

I lent him the seven-league boots and the cloak of invisibility, taught him a few enchantments, and thereafter he came and went many times each day. I, meantime, kept the fire burning and food hot in the kettle, and stood ready to admire each acquisition as he brought it in.

Giraffes and lions and rhinoceri. Auks and dodos and passenger pigeons. Elephants, okapis, and pandas. Snow leopards, tigers, and ocelots.

Seeds of great trees and small. Shrubs and flowers and mere herbage, shoot and root, leaf and branch. Robin and sparrow, goldfinch and wren, eagle and falcon and kestrel, and all the birds of the sea.

Those creatures too large to be transported *in statu quo,* as Father Raymond would have said, were diminished. I taught my great-grandson the spell and he had no trouble with it whatsoever. Evidently even one-sixteenth fairy blood is sufficient for such elementary magic. Once the creatures were in Westfaire, I removed the spell while they lay sleeping two by two, or one by six, or however they properly divided themselves. Herd beasts came by severals, others by pairs, at least two pairs of each, for Giles Edward Vincent Charming had learned his husbandry well. "You have to allow extra so you don't get too much inbreeding," he told me. And "I only picked the ones with young, for they have proven fertility."

Such a good, sensible, intelligent boy.

One day as I sat by the kitchen fire, waiting for his return, I heard a voice calling my name. I tottered out into the garden and found Sariel there among the cabbages. She looked worn and tired. I was afraid to ask her how the battle had gone, but she took me by the hand and told me without my asking.

"We weakened him, but we have not yet killed him," she said. "All those creatures of horror that men invented have gained strength and a terrible life of their own. We are not fighting only our own darkness. We are fighting men's darkness as well. Oh, Beauty,

the things we found down there! The engines of anni-
hilation! The machines of destruction! The human en-
gineers of hate, laboring in their dens to make greater
horrors yet. The human writers, hovering over their
pens, creating baser terrors of bigotry and persecution.
Oh, we could not have made these things, Beauty.
Only God and man can create. All that God makes is
beautiful. Why did He give man the choice? In the
labyrinth of the Dark Lord, man is his ally. Only time
can kill him, and them."

"Our side?" I asked, barely able to get the words
out. "What about our side?"

She smiled, a remote, bitter smile. "Horror is
stronger than joy, Beauty. Particularly when it is encouraged to flourish. Still, we have beat him back. He
has fled from us, out of Faery and into some other
dimension of terror. We are pursuing him with what
strength is left. Many of our people are gone."

"Mama?"

"Your mama. Yes. She perished bravely fighting a
thing none of us could have imagined. And Oberon
and Mab. And Israfel. And many more."

Israfel! Oh, such a pain by my heart.

"But not the Bogles?"

"No. Not the Bogles. Sensibly, they stayed out of
it. Sturdy. Independent. A little cynical. They do not
let pride lead them into folly. They have come behind
us, blocking the earths as it were, to keep the horror
from returning. They will live a long, long time yet."

"And Carabosse."

"When Carabosse saw there could be no victory in
time, she left us. She said she had a greater task before
her."

"But some survive."

"Some survive, yes. But it is the end of Faery. We
must leave the world. We must pursue the Dark Lord
into whatever place he goes, however long it takes. In
the end, we pray the victory will be ours. . . ."

"Then Bill and Janice were right. It was the last
ride."

"They were right."

"Will you ever go back to Baskarone? Those of you who are left?"

That remote smile again. "Who knows if we will ever come there again. Or, if we do, who knows whether it will be there to receive us."

"May I have it?" I asked her.

She was astonished when I told her why, but she smiled and told me I might have it if I liked.

Then she was gone. I wept a time for Mama and for Israfel, but weeping does no good, does it? Sitting down and weeping is what women have done for centuries, and it has done us no good at all. Nor praying. God has given us the earth. He is not waiting in the next room, ready to fix it for us if we ruin it. If we do not care for it, no one will. On other worlds, other races of men perhaps do better than we have done. He cares for us, but he does not control what we do.

So. So. I called Fenoderee, and he was there, with Puck, and a dozen other Bogles as well. I told them what Sariel had said.

"We know," said Puck. "We heard."

"Baskarone won't last. Faery is gone. Mortal men will trash all life by the end of the twenty-first. That means . . ."

"It means this is the only hope," said Puck. "We know. We've come to help."

And so they have. They have brought beetles and butterflies and moths. Orchids and hibiscus and frangipani. Tropical fruits and desert plants. Things that fly and crawl. They bring them all to sleep in my gardens, my orchards, my stables, my hallways. Every sconce is hung with spiders. The moat is filled with fish, there are mice in Papa's pockets and moles under Father Raymond's skirts.

The library is littered with great buildings made small, with bridges and monuments, all those from Baskarone, made small. We could not bring the gardens or the forests, so we have settled for seeds.

On two of their return trips, I asked Giles and Puck to take Weasel-Rabbit and her mama out into the world once more. They are doing no good here;

they would not be good breeding stock; and we desperately need the space.

Days go by, and they shuttle back and forth. My
grandson with them, they alone, they in pairs or trip-
lets, coming and going. The grounds of Westfaire are
capacious, but they are beginning to fill up. Sleeping
bodies are everywhere, perched, sprawled, flopped.
Bats and sloths are hanging upside down in the buttery. I put the koalas in my tower bedroom, clinging to
the bedpost, and four kinds of foxes are curled at the
foot of my bed, next to the Taj Mahal.

Giles Edward has emptied the fountain and filled it
with saltwater from the sea. It took all of them to bring
the whales, though when they arrived they were no
larger than goldfish. Sperm whales and right whales
and blue whales and white whales. Killer whales and
dolphins. Gray whales and pilot fish. Sharks. I thought
perhaps we could leave sharks out, them and mosquitoes, but Puck said no, the Holy One made it beautiful in its entirety, and it had to be all or nothing. I sit
on the edge of the fountain and watch the whales
sleeping on the water, blowing spray from their blow-
holes and dreaming of the songs they will sing. Perhaps. Someday.

Grumpkin IV is on my bed. Or perhaps he is
Grumpkin V or VI. He sleeps on his back with his
paws curled over his belly. His wife is curled on my
pillow, with the kittens. Such pretty kittens.

And at last it is all done. There is not a species
alive between year one of mankind and the twentieth
that they have not found and brought here, alive or in
seed. Mammoths and mastodons and all. There is not
a creation Israfel and his kinfolk included in Baskarone which is not here. And beneath my breastbone
the seed of beauty burns and burns and burns,
stronger with each thing that comes. It will not burn
out. It will never burn out.

Now is only the last bit.

"Where will you go?" I asked Puck.

"Here," he said. "A few of us are going to stay

here. If the time ever comes, you'll need help with this lot."

"Grandmother," said Giles Edward, a youth worn and tired from his long effort, "I can stay, too."

I shook my head at him. "Oh, child, of course not. There's Beloved up there in the tower all this long time, waiting for her prince. We can't let her go on sleeping forever. That wasn't the idea at all."

"But . . ."

"But me no buts, child. No. Tonight we will all have a celebratory dinner. Ham and cheese and ale and wine, and fresh baked bread—Fenoderee has someone to do that—and we will sing songs and laugh. And then you will take Beloved out with you, well away from here, and kiss her awake." Once out of Westfaire, she would wake on her own, but why shouldn't he have the pleasure.

"And then?"

"And then you will apply all your alphabet of industry and intelligence to living a long, prolific, and pleasant life." God grant that it is so.

"And then? What will happen here?"

I shook my head at him again. Who knows for sure?

I was getting ready for our celebration when Carabosse showed up, suddenly, sidling out of nothing.

"So here you are," she said.

I mumbled something at her, something about how hard I'd been working and everything we'd done, and offered to take her about the place and show her.

She looked at the animals in the corners and the bats hanging from the wardrobe door and laughed. She toured the stables and the gardens. Then she sat down in a corner and laughed, the tears running out of her eyes.

"I thought you knew," she said. "I thought you had guessed."

"Knew what?" I asked her. "Guessed what?"

"All this. This," she said, pointing at all of it, ani-

mals, fish, birds, Baskarone shrunken to tiny size.
"You didn't need to do this. We already did it."

"You . . . ?" I couldn't figure out what she was
saying.

"Israfel. And his kindred. They already did it.
Long ago. Before you were born." She leaned forward
to tap me on my chest. "What did you think was in
there, silly girl?" And she went off laughing again.

After a time, I laughed with her.

"Beauty's in there," she said. "In Beauty, beauty.
All of it. Here in Westfaire. In the beautiful is Beauty,
and in Beauty, beauty. Silly girl." And her head
sagged, just for a moment, as though she was too tired
to go on. "Everything you have collected is beautiful,
girl. But it was already inside you. All inside you,
made tiny, like a seed. For you to keep safe, forever."

Well, I had known that, of course. But it wasn't
enough merely to take their word for it. They might
have missed something! It felt better to have done it
myself.

A little redundancy never hurts. Someone told me
that once. I can't remember who.

Carabosse joined us for our celebration.

Candles. Every candle in the place alight. Music.
The Bogles came from everywhere for that. Wild
things. Benevolent monsters. They are a very musical
people. Food, and wine, and dancing, and games. I sat
quietly in the corner, writing in my book, watching
them all.

It went on until dawn. Somewhere out in the world
a cock crowed. Silence came, and most of the Bogles
went.

Giles Edward Vincent Charming brought the
sleeping Beloved downstairs and out into the courtyard. He put on my boots. He was crying as he told me
goodbye, but he was sneaking glances at her, too. He
will not grieve for long. He kissed me and then he
went.

Carabosse kissed me. It felt like a mother's kiss.

She didn't tell me where she was going, but I have a feeling it will not be far. She sidled into somewhere else and was gone.

Fenoderee and the others who are staying are out with the animals. Puck carried my Giles up to the tower and laid him on my bed. Giles looks much better, much stronger. This long sleep has done him good. Then Puck helped me to climb all these stairs to be with my love. Since I've been back this time, my legs have hurt such a lot, and of course I am very, very old. One hundred and sixteen! Think of it! I could not have climbed here without him.

From the balcony I can see the light of dawn and bright wings circling straight above. A dove, I think. Very high. On my bed, Giles snores and Grumpkin snores, little breathy sounds in the silence. When I stroke either of them, they move as though to tell me they know I am here. I sit on the edge of the bed to write, remembering Giles Edward's question.

What will happen?

Beloved will awaken once she is out of Westfaire. He will kiss her, of course, but that has nothing to do with anything. No matter what Joyeause said about a hundred years, this spell was laid forever. Westfaire will go on sleeping. Papa will sleep, and Doll, and Martin. The aunts will sleep, and the young maids, and the young footmen and stable hands, all will sleep until the conditions of this enchantment are fulfilled and someone or something wondrous arrives to kiss beauty awake once more. Not a prince. Or not merely a prince. More than a prince. A rebirth of some kind. And not soon. Not until long after Carabosse's clock has run down. Long after the twenty-third, I should imagine. Long after Baskarone is gone and all of Faery vanished. Long after the Dark Lord and all his minions have perished from the weight of time. The inanition of age will get him, finally, where nothing else can, and having no victims except each other will kill the rest. Perhaps in the twenty-fourth or the twenty-fifth, or perhaps long after that, life will come again. I have done everything a half fairy can to preserve it. Carabosse and I make a good pair.

And if it happens—why, then everything is here. The whales and the elephants and the radishes and the trees. Magic is here. And man, too. All those randy stable boys and giggling maids. And the Bogles. Ready to begin again. Ready to recreate what God created. And Giles, to greet me again in the morning; and I, to greet him.

And if it does not happen?

Then everything is here. Sleeping. Dreaming, perhaps, of what might have been. Perhaps others, on some other world will catch the dream, will wake from it astonished at its marvel, at its complicated wonder. Perhaps someone or something will dream who can create once more.

There is a bedtime prayer Aunt Terror taught me when I was a child. "Now I lay me down to sleep; I pray the Lord my soul to keep." Such an arrogant idea to go to sleep on, I have always thought. Why should God do any such thing, except that I've always loved His beauty passionately. All God's beauty passionately.

That time, so long ago, I would not allow the Curse to touch me. I did not want to spend a hundred years sleeping. I thought it unworthy of me. I thought it monstrously unfair that Papa had let me in for such a fate. I evaded it. I escaped it, so I thought. Escaping destiny is not so easy as that. Funny, the way things work out. Even Carabosse and Israfel couldn't quite keep it from happening the way it did. As though someone else had done the planning.

Puck is holding out his hand for my pen. And my cap. He says he will sit by me, and rub the pains out of my poor old legs. Until I sleep.

"I pray the Lord my soul to keep."

Perhaps, instead, He will keep the fire that burns here; the fire that Israfel and Carabosse set here.

Perhaps that has always been my soul.

ABOUT THE AUTHOR

Sheri S. Tepper was born in 1929 in Denver, Colorado, and has lived in Colorado all her life. She worked in the administration of a multi-state non-profit organization until her retirement in 1986. Currently, she divides her time between writing and—in association with the American Minor Breeds Conservancy—raising various minor and rare breeds of domestic livestock and poultry on a ranch in the foothills of the Rockies. She is married, has two adult children and one grandchild.

In the few short years Ms. Tepper has been publishing, she has written over a dozen novels which have garnered the respect and admiration of both readers and critics. In addition to *After Long Silence*, her works include *The Gate to Women's Country*, *Grass*, *The Awakeners* (published in two volumes as *Northshore* and *Southshore*), *Beauty*, (winner of the *Locus* award for best fantasy novel), *Sideshow*, *A Plague of Angels*, and *Shadow's End*. Her most recent novel is *Gibbon's Decline and Fall*.

A preview of
GIBBON'S DECLINE AND FALL

"A provocative, devastating, enthralling,
consciousness-raiser"
by Sheri S. Tepper

"Tepper is a masterful storyteller . . . the passions
that infuse and enliven her characters, her compelling use of prose, and the fast pace of her plots, usually keep a reader entranced . . . But what makes
Tepper such a compelling and popular read in the
SF community is her frequently expressed desire for
people to think through the things they do and take
responsibility for their actions . . . Tepper handles
her points, and her plots, exquisitely well."

—LOCUS

Continue for an excerpt from this remarkable novel:

Read Sheri S. Tepper's
GIBBON'S DECLINE AND FALL,
on sale wherever Bantam books are sold.

FALL 1959

The campus sprawled rosy brick over a hundred acres and buzzed with a thousand new students making their way through room assignments and registration. Extracurricular activities were posted on the bulletin boards in front of Old Main. Drama-club meeting on Saturday morning. Orchestra tryouts for non-music majors, also on Saturday morning. Women's-chorus tryouts, Tuesday and Wednesday evenings.

Carolyn had an unencumbered hour on Tuesday, so she decided to sit in on the chorus tryouts. She sang some, and if the standard wasn't too high, it might be fun to try out. She sat down next to a plainly dressed young woman with a strong, rather horsey face and offered her hand.

"Carolyn Crespin, from New York."

"I'm Agnes McGann. I'm from Louisiana."

An improbably perfect blond on the other side of Agnes leaned forward. "Hi, I'm Bettiann Bromlet, from Fort Worth."

She smiled, rather shyly. Carolyn, looking at the careful grooming and wealth of tumbled curls, wondered what she had to be shy about.

"Sopranos," called a woman in gray from the front of the room. "Please pick up a copy of the audition music from the table to your left. Contraltos, the table to your right, please. The accompanist's music is clipped to yours. This is for reading ability, ladies—we'll do you alphabetically. Be sure your name is on a sign-up card."

"I'll be near the front," said Bettiann. "Just for once I wish they'd do it backward. It makes me nervous, being first."

"Bound to be a few Adamses or Abrahams before you," Agnes McGann muttered.

But there weren't. Bettiann was called first. She handed the piano music to the person at the keyboard, went to the front of the dais, and sang competently. She read the music easily, and though her voice was small, it was true. Considering the shy smile, and the nervousness, Carolyn was surprised at the amount of personality she displayed, a bit too much pizzazz for Carolyn's taste. If Bettiann Bromlet was the general standard, Carolyn herself might decide to try out.

"Very nice," said the woman in gray. "Lily Charnes?"

"You've done that before," said Carolyn when Bettiann returned to her seat.

"Beauty contests," Bettiann murmured, flushing hotly. "My mom was all the time entering me in these pageants. Last time around I won a scholarship."

"Congratulations," said Carolyn.

The blond shook her head. "It's crazy that I won, I'm not that goodlooking. It's all pretending. . . ."

Carolyn found this an interesting idea. She hadn't thought before that one could pretend to beauty, though of course it made sense. Certainly Bettiann's stage personality was not the same as that of the rather hesitant girl sitting beside her.

It was a while before they got to McGann. Carolyn asked her if she was nervous, but Agnes said no, not particularly. She'd had a good voice teacher at St. Monica's. They'd had a choir they were proud of and paid a good deal of attention to.

"Catholic school?" Carolyn asked. "Me, too."

"Really? I've been in boarding schools since I was six. My family was killed when a truck hit their car, and the settlement was put in trust for my education and keep. I've spent my life in Catholic school. Too long, Mother Elias says. She's the abbess at the Sisters of St. Clare near

New Orleans, where I'm going to be a nun. I wanted to enter right away, but she wants me to get through college and take an M.B.A. first."

"An M.B.A.? For a nun?"

"They want to start an oyster farm, to make money for the abbey school, but there's no one in the order with business training—"

"Agnes McGann?" called the woman in gray.

Agnes had a voice better than Bettiann's, with a good deal more range. She, too, sang competently, though almost without emotion. Carolyn identified the style as churchy: angelic voices conveying as little human emotion as possible.

"Very nice," said the woman in gray. By this time Carolyn had it figured out. "Very nice" meant you were in. "Thank you very much" meant you were out. Hmm, "thank you" meant "maybe." When Agnes returned, the three of them went on sitting, curious about all the other putative singers.

"Faye Whittier," the woman called at last. The final one.

Faye was colored—tall, graceful, with her hair cut very short. Agnes had never seen hair worn like that, just a cap of it, natural. She thought colored people straightened their hair. The maids at St. Monica's had. The pianist tinkled through an introduction as Faye clasped her hands loosely in front of her, holding the music almost negligently. Either she knew this composition or she'd already memorized it.

The voice came like velvet, smooth throughout its register, organlike on a low note, whispering on a high one, easy, fluid, capable of infinite shading and power.

Carolyn decided she would skip trying out for chorus.

"Oh, God," whispered Bettiann, "If that's what they want! I'll never make it. I shouldn't even have tried. . . ."

Agnes shook her head, put her hand firmly atop Bettiann's hand and said, "No. You and I are fine for the chorus, but that girl will get all the solos."

When Faye had finished, "Oh, my, yes, " said the woman in gray, conveying a fourth degree of judgment, one heretofore unexpressed.

Agnes, who was on the aisle, had a little fight with herself as Faye came from the dais. On the one hand, she was colored, and Agnes had no experience with colored people except for the maids and cooks at school. On the other hand, she was colored, and there'd been the recent Supreme Court decision on equal education. One should err, if one did err, on the side of friendliness—especially a nun should, or a person intending to become one. Besides, Faye was elegant looking.

Agnes offered her hand. "You have a beautiful voice," she said. "I'm very envious." Which was perfectly true, and she'd have to confess it, too.

"Don't be," Faye said with a flashing grin. "So far all it's done is get me in trouble."

Fifteen minutes later the four of them walked out together, down the sidewalk, turning at the same place toward the same dormitory, found they were all living in Harrigan Hall (Harridan Hall, said Faye, laughing) and were even in the same wing.

"Must be the new-girl wing," said Agnes. "Who's your roommate, Bettiann?"

"I haven't met her yet. Her name is Ophelia Weisman, and she's from New York."

"And yours?" Agnes turned to Faye.

"I thought they might put me with Jessamine Ortiz, because we already knew each other from school in San Francisco, but they didn't."

They met Ophelia, Bettiann's roommate, in the dorm lounge, a skinny gamine with dark tattered hair and enormous gray eyes behind huge glasses. Faye introduced them, first names only, to her friend Jessamine Ortiz, a slender Eurasian girl with a face so calm and shuttered it did not seem as lovely as it was. Jessamine was majoring in science and math, and so was Ophelia; Jessy had a landscaper father and a passion for biology; Ophy had a physician father and a passion for medicine. Both their fathers thought it was silly to waste college educations on girls.

"Dr. Dad thinks I should go to nursing school," Ophy announced, wrinkling her nose. "My mother was a nurse. She put Dad through med school, and then he divorced her and married a girl about my age. I do not like my father."

"Interesting," said Faye. "I think that must be a white thing. With some black people, it's the men who think they don't need an education." She turned to Jessamine. "All through high school we knew each other. You never said anything about your father's not wanting you to come to college."

Jessamine flushed. "My father is a really nice man, but he has this sort of traditional picture of women's place in the world. He says men are made to take care of women, that women are happier not knowing very much, because if they did, it might make them dissatisfied being wives and mothers."

Agnes silently agreed. Men should take care of women. They were stronger and larger and it was their proper role. And there was entirely too much fiddling about with women's proper roles. Still, women doctors were needed. So much more . . . modest to be treated by a woman physician.

Faye snorted, a sound that could have been outrage, or simple amusement.

"So how'd you get here?"

Jessy laughed, too, rather wryly. "My mother wasn't educated, but she's still dissatisfied being only wife and mother, so she started saving up for my education the day I was born. She had a father who felt the way my father does, and she always hated it. We never told my father. He thinks I won a scholarship."

"So who's your roommate?" Faye asked.

"She's from New York. Her name is . . . let's see, Crespin."

"I'm it," said Carolyn, offering a hand.

"And yours?" Faye asked Agnes.

"I haven't met her yet. I can't pronounce her name. It's spelled S-o-v-a-w-a-n-e-a a-T-c-s-u-a-w-a-n-e."

They puzzled over that for a moment, deciding it was probably Hawaiian. "Who's rooming with you, Faye?" Jessamine asked.

"They haven't assigned anyone," she replied, her eyes very watchful. "I been asking myself whether that's because I'm black or because I'm majoring in art."

"I doubt it's because you're an artist," Carolyn said matter-of-factly. "I suppose it could be because you're black. Or it could be they just haven't assigned anyone yet."

All of which made the subject of blackness all right to acknowledge, along with advanced education for women, which joined other subjects of conversation when Agnes invited them all into her room. They were still there, chattering away, when someone came to the open door and stood shyly looking in as their heads came up, one by one.

She was the most unusually beautiful creature they had ever seen, beautiful in a way they could neither dismiss nor envy, any more than they would dismiss or envy a glorious sunrise.

"Is one of you Agnes?" the beauty asked in an enchanting voice, low and rich, with a slight, indefinable accent. "Agnes McGann?"

Agnes raised her hand, gargled, could not get the words out.

The new arrival smiled. "I'm your roommate. SOvawah-NAYah ah'TAYsoo-ahWAHnay," she said. "Please, call me Sova."

Jessamine was invited to a fraternity party by a boy she'd met in biology class. He told her to bring her friends.

"It's a Halloween party, let's all go," Jessamine suggested to Aggie.

"I don't know," said Agnes doubtfully. "We weren't invited."

"They said bring friends. You're my friends. Ophy talked Bettiann into coming."

"Doesn't Bettiann like parties?"

"She's got this eating problem. She thinks she's fat."

"Bettiann?" Agnes laughed.

"Right, but don't laugh. Ophy says it isn't funny. It isn't logical, either. It's a psychological thingy that comes from trying to stay thin for all those contests her mother put her in. She feels guilty about eating. Sometimes she eats and then makes herself throw up. Or she starves herself. Anyhow, Ophy's read up on it, and she's made Bettiann into a project. Part of the therapy is to go places and act normal. Carolyn's coming. And I've asked Faye. Come on, Aggie, Sophy." They had tried calling her Sova, but it had inevitably become Sophy as all their names had transmogrified. The ABCs: Aggie-Betti-Cara. Plus Ophy-Sophy and Jessy-Faye.

Oh, very well, Agnes grumbled to herself. She hated parties, she always ended up by herself in a corner. Still, the others were going, so come evening she went with them. It was the first time all seven of them had gone anywhere together, but there was such a mob at the party, they didn't add appreciably to the crowd. There was beer. There was punch, which was made of brandy and several kinds of wine, had peaches in it, and didn't taste as lethal as it was. By eleven most of the people present were either unconscious, very drunk, or well on their way.

At which juncture two young men decided to escort Sophy home after the bash.

"No, thank you," she murmured soberly, though she'd

had several cups of the lethal punch. "I will walk back with my friends."

But they wouldn't take no for an answer. One thing led to another, and a fight broke out. Agnes, who was always abstemious, pulled Sophy away from the fray, went in search of the others, gathered them up—even Carolyn, who was inclined to stay and see what happened—and the seven of them departed while the two combatants were still rolling around amid spilled punch and broken crockery. They were well down the block before the police car pulled up in front of the frat house, and soon thereafter they were all in Agnes and Sophy's room, drinking cocoa, eating popcorn, and laughing immoderately at nothing much.

"You certainly made a hit," said Faye to Sophy. "Cut quite a swath through the male population, you did."

"I don't like it," said Sophy. "It's really very disturbing." Her voice sounded more than merely disturbed: it quavered with outrage or shock. "I don't understand men."

"Do any of us understand men?" Jessamine asked in a faraway, cold voice. "I never have."

Carolyn glanced curiously at Jessamine and said, "It's not just men. Do any of us understand people? Including us? I don't understand me!"

That started them all off. Agnes, in a sober confessional mood, told them she had first decided to be a nun when Father Conley had told her she was fortunate to be plain and gawky because she would not therefore be an occasion of sin. Though calmly pale during the telling, she became flushed and agitated when the others told her she was not gawky, and this led to a discussion of female beauty, during which Bettiann told them about pretending to be beautiful, how it often worked just to pretend, and about judges who looked at little girls like so many pet puppies and tried to put their hands down her panties.

Faye erupted in outrage, saying the judges must all be

Humbert Humberts, like in Nabokov's book *Lolita,* the one that had been banned, and Jessamine started to tell them something about herself but then broke off, very pale, and ran for the bathroom. Ophy told about her father's not wanting to pay for her education even though he could afford it, and how her mom had to go to court to make him do it, and Carolyn picked up the true confessions, tipsily telling them about Albert. Somehow she got off onto Hal's infectious grin and warm brown eyes. She couldn't put him out of her mind, she said, which wouldn't do, of course. Catholics did not get divorces or break up other people's homes. Neither did Crespins. In any case, she, Carolyn, was already promised to Albert. . . .

"Who promised you?" Faye asked, jeering. "I don't remember your saying you promised you."

Carolyn paused woozily, trying to remember who had promised her to Albert. "I don't know," she confessed with a pixilated giggle. "He's just . . . he's always been there. I don't want Albert, but I guess I think I will want Albert, because everyone always tells me I'll want Albert."

"You know what they're doing to you, don't you?" Faye asked, her voice slurred velvet, furry at the edges from the punch they'd all drunk. "They're cutting and pasting you, Car-o-line. They're taking everything that pleasures you and cutting it off. There's a thing they do to girls in Africa, cutting off they little clits so they can't ever get any pleasure there. It's a mutilation. Maybe yours dohn hurt so much right now, but it's the same thing. That's what they're doing to you. Mutilation."

The word was only a word, but it stayed with Carolyn like a mantra. She told herself later it was just that she was drunk, very un-Crespinly drunk, so drunk she hadn't even been offended by Faye's vulgar language, but it wasn't only that. It was true. The aunts were trying to mutilate her, and so was Albert. It was a revelation. Damn the aunts. Damn Albert.

The conversation went on to other things, and during all of it Sophy listened and listened, very much, Carolyn thought, like an anthropologist in a native environment, her ears positively quivering.

"Where were you brought up?" Carolyn asked her during a lull in the conversation.

"Oh, here and there," Sophy said, flushing a little. "Nowhere in particular."

"Country or city?"

"Oh, country! Yes, very rural, my people. My upbringing was all very ordinary and dull, really. Farm life is very much the same from day to day. That's why I'm so excited about being here, learning all your stories."

"Our stories?" Carolyn laughed. "We don't even have stories."

"Oh, you do! You've been telling them tonight! I want to hear everything, all about you, all about women everywhere. . . ."

She gave a similar answer every time they asked about her. Sometimes she looked uncomfortable, sometimes she smiled, but she never said anything definite. Carolyn thought she was probably part European, part Native American, or even South American, basing that idea on the panpipes Sophy sometimes played—a very Andean instrument, Jessamine remarked that Sophy played the drum, too, which was Indian or maybe Asian. They asked Agnes, who, being Sophy's roommate, should know, but Agnes only shrugged. "She won't tell me. She meditates sometimes, usually early in the morning. She says she's invoking a guardian spirit, but that's all she'll say."

In anyone else it would have been infuriating. In anyone else it would have led to suspicion, or ill feeling. In Sophy it was part of her charm. Her drumming and piping were mysterious, her meditative exercises unfathomable, but they were part of Sophy, whom they loved, even though they did not understand her. They particularly did not understand why Sophy was constantly so troubled over men.

The defining incident happened in early November. Despite Faye's marvelous voice, she wanted a career in art, not music, and even so early in her studies she visualized things as artworks. This defining incident was remembered as a painting—perhaps of the Dutch or Flemish school, dramatically sidelit: *Interior with Figures*. The interior was the room that she and Sophy shared, full of the golden light of an autumn afternoon, amber sun-fingers reaching toward dark corners and along dusky walls. The figures were themselves: Carolyn crouched on the window seat, the slanting light making a ruddy aureole of her hair, the dorm cat sprawled bonelessly across her lap. Faye herself, wild hair bushing upward, walnut skin, eyes glittering like a jungle creature, catching glimpses of herself in the mirror as she stalked back and forth. Ophy, heaped on a corner of the bed like a disjointed marionette, wide mouth pulled into a jester's gape. And Agnes, sitting solemnly, straight-legged, against the door, staring at the trio before the mirror: Jessamine's sleek olive-brown presence at one side. Bettiann's tousled blondness at the other, and between them, staring into the mirror as into a crystal ball. Sophy.

She was like a rising star, lovely as the morning. Where had she come by that lovesome body, that perfect face? Doe-eyed Sophy. Night-haired Sophy. Sweet-lipped Sophy. Closemouthed Sophy.

Sophy at that particular moment with swollen eyes, an angry mouth, and burning cheeks. "What do I say to discourage him?" she cried into the mirror at their reflected presences. "Think of something."

Ophy threw up her hands. "Sophy, he's the best catch in the whole school! He's good-looking. He's rich! Have you seen that car of his? Besides, he didn't try to rape you! All he asked you to do was go on a date with him!"

Sophy's head went down, her eyes spilling, while Agnes sprang to her roommate's defense.

"What *he* wants isn't the point. Sophy doesn't want to go on a date. That's the point. She doesn't want to be asked to go. That's the point. She doesn't want to be begged, harassed, chivied, or wooed. She wants to be let alone."

"Then she should have gone to a religious college," opined Bettiann. "Or some girl's school."

"My . . . my scholarship was to this place!" cried Sophy, tested past endurance. "I didn't have a choice!"

There was a metallic quality to her voice, rather like a hammer striking an anvil to make first a clang, then a lingering reverberation that faded slowly into silence, an inhuman hardness coupled with an all-too-human desperation, as though two people . . . two creatures spoke at once. Faye stopped pacing; Ophy stopped grinning; Carolyn's stroking hand stilled. Even the lazy cat looked up, suddenly alert to a tension, a presence in the room that had not been there a moment ago. They all ceased breathing as they searched Sophy's tear-streaked face staring at them from the mirror, surprised to see only her face when that Gorgon's voice should have come from another, more terrible creature.

In later years Carolyn occasionally wakened from a sound sleep or turned from a present task, thinking she had heard the clang of that voice, like the door of a distant vault being closed, shutting something in, or out, a ringing adamant, weighty as fate itself. Yet, so she told herself, the sound was not unnatural. It had force, like the roaring of cataracts or the spume of a geyser, and it was earthly, not alien. So she felt when they heard that voice for the first time, when Sophy cried woe into the mirror:

"I don't want men to ask me out. I don't want them to

think of me that way. I can feel their thoughts. It's like being raped inside their heads, little pieces of me ripped off and taken into them, used up. I want them not to think of me, not to discuss me, not to make bets with each other, can they get me to go out with them, can they kiss me, can they take me to bed!"

A silence came while the reverberations stilled. Then Bettiann said:

"It's only words and thoughts, Sophy. Words can't hurt you."

"Words can't hurt?" Sophy cried. "Why do you believe they can't? Words have hurt all of us! It's your mother's words that make you throw up your dinner almost every night, Bettiann. Words made you believe you're unattractive, Aggie! Words may make you marry a man you don't love, Carolyn! Words are as powerful as weapons, as useful as tools. They can injure like a flung stone, cut like a knife, batter like a club. They can open heaven or they can ruin and destroy!"

"Shh, now," Carolyn cried in sudden inexplicable terror, afraid to let silence settle upon that outcry, afraid to let it go on to another word, phrase, sentence. That voice, that particular voice of Sophy's, had to be stilled, quieted, put at rest, or it could destroy them. "You don't need to fight with us, Sophy. We're with you. Just explain what you mean."

Sophy wiped the tears angrily, using the back of her hand. "I . . . look at the lives of those who are greatly desired. I see pretty girls who burn hot, with sunny faces, their bodies like flame. They sing. They dance. They appear on the covers of magazines. I ask myself if it is merely coincidence that so many of them have such great troubles, so many die so young. It is as if they are eaten up alive, their souls nibbled away by all those who have fantasized about them, leered at them, used words and thoughts on them. In my people's stories maidens lean against the dragon's great scaled side under the shelter of a wing and learn secrets. In your stories maidens are chained to a stake for the dragon to burn or devour! The maiden may be mythical and the dragon invisible, but there is still truth in that. I don't want your dragons devouring me."

Agnes, lost, ventured. "Like . . . when someone takes a picture of a primitive person? They're stealing the soul?"

"Like that, perhaps," said Sophy, shaking her head in confusion. "If you cannot feel it as I do, then pretend for my sake that it's real. Pretend it's possible. I don't want them using me that way."

Carolyn nodded. "Then you want to be invisible."

"Exactly," Sophy whispered. "Oh, if I could be invisible."

Carolyn rose to her feet, hands on her hips, jaw jutted. "Then we'll help you become so."

It took the others a few moments to catch up with her.

"She doesn't have to be beautiful," Carolyn said scornfully in the face of their doubt. "No law says she has to be beautiful."

And she gathered the five of them up into her hands like a deck of cards and dealt them out again: You go here, you go there, fetch this, fetch that, supervising Sophy's makeover without a moment's hesitation. Clothing first, baggy skirts and too-large tops, shapeless and of indeterminate colors, borrowed from Carolyn herself; a little liquid makeup on the lips and brows, fading them into the face; a little more on the lashes, making her eyes look bald. Faye saw to that. Hair pulled straight back into a knot. Bettiann's contribution. A touch of olive base, Jessamine's, to take the bloom from those cheeks. Ophy provided the glasses, frames only at first.

It was Agnes who suggested the book. "You need a heavy book," she said. "You can carry it up against your chest and walk sort of bent over. You'll look like a brain, armed with the shield and buckler of the female intelligentsia."

"I've got a thick book," said Jessamine. "I found it in the bottom of the cupboard in my room, with about fifty years' worth of dust on it. I'll get it."

She returned moments later bearing Edward Gibbons's *The Decline and Fall of the Roman Empire,* volume one. An old leather-bound library book, checked out years before by a feckless student, never returned. Sophy rose, took it into her arms, stooped slightly over it, and shuffled across the room. They all burst into laughter, even Sophy, though hers was a sound of honest joy floating on the sea of derision. What the rest of them took as a joke Sophy accepted as a reprieve.

In time her new self became familiar to them. With them, after a shower, her robe belted loosely around her, she was lovely as the dawn, but in public Sophy wore borrowed clothing, was camouflaged like a hermit crab, no longer the object of male fascination and desire.

It was a shared secret, one that made them more than merely friends. They became a club: the Decline and Fall Club. They swore an oath to one another. Even after they left school, they would stay close to one another. They would meet every year, and each of them would find a place to stand where she could be woman as woman was meant to be, and thereafter she would never decline or fall from that place.

Worlds of Wonder:
The Classic Fantasies of

URSULA K. LEGUIN

The Novels of Earthsea

The windswept world of Earthsea is one of the greatest creations in all fantasy literature, comparable to Tolkien's Middle Earth or C. S. Lewis's Narnia. The adventures of the powerful Archmage Ged, from his willful youth through his grand destiny, continue to captivate new generations of readers.

A Wizard of Earthsea	___26250-5	$6.50/NCR
The Tombs of Atuan	___27331-0	$6.50/$8.99
The Farthest Shore	___26847-3	$6.50/$8.99
Tehanu	___28873-3	$6.50/$8.99

Ask for these books at your local bookstore or use this page to order.

Please send me the books i have checked above. I am enclosing $____ (add $2.50 to cover postage and handling). Send check or money order, no cash or C.O.D.'s, please.

Name _____

Address _____

City/State/Zip _____

Send order to: Bantam Books, Dept. SF 105, 2451 S. Wolf Rd., Des Plaines, IL 60018
Allow four to six weeks for delivery.

Prices and availability subject to change without notice.   SF 105 4/96

...a invites you to join us in our new on-line forum.

< Interviews with your favorite authors and excerpts from their latest books

< Bulletin boards that put you in touch with other science fiction fans, with Spectra authors, and with the Bantam editors who bring them to you

< A guide to the best science fiction resources on the Internet

Join us as we catch you up with all of Spectra's finest authors, featuring monthly listings of upcoming titles and special previews, as well as contests, interviews, and more! We'll keep you in touch with the field, both its past and its future—and everything in between.

Look for the Spectra Science Fiction Forum on the World Wide Web at:

http://www.bdd.com

SF 30 7/96

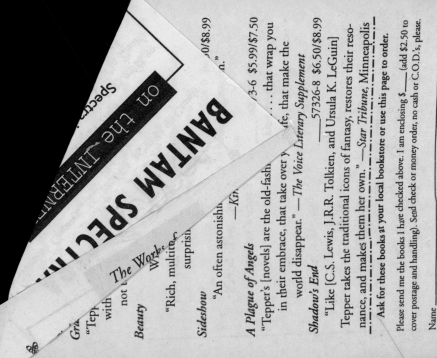

0/$8.99
n."

on the Spectr...

BANTAM SPECTRA
BANTAM INTERN...

3-6 $5.99/$7.50

57326-8 $6.50/$8.99

The Works...
Work...
"Rich, multifac...
surprisi...

Beauty Work...

Sideshow
"An often astonishin...
—Ki...

Gr...
"Tepp...
with...
not...

... that wrap you in their embrace, that take over y... life, that make the world disappear." — *The Voice Literary Supplement*

A Plague of Angels
"Tepper's [novels] are the old-fash...

Shadow's End
"Like [C.S. Lewis, J.R.R. Tolkien, and Ursula K. LeGuin] Tepper takes the traditional icons of fantasy, restores their reso-nance, and makes them her own." — *Star Tribune*, Minneapolis

Ask for these books at your local bookstore or use this page to order.

Please send me the books I have checked above. I am enclosing $_____ (add $2.50 to cover postage and handling). Send check or money order, no cash or C.O.D.'s, please.

Name _____

Address _____

City/State/Zip _____

Send order to: Bantam Books, Dept. SF 25, 2451 S. Wolf Rd., Des Plaines, IL 60018
Allow four to six weeks for delivery.
Prices and availability subject to change without notice.

SF 25 6/96